MEDLEY MACABRE

Medley Macabre

An Anthology of Stories of the Supernatural, Being Ghosts, Psychical Phenomena, Uncanny Mysteries

edited and compiled

by Bryan A. Netherwood

LONDON
HAMMOND, HAMMOND AND COMPANY

First published in Great Britain 1966

Reprinted 1970
" " 1971
" " 1972

ISBN 0.242.78533.6

Printed in Great Britain by
Morrison & Gibb Ltd Edinburgh
for Hammond Hammond Ltd
2 Clement's Inn London WC2

Dedication

RESPECTFULLY, to all those mystical souls who, while favouring the increase of enlightened knowledge, prefer simultaneously that man's reach for the remoter things of the unknown and the unseen shall remain fascinatingly, tantalisingly, and perpetually, if ever so slightly, beyond his grasp.

The authors represented in this collection are:

E. F. Benson 1867–1940
R. H. Benson 1871–1914
Ambrose Bierce 1838–1914?
Algernon Blackwood 1869–1951
Thomas Burke 1887–1945
A. M. Burrage (years not known)
Sir Andrew Caldecott (b.1884)
Ralph A. Cram 1863–1942
F. Marion Crawford 1854–1909
Mrs. Catherine Crowe 1800–1876
M. P. Dare 1902–
William C. Dickinson 1897–
Sir Arthur Conan Doyle 1859–1930
L. P. Hartley 1895–
W. F. Harvey 1885–1937
E. & H. Heron 1876–1922
Robert Hichens 1864–1950
Violet Hunt 1866–1942
M. R. James 1862–1936
Nigel Kneale 1922–
Noel Langley 1911–
H. P. Lovecraft 1890–1937
Arthur Machen 1863–1947
R. H. Malden 1879–1951
Amyas Northcote (years not known)
Elliott O'Donnell (b.1872)
Oliver Onions 1873–1961
J. B. Priestley 1894–
Sir Arthur Quiller-Couch 1863–1944
R. Ellis Roberts 1879–1953
H. R. Wakefield (b.1889)
H. G. Wells 1866–1946
Edith Wharton 1862–1937
Dennis Wheatley 1897–

CONTENTS

		Page
ACKNOWLEDGEMENTS		11
INTRODUCTION		13

MALIGN INFLUENCES, SORCERIES, EVIL POWERS

THE STALLS OF BARCHESTER CATHEDRAL	*M. R. James*	27
NO. 252 RUE M. LE PRINCE	*Ralph A. Cram*	40
OUT OF THE PICTURE	*Arthur Machen*	52
THE RED ROOM	*H. G. Wells*	73
NEGOTIUM PERAMBULANS	*E. F. Benson*	81
SMITH: AN EPISODE IN A LODGING-HOUSE	*Algernon Blackwood*	94
THE ANKARDYNE PEW	*W. F. Harvey*	108
LUCKY'S GROVE	*H. R. Wakefield*	118
OR PERSONS UNKNOWN	*H. R. Wakefield*	137
"BRING OUT YOUR DEAD"	*M. P. Dare*	151
THE BONE BEAD NECKLACE	*Noel Langley*	160
MINUKE	*Nigel Kneale*	171

PHANTOMS AND GHOSTLY VISITATIONS

THE GREEN SCARF	*A. M. Burrage*	183
SEVENTH EVENING	*Mrs. Catherine Crowe*	196
THE EYES	*Edith Wharton*	206
A PAIR OF HANDS	*Sir Arthur Quiller-Couch*	222
FATHER MACCLESFIELD'S TALE	*R. H. Benson*	234
THE GREY PIPER AND THE HEAVY COACH OF DONALDGOWERIE HOUSE, PERTH	*Elliott O'Donnell*	241
THE HOUSE OF THE GHOSTLY TAP-DANCING	*Elliott O'Donnell*	250
THE CIGARETTE CASE	*Oliver Onions*	256
THE LONELY INN	*Thomas Burke*	267
RETURN AT DUSK	*William Croft Dickinson*	274

POSSESSION BY SPIRIT INFLUENCES

		Page
FOR THE BLOOD IS THE LIFE	*F. Marion Crawford*	287
THE STORY OF THE GREY HOUSE	*E. & H. Heron*	301
FEET FOREMOST	*L. P. Hartley*	312
THE CASE OF THE LONG-DEAD LORD	*Dennis Wheatley*	339

PREDICTION AND DOOM

DEMETRIADI'S DREAM	*Robert Hichens*	353
THE BAROMETER	*Violet Hunt*	371
THE BUS-CONDUCTOR	*E. F. Benson*	381
SEATED ONE DAY AT THE ORGAN	*Sir Andrew Caldecott*	389
AUGUST HEAT	*W. F. Harvey*	396

SPIRITUALISM AND MAGIC

THE REALM OF THE UNREAL	*Ambrose Bierce*	403
PLAYING WITH FIRE	*Sir Arthur Conan Doyle*	409
THE OTHER PLACE	*J. B. Priestley*	421

WITCHCRAFT AND SATANISM

THE ASH-TREE	*M. R. James*	445
THE SANCTUARY	*E. F. Benson*	457
MAY DAY EVE	*Algernon Blackwood*	474
A COLLECTOR'S COMPANY	*R. H. Malden*	493
THE LATE MRS. FOWKE	*Amyas Northcote*	504
THE HILL	*R. Ellis Roberts*	513
THE HAUNTER OF THE DARK	*H. P. Lovecraft*	525

ACKNOWLEDGEMENTS

For the right to reprint the copyrighted stories in this volume, the publishers are indebted to the following authors, publishers and agents.

ARKHAM HOUSE

For "The Haunter of the Dark", by H. P. Lovecraft. From *The Haunter of the Dark and Others.* Victor Gollancz, 1951

EDWARD ARNOLD LTD.

For "Seated One Day at the Organ", by Sir Andrew Caldecott. From *Fires Burn Blue.*

For "'Bring Out Your Dead'", by M. P. Dare. From *Unholy Relics.*

For "The Stalls of Barchester Cathedral", by M. R. James. From *Collected Ghost Stories.*

For "A Collector's Company", by R. H. Malden. From *Nine Ghosts.*

THE BODLEY HEAD LTD.

For "The Late Mrs. Fowke", by Amyas Northcote. From *In Ghostly Company.*

CURTIS BROWN LTD.

For "Lucky's Grove", by H. R. Wakefield. From *The Clock Strikes Twelve.*

JONATHAN CAPE LTD.

For "The Realm of the Unreal", by Ambrose Bierce. From *Can Such Things Be?*

CHATTO AND WINDUS LTD.

For "No. 252 Rue M. Le Prince", by Ralph A. Cram. From *Black Spirits and White.*

J. M DENT & SONS LTD.

For "August Heat", by W. F. Harvey. From *Midnight House.*

For "The Ankardyne Pew", by W. F. Harvey. From *The Beast With Five Fingers.*

For "A Pair of Hands" by Sir Arthur Quiller-Couch. From *Old Fires and Profitable Ghosts.*

JOHN FARQUHARSON LTD.

For "The Lonely Inn", by Thomas Burke. From *Night-Pieces.* Published by Constable, 1935.

HAMISH HAMILTON LTD.

For "Feet Foremost", by L. P. Hartley. From *The Travelling Grave.*

A. M. HEATH & CO. LTD.

For "Minuke", by Nigel Kneale. From *Tomato Caine and Others.*

For "Out of the Picture", by Arthur Machen. From *The Children of the Pool.*

WILLIAM HEINEMANN LTD.

For "The Barometer", by Violet Hunt. From *Tales of the Uneasy.*

DAVID HIGHAM ASSOCIATES LTD.

For "The Bone Bead Necklace", by Noel Langley. From *Tales of Mystery and Revenge.*

THE HUTCHINSON PUBLISHING GROUP

For "The Case of the Long-Dead Lord", by Dennis Wheatley. From *Gunmen, Gallants & Ghosts.*

JOHN MURRAY LTD.

For "Playing With Fire", by Sir Arthur Conan Doyle. From *Tales of Twlight and the Unseen.*

OLIVER & BOYD LTD.

For "Return at Dusk", by William C. Dickinson. From *The Sweet Singers and Three Other Remarkable Occurrents.*

C. ARTHUR PEARSON LTD.

For "The Story of the Grey House", by E. & H. Heron. From *Ghost Stories.*

A. D. PETERS & CO.

For "The Other Place", by J. B. Priestley. From *The Other Place and Others.*

SIR ISAAC PITMAN & SONS LTD.

For "Father Macclesfield's Tale", by R. H. Benson. From *A Mirror of Shalott.*

ROUTLEDGE & KEGAN PAUL LTD.

For "The Grey Piper and the Heavy Coach of Donaldgowrie House, Perth", by Elliott O'Donnell. From *Scottish Ghost Stories.*

THE OWNER OF THE COPYRIGHT
AND A. P. WATT & SON

For "The Bus Conductor", by E. F. Benson. From *The Room in the Tower.*

For "The Sanctuary", by E. F. Benson. From *More Spook Stories.*

For "Negotium Perambulans", by E. F. Benson. From *Visible and Invisible.*

THE PUBLIC TRUSTEE, JOHN BAKER LTD.,
THE RICHARDS PRESS AND A. P. WATT & SON

For "May Day Eve", by Algernon Blackwood. From *Selected Tales of Algernon Blackwood.*

For "Smith: An Episode in a Lodging-House", by Algernon Blackwood. From *The Empty House.*

THE OWNER OF THE COPYRIGHT, CASSELL & CO. LTD.
AND A. P. WATT & SON

For "Demetriadi's Dream", by Robert Hichens. From *The Afterglow and Others.*

MRS. GEORGE OLIVER
AND A. P. WATT & SON

For "The Cigarette Case", by Oliver Onions. From *Widdershins.*

THE EXECUTORS OF THE LATE H. G. WELLS
AND A. P. WATT & SON

For "The Red Room", by H. G. Wells. From *The Plattner Story and Others.*

A. WATKINS, INC.

For "The Eyes", by Edith Wharton. From *Tales of Men and Ghosts.*

INTRODUCTION

I

Mystery and Horror! The Uncanny and the Supernatural!

What galaxies of fascination lie in these words! What wonderfully frightening possibilities!

What kind of mystery enthrals us most? Not the tenebrous abysses of some unknown sea and what may exist down there; not the strange worlds encircling some unknown sun at an unimaginably remote vastness of light-years and what may be found on them; not the distant beginnings of an inchoate world without life or order, nor the when and how of the first stirrings of life in the Chaos; none of these, nor many similar; but simply a mystery *for which no natural or rational explanation can be found,* or one having no single solution but capable of many solutions—a mystery which gives more joy unsolved than solved. Arthur Machen, the Welsh writer, put it ideally and concisely in this way: "Man is so made that all his true delight arises from the contemplation of mystery, and save by his own frantic and invincible folly, mystery is never taken from him; it rises within his soul, a well of joy unending." In fact, avoid being enlightened where you find it more enjoyable to be mystified; or, to paraphrase the author's metaphor, the well tastes most refreshing with the waters of mystery unsullied and the dregs of unwanted knowledge left unstirred.

Consider the following weird and uncanny episode reported from Devon in February, 1855: one morning strange imprints of a most unusual kind were seen in the snow. These marks, seemingly cloven-footed and quite small, were spaced apart with amazing exactitude, and meandered in undeviating single file, *not staggered like those of any animal known to naturalists,* in all directions athwart the whole county on both sides of the broad Exe estuary—the total length of all the tracks was probably as much as a hundred miles, *and this in one single night during which, apparently, nothing out of the ordinary had been seen or heard by a living soul!* The prints appeared not only on the ground, but on high walls, house-tops, in enclosed grounds, on the narrowest of ledges, and many other unlikely and inaccessible places, and it was noticed that *the indentation of each mark had cleared the snow, as if by excision, leaving it intact on the outside.* Theory, speculation, and more than a modicum of fear, all buzzed like excited bees; the superstitious postulated the peregrinations of the Devil and feared to venture out of doors after dark, the theorists visualised their zoological chimeras of the rare unknown; but the mystery of the "Satanic" foot-tracks was never solved, and to this day remains unsolved. Fantastic! What better calculated to arouse interest in the occult side of life, of which this surely savours? There *could* be, of course, as the theorists imply, some unexpected and ingenious explanation founded wholly upon natural phenomena, but who cares about *that*—or *them!*

Then there is the theme (familiar enough): "Nobody ever sleeps in that room now; many people have died in it. With one exception, all were found dead the next morning, their faces contorted in an expression of agonised fright and terror; consequently, none was able to report what had been seen there in the dead of night. The sole survivor is now permanently insane, his mind and power of speech alike irretrievably destroyed by some appalling shock...." A fusion of mystery and horror! And our not knowing its nature *endears* it to us, however dreadful and terrifying it may be!

The wonder is that, amid the clamour and distractions and matter-of-fact materialism of this latter-half twentieth century, these fears and dreads of some ancient primordial origin should still linger somewhere below the surface of life; but they do, although the enhanced security of modern times has somehow alchemised them into a form of pleasure: people enjoy nothing better than being frightened—*from a safe position!* And when all is said, I wonder if it would be *too* platitudinous to hint at Hamlet's aphorism to Horatio—that which begins "There are more things in heaven and earth..."

II

I can't write from the first-hand personal experience of one who has had glimpses of the invisible world, as I have never seen anything that could be called extra-physical, or had any extra-sensory perceptions akin to telepathy. But I would refute any suggestion from any quarter that, in an age such as our own when science in all its spheres is leaping ahead with such alacrity, ghosts and the supernatural have been altogether debunked. Obviously it is given to only a few to prise open, by the merest chink, the fast ponderous door that shuts off the abode of spiritual things from the material, physical world. But it *does happen*. Only comparatively recently* a high dignitary of the Church performed a service of exorcism at a house in Newton Abbot, Devon, where a young married couple re-

* at the time of writing—ED

ported to have seen a white form or figure gliding through the rooms of the ground floor flat which they occupied, and found furniture moved round and the radio switched on in their absence. Eventually the couple were unable to sleep there. A thorough investigation was made, and the bishop, in performing the rites, confirmed that he himself had the chilling sensation of some extra-physical influence present in the place. The house has since been reported quiet and untroubled.

Another curious but apparently well authenticated incident dates back to 1924. Sir Shane Leslie once related how, one day in that year, he was at a main-line station in Paris where he boarded the Riviera Express en route for Marseille. As there was a longish wait before the train pulled out, he decided to take a few turns about the platform and while he was engaged in this he noticed the figure of a woman dressed in deep mourning standing some little distance away. His promenade brought him close to where the woman stood, and at this moment, when he met her gaze, he became aware of her grave mien and was almost transfixed by her penetrating eyes. Then he heard her voice, and although she spoke in French he grasped the meaning of her words without much difficulty. She seemed to have some urgent message which she repeated more than once, her mandate being that he must change his train, *must change his train....* What impressed Sir Shane most at the time (as he afterwards told) was the feeling, partly instinctive, that *nobody else on the station platform could see the woman*, and also the weird sensation he had in that instant of being *several minutes outside the time dimension of mortal beings....* Acting upon impulse rather than obedience (his place on the express being a makeshift one in default of an advance booking), he removed his baggage and switched trains, transferring to a slower one. Arrived in Marseille, he was asked how he came there, and insisted that he'd come on the Riviera Express—the *Rapide*—but was told, "You haven't, you know; or you wouldn't be here," and the speaker then disclosed how the express had met with disaster soon after leaving Paris—a disaster involving the loss of a number of lives, including those of some English people. On his return to London Sir Shane Leslie reported this episode, for the record, to a society of spiritualists.

There would seem to be ample justification for believing, as some do, that spiritual beings strive at times to establish contact with mortals, and that only the very limited range of our imperfect senses hinders them from doing so more often than seldom.

In the present collection, the most striking example of a spirit warning is given with the macabre civility of *The Bus-Conductor,* a tale by E. F. Benson which was once used for an episode in a horror film called "Dead of Night". Some readers may remember it.

Having therefore shed the close-packed outer layers of rumour and sensation-mongering, there yet remains a small hard core of indisputable fact: that strange things do still happen in the time of this mortal life, things that no scientist has so far explained; strange legends linger, old superstitions die hard. Undeniably, hauntings and apparitions are reported from time to time, as we've already seen; and one of the most eminent authorities on the supernatural, Elliott O'Donnell, has cited many well-attested instances in this, and other centuries. So far from being restricted to the more obvious stamping-grounds of old residences such as ancient castles, senescent houses and the like, ghosts seem to be as ubiquitous as the human race itself: neither the theatre nor the stage, nor old inns nor sailing ships, nor caves nor mountains, nor lakes nor rivers, nor unfrequented dilapidated thoroughfares of one kind and another, nor (for that matter) a certain R.A.F. Station in Buckinghamshire, are exclusive of them. Again, in this anthology, at least one of the above features has its fictional counterpart: *The Lonely Inn,* of Thomas Burke, distils its own special brew of ghostly lore.

Memories probably still persist of the notorious Borley Rectory, rightly dubbed "the most haunted house in England", which was located in a corner of Essex. Some readers may still remember its destruction by fire in February 1939, a conflagration started in some way apparently never satisfactorily ascertained. This followed some ten years of thoroughgoing investigations, headed by one Mr. Harry Price, into its strange, often startling, not to say frightening manifestations observed by a long line of witnesses who included many successive residents and not a few visitors. Details which would separately occupy whole pages and even chapters must be summarised with as much brevity as possible in the limited space available here; suffice it that in the long catalogue of the phenomena usually associated with phantasmal influences, including the more violent poltergeists, the discarnate voices (of singing as well as speech), footsteps, banging of doors, inexplicible displacement of movables within the house and the equally baffling disappearance and reappearance of household effects, mysterious wall-writings tactile sensations felt by some observers, and so forth, some rather more striking things—literally *striking*—can be singled out. The wife of one incumbent who happened to have the living of that parish at the time, a Mrs. Foyster, was *struck*—full in the eye, seemingly by an invisible fisticuff that launched itself out of the void! Her eye bled, and remained blackened for some days. Objects sometimes hurled themselves violently at the rector, the Rev. L. A. Foyster, or his wife, or both together. On one occasion Mr. Price himself, with a companion, had a bombardment of hardware—a candlestick, slate, pebbles and the like—hurtled down the stairs at them by no visible agency. And it was not only intimidating sounds—tappings, rumblings, soft shuffling noises, and the like—that harassed residents, but *sights* also: one of the daughters of another rector of Borley was startled in the dead of night by the figure of an old man in dark, old-fashioned clothes topped by a tall hat, standing by her bed; another resident, a gardener, reported to have seen one night a massive archaic black coach approach the Rectory without making the least sound, the moonlight bringing out the gleaming head-lamps and also revealing two top-hatted figures seated on the box, then sweep past into the farmyard and disappear; the Foysters' chauffeur, seated one day in the kitchen, chanced to look up from his newspaper and saw what he described as a grisly black hand moving slowly up and down near the door, and Mrs. Foyster herself reported seeing what she was pleased to call "a monstrosity" near the kitchen door, which laid hold on her shoulder with an iron touch; and Captain W. H. Gregson, a later occupant of the Rectory, has told how one day his cocker spaniel, accompanying him through the courtyard, saw something which was invisible to himself, at which it began to whine and shriek—and then bolted, and vanished without trace for all time.

At times the manifestations took the form of pranks, mischievous and even injurious, calculated to cause yet more fright and consternation! However, I will pass over these.

But perhaps the most bizarre and startling vision of all, and one which deserves special mention in preference to its fellows, was the lot of Mrs. Margaret Wilson, an artist who, in the late summer of 1938, having got permission to paint a picture of Borley Rectory, duly arrived there and set up her equipment in the grounds.

She set to work; but as the hours slipped by, she began to be aware of a grim, forbidding quality in the dead silence which had gradually seized upon everything with a tense, dreadful fear ... she had the uneasy feeling of the close presence of invisible watchers. About three o'clock in the afternoon she heard a sound like the sudden onrush of wind or of whirring wings very close, erupting suddenly out of the silence. Looking up from her easel, she saw an exceedingly queer entomoid creature bearing down upon her at near eye level, strangely appearing to issue forth out of a mist and accompanied by a wasp, as if for guidance. Not one second too soon she ducked adroitly, and simultaneously struck out with her mahlstick at the thing. The wasp disappeared in a normal way, but the most careful search revealed no trace of the weird creature she had just struck. Having completed her painting of the Rectory and returned home,

Mrs. Wilson, with a vivid and accurate impression of the above-mentioned chimera still fresh in her memory, made a realistic rendering of it in the materials at her disposal (which, being an artist, she was in the position to do). Apparently it had been a thing with a tapering segmented body three inches or more in length, completely black and somewhat flat in the base; it had huge filmy goggle eyes rather like black grapes with the bloom on them.

Having seen the carefully prepared rendering, none of the several naturalists and entomologists to whom it was referred could identify the strange thing, their general verdict on it being that it was "out of this world", or "like nothing on earth".

Mrs. Wilson's testimony was accepted as having particular value, not only because she was well acquainted with insects herself, especially in connection with art studies and still life, but also because she was essentially practical by nature and would admit to neither psychical nor spiritualistic powers. Her vision could possibly have been pure and simple hallucination, and nothing more; on the other hand, some notions of elemental spirit forms might be admissible. (Incidentally, the most outstanding example of an "elemental" in these present tales is E. F. Benson's grim and fearful *Negotium Perambulans*....)

Investigators at Borley were all agreed on two features of the Rectory: its self-contained coldness, which even warm weather failed to ameliorate entirely, and, in the absence of any "happenings", its profound quietness. This cold was localised with peculiar intensity in one particular place, which was given the title of "The Cold Spot", just outside the infamous Blue Room: one witness who happened one night to be on this spot, felt an inexplicable terror, a sensation of icy cold, particularly in the hands (and this on a warm summer evening), and of "pins and needles" all over.

At least one, and probably more than one, attempt was made to throw light on the mysteries—and the previous history—of Borley Rectory (it was built in 1863 on the foundations of two or more earlier habitations which were said to include a 14th century monastery). Inevitably, these attempts produced the expected crop of séances and their attendant mediums (we can safely assume that one or two of these, at least, were genuine) and, as might be expected, the information so gained was fragmentary; but, pieced together, the emergent picture was one of influences emanating not all from one place, but from many places, some from afar and even involving another continent; of a small island, with people coming and going; of no peace or rest, and feuds, quarrels, between familes; of one of the last owners of the Rectory who died very lonely, disappointed and unappreciated ... during his life he was a public man who played a prominent part in public life ... blame was heaped upon him over many things ... he was very disappointed with life and with his work ... in the last few years of his life he became very queer in his mind and in his ways.... But a miscellany of mediums' soundings is a superfluous rigmarole which it isn't necessary to enlarge upon here.

From the foregoing, at any rate, it is clear how theories held by some spiritualists about "vibrations" from the past can hold their own; how dire deeds and evil passions are believed to generate, in the space and time dimensions, tremendous and enduring ripples which can outspan a long lapse of years, baleful forces that cling to an original abode and may inflict terrible harm: a stone dropped in still water provides the common analogy. Nothing, so it is said, ever *really dies*—in mind, memory, or the macrocosm. It wouldn't be surprising, in this vein, if something indefinably but unmistakably malignant does *still* lurk and brood about the site of some worst of the former wartime concentration camps, and if the lone wayfarer finds the uneasy sensations he had at that spot by day heightened into tremors of a positively palpable evil when he passed that way by night, and longed for company—of the right kind.

Superb examples of waves or ripples out of the past, in these pages, include *The Ankardyne Pew*, *The House of the Ghostly Tap-Dancing*, *Return at Dusk*, and that magnificently styled *"Bring Out Your Dead"*, a strikingly effective tale calculated to make even the boldest quake in the very witching time of night—and by no means alone in this! Other vibrations of a historic kind are woven to strange and startling effect into the old fabric of *The Green Scarf*, from the pen of A. M. Burrage.

All things considered, and all due allowance made for possible fluctuations in the accuracy or probity of eye-witnesses, investigators and other seekers, we are drawn to one inevitable, unalterable conclusion about the supernatural: that there must be *something* in it. "Rubbish!" scoffs the sceptic, still unconvinced. "Pure imagination! Ghosts exist only in the mind." "Of course!" says the bright wit brightly, "that's why they *do* exist." "I'll believe in ghosts when I see one," chimes in another soul, well up in the seeing-is-believing stance.

But the lure of the occult survives the objectors; and ultimately, the efficacy of the stories and legends surrounding ghosts lies with the muse that beckons and leads us, step by step, down into an abyss of fear to the brink of that inmost chasm where the pleasurable horror of the onlooker *plunges steeply down to that full consummation of horror which is the agony of the victim.*

III

Quite a number of years ago, in the autumn of 1943, there was a radio series called "Appointment with Fear". In all probability it was an appointment kept more punctiliously by more people than anything jotted down in a diary. It is in that same spirit that I would recommend you to sample these stories, and there are some, at least, of which I'll even go so far as to say that *I dare you to read them the last thing at night!* No doubt of it, these are tales not for the light summer evenings, but for the fall of the year when the shadows lengthen and the nights close in, when the equinoctial gales lower and rage and awaken ominous stirrings about the house, and taut nerves are hammered on the anvil of suspense, and it is a night on which anything ... *anything* might happen.... It could, of course.

It will have been noted already that these are categorised as stories of the supernatural, dealing with things that transcend natural knowledge, not of terror or horror in its own right; although, naturally, the supernatural is deemed to take horror in its stride. Nevertheless, the idea of the supernatural always having to be unerringly horrific and terrifying is, to me at any rate, a fallacy: two among these, for certain—*A Pair of Hands* and *The Cigarette Case*—so far from imbibing terror of the hair-raising kind, have a distinct flavour of pathos and kindliness, while not dispensing with the supernatural element; others, such as *No. 252 Rue M. Le Prince, The Sanctuary, Or Persons Unknown,* and *The Grey House,* exemplify sheer horror, formidable, malevolent, and of great impact; all intended to bring you as close as possible to *that brink,* if not over the edge....

Compiling an anthology is not merely the lumping together of literary extracts, be they stories or verse; and as the word itself derives from two Greek words which mean the gathering of flowers, it may not be too presumptuous to suppose that the beauty of the individual blooms is as much in the eye of the gatherer as in that of the beholder, and that those of lesser calibre serve to emphasise the essential contrast by which the more showy heads will stand out. Using the most eclectic methods, it is still possible, even with this heterogeneous assembly, to fall short of your avowed aim to please everyone; therefore you are left with no alternative but to please yourself in your final choice, and hope that *that* will please everyone. It is just as easy to court disappointment where you had expected gratification as it is to unearth unexpected gems among the indifferent gravel; but remember, too, that one man's treasure is another man's trash.

My tactic has been to put each story in chronological order of its author's year of birth, under each sub-title, except in the very few cases where such detail has not been forthcoming; in that event I have found it convenient to fall back on an alphabetical sequence based on initial letters of surnames, and fit in the stragglers that way.

IV

Well then, what's your attitude towards the supernatural?

Perhaps you are conditioned to visualise ghosts in, say, a candle-lit setting amid period furnishings in some hoary old mansion hallowed by the history and usages of a couple of centuries and more; or in some derelict, weed-choked, yew-shadowed burial ground whose headstones the erasing touch of time has crumbled to near illegibility: it is more natural, though not necessarily more logical, that ghosts should seem to look more at ease and in their element in such settings than they do in the trappings of modernity, such as electrical appliances, functional design, mechanisation, and so forth. For all that, and for good measure. we have here some restless, destructive spirits in as unlikely and "unspooky" a setting as a modern housing estate, in Nigel Kneale's *Minuke*.

Again, perhaps you will generalise by regarding all ghosts and apparitions as a very highly intensified form of telepathy, the seeing of which must depend on the sensitivity and receptivity of the person affected. That such sensitivity at the psychical level varies enormously between different subjects, human and animal, is beyond dispute. (I must digress here to mention the most remarkable fictional example of telepathic thought transference, that perennial favourite, W. F. Harvey's *August Heat*, which turns up time and again as having a secure place in the affections of anthologists, and has not eluded my embrace.) You are willing to concede, I dare say, that presumably societies for psychical research don't exist solely for their own amusement.

Possibly you are inclined to attribute the alleged powers of witches and witch-doctors and their arcana, survivals of strange esoteric cults of bygone times, for the most part to sheer auto-suggestion amounting almost to mesmerism, carried up to the point where it assails the subconscious mind, but only effective *in direct proportion to the power of subconscious belief in it.* (A particularly fine, gruesome tale of a witch's curse herein is *The Ash-Tree* by that master of the medieval mode, M. R. James, lacking whom no anthology of this genre would be complete.) And of course, it goes without saying that genuine powers of clairvoyance and clair-audience must be quite rare among the professed occultists; indeed it can be said of far the greater number that no more resourceful turn-out of cheats and charlatans ever graduated from the School of Deceits, and that to be fooled by them is the price payable for a puerile, over-eager credulity; equally, it is painfully true that the never-failing ingenuity of science and technology in the manner of gadgets and micro-equipment has given the brigade of hoaxers more scope for imposture than ever before. On the other hand, honest true mediums *have* proved their worth—and their point.

And have you also written off the phenomena of Borley Rectory as being in some part attributable to agencies perfectly natural, if peculiar and unexplained? In some spheres of investigation (not connected with Borley Rectory) curious accounts are given of observers dodging a great stone which appeared suddenly out of nothing and descended upon them, and being drenched by a shower of rain coming quite out of the void—*indoors!* In terms of transcendental physics, the existence of occasional pockets or bubbles of an odd kind of counter-gravitational force, evidenced in rare moments, might be considered—by those intent on accepting only a scientific explanation—to account amply for such spontaneous phenomena as telekinesis (the movement of objects by contacts other than physical); teleportation (the transporting of objects to distant or farther places by conveyances other than physical); levitation (the lifting or floating in the air of bulky or non-buoyant objects, and even of the human body).

On all counts—partially at least—you would be right.

All the same, is there not somewhere a small door of doubt which cannot help but drift open, though you press with all your might against it? There is Mrs. Wilson's strange "insect", for example—what *are* you to make of that? Subjective hallucination? Perhaps. "Pure imagination"? Hardly. And there are others....

True, that lady's vision is scarcely more, and probably a good deal less, frightful than some of the foul, teramorphous beings that are dreamed of once in a while, surrealist beasts and insects among them, ghastly nameless monsters that harass and molest in the rough-house of nightmare. "...I confess an occasional nightmare," wrote Charles Lamb, "but I do not, as in early youth, keep a stud of them. Fiendish faces, with the extinguished taper, will come and look at me; but I know them for mockeries, even while I cannot elude their presence, and I fight and grapple with them...." Dreams, oppressive, portentous, menacing, certainly feature in some few of the following stories.

At all events, the simulacra of Borley Rectory prompt two pertinent questions: first, are there truly existences in other dimensions, spiritual realms and conditions, of which our physical and sensual limitations render us ignorant? The sixteenth-century poet Robert Southwell drops an interesting hint of this in the couplet

> So may there be by gifts of ghostly grace,
> One man in many rooms, yet filling none;

and in the same context gives an apt reflection on the perpetuity of spiritual existence in "Dead forms a never-dying life do shroud".... And second, can we ever know, or so much as imagine, the thousand-millionth part of all that exists, or has existed, in the material universe since tangible matter became formed?

The questions must remain open.

And in all matters impinging on the supernatural, a mind of the same quality—an open mind—is, when all is said, your safest cue, parade or repudiate superstition as you will. And here's the advice of Confucius for what it is worth: "Treat all supernatural beings with respect, but keep aloof from them—then you may be called wise."

Finally, do *I* believe in ghosts? Perhaps up to a point, though by no means in an unquestioning child-like way; and if the apparitions were claimed to be innocuous and no corpse-candles were involved, then I should very likely be more amused than alarmed, and more preoccupied with possible psychical side effects than with the appearance of the wraith itself.

But if, as it seems, I stand in the ranks of believers or at any rate of compromisers, how do I begin to *prove* the existence of a ghost?

Frankly, I haven't the *ghost* of an idea. I can only reiterate: *strange things do happen.*

MALIGN INFLUENCES
SORCERIES
EVIL POWERS

THE STALLS OF BARCHESTER CATHEDRAL

THIS matter began, as far as I am concerned, with the reading of a notice in the obituary section of the *Gentleman's Magazine* for an early year in the nineteenth century:

"On February 26th, at his residence in the Cathedral Close of Barchester, the Venerable John Benwell Haynes, D.D., aged 57, Archdeacon of Sowerbridge and Rector of Pickhill and Candley. He was of —— College, Cambridge, and where, by talent and assiduity, he commanded the esteem of his seniors; when, at the usual time, he took his first degree, his name stood high in the list of *wranglers*. These academical honours procured for him within a short time a Fellowship of his College. In the year 1783 he received Holy Orders, and was shortly afterwards presented to the perpetual Curacy of Ranxton-sub-Ashe by his friend and patron the late truly venerable Bishop of Lichfield.... His speedy preferments, first to a Prebend, and subsequently to the dignity of Precentor in the Cathedral of Barchester, form an eloquent testimony to the respect in which he was held and to his eminent qualifications. He succeeded to the Archdeaconry upon the sudden decease of Archdeacon Pulteney in 1810. His sermons, ever conformable to the principles of the religion and Church which he adorned, displayed in no ordinary degree, without the least trace of enthusiasm, the refinement of the scholar united with the graces of the Christian. Free from sectarian violence, and informed by the spirit of the truest charity, they will long dwell in the memories of his hearers. (Here a further omission.) The productions of his pen include an able defence of Episcopacy, which, though often perused by the author of this tribute to his memory, afford but one additional instance of the want of liberality and enterprise which is a too common characteristic of the publishers of our generation. His published works are, indeed, confined to a spirited and elegant version of the *Argonautica* of Valerius Flaccus, a volume of *Discourses upon the Several Events in the Life of Joshua*, delivered in his Cathedral, and a number of the charges which he pronounced at various visitations to the clergy of his Archdeaconry. These are distinguished by etc., etc. The urbanity and hospitality of the subject of these lines will not readily be forgotten by those who enjoyed his acquaintance. His interest in the venerable and awful pile under whose hoary vault he was so punctual an attendant, and particularly in the musical portion of its rites, might be termed filial, and formed a strong and delightful contrast to the polite indifference displayed by too many of our Cathedral dignitaries at the present time."

The final paragraph, after informing us that Dr. Haynes died a bachelor, says:

"It might have been augured that an existence so placid and benevolent would have been terminated in a ripe old age by a dissolution equally gradual and calm. But how unsearchable are the workings of Providence! The peaceful and retired seclusion amid which the honoured evening of Dr. Haynes's life was mellowing to its close was destined to be disturbed, nay, shattered, by a tragedy as appalling as it was unexpected. The morning of the 26th of February—"

But perhaps I shall do better to keep back the remainder of the narrative until I have told the circumstances which led up to it. These, as far as they are now accessible, I have derived from another source.

I had read the obituary notice which I have been quoting, quite by chance, along with a great many others of the same period. It had excited some little speculation in my mind, but, beyond thinking that, if I ever had an opportunity of examining the local records of the period indicated, I would try to remember Dr. Haynes, I made no effort to pursue his case.

Quite lately I was cataloguing the manuscripts in the library of the college to which he belonged. I had reached the end of the numbered volumes on the shelves, and I proceeded to ask the librarian whether there were any more books which he thought I ought to include in my description. "I don't think there are," he said, "but we had better come and look at the manuscript class and make sure. Have you time to do that now?" I had time. We went to the library, checked off the manuscripts, and, at the end of our survey, arrived at a shelf of which I had seen nothing. Its contents consisted for the most part of sermons, bundles of fragmentary papers, college exercises, *Cyrus*, an epic poem in several cantos, the product of a country clergyman's leisure, mathematical tracts by a deceased professor, and other similar material of a kind with which I am only too familiar. I took brief notes of these. Lastly, there was a tin box, which was pulled out and dusted. Its label, much faded, was thus inscribed: "Papers of the Ven. Archdeacon Haynes. Bequeathed in 1834 by his sister, Miss Letitia Haynes."

I knew at once that the name was one which I had somewhere encountered, and could very soon locate it. "That must be the Archdeacon Haynes who came to a very odd end at Barchester. I've read his obituary in the *Gentleman's Magazine*. May I take the box home? Do you know if there is anything interesting in it?"

The librarian was very willing that I should take the box and examine it at leisure. "I never looked inside it myself," he said, "but I've always been meaning to. I am pretty sure that is the box which our old Master once said ought never to have been accepted by the college. He said that to Martin years ago; and he said also that as long as he had control over the library it should never be opened. Martin told me about it, and said that he wanted terribly to know what was in it; but the Master was librarian, and always kept the box in the lodge, so there was no getting at it in his time, and when he died it was taken away by mistake by his heirs, and only returned a few years ago. I can't think why I haven't opened it; but, as I have to go away from Cambridge this afternoon, you had better have first go at it. I think I can trust you not to publish anything undesirable in our catalogue."

I took the box home and examined its contents, and thereafter consulted the librarian as to what should be done about publication, and, since I have his leave to make a story out of it, provided I disguise the identity of the people concerned, I will try what can be done.

The materials are, of course, mainly journals and letters. How much I shall quote and how much epitomise must be determined by considerations of space. The proper understanding of the situation has necessitated a little—not very arduous—research, which has been greatly facilitated by the excellent illustrations and text of the Barchester volume in Bell's *Cathedral Series*.

When you enter the choir of Barchester Cathedral now, you pass through a screen of metal and coloured marbles, designed by Sir Gilbert Scott, and find yourself in what I must call a very bare and odiously furnished place. The stalls are modern, without canopies. The place of the dignitaries and the names of the prebends have fortunately been allowed to survive, and are inscribed on small brass plates affixed to the stalls. The organ is in the triforium, and what is seen of the case is Gothic. The reredos and its surroundings are like every other.

Careful engravings of a hundred years ago show a very different state of things. The organ is on a massive classical screen. The stalls are also classical and very massive. There is a baldacchino of wood over the altar, with urns upon its corners. Farther east is a solid altar screen, classical in design, of wood, with a pediment, in which is a triangle surrounded by rays, enclosing certain Hebrew letters in gold. Cherubs contemplate these. There is a pulpit with a great sounding-board at the eastern end of the stalls on the north side, and there is a black and white marble pavement. Two ladies and a gentleman are admiring the general effect. From other sources I gather that the archdeacon's stall then, as now, was next to the bishop's throne at the south-eastern end of the stalls. His house almost faces the west front of the church, and is a fine red-brick building of William the Third's time.

Here Dr. Haynes, already a mature man, took up his abode with his sister in the year 1810. The dignity had long been the object of his wishes, but his predecessor refused to depart until he had attained the age of ninety-two. About a week after he had held a modest festival in celebration of that ninety-second birthday, there came a morning, late in the year, when Dr. Haynes, hurrying cheerfully into his breakfast-room, rubbing his hands and humming a tune, was greeted, and checked in his genial flow of spirits, by the sight of his sister, seated, indeed, in her usual place behind the tea-urn, but bowed forward and sobbing unrestrainedly into her handkerchief. "What—what is the matter? What bad news?" he began. "Oh, Johnny, you've not heard? The poor dear archdeacon!" "The archdeacon, yes? What is it—ill, is he?" "No, no; they found him on the staircase this morning; it is so shocking." "Is it possible! Dear, dear, poor Pulteney! Had there been any seizure?" "They don't think so, and that is almost the worst thing about it. It seems to have been all the fault of that stupid maid of theirs, Jane." Dr. Haynes paused. "I don't quite understand, Letitia. How was the maid at fault?" "Why, as far as I can make out, there was a stair-rod missing, and she never mentioned it, and the poor archdeacon set his foot quite on the edge of the step—you know how slippery that oak is—and it seems he must have fallen almost the whole flight and broken his neck. It *is* so sad for poor Miss Pulteney. Of course, they will get rid of the girl at once. I never liked her." Miss Haynes's grief resumed its sway, but eventually relaxed so far as to permit of her taking some breakfast. Not so her brother, who, after standing in silence before the window for some minutes, left the room, and did not appear again that morning.

I need only add that the careless maid-servant was dismissed forthwith, but that the missing stair-rod was very shortly afterwards found *under* the stair-carpet—an additional proof, if any were needed, of extreme stupidity and carelessness on her part.

For a good many years Dr. Haynes had been marked out by his

ability, which seems to have been really considerable, as the likely successor of Archdeacon Pulteney, and no disappointment was in store for him. He was duly installed, and entered with zeal upon the discharge of those functions which are appropriate to one in his position. A considerable space in his journals is occupied with exclamations upon the confusion in which Archdeacon Pulteney had left the business of his office and the documents appertaining to it. Dues upon Wringham and Barnswood have been uncollected for something like twelve years, and are largely irrecoverable; no visitation has been held for seven years; four chancels are almost past mending. The persons deputised by the archdeacon have been nearly as incapable as himself. It was almost a matter for thankfulness that this state of things had not been permitted to continue, and a letter from a friend confirms this view. "ὁ κατέχων," it says (in rather cruel allusion to the Second Epistle to the Thessalonians), "is removed at last. My poor friend! Upon what a scene of confusion will you be entering! I give you my word that, on the last occasion of my crossing his threshold, there was no single paper that he could lay hands upon, no syllable of mine that he could hear, and no fact in connection with my business that he could remember. But now, thanks to a negligent maid and a loose stair-carpet, there is some prospect that necessary business will be transacted without a complete loss alike of voice and temper." This letter was tucked into a pocket in the cover of one of the diaries.

There can be no doubt of the new archdeacon's zeal and enthusiasm. "Give me but time to reduce to some semblance of order the innumerable errors and complications with which I am confronted, and I shall gladly and sincerely join with the aged Israelite in the canticle which too many, I fear, pronounce but with their lips." This reflection I find, not in a diary, but in a letter; the doctor's friends seem to have returned his correspondence to his surviving sister. He does not confine himself, however, to reflections. His investigation of the rights and duties of his office are very searching and business-like, and there is a calculation in one place that a period of three years will just suffice to set the business of the Archdeaconry upon a proper footing. The estimate appears to have been an exact one. For just three years he is occupied in reforms; but I look in vain at the end of that time for the promised *Nunc dimittis.* He has now found a new sphere of activity. Hitherto his duties have precluded him from more than an occasional attendance at the Cathedral services. Now he begins to take an interest in the fabric and the music. Upon his struggles with the organist, an old gentleman who had been in office since 1786, I have no time to dwell; they were not attended with any marked success. More to the purpose is his sudden growth of enthusiasm for the Cathedral itself and its furniture. There is a draft of a letter to Sylvanus Urban (which I do not think was ever sent) describing the stalls in the choir. As I have said, these were of fairly late date—of about the year 1700, in fact.

"The archdeacon's stall, situated at the south-east end, west of the episcopal throne (now so worthily occupied by the truly excellent prelate who adorns the See of Barchester), is distinguished by some curious ornamentation. In addition to the arms of Dean West, by whose efforts the whole of the internal furniture of the choir was completed, the prayer-desk is terminated at the eastern extremity by three small but remarkable statuettes in the grotesque manner. One is an exquisitely modelled figure of a cat, whose crouching posture suggests with admirable spirit the suppleness, vigilance, and craft of the redoubted adversary of the genus *Mus*. Opposite to this is a figure seated upon a throne and invested with the attributes of royalty; but it is no earthly monarch whom the carver has sought to portray. His feet are studiously concealed by the long robe in which he is draped; but neither the crown nor the cap which he wears suffices to hide the prick-ears and curving horns which betray his Tartarean origin; and the hand which rests upon his knee is armed with talons of horrifying length and sharpness. Between these two figures stands a shape muffled in a long mantle. This might at first sight be mistaken for a monk or 'friar of orders gray', for the head is cowled and a knotted cord depends from somewhere about the waist. A slight inspection, however, will lead to a very different conclusion. The knotted cord is quickly seen to be a halter, held by a hand all but concealed within the draperies; while the sunken features and, horrid to relate, the rent flesh upon the cheek-bones, proclaim the King of Terrors. These figures are evidently the production of no unskilled chisel; and should it chance that any of your correspondents are able to throw light upon their origin and significance, my obligations to your valuable miscellany will be largely increased."

There is more description in the paper, and, seeing that the woodwork in question has now disappeared, it has a considerable interest. A paragraph at the end is worth quoting:

"Some late researches among the Chapter accounts have shown me that the carving of the stalls was not, as was very usually reported, the work of Dutch artists, but was executed by a native of this city or district named Austin. The timber was procured from an oak copse in the vicinity, the property of the Dean and Chapter, known as Holywood. Upon a recent visit to the parish within whose boundaries it is situated, I learned from the aged and truly respectable incumbent that traditions still lingered amongst the inhabitants of the great size and age of the oaks employed to furnish the materials of the stately structure which has been, however imperfectly, described in the above lines. Of one in particular, which stood near the centre of the grove, it is remembered that it was known as the Hanging Oak. The propriety of that title is confirmed by the fact that a quantity of human bones was found in the soil about its roots, and that at certain times of the year it was the custom for those who wished to secure a successful issue to their affairs, whether of love or the ordinary business of life, to suspend from its boughs small images or puppets rudely fashioned of straw, twigs, or the like rustic materials."

So much for the archdeacon's archaeological investigations. To return to his career as it is to be gathered from his diaries. Those of his first three years of hard and careful work show him throughout in high spirits, and, doubtless, during this time, that reputation for hospitality and urbanity which is mentioned in his obituary notice was well deserved. After that, as time goes on, I see a shadow coming over him—destined to develop into utter blackness—which I cannot but think must have been reflected in his outward demeanour. He commits a good deal of his fears and troubles to his diary; there was no other outlet for them. He was unmarried, and his sister was not always with him. But I am much mistaken if he has told all that he might have told. A series of extracts shall be given:

> *Aug.* 30, 1816.—The days begin to draw in more perceptibly than ever. Now that the Archdeaconry papers are reduced to order, I must find some further employment for the evening hours of autumn and winter. It is a great blow that Letitia's health will not allow her to stay through these months. Why not go on with my *Defence of Episcopacy*? It may be useful.
>
> *Sept.* 15.—Letitia has left me for Brighton.
>
> *Oct.* 11.—Candles lit in the choir for the first time at evening prayers. It came as a shock: I find that I absolutely shrink from the dark season.
>
> *Nov.* 17.—Much struck by the character of the carving on my desk: I do not know that I had ever carefully noticed it before. My attention was called to it by an accident. During the *Magnificat* I was, I regret to say, almost overcome with sleep. My hand was resting on the back of the carved figure of a cat which is the nearest to me of the three figures on the end of my stall. I was not aware of this, for I was not looking in that direction, until I was startled by what seemed a softness, a feeling as of rather rough and coarse fur, and a sudden movement, as if the creature were twisting round its head to bite me. I regained complete conscious-

ness in an instant, and I have some idea that I must have uttered a suppressed exclamation, for I noticed that Mr. Treasurer turned his head quickly in my direction. The impression of the unpleasant feeling was so strong that I found myself rubbing my hand upon my surplice. This accident led me to examine the figures after prayers more carefully than I had done before, and I realised for the first time with what skill they are executed.

Dec. 6.—I do indeed miss Letitia's company. The evenings, after I have worked as long as I can at my *Defence*, are very trying. The house is too large for a lonely man, and visitors of any kind are too rare. I get an uncomfortable impression when going to my room that there *is* company of some kind. The fact is (I may as well formulate it to myself) that I hear voices. This, I am well aware, is a common symptom of incipient decay of the brain—and I believe that I should be less disquieted than I am if I had any suspicion that this was the cause. I have none—none whatever, nor is there anything in my family history to give colour to such an idea. Work, diligent work, and a punctual attention to the duties which fall to me is my best remedy, and I have little doubt that it will prove efficacious.

Jan. 1.—My trouble is, I must confess it, increasing upon me. Last night, upon my return after midnight from the Deanery, I lit my candle to go upstairs. I was nearly at the top when something whispered to me, "Let me wish you a happy New Year." I could not be mistaken: it spoke distinctly and with a peculiar emphasis. Had I dropped my candle, as I all but did, I tremble to think what the consequences must have been. As it was, I managed to get up the last flight, and was quickly in my room with the door locked, and experienced no other disturbance.

Jan. 15.—I had occasion to come downstairs last night to my workroom for my watch, which I had inadvertently left on my table when I went up to bed. I think I was at the top of the last flight when I had a sudden impression of a sharp whisper in my ear "*Take care*". I clutched the balusters and naturally looked round at once. Of course, there was nothing. After a moment I went on—it was no good turning back—but I had as nearly as possible fallen: a cat—a large one by the feel of it—slipped between my feet, but again, of course, I saw nothing. It *may* have been the kitchen cat, but I do not think it was.

Feb. 27.—A curious thing last night, which I should like to forget. Perhaps if I put it down here I may see it in its true proportion. I worked in the library from about 9 to 10. The hall and staircase seemed to be unusually full of what I can only call movement without sound: by this I mean that there seemed to be continuous going and coming, and that whenever I ceased writing to listen, or looked out into the hall, the stillness was absolutely unbroken. Nor, in going to my room at an earlier hour than usual —about half-past ten—was I conscious of anything that I could call a noise. It so happened that I had told John to come to my room for the letter to the bishop which I wished to have delivered early in the morning at the Palace. He was to sit up, therefore, and come for it when he heard me retire. This I had for the moment forgotten, though I had remembered to carry the letter with me to my room. But when, as I was winding up my watch, I heard a light tap at the door, and a low voice saying, "May I come in?" (which I most undoubtedly did hear), I recollected the fact, and took up the letter from my dressing-table, saying, "Certainly: come in." No one, however, answered my summons, and it was now that, as I strongly suspect, I committed an error: for I opened the door and held the letter out. There was certainly no one at that moment in the passage, but, in the instant of my standing there, the door at the end opened and John appeared carrying a candle. I asked him whether he had come to the door earlier; but am satisfied that he had not. I do not like the situation; but although my senses were very much on the alert, and though it was some time before I could sleep, I must allow that I perceived nothing further of an untoward character.

With the return of spring, when his sister came to live with him for some months, Dr. Haynes's entries become more cheerful, and, indeed, no symptom of depression is discernible until the early part of September, when he was again left alone. And now, indeed, there is evidence that he was incommoded again, and that more pressingly. To this matter I will return in a moment, but I digress to put in a document which, rightly or wrongly, I believe to have a bearing on the thread of the story.

The account-books of Dr. Haynes, preserved along with his other papers, show, from a date but little later than that of his institution as archdeacon, a quarterly payment of £25 to J.L. Nothing could have been made of this, had it stood by itself. But I connect with it a very dirty and ill-written letter, which, like another that I have quoted, was in a pocket in the cover of a diary. Of date or postmark there is no vestige, and the decipherment was not easy. It appears to run:

Dr Sr.

I have bin expctin to her off you theis last wicks, and not Haveing done so must supose you have not got mine witch was saying how me and my man had met in with bad times this season all seems to go cross with us on the farm and which way to look for the rent we have no knowledge of it this been the sad case with us if you would have the great (liberality *probably, but the exact spelling defies reproduction*) to send fourty pounds otherwise steps will have to be took which I should not wish. Has you was the Means of me losing my place with Dr. Pulteney I think it is only just what I am asking and you know best what I could say if I was Put to it but I do not wish anything of that unpleasant Nature being one that always wish to have everything Pleasant about me.

Your obedt Servt,

JANE LEE.

About the time at which I suppose this letter to have been written there is, in fact, a payment of £40 to J.L.

We return to the diary:

Oct. 22.—At evening prayers, during the Psalms, I had that same experience which I recollect from last year. I was resting my hand on one of the carved figures, as before (I usually avoid that of the cat now), and—I was going to have said—a change came over it, but that seems attributing too much importance to what must, after all, be due to some physical affection in myself: at any rate, the wood seemed to become chilly and soft as if made of wet linen. I can assign the moment at which I became sensible of this. The choir were singing the words (*Set thou an ungodly man to be ruler over him and*) *let Satan stand at his right hand.*

The whispering in my house was more persistent to-night. I seemed not to be rid of it in my room. I have not noticed this before. A nervous man, which I am not, and hope I am not becoming, would have been much annoyed, if not alarmed, by it. The cat was on the stairs to-night. I think it sits there always. There *is* no kitchen cat.

Nov. 15.—Here again I must note a matter I do not understand. I am much troubled in sleep. No definite image presented itself, but I was pursued by the very vivid impression that wet lips were whispering into my ear with great rapidity and emphasis for some time together. After this, I suppose, I fell asleep, but was awakened with a start by a feeling as if a hand were laid on my shoulder. To my intense alarm I found myself standing at the top of the lowest flight of the first staircase. The moon was shining brightly enough through the large window to let me see that there was a large cat on the second or third step. I can make no comment. I crept up to bed again, I do not know how. Yes, mine is a heavy burden. (Then follows a line or two which has been scratched out. I fancy I read something like "acted for the best".)

Not long after this it is evident to me that the archdeacon's firmness began to give way under the pressure of these phenomena. I omit as unnecessarily painful and distressing the ejaculations and prayers which, in the months of December and January, appear for the first time and become increasingly frequent. Throughout this time, however, he is obstinate in clinging to his post. Why he did not plead ill-health and take refuge at Bath or Brighton I cannot tell; my impression is that it would have done him no good; that he was a man who, if he had confessed himself beaten by the annoyances, would have succumbed at once, and that he was conscious of this. He did seek to palliate them by inviting visitors to his house. The result he has noted in this fashion:

> *Jan.* 7.—I have prevailed to my cousin Allen to give me a few days, and he is to occupy the chamber next to mine.
>
> *Jan.* 8.—A still night. Allen slept well, but complained of the wind. My own experiences were as before: still whispering and whispering: what is it that he wants to say?
>
> *Jan.* 9.—Allen thinks this a very noisy house. He thinks, too, that my cat is an unusually large and fine specimen, but very wild.
>
> *Jan.* 10.—Allen and I in the library until 11. He left me twice to see what the maids were doing in the hall: returning the second time he told me he had seen one of them passing through the door at the end of the passage, and said if his wife were here she would soon get them into better order. I asked him what coloured dress the maid wore; he said grey or white. I supposed it would be so.
>
> *Jan.* 11.—Allen left me to-day. I must be firm.

These words, *I must be firm,* occur again and again on subsequent days; sometimes they are the only entry. In these cases they are in an unusually large hand, and dug into the paper in a way which must have broken the pen that wrote them.

Apparently the archdeacon's friends did not remark any change in his behaviour, and this gives me a high idea of his courage and determination. The diary tells us nothing more than I have indicated of the last days of his life. The end of it all must be told in the polished language of the obituary notice:

> The morning of the 26th of February was cold and tempestuous. At an early hour the servants had occasion to go into the front hall of the residence occupied by the lamented subject of these lines. What was their horror upon observing the form of their beloved and respected master lying upon the landing of the principal staircase in an attitude which inspired the gravest fears. Assistance was procured, and an universal consternation was experienced upon the discovery that he had been the object of a brutal and murderous attack. The vertebral column was fractured in more that one place. This might have been the result of a fall: it appeared that the stair-carpet was loosened at one point. But, in addition to this, there were the injuries inflicted upon the eyes, nose and mouth, as if by the agency of some savage animal, which,

dreadful to relate, rendered those features unrecognisable. The vital spark was, it is needless to add, completely extinct, and had been so, upon the testimony of respectable medical authorities, for several hours. The author or authors of this mysterious outrage are alike buried in mystery, and the most active conjecture has hitherto failed to suggest a solution of the melancholy problem afforded by this appalling occurrence.

The writer goes on to reflect upon the possibility that the writings of Mr. Shelley, Lord Byron, and M. Voltaire may have been instrumental in bringing about the disaster, and concludes by hoping, somewhat vaguely, that this event may "operate as an example to the rising generation"; but this portion of his remarks need not be quoted in full.

I had already formed the conclusion that Dr. Haynes was responsible for the death of Dr. Pulteney. But the incident connected with the carved figure of death upon the archdeacon's stall was a very perplexing feature. The conjecture that it had been cut out of the wood of the Hanging Oak was not difficult, but seemed impossible to substantiate. However, I paid a visit to Barchester, partly with the view of finding out whether there were any relics of the woodwork to be heard of. I was introduced by one of the canons to the curator of the local museum, who was, my friend said, more likely to be able to give me information on the point than anyone else. I told this gentleman of the description of certain carved figures and arms formerly on the stalls, and asked whether any had survived. He was able to show me the arms of Dean West and some other fragments. These, he said, had been got from an old resident. who had also once owned a figure—perhaps one of those which I was inquiring for. There was a very odd thing about that figure, he said. "The old man who had it told me that he picked it up in a woodyard, whence he had obtained the still extant pieces, and had taken it home for his children. On the way home he was fiddling about with it and it came in two in his hands, and a bit of paper dropped out. This he picked up and, just noticing that there was writing on it, put it into his pocket, and subsequently into a vase on his mantelpiece. I was at his house not very long ago, and happened to pick up the vase and turn it over to see whether there were any marks on it, and the paper fell into my hand. The old man, on my handing it to him, told me the story I have told you, and said I might keep the paper. It was crumpled and rather torn, so I have mounted it on a card, which I have here. If you can tell me what it means I shall be very glad, and also, I may say, a good deal surprised."

He gave me the card. The paper was quite legibly inscribed in an old hand, and this is what was on it:

When I grew in the Wood
I was water'd wth Blood
Now in the Church I stand
Who that touches me with his Hand
If a Bloody hand he bear
I councell him to be ware
Lest he be fetcht away
Whether by night or day,
But chiefly when the wind blows high
In a night of February.

This I drempt, 26 Febr. A° 1699. JOHN AUSTIN.

"I suppose it is a charm or a spell: wouldn't you call it something of that kind?" said the curator.

"Yes," I said, "I suppose one might. What became of the figure in which it was concealed?"

"Oh, I forgot," said he. "The old man told me it was so ugly and frightened his children so much that he burnt it."

NO. 252 RUE M. LE PRINCE

WHEN in May, 1886, I found myself at last in Paris, I naturally determined to throw myself on the charity of an old chum of mine, Eugene Marie d'Ardeche, who had forsaken Boston a year or more ago on receiving word of the death of an aunt who had left him such property as she possessed. I fancy this windfall surprised him not a little, for the relations between the aunt and nephew had never been cordial, judging from Eugene's remarks touching the lady, who was, it seems, a more or less wicked and witch-like old person, with a penchant for black magic, at least such was the common report.

Why she should leave all her property to d'Ardeche, no one could tell, unless it was that she felt his rather hobbledehoy tendencies towards Buddhism and occultism might some day lead him to her own unhallowed height of questionable illumination. To be sure d'Ardeche reviled her as a bad old woman, being himself in that state of enthusiastic exaltation which sometimes accompanies a boyish fancy for occultism; but in spite of his distant and repellent attitude, Mlle. Blaye de Tartas made him her sole heir, to the violent wrath of a questionable old party known to infamy as the Sar Torrevieja, the "King of the Sorcerers". This malevolent old portent, whose grey and crafty face was often seen in the Rue M. Le Prince during the life of Mlle. de Tartas, had, it seems, fully expected to enjoy her small wealth after her death; and when it appeared that she had left him only the contents of the gloomy old house in the Quartier Latin, giving the house itself and all else of which she died possessed to her nephew in America, the Sar proceeded to remove everything from the place, and then to curse it elaborately and comprehensively, together with all those who should ever dwell therein.

Whereupon he disappeared.

This final episode was the last word I received from Eugene, but I knew the number of the house, 252 Rue M. Le Prince. So, after a day or two given to a first cursory survey of Paris, I started across the Seine to find Eugene and compel him to do the honours of the city.

Everyone who knows the Latin Quarter knows the Rue M. Le

Prince, running up the hill towards the Garden of the Luxembourg. It is full of queer houses and odd corners—or was in '86—and certainly No. 252 was, when I found it, quite as queer as any. It was nothing but a doorway, a black arch of old stone between and under two new houses painted yellow. The effect of this bit of seventeenth century masonry, with its dirty old doors, and rusty broken lantern sticking gaunt and grim out over the narrow sidewalk, was, in its frame of fresh plaster, sinister in the extreme.

I wondered if I had made a mistake in the number; it was quite evident that no one lived behind those cobwebs. I went into the doorway of one of the new hotels and interviewed the concierge.

No, M. d'Ardeche did not live there, though to be sure he owned the mansion; he himself resided in Meudon, in the country house of the late Mlle. de Tartas. Would Monsieur like the number and the street?

Monsieur would like them extremely, so I took the card that the concierge wrote for me, and forthwith started for the river, in order that I might take a steamboat for Meudon. By one of those coincidences which happen so often, being quite inexplicable, I had not gone twenty paces down the street before I ran directly into the arms of Eugene d'Ardeche. In three minutes we were sitting in the queer little garden of the Chien Bleu, drinking vermouth and absinthe, and talking it all over.

"You do not live in your aunt's house?" I said at last, interrogatively.

"No, but if this sort of thing keeps on I shall have to. I like Meudon much better, and the house is perfect, all furnished, and nothing in it newer than the last century. You must come out with me tonight and see it. I have got a jolly room fixed up for my Buddha. But there is something wrong with this house opposite. I can't keep a tenant in it—not four days. I have had three, all within six months, but the stories have gone around and a man would as soon think of hiring the Cour des Comptes to live in as Number 252. It is notorious. The fact is, it is haunted the worst way."

I laughed and ordered more vermouth.

"That is all right. It is haunted all the same, or enough to keep it empty, and the funny part is that no one knows *how* it is haunted. Nothing is ever seen, nothing heard. As far as I can find out, people just have the horrors there, and have them so bad they have to go to the hospital afterwards. I have one ex-tenant in the Bicêtre now. So the house stands empty, and as it covers considerable ground and is taxed for a lot, I don't know what to do about it. I think I'll either give it to that child of sin, Torrevieja, or else go and live in it myself. I shouldn't mind the ghosts, I am sure."

"Did you ever stay there?"

"No, but I have always intended to, and in fact I came up here today to see a couple of rake-hell fellows I know, Fargeau and Duchesne, doctors in the Clinical Hospital beyond here, up by the Parc Mont Souris. They promised that they would spend the night with me some time in my aunt's house—which is called around here, you must know, 'la Bouche d'Enfer'—and I thought perhaps they would make it this week, if they can get off duty. Come up with me while I see them, and then we can go across the river to Véfour's and have some luncheon, you can get your things at the Chatham, and we will go out to Meudon, where of course you will spend the night with me."

The plan suited me perfectly, so we went up to the hospital, found Fargeau, who declared that he and Duchesne were ready for anything, the nearer the real "bouche d'enfer" the better; that the following Thursday they would both be off duty for the night, and that on that day they would join in an attempt to outwit the devil and clear up the mystery of No. 252.

"Does M. l'Américain go with us?" asked Fargeau.

"Why of course," I replied, "I intend to go, and you must not refuse me, d'Ardeche; I decline to be put off. Here is a chance for you to do the honours of your city in a manner which is faultless. Show me a real live ghost, and I will forgive Paris for having lost the Jardin Mabille."

So it was settled.

Later we went down to Meudon and ate dinner in the terrace room of the villa, which was all that d'Ardeche had said, and more, so utterly was its atmosphere that of the seventeenth century. At dinner Eugene told me more about his late aunt, and the queer goings on in the old house.

Mlle. Blaye lived, it seems, all alone, except for one female servant of her own age; a severe, taciturn creature, with massive Breton features and a Breton tongue, whenever she vouchsafed to use it. No one was ever seen to enter the door of No. 252 except Jeanne the servant and the Sar Torrevieja, the latter coming constantly from none knew whither, and always entering, *never leaving*. Indeed, the neighbours, who for eleven years had watched the old sorcerer sidle crab-wise up to the bell almost every day, declared vociferously that *never* had he been seen to leave the house. Once, when they decided to keep absolute guard, the watcher, none other than Maître Garceau of the Chien Bleu, after keeping his eyes fixed on the door from ten o'clock one morning when the Sar arrived until four in the afternoon, during which time the door was unopened (he knew this, for had he not gummed a ten-centime stamp over the joint and was not the stamp unbroken?) nearly fell down when the sinister figure of Torrevieja slid wickedly by him with a dry "Pardon, Monsieur!" and disappeared again through the black doorway.

This was curious, for No. 252 was entirely surrounded by houses, its only windows opening on a courtyard into which no eye could look from the hotels of the Rue M. Le Prince and the Rue de l'École, and the mystery was one of the choice possessions of the Latin Quarter.

Once a year the austerity of the place was broken, and the denizens of the whole quarter stood open-mouthed watching many carriages drive up to No. 252, many of them private, not a few with crests on the door panels, from all of them descending veiled female figures and men with coat collars turned up. Then followed curious sounds of music from within, and those whose houses joined the blank walls of No. 252 became for the moment popular, for by placing the ear against the wall strange music could distinctly be heard, and the sound of monotonous chanting voices now and then. By dawn the last guest would have departed, and for another year the hotel of Mlle. de Tartas was ominously silent.

Eugene declared that he believed it was a celebration of "Walpurgisnacht", and certainly appearances favoured such a fancy.

"A queer thing about the whole affair is," he said, "the fact that everyone in the street swears that about a month ago, while I was out in Concarneau for a visit, the music and voices were heard again, just as when my revered aunt was in the flesh. The house was perfectly empty, as I tell you, so it is quite possible that the good people were enjoying an hallucination."

I must acknowledge that these stories did not reassure me; in fact, as Thursday came near, I began to regret a little my determination to spend the night in the house. I was too vain to back down, however, and the perfect coolness of the two doctors, who ran down Tuesday to Meudon to make a few arrangements, caused me to swear that I would die of fright before I would flinch. I suppose I believed more or less in ghosts, I am sure now that I am older I believe in them, there are in fact few things I can *not* believe. Two or three inexplicable things had happened to me, and, although this was before my adventure with Rendel in Paestum I had a strong predisposition to believe some things that I could not explain, wherein I was out of sympathy with the age.

Well, to come to the memorable night of the twelfth of June, we had made our preparations, and after depositing a big bag inside the doors of No. 252, went across to the Chien Bleu, where Fargeau and Duchesne turned up promptly, and we sat down to the best dinner Père Garceau could create.

I remember I hardly felt that the conversation was in good taste. It began with various stories of Indian fakirs and Oriental jugglery, matters in which Eugene was curiously well read, swerved to the horrors of the great Sepoy mutiny, and thus to reminiscences of the dissecting-room. By this time we had drunk more or less, and Duchesne launched into a photographic and Zolaesque account of the only time (as he said) when he was possessed of the panic of fear; namely, one night many years ago, when he was locked by accident into the dissecting-room of the Loucine, together with several cadavers of a rather unpleasant nature. I ventured to protest mildly against the choice of subjects, the result being a perfect carnival of horrors, so that when we finally drank our last *crème de cacao* and started for "la Bouche d'Enfer", my nerves were in a somewhat rocky condition.

It was just ten o'clock when we came into the street. A hot dead wind drifted in great puffs through the city, and ragged masses of vapour swept the purple sky; an unsavoury night altogether, one of those nights of hopeless lassitude when one feels, if one is at home, like doing nothing but drink mint juleps and smoke cigarettes.

Eugene opened the creaking door, and tried to light one of the lanterns; but the gusty wind blew out every match, and we finally had to close the outer doors before we could get a light. At last we had all the lanterns going, and I began to look around curiously. We were in a long, vaulted passage, partly carriageway, partly footpath, perfectly bare but for the street refuse which had drifted in with eddying winds. Beyond lay the courtyard, a curious place rendered more curious still by the fitful moonlight and the flashing of four dark lanterns. The place had evidently been once a most noble palace. Opposite rose the oldest portion, a three-storey wall of the time of Francis I., with a great wisteria vine covering half. The wings on either side were more modern, seventeenth century, and ugly, while towards the street was nothing but a flat unbroken wall.

The great bare court, littered with bits of paper blown in by the wind, fragments of packing cases, and straw, mysterious with flashing lights and flaunting shadows, while low masses of torn vapour drifted overhead, hiding, then revealing, the stars, and all in absolute silence, not even the sounds of the streets entering this prison-like place, was weird and uncanny in the extreme. I must confess that already I began to feel a slight disposition towards the horrors, but with that curious inconsequence which so often happens in the case of those who are deliberately growing scared, I could think of nothing more reassuring than those delicious verses of Lewis Carroll's—

Just the place for a Snark! I have said it twice,
That alone should encourage the crew.
Just the place for a Snark! I have said it thrice,
What I tell you three times is true—

which kept repeating themselves over and over in my brain with feverish insistence.

Even the medical students had stopped their chaffing, and were studying the surroundings gravely.

"There is one thing certain," said Fargeau, "*anything* might have happened here without the slightest chance of discovery. Did ever you see such a perfect place for lawlessness?"

"And *anything* might happen here now, with the same certainty of impunity," continued Duchesne, lighting his pipe, the snap of the match making us all start. "D'Ardeche, your lamented relative was certainly well fixed; she had full scope here for her traditional experiments in demonology."

"Curse me if I don't believe that those same traditions were more or less founded on fact," said Eugene. "I never saw this court under these conditions before, but I could believe anything now. What's that?"

"Nothing but a door slamming," said Duchesne, loudly.

"Well, I wish doors wouldn't slam in houses that have been empty for eleven months."

"It is irritating"—and Duchesne slipped his arm through mine—"but we must take things as they come. Remember we have to deal not only with the spectral lumber left here by your scarlet aunt, but as well with the supererogatory curse of that hell-cat Torrevieja. Come on! Let's get inside before the hour arrives for the sheeted dead to squeak and gibber in these lonely halls. Light your pipes, your tobacco is a sure protection against 'your whoreson dead bodies'; light up and move on."

We opened the hall door and entered a vaulted stone vestibule, full of dust, and cobwebby.

"There is nothing on this floor," said Eugene, "except servants' rooms and offices, and I don't believe there is anything wrong with them. I never heard that there was, anyway. Let's go upstairs."

So far as we could see, the house was apparently perfectly uninteresting inside, all eighteenth century work, the façade of the main building being, with the vestibule, the only portion of the Francis I. work.

"The place was burned during the Terror," said Eugene, "for my great-uncle, from whom Mlle. de Tartas inherited it, was a good and true Royalist; he went to Spain after the Revolution, and did not come back until the accession of Charles the Tenth, when he restored the house, and then died, enormously old. This explains why it is all so new."

The old Spanish sorcerer to whom Mlle. de Tartas had left her personal property had done his work thoroughly. The house was absolutely empty, even the wardrobes and bookcases built in had been carried away; we went through room after room, finding all absolutely dismantled, only the windows and doors with their casings, the parquet floors, and the florid Renaissance mantels remaining.

"I feel better," remarked Fargeau. "The house may be haunted, but it don't look it, certainly; it is the most respectable place imaginable."

"Just you wait," replied Eugene. "These are only the state apartments, which my aunt seldom used, except, perhaps, on her annual 'Walpurgisnacht'. Come upstairs and I will show you a better *mise en scène*."

On this floor, the rooms fronting the court—the sleeping-rooms—were quite small ("They are the bad rooms all the same," said Eugene); four of them, all just as ordinary in appearance as those below. A corridor ran behind them connecting with the wing corridor, and from this opened a door, unlike any of the other doors in that it was covered with green baize, somewhat moth-eaten. Eugene selected a key from the bunch he carried, unlocked the door, and with some difficulty forced it to swing inward; it was as heavy as the door of a safe.

"We are now," he said, "on the very threshold of hell itself; these rooms in here were my scarlet aunt's unholy of unholies. I never let them with the rest of the house, but keep them as a curiosity. I only wish Torrevieja had kept out; as it was, he looted them, as he did the rest of the house, and nothing is left but the walls and ceiling and floor. They are something, however, and may suggest what the former condition must have been. Tremble and enter."

The first apartment was a kind of anteroom, a cube of perhaps twenty feet each way, without windows, and with no doors except that by which we entered, and another to the right. Walls, floor, and ceiling were covered with a black lacquer, brilliantly polished, that flashed the light of our lanterns in a thousand intricate reflections. It was like the inside of an enormous Japanese box, and about as empty. From this we passed to another room, and here we nearly dropped our lanterns. The room was circular, thirty feet or so in diameter, covered by a hemispherical dome; walls and ceiling were dark blue, spotted with gold stars; and reaching from floor to floor across the dome stretched a colossal figure in red lacquer of a nude woman kneeling, her head touching the lintel of the door through which we had entered, her arms forming its sides, with the forearms extended and stretching along the walls until they met the long feet. The most astounding, misshapen, absolutely terrifying thing, I think, I ever saw. From the navel hung a great white object, like the traditional roc's egg of the Arabian Nights. The floor was of red lacquer, and in it was inlaid a pentagram the size of the room, made of wide strips of brass. In the centre of this pentagram was a circular disk of black stone, slightly saucer-shaped, with a small outlet in the middle.

The effect of the room was simply crushing, with this gigantic red figure crouched over it all; the staring eyes fixed no one, no matter what his position. None of us spoke, so oppressive was the whole thing.

The third room was like the first in dimensions, but instead of being black it was entirely sheathed with plates of brass, walls, ceiling, and floor—tarnished now, and turning green, but still brilliant under the lantern light. In the middle stood an oblong altar of porphyry, its longer dimensions on the axis of the suite of rooms, and at one end, opposite the range of doors, a pedestal of black basalt.

This was all. Three rooms stranger than these, even in their emptiness, it would be hard to imagine. In Egypt, in India, they would not be entirely out of place, but here in Paris, in a commonplace hotel, in the Rue M. Le Prince, they were incredible.

We retraced our steps, Eugene closed the iron door with its baize covering, and we went into one of the front chambers and sat down, looking at each other.

"Nice party, your aunt," said Fargeau. "Nice old party, with amiable tastes; I am glad we are not to spend the night in *those* rooms."

"What do you suppose she did in there?" inquired Duchesne. "I know more or less about black art, but that series of rooms is too much for me."

"My impression is," said d'Ardeche, "that the brazen room was a kind of sanctuary containing some image or other on the basalt base, while the stone in front was really an altar—what the nature of the sacrifice might be I don't even guess. The round room may have been used for invocations and incantations. The pentagram looks like it. Anyway it is all just as queer and *fin de siècle* as I can well imagine. Look here, it is nearly twelve, let's dispose of ourselves, if we are going to hunt this thing down."

The four chambers on this floor of the old house were those said to be haunted, the wings being quite innocent, and, so far as we knew, the floors below. It was arranged that we should each occupy a room, leaving the doors open with the lights burning, and at the slightest cry or knock we were all to rush at once to the room from which the warning sound might come. There was no communication between the rooms, to be sure, but, as the doors all opened into the corridor, every sound was plainly audible.

The last room fell to me, and I looked it over carefully.

It seemed innocent enough, a commonplace, square, rather lofty Parisian sleeping-room, finished in wood painted white, with a small marble mantel, a dusty floor of inlaid maple and cherry, walls hung with an ordinary French paper, apparently quite new, and two deeply embrasured windows looking out on the court.

I opened the swinging sash with some trouble, and sat down in the window seat with my lantern beside me trained on the only door, which gave on the corridor.

The wind had gone down, and it was very still without—still and hot. The masses of luminous vapour were gathering thickly overhead, no longer urged by the gusty wind. The great masses of rank wisteria leaves, with here and there a second blossoming of purple flowers, hung dead over the window in the sluggish air. Across the roofs I could hear the sound of a belated *fiacre* in the streets below. I filled my pipe again and waited.

For a time the voices of the men in the other rooms were a companionship, and at first I shouted to them now and then, but my voice echoed rather unpleasantly through the long corridors, and had a suggestive way of reverberating around the left wing beside me, and coming out at a broken window at its extremity like the voice of another man. I soon gave up my attempts at conversation, and devoted myself to the task of keeping awake.

It was not easy; why did I eat that lettuce salad at Père Garceau's? I should have known better. It was making me irresistibly sleepy, and wakefulness was absolutely necessary. It was certainly gratifying to know that I could sleep, that my courage was by me to that extent, but in the interests of science I must keep awake. But almost never, it seemed, had sleep looked so desirable. Half a hundred times, nearly, I would doze for an instant, only to awake with a start, and find my pipe gone out. Nor did the exertion of relighting it pull me together. I struck my match mechanically, and with the first puff dropped off again. It was most vexing. I got up and walked around the room. It was most annoying. My cramped position had almost put both legs to sleep. I could hardly stand. I felt numb, as though with cold. There was no longer any sound from the other rooms, nor from without. I sank down in my window seat. How dark it was growing! I turned up the lantern. That pipe again, how obstinately it kept going out! And my last match was gone. The lantern, too, was *that* going out? I lifted my hand to turn it up again. It felt like lead, and fell beside me.

Then I awoke—absolutely. I remembered the story of "The Haunters and the Haunted". *This* was the Horror. I tried to rise, to cry out. My body was like lead, my tongue was paralysed. I could hardly move my eyes. And the light was going out. There was no question about that. Darker and darker yet; little by little the pattern of the paper was swallowed up in the advancing night. A prickling numbness gathered in every nerve, my right arm slipped without feeling from my lap to my side, and I could not raise it—it swung helpless. A thin, keen humming began in my head, like the cicadas on a hillside in September. The darkness was coming fast.

Yes, this was it. Something was subjecting me, body and mind, to slow paralysis. Physically I was already dead. If I could only hold my mind, my consciousness, I might still be safe, but could I? Could I resist the mad horror of this silence, the deepening dark, the creeping numbness? I knew that, like the man in the ghost story, my only safety lay here.

It had come at last. My body was dead, I could no longer move my eyes. They were fixed in that last look on the place where the door had been, now only a deepening of the dark.

Utter night: the last flicker of the lantern was gone. I sat and waited; my mind was still keen, but how long would it last? There was a limit even to the endurance of the utter panic of fear.

Then the end began. In the velvet blackness came two white eyes, milky, opalescent, small, far away—awful eyes, like a dead dream. More beautiful than I can describe, the flakes of white flame moving from the perimeter inward, disappearing in the centre, like a never ending flow of opal water into a circular tunnel. I could not have moved my eyes had I possessed the power: they devoured the fearful, beautiful orbs that grew slowly, slowly larger, fixed on me, advancing, growing more beautiful, the white flakes of light sweeping more swiftly into the blazing vortices, the awful fascination deepening in its insane intensity as the white, vibrating eyes grew nearer, larger.

Like a hideous and implacable engine of death the eyes of the unknown Horror swelled and expanded until they were close before me, enormous, terrible, and I felt a slow, cold, wet breath propelled with mechanical regularity against my face, enveloping me in its fetid mist, in its charnel-house deadliness.

With ordinary fear goes always a physical terror, but with me in the presence of this unspeakable Thing was only the utter and awful terror of the mind, the mad fear of a prolonged and ghostly nightmare. Again and again I tried to shriek, to make some noise, but physically I was utterly dead. I could only feel myself go mad with the terror of hideous death. The eyes were close on me—their movement so swift that they seemed to be but palpitating flames, the dead breath was around me like the depths of the deepest sea.

Suddenly a wet, icy mouth, like that of a dead cuttle-fish, shapeless, jelly-like, fell over mine. The horror began slowly to draw my life from me, but, as enormous and shuddering folds of palpitating jelly swept sinuously around me, my will came back, my body awoke with the reaction of final fear, and I closed with the nameless death that enfolded me.

What was it that I was fighting? My arms sank through the unresisting mass that was turning me to ice. Moment by moment new folds of cold jelly swept round me, crushing me with the force of Titans. I fought to wrest my mouth from this awful Thing that sealed it, but, if ever I succeeded and caught a single breath, the wet, sucking mass closed over my face again before I could cry out. I think I fought for hours, desperately, insanely, in a silence that was more hideous than any sound—fought until I felt final death at hand, until the memory of all my life rushed over me like a flood, until I no longer had strength to wrench my face from that hellish succubus, until with a last mechanical struggle I fell and yielded to death.

Then I heard a voice say, "If he is dead, I can never forgive myself; I was to blame."

Another replied, "He is not dead, I know we can save him if only we reach the hospital in time. Drive like hell, *cocher!* Twenty francs for you, if you get there in three minutes."

Then there was night again, and nothingness, until I suddenly awoke and stared around. I lay in a hospital ward, very white and sunny, some yellow *fleurs-de-lis* stood beside the head of the pallet, and a tall sister of mercy sat by my side.

To tell the story in a few words, I was in the Hotel Dieu, where the men had taken me that fearful night of the twelfth of June. I asked for Fargeau or Duchesne, and by-and-by the latter came, and sitting beside the bed told me all that I did not know.

It seems that they had sat, each in his room, hour after hour, hearing nothing, very much bored, and disappointed. Soon after two o'clock Fargeau, who was in the next room, called to me to ask if I was awake. I gave no reply, and, after shouting once or twice, he took his lantern and came to investigate. The door was locked on the inside! He instantly called d'Ardeche and Duchesne, and together they hurled themselves against the door. It resisted. Within they could hear irregular footsteps dashing here and there, with heavy breathing. Although frozen with terror, they fought to destroy the door and finally succeeded by using a great slab of marble that formed the shelf of the mantel in Fargeau's room. As the door crashed in, they were suddenly hurled back against the walls of the corridor, as though by an explosion, the lanterns were extinguished, and they found themselves in utter silence and darkness.

As soon as they recovered from the shock, they leaped into the room and fell over my body in the middle of the floor. They lighted one of the lanterns, and saw the strangest sight that can be imagined. The floor and walls to the height of about six feet were running with something that seemed like stagnant water, thick, glutinous, sickening. As for me, I was drenched with the same cursed liquid. The odour of musk was nauseating. They dragged me away, stripped off my clothing, wrapped me in their coats, and hurried to the hospital, thinking me perhaps dead. Soon after sunrise d'Ardeche left the hospital, being assured that I was in a fair way to recovery, with time, and with Fargeau went up to examine by daylight the traces of the adventure that was so nearly fatal. They were too late. Fire engines were coming down the street as they passed the Académie. A neighbour rushed up to d'Ardeche: "Oh Monsieur! What misfortune, yet what fortune! It is true *la Bouche d'Enfer*—I beg pardon, the residence of the lamented Mlle. de Tartas—was burned, but not wholly, only the ancient building. The wings were saved, and for that great credit is due to the brave firemen. Monsieur will remember them, no doubt."

It was quite true. Whether a forgotten lantern, overturned in the excitement, had done the work, or whether the origin of the fire was more supernatural, it was certain that "the Mouth of Hell" was no more. A last engine was pumping slowly as d'Ardeche came up; half a dozen limp, and one distended hose stretched through the *porte cochère*, and within, only the façade of Francis I. remained, draped still with the black stems of the wisteria. Beyond lay a great vacancy, where thin smoke was rising slowly. Every floor was gone, and the strange halls of Mlle. Blaye de Tartas were only a memory.

With d'Ardeche I visited the place last year, but in the stead of the ancient walls was then only a new and ordinary building, fresh and respectable; yet the wonderful stories of the old *Bouche d'Enfer* still lingered in the Quarter, and will hold there, I do not doubt, until the Day of Judgement.

OUT OF THE PICTURE

I

In the old days—which means anything from ten to thirty years ago*—there was a question which used to be asked now and then at studio parties and Chelsea pubs. The question was:

"But who was the twisted man?"

And it was often followed by another:

"But where did M'Calmont take himself off to?"

Neither interrogation ever got an answer; save that to the second query, a young man in very full dark green corduroy trousers is reported to have said once on a time:

"Somebody told me he had been seen in Quito."

But to this neither credit nor attention was given. And it is probable from what follows that the double enigma is to be reckoned with that question as to what song the Sirens sang; if, indeed, it is not past all solution.

Going back, then, to those old days aforesaid, and rather to the earlier portion of them, when, as a journalist, I saw many strange things and people; I was once sent to view an exhibition of pictures at the Molyneux Galleries in Danby Place. Perhaps the event may be sufficiently dated by saying that the Exhibition was opened somewhere between the Battle of Sidney Street and the Coronation of King George V; and I have a feeling that it was a misty May morning when I went to see it. It was not a large exhibition: all the pictures were contained in two sizeable rooms, and as soon as I got into them I saw at once that I could make nothing of it—that is, from any serious standpoint. I cared nothing; my point of view in that instance, as in all others like it, was, that if the paper chose to send an outsider and an ignoramous to criticise works of art—especially the works of a new and tentative and experimental school—then, on the head of the paper let the just doom fall. And the school represented on this particular occasion at the Molyneux Galleries evidently represented a fierce revolt against the traditions and conventions of the elders. To begin with; my eye was caught by

* Before the time when this story was written—*Ed.*

"The Old Harbour". There were buildings in vertical perspective, their walls appearing to incline together and to aspire to meet in the upper part of the canvas, and with a sense about them as if the whole mass were unstable, impermanent, void of true solidity and settlement on the earth. A mystic once told me that after he had finished his meditation and gone out into the street, he had seen the grey bulk of the houses opposite suddenly melt, evaporate, go up like smoke, leaving void nothingness in their place. And so the painter with his art had made these warehouses and Customs buildings, or whatever they were, in such a fashion that they seemed as if they also were on the very point to turn to mist, to float into the air, and to disappear. And then, for the rest, there was grey water, and segments, and portions, and particles of keels, sails, masts, ropes, decks, and deck furniture, not cohering, or fitting together, but dispersed and apart. Here, I could see, was choice matter on which the expert and the art critic could exercise their knowledge and judgement. As I had neither, I made an experiment or two, and was able to inform the readers of the paper that if you walked briskly past the picture, winking both eyes as fast as possible, you really got a sort of impression of movement and activity, of ships and boats coming into harbour and sailing out of it, of sails lowered and hoisted, of an uncertain background, now obscured, now left visible as a ship in full sail passed before it. It struck me that, in my hands, art criticism was in a fair way to become a popular sport.

And then there was another picture that both attracted and distracted me. It was a big canvas, and the subject was a number of geometrical figures of all kinds, most ingeniously fitted into one another, and rainbow painted, no doubt on some occult principle of contrast and complement and correspondence. It was called "King Solomon's Cargoes". I murmured: "Gold and silver and ivory and apes and peacocks," and looked for them. I could not see any of them, and I thought I would go back to Fleet Street, relying on my impressions of "The Old Harbour", which would just fill the "two sticks" that had been allotted to the story. It was, decidedly, a case of least said, soonest mended. In spite of the defence which, as I have mentioned, I had ready, I felt I was on unsafe and treacherous ground. Who was I to sit in judgement on the work of painters? No doubt, I might say that I had looked for apes and peacocks in that picture and had found none; and, likely enough, that remark might merely serve to display my utter ignorance of the subject I was pretending to treat. But it was not written that I should escape "King Solomon's Cargoes" so easily.

It was some years after the exhibition at the Molyneux Galleries that I found myself in a various company one evening. I saw a few people that I knew, and was talking to one of them, when the friend who had brought me along came and said:

"Do you mind if I introduce you to a man? It's M'Calmont, the painter, who says he's been wanting to meet you for years. Some criticism of yours that he read seems to have made a great impression on him."

He took me up to a dark, slight man with a black moustache, and left me. M'Calmont made room on the settee, and began at once:

"I've been wanting to thank you for a long time for that notice you wrote in your paper about the Exhibition in the Molyneux Galleries. You'll remember? It was in Coronation year."

I told him I thought I did remember something about it. But I wondered, internally, what sort of thanks I was going to get from a painter for my vain ribaldry. He went on:

"I said to myself at the time: 'This A.M., whoever he may be, has got an eye to detect the falsities and fallacies, and I'd like to have a talk with him. Then somebody told me your name, but I left town soon after, and this is the first chance I've had."

And, finally, it came to this: that the falsities and fallacies were the picture of "The Old Harbour", by Frank Guildford, and M'Calmont had enjoyed the way I had stuck my knife into the fellow.

I explained. I said I knew nothing about painting, and had been afraid that I had been guilty of ill-placed and unmannerly humour. He wouldn't hear of this.

"It was just instinct, pure instinct. You may not have the technical knowledge, but you know a silly man when you see him."

I asked what had become of this unhappy man.

"He's what they call a fashionable painter, and makes his eight thousand a year by painting grocers and their wives—damn him!"

And he went on:

"I don't know whether you happened to see a thing I had in that Exhibition? I called it 'King Solomon's Cargoes'."

I lied. I dwelt again and more forcibly on the utter unscrupulousness of my character when simulating an art critic. I said I had not seen his canvas. I had just dashed into the galleries, invented my silly game with the ships in the harbour, and run out again as soon as I had got material for my two or three paragraphs. But, in fact, I remembered those purple squares, scarlet triangles, sky-blue circles very well.

M'Calmont nodded his head gloomily.

"I'm glad it didn't catch your eye. You might have had something to say to me too. You'd have been right, and you'd have been wrong. I was never a faker like Guildford. I never pretended that if you painted a bit of mast here and a scrap of sail there and a deck in another part of the canvas you could call it painting a ship. But I did believe in abstract painting—and I do still in a way."

I asked him to tell me all about it.

"I'd like to explain what I was after in those days. You say you know nothing about the technical side of painting. You won't want to know anything about it: it's not a technical question. It's behind all that and beyond it. But you can't talk sense in the middle of all these havers. Come away."

I followed him out, and by devious and obscure ways he led me to an obscure tavern, where we sat down together in a quiet corner of a bulging and old-fashioned bar. They spoke his language there, since his order for "two wee halfyins" was fulfilled without comment. But I looked at the stuff in my glass, and remembered how the poet had said long ago that the half is greater than the whole—"greater," I corrected mentally, "than the double." I added water.

"Don't kill good drink," M'Calmont said reproachfully. "*Scelus est jugulare Falernum,* and this is better. It's the genuine Lagavulin, not the trash they sell in London for whisky. But you were asking about abstract painting. It will be necessary to go back and away a little if we're to see what we're after. They say distance lends enchantment to the view; I'd put it myself, 'lends vision,' *theoria.* It may turn out, of course, that when you do see, you see enchantment, but that is just secondary; a kind of by-product, you might say, of the proposition. I'll ask you, then, if you know anything about the Kabbala of the Hebrews?"

Whatever I knew of that matter, I dissembled. I am a lover of the rich improbabilities, and I would not check this rare manifestation of them.

"Well, I don't want you to feel like a cow in a fremd loaming; so we won't go deeply into those dark mysteries. But the Kabbalists tell us that at the Fall of Man, the Serpent did not ascend to Kether in the Tree of Life. It stopped at Daath. And that's their way of saying that the nature of man was not entirely corrupted. The Serpent poisoned and infected the logical understanding, but there was a pure, spiritual region above that which remained untouched.

"Very good. You see that? And there you have the reason why a man that's sunk deep in the blackest mud of materialism may very possibly be overcome with delight at the Fugues of Bach. You'll see how that may be? That's absolute music. It has nothing to do with Daath, the logical understanding. I'm speaking, you understand, of the pattern of sounds that reaches the ears of the hearer; just the ordered noise that he hears, if you like to put it that way. In the making of the music, no doubt, in the technical part of the creation, the understanding had its share, as the slave of the spirit. If you want to build Jerusalem with its Temple you must have your hewers of wood and stone, and drawers of water. You're a writer yourself, and you know you can't do much in that way without calling in the aid of the pen-makers and the ink manufacturers and the paper merchants; but you don't allow them to teach you how to turn the phrase.

"But the way the thing is fashioned is nothing to do with us. What we're concerned with is the thing we hear; and with that thing the logical understanding has just no concern at all. You'll note there's no tongue or language in which we can speak of it. There's no answer to the question: 'But what does it mean?' when that question is asked of pure music. Bach, you may say, had the gift of tongues; but in his case there's no legitimate gift of the interpretation of tongues. It's impossible to translate the language of Kether into the speech of Daath. I remember well going to hear *Lohengrin,* and there was a manner of commentary attached to the bill of the opera. I just glanced at it and saw that when the overture began I was to picture to myself a blue sky, and then to watch the wee white clouds forming on it. There you have your music critic calling in nature, and I saw in the paper, there was another of them puzzling his head over Berlioz, and deciding that he was a 'pictural', not a 'linear' composer—calling in the terms of another art. And you'll hear often enough of the 'magnificent colour' of this or that passage of music. And I don't say they can do better. But it proves what I am telling you: that the understanding has nothing to do with absolute music, and nothing to say to it.

"Aye, and what about painting? That's the question I asked myself years ago. You know Aristotle says that all art is imitation. It's a very questionable pronouncement. If I'm not mistaken, he had the drama chiefly in his mind when he made it. But the drama is just an impure or mixed development of the dance. In its primitive, original form, the dance was not an imitation of anything. It was, like music, an expression of something; but that's different. You may say that the drama of the Greeks was the dance set to words. And then, there's architecture. You can't say that the Parthenon is an imitation of anything, or that Rheims Cathedral is an imitation of anything. And literature. I shan't need to tell you that all the things we value most in the finest literature are just the things that soar above the sense—that is the logical understanding of it. If you turn to the Book and read Second Samuel, one, seventeen, you'll find a statement to the effect that David lamented the decease of Saul and Jonathan; but you'll not tell me that the vital interest and value of that proposition is to be discovered in the logical sense of it. And if you read Coleridge's *Kubla Khan,* I think you'll be puzzled to find out the logical sense in it and to tell me what it is. But there you have literature almost becoming music.

"And now you see what I've been getting at all the while."

I did not; but I forbore to say so.

"It was just this: that I asked myself why should there not be abstract or absolute painting, as well as absolute music and architecture? In the past, painting has been almost entirely Aristotelian, imitative. Why should it continue wholly on those lines? And you'll have gathered that I don't consider you solve the problem by cracking an object up into bits and scraps and pieces, and then painting the bits as they lie abroad. And if you paint a man's hands three times their natural size and draw a jackass with five legs, I'm not thinking you're any nearer to a solution. And that's how I came to paint the picture that I sent into those Galleries, that I'm glad now you didn't see. I was on the wrong track."

He lapsed at last into silence. I broke it by making a proposition remote from pure aesthetics. He declined to accede to it.

"No, no," said M'Calmont, "I'll not hear of it. In the 'Crown and Thistle', I'm in Scotland, and you're my guest. Where's the Macfarlane creature?"

When we parted soon after, he wrote his address on a scrap of paper torn from his note-book, and begged me to come and see him some evening.

"I'd like to show you the new track I've found," he said, and vanished into the night, as we came out together.

II

It may be as well to make it clear at once that I am not the man to be daunted by the unusual. I have seen too much of it for that. I know that there are quarters, and very influential quarters, in which it is considered improper to mention such things. Every age has its conventions of propriety and impropriety: every age and every race. The missionary's wife in Africa shocked her two black servants horribly and unspeakably when she said that she was afraid the fruit was too green for a tart. Her husband's name was Green, and every (black) body knows that for a wife to utter her husband's name is both impious and obscene in the highest degree. We talk quite freely in the drawing-room in a style that would have made Dickens run out of the smoking-room, and when we write books we set down boldly words that were only forced out of the policeman of yesterday by the strict order of the Bench. It is all a matter of convention and taboo, and perhaps it is idle to ask for reasons. Mrs. Green, I dare say, couldn't understand why on earth she shouldn't utter the word "green"; and I suppose I am in much the same case when I say that I have no notion why I shouldn't mention the unusual, the odd, the extraordinary, when I come across it. At any rate, I propose to defy this particular convention, here and elsewhere and always. As I was saying, I have seen too much of it to affect disbelief in its existence. I heard from the brassfounders of Clerkenwell about a former member of their craft who had confuted Darwin by the Hebrew alphabet and by the stars, and had buried the pot of gold in the field, where it was found by the navvies who were making the cutting for the Midland Railway. I have discussed with a solicitor, in his London office, the affairs of the J.H.V.S. Syndicate, who were seeking for the Ark of the Covenant from the directions of a cypher contained in that chapter of the Prophet Ezekiel which is called Mercabah. I know all about Campo Tosto, of Burnt Green, near Reigate, who defended his treasures with the bow and arrow. Why, then, should I hush up M'Calmont the painter, who drew his artistic principles from the Hebrew Kabbala?

As a matter of fact, I thought him an interesting man, and determined that I would see more of him. And so, one windy night in October, a few weeks after our meeting, I set out from somewhere in the west and made up the Gray's Inn Road. I am not certain by which street I turned from it. I think, but I am not sure, that it was by Acton Street. I know I had gone too far north, and that when I came to the bottom of the street, and traversed the King's Cross Road, I found out my mistake, and had to incline somewhat to the right in climbing the hill. It is a district both devious and obscure, and I suppose that its twisting streets and unexpected squares of dusty trees will all come to ruin before they are intelligently explored. I had trod these mazes before, and thought I knew them tolerably well, but it was some years since I had been in that region, and I found myself perplexed and at fault, while the great wind blew the leaves of shadowy trees about my head and at my feet. At last I entered a black passage at a venture, and came down a short flight of steps into an irregular open space, on which there abutted a chapel of the Countess of Huntingdon's Connexion. I went round and about this square or triangle or trapezium, which was sparsely lit, till I found the green door in a wall to which I was directed, and rang the bell under the name M'Calmont. It was M'Calmont who opened the door and, taking hold of my arm, led me down a passage, past a house all lit up, where they were singing, and so to his studio, wih trees all about it, bending and tossing and straining in the wind. Inside, there was a hanging lamp, and though it was not cold, the blaze of the fire was cheerful; the lamplight and firelight glittered on the carved and gilded frames of the pictures that hung on the walls. We sat down on a big settee at a comfortable distance from the fire; and he pressed on my attention what he called "Eela" —which is spelt, I found, "Islay".

And then there was more of it. Not of the spirit of the western isle, but of art, as he expounded it. It seemed that he had been forced to modify, one might say, to abandon his earlier views.

"I found out, and I was not so long about it, that you can't have absolute painting any more than you can have absolute literature. There are people, as you know, who are trying their hands at that—by writing gibberish without grammar. And *that* won't do. And I discovered that my endeavours in the direction of pure painting wouldn't do either. The principle of it is all right; but it's not for pigments. If you would carry it out, you must turn Eastern carpet-maker. And I'll maintain that there are Persian carpets as fine as any symphony of Beethoven's. They are the very analogy in colour and form of pure music.

"As it seemed that I couldn't go forward, I went back. And there, as you'll no doubt be well aware, I was in the height of the fashion. The sculptors and the painters too have been trying back for the last quarter of a century. There are men who do their best to forget all the bare elements of their art, their drawing and their perspective and all the rest of it, that they may paint as if they were five years old. Another lot are off to Borrioboolah Gha, to learn the principles of sculpture from black savages. And I've no doubt there's a weary band trying to tramp back all the way to the Stone Age to see what they can find there. It's all very interesting. I'd like it fine—if they'd not call their imitations of barbarism Modern Art. And now I shall show you where I've gone back myself, so as to be in the movement."

He barked derisively, and turning up the lamp a little, proceeded to guide me round the studio. And I felt as helpless and as futile as I had been in the old days, when I was an art critic *pour rire*.

For I was not at all sure where he had gone back, to use his own phrase. The pictures were all landscapes, painted, I conjecture, in the manner of the eighteenth century. There seemed to me, the un-instructed, as it were a dark shadow that hung over them all. Now and again there were patches of an intense and glowing blue in M'Calmont's skies; but these were contrasted with purple cloud masses rimmed with fire, with huge white clouds blown up into the sky by gathering thunder, with cloudy walls of black streaked with coppery flame. The green of the trees and of the grass was dark and livid, and the water of pools and streams reflected something of the threat of the skies. M'Calmont had depicted open spaces in the midst of mysterious woods, narrow valleys edged with grim rocks, paths that wound in and out by lonely lands to shattered walls on a far height, trees of strange growth hanging over a well, glades glooming with twilight and the coming storm. There was an enchantment; but the incantation was of oppression and terror. There were three things that I noted as curious: the first was that in every picture M'Calmont had introduced fire—logs burning under a broken wall, flames breaking out of yellowish smoke in the forest clearing, a fire by the well, a fire on the far hill-side. Water, also, was represented in each canvas; well, or brook, or pool in the woods; and in every one of them there was the figure of a man, the same man, so far as I could judge. The figure was roughly dressed in the costume of an eighteenth-century countryman, in ragged clothes, with a scarlet cap on his head. He was depicted as tending the invariable fire, perhaps, or leaning on his staff, or half hidden behind the trunk of a tree, or crouching among thorns on the border of a broken road. As I passed slowly from picture to picture, I noticed that the figure became more prominent. At first, it was barely seen in the background. Then it came forward into the middle distance, and at the end of the tour, the recently painted pictures, as M'Calmont told me, it was prominent in the foreground. In one picture he led a procession of torch-bearers into a wood as the night came on; but mostly he was alone in these desolate places that M'Calmont had made. And there was about this figure an impression of distortion. There was no specific deformity, as of hunched back or misshapen limbs; but yet a distinct sense of a form twisted and awry. And the face, where it could be clearly seen, was at once piteous and malignant, as of a stricken snake, wounded and dying.

Whatever my feeling about this odd gallery of paintings may have been, I kept it to myself. I reminded M'Calmont that I was an outsider and (perhaps exaggerating a little) that I could never be an admirer of the famous slaughterhouse, since it told no story.

"You're an awful liar," he said with an engaging directness as we sat down again, "but let that flee stick to the wa'. I told you I was going back, like the rest, but not to the ignorance of childhood or savagery. I'm returning to a great art, and exploring its possibilities. You know that the Gothic architecture was the result of the builders, first of the dark ages and then of the middle ages, exploring the possibilities of the architecture of the Romans?"

"I have heard that theory advanced," I said, "but I don't know that it holds the field so decisively as you seem to think. I believe that some authorities would tell you that the gothicosity of Gothic derives, to a great extent at least, from the East."

"I wouldn't believe a word of that tale—not that it signifies one way or the other in the argument. But I've seen churches down on the Rhone where the Gothic seems growing out of the Classic before your very eyes. There's one such at Valence: a regular Classic pediment, and all the detail of it one would call Norman, if one saw it in England. And anyone who will cast an eye over a First Pointed capital will see in a moment that it's a Corinthian capital in disguise; especially if it's got the square abacus."

"Very good, then," I assented, "let us grant your doctrine of Gothic. You're applying it to painting?"

"That is so. As I said; I'm exploring the possibilities of an old school of landscape. I don't know whether it's ever struck you; but there's no doubt that some of the painters of that age anticipated the word that came to Coleridge and Wordsworth. The eighteenth-century literature was Pope. It belonged to Daath, the region of the logical understanding. To the men of that age, the poetry of the sixteenth century and the first half of the seventeenth century was just Egyptian hieroglyphics. They could not interpret a single word of it; they'd forgotten what it meant. And, naturally, they could not dream of what was to come after them. But if you'll look at some of their painting: you'll see the landscapes of *Kubla Khan*—the awe, and the terror, and the hidden mysteries of earth and air, water and fire. And I just meant to find out what's beyond the turn of those paths they made."

He paused for a moment. "But that's not painter's talk," he went on. "I mean, of course, that I've taken a certain school of landscape painting as my starting-point; and I will see if I can't develop it on its own lines. I hope to draw something new out of the old."

"You have a figure, I notice, in all your pictures."

"You must have the human figure. Without that, all your scenery would dissolve and melt away. It would be just nothing at all."

I did not ask if it was necessary that this human figure should be abhorrent of aspect. For that, I was certain, would not be painter's talk. And soon after, I went out into the labyrinth on the hill-side. It was late, and the night had grown misty, and the sound of the streets below came faintly, with strange voices.

III

I remember being told a good many years ago in the course of a cheerful evening that the one thing fatal to an actor was intelligence.

"Or if you like it better," said the speaker, "I will say intellect. Or, better still, that something or other in a man that can pick a character to pieces, and analyse it, and find out why it does this, that or the other, and relate it to the plot and the other parts in the cast; and then, continuing the process, build up by careful reasoning, the impersonation out of tones of the voice, facial expression, gesture, habit of body, and so forth."

"But," said a gentleman in company, "isn't that the way to act? I thought that was how it was done."

"That's how I do it," replied the lecturer. "But I haven't any illusions. The man who depicts by that method will never be a 'feerest actor', as the German producer called it when I was in *Old Heidelberg* with Alexander. You know the story of Irving and poor Bill Terriss. Bill was ponging away for all he was worth as Henry VIII. Irving stopped him.

"'Very good, Terriss; very good indeed. I suppose you don't understand the meaning of one single word that you have uttered?'

"'No, guv'nor,' said Terriss, not in the least put out. 'But it'll go all right on the night.'

"That's the way to act."

"But, excuse me," said the man who wanted to know, "I'm afraid I don't quite grasp your meaning. *What* is the way to act?"

"You begin by not being able to give a single reason for anything you do or for your particular style of doing it. The rest comes along by itself. And I think I will help myself to another drink ere I go to that bourne . . . I don't want to miss the twelve-forty."

It was probably, I considered, that the old actor—a dignified Priest in *Hamlet*—was right in the main. Creative work, even such secondary creative work as the actor's, is not achieved by theories or by taking thought. A man must know the grammar of his business, whatever it is; the rest, if it is to be of the first order, must be the work of the hidden flame within. And, therefore, I had grave doubts of the validity of M'Calmont's art, when I thought of the elaboration of his theories. I remembered Claude Lantier in *L'OEuvre*. He made up his mind to be a stark realist, to paint bunches of carrots with sincerity. But he listened to theories, and ended by hanging himself before his symbolical picture of Paris as a nude woman, whose flesh glowed with jewels, like a Byzantine icon. It was some time before I went to see him again in that retired and secret studio. I met him in Holborn a few weeks after my visit, and he asked me in a very cheerful manner whether I was recovering from his pictures by degrees—giving his short bark of laughter. I told him that I had been allowed out for the last week.

"But," said I, willing to continue the vein of mild facetiousness, "you know art without a story is no good to me. Do tell me the story of that figure in all your paintings—the figure of the twisted man."

He stared at me blankly as if he hadn't a notion what I was talking about. Then he caught sight of an eastbound bus in a slowly moving press of traffic, ran for it, and shook a jocular fist at me from the top of the stair. And that was the last I saw of M'Calmont for a considerable time.

I was occupied, as a matter of fact, all through that winter with affairs and interests of my own. What is generally and conveniently known as psychical research has always had a strong attraction for me, in spite, or perhaps because, of the obscurities, difficulties and drawbacks of the pursuit. I must say that the usual demand of the men of physical science does not strike me as in the least rational. This demand is, I believe, that psychical phenomena should be made to conform to the laws of laboratory experiment. The man of science says: "I can make hydrogen by a simple process of mixing acid and water and zinc. If you don't believe me, come along now to my laboratory, and I will make hydrogen in three of four minutes, and show you how it is done, so that you can make it yourself—and blow yourself up, too, if you don't follow the direction. Or, if you like, I will make hydrogen to-morrow morning at eleven, or to-morrow night at twelve, or on Saturday by written appointment." You confess your belief in the validity and efficacy of the hydrogen process; and your scientific friend goes on: "Very good; but you were telling me of a woman who looked in a crystal one morning, and saw and foretold correctly certain things that happened fifty miles away four hours later. Then find that woman and bring her along to the laboratory, and let me see and hear her doing it again, and let her explain to me how she does it." And here, I say, physical science strikes me as profoundly irrational. A great poet cannot guarantee a masterpiece to be written on demand, under the eye of the observer, by 6.50 p.m. Shillaker, the famous bat, would never undertake to reproduce his 250 not out and no chances given, against the Patagonians. He knows that when he next meets that famous eleven, he may be out for a duck in the first over. And what painter can explain how he does it? Can Dick, Tom and Harry go to the Master, listen to a demonstration, and come away, fully prepared to equal his immortal works? Clearly, men are capable of all sorts of performances of body and spirit which are not in the least amenable to the law of the laboratory. Let us remember the historic case of one of whom it is recorded: "at tip-cheese, or odd and even, his hand is out". If Master Tommy Bardell had been required to demonstrate his skill at tip-cheese then and there in Court, under the immediate eye of Mr. Justice Stareleigh, he would, very likely, have made a miserable fiasco.

So I have always ruled out the scientific demand and its implied conclusion as void and vain and foolish. The real difficulties in these enquiries are to be found, partly in the exquisite skill to which the art of the conjuror is sometimes brought, partly to the rarity of the faculty of keen and clear observation, partly to inaccurate and unreliable memory, a little to the commonness of lying: but most of all to the vast and bottomless credulity of the race of men. It is not a case of a plausible tale deceiving a simpleton; it is a case of homely strangers going to an hotel in a busy seaside town, telling the managing director of the concern that they are leaving him a couple of million in their wills, and living at the hotel free of payment for eight or nine months. What is to be expected when the managing director—the type is common—devotes his talents to psychical research?

Still, with all this in my mind, I persevered; perhaps not altogether displeased at the thought that, so far as clear and final and general conclusions were concerned, the quest was a hopeless one. After all, there is something eminently human in the desire of impossible things. To seek for possibilities is rather the business of the lower animals than of man. To be more specific: it had often struck me that from the singular phenomena grouped together under the heading of *poltergeist* there might, possibly or even probably, emerge a good deal of light on the doings and showings of modern spiritualism. In both cases, naturally, a huge discount had to be made. No doubt the poltergeist was often a bad child, delighting in annoying, alarming, and humbugging its elders, delighting also in playing the leading part in the comedy. Sometimes hysteria was to be expected; and hysteria is capable of anything. But it seemed to me that there was a very considerable remanet of poltergeist cases in which mischief and trickery and ordinary hysteria were necessarily excluded from consideration. As to the other end of the enquiry, spiritualism; its history might, in a sense, be called a sad one. The last time I looked into the leading spiritualist journal I saw on one page a description of the unpleasing methods by which the medium had hidden the flowers that were to drop later from the spirit world on to the séance table; on another page was a brief announcement that an eminent spiritualist had declared the equally eminent Mr. X, the spirit photographer, to be a highly fraudulent person. For the time, at all events, I decided on occupying myself with the manifestations of the simple poltergeist.

And, as it happened, a favourable opportunity came in my way. Soon after my encounter with M'Calmont in Holborn, I ran across an old acquaintance of mine, Manning, who was something in the British Museum. A few years before, when he had been a lodger in a Bloomsbury street, I had been accustomed to see a good deal of him; but he had married and had gone to live with his wife on some remote heights up at Hornsey, and we had not encountered one another for some time. We found a nook in which we could exchange such news as we had, and I heard a good deal about the fine old garden, "above the London smoke," and of great success with roses. Then came something interesting.

"Six months ago," Manning began, "we took a boarder. He's a boy of fifteen, and his father, Richards, an old friend of mine, has got a job in the East, which will keep him there for some years. He asked me if my wife and I would take charge of the lad for the next year or two, anyhow. The mother is dead, and, as Richards put it, he didn't want to leave his son with strangers. The young fellow is a day boy at Westminster, so we don't see too much of him, in term-time at all events.

"Well, he came along and seemed a decent young chap enough, and didn't give any trouble—till the last week or so. And now we don't know what to do about him."

"What's wrong?" I asked. "Stays out late at night and comes home drunk? That sort of thing?"

"Not a bit of it. He sticks to his work all the evening and goes to bed soon after ten. But, wherever he is, things go smash. It began with a stone coming through the dining-room window. I thought, naturally, some hooligan had thrown it from the street, and rushed out. The only people near enough to have done it were a couple of quiet old ladies walking along and chattering to each other about the vicar. Another night the clock jumped from the shelf on to the table. Then he went into the kitchen to get me a box of matches, and the plates on the dresser began falling about. It worries my wife—and it bothers me too. Young Richards says he doesn't do it. No doubt he does, all the same; but I haven't succeeded in catching him at it, so far. I suppose I shall have to write to his father, and that won't be pleasant."

I saw my chance. I told Manning that young Richards must be regarded, not as an infernal nuisance, but as an interesting case. On my earnest petition, Mrs. Manning being, I believe, rather glad to have another man on the premises, I became the second paying guest at the Hornsey house, promising myself important and first-hand evidence. And I had better say at once that I was disappointed. As young Richards pored over his homework at a side table, I saw a small piece of Samian ware rise up from a table at the other end of the room, hover, or seem to hover, for an instant, and then fall to the floor, breaking into fragments. I could not see how Richards could possibly be the conscious agent in this event. There was certainly no apparatus of threads or wires concerned in the destruction of the Samian bowl. The boy looked frightened and furious; and I found out that he had been thrashed at his preparatory school for "wilful destruction". But, from the enquirer's point of view, "what next?" It seemed that one was reduced to posit an unknown force, devoid of conscious or intelligent direction, and wholly outside and beyond the sphere of physical science. And yet—this was something.

Richards in himself was an entirely ordinary and normal boy; a very decent fellow, I should say, neither too stupid nor too intelligent. It was only in his appearance that there was something not quite ordinary. I do not know that he was short for his age, but his breadth of chest made him appear short, and gave a certain vague impression of deformity, and also of considerable strength.

I had been staying with the Mannings for six or seven weeks, and it was drawing towards the darkest and shortest days in the year. There was a succession of heavy fogs, and it was after one of these that the "Horrible Dwarf" scare began its course in the papers. A small child, living with its parents in a back street of Westminster, had been sent on some errand to a shop round the corner. The fog was thick down there by the river, but the distance was short, the little girl went to the shop for her mother every other day, and there were no roads to be crossed. She came back crying, and evidently badly frightened, having dropped the sixpenn'orth of tea, or whatever it was. When she had been soothed into coherence, she told a tale of a "dreadful little man", who came out of a passage, and bent down with all his teeth showing, and put out his hands as if he would take her by the throat and kill her—and then disappeared into the fog, without saying a word. Of course the neighbours came swarming to hear all about it, and deafened each other with conjectures of an impossible kind, and proposed moves and measures which led nowhere. On the whole, it was to be gathered that the horrible little man must be a stranger, since no dwarfs were known to inhabit the neighbourhood. The police were called in, and made very little of the business, ranking the offender with those tiresome but not dangerous semi-lunatics who cut off girls' hair on the bus, or slash their clothes in the street. The paragraphs in the press were brief; and some people were inclined to think that the small messenger had let the tea or the sugar spill into the gutter and had invented the dwarf in order to escape punishment.

But then, in a couple of days, there was something more serious. Late on a dismal afternoon, a man who was taking a short cut through an unfrequented by-street off the Tottenham Court Road, felt, as he said, a violent punch in the back, and found himself at the bottom of a flight of area stairs. He was bruised and shaken, but conscious, and as he looked up, he saw an ugly little man grinning at him through the railings. He struggled to his feet, and ran up the steps, shouting: "Stop thief!" There were two or three people about, who came running; but they had seen nothing.

Then, on another evening, five or six days later, a girl looking into a shop window in Camden Town, became aware that there was a short man, "with a nasty look on his face", standing beside her, and the next moment she felt a piercing pain in her arm, screamed out in agony and fear, and fainted. There was hurry and bustle, shouting and confusion, running here and there from all quarters, but by the time the girl had come to herself and was able to say what had happened to her, the assailant had disappeared. A doctor came up and found a long needle almost buried in her arm. The newspaper paragraphs had become half-columns, and people began to be afraid.

And the next outrage of the "Horrible Dwarf" was again at Westminster; and close to the place where the small messenger had been frightened. Again there was a dense fog; rather a thick white mist, deadening to sound, so that in those narrow streets where there is little wheeled traffic on the brightest days, such noises as these were could hardly be heard, and seemed dull and muffled as if they came from a place far off. But through this thick, stilled silence there broke a lamentable complaint. A man, making his way homeward, cautiously, warily, and slowly, passed through one of these by-streets where, for some years, there had been a patch of wretched and wasted land. Four or five cottages had been pulled down, and for some reason or another the plans for re-building had fallen through, and the plot where the houses had stood lay as the housebreakers had left it. There were cavernous remains of underground rooms or cellars, brickbat mountains, plaster valleys, all scattered over with fragments of mouldering beams and jagged with shattered slates; a very dismal and ruined place, separated from the pavement by a line of broken-down palings. As the homeward bound man felt his way along the street, he thought he heard a noise of crying, a very faint, sad sound. He stopped and listened by a window, where the light from within was barely apparent through the thick, white folds of mist, and wondered whether the sound came from a child, shut up alone and frightened. He could not satisfy himself that this was so, and walked on a few paces, still listening, and thinking that he was drawing nearer to the noise of crying.

He was now by the palings that hedged off the waste land, and he became sure that here was the scene of the trouble. He broke through the rotten fence, and went prowling and stumbling about, well aware, as he had often passed that way, that he might very well come to grief himself in the broken-down ruin and confusion of the place. But, with good fortune, he came without disaster to a wretched child lying on his back amidst the rubbish, sobbing and wailing most piteously. The man gave him a cheerful "What's the matter, Tommy? Come along, and we'll make it all right," and tried to lift the child to his feet. But the poor misery cried out in sharper anguish, and the man raised him as gently as he could and bore him away, dreadfully afraid all the while that he might stumble and fall and, as he said afterwards, do the poor little beggar in.

However, he brought his burden safely out of the horrible pits, and rang the bell at the first house he came to. The rescuer and the people of the house saw a terrible sight. It was a poor place, with a bed in the sitting-room, and on this they laid the wreckage. It was a boy of nine or ten. One leg seemed bent under him, and when they tried to straighten it the child screamed with pain. But it was the boy's face that frightened them. It was all swollen and bloody, and black with bruises, and the blood was still gushing from the nostrils, which were as if they had been stamped on by the hoof of a horse. One went out and shouted through the fog for the police; and in time the poor boy was taken in an ambulance to the hospital. In a day or two, a little mended and recovered, he told his tale of a twisted man that came out of the mist, and took him up as if he would have broken him, and carried him over the fence and threw him down, and then stamped with his feet on his face.

The newspapers altered their headline to "Devilish Dwarf", and cursed the police—and so forth.

And it was after this most detestable outrage that Manning horrified me one night, as we sat by the fire with the rest of the house abed. He told me that he was seriously afraid that young Richards was guilty of these abominations. He urged that they had all taken place at a time when the boy was on his way from Westminster to Hornsey, that he had certainly been late home on the occasions of the first and last of the outrages. He dwelt on his dwarfish appearance, on his great strength, but above all on those abnormal activities which had interested me in the first place.

"You know yourself there's something queer about the fellow. Upon my word, I'm afraid he's the man. And if we don't do something, it will come to murder."

I was, indeed, horrified for a moment when he began, but at the end I laughed, I am glad to remember. I told him that the fog would amply account for Richards's late return on the two occasions he had mentioned; that to the best of my recollection he had been back in good time on the other two evenings of outrage; and finally, and most conclusively, that he was talking nonsense. "Excepting only that singular faculty or fatality of his, he's a very ordinary boy, and a good sort."

In short, I laughed him out of it. Happily, there were no more horrors of the "Devilish Dwarf" order for the rest of the winter. They stopped as suddenly as they had begun; and in the succeeding calm somebody found sense enough to write an article pointing out the helplessness of the police when confronted with the motiveless outrages of a maniac. The new generation heard all about the doings of Jack the Ripper, and the analogy seemed fair enough. And at the same time—it was, of course, pure coincidence—the poltergeist activity, or possession, or whatever it was, of young Richards, dwindled and ceased. The house on the Hornsey heights was in all respects at peace with itself when I left it for the valley of London in the early spring.

IV

Extract from a letter received about eighteen months after "the early spring" mentioned above.

...Now, as to this M'Calmont business. In your place, I should certainly go no farther—or "further"—I never know which is right and which is wrong. There's no question of bringing the story to its logical conclusion, because there isn't one. Your theories and conjectures and the rest of it may be all right—and they may be all wrong. And just remember that for all we know M'Calmont may turn up any day, and that might be a nasty business for you. I remember Sandy M'Calmont very well, and he always struck me as a man who would be extremely (shall we say) tenacious, if he got in a temper.

I note what you say about your visit to his studio in the spring of last year. In the first place; as to the man himself. You say he struck you as very much changed: "silent, morose, and apparently not in the least glad to see me." And I gather that the Lagavulin touch was conspicuous by its absence. I don't think there's much significance in that. There are genial Scotsmen and frozen Scotsmen, and sometimes, and naturally enough, you have samples of both temperatures in one man. And, as I've just said, he always struck me as having a reserve of grimness. One of his race gave me a most cordial invitation to dine with him at his club, and when the evening came, I was going to say, he didn't speak half a dozen words. That's a figure of speech; but, to be strictly accurate, if he had been "measured up", I don't think his remarks all through the evening would have exceeded a hundred words. He was all right the next time we met. Some of them are like that.

You say that all the pictures you had seen when you went to the studio the autumn before had been cleared away, and that there was a new lot on the walls. The change you noticed is certainly interesting: the reduction of the elaborate landscapes into mere backgrounds, the trees barely indicated, the detail shadowy, and so forth: the Twisted Man promoted from a sort of super to be the real subject of the picture—"a devilish figure", as you say, with, I gather, minor demons grouped about him, being instructed in strange traps and chases, in obscure employments, in pastimes that did not strike you as too agreeable. I was rather reminded of an old lacquer bureau I grew up with. I remember one of the drawers was decorated with a design of a golden garden of unearthly trees, in which Chinamen in golden robes tormented a porcupine with long wands of gold. All this was certainly very odd. You didn't like M'Calmont's manner when he said: "You asked me for the story of the Twisted Man and here it is"? I don't see much in that. But that particular gesture in one of the pictures: the man pointing to an indistinct figure on the ground, and lifting up his foot above it: well... Still, as you can see for yourself, there's nothing you can fasten on in that. You can't charge a painter with the crimes he chooses to paint. And that's the fatal flaw in the whole of your case; if you think you have a case.

Of course I remember that awful business of the poor girl in the July following. It was one of the most hideous and revolting things that have happened in my time; and I think we should both agree that Fleet Street, with all its faults, rendered a public service by its suppression of most of the facts. I knew Selwyn of the *Gazette,* who was put on the country end of the story. He managed to see a sort of diary the girl had kept—about her visits to London and all that. I don't care to recall what he told me. But there again, when you try to put two and two together, you'll find it can't be done. There was nothing in those papers that Selwyn looked at to connect the unfortunate wretch with the studio. As you say, that square in Bloomsbury where the body was found is not a great distance off; but that's nothing to go on.

And, after all, it seems to me that either way, you would be well advised to let it alone. The man has gone away, and it seems likely that he will stay away, so there's no fear of any recurrence of these abominations. But, on the other hand, he *may* come back, and if he did, you might find yourself in the dock on a charge of criminal libel. And I don't think that such evidence as you have is anything like strong enough for you to put up a good defence. I say again: drop it.

I took this advice, so far as making any representations to the police authorities was concerned. After some years—nine, getting on for ten—nothing has been heard of M'Calmont. A cousin of his eventually received authority to deal with the pictures in the studio. Some of the earlier canvases appeared in due course in the dealers' shops round St. James's and Bond Street, and others went to the auction rooms, and realised very fair prices. There is a movement, I have gathered, in certain circles of art criticism, to appreciate M'Calmont's work very highly. One critic wrote lately: "It is all old school, if you like, but there is something there that the old school never had; and I don't think that any of us quite know what it is. And I am convinced that collectors, public and private, will do well to keep a very keen eye on M'Calmonts. At the present prices they are undoubted bargains."

And the studios are still asking where M'Calmont got his model for the wonderful Twisted Man.

There was one circumstance which I failed to mention, when I consulted the friend who wrote me the letter of advice. I am not sure why I left it out of my story; possibly from a whimsical dislike of making the case too complete, possibly from a feeling, equally whimsical, that it was as well to keep one card at least safe and secret in my own hand.

But, two nights after the discovery of the package in Irving Square, when horror was still black and raging, I felt that I must visit that secret studio on the hill-side. It was a clear night with a red moon, just past the full, rising out of a low band of clouds, and this time I found my way without any difficulty. And just as I came down the flight of steps that led into the open square, I saw the green door of M'Calmont's studio open; very cautiously at first, inch by inch, and then wider, and a figure, vague against the darkness behind it, seemed to peer about for a moment. Then, the door was opened wide, and as quickly shut, and I saw a man, all twisted and bent so as to be dwarf-like, go capering with fantastic and extravagant gestures across the scene of light, and vanish into a narrow passage which led down the hill between garden walls and the shadowy boughs of trees. I stood still, beaten back into the shelter of my steps, drawing a long breath. I had recognised very well that dancing and terrible figure, and I was quite overcome by the utter impossibility of that which I had certainly seen. I had been living for some time with gathering suspicions of some dreadful and mysterious connection between the work of the studio and the horror of the waste place in Westminster; but they had been vague surmises and unshapen fears. But this was delirium; nightmare walking visibly abroad. I shook myself out of my terror and went briskly up to the studio door and rang the bell.

The door was opened by M'Calmont's handy man whom I had seen pottering about on my last visit. I asked him if Mr. M'Calmont were at home.

"Not at the moment, sir," he replied. "But please to step in. Mr. M'Calmont told me he'd be back in a minute; he's only gone to post a letter—and I'm sure he'd be very sorry to miss you."

I followed the man to the studio, which was all lit up. I stood there in a great bewilderment.

"But, William," I said, "I saw somebody come out by that door just as I was coming down the steps. But it was a twisted sort of man, like that man in all Mr. M'Calmont's pictures. I thought it must be the model." The notion had flashed into my mind that moment, as with a deep sigh of relief.

William looked puzzled.

"It must have been Mr. M'Calmont, sir. There's nobody else been here to-night. He went out a couple of minutes ago."

"But the man I saw was twisted; crooked. And he was dancing about like a lunatic."

"Then, sir, I think that was Mr. M'Calmont all right. I expect he was doing what he calls his Physical Jerks, thinking there would be nobody about to see him. He says it's strongly recommended by the doctors. But do be seated, sir, if you please."

I was staring at a great sheet of paper on an easel. It was covered with black charcoal outlines, to me significant and most awful. I had heard something of the contents of the package that had been found under the bushes of Irving Square.

I told the man I really could not wait. I hurried out of the place, and struck away up to the north, and made as quickly as I could for the broad and jangling streets, and so got home at last, avoiding dark narrows and short cuts all the way.

I do not know how long William waited for his master to return. But he waited vainly.

THE RED ROOM

"I CAN assure you," said I, "that it will take a very tangible ghost to frighten me." And I stood up before the fire with my glass in my hand.

"It is your own choosing," said the man with the withered arm, and glanced at me askance.

"Eight-and-twenty years," said I, "I have lived, and never a ghost have I seen as yet."

The old woman sat staring hard into the fire, her pale eyes wide open. "Ay," she broke in; "and eight-and-twenty years you have lived and never seen the likes of this house, I reckon. There's a many things to see, when one's still but eight-and-twenty." She swayed her head slowly from side to side. "A many things to see and sorrow for."

I half suspected the old people were trying to enhance the spiritual terrors of their house by their droning insistence. I put down my empty glass on the table and looked about the room, and caught a glimpse of myself, abbreviated and broadened to an impossible sturdiness, in the queer old mirror at the end of the room. "Well," I said, "if I see anything to-night, I shall be so much the wiser. For I come to the business with an open mind."

"It's your own choosing," said the man with the withered arm once more.

I heard the sound of a stick and a shambling step on the flags in the passage outside, and the door creaked on its hinges as a second old man entered, more bent, more wrinkled, more aged even than the first. He supported himself by a single crutch, his eyes were covered by a shade, and his lower lip, half-averted, hung pale and pink from his decaying yellow teeth. He made straight for an armchair on the opposite side of the table, sat down clumsily, and began to cough. The man with the withered arm gave this new-comer a short glance of positive dislike; the old woman took no notice of his arrival, but remained with her eyes fixed steadily on the fire.

"I said—it's your own choosing," said the man with the withered arm, when the coughing had ceased for a while.

"It's my own choosing," I answered.

The man with the shade became aware of my presence for the first time, and threw his head back for a moment and sideways, to see me. I caught a momentary glimpse of his eyes, small and bright and inflamed. Then he began to cough and splutter again.

"Why don't you drink?" said the old man with the withered arm, pushing the beer towards him. The man with the shade poured out a glassful with a shaky arm that splashed half as much again on the deal table. A monstrous shadow of him crouched upon the wall and mocked his action as he poured and drank. I must confess I had scarce expected these grotesque custodians. There is to my mind something inhuman in senility, something crouching and atavistic; the human qualities seem to drop from old people insensibly day by day. The three of them made me feel uncomfortable, with their gaunt silences, their bent carriage, their evident unfriendliness to me and to one another.

"If," said I, "you will show me to this haunted room of yours, I will make myself comfortable there."

The old man with the cough jerked his head back so suddenly that it startled me, and shot another glance of his red eyes at me from under the shade; but no one answered me. I waited a minute, glancing from one to the other.

"If," I said a little louder, "if you will show me to this haunted room of yours, I will relieve you from the task of entertaining me."

"There's a candle on the slab outside the door," said the man with the withered arm, looking at my feet as he addressed me. "But if you go to the red room to-night—"

("This night of all nights!" said the old woman.)

"You go alone."

"Very well," I answered. "And which way do I go?"

"You go along the passage for a bit," said he, "until you come to a door, and through that is a spiral staircase, and half-way up that is a landing and another door covered with baize. Go through that and down the long corridor to the end, and the red room is on your left up the steps."

"Have I got that right?" I said, and repeated his directions. He corrected me in one particular.

"And are you really going?" said the man with the shade, looking at me again for the third time, with that queer, unnatural tilting of the face.

("This night of all nights!" said the old woman.)

"It is what I came for," I said, and moved towards the door. As I did so, the old man with the shade rose and staggered round the table, so as to be closer to the others and to the fire. At the door I turned and looked at them, and saw they were all close together, dark against the firelight, staring at me over their shoulders, with an intent expression on their ancient faces.

"Good-night," I said, setting the door open.

"It's your own choosing," said the man with the withered arm.

I left the door wide open until the candle was well alight, and then I shut them in and walked down the chilly, echoing passage.

I must confess that the oddness of these three old pensioners in whose charge her ladyship had left the castle, and the deep-toned, old fashioned furniture of the house-keeper's room in which they foregathered, affected me in spite of my efforts to keep myself at a matter-of-fact phase. They seemed to belong to another age, an older age when things spiritual were different from this of ours, less certain; an age when omens and witches were credible, and ghosts beyond denying. Their very existence was spectral; the cut of their clothing, fashions born in dead brains. The ornaments and conveniences of the room about them were ghostly—the thoughts of vanished men, which still haunted rather than participated in the world of to-day. But with an effort I sent such thoughts to the right-about. The long, draughty subterranean passage was chilly and dusty, and my candle flared and made the shadows cower and quiver. The echoes rang up and down the spiral staircase, and a shadow came sweeping up after me, and one fled before me into the darkness overhead. I came to the landing and stopped there for a moment, listening to a rustling that I fancied I heard; then, satisfied of the absolute silence, I pushed open the baize-covered door and stood in the corridor.

The effect was scarcely what I expected, for the moonlight, coming in by the great window on the grand staircase, picked out everything in vivid black shadowy or silvery illumination. Everything was in its place: the house might have been deserted on the yesterday instead of eighteen months ago. There were candles in the sockets of the sconces, and whatever dust had gathered on the carpets or upon the polished flooring was distributed so evenly as to be invisible in the moonlight. I was about to advance, and stopped abruptly. A bronze group stood upon the landing, hidden from me by the corner of the wall, but its shadow fell with marvellous distinctness upon the white panelling, and gave me the impression of someone crouching to waylay me. I stood rigid for half a minute perhaps. Then, with my hand in the pocket that held my revolver, I advanced, only to discover a Ganymede and Eagle glistening in the moonlight. That incident for a time restored my nerve, and a porcelain Chinaman on a buhl table, whose head rocked silently as I passed him, scarcely startled me.

The door to the red room and the steps up to it were in a shadowy corner. I moved my candle from side to side, in order to see clearly the nature of the recess in which I stood before opening the door. Here it was, thought I, that my predecessor was found, and the memory of that story gave me a sudden twinge of apprehension. I glanced over my shoulder at the Ganymede in the moonlight, and opened the door of the red room rather hastily, with my face half turned to the pallid silence of the landing.

I entered, closed the door behind me at once, turned the key I found in the lock within, and stood with the candle held aloft, surveying the scene of my vigil, the great red room of Lorraine Castle, in which the young duke had died. Or, rather, in which he had begun his dying, for he had opened the door and fallen headlong down the steps I had just ascended. That had been the end of his vigil, of his gallant attempt to conquer the ghostly tradition of the place; and never, I thought, had apoplexy better served the ends of superstition. And there were other and older stories that clung to the room, back to the half-credible beginning of it all, the tale of a timid wife and the tragic end that came to her husband's jest of frightening her. And looking around that large shadowy room, with its shadowy bays, its recesses and alcoves, one could well understand the legends that had sprouted in its black corners, it germinating darkness. My candle was a little tongue of flame in its vastness, that failed to pierce the opposite end of the room, and left an ocean of mystery and suggestion beyond its island of light.

I resolved to make a systematic examination of the place at once, and dispel the fanciful suggestions of its obscurity before they obtained a hold upon me. After satisfying myself of the fastening of the door, I began to walk about the room, peering round each article of furniture, tucking up the valances of the bed, and opening its curtains wide. I pulled up the blinds and examined the fastenings of the several windows before closing the shutters, leant forward and looked up the blackness of the wide chimney, and tapped the dark oak panelling for any secret opening. There were two big mirrors in the room, each with a pair of sconces bearing candles, and on the mantelshelf, too, were more candles in china candlesticks. All these I lit one after the other. The fire was laid—an unexpected consideration from the old housekeeper—and I lit it, to keep down any disposition to shiver, and when it was burning well, I stood round with my back to it and regarded the room again. I had pulled up a chintz-covered arm-chair and a table, to form a kind of barricade before me, and on this lay my revolver ready to hand. My precise examination had done me good, but I still found the remoter darkness of the place, and its perfect stillness, too stimulating for the imagination. The echoing of the stir and crackling of the fire was no sort of comfort to me. The shadow in the alcove, at the end in particular, had that undefinable quality of a presence, that odd suggestion of a lurking living thing, that comes so easily in silence and solitude. At last, to reassure myself, I walked with a candle into it, and satisfied myself that there was nothing tangible there. I stood that candle upon the floor of the alcove, and left it in that position.

By this time I was in a state of considerable nervous tension, although to my reason there was no adequate cause for the condition. My mind, however, was perfectly clear. I postulated quite unreservedly that nothing supernatural could happen, and to pass the time I began to string some rhymes together, Ingoldsby fashion, of the original legend of the place. A few I spoke aloud, but the echoes were not pleasant. For the same reason I also abandoned, after a time, a conversation with myself upon the impossibility of ghosts and haunting. My mind reverted to the three old and distorted people downstairs, and I tried to keep it upon that topic. The sombre reds and blacks of the room troubled me; even with seven candles the place was merely dim. The one in the alcove flared in a draught, and the fire-flickering kept the shadows and penumbra perpetually shifting and stirring. Casting about for a remedy, I recalled the candles I had seen in the passage, and, with a slight effort, walked out into the moonlight, carrying a candle and leaving the door open, and presently returned with as many as ten. These I put in various knick-knacks of china with which the room was sparsely adorned, lit and placed where the shadows had lain deepest, some on the floor, some in the window recesses, until at last my seventeen candles were so arranged that not an inch of the room but had the direct light of at least one of them. It occurred to me that when the ghost came, I could warn him not to trip over them. The room was now quite brightly illuminated. There was something very cheery and reassuring in these little streaming flames, and snuffing them gave me an occupation, and afforded a reassuring sense of the passage of time.

Even with that, however, the brooding expectation of the vigil weighed heavily upon me. It was after midnight that the candle in the alcove suddenly went out, and the black shadow sprang back to its place. I did not see the candle go out; I simply turned and saw that the darkness was there, as one might start and see the unexpected presence of a stranger. "By Jove!" said I aloud; "that draught's a strong one!" and, taking the matches from the table, I walked across the room in a leisurely manner to relight the corner again. My first match would not strike, and as I succeeded with the second, something seemed to blink on the wall before me. I turned my head involuntarily, and saw that the two candles on the little table by the fireplace were extinguished. I rose at once to my feet.

"Odd!" I said. "Did I do that myself in a flash of absent-mindedness?"

I walked back, relit one, and as I did so, I saw the candle in the right sconce of one of the mirrors wink and go right out, and almost immediately its companion followed it. There was no mistake about it. The flame vanished, as if the wicks had been suddenly nipped between a finger and a thumb, leaving the wick neither glowing nor smoking, but black. While I stood gaping, the candle at the foot of the bed went out, and the shadows seemed to take another step towards me.

"This won't do!" said I, and first one and then another candle on the mantelshelf followed.

"What's up?" I cried, with a queer high note getting into my voice somehow. At that the candle on the wardrobe went out, and the one I had relit in the alcove followed.

"Steady on!" I said. "These candles are wanted," speaking with a half-hysterical facetiousness, and scratching away at a match the while for the mantel candlesticks. My hands trembled so much that twice I missed the rough paper of the matchbox. As the mantel emerged from darkness again, two candles in the remoter end of the window were eclipsed. But with the same match I also relit the larger mirror candles, and those on the floor near the doorway, so that for the moment I seemed to gain on the extinctions. But then in a volley there vanished four lights at once in different corners of the room, and I struck another match in quivering haste, and stood hesitating whither to take it.

As I stood undecided, an invisible hand seemed to sweep out the two candles on the table. With a cry of terror, I dashed at the alcove, then into the corner, and then into the window, relighting three, as two more vanished by the fireplace; then, perceiving a better way, I dropped the matches on the iron-bound deed-box in the corner, and caught up the bedroom candlestick. With this I avoided the delay of striking matches; but for all that the steady process of extinction went on, and the shadows I feared and fought against returned, and crept in upon me, first a step gained on this side of me and then on that. It was like a ragged storm-cloud sweeping out the stars. Now and then one returned for a minute, and was lost again. I was now almost frantic with the horror of coming darkness, and my self-possession deserted me. I leaped panting and dishevelled from candle to candle, in a vain struggle against that remorseless advance.

I bruised myself on the thigh against the table, I sent a chair headlong, I stumbled and fell and whisked the cloth from the table in my fall. My candle rolled away from me, and I snatched another as I rose. Abruptly this was blown out, as I swung it off the table, by the wind of my sudden movement, and immediately the two remaining candles followed. But there was light still in the room, a red light that staved off the shadows from me. The fire! Of course, I could thrust my candle between the bars and relight it!

I turned to where the flames were dancing between the glowing coals, and splashing red reflections upon the furniture, made two steps towards the grate, and incontinently the flames dwindled and vanished, the glow vanished, the reflections rushed together and vanished, and as I thrust the candle between the bars, darkness closed upon me like the shutting of an eye, wrapped about me in a stifling embrace, sealed my vision, and crushed the last vestige of reason from my brain. The candle fell from my hand. I flung out my arms in a vain effort to thrust that ponderous blackness away from me, and, lifting up my voice, screamed with all my might—once, twice, thrice. Then I think I must have staggered to my feet. I know I thought suddenly of the moonlit corridor, and, with my head bowed and my arms over my face, made a run for the door.

But I had forgotten the exact position of the door, and struck myself heavily against the corner of the bed. I staggered back, turned, and was either struck or struck myself against some other bulky furniture. I have a vague memory of battering myself thus, to and fro in the darkness, of a cramped struggle, and of my own wild crying as I darted to and fro, of a heavy blow at last upon my forehead, a horrible sensation of falling that lasted an age, of my last frantic effort to keep my footing, and then I remember no more.

I opened my eyes in daylight. My head was roughly bandaged, and the man with the withered arm was watching my face. I looked about me, trying to remember what had happened, and for a space I could not recollect. I turned to the corner, and saw the old woman, no longer abstracted, pouring out some drops of medicine from a little blue phial into a glass. "Where am I?" I asked. "I seem to remember you, and yet I cannot remember who you are."

They told me then, and I heard of the haunted Red Room as one who hears a tale. "We found you at dawn," said he, "and there was blood on your forehead and lips."

It was very slowly I recovered my memory of my experience. "You believe now," said the old man, "that the room is haunted?" He spoke no longer as one who greets an intruder, but as one who grieves for a broken friend.

"Yes," said I; "the room is haunted."

"And you have seen it. And we, who have lived here all our lives, have never set eyes upon it. Because we have never dared.... Tell us, is it truly the old earl who—"

"No," said I; "it is not."

"I told you so," said the old lady, with the glass in her hand. "It is his poor young countess who was frightened—"

"It is not," I said. "There is neither ghost of earl nor ghost of countess in that room, there is no ghost there at all; but worse, far worse—"

"Well?" they said.

"The worst of all the things that haunt poor mortal man," said I; "and that is, in all its nakedness—*Fear!* Fear that will not have light nor sound, that will not bear with reason, that deafens and darkens and overwhelms. It followed me through the corridor, it fought against me in the room—"

I stopped abruptly. There was an interval of silence. My hand went up to my bandages.

Then the man with the shade sighed and spoke. "That is it," said he. "I knew that was it. A Power of Darkness. To put such a curse upon a woman! It lurks there always. You can feel it even in the daytime, even of a bright summer's day, in the hangings, in the curtains, keeping behind you however you face about. In the dusk it creeps along the corridor and follows you, so that you dare not turn. There is Fear in that room of hers—black Fear, and there will be—so long as this house of sin endures."

EDWARD FREDERIC BENSON

NEGOTIUM PERAMBULANS

THE casual tourist in West Cornwall may just possibly have noticed, as he bowled along over the bare high plateau between Penzance and the Land's End, a dilapidated signpost pointing down a steep lane and bearing on its battered finger the faded inscription "Polearn 2 miles", but probably very few have had the curiosity to traverse those two miles in order to see a place to which their guide-books award so cursory a notice. It is described there, in a couple of unattractive lines, as a small fishing village with a church of no particular interest except for certain carved and painted wooden panels (originally belonging to an earlier edifice) which form an altar-rail. But the church of St. Creed (the tourist is reminded) has a similar decoration far superior in point of preservation and interest, and thus even the ecclesiastically disposed are not lured to Polearn. So meagre a bait is scarce worth swallowing, and a glance at the very steep lane which in dry weather presents a carpet of sharp-pointed stones, and after rain a muddy watercourse, will almost certainly decide him not to expose his motor or his bicycle to risks like these in so sparsely populated a district. Hardly a house has met his eye since he left Penzance, and the possible trundling of a punctured bicycle for half a dozen weary miles seems a high price to pay for the sight of a few painted panels.

Polearn, therefore, even in the high noon of the tourist season, is little liable to invasion, and for the rest of the year I do not suppose that a couple of folk a day traverse those two miles (long ones at that) of steep and stony gradient. I am not forgetting the postman in this exiguous estimate, for the days are few when, leaving his pony and cart at the top of the hill, he goes as far as the village, since but a few hundred yards down the lane there stands a large white box, like a sea-trunk, by the side of the road, with a slit for letters and a locked door. Should he have in his wallet a registered letter or be the bearer of a parcel too large for insertion in the square lips of the sea-trunk, he must needs trudge down the hill and deliver the trouble-some missive, leaving it in person on the owner, and receiving some small reward of coin or refreshment for his kindness. But such occasions are rare, and his general routine is to take out of the box such letters as may have been deposited there, and insert in their place such letters as he has brought. These will be called for, perhaps that day or perhaps the next, by an emissary from the Polearn post-office. As for the fishermen of the place, who, in their export trade, constitute the chief link of movement between Polearn and the outside world, they would not dream of taking their catch up the steep lane and so, with six miles farther of travel, to the market of Penzance. The sea route is shorter and easier, and they deliver their wares to the pier-head. Thus, though the sole industry of Polearn is sea-fishing, you will get no fish there unless you have bespoken your requirements to one of the fishermen. Back come the trawlers as empty as a haunted house, while their spoils are in the fish-train that is speeding to London.

Such isolation of a little community, continued, as it has been, for centuries, produces isolation in the individual as well, and nowhere will you find greater independence of character than among the people of Polearn. But they are linked together, so it has always seemed to me, by some mysterious comprehension: it is as if they had all been initiated into some ancient rite, inspired and framed by forces visible and invisible. The winter storms that batter the coast, the vernal spell of the spring, the hot, still summers, the season of rains and autumnal decay, have made a spell which, line by line, has been communicated to them, concerning the powers, evil and good, that rule the world, and manifest themselves in ways benignant or terrible....

I came to Polearn first at the age of ten, a small boy, weak and sickly, and threatened with pulmonary trouble. My father's business kept him in London, while for me abundance of fresh air and a mild climate were considered essential conditions if I was to grow to manhood. His sister had married the vicar of Polearn, Richard Bolitho, himself native to the place, and so it came about that I spent three years, as a paying guest, with my relations. Richard Bolitho owned a fine house in the place, which he inhabited in preference to the vicarage, which he let to a young artist, John Evans, on whom the spell of Polearn had fallen, for from year's beginning to year's end he never left it. There was a solid roofed shelter, open on one side to the air, built for me in the garden, and here I lived and slept, passing scarcely one hour out of the twenty-four behind walls and windows. I was out on the bay with the fisher-folk, or wandering along the gorse-clad cliffs that climbed steeply to right and left of the deep combe where the village lay, or pottering about on the pier-head, or bird's-nesting in the bushes with the boys of the village. Except on Sunday and for the few daily hours of my lessons, I might do what I pleased so long as I remained in the open air. About the lessons there was nothing formidable; my uncle conducted me through the flowering bypaths among the thickets of arithmetic, and made pleasant excursions into the elements of Latin grammar, and above all, he made me daily give him an account, in clear and grammatical sentences, of what had been occupying my mind or my movements. Should I select to tell him about a walk along the cliffs, my speech must be orderly, not vague, slip-shod notes of what I had observed. In this way, too, he trained my observation, for he would bid me tell him what flowers were in bloom, and what birds hovered fishing over the sea or were building in the bushes. For that I owe him a perennial gratitude, for to observe and to express my thoughts in the clear spoken word became my life's profession.

But far more formidable than my weekday tasks was the prescribed routine for Sunday. Some dark embers compounded of Calvinism and mysticism smouldered in my uncle's soul, and made it a day of terror. His sermon in the morning scorched us with a foretaste of the eternal fires reserved for unrepentant sinners, and he was hardly less terrifying at the children's service in the afternoon. Well do I remember his exposition of the doctrine of guardian angels. A child, he said, might think himself secure in such angelic care, but let him beware of committing any of those numerous offences which would cause his guardian to turn his face from him, for as sure as there were angels to protect us, there were also evil and awful presences which were ready to pounce; and on them he dwelt with peculiar gusto. Well, too, do I remember in the morning sermon his commentary on the carved panels of the altar-rails to which I have already alluded. There was the angel of the Annunciation there, and the angel of the Resurrection, but not less was there the witch of Endor, and, on the fourth panel, a scene that concerned me most of all. This fourth panel (he came down from his pulpit to trace its time-worn features) represented the lych-gate of the churchyard at Polearn itself, and indeed the resemblance when thus pointed out was remarkable. In the entry stood the figure of a robed priest holding up a Cross, with which he faced a terrible creature like a gigantic slug, that reared itself up in front of him. That, so ran my uncle's interpretation, was some evil agency, such as he had spoken about to us children, of almost infinite malignity and power, which could alone be combated by firm faith and a pure heart. Below ran the legend *"Negotium perambulans in tenebris"* from the ninety-first Psalm. We should find it translated there, "the pestilence that walketh in darkness," which but feebly rendered the Latin. It was more deadly to the soul than any pestilence that can only kill the body: it was the Thing, the Creature, the Business that trafficked in the outer Darkness, a minister of God's wrath on the unrighteous. . . .

I could see, as he spoke, the looks which the congregation exchanged with each other, and knew that his words were evoking a surmise, a remembrance. Nods and whispers passed between then, they understood to what he alluded, and with the inquisitiveness of boyhood I could not rest till I had wormed the story out of my friends among the fisher-boys, as, next morning, we sat basking and naked in the sun after our bathe. One knew one bit of it, one another, but it pieced together into a truly alarming legend. In bald outline it was as follows:

A church far more ancient than that in which my uncle terrified us every Sunday had once stood not three hundred yards away, on the shelf of level ground below the quarry from which its stones were hewn. The owner of the land had pulled this down, and erected for himself a house on the same site out of these materials, keeping, in a very ecstasy of wickedness, the altar, and on this he dined and played dice afterwards. But as he grew old some black melancholy seized him, and he would have lights burning there all night, for he had deadly fear of the darkness. On one winter evening there sprang up such a gale as was never before known, which broke in the windows of the room where he had supped, and extinguished the lamps. Yells of terror brought in his servants, who found him lying on the floor with the blood streaming from his throat. As they entered some huge black shadow seemed to move away from him, crawled across the floor and up the wall and out of the broken window.

"There he lay a-dying," said the last of my informants, "and him that had been a great burly man was withered to a bag o' skin, for the critter had drained all the blood from him. His last breath was a scream, and he hollered out the same words as passon read off the screen."

"Negotium perambulans in tenebris," I suggested eagerly.

"Thereabouts. Latin anyhow."

"And after that?" I asked.

"Nobody would go near the place, and the old house rotted and fell in ruins till three years ago, when along comes Mr. Dooliss from Penzance, and built the half of it up again. But he don't care much about such critters, nor about Latin neither. He takes his bottle of whisky a day and gets drunk's a lord in the evening. Eh, I'm gwine home to my dinner."

Whatever the authenticity of the legend, I had certainly heard the truth about Mr. Dooliss from Penzance, who from that day became an object of keen curiosity on my part, the more so because the quarry-house adjoined my uncle's garden. The Thing that walked in the dark failed to stir my imagination, and already I was so used to sleeping alone in my shelter that the night had no terrors for me. But it would be intensely exciting to wake at some timeless hour and hear Mr. Dooliss yelling, and conjecture that the Thing had got him.

But by degrees the whole story faded from my mind, overscored by the more vivid interests of the day, and, for the last two years of my outdoor life in the vicarage garden, I seldom thought about Mr. Dooliss and the possible fate that might await him for his temerity in living in the place where the Thing of darkness had done business. Occasionally I saw him over the garden fence, a great yellow lump of a man, with slow and staggering gait, but never did I set eyes on him outside his gate, either in the village street or down on the beach. He interfered with none, and no one interfered with him. If he wanted to run the risk of being the prey of the legendary nocturnal monster, or quietly drink himself to death, it was his affair. My uncle, so I gathered, had made several attempts to see him when first he came to live at Polearn, but Mr. Dooliss appeared to have no use for parsons, said he was not at home and never returned the call.

After three years of sun, wind, and rain, I had completely outgrown my early symptoms and had become a tough, strapping youngster of thirteen. I was sent to Eton and Cambridge, and in due course ate my dinners and became a barrister. In twenty years from that time I was earning a yearly income of five figures, and had already laid by in sound securities a sum that brought me dividends which would, for one of my simple tastes and frugal habits, supply me with all the material comforts I needed on this side of the grave. The great prizes of my profession were already within my reach, but I had no ambition beckoning me on, nor did I want a wife and children, being, I must suppose, a natural celibate. In fact there was only one ambition which through these busy years had held the lure of blue and far-off hills to me, and that was to get back to Polearn, and live once more isolated from the world with the sea and the gorse-clad hills for playfellows, and the secrets that lurked there for exploration. The spell of it had been woven about my heart, and I can truly say that there had hardly passed a day in all those years in which the thought of it and the desire for it had been wholly absent from my mind. Though I had been in frequent communication with my uncle there during his lifetime, and, after his death, with his widow who still lived there, I had never been back to it since I embarked on my profession, for I knew that if I went there, it would be a wrench beyond my power to tear myself away again. But I had made up my mind that when once I had provided for my own independence, I would go back there not to leave it again. And yet I did leave it again, and now nothing in the world would induce me to turn down the lane from the road that leads from Penzance to the Land's End, and see the sides of the combe rise steep above the roofs of the village and hear the gulls chiding as they fish in the bay. One of the things invisible, of the dark powers, leaped into light, and I saw it with my eyes.

The house where I had spent those three years of boyhood had been left for life to my aunt, and when I made known to her my intentions of coming back to Polearn, she suggested that, till I found a suitable house or found her proposal unsuitable, I should come to live with her.

"The house is too big for a lone old woman," she wrote, "and I have often thought of quitting and taking a little cottage sufficient for me and my requirements. But come and share it, my dear, and if you find me troublesome, you or I can go. You may want solitude—most people in Polearn do—and will leave me. Or else I will leave you: one of the main reasons of my stopping here all these years was a feeling that I must not let the old house starve. Houses starve, you know, if they are not lived in. They die a lingering death; the spirit in them grows weaker and weaker, and at last fades out of them. Isn't this nonsense to your London notions . . . ?"

Naturally I accepted with warmth this tentative arrangement, and on an evening in June found myself at the head of the lane leading down to Polearn, and once more I descended into the steep valley between the hills. Time had stood still apparently for the combe, the dilapidated signpost (or its successor) pointed a rickety finger down the lane, and a few hundred yards farther on was the white box for the exchange of letters. Point after remembered point met my eye, and what I saw was not shrunk, as is often the case with the revisited scenes of childhood, into a smaller scale. There stood the post-office, and there the church and close beside it the vicarage, and beyond, the tall shrubberies which separated the house for which I was bound from the road, and beyond that again the grey roofs of the quarry-house damp and shining with the moist evening wind from the sea. All was exactly as I remembered it, and, above all, that sense of seclusion and isolation. Somewhere above the tree-tops climbed the lane which joined the main road to Penzance, but all that had become immeasurably distant. The years that had passed since last I turned in at the well-known gate faded like a frosty breath, and vanished in this warm, soft air. There were law courts somewhere in memory's dull book which, if I cared to turn the pages, would tell me that I had made a name and a great income there. But the dull book was closed now, for I was back in Polearn, and the spell was woven around me again.

And if Polearn was unchanged, so too was Aunt Hester, who met me at the door. Dainty and china-white she had always been, and the years had not aged but only refined her. As we sat and talked after dinner she spoke of all that had happened in Polearn in that score of years, and yet somehow the changes of which she spoke seemed but to confirm the immutability of it all. As the recollection of names came back to me, I asked her about the quarry-house and Mr. Dooliss, and her face gloomed a little as with the shadow of a cloud on a spring day.

"Yes, Mr. Dooliss," she said, "poor Mr. Dooliss, how well I remember him, though it must be ten years and more since he died. I never wrote to you about it, for it was all very dreadful, my dear, and I did not want to darken your memories of Polearn. Your uncle always thought that something of the sort might happen if he went on in his wicked, drunken ways, and worse than that, and though nobody knew exactly what took place, it was the sort of thing that might have been anticipated."

"But what more or less happened, Aunt Hester?" I asked.

"Well, of course I can't tell you everything, for no one knew it. But he was a very sinful man, and the scandal about him at Newlyn was shocking. And then he lived, too, in the quarry-house.... I wonder if by any chance you remember a sermon of your uncle's when he got out of the pulpit and explained that panel in the altar-rails, the one, I mean, with the horrible creature rearing itself up outside the lych-gate?"

"Yes, I remember perfectly," said I.

"Ah. It made an impression on you, I suppose, and so it did on all who heard him, and that impression got stamped and branded on us all when the catastrophe occurred. Somehow Mr. Dooliss got to hear about your uncle's sermon, and in some drunken fit he broke into the church and smashed the panel to atoms. He seems to have thought that there was some magic in it, and that if he destroyed that he would get rid of the terrible fate that was threatening him. For I must tell you that before he committed that dreadful sacrilege he had been a haunted man: he hated and feared darkness, for he thought that the creature on the panel was on his track, but that as long as he kept lights burning it could not touch him. But the panel, to his disordered mind, was the root of his terror, and so, as I said, he broke into the church and attempted—you will see why I said 'attempted'—to destroy it. It certainly was found in splinters next morning, when your uncle went into church for matins, and knowing Mr. Dooliss's fear of the panel, he went across to the quarry-house afterwards and taxed him with its destruction. The man never denied it; he boasted of what he had done. There he sat, though it was early morning, drinking his whisky.

" 'I've settled your Thing for you,' he said, 'and your sermon too. A fig for such superstitions.'

"Your uncle left him without answering his blasphemy, meaning to go straight into Penzance and give information to the police about this outrage to the church, but on his way back from the quarry-house he went into the church again, in order to be able to give details about the damage, and there in the screen was the panel, untouched and uninjured. And yet he had himself seen it smashed, and Mr. Dooliss had confessed that the destruction of it was his work. But there it was, and whether the power of God had mended it or some other power, who knows?"

This was Polearn indeed, and it was the spirit of Polearn that made me accept all Aunt Hester was telling me as attested fact. It had happened like that. She went on in her quiet voice.

"Your uncle recognised that some power beyond police was at work, and he did not go to Penzance or give information about the outrage, for the evidence of it had vanished."

A sudden spate of scepticism swept over me.

"There must have been some mistake," I said. "It hadn't been broken..."

She smiled.

"Yes, my dear, but you have been in London so long," she said. "Let me, anyhow, tell you the rest of my story. That night, for some reason, I could not sleep. It was very hot and airless; I dare say you will think that the sultry conditions accounted for my wakefulness. Once and again, as I went to the window to see if I could not admit more air, I could see from it the quarry-house, and I noticed the first time that I left my bed that it was blazing with lights. But the second time I saw that it was all in darkness, and as I wondered at that, I heard a terrible scream, and the moment afterwards the steps of someone coming at full speed down the road outside the gate. He yelled as he ran; 'Light, light!' he called out. 'Give me light, or it will catch me!' It was very terrible to hear that, and I went to rouse my husband, who was sleeping in the dressing-room across the passage. He wasted no time, but by now the whole village was aroused by the screams, and when he got down to the pier he found that all was over. The tide was low, and on the rocks at its foot was lying the body of Mr. Dooliss. He must have cut some artery when he fell on those sharp edges of stone, for he had bled to death, they thought, and though he was a big burly man, his corpse was but skin and bones. Yet there was no pool of blood round him, such as you would have expected. Just skin and bones as if every drop of blood in his body had been sucked out of him!"

She leaned forward.

"You and I, my dear, know what happened," she said, "or at least can guess. God has His instruments of vengeance on those who bring wickedness into places that have been holy. Dark and mysterious are His ways."

Now what I should have thought of such a story if it had been told me in London I can easily imagine. There was such an obvious explanation: the man in question had been a drunkard, what wonder if the demons of delirium pursued him? But here in Polearn it was different.

"And who is in the quarry-house now?" I asked. "Years ago the fisher-boys told me the story of the man who first built it and of his horrible end. And now again it has happened. Surely no one has ventured to inhabit it once more?"

I saw in her face, even before I asked that question, that somebody had done so.

"Yes, it is lived in again," said she, "for there is no end to the blindness.... I don't know if you remember him. He was tenant of the vicarage many years ago."

"John Evans," said I.

"Yes. Such a nice fellow he was too. Your uncle was pleased to get so good a tenant. And now—"

She rose.

"Aunt Hester, you shouldn't leave your sentences unfinished," I said.

She shook her head.

"My dear, that sentence will finish itself," she said. "But what a time of night! I must go to bed, and you too, or they will think we have to keep lights burning here through the dark hours."

Before getting into bed I drew my curtains wide and opened all the windows to the warm tide of the sea air that flowed softly in. Looking out into the garden I could see in the moonlight the roof of the shelter, in which for three years I had lived, gleaming with dew. That, as much as anything, brought back the old days to which I had now returned, and they seemed of one piece with the present, as if no gap of more than twenty years sundered them. The two flowed into one like globules of mercury uniting into a softly shining globe, of mysterious lights and reflections. Then, raising my eyes a little, I saw against the black hill-side the windows of the quarry-house still alight.

Morning, as is so often the case, brought no shattering of my illusion. As I began to regain consciousness, I fancied that I was a boy again waking up in the shelter in the garden, and though, as I grew more widely awake, I smiled at the impression, that on which it was based I found to be indeed true. It was sufficient now as then to be here, to wander again on the cliffs, and hear the popping of the ripened seed-pods on the gorse bushes; to stray along the shore to the bathing-cove, to float and drift and swim in the warm tide, and bask on the sand, and watch the gulls fishing, to lounge on the pier-head with the fisher-folk, to see in their eyes and hear in their quiet speech the evidence of secret things not so much known to them as part of their instincts and their very being. There were powers and presences about me; the white poplars that stood by the stream that babbled down the valley knew of them, and showed a glimpse of their knowledge sometimes, like the gleam of their white under-leaves; the very cobbles that paved the street were soaked in it.... All that I wanted was to lie there and grow soaked in it too; unconsciously, as a boy, I had done that, but now the process must be conscious. I must know what stir of forces, fruitful and mysterious, seethed along the hill-side at noon, and sparkled at night on the sea. They could be known, they could even be controlled by those who were masters of the spell, but never could they be spoken of, for they were dwellers in the innermost, grafted into the eternal life of the world. There were dark secrets as well as these clear, kindly powers, and to these no doubt belonged the *negotium perambulans in tenebris* which, though of deadly malignity, might be regarded not only as evil, but as the avenger of sacrilegious and impious deeds.... All this was part of the spell of Polearn, of which the seeds had long lain dormant in me. But now they were sprouting, and who knew what strange flower would unfold on their stems?

It was not long before I came across John Evans. One morning, as I lay on the beach, there came shambling across the sand a man stout and middle-aged with the face of Silenus. He paused as he drew near and regarded me from narrow eyes.

"Why, you're the little chap that used to live in the parson's garden," he said. "Don't you recognise me?"

I saw who it was when he spoke: his voice, I think, instructed me, and recognising it, I could see the features of the strong, alert young man in this gross caricature.

"Yes, you're John Evans," I said. "You used to be very kind to me: you used to draw pictures for me."

"So I did, and I'll draw you some more. Been bathing? That's a risky performance. You never know what lives in the sea, nor what lives on the land for that matter. Not that I heed them. I stick to work and whisky. God! I've learned to paint since I saw you, and drink too for that matter. I live in the quarry-house, you know, and it's a powerful thirsty place. Come and have a look at my things if you're passing. Staying with your aunt, are you? I could do a wonderful portrait of her. Interesting face; she knows a lot. People who live at Polearn get to know a lot, though I don't take much stock in that sort of knowledge myself."

I do not know when I have been at once so repelled and interested. Behind the mere grossness of his face there lurked something which, while it appalled, yet fascinated me. His thick lisping speech had the same quality. And his paintings, what would they be like? . . .

"I was just going home," I said. "I'll gladly come in, if you'll allow me."

He took me through the untended and overgrown garden into the house which I had never yet entered. A great grey cat was sunning itself in the window, and an old woman was laying lunch in a corner of the cool hall into which the door opened. It was built of stone, and the carved mouldings let into the walls, the fragments of gargoyles and sculptured images, bore testimony to the truth of its having been built out of the demolished church. In one corner was an oblong and carved wooden table littered with a painter's apparatus and stacks of canvases leaned against the walls.

He jerked his thumb towards a head of an angel that was built into the mantelpiece and giggled.

"Quite a sanctified air," he said, "so we tone it down for the purposes of ordinary life by a different sort of art. Have a drink? No? Well, turn over some of my pictures while I put myself to rights."

He was justified in his own estimate of his skill: he could paint (and apparently he could paint anything), but never have I seen pictures so inexplicably hellish. There were exquisite studies of trees, and you knew that something lurked in the flickering shadows. There was a drawing of his cat sunning itself in the window, even as I had just now seen it, and yet it was no cat but some beast of awful malignity. There was a boy stretched naked on the sands, not human, but some evil thing which had come out of the sea. Above all there were pictures of his garden overgrown and jungle-like, and you knew that in the bushes were presences ready to spring out on you. . . .

"Well, do you like my style?" he said as he came up, glass in hand. (The tumbler of spirits that he held had not been diluted.) "I try to paint the essence of what I see, not the mere husk and skin of it, but its nature, where it comes from and what gave it birth. There's much in common between a cat and a fuchsia-bush if you look at them closely enough. Everything came out of the slime of the pit, and it's all going back there. I should like to do a picture of you some day. I'd hold the mirror up to Nature, as that old lunatic said."

After this first meeting I saw him occasionally throughout the months of that wonderful summer. Often he kept to his house and to his painting for days together, and then perhaps some evening I would find him lounging on the pier, always alone, and every time we met thus the repulsion and interest grew, for every time he seemed to have gone farther along a path of secret knowledge towards some evil shrine where complete initiation awaited him.... And then suddenly the end came.

I had met him thus one evening on the cliffs while the October sunset still burned in the sky, but over it with amazing rapidity there spread from the west a great blackness of cloud such as I have never seen for denseness. The light was sucked from the sky, the dusk fell in ever thicker layers. He suddenly became conscious of this.

"I must get back as quick as I can," he said. "It will be dark in a few minutes, and my servant is out. The lamps will not be lit."

He stepped out with extraordinary briskness for one who shambled and could scarcely lift his feet, and soon broke out into a stumbling run. In the gathering darkness I could see that his face was moist with the dew of some unspoken terror.

"You must come with me," he panted, "for we shall get the lights burning the sooner. I cannot do without light."

I had to exert myself to the full to keep up with him, for terror winged him, and even so I fell behind, so that when I came to the garden gate, he was already halfway up the path to the house. I saw him enter, leaving the door wide, and found him fumbling with matches. But his hand so trembled that he could not transfer the light to the wick of the lamp.

"But what's the hurry about?" I asked.

Suddenly his eyes focused themselves on the open door behind me, and he jumped from his seat beside the table which had once been the altar of God, with a gasp and a scream.

"No, no!" he cried. "Keep it off . . . !"

I turned and saw what he had seen. The Thing had entered and now was swiftly sliding across the floor towards him, like some gigantic caterpillar. A stale phosphorescent light came from it, for though the dusk had grown to blackness outside, I could see it quite distinctly in the awful light of its own presence. From it, too, there came an odour of corruption and decay, as from slime that has long lain below water. It seemed to have no head, but on the front of it was an orifice of puckered skin which opened and shut and slavered at the edges. It was hairless, and slug-like in shape and texture. As it advanced its fore-part reared itself from the ground, like a snake about to strike, and it fastened on him....

At that sight, and with the yells of his agony in my ears, the panic which had struck me relaxed into a hopeless courage, and with palsied, impotent hands I tried to lay hold of the Thing. But I could not: though something material was there, it was impossible to grasp it; my hands sank in it as in thick mud. It was like wrestling with a nightmare.

I think that but a few seconds elapsed before it was over. The screams of the wretched man sank to moans and mutterings as the Thing fell on him: he panted once or twice and was still. For a moment longer there came gurglings and sucking noises, and then it slid out even as it had entered. I lit the lamp which he had fumbled with, and there on the floor he lay, no more than a rind of skin in loose folds over protruding bones.

SMITH: AN EPISODE IN A LODGING-HOUSE

"When I was a medical student," began the doctor, half turning towards his circle of listeners in the firelight, "I came across one or two very curious human beings; but there was one fellow I remember particularly, for he caused me the most vivid, and I think the most uncomfortable, emotions I have ever known.

"For many months I knew Smith only by name as the occupant of the floor above me. Obviously his name meant nothing to me. Moreover I was busy with lectures, reading, cliniques and the like, and had little leisure to devise plans for scraping acquaintance with any of the other lodgers in the house. Then chance brought us curiously together, and this fellow Smith left a deep impression upon me as the result of our first meeting. At the time the strength of this first impression seemed quite inexplicable to me, but looking back at the episode now from a standpoint of greater knowledge I judge the fact to have been that he stirred my curiosity to an unusual degree, and at the same time awakened my sense of horror—whatever that may be in a medical student—about as deeply and permanently as these two emotions were capable of being stirred at all in the particular system and set of nerves called ME.

"How he knew that I was interested in the study of languages was something I could never explain, but one day, quite unannounced, he came quietly into my room in the evening and asked me point-blank if I knew enough Hebrew to help him in the pronunciation of certain words.

"He caught me along the line of least resistance, and I was greatly flattered to be able to give him the desired information; but it was only when he had thanked me and was gone that I realised I had been in the presence of an unusual individuality. For the life of me I could not quite seize and label the peculiarities of what I felt to be a very striking personality, but it was borne in upon me that he was a man apart from his fellows, a mind that followed a line leading away from ordinary human intercourse and human interests, and into regions that left in his atmosphere something remote, rarefied, chilling.

"The moment he was gone I became conscious of two things—an

intense curiosity to know more about this man and what his real interests were, and secondly, the fact that my skin was crawling and that my hair had a tendency to rise."

The doctor paused a moment here to puff hard at his pipe, which, however, had gone out beyond recall without the assistance of a match; and in the deep silence, which testified to the genuine interest of his listeners, someone poked the fire up into a little blaze, and one or two others glanced over their shoulders into the dark distances of the big hall.

"On looking back," he went on, watching the momentary flames in the grate, "I see a short, thick-set man of perhaps forty-five, with immense shoulders and small, slender hands. The contrast was noticeable, for I remember thinking that such a giant frame and such slim finger bones hardly belonged together. His head, too, was large and very long, the head of an idealist beyond all question, yet with an unusually strong development of the jaw and chin. Here again was a singular contradiction, though I am better able now to appreciate its full meaning, with a greater experience in judging the values of physiognomy. For this meant, of course, an enthusiastic idealism balanced and kept in check by will and judgement—elements usually deficient in dreamers and visionaries.

"At any rate, here was a being with probably a very wide range of possibilities, a machine with a pendulum that most likely had an unusual length of swing.

"The man's hair was exceedingly fine, and the lines about his nose and mouth were cut as with a delicate steel instrument in wax. His eyes I have left to the last. They were large and quite changeable, not in colour only, but in character, size, and shape. Occasionally they seemed the eyes of someone else, if you can understand what I mean, and at the same time, in their shifting shades of blue, green, and a nameless sort of dark grey, there was a sinister light in them that lent to the whole face an aspect almost alarming. Moreover, they were the most luminous optics I think I have ever seen in any human being.

"There, then, at the risk of a wearisome description, is Smith as I saw him for the first time that winter's evening in my shabby student's rooms in Edinburgh. And yet the real part of him, of course, I have left untouched, for it is both indescribable and un-getatable. I have spoken already of an atmosphere of warning and aloofness he carried about with him. It is impossible further to analyse the series of little shocks his presence always communicated to my being; but there was that about him which made me instantly on the *qui vive* in his presence, every nerve alert, every sense strained and on the watch. I do not mean that he deliberately suggested danger, but rather that he brought forces in his wake which automatically warned the nervous centres of my system to be on their guard and alert.

"Since the days of my first acquaintance with this man I have lived through other experiences and have seen much I cannot pretend to explain or understand; but, so far in my life, I have only once come across a human being who suggested a disagreeable familiarity with unholy things, and who made me feel uncanny and 'creepy' in his presence; and that unenviable individual was Mr. Smith.

"What his occupation was during the day I never knew. I think he slept until sun set. No one ever saw him on the stairs, or heard him move in his room during the day. He was a creature of the shadows, who apparently preferred darkness to light. Our landlady either knew nothing, or would say nothing. At any rate she found no fault, and I have since wondered often by what magic this fellow was able to convert a common landlady of a common lodging-house into a discreet and uncommunicative person. This alone was a sign of genius of some sort.

" 'He's been here with me for years—long before you come, an' I don't interfere or ask no questions of what doesn't concern me, as long as people pays their rent,' was the only remark on the subject that I ever succeeded in winning from that quarter, and it certainly told me nothing nor gave me any encouragement to ask for further information.

"Examinations, however, and the general excitement of a medical student's life for a time put Mr. Smith completely out of my head. For a long period he did not call upon me again, and for my part, I felt no courage to return his unsolicited visit.

"Just then, however, there came a change in the fortunes of those who controlled my very limited income, and I was obliged to give up my ground-floor and move aloft to more modest chambers on the top of the house. Here I was directly over Smith, and had to pass his door to reach my own.

"It so happened that about this time I was frequently called out at all hours of the night for the maternity cases which a fourth-year student takes at a certain period of his studies, and on returning from one of these visits at about two o'clock in the morning I was surprised to hear the sound of voices as I passed his door. A peculiar sweet odour, too, not unlike the smell of incense, penetrated into the passage.

"I went upstairs very quietly, wondering what was going on there at this hour of the morning. To my knowledge Smith never had visitors. For a moment I hesitated outside the door with one foot on the stairs. All my interest in this strange man revived, and my curiosity rose to a point not far from action. At last I might learn something of the habits of this lover of the night and the darkness.

"The sound of voices was plainly audible, Smith's predominating so much that I never could catch more than points of sound from the other, penetrating now and then the steady stream of his voice. Not a single word reached me, at least, not a word that I could understand, though the voice was loud and distinct, and it was only afterwards that I realised he must have been speaking in a foreign language.

"The sound of footsteps, too, was equally distinct. Two persons were moving about the room, passing and repassing the door, one of them a light, agile person, and the other ponderous and somewhat awkward. Smith's voice went on incessantly with its odd, monotonous droning, now loud, now soft, as he crossed and re-crossed the floor. The other person was also on the move, but in a different and less regular fashion, for I heard rapid steps that seemed to end sometimes in stumbling, and quick sudden movements that brought up with a violent lurching against the walls or furniture.

"As I listened to Smith's voice, moreover, I began to feel afraid. There was something in the sound that made me feel intuitively he was in a tight place and, an impulse stirred faintly in me—very faintly, I admit—to knock at the door and inquire if he needed help.

"But long before the impulse could translate itself into an act, or even before it had been properly weighed and considered by the mind, I heard a voice close beside me in the air, a sort of hushed whisper which I am certain was Smith speaking, though the sound did not seem to have come to me through the door. It was close in my very ear, as though he stood beside me, and it gave me such a start, that I clutched the banisters to save myself from stepping backwards and making a clatter on the stairs.

" 'There is nothing you can do to help me,' it said distinctly, 'and you will be much safer in your own room.'

"I am ashamed to this day of the pace at which I covered the flight of stairs in the darkness to the top floor, and of the shaking hand with which I lit my candles and bolted the door. But, there it is, just as it happened.

"This midnight episode, so odd and yet so trivial in itself, fired me with more curiosity than ever about my fellow lodger. It also made me connect him in my mind with a sense of fear and distrust. I never saw him, yet I was often, and uncomfortably, aware of his presence in the upper regions of that gloomy lodging-house. Smith and his secret mode of life and mysterious pursuits, somehow contrived to awaken in my being a line of reflection that disturbed my comfortable condition of ignorance. I never saw him, as I have said, and exchanged no sort of communication with him, yet it seemed to me that his mind was in contact with mine, and some of the strange forces of his atmosphere filtered through into my being and disturbed my equilibrium. Those upper floors became haunted for me after dark, and, though outwardly our lives never came into contact, I became unwillingly involved in certain pursuits on which his mind was centred. I felt that he was somehow making use of me against my will, and by methods which passed my comprehension.

"I was at that time, moreover, in the heavy, unquestioning state of materialism which is common to medical students when they begin to understand something of the human anatomy and nervous system, and jump at once to the conclusion that they control the universe and hold in their forceps the last word of life and death. I 'knew it all', and regarded a belief in anything beyond matter as the wanderings of weak, or at best, untrained minds. And this condition of mind, of course, added to the strength of this upsetting fear which emanated from the floor below and began slowly to take possession of me.

"Though I kept no notes of the subsequent events in this matter, they made too deep an impression for me ever to forget the sequence in which they occurred. Without difficulty I can recall the next step in the adventure with Smith, for adventure it rapidly grew to be."

The doctor stopped a moment and laid his pipe on the table behind him before continuing. The fire had burned low, and no one stirred to poke it. The silence in the great hall was so deep that when the speaker's pipe touched the table the sound woke audible echoes at the far end among the shadows.

"One evening, while I was reading, the door of my room opened and Smith came in. He made no attempt at ceremony. It was after ten o'clock and I was tired, but the presence of the man immediately galvanised me into activity. My attempts at ordinary politeness he thrust on one side at once, and began asking me to vocalise, and then pronounce for him, certain Hebrew words; and when this was done he abruptly inquired if I was not the fortunate possessor of a very rare Rabbinical Treatise, which he named.

"How he knew that I possessed this book puzzled me exceedingly; but I was still more surprised to see him cross the room and take it out of my book-shelf almost before I had had time to answer in the affirmative. Evidently, he knew exactly where it was kept. This excited my curiosity beyond all bounds, and I immediately began asking him questions; and though, out of sheer respect for the man,

I put them very delicately to him, and almost by way of mere conversation, he had only one reply for the lot. He would look up at me from the pages of the book with an expression of complete comprehension on his extraordinary features, would bow his head a little and say very gravely, 'That, of course, is a perfectly proper question' —which was absolutely all I could ever get out of him.

"On this particular occasion he stayed with me perhaps ten or fifteen minutes. Then he went quickly downstairs to his room with my Hebrew Treatise in his hand, and I heard him close and bolt his door.

"But a few moments later, before I had time to settle down to my book again, or to recover from the surprise his visit had caused me, I heard the door open, and there stood Smith once again beside my chair. He made no excuse for his second interruption, but bent his head down to the level of my reading lamp and peered across the flame straight into my eyes.

" 'I hope,' he whispered, 'I hope you are never disturbed at night?'

" 'Eh?' I stammered, 'disturbed at night? Oh no, thanks, at least, not that I know of—'

" 'I'm glad,' he replied gravely, appearing not to notice my confusion and surprise at his question. 'But, remember, should it ever be the case, please let me know at once.'

"And he was gone down the stairs and into his room again.

"For some minutes I sat reflecting upon his strange behaviour. He was not mad, I argued, but was the victim of some harmless delusion that had gradually grown upon him as a result of his solitary mode of life; and from the books he used, I judged that it had something to do with medieval magic, or some system of ancient Hebrew mysticism. The words he asked me to pronounce for him were probably 'Words of Power', which, when uttered with the vehemence of a strong will behind them, were supposed to produce physical results, or set up vibrations in one's own inner being that had the effect of a partial lifting of the veil.

"I sat thinking about the man, and his way of living, and the probable effects in the long run of his dangerous experiments, and I can recall perfectly well the sensation of disappointment that crept over me when I realised that I had labelled his particular form of aberration, and that my curiosity would therefore no longer be excited.

"For some time I had been sitting alone with these reflections—it may have been ten minutes or it may have been half an hour—when I was aroused from my reverie by the knowledge that someone was again in the room standing close beside my chair. My first thought was that Smith had come back again in his swift, unaccountable manner, but almost at the same moment I realised that this could not be the case at all. For the door faced my position, and it certainly had not been opened again.

"Yet someone was in the room, moving cautiously to and fro, watching me, almost touching me. I was as sure of it as I was of myself, and though at the moment I do not think I was actually afraid, I am bound to admit that a certain weakness came over me and that I felt that strange disinclination for action which is probably the beginning of the horrible paralysis of real terror. I should have been glad to hide myself, if that had been possible, to cower into a corner, or behind a door, or anywhere so that I could not be watched and observed.

"But, overcoming my nervousness with an effort of the will, I got up quickly out of my chair and held the reading lamp aloft so that it shone into all the corners like a searchlight.

"The room was utterly empty! It was utterly empty, at least, to the *eye,* but to the nerves, and especially to that combination of sense perception which is made up by all the senses acting together, and by no *one* in particular, there was a person standing there at my very elbow.

"I say 'person', for I can think of no appropriate word. For, if it *was* a human being, I can only affirm that I had the overwhelming conviction that it was *not,* but that it was some form of life wholly unknown to me both as to its essence and its nature. A sensation of gigantic force and power came with it, and I remember vividly to this day my terror on realising that I was close to an invisible being who could crush me as easily as I could crush a fly, and who could see my every movement while itself remaining invisible.

"To this terror was added the certain knowledge that the 'being' kept in my proximity for a definite purpose. And that this purpose had some direct bearing upon my well-being, indeed upon my life, I was equally convinced; for I became aware of a sensation of growing lassitude as though the vitality were being steadily drained out of my body. My heart began to beat irregularly at first, then faintly. I was conscious, even within a few minutes, of a general drooping of the powers of life in the whole system, an ebbing away of self-control, and a distinct approach of drowsiness and torpor.

"The power to move, or to think out any mode of resistance, was fast leaving me, when there rose, in the distance as it were, a tremendous commotion. A door opened with a clatter, and I heard the peremptory and commanding tones of a human voice calling aloud in a language I could not comprehend. It was Smith, my fellow lodger, calling up the stairs; and his voice had not sounded for more than a few seconds, when I felt something withdrawn from my presence, from my person, indeed from my *very skin*. It seemed as if there was a rushing of air and some large creature swept by me at about the level of my shoulders. Instantly the pressure on my heart was relieved, and the atmosphere seemed to resume its normal condition.

"Smith's door closed quietly downstairs, as I put the lamp down with trembling hands. What had happened I do not know; only, I was alone again and my strength was returning as rapidly as it had left me.

"I went across the room and examined myself in the glass. The skin was very pale, and the eyes dull. My temperature, I found, was a little below normal and my pulse faint and irregular. But these smaller signs of disturbance were as nothing compared with the feeling I had—though no outward signs bore testimony to the fact—that I had narrowly escaped a real and ghastly catastrophe. I felt shaken, somehow, shaken to the very roots of my being."

The doctor rose from his chair and crossed over to the dying fire, so that no one could see the expression on his face as he stood with his back to the grate, and continued his weird tale.

"It would be wearisome," he went on in a lower voice, looking over our heads as though he still saw the dingy top floor of that haunted Edinburgh lodging-house; "it would be tedious for me at this length of time to analyse my feelings, or attempt to reproduce for you the thorough examination to which I endeavoured then to subject my whole being, intellectual, emotional and physical. I need only mention the dominant emotion with which this curious episode left me—the indignant anger against myself that I could ever have lost my self-control enough to come under the sway of so gross and absurd a delusion. This protest, however, I remember making with all the emphasis possible. And I also remember noting that it brought me very little satisfaction, for it was the protest of my reason only, when all the rest of my being was up in arms against its conclusions.

"My dealings with the 'delusion', however, were not yet over for the night; for very early next morning, somewhere about three o'clock, I was awakened by a curiously stealthy noise in the room, and the next minute there followed a crash as if all my books had been swept bodily from their shelf on to the floor.

"But this time I was not frightened. Cursing the disturbance with all the resounding and harmless words I could accumulate, I jumped out of bed and lit the candle in a second, and in the first dazzle of the flaring match—but before the wick had time to catch—I was certain I *saw* a dark grey shadow, of ungainly shape, and with something more or less like a human head, drive rapidly past the side of the wall furthest from me and disappear into the gloom by the angle of the door.

"I waited one single second to be sure the candle was alight, and then dashed after it, but before I had gone two steps, my foot stumbled against something hard piled up on the carpet and I only just saved myself from falling headlong. I picked myself up and found that all the books from what I called my 'language shelf' were strewn across the floor. The room, meanwhile, as a minute's search revealed, was quite empty. I looked in every corner and behind every stick of furniture, and a student's bedroom on a top floor, costing twelve shillings a week, did not hold many available hiding-places, as you may imagine.

"The crash, however, was explained. Some very practical and physical force had thrown the books from their resting-place. That, at least, was beyond all doubt. And as I replaced them on the shelf and noted that not one was missing, I busied myself mentally with the sore problem of how the agent of this little practical joke had gained access to my room, and then escaped again. *For my door was locked and bolted.*

"Smith's odd question as to whether I was disturbed in the night, and his warning injunction to let him know at once if such were the case, now of course returned to affect me as I stood there in the early morning, cold and shivering on the carpet; but I realised at the same moment how impossible it would be for me to admit that a more than usually vivid nightmare could have any connection with himself. I would rather stand a hundred of these mysterious visitations than consult such a man as to their possible cause.

"A knock at the door interrupted my reflections, and I gave a start that sent the candle grease flying.

" 'Let me in,' came in Smith's voice.

"I unlocked the door. He came in fully dressed. His face wore a curious pallor. It seemed to me to be under the skin and to shine through and almost make it luminous. His eyes were exceedingly bright.

"I was wondering what in the world to say to him, or how he would explain his visit at such an hour, when he closed the door behind him and came close up to me—uncomfortably close.

" 'You should have called me at once,' he said in his whispering voice, fixing his great eyes on my face.

"I stammered something about an awful dream, but he ignored my remark utterly, and I caught his eye wandering next—if any movement of those optics can be described as 'wandering'—to the book-shelf. I watched him, unable to move my gaze from his person. The man fascinated me horribly for some reason. Why, in the devil's name, was he up and dressed at three in the morning? How did he know anything had happened unusual in my room? Then his whisper began again.

" 'It's your amazing vitality that causes you this annoyance,' he said, shifting his eyes back to mine.

"I gasped. Something in his voice or manner turned my blood into ice.

" 'That's the real attraction,' he went on. 'But if this continues one of us will have to leave, you know.'

"I positively could not find a word to say in reply. The channels of speech dried up within me. I simply stared and wondered what he would say next. I watched him in a sort of dream, and as far as I can remember, he asked me to promise to call him sooner another time, and then began to walk round the room, uttering strange sounds, and making signs with his arms and hands until he reached the door. Then he was gone in a second, and I had closed and locked the door behind him.

"After this, the Smith adventure drew rapidly to a climax. It was a week or two later, and I was coming home between two and three in the morning from a maternity case, certain features of which for the time being had very much taken possession of my mind, so much so, indeed, that I passed Smith's door without giving him a single thought.

"The gas jet on the landing was still burning, but so low that it made little impression on the waves of deep shadow that lay across the stairs. Overhead, the faintest possible gleam of grey showed that the dawn was not far away. A few stars shone down through the skylight. The house was still as the grave, and the only sound to break the silence was the rushing of the wind round the walls and over the roof. But this was a fitful sound, suddenly rising and as suddenly falling away again, and it only served to intensify the silence.

"I had already reached my own landing when I gave a violent start. It was automatic, almost a reflex action in fact, for it was only when I caught myself fumbling at the door handle and thinking where I could conceal myself quickest that I realised a voice had sounded close beside me in the air. It was the same voice I had heard before, and it seemed to me to be calling for help. And yet the very same minute I pushed on into the room, determined to disregard it, and seeking to persuade myself it was the creaking of the boards under my weight or the rushing noise of the wind that had deceived me.

"But hardly had I reached the table where the candles stood when the sound was unmistakably repeated: 'Help! Help!' And this time it was accompanied by what I can only describe as a vivid tactile hallucination. I was touched: the *skin* of my arm was clutched by fingers.

"Some compelling force sent me headlong downstairs as if the haunting forces of the whole world were at my heels. At Smith's door I paused. The force of his previous warning injunction to seek his aid without delay acted suddenly and I leant my whole weight against the panels, little dreaming that I should be called upon to give help rather than to receive it.

"The door yielded at once, and I burst into a room that was so full of choking vapour, moving in slow clouds, that at first I could distinguish nothing at all but a set of what seemed to be huge shadows passing in and out of the mist. Then, gradually, I perceived that a red lamp on the mantelpiece gave all the light there was, and that the room which I now entered for the first time was almost empty of furniture.

"The carpet was rolled back and piled in a heap in the corner, and upon the white boards of the floor I noticed a large circle drawn in black of some material that emitted a faint glowing light and was apparently smoking. Inside this circle, as well as at regular intervals outside it, were curious-looking designs, also traced in the same black, smoking substance. These, too, seemed to emit a feeble light of their own.

"My first impression on entering the room had been that it was full of—*people*, I was going to say; but that hardly expresses my meaning. *Beings*, they certainly were, but it was borne in upon me beyond the possibility of doubt, that they were not human beings. That I had caught a momentary glimpse of living, intelligent entities I can never doubt, but I am equally convinced, though I cannot prove it, that these entities were from some other scheme of evolution altogether, and had nothing to do with the ordinary human life, either incarnate or discarnate.

"But, whatever they were, the visible appearance of them was exceedingly fleeting. I no longer saw anything, though I still felt convinced of their immediate presence. They were, moreover, of the same order of life as the visitant in my bedroom of a few nights before, and their proximity to my atmosphere in numbers, instead of singly as before, conveyed to my mind something that was quite terrible and overwhelming. I fell into a violent trembling, and the perspiration poured from my face in streams.

"They were in constant motion about me. They stood close to my side; moved behind me; brushed past my shoulder; stirred the hair on my forehead; and circled round me without ever actually touching me, yet always pressing closer and closer. Especially in the air just over my head there seemed ceaseless movement, and it was accompanied by a confused noise of whispering and sighing that threatened every moment to become articulate in words. To my intense relief, however, I heard no distinct words, and the noise continued more like the rising and falling of the wind than anything else I can imagine.

"But the characteristic of these 'Beings' that impressed me most strongly at the time, and of which I have carried away the most permanent recollection, was that each one of them possessed what seemed to be a *vibrating centre* which impelled it with tremendous force and caused a rapid whirling motion of the atmosphere as it passed me. The air was full of these little vortices of whirring, rotating force, and whenever one of them pressed me too closely I felt as if the nerves in that particular portion of my body had been literally drawn out, absolutely depleted of vitality, and then immediately replaced—but replaced dead, flabby, useless.

"Then, suddenly, for the first time my eyes fell upon Smith. He was crouching against the wall on my right, in an attitude that was obviously defensive, and it was plain he was in extremities. The terror on his face was pitiable, but at the same time there was another expression about the tightly clenched teeth and mouth which showed that he had not lost all control of himself. He wore the most resolute expression I have ever seen on a human countenance, and, though for the moment at a fearful disadvantage, he looked like a man who had confidence in himself, and, in spite of the working of fear, was waiting his opportunity.

"For my part, I was face to face with a situation so utterly beyond my knowledge and comprehension, that I felt as helpless as a child, and as useless.

" 'Help me back—quick—into that circle,' I heard him half cry, half whisper to me across the moving vapours.

"My only value appears to have been that I was not afraid to act. Knowing nothing of the forces I was dealing with I had no idea of the deadly perils risked, and I sprang forward and caught him by the arms. He threw all his weight in my direction, and by our combined efforts his body left the wall and lurched across the floor towards the circle.

"Instantly there descended upon us, out of the empty air of that smoke-laden room, a force which I can only compare to the pushing, driving power of a great wind pent up within a narrow space. It was almost explosive in its effect, and it seemed to operate upon all parts of my body equally. It fell upon us with a rushing noise that filled my ears and made me think for a moment the very walls and roof of the building had been torn asunder. Under its first blow we staggered back against the wall, and I understood plainly that its purpose was to prevent us getting back into the circle in the middle of the floor.

"Pouring with perspiration, and breathless, with every muscle strained to the very utmost, we at length managed to get to the edge of the circle, and at this moment, so great was the opposing force, that I felt myself actually torn from Smith's arms, lifted from my feet, and twirled round in the direction of the windows as if the wheel of some great machine had caught my clothes and was tearing me to destruction in its revolution.

"But, even as I fell, bruised and breathless, against the wall, I saw Smith firmly upon his feet in the circle and slowly rising again to an upright position. My eyes never left his figure once in the next few minutes.

"He drew himself up to his full height. His great shoulders squared themselves. His head was thrown back a little, and as I looked I saw the expression on his face change swiftly from fear to one of absolute command. He looked steadily round the room and then his voice began to *vibrate*. At first in a low tone, it gradually rose till it assumed the same volume and intensity I had heard that night when he called up the stairs into my room.

"It was a curiously increasing sound, more like the swelling of an instrument than a human voice; and as it grew in power and filled the room, I became aware that a great change was being effected slowly and surely. The confusion of noise and rushings of air fell into the roll of long, steady vibrations not unlike those caused by the deeper pedals of an organ. The movements in the air became less violent, then grew decidedly weaker, and finally ceased altogether. The whisperings and sighings became fainter and fainter, till at last I could not hear them at all; and, strangest of all, the light emitted by the circle, as well as by the designs round it, increased to a steady glow, casting their radiance upwards with the weirdest possible effect upon his features. Slowly, by the power of his voice, behind which lay undoubtedly a genuine knowledge of the occult manipulation of sound, this man dominated the forces that had escaped from their proper sphere, until at length the room was reduced to silence and perfect order again.

"Judging by the immense relief which also communicated itself to my nerves I then felt that the crisis was over and Smith was wholly master of the situation.

"But hardly had I begun to congratulate myself upon this result, and to gather my scattered senses about me, when, uttering a loud cry, I saw him leap out of the circle and fling himself into the air—as it seemed to me, into the empty air. Then, even while holding my breath for dread of the crash he was bound to come upon the floor, I saw him strike with a dull thud against a solid body in mid-air, and the next instant he was wrestling with some ponderous thing that was absolutely invisible to me, and the room shook with the struggle.

"To and fro *they* swayed, sometimes lurching in one direction, sometimes in another, and always in horrible proximity to myself, as I leaned trembling against the wall and watched the encounter.

"It lasted at most but a short minute or two, ending as suddenly as it had begun. Smith, with an unexpected movement, threw up his arms with a cry of relief. At the same instant there was a wild, tearing shriek in the air beside me and something rushed past us with a noise like the passage of a flock of big birds. Both windows rattled as if they would break away from their sashes. Then a sense of emptiness and peace suddenly came over the room, and I knew that all was over.

"Smith, his face exceedingly white, but otherwise strangely composed, turned to me at once.

" 'God!—if you hadn't come.... You deflected the stream—broke it up...' he whispered. 'You saved me.' "

The doctor made a long pause. Presently he felt for his pipe in the darkness, groping over the table behind us with both hands. No one spoke for a bit, but all dreaded the sudden glare that would come when he struck the match. The fire was nearly out and the great hall was pitch dark.

But the story-teller did not strike that match. He was merely gaining time for some hidden reason of his own. And presently he went on with his tale in a more subdued voice.

"I quite forget," he said, "how I got back to my own room. I only know that I lay with two lighted candles for the rest of the night, and the first thing I did in the morning was to let the landlady know I was leaving her house at the end of the week.

"Smith still has my Rabbinical Treatise. At least he did not return it to me at the time, and I have never seen him since to ask for it."

THE ANKARDYNE PEW

THE following narrative of the occurrences that took place at Ankardyne House in February 1890, is made up chiefly of extracts from letters written by my friend, the Rev. Thomas Prendergast, to his wife, immediately before taking up residence at the vicarage, together with transcripts from the diary which I kept at the time. The names throughout are, of course, fictitious.

February 9th. I am sorry that I had no opportunity yesterday of getting over to the vicarage, so your questions—I have not lost the list—must remain unanswered. It is almost a quarter of a mile away from the church, in the village. You see, the church, unfortunately, is in the grounds of the park, and there is a flagged passage, cold and horribly draughty, that leads from Ankardyne House to the great loose box of the Ankardyne pew. The squires in the old days could come in late and go out early, or even stay away altogether, without anyone being the wiser. The whole situation of the church is bad and typically English—the House of God in the squire's pocket. Why should he have right of secret access? I haven't had time to examine the interior—early eighteenth-century, I should guess—but as we drove up last evening in the dusk, the tall gloomy façade of Ankardyne House, with the elegant little church—a Wren's nest—adjoining it, made me think of a wicked uncle, setting off for a walk in the woods with one of the babes. The picture is really rather apt, as you will agree, when you see the place. It's partly a question of the height of the two buildings, partly a question of the shape of the windows, those of the one square, deep set, and grim; of the other round—the raised eyebrows of startled innocence.

We were quite wrong about Miss Ankardyne. She is a charming little lady, not a trace of Lady Catherine De Bourgh, and is really looking forward to having you as her nearest neighbour. I will write more of her to-morrow, but the stable clock has struck eleven and my candle is burning low.

February 10th. I measured the rooms as you asked me to. They are, of course, larger than ours at Garvington, and will swallow all our furniture and carpets. But you will like the vicarage. It, at least, is a cheerful house; faces south, and isn't, like this place, surrounded by woods. I suppose familiarity with the skies and wide horizons of the fens accounts for the shut-in feeling one gets here. But I have never seen such cedars!

And now to describe Miss Ankardyne. She is perhaps seventy-five, *petite* and bird-like, with the graceful, alert poise of a bird. I should say that sight and hearing are abnormally acute and have helped to keep her young. She is a good talker, well read and interested in affairs, and a still better listener. Parson's pride! you will exclaim; since we are only two, and if she listens, I must talk. But I mean what I say. All that the archdeacon told is true; you are conscious in her presence of a living spirit of peace. By the way, she is an interesting example of your theory that there are some people for whom animals have an instinctive dislike—indeed, the best example I have met. For Miss Ankardyne tells me that, though since childhood she has had a fondness for all living creatures, especially for birds, it is one which is not at first reciprocated. She can, after assiduous, continuous persevering, win their affection; her spaniel, her parrot, and Karkar, the tortoiseshell cat, are obviously attached to her. But strange dogs snarl, if she attempts to fondle them; and she tells me that, when she goes to the farm to feed the fowls, the birds seem to sense her coming and *run from the scattered corn.* I have heard of cows showing this antipathy to individuals, but never before of birds. There is an excellent library here, that badly needs cataloguing. The old vicar had, I believe, begun the task at the time of his fatal seizure.

I have been inside the church. Anything less like dear old Garvington it would be impossible to find. Architecturally, it has its points, but the unity of design, on which everything here depends, is broken by the Ankardyne pew. Its privacy is an abomination. Even from the pulpit it is impossible to see inside, and I can well believe the stories of the dicing squires and their Sunday play. Miss Ankardyne refuses to use it. The glass is crude and uninteresting; but there is an uncommon chancel screen of Spanish workmanship, which somehow seems in keeping with the place. I wish it didn't.

We shall miss the old familiar monuments. There is no snub-nosed crusader here, no worthy Elizabethan knight, like our Sir John Parkington, kneeling in supplication, with those nicely balanced families on right and left. The tombs are nearly all Ankardyne tombs—urns, weeping charities, disconsolate relicts, and all the cold Christian virtues. You know the sort. The Ten Commandments are painted on oak panels on either side of the altar. From the Ankardyne pew I doubt if you can see them.

February 11th. You ask about my neuritis. It is better, despite the fact that I have been sleeping badly. I wake up in the morning, sometimes during the night, with a burning headache and a curious tingling feeling about the tongue, which I can only attribute to indigestion. I am trying the effect of a glass of hot water before retiring. When we move into the vicarage, we shall at least be spared the attention of the owls, which make the nights so dismal here. The place is far too shut in by trees, and I suppose, too, that the disused out-buildings give them shelter. Cats are bad enough, but I prefer the sound of night-walkers to night-fliers. It won't be long now before we meet. They are getting on splendidly with the vicarage. The painters have already started work; the new kitchen range has come, and is only waiting for the plumbers to put it in. Miss Ankardyne is leaving for a visit to friends in a few days' time. It seems that she always goes away about this season of the year—wise woman!—so I shall be alone next week. She said Dr. Hulse would be glad to put me up. if I find the solitude oppressive, but I shan't trouble him. You would like the old butler. His name is Mason, and his wife—a Scotchwoman—acts as housekeeper. The three maids are sisters. They have been with Miss Ankardyne for thirty years, and are everything that maids should be. They belong to the Peculiar People. I cannot desire that they should be orthodox. If I could be sure that Dr. Hulse was as well served....

February 13th. I had an experience last night which moved me strangely. I hardly know what to make of it. I went to bed at half-past ten after a quiet evening with Miss Ankardyne. I thought she seemed in rather poor spirits, and tried to cheer her by reading aloud. She chose a chapter from the *Vicar of Wakefield*. I awoke soon after one with an intolerable feeling of oppression, almost of dread. I was conscious, too—and in some way my alarm was associated with this—of a burning, tingling, piercing pain in my tongue. I got up from bed and was about to pour myself out a glass of water, when I heard the sound of someone speaking. The voice was low and continuous, and seemed to come from an adjoining room. I slipped on my dressing-gown and, candle in hand, went out into the corridor. For a moment I stood in silence. Frankly, I was afraid. The voice proceeded from a room two doors away from mine. As I listened, I recognised it as Miss Ankardyne's. She was repeating the Benedicite.

There were such depths of sadness, so much of the weariness of defeat in this song of triumph of the Three Children saved from the furnace of fire, that I felt I could not leave her. I should have spoken before knocking, for I could almost feel that gasp of fear. "Oh, no!" she said, "Oh, no! Not now!" and then, as if bracing herself for a great effort, "Who is it?"

I told her and she bade me enter. The poor little woman had risen from her knees and was trembling from head to foot. I spent about an hour with her and left her sleeping peacefully. I did not wish to rouse the house, but I managed to find the Masons' room and arranged for Mrs. Mason to sit by the old lady.

I can't say what happened in that hour we spent together in talk and in prayer. There is something very horrible about this house, that Miss Ankardyne is dimly aware of. Something connected with pain and fire and a bird, and something that was human too. I was shaken to the very depths of my being. I don't think I ever felt the need for prayer and the power of prayer as I did last night. The stable clock had just struck five.

February 14th. I have arranged for Miss Ankardyne to go away to-morrow. She is fit to travel, and is hardly fit to stay. I had a long talk with her this morning. I think she is the most courageous woman I know. All her life she has felt that the house is haunted, and all her life she has felt pity for that which haunts it. She says that she is sure that she is living it down; that the house is better than it was; but that at this season of the year it is almost too much for her. She is anxious that I should stay with Dr. Hulse. I feel, however, that I must see this business through. She then suggested that I should invite a friend to stay with me. I thought of Pellow. You remember how we were obliged to postpone his visit last September. I had a letter from him only last Friday. He is living in this part of the world and could probably run over for a day or two.

The extracts from Mr. Prendergast's letters end here. The following are excerpts from my diary.

February 16th. Arrived at Ankardyne House at midday. Prendergast had meant to meet me at the station, but had been suddenly called away to visit a dying parishioner. I had in consequence a couple of hours by myself in which to form an impression of the place. The house dates from the early eighteenth century. It is dignified though sombre, and is closely surrounded on three sides by shrubberies of rhododendrons and laurel, that merge into thick woods. The cedars in the park must be older than any of the buildings. Miss Ankardyne, I gather, has lived here all her life, and the house gives you the impression of having been lived in, a slightly sinister mansion, well aired by a kindly soul. There is a library that should be well worth exploring. The family portraits are in the dining-room. None are of outstanding interest. The most unusual feature of the house is its connection with the church, which has many of the characteristics of a private chapel. It does not actually abut on the building, but is joined to it by a low, curved façade, unpierced by windows.

A corridor, lighted from above, runs behind the façade and gives a private entry from the house to the church. The door into this corridor opens into the spacious hall of Ankardyne House; but there is a second mode of access (of which Prendergast seemed unaware) from Miss Ankardyne's bed-chamber down a narrow stair. This door is kept locked and has never been opened, as far as Mason, the butler, can recollect. The church, with the curved façade connecting it to the house, is balanced on the other side by the coach-house and stables, which can be approached in a similar manner from the kitchens. The architect has certainly succeeded in conveying the idea that religion and horseflesh can be made elegant adjuncts to the life of a country gentleman. Prendergast came in just before luncheon. He does not look well, and was obviously glad to see me and to unburden himself. In the afternoon I had a long talk with Mason, the butler, a very level-headed man.

From what Prendergast tells me I gather that Miss Ankardyne's experiences have been both auditory and visual. They are certainly vague.

Auditory. The cry of a bird—sometimes she thinks it is an owl, sometimes a cock—sometimes a human cry with something bird-like in it. This she has heard almost as long as she can remember, both outside the house and inside her room, but most frequently in the direction of the corridor that leads to the church. The cry is chiefly heard at night, hardly ever before dusk. (This would point to an owl.) It has become less frequent of recent years, but at this particular season is most persistent. Mason confirms this. He doesn't like the sound, and doesn't know what to make of it. The maids believe that it is an evil spirit; but, as it can have no power over them—they belong to the Peculiar People—they take no notice of it.

Visual and Sensory. From time to time—less frequently, again, of recent years—Miss Ankardyne wakes up "with her eyes balls of fire". She can distinguish nothing clearly for several minutes. Then the red spheres slowly contract to pin-pricks; there is a moment of sharp pain; and normal vision is restored. At other times she is aroused from sleep by a sharp, piercing pain in her tongue. She has consulted several oculists, who find that her sight is perfectly normal. I believe she has never known a day's illness. Prendergast seems to have had a similar, though less vivid, experience; he used the term "burning" headache.

I have elicited from Mason the statement that animals dislike the house, with the exception of Karkar, Miss Ankardyne's cat, who seems entirely unaffected. The spaniel refuses to sleep in Miss

Ankardyne's bedroom; and on one occasion, when the parrot's cage was brought up there, the bird, "fell into such a screaming fit, that it nearly brought the house down". This I believe, for I tried the experiment myself with the reluctant consent of Mrs. Mason. The feathers of the bird lay back flat on its head and neck with rage, and then it began to shriek in a really horrible way.

All this, of course, is very vague. We have no real evidence of anything supernatural. What impresses me most is the influence of the house on a woman of Miss Ankardyne's high character and courage.

February 18th. Certainly an interesting night. After a long walk with Prendergast in the afternoon I went to bed early with a volume of Trollope and a long candle. I did what I have never done before —fell asleep with the candle burning. When I awoke, it was within an inch of the socket; the fire had settled into a dull glow. Close to the candle-stick on the table by my bedside stood a carafe of water. As I lay in bed, too sleepy to move, I was conscious of the hypnotic effect induced by gazing into a crystal. Slowly the surface of the glass grew dim and then gradually cleared from the centre. I was looking into the interior of a building, which I at once recognised as Ankardyne Church. I could make out the screen and the Ankardyne pew. It seemed to be night, though I could see more clearly than if it had been night—the monuments in the aisle, for example. There were not as many as there are now. Presently the door of the Ankardyne pew opened and a man stepped out. He was dressed in black coat and knee-breeches, such as a clergyman might have worn a century or more ago. In one hand he held a lighted candle, the flame of which he sheltered with the other. I judged him to be of middle age. His face wore an expression of extreme apprehension. He crossed the church, casting backward glances as he went, and stopped before one of the mural monuments in the south aisle. Then, placing his candle on the ground, he drew from his pocket a hammer and some tools and, kneeling on the ground, began to work feverishly at the base of the inscription. When he had finished, and the task was not long, he seemed to moisten a finger and, running it along the floor, rubbed the dust into the newly cut stone. He then picked up his tools and began to retrace his steps. But the wind seemed to have risen; he had difficulty in shielding the flame of the candle, and just before he regained the door of the Ankardyne pew, it went out.

That was all that I saw in the crystal. I was now wide awake. I got out of bed, put fresh fuel on the fire, and wrote this account in my diary, while the picture was still vivid.

February 19th. Slept splendidly, despite the fact that I was prepared to spend a wakeful night. After a late breakfast I went with

Prendergast into the church and had no difficulty in identifying the monument. It is in the east end of the south aisle, immediately opposite the Ankardyne pew and partly hidden by the American organ. The inscription reads:

IN MEMORY OF
FRANCIS ANKARDYNE, ESQUIRE,
of Ankardyne Hall, in the County of Worcester,
late Captain in His Majesty's 42nd Regiment of
Foot.
He departed this life February 27th, 1781.
Rev. xiv. 12, 13.

I brought the Bible from the lectern. "There are lives," said Prendergast, "which can fitly be commemorated by such verses: 'Here is the patience of the saints; here are they that keep the commandments of God.' Miss Ankardyne's is one. And I suppose," he added, "that there may be some of whom the eleventh verse is true." He read it out to me: "And the smoke of their torment ascendeth for ever and ever; and they have no rest day nor night, who worship the beast and his image, and whosoever receiveth the mark of his name."

I thought at first that he was right; that the 12 might originally have been engraved as 11. But closer scrutiny showed that, though some of the figures had certainly been tampered with, it was not either the 2 or the 3. Prendergast hit on what I believe is the right solution. "That R," he said, "has been superimposed on an L, and the 1 was originally 5. The reference is to Leviticus xiv. 52, 53." If he is correct, we have still far to go. I have read and re-read those verses so often during the day, that I can write them down from memory:

"And he shall cleanse the house with the blood of the bird, and with the running water, and with the living bird, and with the cedar wood, and with the hyssop, and with the scarlet:

"But he shall let go the living bird out of the city into the open fields, and make an atonement for the house; and it shall be clean."

Miss Ankardyne told Prendergast that she was dimly aware of something connected with pain and fire and a bird. It is at least a curious coincidence.

Mason knows nothing about Francis Ankardyne except his name. He tells me that the Ankardyne squires of a hundred years ago had a reputation for evil living; in that, of course, they were not peculiar.

Spent the afternoon in the library in a rather fruitless search for clues. I found two books with the name "Francis Ankardyne" written on the fly-leaf. It was perhaps just as well that they should be tucked away on one of the upper shelves. One was inscribed as the gift of his cousin, Cotter Crawley. Query: Who is Crawley, and can he be identified with my man in black?

I tried to reproduce the crystal-gazing under conditions similar to those of the other night, but without success. I have twice heard the bird. It might be either an owl or a cock. The sound seemed to come from outside the house, and was not pleasant.

February 19th. To-morrow Prendergast moves into the vicarage and I return home. Miss Ankardyne prolongs her stay at Malvern for another fortnight, and is then to visit friends on the South Coast. I should like to have seen and questioned her, and so have discovered something more of the family history. Both Prendergast and I are disappointed. It seemed as if we were on the point of solving the mystery, and now it is as dark as ever. This new society in which Myers is interested should investigate the place.

So ends my diary, but not the story. Some four months after the events narrated I managed to secure through a second-hand book dealer four bound volumes of the *Gentleman's Magazine*. They had belonged to a Rev. Charles Phipson, once Fellow of Brasenose College and incumbent of Norton-on-the-Wolds. One evening, as I was glancing through them at my leisure, I came upon the following passage, under the date April, 1789:

> At Tottenham, John Ardenoif, Esq., a young man of large fortune and in the splendour of his carriages and horses rivalled by few country gentlemen. His table was that of hospitality, where, it may be said, he sacrificed too much to conviviality; but, if he had his foibles, he had his merits also, that far outweighed them. Mr. A. was very fond of cock-fighting and had a favourite cock upon which he won many profitable matches. The last bet he laid upon this cock he lost, which so enraged him that he had the bird tied to a spit and roasted alive before a large fire. The screams of the miserable bird were so affecting, that some gentlemen who were present attempted to interfere, which so enraged Mr. A. that he seized a poker and with the most furious vehemence declared that he would kill the first man who interposed; but, in the midst of his passionate asseverations, he fell down dead upon the spot. Such, we are assured, were the circumstances which attended the death of this great pillar of humanity.

Beneath was written:

> See also the narrative of Mr. C—— at the end of this volume.

I give the story as I found it, inscribed in minute handwriting on the terminal fly-leaves:

> During his last illness the Rev. Mr. C—— gave me the following account of a similar instance of Divine Judgment. Mr. A—— of A—— House, in the county of W——, was notorious for his open practice of infidelity. He was an ardent votary of the chase, a reckless gamester, and was an enthusiast in his love of cock-fighting. After carousing one evening with a boon companion, he proposed that they should then and there match the birds which they had entered for a contest on the morrow. His friend, declaring that his bird should fight only in a cockpit, Mr. A—— announced that he had one adjoining the very room in which they were. The birds were brought, lights called for, and Mr. A——, opening the door, led his guest down a flight of stairs and along a corridor to what he at first supposed were the stables. It was only after the match had begun, that he realised to his horror that they were in the family pew of A—— Church, to which A—— House had private access. His expostulations only enraged his host, who commenced to blaspheme, wagering his very soul on the success of his bird, the victor of fifty fights. On this occasion the cock was defeated. Beside himself with frenzy, Mr. A—— rushed back to his bedchamber and, declaring that the Judgment Day had come and that the bird should never crow again, thrust a wire into the embers, burned out its eyes, and bored through its tongue. He then fell down in some form of apoplectic fit. He recovered and continued his frenzied course of living for some years. It was noticed, however, that he had an impediment in his speech, especially remarkable when he was enraged, the effect of which was to make him utter a sound like the crowing of a cock. It became a cant phrase in the neighbourhood: "When A—— crows, honest men must move." Two years after this awful occurrence, his sight began to fail. He was killed in the hunting field. His horse took fright and, bolting, carried him for over a mile across bad country to break his neck in an attempt to leap a ten-foot wall. At each obstacle they encountered, Mr. A—— called out, but the noise that came from his throat only seemed to terrify his horse the more. Mr. C—— vouches for the truth of the story, having had personal acquaintance with both the parties.

The supposition that the Rev. Mr. C—— was none other than the boon companion of Francis Ankardyne did not seem to occur to the mind of the worthy Mr. Phipson. That such was the case, I have no doubt. I saw him once in a glass darkly; and I saw later at Ankardyne House a silhouette of Cotter Crawley in an old album, and recognised the weak, foolish profile.

Who it was who drew up the wording of the monument in

Ankardyne Church I do not know. Probably the trustees of the heir, a distant kinsman and a mere boy. Perhaps the mason mistook the R for an L, the 1 for a 5. Perhaps he was a grim jester; perhaps the dead man guided the chisel. But I can picture the horror of Cotter Crawley in being confronted with those suggestive verses. I see him stealing from the house, which after years of absence he has brought himself to revisit, at night. I see him at work, cold, yet feverish, on the tell-tale stone. I see him stricken by remorse and praying, as the publican prayed, without in the shadow.

Part of this story Prendergast and I told to Miss Ankardyne. The family pew is pulled down, and of the passage that connected the church with the house, only the façade is left. The house itself is quieter than it has been for years. A nephew of Miss Ankardyne from India is coming to live there soon. He has children, but I do not think there is anything of which they need be afraid. As I wrote before, it has been well aired by a kindly soul.

LUCKY'S GROVE

And Loki begat Hel, Goddess of the Grave, Fenris, the Great Wolf, and the Serpent, Nidnogg, who lives beneath The Tree.

MR. BRAXTON strolled with his land-agent, Curtis, into the Great Barn.

"There you are," said Curtis, in a satisfied tone, "the finest little larch I ever saw, and the kiddies will never set eyes on a lovelier Christmas tree."

Mr. Braxton examined it; it stood twenty feet from huge green pot to crisp, straight peak, and was exquisitely sturdy, fresh and symmetrical.

"Yes, it's a beauty," he agreed. "Where did you find it?"

"In that odd little spinney they call Lucky's Grove in the long meadow near the river boundary."

"Oh!" remarked Mr. Braxton uncertainly. To himself he was saying vaguely, "He shouldn't have got it from there, of course he wouldn't realise it, but he shouldn't have got it from there."

"Of course we'll replant it," said Curtis, noticing his employer's diminished enthusiasm. "It's a curious thing, but it isn't a young tree; it's apparently full-grown. Must be a dwarf variety, but I don't know as much about trees as I should like."

Mr. Braxton was surprised to find there was one branch of country lore on which Curtis was not an expert; for he was about the best-known man at his job in the British Isles. Pigs, bees, chickens, cattle, crops, running a shoot, he had mastered them one and all. He paid him two thousand a year with house and car. He was worth treble.

"I expect it's all right," said Mr. Braxton; "it's just that Lucky's Grove is—is—well, 'sacred' is perhaps too strong a word. Maybe I should have told you, but I expect it's all right."

"That accounts for it then," laughed Curtis. "I thought there seemed some reluctance on the part of the men while we were yanking it up and getting it on the lorry. They handled it a bit gingerly; on the part of the older men, I mean; the youngsters didn't worry."

"Yes, there would be," said Mr. Braxton. "But never mind, it'll be back in a few days and it's a superb little tree. I'll bring Mrs. Braxton along to see it after lunch," and he strolled back into Abingdale Hall.

Fifty-five years ago Mr. Braxton's father had been a labourer on this very estate, and in that year young Percy, aged eight, had got an errand boy's job in Oxford. Twenty years later he'd owned one small shop. Twenty-five years after that fifty big shops. Now, though he had finally retired, he owned two hundred and eighty vast shops and was a millionaire whichever way you added it up. How had this happened? No one can quite answer such questions. Certainly he'd worked like a brigade of Trojans, but midnight oil has to burn in Aladdin's Lamp before it can transform ninepence into one million pounds. It was just that he asked no quarter from the unforgiving minute, but squeezed from it the fruit of others' many hours. Those like Mr. Braxton seem to have their own time-scale; they just say the word and up springs a fine castle of commerce, but the knowledge of that word cannot be imparted; it is as mysterious as the Logos. But all through his great labours he had been moved by one fixed resolve—to avenge his father—that fettered spirit—for he had been an able, intelligent man who had had no earthly chance of revealing the fact to the world. Always the categorical determination had blazed in his son's brain, "I will own Abingdale Hall, and, where my father sweated, I will rule and be lord." And of course it had happened. Fate accepts the dictates of such men as Mr. Braxton, shrugs its shoulders, and leaves its revenge to Death. The Hall had come on the market just when he was about to retire, and with an odd delight, an obscure sense of home-coming, the native returned, and his riding boots, shooting boots, golf shoes, and all the many glittering guineas' worth, stamped in and obliterated the prints of his father's hob-nails.

That was the picture he often re-visualised, the way it amused him to "put it to himself", as he roamed his broad acres and surveyed the many glowing triumphs of his model husbandry.

Some credit was due to buxom, blithe and debonair Mrs. Braxton, kindly, competent and innately adaptable. She was awaiting him in the morning-room and they went in solitary state, to luncheon. But it was the last peaceful lunch they would have for a spell—"the Families" were pouring in on the morrow.

As a footman was helping them to Sole Meunière Mr. Braxton said, "Curtis has found a very fine Christmas tree. It's in the barn. You must come and look at it after lunch."

"That *is* good," replied his wife. "Where did he get it from?"

Mr. Braxton hesitated for a moment.

"From Lucky's Grove."

Mrs. Braxton looked up sharply.

"From the grove!" she said, surprised.

"Yes, of course he didn't realise—anyway it'll be all right, it's all rather ridiculous, and it'll be replanted before the New Year."

"Oh, yes," agreed Mrs. Braxton. "After all it's only just a clump of trees."

"Quite. And it's just the right height for the ballroom. It'll be taken in there to-morrow morning and the electricians will work on it in the afternoon."

"I heard from Lady Pounser just now," said Mrs. Braxton. "She's bringing six over, that'll make seventy-four; only two refusals. The presents are arriving this afternoon."

They discussed the party discursively over the cutlets and Peach Melba and soon after lunch walked across to the barn. Mr. Braxton waved to Curtis, who was examining a new tractor in the garage fifty yards away, and he came over.

Mrs. Braxton looked the tree over and was graciously delighted with it, but remarked that the pot could have done with another coat of paint. She pointed to several streaks, rust-coloured, running through the green. "Of course it won't show when it's wrapped, but they didn't do a very good job."

Curtis leant down. "They certainly didn't," he answered irritably. "I'll see to it. I think it's spilled over from the soil; that copse is on a curious patch of red sand—there are some at Frilford too. When we pulled it up I noticed the roots were stained a dark crimson." He put his hand down and scraped at the stains with his thumb. He seemed a shade puzzled.

"It shall have another coat at once," he said. "What did you think of Lampson and Colletts' scheme for the barn?"

"Quite good," replied Mrs. Braxton, "but the sketches for the chains are too fancy."

"I agree," said Curtis, who usually did so in the case of unessentials; reserving his tactful vetoes for the others.

The Great Barn was by far the most aesthetically satisfying, as it was the oldest feature of the Hall buildings, it was vast, exquisitely proportioned, and mellow. That could hardly be said of the house itself, which the 4th Baron of Abingdale had rebuilt on the cinders of its predecessor in 1752.

This nobleman had travelled abroad extensively and returned with most enthusiastic, grandiose and indigestible ideas of architecture. The result was a gargantuan piece of rococo-jocoso which only an entirely humourless pedant could condemn. It contained forty-two bedrooms and eighteen reception rooms—so Mrs. Braxton had made it at the last recount. But Mr. Braxton had not repeated with the interior the errors of the 4th Baron. He'd briefed the greatest expert in Europe with the result that that interior was quite tasteful and sublimely comfortable.

"Ugh!" he exclaimed, as they stepped out into the air, "it *is* getting nippy!"

"Yes," said Curtis, "there's a nor'-easter blowing up—may be snow for Christmas."

On getting back to the house Mrs. Braxton went into a huddle with butler and housekeeper and Mr. Braxton retired to his study for a doze. But instead his mind settled on Lucky's Grove. When he'd first seen it again after buying the estate, it seemed as if fifty years had rolled away, and he realised that Abingdale was far more summed up to him in the little copse than in the gigantic barracks two miles away. At once he felt at home again. Yet, just as when he'd been a small boy, the emotion the Grove had aroused in him had been sharply tinged with awe, so it had been now, half a century later. He still had a sneaking dread of it. How precisely he could see it, glowing darkly in the womb of the fire before him, standing starkly there in the centre of the big, fallow field, a perfect circle; and first, a ring of holm-oaks and, facing east, a breach therein to the larches and past them on the west a gap to the yews. It had always required a tug at his courage—not always forthcoming—to pass through them and face the mighty Scotch fir, rearing up its great bole from the grass mound. And when he stood before it, he'd always known an odd longing to fling himself down and—well, worship—it was the only word—the towering tree. His father had told him his forebears had done that very thing, but always when alone and at certain seasons of the year; and that no bird or beast was ever seen there. A lot of traditional nonsense, no doubt, but he himself had absorbed the spirit of the place and knew it would always be so.

One afternoon in late November, a few weeks after they had moved in, he'd gone off alone in the drowsing misty dusk; and when he'd reached the holm-oak bastion and seen the great tree surrounded by its sentinels, he'd known again that quick turmoil of confused emotions. As he'd walked slowly towards it, it had seemed to quicken and be aware of his coming. As he passed the shallow grassy fosse and entered the oak ring he felt there was something he ought to say, some greeting, password or prayer. It was the most aloof, silent little place under the sun, and oh, so old. He'd tiptoed past the larches and faced the barrier of yews. He'd stood there for a long musing minute, tingling with the sensation that he was being watched and regarded. At length he stepped forward and stood before the God—that mighty word came abruptly and unforeseen—and he felt a wild desire to fling himself down on the mound and do obeisance. And then he'd hurried home. As he recalled all this most vividly and minutely, he was seized with a sudden gust of uncontrollable anger at the thought of the desecration of the grove. He knew now that if he'd had the slightest idea of Curtis's purpose he'd have resisted and opposed it. It was too late now. He realised he'd "worked himself up" rather absurdly. What could it matter! He was still a superstitious bumpkin at heart. Anyway it was no fault of Curtis. It was the finest Christmas tree anyone could hope for, and the whole thing was too nonsensical for words. The general tone of these cadentic conclusions did not quite accurately represent his thoughts—a very rare failing with Mr. Braxton.

About dinner-time the blizzard set furiously in, and the snow was lying.

"Chains on the cars to-morrow," Mrs. Braxton told the head chauffeur.

"Boar's Hill'll be a beggar," thought that person.

Mr. and Mrs. Braxton dined early, casually examined the presents, and went to bed. Mr. Braxton was asleep at once as usual, but was awakened by the beating of a blind which had slipped its moorings. Reluctantly he got out of bed and went to fix it. As he was doing so he became conscious of the frenzied hysterical barking of a dog. The sound, muffled by the gale, came, he judged, from the barn. He believed the underkeeper kept his whippet there. Scared by the storm, he supposed, and returned to bed.

The morning was brilliantly fine and cold, but the snowfall had been heavy.

"I heard a dog howling in the night, Perkins," said Mr. Braxton to the butler at breakfast; "Drake's, I imagine. What's the matter with it?"

"I will ascertain, sir," replied Perkins.

"It *was* Drake's dog," he announced a little later. "Apparently something alarmed the animal, for when Drake went to let it out this morning, it appeared to be extremely frightened. When the barn door was opened, it took to its heels and, although Drake pursued it, it jumped into the river and Drake fears it was drowned."

"Um," said Mr. Braxton, "must have been the storm; whippets are nervous dogs."

"So I understand, sir."

"Drake was so fond of it," said Mrs. Braxton, "though it always looked so naked and shivering to me."

"Yes, madam," agreed Perkins, "it had that appearance."

Soon after, Mr. Braxton sauntered out into the blinding glitter. Curtis came over from the garage. He was heavily muffled up.

"They've got chains on all the cars," he said. "Very seasonable and all that, but farmers have another word for it." His voice was thick and hoarse.

"Yes," said Mr. Braxton. "You're not looking very fit."

"Not feeling it. Had to get up in the night. Thought I heard someone trying to break into the house; thought I saw him, too."

"Indeed," said Mr. Braxton. "Did you see what he was like?"

"No," replied Curtis uncertainly. "It was snowing like the devil. Anyway, I got properly chilled to the marrow, skipping around in my nightie."

"You'd better get to bed," said Mr. Braxton solicitously. He had affection and a great respect for Curtis.

"I'll stick it out to-day and see how I feel to-morrow. We're going to get the tree across in a few minutes. Can I borrow the two footmen? I want another couple of pullers and haulers."

Mr. Braxton consented, and went off on his favourite little stroll across the sparkling meadows to the river and the pool where the big trout set their cunning noses to the stream.

Half an hour later Curtis had mobilised his scratch team of sleeve-rolled assistants and, with Perkins steering and himself breaking, they got to grips with the tree and bore it like a camouflaged battering-ram towards the ballroom, which occupied the left centre of the frenetic frontage on the ground floor. There was a good deal of bumping and boring and genial blasphemy before the tree was manoeuvred into the middle of the room and levered by rope and muscle into position. As it came up its pinnacle just cleared the ceiling. Sam, a cow-man, whose ginger mop had been buried in the foliage for some time, exclaimed tartly as he slapped the trunk, "There ye are, ye old sod! Thanks for the scratches on me mug, ye old—!"

The next moment he was lying on his back, a livid weal across his right cheek.

This caused general merriment, and even Perkins permitted himself a spectral smile. There was more astonishment than pain on the face of Sam. He stared at the tree in a humble way for a moment, like a chastised and guilty dog, and then slunk from the room. The merriment of the others died away.

"More spring in these branches than you'd think," said Curtis to Perkins.

"No doubt, sir, that is due to the abrupt release of the tension," replied Perkins scientifically.

The "Families" met at Paddington and travelled down together, so at five o'clock three car-loads drew up at the Hall. There were Jack and Mary with Paddy aged eight, Walter and Pamela with Jane and Peter, seven and five respectively, and George and Gloria with Gregory and Phyllis, ten and eight.

Jack and Walter were sons of the house. They were much of a muchness, burly, handsome and as dominating as their sire; a fine pair of commercial kings, entirely capable rulers, but just lacking that something which founds dynasties. Their wives conformed equally to the social type to which they belonged, good-lookers, smart dressers, excellent wives and mothers; but rather coolly colourless, spiritually. Their offspring were "charming children", flawless products of the English matrix, though Paddy showed signs of some obstreperous originality. "George" was the Honourable George, Calvin, Roderick, etcetera Penables, and Gloria was Mr. and Mrs. Braxton's only daughter. George had inherited half a million and had started off at twenty-four to be something big in the City. In a sense he achieved his ambition, for two years later he was generally reckoned the biggest "Something" in the City, from which he then withdrew, desperately clutching his last hundred thousand and vowing lachrymose repentance. He had kept his word and his wad, hunted and shot six days a week in the winter, and spent most of the summer wrestling with the two dozen devils in his golf bag. According to current jargon he was the complete extrovert, but what a relief are such, in spite of the pitying shrugs of those who for ever are peering into the septic recesses of their souls.

Gloria had inherited some of her father's force. She was rather overwhelmingly primed with energy and pep for her opportunities of releasing it. So she was always rather pent up and explosive, though maternity had kept the pressure down. She was dispassionately fond of George who had presented her with a nice little title and aristocratic background and two "charming children". Phyllis gave promise of such extreme beauty that, beyond being the cynosure of every press-camera's eye, and making a resounding match, no more was to be expected of her. Gregory, however, on the strength of some artistic precocity and a violent temper was already somewhat prematurely marked down as a genius to be.

Such were the "Families".

During the afternoon four engineers arrived from one of the Braxton factories to fix up the lighting of the tree. The fairy lamps for this had been specially designed and executed for the occasion. Disney figures had been grafted upon them and made to revolve by an ingenious mechanism; the effect being to give the tree, when illuminated, an aspect of whirling life meant to be very cheerful and pleasing.

Mr. Braxton happened to see these electricians departing in their lorry and noticed one of them had a bandaged arm and a rather white face. He asked Perkins what had happened.

"A slight accident, sir. A bulb burst and burnt him in some manner. But the injury is, I understand, not of a very serious nature."

"He looked a bit white."

"Apparently, sir, he got a fright, a shock of some kind, when the bulb exploded."

After dinner the grown-ups went to the ballroom. Mr. Braxton switched on the mechanism and great enthusiasm was shown. "Won't the kiddies love it," said George, grinning at the kaleidoscope. "Look at the Big Bad Wolf. He looks so darn realistic I'm not sure I'd give him a 'U' certificate."

"It's almost frightening," said Pamela, "they look incredibly real. Daddie, you really are rather bright, darling."

It was arranged that the work of decoration should be tackled on the morrow and finished on Christmas Eve.

"All the presents have arrived," said Mrs. Braxton, "and are being unpacked. But I'll explain about them to-morrow."

They went back to the drawing-room. Presently Gloria puffed and remarked: "Papa, aren't you keeping the house rather too hot?"

"I noticed the same thing," said Mrs. Braxton.

Mr. Braxton walked over to a thermometer on the wall. "You're right," he remarked, "seventy." He rang the bell.

"Perkins," he asked, "who's on the furnace?"

"Churchill, sir."

"Well, he's overdoing it. It's seventy. Tell him to get it back to fifty-seven."

Perkins departed and returned shortly after.

"Churchill informs me he has damped down and cannot account for the increasing warmth, sir."

"Tell him to get it back to fifty-seven at once," rapped Mr. Braxton.

"Very good, sir."

"Open a window," said Mrs. Braxton.

"It is snowing again, madam."

"Never mind."

"My God!" exclaimed Mary, when she and Jack went up to bed. "That furnace-man is certainly stepping on it. Open all the windows."

A wild flurry of snow beat against the curtains.

Mr. Braxton did what he very seldom did, woke up in the early hours. He awoke sweating from a furtive and demoralising dream. It had seemed to him that he had been crouching down in the fosse round Lucky's Grove and peering beneath the holm-oaks, and that there had been activity of a sort vaguely to be discerned therein, some quick, shadowy business. He knew a very tight terror at the thought of being detected at this spying, but he could not wrench himself away. That was all, and he awoke still trembling and troubled. No wonder he'd had such a nightmare, the room seemed like a stokehold. He went to the windows and flung another open, and as he did so glanced out. His room looked over the rock garden and down the path to the maze. Something moving just outside it caught his eye. He thought he knew what it was, that big Alsatian which had been sheep-worrying in the neighbourhood. What an enormous brute! Or was it just because it was outlined against the snow? It vanished suddenly, apparently into the maze. He'd organise a hunt for it after Christmas; if the snow lay, it should be easy to track.

The first thing he did after breakfast was to send for Churchill, severely reprimand him and threaten him with dismissal from his ship. That person was almost tearfully insistent that he had obeyed orders and kept his jets low. "I can't make it out, sir. It's got no right to be as 'ot as what it is."

"That's nonsense!" said Mr. Braxton. "The system has been perfected and cannot take charge, as you suggest. See to it. You don't want me to get an engineer down, do you?"

"No, sir."

"That's enough. Get it to fifty-seven and keep it there."

Shortly after, Mrs. Curtis rang up to say her husband was quite ill with a temperature and that the doctor was coming. Mr. Braxton asked her to ring him again after he'd been.

During the morning the children played in the snow. After a pitched battle in which the girls lost their tempers, Gregory organised the erection of a snowman. He designed, the others fetched the material. He knew he had a reputation for brilliance to maintain and he produced something Epsteinish, huge and squat. The other children regarded it with little enthusiasm, but, being Gregory, they supposed it must be admired. When it was finished Gregory wandered off by himself while the others went in to dry. He came in a little ate for lunch, during which he was silent and pre-occupied. Afterwards the grown-ups sallied forth.

"Let's see your snowman, Greg," said Gloria, in a mother-of-genius tone.

"It isn't all his, we helped," said Phyllis, voicing a point of view which was to have many echoes in the coming years.

"Why, he's changed it!" exclaimed a chorus two minutes later.

"What an ugly thing!" exclaimed Mary, rather pleased at being able to say so with conviction.

Gregory had certainly given his imagination its head, for now the squat, inert trunk was topped by a big wolf's head with open jaw and ears snarlingly laid back, surprisingly well modelled. Trailing behind it was a coiled, serpentine tail.

"Whatever gave you the idea for that?" asked Jack.

Usually Gregory was facile and eloquent in explaining his inspiration, but this time he refused to be drawn, bit his lip and turned away.

There was a moment's silence and then Gloria said with convincing emphasis, "I think it's wonderful, Greg!"

And then they all strolled off to examine the pigs and the poultry and the Suffolk punches.

They had just got back for tea when the telephone rang in Mr. Braxton's study. It was Mrs. Curtis. The patient was no better and Doctor Knowles had seemed rather worried, and so on. So Mr. Braxton rang up the doctor.

"I haven't diagnosed his trouble yet," he said. "And I'm going to watch him carefully and take a blood-test if he's not better tomorrow. He has a temperature of a hundred and two, but no other superficial symptoms, which is rather peculiar. By the way, one of your cow-men, Sam Colley, got a nasty wound on the face yesterday and shows signs of blood poisoning. I'm considering sending him to hospital. Some of your other men have been in to see me—quite a little outbreak of illness since Tuesday. However, I hope we'll have a clean bill again soon. I'll keep you informed about Curtis."

Mr. Braxton was one of those incredible people who never have a day's illness—till their first and last. Consequently his conception of disease was unimaginative and mechanical. If one of his more essential human machines was running unsatisfactorily, there was a machine-mender called a doctor whose business it was to ensure that all the plug leads were attached firmly and that the manifold drain-pipe was not blocked. But he found himself beginning to worry about Curtis, and this little epidemic amongst his henchmen affected him disagreeably—there was something disturbing to his spirit about it. But just what and why, he couldn't analyse and decide.

After dinner, with the children out of the way, the business of decorating the tree was begun. The general scheme had been sketched out and coloured by one of the Braxton display experts and the company consulted this as they worked, which they did rather silently; possibly Mr. Braxton's palpable anxiety somewhat affected them.

Pamela stayed behind after the others had left the ballroom to put some finishing touches to her section of the tree. When she rejoined the others she was looking rather white and tight-lipped. She said good-night a shade abruptly and went to her room. Walter, a very, very good husband, quickly joined her.

"Anything the matter, old girl?" he asked anxiously.

"Yes," replied Pamela, "I'm frightened."

"Frightened! What d'you mean?"

"You'll think it's all rot, but I'll tell you. When you'd all left the ballroom, I suddenly felt very uneasy—you know the sort of feeling when one keeps on looking round and can't concentrate. However, I stuck at it. I was a little way up the steps when I heard a sharp hiss from above me in the tree. I jumped back to the floor and looked up; now, of course, you won't believe me, but the trunk of the tree was moving—it was like the coils of a snake writhing upward, and there was something at the top of the tree, horrid-looking, peering at me. I know you won't believe me."

Walter didn't, but he also didn't know what to make of it. "I know what happened!" he improvised lightly. "You'd been staring in at that trunk for nearly two hours and you got dizzy—like staring at the sun on the sea; and that snow dazzle this afternoon helped it. You've heard of snow-blindness—something like that, it still echoes from the retina or whatever..."

"You think it might have been that?"

"I'm sure of it."

"And that horrible head?"

"Well, as George put it rather brightly, I don't think some of those figures on the lamps should get a 'U' certificate. There's the wolf to which he referred, and the witch."

"Which witch?" laughed Pamela a little hysterically. "I didn't notice one."

"I did. I was working just near it, at least, I suppose it's meant to be a witch. A figure in black squinting round from behind a tree. As a matter of fact fairies never seemed all fun and frolic to me, there's often something diabolical about them—or rather casually cruel. Disney knows that."

"Yes, there is," agreed Pamela. "So you think that's all there was to it?"

"I'm certain. One's eyes can play tricks on one."

"Yes," said Pamela, "I know what you mean, as if they saw what one knew wasn't there or was different. Though who would 'one' be then?"

"Oh, don't ask me that sort of question!" laughed Walter. "Probably Master Gregory will be able to tell you in a year or two."

"He's a nice little boy, really," protested Pamela. "Gloria just spoils him and it's natural."

'I know he is, it's not his fault, but they will *force* him. Look at that snow-man—and staying behind to do it. A foul-looking thing!"

"Perhaps his eyes played funny tricks with him," said Pamela.

"What d'you mean by that?"

"I don't know why I said it," said Pamela, frowning. "Sort of echo, I suppose. Let's go to bed."

Walter kissed her gently but fervently, as he loved her. He was a one-lady's-man and had felt a bit nervous about her for a moment or two.

Was the house a little cooler? wondered Mr. Braxton, as he was undressing, or was it that he was getting more used to it? He was now convinced there was something wrong with the installation; he'd get an expert down. Meanwhile they must stick it. He yawned, wondered how Curtis was, and switched off the light.

Soon all the occupants were at rest and the great house swinging silently against the stars. Should have been at rest, rather, for one and all recalled that night with reluctance and dread. Their dreams were harsh and unhallowed, yet oddly related, being concerned with dim, uncertain and yet somehow urgent happenings in and around the house, as though some thing or things were stirring while they slept and communicated their motions to their dreaming consciousness. They awoke tired with a sense of unaccountable malaise.

Mrs. Curtis rang up during breakfast and her voice revealed her distress. Timothy was delirious and much worse. The doctor was coming at 10.30.

Mr. and Mrs. Braxton decided to go over there, and sent for the car. Knowles was waiting just outside the house when they arrived.

"He's very bad," he said quietly. "I've sent for two nurses and Sir Arthur Galley; I want another opinion. Has he had some trouble with a tree?"

"Trouble with a tree!" said Mr. Braxton, his nerves giving a flick.

"Yes, it's probably just a haphazard, irrational idea of delirium, but he continually fusses about some tree."

"How bad is he?" asked Mrs. Braxton.

The doctor frowned. "I wish I knew. I'm fairly out of my depth. He's keeping up his strength fairly well, but he can't go on like this."

"As bad as that!" exclaimed Mr. Braxton.

"I'm very much afraid so. I'm anxiously awaiting Sir Arthur's verdict. By the way, that cow-man is very ill indeed; I'm sending him into hospital."

"What happened to him?" asked Mr. Braxton, absently, his mind on Curtis.

"Apparently a branch of your Christmas tree snapped back at him and struck his face. Blood-poisoning set in almost at once."

Mr. Braxton felt that tremor again, but merely nodded.

"I was just wondering if there might be some connection between the two, that Curtis is blaming himself for the accident. Seems an absurd idea, but judging from his ravings he appears to think he is lashed to some tree and that the great heat he feels comes from it."

They went into the house and did their best to comfort and reassure Mrs. Curtis, instructed Knowles to ring up as soon as Sir Arthur's verdict was known, and then drove home.

The children had just come in from playing in the snow.

"Grandpa, the snow-man's melted," said Paddy, "did it thaw in the night?"

"Must have done," replied Mr. Braxton, forcing a smile.

"Come and look, Grandpa," persisted Paddy, "there's nothing left of it."

"Grandpa doesn't want to be bothered," said Mary, noticing his troubled face.

"I'll come," said Mr. Braxton. When he reached the site of the snow-man his thoughts were still elsewhere, but his mind quickly refocused itself, for he was faced with something a little strange. Not a vestige of the statue remained, though the snow was frozen crisp and crunched hard beneath their feet; and yet that snow-man was completely obliterated and where it had stood was a circle of bare, brown grass.

"It must have thawed in the night and then frozen again," he said uncertainly.

"Then why—" began Paddy.

"Don't bother Grandpa," said Mary sharply. "He's told you what happened."

They wandered off towards the heavy, hurrying river.

"Are those dog-paw marks?" asked Phyllis.

That reminded Mr. Braxton. He peered down. "Yes," he replied. "And I bet they're those of that brute of an Alsatian; it must be a colossal beast."

"And it must have paws like a young bear," laughed Mary. "They're funny dogs, sort of Jekyll-and-Hydes. I rather adore them."

"You wouldn't adore this devil. He's all Hyde." (I'm in the wrong mood for these festivities, he thought irritably.)

During the afternoon George and Walter took the kids to a cinema in Oxford; the others finished the decoration of the tree.

The presents, labelled with the names of their recipients, were arranged on tables round the room and the huge cracker, ten feet long and forty inches in circumference, was placed on its gaily decorated trestle near the tree. Just as the job was finished, Mary did a three-quarters faint, but was quickly revived with brandy.

"It's the simply ghastly heat in the house!" exclaimed Gloria, who was not looking too grand herself. "The installation must be completely diseased. Ours always works perfectly." Mary had her dinner in bed and Jack came up to her immediately he had finished his.

"How are you feeling, darling?" he asked.

"Oh, I'm all right."

"It *was* the heat, of course?"

"Oh, yes," replied Mary with rather forced emphasis.

"Scared you a bit, going off like that?" suggested Jack, regarding her rather sharply.

"I'm quite all right, thank you," said Mary in the tone she always adopted when she's had enough of a subject. "I'd like to rest. Switch off the light."

But when Jack had gone, she didn't close her eyes, but lay on her back staring up at the faint outline of the ceiling. She frowned and lightly chewed the little finger of her left hand, a habit of hers when unpleasantly puzzled. Mary, like most people of strong character and limited imagination, hated to be puzzled. Everything, she considered, ought to have a simple explanation if one tried hard enough to find it. But how could one explain this odd thing that had happened to her? Besides the grandiose gifts on the tables which bore a number, as well as the recipient's name, a small present for everyone was hung on the tree. This also bore a number, the same one as the lordly gift, so easing the Braxtons' task of handing these out to the right people. Mary had just fixed Curtis's label to a cigarette lighter and tied it on the tree when it swung on its silk thread, so that the back of the card was visible; and on it was this inscription: "Died, December 25th, 1938". It spun away again and back and the inscription was no longer there.

Now Mary came of a family which rather prided itself on being unimaginative. Her father had confined his flights of fancy to the Annual Meeting of his Shareholders, while, to her mother, imagination and mendacity were at least first cousins. So Mary could hardly credit the explanation that, being remotely worried about Mr. Curtis, she had subconsciously concocted that sinister sentence. On the other hand she knew poor Mr. Curtis was very ill and, therefore, perhaps, if her brain had played that malign little trick on her, it might have done so in "tombstone writing".

This was a considerable logical exercise for Mary, the effort tired her, the impression began to fade and she started wondering how much longer Jack was going to sit up. She dozed off and there, as if flashed on the screen "inside her head" was "Died, December 25th, 1938". This, oddly enough, completely reassured her. There was "nothing there" this time. There had been nothing that other time. She'd been very weak and imaginative even to think otherwise.

While she was deciding this, Dr. Knowles rang up. "Sir Arthur has just been," he said. "And I'm sorry to say he's pessimistic. He says Curtis is very weak."

"But what's the matter with him?" asked Mr. Braxton urgently.

"He doesn't know. He calls it P.U.O., which really means nothing."

"But what's it stand for?"

"Pyrexia unknown origin. There are some fevers which cannot be described more precisely."

"How ill is he really?"

"All I can say is, we must hope for the best."

"My God!" exclaimed Mr. Braxton. "When's Sir Arthur coming again?"

"At eleven to-morrow. I'll ring you up after he's been."

Mr. Braxton excused himself and went to his room. Like many men of his dominating, sometimes ruthless type, he was capable of an intensity of feeling, anger, resolution, desire for revenge, but also affection and sympathy, unknown to more superficially Christian and kindly souls. He was genuinely attached to Curtis and his wife and very harshly and poignantly moved by this news which, he realised, could hardly have been worse. He would have to exercise all his will power if he was to sleep.

If on the preceding night the rest of the sleepers had been broken by influences which had insinuated themselves into their dreams, that which caused the night of that Christmas Eve to be unforgettable was the demoniacal violence of the elements. The north-easter had been waxing steadily all the evening and by midnight reached hurricane force, driving before it an almost impenetrable wall of snow. Not only so, but continually all through the night the wall was enflamed, and the roar of the hurricane silenced, by fearful flashes of lightning and raffales of thunder. The combination was almost intolerably menacing. As the great house shook from the gale and trembled at the blasts and the windows blazed with strange polychromatic balls of flame, all were tense and troubled. The children fought or succumbed to their terror according to their natures; their parents soothed and reassured them.

Mr. Braxton was convinced the lightning conductors were struck three times within ten minutes, and he could imagine them recoiling from the mighty impacts and seething from the terrific charges.

Not till a dilatory, chaotic dawn staggered up the sky did the storm temporarily lull. For a time the sky cleared and the frost came hard. It was a yawning and haggard company which assembled at breakfast. But determined efforts were made to engender a communal cheerfulness. Mr. Braxton did his best to contribute his quota of seasonable bonhomie, but his mind was plagued by thoughts of Curtis. Before the meal was finished the vicar rang up to say the church tower had been struck and almost demolished, so there could be no services. It rang again to say that Brent's farmhouse had been burnt to the ground.

While the others went off to inspect the Church Mr. Braxton remained in the study. Presently Knowles rang to say Sir Arthur had been and pronounced Curtis weaker, but his condition was not quite hopeless. One of the most ominous symptoms was the violence of the delirium. Curtis appeared to be in great terror and sedatives had no effect.

"How's that cow-man?" asked Mr. Braxton.

"He died in the night, I'm sorry to say."

Whereupon Mr. Braxton broke one of his strictest rules by drinking a very stiff whisky with very little soda.

Christmas dinner was tolerably hilarious, and after it, the children, bulging and incipiently bilious, slept some of it off, while their elders put the final touches to the preparations for the party.

In spite of the weather, not a single "cry-off" was telephoned. There was a good reason for this; Mr. Braxton's entertainments were justly famous.

So from four-thirty onwards the "Cream of North Berkshire Society" came ploughing through the snow to the Hall; Lady Pounser and party bringing up the rear in her heirloom Rolls which was dribbling steam from its ancient and aristocratic beak. A tea of teas, not merely a high-tea, an Everest tea, towering, sky-scraping, was then attacked by the already stuffed juveniles who, by the end of it, were almost livid with repletion, finding even the efforts of cracker-pulling almost beyond them.

They were then propelled into the library where rows of chairs had been provided for them. There was a screen at one end of the room, a projector at the other. Mr. Braxton had provided one of his famous surprises! The room was darkened and on the screen was flashed the sentence: *"The North Berks News Reel."*

During the last few weeks Mr. Braxton had had a sharp-witted and discreetly furtive camera-man at work shooting some of the guests while busy about their more or less lawful occasions.

For example, there was a sentence from a speech by Lord Gallen, the Socialist Peer: "It is a damnable and calculated lie for our opponents to suggest we aim at a preposterous and essentially *inequitable* equalisation on income—" And then there was His Lordship just entering his limousine, and an obsequious footman, rug in hand, holding the door open for him.

His Lordship's laughter was raucous and vehement, though he *would* have liked to have said a few words in rebuttal.

And there was Lady Pounser's Rolls, locally known as "the hippogriffe", stuck in a snow-drift and enveloped in steam, with the caption, "Oh, Mr. Mercury, *do* give me a start!" And other kindly, slightly sardonic japes at the expense of the North Berks Cream.

The last scene was meant as an appropriate prelude to the climax of the festivities. It showed Curtis and his crew digging up the tree from Lucky's Grove. Out they came from the holm-oaks straining under their load, but close observers noticed there was one who remained behind, standing menacing and motionless, a very tall, dark, brooding figure. There came a blinding lightning flash which seemed to blaze sparking round the room, and a fearsome metallic bang. The storm had returned with rasping and imperious salute.

The lights immediately came on and the children were marshalled to the ballroom. As they entered and saw the high tree shining there and the little people so lively upon its branches a prolonged "O—h!" of astonishment was extorted from the blasé brats. But there was another wave of flame against the windows which rattled wildly at the ensuing roar, and the cries of delight were tinged with terror. And, indeed, the hard, blue glare flung a sinister glow on the tree and its whirling throng.

The grown-ups hastened to restore equanimity and, forming rings of children, circled round the tree.

Presently Mrs. Braxton exclaimed: "Now then, look for your names on the cards and see what Father Christmas has brought you.

Though hardly one of the disillusioned infants retained any belief in that superannuated Deliverer of Goods, the response was immediate. For they had sharp ears which had eagerly absorbed the tales of Braxton munificence. At the same time it was noticeable that some approached the tree with diffidence, almost reluctance, and started back as a livid flare broke against the window-blinds and the dread peals shook the streaming snow from the eaves.

Mary had just picked up little Angela Rayner so that she could reach her card, when the child screamed and pulled away her hand.

"The worm!" she cried, and a thick, black-grey squirming maggot fell from her fingers to the floor and writhed away. George, who was near, put his shoe on it with a squish.

One of the Pounser tribe, whose card was just below the Big Bad

Wolf, refused to approach it. No wonder, thought Walter, for it looked horribly hunting and alive. There were other mischances too. The witch behind the sombre tree seemed to pounce out at Clarissa Balder, so she tearfully complained, and Gloria had to pull off her card for her. Of course Gregory was temperamental, seeming to stare at a spot just below the taut peak of the tree, as if mazed and entranced. But the presents were wonderful and more than worth the small ordeal of finding one's card and pretending not to be frightened when the whole room seemed full of fiery hands and the thunder cracked against one's ear-drums and shook one's teeth. Easy to be afraid!

At length the last present had been bestowed and it was time for the *pièce de résistance*, the pulling of the great cracker. Long, silken cords streamed from each end with room among them for fifty chubby fists, and a great surprise inside, for sure. The languid, uneasy troop were lined up at each end and took a grip on the silken cords.

At that moment a footman came in and told Mr. Braxton he was wanted on the telephone.

Filled with foreboding he went to his study. He heard the voice of Knowles—

"I'm afraid I have very bad news for you...."

The chubby fists gripped the silken cords.

"Now pull!" cried Mrs. Braxton.

The opposing teams took the strain.

A leaping flash and a blasting roar. The children were hurled, writhing and screaming over each other.

Up from the middle of the cracker leapt a rosy shaft of flame which, as it reached the ceiling, seemed to flatten its peak so that it resembled a great snake of fire which turned and hurled itself against the tree in a blinding embrace. There was a fierce sustained "Hiss", the tree flamed like a torch, and all the fairy globes upon it burst and splintered. And then the roaring torch cast itself down amongst the screaming chaos. For a moment the great pot, swathed in green, was a carmine cauldron and its paint streamed like blood upon the floor. Then the big room was a dream of fire and those within it driven wildly from its heat.

Phil Tangler, whose farmhouse, on the early slopes of Missen Rise, overlooked both Lucky's Grove and the Hall, solemnly declared that at 7.30 on Christmas Day, 1938, he was watching from a window and marvelling at the dense and boiling race of snow, the bitter gale, and the wicked flame and fury of the storm, when he saw a huge fist of fire form a rift in the cloud-rack, a fist with two huge blazing fingers, one of which speared down on the Hall, another touched and kindled the towering fir in Lucky's Grove, as though saluting it. Five minutes later he was racing through the hurricane to join in a vain night-long fight to save the Hall, already blazing from stem to stern.

OR PERSONS UNKNOWN

Mr James Ponders rubbed his nose, and then read again his brother's letter:

Dear Jim,

I've just got back from Madeira, and am so sorry to hear about poor old Reynolds. How you must miss him! Have you got anyone else yet? If not, I have someone I can recommend with perfect confidence. He is a man of the name of Millin, who was my valet for a time many years ago; I don't suppose you remember him. He left me to take up "butling", and was with Harry Roper till his death. He then went to Sir Roger Wallington, a very curious cove. You may remember that there was a mighty mystery about his passing. Well, Millin was suspected of having murdered him, not that there was any motive brought forward, but simply because he was sleeping in a room near by, and there was no other man in the house. Superficially it looked fishy. However, there was no real evidence against him, and he was never arrested. Now when I read the case I *knew* quite positively that Millin was innocent. He is one of the best fellows in the world, kind, thoughtful, a gentleman if ever there was one, besides being as efficient and hard-working as they're made. So I asked him to come to see me. When he came, looking very weary and worn, he suddenly blurted out the very curicus story which I hope you'll permit him to tell to you.

Now you know what an arrant old sceptic I am; nevertheless I believed every word of this very curious story, though it tends to drive a hole clean through all my scandalous and antediluvian materialism.

Now there are many more things in *your* heaven and earth than in mine, so if I can believe it, you should have no difficulty in doing likewise. If you can, that act of faith will give you the finest servant in Europe, and a charming companion. His past has made it impossible for him to get a decent job, so I have been looking after him for the past two years. This seems a heaven-sent opportunity to do you and him a very good turn. At any rate see him. He is 46 and a bachelor. I hope you're flourishing; I should like to pay you a visit in June some time, if you'd like to have me.

LEONARD

P.S.—His address is 38, Mustard Row, Clapham.

Certainly Mr. Ponders missed Reynolds, his devoted companion for 25 years. To middle-aged bachelors with large Tudor houses, dwarfed social senses and a great appreciation of personal comfort, to perhaps a little bit selfish gentry of this sort, their butlers are, next to themselves, the most important people in the world. Mrs. Dupine did her best, Mr. Ponders conceded, but he had noted several little unpleasant omissions during the last three weeks. He had interviewed several highly recommended and rotund individuals since Reynold's death, but none of them had really appealed to him.

But was there anything less appealing than to have always near one somebody who had been seriously suspected of having cut his master's throat! For that was how Sir Roger had come to his end, as he remembered. Might not such a one, encouraged by the success of his first—if it were his first—butchery, proceed with careful and cunning planning to commit another!

Had these questions been raised by anyone but his brother Leonard, Mr. Ponders would have scorned to put himself to the trouble of answering them. But his brother Leonard was without exception the finest judge of character he knew. He was *inspired*, his instinct flawless. He *could* not disregard his opinion in this case. Mr. Ponders was rather a timid, and perhaps a little old-fashioned and prejudiced person, but he prided himself on his courage and open-mindedness. Would he have a claim to either if he refused to see this Mr. Millin? He would not. Besides, it sounded as though his story might be of interest to an earnest student of psychic phenomena. And he *did* want a butler. So he straightway sat down at his bureau in that glorious study, the pride of that famous show-place, Ponders Manor, in the County of Bucks, the ancestral seat of the Ponders line, and wrote a note to Mr. Millin in his flowing yet staccato script, asking him, were it convenient to him, to come down the following Thursday. He suggested the 11.30 train from Marylebone. A car would meet him at Great Missenden. All this would be, of course, at his, Mr. Ponders's, expense.

He also wrote to his brother Leonard. Then he looked at his watch and found it was 4.30. Chess-time for a man of habit, so out came the ivory pieces, the chequered board, and the book of the New York Tourney, and he began studiously analysing that mighty tilt, "Capablanca *v.* Alechin, Round I."

On the next evening he received a note from Mr. Millin, respectfully announcing his intention of catching the 11.30 next Thursday.

Mr. Ponders looked forward to this interview with controlled trepidation. Fancy meeting someone—all alone in his study—who but for the lack of a little evidence might have been hanged—might have been "jerked", they called it, didn't they?

Certainly, but for Leonard, he would not have put himself in such a position.

However, when 12.40 saw Mr. Millin entering the study his trepidation wavered and died. He saw an erect and rather lean figure appropriately garbed in black with a gold watch-chain. But it was Mr. Millin's face that almost persuaded Mr. Ponders forthwith to engage him without further ado. His features were nondescript, but there was something in his expression, so candid, benign, if a little dejected, the expression of one who had known terror and danger, which encountering, he had conquered—at a cost, that went straight to Mr. Ponders's really kind little heart.

He opened the conversation with a conventional gambit, describing the circumstances—already well known to Mr. Millin—by which the latter found himself there.

Mr. Millin paid murmured thanks to the kindness of all concerned.

"And now, Mr. Millin," said Mr. Ponders, "I will be frank with you. My brother has told me about your connection with Sir Roger Wallington, the difficult position in which you were placed, and your explanation. The latter, I understand, takes the form of a rather remarkable story which my brother believed implicitly. In some way, I take it, it explains the mystery of Sir Roger's death?"

"In some way, I suppose it does, sir," replied Mr. Millin, "but it is so unlikely a tale that I wouldn't have had the courage to tell it to anyone but Sir Leonard. But he's always been so good to me that I dared to tell it to him. You can imagine my relief, sir, when he believed it. I quite understand that you, sir, wouldn't dream of taking me into your service unless you believed it too, and thought it freed me from all suspicion concerning Sir Roger's death."

"That is so," said Mr. Ponders. "Let me hear it."

"Well, sir, after Mr. Roper's death I was out of a position, and seeing Sir Roger's advertisement in the *Morning Post* I answered it, and received a request from Sir Roger to go down to see him.

"Sir Roger was a remarkable-looking gentleman, sir—very tall and strong, with very hard blue eyes, and a contemptuous, nervous, fighting look about him; yet somehow I took a fancy to him.

" 'Well, Millin,' he said, 'so you think you'd like to be my butler. Five strong men have thought that in the last eighteen months, and then—they have decided otherwise. The fellow who's here now, for example, Mr. Peters, well—*he's* decided otherwise. He spent some time in America, Millin. The United States have much to be said for them, but they're not good for British butlers. Have you been abroad?'

"'Only for one day, sir,' I said, 'from Brighton to Boulogne and back.'

"'I shan't hold that up against you. I rather like the look of you—you look *soothing*. I want someone soothing. Would you like to try it?'

"I said I would, sir (for one thing, the wages Sir Roger offered were much above the average).

"'Very well,' he said, 'come next Wednesday and stay as long as you can stick it.'

"I had some dinner with the servants before leaving, and what I heard made me realise I was taking something on. Apparently Sir Roger had always been famous for his tempers; during the War he had been wounded in the head, and still had a good deal of pain, and his rages had become very hot indeed, sir.

"'Well, old man, I wish you luck,' said Peters, 'take out some All-Risk insurance, and when you see his chin go kind of down and back and his mouth open, and his left hand begin to twitch, and his eyes begin to spit blood, you'll know you were the wise guy; isn't that so, Mary?' (Mary was one of the housemaids, sir, with whom, I found, this Peters had been too free.)

"'How often does he get that way?' I asked.

"'Ordinary times about once a month. Depends how things are. But when this poacher bird Black Jack gets busy—well, I won't pump the breeze up you, one of these sunny days you'll know what I haven't said! Anyway, I'm through, thank Theodore! Last Monday he threw a four-pound vase at my head, and I only side-stepped it by a millimetre. I'm not as young as I was. I'm off to Philadelphia next Thursday morning, so I should worry! Anyway, just remember when Black Jack is working his nets you watch his Lordship's eyes when you take in his early morning brandy and soda, and *keep on your toes*!'

"Well, sir, I didn't like this chap's way of carrying on, though his obvious relief at leaving his job made me think twice, but I am easy to get on with as a rule, I wanted work badly, and the pay was very tempting. Also I thought this Peters was the wrong sort of person for Sir Roger, with all his American slang and loud ways. There was another thing which helped to persuade me to accept. Elm Court is a very beautiful place, and I'm very partial to good surroundings."

"It is!" said Mr. Ponders. "The finest medium-sized Tudor House in Great Britain, and the grounds are perfection."

"Yes, sir. After I had been in Sir Roger's service for a week or so, I found out, sir, that he was subject to fits of heavy drinking. He was fairly moderate most of the time, sir, but about once a week he'd drink nearly a bottle of whisky besides other things. The housekeeper, Mrs. Miles, who had been with him many years, told me the habit was growing upon him. I was glad to find, sir, he seemed to take a liking to me; in fact, he quite made a friend of me. He saw very few people; it seemed he had got the wrong side of many of the gentry in the neighbourhood through rubbing them up the wrong way; it was as if he enjoyed doing it.

"Now and again he'd have some friends down from London, but he only entertained the local people, sir, when the Judge came down for the Assizes at Lewes. Otherwise he kept to himself, spending his time riding, looking after the farms on the estate, and, in the season, shooting. Peters had been right about the poachers. Sir Roger had the finest shoot in that part of the world, and the poachers were always at it. It was partly because he was so badly liked, for I found out that a lot of the local chaps were on the poachers' side and helped them. This Black Jack was the worst. The local people seemed to be very much afraid of him, and didn't like to talk about him. They were superstitious about him and very careful to keep on his right side. They told some funny tales. The first time I saw him was in the village about three weeks after I arrived. He was tall and slim and very dark, a good bit of the gipsy in him, I should say, sir. His face was like a hawk's, and he had a very piercing look, a nasty customer to get up against, he seemed to me. He had his dog, Scottie, with him, a big mongrel, a mixture of collie and lurcher he looked, who'd got the name of being the cleverest at his job in the county, a savage, cunning-looking brute. Well, Black Jack came up to me with a cheeky contemptuous look on his face. 'You're the new bottle-washer at the Hall, aren't you?' he said. He had almost a gentleman's voice, sir. 'Well, I don't suppose you'll stay any longer than the other bottle-washers. You haven't met Scottie, have you?' The dog bared its teeth and snarled and growled. 'Doesn't seem to like you, never does seem to like Hall folk, somehow; can't think where he learnt to hate 'em. Well, tell that old —— of yours I shall be working the East Side for the next week or so,' and he sauntered off.

"I gave Wilkins, the head-keeper, the tip. 'That's like his blasted sauce,' he said. 'I'll get that fine gentleman one of these days! I've had enough of him. It'll mean a new job for me if I miss him this time. I sometimes think he's got the Devil on his side. Say nothing to the master if you like a quiet life.'

"Well, Black Jack started his business as he said he would. He and his gang cleaned up the coverts on the East Side, but none of them was caught. Directly the poaching began the master began to drink. He was out every night, and his temper was something I'd never seen before, but he never actually went for me—Wilkins got it, though, sir. He and three other keepers got the sack, and a new lot came in. Wilkins didn't seem sorry to go. He told me he'd had enough of it, and that the master's cursing was too bad to put up with.

"It was a difficult time for me, sir. Sir Roger was drinking hard and up most of the night, chasing after Black Jack, and he'd come in at four and five in the morning, and I had to wait up for him. The servants were a great trouble. Sir Roger hated to see any of the maids about the house, and when he sacked one of the girls he found dusting his study at seven one morning all of them gave notice. However, I calmed them down and got Sir Roger to raise their wages. After a time Black Jack took his gang elsewhere, and things were a bit more peaceful for a few days.

"One day, early in February, Sir Roger drove up to town, taking Godson, the chauffeur, with him. He had said he'd be back about five, but it was a quarter past eight when they arrived—on foot. When I opened the door I knew that something had happened and that he'd had one of his rages. His face was always white and heavily lined after them, and his eyes looked swollen and red. He pushed past me without saying a word and began drinking whisky in his study. Presently he rang and said he would not dine, but that I was to bring him some sandwiches. When I got down to the servants' hall I found Godson sitting at the table, his head in his hands. He looked up at me, and his face was haggard.

"'I'm through!' he said. 'The ——'s mad, bloody mad'—he was never one to swear as a rule, sir.

"'What's up?' I asked, 'where's the car?'

"'What's up!' he cried; 'that ——'s up the pole! I tell you I'm through. I'll tell you what sort of a blasted, bloody lunatic he is! When I met him at the Club I could see he'd been drinking, but he *would* drive coming home. I've never seen him wilder, we ought to have been killed ten times. I was just beginning to think we'd get through when we reached that switchback in the woods near Ollen. I should think we touched ninety on the way down. As we reached the bottom I saw there was someone standing at the side of the road halfway up the hill. Suddenly he began braking hard and peering ahead. It was then I could see the chap in the road was Black Jack. Just as we were drawing up to him that dog of his bounded out into the road behind him. Then I felt the car swing. He drove her straight at Black Jack, missed him by a foot, and then swung back and caught the dog fair and square. The next thing I knew was that I was lying on my ear in a field. Both front tyres had gone, and we'd bust clean through a gate, bounced on the plough, and then turned half over in a dew-pond.'

"'Well, His Highness was out in a flash, and I followed him back to the road. When we got there Black Jack was bending over the dog. When he saw us he picked it up and walked towards us. Sir Ruddy Roger went to meet him. Black Jack lifted his cap, and then held up the dog by the back of his neck. It's face was all bloody and dusty and smashed up.

"'Good evening, Sir Roger,' said Black Jack. 'Scottie's dead all right, you got him at last, you got him!'

"'Get to hell from here, you poaching blackguard!' cried the Guv'nor. 'Certainly I've got one of you, and if you come on my land again I'll get you, too!'

"'I was rather fond of Scottie,' said Black Jack, 'and knew all his tricks. He'd got some funny tricks, too; don't be too sure you've done with him!' Then suddenly his face went hard and fierce, and there were tears in his eyes. He shoved the dog's muzzle right into the Guv-nor's face and gave a funny little sharp whistle which seemed to scream in one's head, and he muttered something in some foreign language, gipsy, I guess, and I got the idea that the dog was listening as if it was alive again, and in a twinkling Jack and the dog had disappeared—into the woods I suppose, but it was quick work.

"'The Guv'nor never said a word, but started off to walk home and here we are, and the ruddy car can drown for all I care! I leave to-morrow. He can get some other stiff to be killed with him. I'm through. Christ, I've got a head!'

"'You go to bed,' I said, 'I'll get the car brought in, in the morning.'

"He was as good as his word, sir; he left before lunch and I never saw him again.

"The next afternoon I had to go down to the village, and at once I noticed a change. Nobody from the Hall was ever much welcomed there, but I had always been treated with civility, and some of them were quite friendly. That day they looked at me out of the corners of their eyes, and were short and abrupt in their manner. It made me feel quite uncomfortable, sir."

"What had Sir Roger done to make himself so unpopular with the local people?" asked Mr. Ponders.

"Well, sir, he was a harsh landlord, and never put himself out to please. In this way he was very unlike his father. I think that's what they hated most about him."

"I remember Fred Wallington," said Mr. Ponders. "A genial, easy-going old fox-hunter. Well, go on."

"Of course I couldn't get anything out of them, but they were behaving so queerly that I sent one of the maids, who had a sweet-heart working in the local public-house, the Bee and Clover, to see if she could pick up anything. When she got back she said that Joe had 'been funny', and that she'd had to make a bit of a scene before she could get anything out of him, and that he'd only mutter that Black Jack had said something the night before. He'd come in for a drink and left almost at once. When she asked what he'd said, he wouldn't answer, but had left her and gone home. She'd never seen him like that, she'd said. So putting two and two together, sir, I made out that Black Jack had made some sort of threat against the master which the local people believed he would carry out, and so they wanted to have as little to do with the Hall as possible. I thought the master seemed a bit uneasy at dinner that night. Sometimes he'd seem to be listening to something, and several times I noticed him giving sudden quick looks into a dark corner there was between the door and the serving table. After dinner he went out on to the lawn and walked in a stealthy sort of way over towards the clump of big cedars.

"Well, my pantry window looked out that way, and I saw the master suddenly come running back, and then I heard him slam the window of the morning-room. When I took in the whisky and soda he was looking a little queer, I thought. His face was flushed and his eyes were sort of screwed up, sir, as if he wasn't sure if he could see something or not.

"The next morning when I went to call him I found him wide awake—which I never remembered him being before.

" 'Whose dog is that?' he asked, as soon as I came in.

" 'What dog, sir?' I asked.

" 'I don't know,' he answered shortly. 'I was restless during the night, and got up, and I saw it on the lawn. Find out whose it is and keep it away. Tell whoever owns it I shall have it shot if I see it again.'

" 'Very good, sir,' I said.

"I made some enquiries, but no one knew anything about it, and the new keeper told me both his dogs had been sleeping in his kitchen from eight o'clock on.

"The master was all right through the day, but as soon as dusk came on he seemed worried and not himself. We were all a bit on edge, sir, for it was then the Noise began.

"It was quite faint at first. Now, sir, I know I shall never be able to explain what it was like, because the strange thing was that we couldn't really say we heard it, not through one's ears, that is to say. It was as if it was going on inside one's head. Also it was as much a shake as a noise; when it got worse it made everything in the house —how would you call it, sir?"

"Vibrate?" suggested Mr. Ponders.

"Yes, sir; as for what sort of sound it was, it reminded one of what Godson had said about Black Jack's whistle, it seemed to scream in one's head. You know that high noise bats make, piercing, but so high one can only hear it. Well, sir, it was like that a thousand times louder, and it never stopped from dusk till dawn for a second. It seemed to cut us at the Hall from the rest of the world, close us in, as it were. I can't tell you, sir, how horrible it was at its worst, but at first it was quite soft, though all the servants noticed it, and kept going to the windows to look out, and wondering what it was.

"At dinner that night Sir Roger was very queer. He had just started on the soup when I saw his eyes go to the dark corner I mentioned before, sir. He never touched another mouthful of anything, but all the time his eyes travelled round the room as if he was following something about. Once or twice when he seemed to follow it right up to his side, he half started from his chair, but he always had great self-control of a sort—that is to say, he hated to make any kind of exhibition of himself before other people, sir, and he held himself in, though I could see his knuckles go white as he hung on to the chair. He got up halfway through dinner and went back to the morning-room. When I took in his coffee he was peeping through the blind on to the lawn.

"When I came in he turned round rather slowly and said, 'You know that dog I spoke to you about. It's here again. Take the rook-rifle and see if you can find it. I thought I heard it barking just now in Grey Fallow.' (Grey Fallow, sir, is a big copse in the Park, up the hill a bit, about three hundred yards from the wild-rose hedge which cuts the Park off from the lawn.)

" 'There,' he said, 'can't you hear it?'

" 'I'll see if I can find it, sir,' I said, and got the rifle out, for I thought it would upset the master if I said I couldn't hear anything. By the time I'd reached the rose-hedge I felt I wanted to turn back, but I went through the gate up towards Grey Fallow. There was just a little moon coming through the clouds. Suddenly I felt I couldn't go any further. It was cowardice, I expect, sir, but there were two shadows which seemed to be coming from something standing, and another one crouching just inside the wood, which were more than I could face up to, sir. And then I found myself walking through the open window into the morning-room.

" 'Well?' asked the master.

" 'I couldn't see anything, sir.'

" 'Damn you,' he said, 'I can hear it now; give me the rifle and pour me out a whisky and soda!'

"Some time later I was working in the pantry when I heard a shot. I looked out, but at first I couldn't see anything. Then the moon came through, and I picked out the master crouching down beside the big cedar. 'What's he up to?' I wondered, and it was then for the first time I felt a sinking, creepy feeling, sir, as if I'd give anything to be up in London with people and lights. But I was fond of the master, sir, and I felt it was up to me to look after him, and I made up my mind to stick it out.

"When I went back to the morning-room to ask about orders for the next day he was on his knees peering through the blind. I went out and knocked loudly, and he was sitting in his chair when I came in again, but his left hand was twitching quickly. I was going to take the rifle out to be cleaned, but he told me to leave it there till the morning.

"It was from then, sir, that the bad time really began. It was all right till dusk came, and the master was quite boisterous and good-humoured during the day, but as soon as the sun was down, and that sound began, and the master started to be funny, and all the maids got agitated and hysterical, it was as much as I could stand.

"When I say the master started to be funny, I mean that he got silent and watchful and absorbed in something. From then on he ate nothing at dinner, though he usually went in and sat down for a time. On the third night, after he had been staring at the dark corner and round the room for a time, he suddenly jumped to his feet and seemed to fling something from him. His face was working, sir, and he pointed his hand to the door. 'Turn that dog out! Turn that dog out!' he shouted.

"I was badly taken aback, but I pretended to drive something out of the door. This finished the footman, who ran away the next morning. I wasn't sorry, as I thought I'd better have the master to myself. It was from then on I had to pretend all the time when I was with him at night, for there was no doubt by now, sir, that he was seeing some dog most of the time and he was scared of it. I had to sit with him in the evening with a whip in my hand and let fly in the direction he pointed to. Then he made me come and sleep in the room next to his. The sound got steadily worse and became something shocking, sir, and the maids went one by one. It seemed to drive them crazy, and they'd sit with their hands to their ears, crying. I replaced them at first and offered every kind of high wages, but it was no good, they wouldn't stay, and very soon Mrs. Miles and I were left alone. She was a brave woman, sir, she said she'd stick till she died, if necessary."

"Did Sir Roger hear this sound?" asked Mr. Ponders.

"Not as we did, sir, but he was always hearing barking and snarling and something scratching at the door. He hated *that* worst of all. Time after time he'd tell me through the tube from his room to mine that there was a dog at his door. I always got up, but, of course, there was nothing there.

"I expect you wonder, sir, why I didn't take it for granted it was D.T.s—delirium tremens I should have said, sir, and fetched a doctor, and I often thought of it, but the master was not drinking so heavily now as before the trouble began. Then again the doctor would have probably come during the day, and found the master almost himself. Besides, I don't believe he would have seen a doctor, he always hated and despised them."

"You didn't think it *was* drink, then?" he asked.

"I didn't know what to think. You see, sir, there was that Sound."

"I wonder you could stick it."

"Well, sir, I did long to go, but if Mrs. Miles could put up with it I could, and I felt I had to stand by the master in the bad time. I was quite attached to him, sir, and I shouldn't have felt right about leaving him in the lurch. I tried to get him to go up to London and stay at the club, but he wouldn't hear of it.

"There began to be a lot of talk in the neighbourhood, for the maids said things before they left, and all the villagers and local people round were certain it had something to do with Black Jack. He had never been seen since that night his dog was killed, but he was believed to be somewhere about. It was a funny thing the local people had a curious knowledge when he was about, and they were always right.

"The master got worse and worse. He couldn't seem to stay in the house after dark unless I was with him. He'd be out all night in the grounds, and I'd sometimes catch a sight of him crouching and hiding, and sometimes he'd come running back as if something was after him. He took to sleeping heavily during the day, but he had bad dreams then, and he said some funny things in his sleep.

"I felt he must be getting near the end of his tether.

"When the Judge came down I never for a moment believed he would attempt to entertain him, but, to my dismay, sir, he insisted, and asked thirty people to meet him. Of course, I had to get a lot of help down from London. The only good thing about it was, I felt, that some of the gentlemen might see what a state he was in and help me to do something for it.

"It was a terrible evening. The Sound was wicked that night. The hired chaps got the wind up, sir, as soon as it began, and kept asking what the hell it was, and several of them tried to slip away. It made all the guests nervous and uneasy.

"The master made an effort for a time; it was a very brave effort, sir, but after a time his eyes went to the corner by the door, and suddenly he gave a sharp movement and then his eyes flitted about as if he was following something. Twice he half rose from his chair as if something was getting at him. Of course, the guests noticed it and, although they made a pretence of talking, I could see them watching the master. The hired men lost their heads and were dropping plates and waiting shockingly. The Noise got so bad that everything was quivering and shaking, and I could see the guests were beginning to get horrified and very uneasy. I felt something was going to happen. Suddenly the master jumped to his feet and began flinging all his glasses and anything he could pick up from the table into the dark corner, shouting, 'Go! go! go! Drive it out, I tell you! Drive it out!' and then he fell in a heap on the floor. Some of the gentlemen helped me to carry him up to his room, and then they left, and glad to go they were. One of them, Sir Marcus O'Reilly, took me aside, and asked if this sort of thing had been going on long. I said for just three weeks. 'Well,' he said, 'it's delirium tremens, and a bad case. I'll do something about it in the morning. He can't go on like this.'

"Would you believe it, sir, the master pulled round about midnight and spent the rest of the night in the Park!"

"Did *you* ever see anything unnatural, except those shadows, I mean?" asked Mr. Ponders.

Mr. Millin paused. "There was just something I did see—marks very like those made by the muddy paws of some animals outside the master's bedroom door several times, and one time, when Sir Roger woke me up and told me the dog was on his bed, there were some marks on the blanket.

"There was one funny little thing. The master was fond of cats, and kept six of them. Well, as soon as the Sound began, they all disappeared and were never seen again, and the keeper told me his dog wouldn't go near the hall after dusk. But I don't *think* I ever saw anything, though the master made it all seem so real that it was enough to make anyone see things.

"Well, sir, the next night it happened—I had managed to get to sleep about two o'clock—the master was out as usual. Suddenly I was awakened by hearing him rushing down the passage. I heard his door slam and then he began shouting, 'Get down! Down, you brute! Down! Down! Down!' and then I heard everything in the room begin crashing about. Just as I reached my door there was a terrible screaming and choking kind of cry—the most awful sound I ever heard, sir.

"I rushed to his room and turned on the light. He was lying across the bed, his throat torn open and the blood pouring out. He was dead already. As I lifted him and tried to staunch the blood I noticed something about his eyes. There was something sort of photographed in them."

"What?" asked Mr. Ponders sharply.

"Well, sir, it might have been the head of a dog smashed up and bleeding.

"When I went to pull down the blinds, my eye was caught by a shadow coming out from the big cedar. It was like the one I had seen in Grey Fallow. And it almost seemed as if I saw another shadow, which was leaping and bounding towards it—and then they both disappeared. And then I noticed the Sound had stopped.

"I got the doctor and the police as soon as I could. The doctor was very puzzled. He said he'd never seen a wound like it, and couldn't imagine how it had been caused.

"Next day the London police came down, and, of course, it began to be a bit unpleasant for me, being so near in the next room like that, and no one else about. They cross-examined me for a long time. All I could say was that the master had been queer for a long time and taken to roaming in the grounds at night, that I had been woken up by hearing him scream and had rushed in to find what I have described, sir. But it sounded weak and fishy. The Inspector heard something in the village about Black Jack, and tried his best to find him, but he was never seen again. The inquest was adjourned several times, and I think everyone expected me to be arrested, but when the doctor had given his evidence it seemed to me that everyone in the Court felt there was something that couldn't be explained about the business, and the verdict was 'Murder by a person or persons unknown'. After that the police left me alone, but I suppose most people still believe I did it. And then I came up to London and saw Sir Leonard. I've never been able to get another place. As soon as they hear I was with Sir Roger they turn me down.

"Well, that's my story, sir, and it's the whole truth and nothing but the truth, though I know how it must sound."

"Did you ever think of telling the whole truth and nothing but the truth to the police?" asked Mr. Ponders.

"They wouldn't have stood for it, sir. I'm sure they wouldn't."

"Well, Mr. Millin," said Mr. Ponders, smiling, "my brother has praised you more than I have known him praise many people, but even he never suggested you had the imagination to invent *that* story. Do you know why—amongst other reasons—I believe every word of it? It's because I've heard it before."

"Heard it before, sir!"

"Well, almost. Do you see that black and red book on the shelf just behind you?"

"Yes, sir."

"Well, that contains an account of a very, very similar happening in the year 1795 in this county, not ten miles away. It is called 'A True Account of the Curious Events connected with the death of Mr. Arthur Pitts'. You shall read it when you are installed here. By the way, how soon can you come?"

Mr. Millin's eyes were very bright as he answered, "Any time which will suit you, sir."

MARCUS PAUL DARE

"BRING OUT YOUR DEAD"

It is not often that the Post Office van favours us with a mid-morning call in our isolated district. On one memorable day last August, however, it swung up our drive in a cloud of dust and deposited a letter whose superscription, addressed to "Messrs. Granville and Wayne" (as though we were a firm of grocers or something) was written in a sufficiently scholarly hand to arouse interest. I happened to be crossing the hall at the time, so took it in from our obliging district postman, and conveyed it to the study, where Alan looked up in surprise.

"What's that in aid of?" he demanded.

"Something in Yorkshire," said I, inspecting the postmark, which was that of Adel, Leeds. "I deduce, my dear Watson," I added, "that it is something to do with our Anglo-Saxon researches, since (a) nobody in Yorkshire is likely to write to *us* for any other reason, and (b) Adel is the 'home' of the famous Anglian gravestones."

"All right, Sherlock," laughed Alan, "when you've finished the forensic lecture, what about opening the thing?"

I did, and proceeded to read:

Dear Sirs.

Having studied with interest your work on the Saxon Kingdoms, I write to introduce myself as a student of the period. I took a First in History at the University, and am now working, for my D. Litt. thesis, on Anglo-Saxon funeral customs—a subject upon which you may possibly have seen a few contributions from my pen in "Archaeologia". As I am proposing to drive down to the Midlands to study the famous bone-crypt of Rawton, and find that my way lies through your district, I wonder if I might call upon you on the way, to discuss one or two technical points in which your knowledge is far superior to mine. If so, I shall be most grateful if you will please intimate, by the enclosed stamped envelope, what day next week would be most convenient to you for me to call.

Yours faithfully,
Martin Latouche.

The signature aroused our interest at once, for Mr. Martin

Latouche, M.A., had already attracted our attention as a young scholar of promise, by virtue of the articles to which he modestly alluded.

"Well," said Alan, "he has a very long journey by car, and if you are agreeable, I suggest we offer him hospitality overnight, both on his way down and on the return trip."

I agreed warmly, feeling also that this visit of fellow-worker would be of mutual advantage, besides being a pleasant break for us; for, though we are in correspondence with scholars all over Europe, we rarely have a visitor to our Wolds stronghold. The invitation was therefore sent off the same day, giving Mr. Latouche a free hand as to his arrangements and pointing out that we should be at home all the next week.

In due course our new acquaintance, who had acknowledged the invitation with prompt courtesy and grace, arrived in an ancient but serviceable four-seater saloon, from which he extracted with great care, in addition to his suitcase, a leather-covered box about a foot square; this, he explained, contained a delicate whole-plate camera, and he insisted on carrying it to his room himself.

Mr. Latouche, who in appearance was the typical lanky, untidy and rather ascetic-looking young University lecturer, proved to be as well-informed as his articles indicated, and by no means a narrow specialist, but a man of wide culture. I need not inflict on the general reader our conversation over the excellent dinner produced by our man, for—as may be supposed—it was highly technical. I may say, however, that our guest had explored some queer byways of knowledge connected with his period and was able to cast light on some matter that had puzzled both Alan and myself, though we were getting on for twice his age. When at last we all did decide to retire, he announced his intention of making a reasonably early start in the morning, so that, as it is not so far across country from our place to Rawton, he could return to us the same night.

Accordingly, 8 a.m. saw him on his way, complete with his precious camera-case. He pressed us to join him in the expedition, but Alan was "up to the eyes" in proof-correcting for a small popular book which a publisher had inveigled him into writing, and I was woefully in arrears with several book-reviews for a learned quarterly, and was near the time-limit through my dilatory habits. Poor Latouche! I wish now that I had laid aside my work and gone with him, for I might then have prevented the tragedy that robbed the world, by a means beyond mortal understanding, of a brilliant young scholar.

However—about an hour after our guest's departure, John, who in addition to his more "butlerian" duties acts as our gardener and odd-job man, interrupted my reviewing to inform me he had just noticed that the head of a rainwater stackpipe from the roof-gutter was dangerously loose, "and please will the guv'nor see what can be done abaht it, for we're going to 'ave 'eavy rine soon."

Looking at the damage from below, I found I could best inspect it by going upstairs and sticking my head out of the guest-room window. Entering, the first thing that met my eye was a fine and expensive whole-plate camera, standing on an occasional table.

"Oh dear!" I thought, "Latouche *will* be annoyed when he gets to Rawton and finds he's left that behind."

I could only vaguely suppose that before retiring, he had been overhauling the camera, had forgotten to put it back, and had seized the case without noticing. "Yet surely," I thought, "he must have seen it, right under his nose, and it seems strange he didn't notice the difference in weight when he picked the case up—still, perhaps he's as absent-minded as I am."

So, after mentioning the fact to Alan, who agreed with me that it was useless to think of pursuing Latouche with the camera in our car, as he had over an hour's start and was, indeed, probably at Rawton by now, I dismissed the matter from my mind and, having given John instructions about the offending spout, returned to my interrupted reviewing.

We dine at seven, and, as we have not yet descended to the modern barbarity of a "cocktail hour", Alan and I were strolling in the garden when, about 6.30, our guest returned. He narrowly missed the gatepost in negotiating the drive entrance, and as he stepped out of the car, I thought from his face that he did not look very well.

"Did you have a tiring drive back?" I asked sympathetically.

"Not so very," replied Latouche, "but I think I've caught a touch of the sun—it's been very hot, you know, and I've been out in the sun taking photographs."

"Photographs!" exclaimed Alan. "Why, you went off and forgot your camera."

Mr. Latouche looked, I thought, slightly sheepish. "Oh," he said after a slight pause, turning at the same time to get his camera-case off the back seat, "I had another camera with me, a small pocket Leica, and decided I didn't want the big one."

Then why on earth, I wondered, as we strolled towards the porch, did he want to lug the whole-plate case about? Something of my thoughts must have been visible on my face (for I am no actor), for Latouche said rather hastily: "I often eject the big camera on a job like this—the case is very useful for carrying my instruments and notebooks."

He went off to his room with his precious case to wash before dinner, while I attended to the ritual of sherry, and our excellent Amontillado put some colour back into his face, though he still complained of feeling a little dizzy; and at dinner he made only the barest pretence of eating.

However, conversation was lively enough, and our guest got us deeply interested in a theory he had developed about Anglo-Saxon racial mixtures. It now came out that one of his chief objects in visiting Rawton had been to test this theory by measurement of a large number of skulls in the parish-church bone-crypt (which, my readers may be aware, is one of the best in England, the others being at Hythe in Kent, and Rothwell in Northants). Latouche's theme was that no anthropologist had yet tried to distinguish between the skulls of the Anglian, Saxon, Jutish, and Frisian peoples who comprised our "Anglo-Saxon" invaders, and he was confident that his own research was casting light on the matter.

"Good gracious!" said Alan, "if you set about measuring dozens of those skulls, I should think the verger wished you in blazes!"

"He did, rather," replied Latouche, "till I thought of giving him a good tip and telling him he could lock me in if he wished, as I should be some hours on the job."

"It is years since I visited Rawton," I put in. "So far as I remember, I always understood that the bone-collection was reputed to contain skulls of every conceivable sort—including even negro—but the only thing I *do* clearly remember about the place is an enormous thigh-bone that must have belonged to a seven-foot giant of a man."

"My own idea," I added, "speaking of course quite without any authority, is that these crypts, like Rawton, Rothwell, and Hythe, were filled up with the bones of medieval or later plague-victims."

"It's a pity we have no written records on the subject," remarked Alan, doing the honours with the port. "Kohler's standard work on the Black Death doesn't mention it, and parish clerks in the seventeenth-century epidemics, for instance, never tell us in their registers *where* they buried plague victims in a heavy mortality—I suppose they must have generally made a communal pit in the churchyard; and later sextons, finding the ground over-full, would regard these rare crypts as a godsend when they wanted to re-bury the surplus bones."

From this somewhat macabre discussion, in which our guest took little part, sitting with a very thoughtful look, we veered round to a highly technical argument about the architecture and dates of these crypts and, as we had lingered long over the table and thoroughly punished the port, I suggested an adjournment to the library.

Latouche, however, on rising, went very queer. His face became a pasty yellow, and perspiration came out on his forehead. He looked as I have seen men look in the first stages of malarial attack, and I summoned James to get him a glass of hot whisky, lemon and aspirin —the best medicine for anyone suffering from fever.

Drinking the concoction gratefully, Latouche went off to bed, declaring that he would be "as right as rain" in the morning; and Alan and I, always late birds, retired to the study and did our respective writings for another couple of hours. I remember noticing, when I decided to pack up for the night, that our grandfather clock registered just 12.30 a.m.

It had been a glorious late-summer day, and the night was equally lovely. A full harvest moon shone through the ancient window of armorial glass as I crossed the hall, and there was hardly a breath of air stirring anywhere. My way to my own room led past the guest-chamber along a rambling, panelled corridor, and as I passed Latouche's door I was surprised to hear what sounded like a window banging violently to and fro. Puzzled, I walked to the end of the corridor, inspecting each of the windows, and finally put my head out of the one at the end and looked to my left along the wall, since from here I could see the whole range of windows containing Latouche's room. His window was open, but firmly kept so by its iron pivot-bar. So, being able to make nothing of the noise, and feeling very sleepy, I turned in.

It must have been an hour later, that I was awakened by the most extraordinary collection of noises. My room was ice-cold, and there was a great roar and rushing as of a freezing wind right through it, though the heavy curtains were absolutely motionless; and at the same time, there came from somewhere within the ancient house a series of unearthly groans, a furious hammering on a door, the deep sound of a throaty, unpleasant voice calling something I could not distinguish, and the clang, clang of a bell.

I leapt out of bed, flung on a dressing-gown, and rushed for the corridor and stairs, thinking—so imperfectly does the whole mind function in an emergency—that the house was on fire and that someone was trying to warn us.

Downstairs, however, all was calm and undisturbed, and as I flung open the porch door, the balmy night floated to me all the scents of the old English garden.

Telling myself I must have had a particularly unpleasant nightmare, I set off back to my room along the corridor; but on passing Latouche's room, I heard again the dreadful groaning and that grim, throaty voice. The door was unlocked, and I burst in, to be confronted by a terrible spectacle, the like of which I hope never to see again.

Our guest lay on his bed, a fearful sight, twisted and arched up as is the victim of cholera. His face and lips were black, and the flesh so sunken that he more resembled a skull than anything living. His pyjama coat was off; he was ice-cold, and all over his torso were weird yellow and black patches of skin, while his armpits were swollen into hideous bulbous lumps. Groaning and muttering inaudibly, he twisted and retched in agony. After one look at him, I rushed to awaken Alan, but he too had been roused, and I met him hurrying along the corridor, with the frightened figure of the manservant in his rear.

Luckily, we had quite recently had the telephone installed in the house; it was the result of a visiting Professor being seized with a heart attack, when our car was out of order and I had to ride three miles into Tilton on a cycle for a doctor. So in a very short time I was through to our own practitioner, Dr. Dolben, who is a neighbour and ranks as a personal friend. Rapidly I described the condition of our guest. The doctor whistled softly, and promised to be with us in ten minutes, for he had only just returned from an emergency call to a farm, and had not even had time to put his car away. Meantime, he ordered, we must get a collection of steaming hot blankets ready by plunging them in boiling water.

Dr. Dolben lost no time; he arrived in the midst of these preparations, and accompanied us straight to Latouche's room. As we opened the door, we were almost knocked back by a dreadful stench, which was not there a few minutes before. The sick man was now sitting up, muttering and gasping, with an arm stretched out pointing to an object on his dressing-table, from which there radiated a weird bluish phosphorescence. It was his camera-case.

As the doctor bent over the patient, there came, from the direction of the camera-case, that horrible, hoarse voice I had heard before, and we could now hear distinctly what it said. It kept croaking, with fiendish relish: *Bring out your dead! Bring out your dead! More chalk for the doors, Master Will. The cart be full.*

At the same time, apparently from mid-air over the head of the bed, there came the deep clanging note of a handbell that I had also already heard.

Henry appeared in the doorway with a zinc bath full of steaming blankets as Dr. Dolben straightened himself up and looked very grave.

"This is incredible, Wayne," he said, addressing me as the nearest to him. "This young man is apparently suffering from cholera plus bubonic plague—every symptom present. I'm not sure we can save him. Quick now, with those blankets—wrap him up and keep him sweating."

We had just got Latouche into the blankets, and succeeded somewhat in easing the rigid tension of his body, when the doctor became aware of the extraordinary phenomena in the room.

Bring out your dead! croaked the voice.

"Where on earth is that coming from?" asked the doctor. "It's not the patient—he can't speak."

His eyes fell on the camera-case.

"God God," he exclaimed, "what's the matter with that box?"

He, too, had noticed the phosphorescent glow it was emitting.

"Look here," he added, "we can do no more for this poor fellow—what's his name, by the way?—for several hours, and if he *has* caught anything infectious, we run a risk staying here. What's more, I don't like the smell of your drains. Let's get downstairs, and tell me what you know about the start of your guest's illness."

So saying, he stepped across and shut the window, and the three of us trooped downstairs to the library. I did not realise until we got there that I had automatically picked up the camera-case. This I placed on the library table while Alan was putting out whisky and cigars.

Dr. Dolben sniffed as we seated ourselves. "If that young man upstairs *has* caught cholera—which I doubt in the English countryside," he said testily, "I imagine your drains have something to do with it. That awful smell's even in here!"

"I rather think," replied Alan quietly, "that we have brought it in with us"—and he gestured towards the leather camera-case on the table.

"I suggest," he added, "that we open it, and see exactly what Latouche brought back in it, since we know he left the camera behind."

"Well," said I rather lamely, "he did say he had his instruments and notebooks in it. Still, perhaps we ought to make sure." Here I mentioned the strange phenomenon of the phosphorescent glow, which Alan had not noticed upstairs, and which had now entirely gone.

Very gingerly, not knowing what might confront us, I lifted the lid of the case, to reveal to our astonished gaze a human skull. As the lid went up, though the skull was itself clean and bleached, that overpowering odour of corruption seemed to fill the whole room.

As I lifted the thing out and placed it on the table, the French windows of the library rattled as though a high storm-wind raged outside, and, right in my ear, the damnable voice I was beginning to dread croaked: *Bring out your dead!*

We all heard it, and exchanged glances; and a few seconds later, there came again, as from a distance, the clang of the handbell.

"Well!" exclaimed Dr. Dolben. "This is the strangest case I've ever attended. It is utterly impossible, yet that man upstairs *is suffering from the Great Plague of 1665*. Incredible as it seems to anyone of scientific training, I can only conclude he got it from that"—jerking a finger at the grinning skull.

Dolben, as his name indicates, is a Cornishman, and the Cornish are a queer, ancient race, with deep-rooted beliefs in occult matters that would astonish the average Englishman. He has often told us, dropping in for a chat and a drink at night, of the queer, nameless things that haunt the Cornish coast churches where, they say, "the dead come up out of the sea"; and my own experiences in the realm of the unknown have rather appealed to the Kelt in him than astonished the scientist.

"You fellows know," he said, reaching out for his glass and a fresh cigar, "better than I (being historians), the circumstances and setting of the Plague. It suddenly dawned on me just now, when I heard that voice and the bell while puzzling over the medical features of the case."

"Yes," I said gravely. "The corpses were too numerous to bury, and, as Defoe's account tells us, men went round with the death-cart, calling out *'Bring out your dead'*, ringing a handbell, and putting a cross in red chalk on the doors of the infected houses. They had to fling the bodies into pits—"

"Or crypts!" put in Alan quickly.

"Good God!" I exclaimed, as the truth dawned on me, "so *that's* why Latouche left his camera behind and took its case. He evidently wanted to abstract what he thought to be an Anglo-Saxon skull from the crypt—but the poor devil got hold of one from the Plague period instead."

The doctor looked a question; remembering that he had not yet been furnished with the facts, I related briefly the circumstances of Latouche's visit and its ostensible purpose.

"Yes," he said calmly, when I had finished. "There is no doubt what happened; the poor fellow has by some occult means become infected with the Plague—though for my reputation's sake I daren't let the narrow-minded General Medical Council know I think so. Observe that none of us three is any the worse, though we have been in dangerous infective contact: all of us with the patient, and you, Wayne, with the skull. Therefore there is nothing inherently infectious about the skull; indeed, it must be scientifically impossible that the germs of the disease could have lurked in the thing for three centuries or so—to say nothing of the fact that the Plague organism attacks the blood and tissues, not the bone structure."

"It seems to me," he added, "that your unfortunate guest has either been singled out by some malignant power because the original Plague victim whose skull it is had been buried in an unconsecrated pit (I remember reading accounts of such pits being outside town ditches) and the bones only later tipped into the church crypt, and that his connection with the skull has released an Elemental dormant all this time; or because he committed sacrilege in taking the thing."

Hardly had Dolben finished speaking, when a dreadful yell of agony rang through the house, and the skull, under our very noses, rose in the air a few inches off the table, and crashed with great violence on to the carpet, where it cracked across, while a thunderous hammering rained on the library door, and above it could be heard the dread call: *Bring out your dead! Bring out your dead!*

Leaping to our feet, Alan and I were for making a concerted rush to the sick-chamber, but Dr. Dolben rose leisurely and put up a hand.

"Best take it calmly," he said. "That was the passing of a soul, by laws science will probably never understand."

Poor Latouche was, of course, beyond our aid by the time we reached his room.

The next day, there fell to me the sad office of telephoning his University to discover and notify his people, while Dr. Dolben specially visited the Coroner, an understanding man, not nearly so officious as most of his tribe—and left him a much-puzzled officer of the Crown.

Dolben did the post-mortem, and at the inquest, for which Latouche's father came down from Leeds, it was given out that on his return to us the young archaeologist had ascribed his feeling ill to his having stopped and drunk water from a wayside pool in the heat. Dolben was consequently able to depose to a condition of acute gastro-enteritis, and a verdict of Death from Natural Causes was returned.

Natural causes, indeed! I wonder what the two bored-looking country reporters who attended the inquest would have written, could they have seen me that very night, after the undertakers had gone, unscrewing the lid of Martin Latouche's coffin to slip in the deadly skull; or if I had let out in evidence that on the fatal morning we went to the guest-room after hearing his last scream of agony, we found a Plague cross in red chalk on its door-post, and another on that of the library—which crosses, rub as we would, could not be entirely eradicated until the day after scholar and skull had been given Christian burial in our country churchyard.

THE BONE BEAD NECKLACE

Lieutenant Torbal Medwin of the Queens Cavalry was twenty-three when the Zulu Rebellion broke out in South Africa. He left a young wife behind him; and the parting seemed vast and everlasting, even before the troop-ship had entered the Biscay. He was a young man of spirit and energy, however, and could so fling himself into his duties that only at night, in the extreme sanctuary of his bunk, did homesickness and loneliness engulf and depress him.

It was this sense of emotional desolation, and the feeling of being too small a cypher in too vast and alien a pattern of surly sea and forbidding coastline, that made him drive himself until he became the most conscientious officer in the company.

When the contingent disembarked at Capetown, he was already in a position of authority and responsibility; and as intolerant of human foibles as an Old Testament prophet. Because of his youth, he overdid it. He was a martinet to his men and a nuisance to his superior officers: he was too efficient; too official, and too untiring.

His Colonel, a weather-beaten campaigner who had mellowed over the years, advised him against one or two of the minor disadvantages of a too proud flesh; but young Torbal Medwin, for all his respectful attention and poker face, nursed by now too pronounced a condescension for his elders to take much of it to heart.

"An officer, God help me for saying it, can be too efficient," the old man said mildly. "Sometimes it's a good thing to think of your men in terms of sore feet and tired bellies and private problems. Don't lose sight of the human element, Medwin: we're all of the same clay, you know. Beware of being too impulsive. It's your only hazard, I think. Otherwise, you've the makings of a fine soldier."

"It's very good of you, sir," said Lieutenant Medwin, with the correct mixture of obsequious gratitude and restraint. "I shall certainly remember what you have said."

"You won't, you know," said his Colonel, "but I dare say I didn't, either, at your age."

Their unit proceeded overland to Natal, slowly and laboriously, following the wagon tracks through the veld, and spiralling down the slopes of the Drakensberg Mountains into the Garden Colony, as rich and lush and brooding as elemental music on a distant drum.

The Zulu regiments, circling out in huge pincer formation, rattling their shields and roaring their battle chants, struck awe and terror into young Medwin's heart by their pure magnificence. They fought with stabbing-spears and huge oxhide shields, with a raging courage and an utter indifference to death; but the first cavalry charge, well covered by rifle fire, cut through their ranks like a knife through butter, and drove them off. Young Medwin had seen nothing like it before, and found his imagination perpetually boggling, like a child's overwhelmed by Arabian Nights fantasia.

The Unit's chief scout was an old Boer hunter called Sannie Verster; nearly seventy, but as wiry and chipper as a thirty-year-old. He shuffled along beside the dapper officers, seated on the saddleless rump of a Basuto pony, with his pipe in his mouth and a flow of white whiskers slaying out over his chest and drifting over his shoulders in the wind. He had no love for the British militia, but he had less for the Zulus, who had ravaged and massacred his own families when they had thrust through from the south on their great trek forty years earlier. He knew every strategy and tactic of the Zulu impi attack: it was upon his advice that the Colonel abandoned the old square and used the Boer laager, a makeshift fort of supply wagons; end to end, like a snake with its tail in its mouth; from behind which his men loaded, fired, and reloaded like automatons.

"It's their witch-doctors," old Verster said. "Their witch-doctors put crazy ideas in their heads. They promise their men that your bullets will turn to water. They promise them that the earth will open and swallow you. Kill their witch-doctors, and you end the war."

"It couldn't be more simple," agreed the Colonel drily.

"Do their doctors come into the fighting line?" asked Medwin, impressed by Sannie Verster's conviction.

"Ya," said Verster. "But they're smart as the baboon. It's no easy job to pick them off. Only a sharp shooter could do it. When *they* die, the Zulus reckon it's all up with them. I've seen a Zulu coming at me with his spear, and me not mounted on my horse, and I fired without looking first to see if my rifle was loaded; nor was it: and the Zulu, he yelled blerry murder and came at me twice as quick, for he thought his witch-doctor had turned my bullet to water. Well, I lep on my horse then, and I galloped till I'd put a little distance between me and his spear, and I reloaded and turned in my saddle and shot him through the stomach; he sat down, he did; and he cried like a child, he did; like a blerry child he cried; because my magic was stronger than his witch-doctor's, and his whole blerry world had come to an end."

"I don't like killing fanatics and holy men," said the Colonel. "I put in twenty years in India, and I wouldn't relish firing on anything other than an armed fighter."

"Do the witch-doctors *really* have powers?" Medwin enquired.

The old scout nodded.

"They got powers," he said flatly. "But a good bullet's got powers too."

"They've got powers all right," the Colonel confirmed. "Tricky stuff it is too. You never know when you're dealing with a humbug or the real thing. I leave them well alone. It pays in the end."

"But if they're at the root of all the trouble," young Medwin protested, "surely that's where we ought to attack first?"

Lieutenant Medwin and two batmen rode down across a clearing in the flat bush veld and proceeded peacefully towards the encampment. Medwin had a buck strapped across his saddle; he had brought it down in mid-leap, drilling it neatly through the chest. The country was still and dry and blue; the sun blazed down on it mercilessly; and four vultures keeled languidly in the sky above. The Zulu impis were far away, in retreat, and a sense of security had begun to steal into Medwin's soul. He was day-dreaming about his wife, and the child that was on its way: his mind was meandering down the rich green lanes of Sussex; and he was feeling happy; and impatient, suddenly, to be back in England.

They skirted a stunted scrubble of thorn trees and came to the foothill of a low kopjie, crowned by ugly stones like a Gothic ruin. As they passed under its shadow, a figure leaped on to the topmost rock and screamed a savage war-cry. It was an old man, acock with bedraggled feathers and scraps of skin, hung about with horns and bones, his face smeared with white and red daubs of clay; and he loped and pranced like a drunken banshee, shuddering his arms and kicking his heels and shrilling his imprecations till the hills were dizzy with his echoes. Five Zulus in full war dress came bounding down the side of the kopjie, taking up his cries and swirling their assegais in the air.

Medwin flung himself off his horse as the batmen did likewise, and stepping back, drew a steady bead on the nightmarish little figure on the rock, and fired.

The witch-doctor gave a jerky spasm, like a toy jerked taut on a spring; his legs seemed to jack-knife up under him; and he back somersaulted ludicrously out of sight.

The batmen brought down two of the Zulus, and Medwin reloaded and shot the third. The other two charged on; their huge, handsome bodies flashing in the sun; until they were in point blank range, and then crumpled and fell under the next volley of bullets.

Medwin remounted and led his men up the kopjie, their rifles cocked, and found the witch-doctor thudding on the ground like a dying fowl, his eyes glazed and glaring, and mouth bleeding. As they drew up near him, he gave one last dreadful heave, arching his back like a bent tree, and then fell on his side with a gasp. As his death rattle bubbled up in his throat, his eyes stared directly into Medwin's.

"Cor!" said the batman under his breath. "Fair gives you the 'orrers, don't it?"

"All 'e needs is a top 'at and a banjo," said the second. "Phew! 'E don't half ponk, does 'e? What's all them decorations round 'is neck? Medals?"

"It's a necklace," said Medwin, who had been momentarily seized with a blank and engulfing elemental terror, and needed now to hear the sound of his own steady voice to reassure himself. "Get it for me, Parker. It'll do as a souvenir."

" 'Oo; *me*?" said the first batman without relish. "Maybe it's unhygienic, sir!"

"You're skeered!" said the second batman cheerfully, and slipped out of his saddle. "I'll get it for you, sir! You'll be able to 'ang it on your Christmas tree, if and when we ever get out of this 'ere land of sunshine!"

He bent over the witch-doctor's body and slipped the necklace over the top of his head. "Blimey, wot a sniff!" he added feelingly. "I bet he never washed since the battle of Trafalgar!" He brought the necklace to Medwin, examining it as he walked. "Lot of nice workmanship in this 'ere," he said admiringly. "They've used bits of bones like beads, to make a pattern. Bit barbaric, mind you; but chick; chick, all right."

Medwin took it and swung it on his finger. "Thanks," he said casually, not particularly enamoured of the necklace, but self-consciously aware that Parker was eyeing him with awe and respect.

The necklace was patterned in red, black and white; the bones were small and neat, about an inch long. It was dirty and evil smelling, but he slipped it in his pocket. "Well, that's one less of 'em," he said briskly. "Something tells me the war'll be over sooner than we expect."

For him, it was.

He died, screaming horribly, of dysentery and fever eight days later, and his effects were conscientiously assembled and sent to his wife with a fitting letter of condolence from his Colonel....

The next Medwin fell at Vimy Ridge in the first world war, leaving a son of eighteen who had been named after his grandfather; and he died in a motor collision in 1934, leaving the last of the Medwins sitting pensively in his nursery, mastering his alphabet.

The Medwin house had stood unchanged and untouched, even though London's suburbia had crept like a fungus around its park walls, and electric trains scuttled past it, roaring its stately silence into oblivion.

Old Mrs. Torbal Medwin had died at eighty-four, and the next Mrs. Medwin at sixty-nine.

Young Sholto Medwin remembered neither of them, though they had interfered ferociously with the method of his upbringing. His mother was weak-willed, and apathetic after the death of his father. He was allowed to be brought up by Calvinistic nannies who harrowed him with tales of ghosts and avenging deities; and he lived a bored, lonely, uneventful life until he was packed off to boarding school. He was to go to Sandhurst from school, and follow the military tradition of the family, though he shrank from the thought. In the holidays he moped disconsolately along the gloomy vastnesses of the old house.

When he was fifteen, however, he brought home with him for the summer holidays one of the few friends he had been able to make; a small, quiet youth called Sean O'Fanlin. They shared the common inability to conform to the extrovert pattern of their school-fellows. They were both reserved and retiring, with the difference that Sean O'Fanlin was perfectly content to be, and nursed an amiable indifference to his contemporaries; and Sholto was *gauche* and inarticulate, and accepted O'Fanlin unquestioningly as his leader.

Sean O'Fanlin was a confirmed mystic. He had heard the banshee wail, and had actually seen the Great Dog; and dreamed strange, coherent dreams of foreign places and people, and was for ever confirming the flora and fauna of his dreams by wading through the *Encyclopaedia Britannica.* He had no fear of the supernatural at all, and was passionately fond of wandering into old churchyards and reeling off the personal history of forgotten bones under crumbled tombstones; giving names, dates, ailments and habits as if he were reading it from an invisible parish register.

Often he would be seized with the desire to prophesy; but grim and bitter experience of the treatment of unsympathetic schoolboys had long ago taught him to keep his mouth shut when he sensed the future wafting against his vision.

He was kindly, and very wise for his age, with a kind of ingrained common sense and tolerance. His passion was dogs; and he never killed anything, not even flies. "If you leave them alone, and they *know* you don't mean them harm, they go away," he would explain;

and surely enough he was never bothered by flies, even when they swarmed over everyone else.

"I once saw a man's fear," he told Sholto, with no desire to over-impress. "The man didn't see it, only I did. It was small, only about as big as a fat baby, and it sat and laughed at him in a nasty way. It was covered with a sort of fur, in patches; mangy sort of fur, and it had little ears like a pig. It was all belly; its arms and legs were too small to do any harm with; but the man didn't know that. He thought he was looking at a man-eating ogre, for he wasn't afraid of *things,* you understand; he was only afraid of his own fear."

"I don't see the difference," Sholto countered.

"Ah, don't you, now? Well, it's the difference between being afraid of a buzz-bomb that's going to hit you, and a buzz-bomb that isn't."

"I still don't see the difference."

"It's because you don't trust the will of God, then."

"I do!"

"Not you, you don't. You think God's a bad-tempered old man; like Moses when he cursed the Israelites; but He's not that way at all. He knows what's to do; and if you trust Him, *you'll* know what's to do, too, and then how can you be afraid of anything? Dogs trust Him sure enough, and certain kinds of cat, and many of the beasts; the elephant in particular."

"Why only certain kinds of cat?"

"Some cats are sluts: they have no decency at all."

Then one rainy afternoon they climbed the stairs into one of the servants' attics, in search of old tennis-racquets, and came across an old tin trunk with shreds of old-fashioned labels from Capetown and Bloemfontein; and when Sholto finally prised the lid open, Sean leaned forward, sniffed once like a clever otter, and then very calmly drew Sholto away by the arm.

"Shut the lid," he said. "There's something in there that should have been left on a yellow-grey hill-top, for the sun to rot it dry, a long way from here. It's a hill with big stones on the top; the stones are bigger than a man with his hands stretched over his head; and you're on a horse, Sholto, in a red coat and a white helmet, and black whiskers. I don't know why you're there, but you are."

"That's daft," said Sholto reasonably. "I don't even shave yet."

"No, but it's you, all the same. It's you in a red coat and a white helmet, older than you are now, yet as old as you'll ever be."

"My great-grandfather was in the Zulu War in South Africa. He had a moustache. He died out there."

"Ah, that he may have done: but something else didn't die, though it should have: it's here, in this attic, in that trunk."

"Well, let's have a look, then," said Sholto decisively.

"No," said Sean.

"What's up? Are you skitsy?"

"I'm never skitsy, but we should go downstairs, and all the things in that trunk should be burned."

"Fat hope! What do you think my mother would say to a thing like that?"

"Your mother isn't a very thinking woman; not meaning it in an unflattering way."

"I'm going to have a look," said Sholto with sudden resolution, and pushed the lid of the trunk back on its rusty hinges.

A padding of old newspapers confronted them, and under that, the tarnished glories of Lieutenant Medwin's mess-kit, badly moth-eaten. Sean sat back on his heels, his jaw set in tight disapproval, and Sholto dug down into the trunk, his eyes bright.

"It's jolly exciting!" he said over his shoulder. "Here's his sword; and piles of old letters ... we could put them together and sell them to a novelist, or something.... And a water-bottle.... It's like Kipling, isn't it?"

"Kipling never went to the Zulu War."

"No; but Gunga Din and all that.... And look at this! It's made of chicken bones."

"It's made of finger-joints," said Sean, without drawing closer, "and it's been cursed black."

"You haven't even looked at it!"

"Put it back where you found it."

"Not likely! It's my property. I'm going to take it back to school with me, and show old Combers. He's always yapping about primitive design and stuff."

"You leave it where it is!" said Sean, with more insistence, his cheeks beginning to flush.

"You mind your own biz," retorted Sholto curtly, and climbed to his feet, slipping the necklace in his pocket.

"Very well," said Sean in a slightly uneven voice. "I've warned you, Sholto. If you refuse to listen, I'm not going to have anything more to do with you. I mean that."

Sholto laughed with a touch of aggressive scorn in his voice.

"You *are* a juggins, Sean!" he said. "You can't go telling people what they *can* do and *can't* do with their own property, you know! It's a free country still, I hope!"

Without answering, Sean turned on his heel and went out of the attic. He made his way purposefully down the stairs and along the dim halls to the drawing-room, where Mrs. Medwin was reading the *Queen*.

"I must speak to you, Mrs. Medwin," he said in an odd, old voice.

"Why, do," Mrs. Medwin invited pleasantly, lowering her magazine and smiling as mechanically as a fan being opened.

"Sholto has found a bone necklace in a trunk in the attic. It must be put in the furnace and burned at once."

"What on earth for?" asked Mrs. Medwin in a tone of tinnily tinkling condescension.

"It was cursed. The curse was made a long time ago, the last time Sholto was on earth, and he will have to keep dying by it until the necklace is destroyed."

"Who cursed him?" asked Mrs. Medwin vaguely.

"A black high-priest."

"Oh really, come now, Sean!"

"He was. At one time he wore robes and made blood-sacrifices; but when he made *this* curse, he was a black savage with his face painted and feathers round his waist, and skins of animals; and he recognised Sholto again—though his name wasn't Sholto, *then*; it was ... it was Torbal—and Sholto shot him, and as he died, he cursed Sholto."

"You know, I don't think this is quite *healthy*, do you, Sean ... in a boy of your age, I mean?"

"But it's true," said Sean simply and calmly. "Why else should I be poking my nose in? You don't follow, Mrs. Medwin. I ought to have explained. When a man curses another man, the curse works; but it binds the curser to the cursed. So if they die, they have to come back together to the earth, and go on with the curse: and the curser has to live as unhappily as the man he cursed because *he himself* can't un-curse his own curse."

"You shall see a doctor, Sean," said Mrs. Medwin with firm resolve. "You've caught a chill of some sort, and you're a little feverish. Why not pop along to bed and I'll tell Brandis to bring you some hot milk and aspirin?"

With a nice attempt to control his impatience and irritability, Sean came closer and talked more earnestly.

"That necklace is the token—the emblem of the curse. Now that Sholto's found it again, it means that the witch-doctor is somewhere near; either alive, in a body, another human being; or he's still an earth-bound spirit. It means he'll kill Sholto. The only way to stop it is to burn the necklace, and get a good exorciser to release Sholto's spirit from the curse; there's many can do it; in a trance they go; an old apple-woman in Balgowdy could do it. She'd go stiff, and break out in a sweat, and talk lost languages; and the earth-bound spirits would be told they were free, and could come back in human bodies again, as long as they behaved in future."

"And did they?"

"Some did, some didn't, according to how far along the path of their own destinies they'd progressed. Nobody hurries a man who dawdles, nor pats a man on the back who goes fast. It's only to ourselves we have to answer, in the end; all evil being temporary, and all good being permanent, when you add it up after thirty or forty lifetimes on this earth; which is only a minor one ... there's others to come."

"I don't like to say this," said Mrs. Medwin carefully, "but I'm not *quite* sure that you're really the best sort of influence for Sholto, if this is the way you talk to him."

"You're to tell him to burn that necklace or I won't be responsible for the consequences," said Sean with sudden vast dignity.

"Then I'm afraid we'll have to take the consequences as we find them," said Mrs. Medwin, fast losing the kindly tone that always floated like a glossy patina on the stagnant pool of her egoistic stupidity.

"Very well," said Sean stiffly. "You're not the first blind and deaf fool that wouldn't heed a warning staring him in the nose, and you won't be the last."

He left the next morning. Mrs. Medwin was having the decorators in and could not offer him further hospitality; and it was the beginning, besides, of the coolness between him and Sholto.

The coolness reached an ugly head when Sholto, a week after the Christmas term had started, reported Sean to his house-master for theft. The case, being a grave one, went instantly before the headmaster, together with the evidence—a bone necklace—and Sean's shameless admission of guilt.

"I confess I am not as surprised as I should be," the headmaster pronounced in awesome tones. "You are not made of the right stuff, O'Fanlin, and as far as I am competent to judge, this school cannot put it there any more than it can make bricks without straw."

"I'm only sorry," retorted the impenitent Sean, "that I didn't have time to burn it."

"I'm sure you are," said the headmaster scathingly. "You are aware, of course, that as you *did* fail to destroy your evidence, that you face the supreme penalty ... expulsion?"

'And what the hell do I care for that, when the fool Medwin faces death if you don't stop it in time?" demanded Sean hotly.

"You have said enough!" the headmaster warned him in an outraged voice. "You may go!"

"No, I won't go!" Sean shouted in a wild rage. "Not till you put that necklace out of his reach for good! 'Tis the same one exactly as killed him before: the curse was breathed into it by the fool that killed him and must go on killing him till the curse be broken, first by burning the necklace, and then by exorcising the unquiet spirits of the both of them; the one being as bad as the other in the matter of taking life, do you see? No; you don't, you donkey-headed old four-eyes! The bust of Caesar behind you has more sense in its head than you ever will! But I tell you this, and I tell you this with God as my judge as I stand here; it's me as tried to save Medwin's skin, and you as is sending him to a silly death that'll mean the coming back and the doing of it all over again!"

"I should flog you," said the headmaster, very red in the face, "had I not already expelled you. You will leave this room and pack your bags!"

The house-master saw Sean on to the four o'clock train, and stood watching it draw out of the station in austere disapproval until Sean's rebellious and unrepentant scowl was a small blur in the carriage window; whereupon he returned to the school to report the exodus to the headmaster.

As he strolled across the playing fields, he paused at the rifle range to watch the school's crack shot, a lanky seventeen-year-old called Hotchkiss, keeping his hand in with a .22.

A group of admiring cronies were standing circumspectly clear of the danger zone, applauding sycophantly every time he drilled a bull's eye. The sun had just set, and a clear twilight lay smoothly on the field. The house-master, observing Medwin beside him, nodded with a patronising amiability.

"Ah, there, Medwin," he said. "I take it we can assume the little matter of that theft to be settled. Where *is* that necklace, by the way? I never really had time to get a good look at it."

"Here, sir," said Medwin willingly and proudly, dragging it from his pocket. "It belonged to my great-grandfather. He picked it up in South Africa in the Zulu Rebellion—"

Hotchkiss's rifle cracked: there was an odd metallic jangle, and something zagged angrily past the house-master's ear. He ducked with instinctive cowardice and felt his heart bolt into his throat: then, realising in a split flash that he had a front to keep up in the presence of his boys, began to straighten again. A wail of husky terror wobbled from Hotchkiss's mouth; a low, gusty "ah" of alarm went up from the group of watchers; and Medwin, a blank, foolish smile on his face, sagged forward so slowly that the house-master was able to catch him easily.

The ricochetted bullet had entered his temple and killed him outright.

"Quick! Boys! Help me!" the house-master cried, with an ineffectual attempt to keep his voice deep and steady. They came up clumsily and awkwardly, gazing at Medwin's sagging body.

"Oh my God!" Hotchkiss said, with hysteria mounting as he spoke. "I aimed straight! I swear, I *swear* I aimed straight! I don't see how it could have—it was the monkey dancing about . . . !"

"Monkey?" said the house-master inanely, bracing himself against the dead weight. "One of you boys—the doctor—get a stretcher from Sick Bay—damn it all, *move! Move,* will you?"

"Over there . . . for a minute . . ." Hotchkiss babbled pitifully ". . . just as I fired . . . it seemed like a sort of big monkey, dancing . . . I wouldn't have aimed wide otherwise! I *never* aim wide! . . . any of these fellows can tell you . . . !"

Two of the bigger boys gingerly helped the house-master with the weight of Medwin's body; between them they laid it clumsily on the grass. It was then that the house-master realised he was still holding the necklace, and that in the general confusion he had gripped it so tight that it had bitten into the palm of his hand and raised blood.

"Trevor," he said thickly to a senior prefect nearby, "Trevor, take this thing to the janitor, and tell him to throw it in the furnace."

"Yes, sir," said Trevor rather blankly, and sped off across the fields. Rather than look at the body at his feet, the house-master stood and watched him running.

He was not clear in his own dusty little mind as to why he had given the order; but a curious half dim sense of relief in the back of his brain assured him that he had done a fitting thing.

He had already dismissed and forgotten Hotchkiss's overwrought mumblings about monkeys as having no bearing on an unlucky accident.

THOMAS NIGEL KNEALE

MINUKE

THE estate agent kept an uncomfortable silence until we reached his car. "Frankly, I wish you hadn't got wind of that," he said. "Don't know how you did: I thought I had the whole thing carefully disposed of. Oh, please get in."

He pulled his door shut and frowned. "It puts me in a rather awkward spot. I suppose I'd better tell you all I know about that case, or you'd be suspecting me of heaven-knows-what kinds of chicanery in your own."

As we set off to see the property I was interested in, he shifted the cigarette to the side of his mouth.

"It's quite a distance, so I can tell you on the way there," he said. "We'll pass the very spot, as a matter of fact, and you can see it for yourself. Such as there is to see."

It was away back before the war (said the estate agent). At the height of the building boom. You remember how it was: ribbon development in full blast everywhere; speculative builders sticking things up almost overnight. Though at least you could get a house when you wanted it in those days.

I've always been careful in what I handle—I want you to understand that. Then one day I was handed a packet of coast-road bungalows, for letting. Put up by one of these gone to-morrow firms, and bought by a local man. I can't say I exactly jumped for joy, but for once the things looked all right, and—business is inclined to be business.

The desirable residence you heard about stood at the end of the row. Actually, it seemed to have the best site. On a sort of natural platform, as it were, raised above road level and looking straight out over the sea. Like all the rest, it had a simple two-bedroom, lounge, living-room, kitchen, bathroom layout. Red-tiled roof, roughcast walls. Ornamental portico, garden strip all round. Sufficiently far from town, but with all conveniences.

It was taken by a man named Pritchard. Cinema projectionist, I think he was. Wife, a boy of ten or so, and a rather younger daughter. Oh—and dog, one of those black, lop-eared animals. They christened the place "Minuke", M-I-N-U-K-E. My Nook. Yes, that's what I said too. And not even the miserable excuse of its being phonetically correct. Still, hardly worse than most.

Well, at the start everything seemed quite jolly. The Pritchards settled in and busied themselves with rearing a privet hedge and shoving flowers in. They'd paid the first quarter in advance, and as far as I was concerned, were out of the picture for a bit.

Then, about a fortnight after they'd moved in, I had a telephone call from Mrs. P. to say there was something odd about the kitchen tap. Apparently the thing had happened twice. The first time was when her sister was visiting them, and tried to fill the kettle: no water would come through for a long time, then suddenly squirted violently and almost soaked the woman. I gather the Pritchards hadn't really believed this—thought she was trying to find fault with their little nest—it had never happened before, and she couldn't make it happen again. Then, about a week later, it did: with Mrs. Pritchard this time. After her husband had examined the tap and could find nothing wrong with it, he decided the water supply must be faulty. So they got on to me.

I went round personally, as it was the first complaint from any of these bungalows. The tap seemed normal, and I remember asking if the schoolboy son could have been experimenting with their main stop, when Mrs. Pritchard, who had been fiddling with the tap, suddenly said, "Quick, look at this! It's off now!" They were quite cocky about its happening when I was there.

It really was odd. I turned the tap to the limit, but—not a drop! Not even the sort of gasping gurgle you hear when the supply is turned off at the main. After a couple of minutes, though, it came on. Water shot out with, I should say, about ten times normal force, as if it had been held under pressure. Then gradually it died down and ran steadily.

Both children were in the room with us until we all dodged out of the door to escape a soaking—it had splashed all over the ceiling—so they couldn't have been up to any tricks. I promised the Pritchards to have the pipes checked. Before returning to town, I called at the next two bungalows in the row: neither of the tenants had had any trouble at all with the water. I thought, well, that localised it at least.

When I reached my office there was a telephone message waiting, from Pritchard. I rang him back and he was obviously annoyed. "Look here," he said, "not ten minutes after you left, we've had something else happen! The wall of the large bedroom's cracked from top to bottom. Big pieces of plaster fell, and the bed's in a terrible mess." And then he said, "You wouldn't have got me in a jerry-built place like this if I'd known!"

I had plasterers on the job next morning, and the whole water supply to "Minuke" under examination. For about three days there was peace. The tap behaved itself, and absolutely nothing was found to be wrong. I was annoyed at what seemed to have been unnecessary expenditure. It looked as if the Pritchards were going to be difficult—and I've had my share of that type: fault-finding cranks occasionally carry eccentricity to the extent of a little private destruction, to prove their points. I was on the watch from now on.

Then it came again.

Pritchard rang me at my home, before nine in the morning. His voice sounded a bit off. Shaky.

"For God's sake can you come round here right away," he said. "Tell you about it when you get here." And then he said, almost fiercely, but quietly and close to the mouthpiece, "There's something damned queer about this place!" Dramatising is a typical feature of all cranks, I thought, but particularly the little mousy kind, like Pritchard.

I went to "Minuke" and found that Mrs. Pritchard was in bed, in a state of collapse. The doctor had given her a sleeping dose.

Pritchard told me a tale that was chiefly remarkable for the expression on his face as he told it.

I don't know if you're familiar with the layout of that type of bungalow? The living-room is in the front of the house, with the kitchen behind it. To get from one to the other you have to use the little hallway, through two doors. But for convenience at meal-times, there's a serving-hatch in the wall between these rooms. A small wooden door slides up and down over the hatch-opening.

"The wife was just passing a big plate of bacon and eggs through from the kitchen," Pritchard told me, "when the hatch door came down on her wrists. I saw it and I heard her yell. I thought the cord must've snapped, so I said, 'All right, all right!' and went to pull it up because it's only a light wooden frame."

Pritchard was a funny colour, and as far as I could judge, it was genuine.

"Do you know, it wouldn't come! I got my fingers under it and heaved, but it might have weighed two hundredweight. Once it gave an inch or so, and then pressed harder. That was it—it was *pressing* down! I heard the wife groan. I said, 'Hold on!' and ripped round through the hall. When I got into the kitchen she was on the floor, fainted. And the hatch-door was hitched up as right as ninepence. That gave me a turn!" He sat down, quite deflated: it didn't appear to be put on. Still, ordinary neurotics can be almost as troublesome as out-and-out cranks.

I tested the hatch, gingerly; and, of course, the cords were sound and it ran easily.

"Possibly a bit stiff at times, being new," I said. "They're apt to jam if you're rough with them." And then, "By the way, just what were you hinting on the phone?"

He looked at me. It was warm sunlight outside, with a bus passing. Normal enough to take the mike out of Frankenstein's monster. "Never mind," he said, and gave a sheepish half-grin. "Bit of—well, funny construction in this house, though, eh?"

I'm afraid I was rather outspoken with him.

Let alone any twaddle about a month-old bungalow being haunted, I was determined to clamp down on this "jerry-building" talk. Perhaps I was beginning to have doubts myself.

I wrote straight off to the building company when I'd managed to trace them, busy developing an arterial road about three counties away. I dare say my letter was on the insinuating side: I think I asked if they had any record of difficulties in the construction of this bungalow. At any rate I got a sniffy reply by return, stating that the matter was out of their hands: in addition, their records were not available for discussion. Blind alley.

In the meantime, things at "Minuke" had worsened to a really frightening degree. I dreaded the phone ringing. One morning the two Pritchards senior awoke to find that nearly all the furniture in their bedroom had been moved about, including the bed they had been sleeping in: they had felt absolutely nothing. Food became suddenly and revoltingly decomposed. All the chimney pots had come down, not just into the garden, but to the far side of the high road, except one which appeared, pulverised, on the living-room floor. The obvious attempts of the Pritchards to keep a rational outlook had put paid to most of my suspicions by this time.

I managed to locate a local man who had been employed during the erection of the bungalows, as an extra hand. He had worked only on the foundations of "Minuke", but what he had to say was interesting.

They had found the going slow because of striking a layer of enormous flat stones, apparently trimmed slate, but as the site was otherwise excellent, they pressed on, using the stone as foundation where it fitted in with the plan, and laying down rubble where it didn't. The concrete skin over the rubble—my ears burned when I heard about that, I can tell you—this wretched so-called concrete had cracked, or shattered, several times. Which wasn't entirely surprising, if it had been laid as he described. The flat stones, he said, had not been seriously disturbed. A workmate had referred to them as "a giant's grave", so it was possibly an old burial mound. Norse, perhaps—those are fairly common along this coast—or even very much older.

Apart from this—I'm no diehard sceptic, I may as well confess—I was beginning to admit modest theories about a poltergeist, in spite of a lack of corroborative knockings and ornament-throwing. There were two young children in the house, and the lore has it that kids are often unconsciously connected with phenomena of that sort, though usually adolescents. Still, in the real-estate profession you have to be careful, and if I could see the Pritchards safely off the premises without airing these possibilities, it might be kindest to the bungalow's future.

I went to "Minuke" the same afternoon.

It was certainly turning out an odd nook. I found a departing policeman on the doorstep. That morning the back door had been burst in by a hundredweight or so of soil, and Mrs. Pritchard was trying to convince herself that a practical joker had it in for them. The policeman had taken some notes, and was giving vague advice about "civil action" which showed that he was out of his depth.

Pritchard looked very tired, almost ill. "I've got leave from my job, to look after them," he said, when we were alone. I thought he was wise. He had given his wife's illness as the reason, and I was glad of that.

"I don't believe in—unnatural happenings," he said.

I agreed with him, non-committally.

"But I'm afraid of what ideas the kids might get. They're both at impressionable ages, y'know."

I recognised the symptoms without disappointment. "You mean, you'd rather move elsewhere," I said.

He nodded. "I like the district, mind you. But what I—"

There was a report like a gun in the very room.

I found myself with both arms up to cover my face. There were tiny splinters everywhere, and a dust of fibre in the air. The door had exploded. Literally.

To hark back to constructional details, it was one of those light, hollow frame-and-plywood jobs. As you'll know, it takes considerable force to splinter plywood: well, this was in tiny fragments. And the oddest thing was that we had felt no blast effect.

In the next room I heard their dog howling. Pritchard was as stiff as a poker.

"I felt it!" he said. "I felt this lot coming. I've got to knowing when something's likely to happen. It's all round!" Of course I began to imagine I'd sensed something too, but I doubt if I had really;

my shock came with the crash. Mrs. Pritchard was in the doorway by this time with the kids behind her. He motioned them out and grabbed my arm.

"The thing is," he whispered, "that I can still feel it! Stronger than ever, by God! Look, will you stay at home to-night, in case I need—well, in case things get worse? I can phone you."

On my way back I called at the town library and managed to get hold of a volume on supernatural possession and what-not. Yes, I was committed now. But the library didn't specialise in that line, and when I opened the book at home, I found it was very little help. "Vampires of south-eastern Europe" type of stuff. I came across references to something the jargon called an "elemental" which I took to be a good deal more vicious and destructive than any poltergeist. A thoroughly nasty form of manifestation, if it existed. Those Norse gravestones were fitting into the picture uncomfortably well; it was fashionable in those days to be buried with all the trimmings, human sacrifice and even more unmentionable attractions.

But I read on. After half a chapter on zombies and Rumanian were-wolves, the whole thing began to seem so fantastic that I turned seriously to working out methods of exploding somebody's door as a practical joke. Even a totally certifiable joker would be likelier than vampires. In no time I'd settled down with a whisky, doodling wiring diagrams, and only occasionally—like twinges of conscience—speculating on contacting the psychic investigation people.

When the phone rang I was hardly prepared for it.

It was a confused, distant voice, gabbling desperately, but I recognised it as Pritchard. "For God's sake, don't lose a second! Get here—it's all hell on earth! Can't you hear it? My God, I'm going crazy!" And in the background I thought I was able to hear something. A sort of bubbling, shushing "wah-wah" noise. Indescribable. But you hear some odd sounds on telephones at any time.

"Yes," I said, "I'll come immediately. Why don't you all leave—" But the line had gone dead.

Probably I've never moved faster. I scrambled out to the car with untied shoes flopping, though I remembered to grab a heavy stick in the hall—whatever use it was to be. I drove like fury, heart belting, straight to "Minuke", expecting to see heaven knows what.

But everything looked still and normal there. The moon was up and I could see the whole place clearly. Curtained lights in the windows. Not a sound.

I rang. After a moment Pritchard opened the door. He was quiet and seemed almost surprised to see me.

I pushed inside. "Well?" I said. "What's happened?"

"Not a thing, so far," he said. "That's why I didn't expect—"

I felt suddenly angry. "Look here," I said, "what are you playing at? Seems to me that any hoaxing round here begins a lot nearer home than you'd have me believe!" Then the penny dropped. I saw by the fright in his face that he knew something had gone wrong. That was the most horrible, sickening moment of the whole affair for me.

"Didn't you ring?" I said.

And he shook his head.

I've been in some tight spots. But there was always some concrete actual business in hand to screw the mind safely down to. I suppose panic is when the subconscious breaks loose and everything in your head dashes screaming out. It was only just in time that I found a touch of the concrete and actual. A kiddie's paintbox on the floor, very watery.

"The children," I said. "Where are they?"

"Wife's just putting the little 'un to bed. She's been restless to-night: just wouldn't go, crying and difficult. Arthur's in the bath-room. Look here, what's happened?"

I told him, making it as short and matter of fact as I could. He turned ghastly.

"Better get them dressed and out of here right away," I said. "Make some excuse, not to alarm them."

He'd gone before I finished speaking.

I smoked hard, trying to build up the idea of "Hoax! Hoax!" in my mind. After all, it could have been. But I knew it wasn't.

Everything looked cosy and normal. Clock ticking. Fire red and mellow. Half-empty cocoa mug on the table. The sound of the sea from beyond the road. I went through to the kitchen. The dog was there, looking up from its sleeping-basket under the sink. "Good dog," I said, and it wriggled its tail.

Pritchard came in from the hall. He jumped when he saw me.

"Getting nervy!" he said. "They won't be long. I don't know where we can go if we—well, if we have to—to leave to-night—"

"My car's outside," I told him. "I'll fix you up. Look here, did you ever 'hear things'? Odd noises?" I hadn't told him that part of the telephone call.

He looked at me so oddly I thought he was going to collapse.

"I don't know," he said. "Can you?"

"At this moment?"

I listened.

"No," I said. "The clock on the shelf. The sea. Nothing else. No."

"The sea," he said, barely whispering. "But you can't hear the sea in this kitchen!"

He was close to me in an instant. Absolutely terrified. "Yes, I have heard this before! I think we all have. I said it was the sea: so as not to frighten them. But it isn't! And I recognised it when I came in here just now. That's what made me start. It's getting louder: it does that."

He was right. Like slow breathing. It seemed to emanate from inside the walls, not at a particular spot, but everywhere. We went into the hall, then the front room: it was the same there. Mixed with it now was a sort of thin crying.

"That's Nellie," Pritchard said. "The dog: she always whimpers when it's on—too scared to howl. My God, I've never heard it as loud as this before!"

"Hurry them up, will you!" I almost shouted. He went.

The "breathing" was ghastly. Slobbering. Stertorous, I think the term is. And faster. Oh, yes, I recognised it. The background music to the phone message. My skin was pure ice.

"Come along!" I yelled. I switched on the little radio to drown the noise. The old National Programme, as it was in those days, for late dance music. Believe it or not, what came through that loudspeaker was the same vile sighing noise, at double the volume. And when I tried to switch off, it stayed the same.

The whole bungalow was trembling. The Pritchards came running in, she carrying the little girl. "Get them into the car," I shouted. We heard glass smashing somewhere.

Above our heads there was an almighty thump. Plaster showered down.

Half-way out of the door the little girl screamed, "Nellie! Where's Nellie? Nellie, Nellie!"

"The dog!" Pritchard moaned. "Oh, curse it!" He dragged them outside. I dived for the kitchen, where I'd seen the animal, feeling a lunatic for doing it. Plaster was springing out of the walls in painful showers.

In the kitchen I found water everywhere. One tap was squirting like a fire-hose. The other was missing, water belching across the window from a torn end of pipe.

"Nellie!" I called.

Then I saw the dog. It was lying near the oven, quite stiff. Round its neck was twisted a piece of painted piping with the other tap on the end.

Sheer funk got me then. The ground was moving under me. I bolted down the hall, nearly bumped into Pritchard. I yelled and shoved. I could actually feel the house at my back.

We got outside. The noise was like a dreadful snoring, with rumbles and crashes thrown in. One of the lights went out. "Nellie's run away," I said, and we all got into the car, the kids bawling. I started up. People were coming out of the other bungalows—they're pretty far apart and the din was just beginning to make itself felt. Pritchard mumbled, "We can stop now. Think it'd be safe to go back and grab some of the furniture?" As if he was at a fire: but I don't think he knew what he was doing.

"Daddy—look!" screeched the boy.

We saw it. The chimney of "Minuke" was going up in a horrible way. In the moonlight it seemed to grow quite slowly, to about sixty feet, like a giant crooked finger. And then—burst. I heard bricks thumping down. Somewhere somebody screamed.

There was a glare like an ungodly great·lightning-flash. It lasted for a second or so.

Of course we were dazzled, but I thought I saw the whole of "Minuke" fall suddenly and instantaneously flat, like a swatted fly. I probably did, because that's what happened, anyway.

There isn't much more to tell.

Nobody was really hurt, and we were able to put down the whole thing to a serious electrical fault. Main fuses had blown throughout the whole district, which helped this theory out. Perhaps it was unfortunate in another respect, because a lot of people changed over to gas.

There wasn't much recognisably left of "Minuke". But some of the bits were rather unusual. Knots in pipes, for instance—I buried what was left of the dog myself. Wood and brick cleanly sliced. Small quantities of completely powdered metal. The bath had been squashed flat, like tinfoil. In fact, Pritchard was lucky to land the insurance money for his furniture.

My professional problem, of course, remained. The plot where the wretched place had stood. I managed to persuade the owner it wasn't ideal for building on. Incidentally, lifting those stones might reveal .something to somebody some day—but not to me, thank you!

I think my eventual solution showed a touch of wit: I let it very cheaply as a scrap-metal dump.

Well? I know I've never been able to make any sense out of it. I hate telling you all this stuff, because it must make me seem either a simpleton or a charlatan. In so far as there's any circumstantial evidence in looking at the place, you can see it in a moment or two. Here's the coast road....

The car pulled up at a bare spot beyond a sparse line of bungalows. The space was marked by a straggling, tufty square of privet bushes. Inside I could see a tangle of rusting iron: springs, a car chassis, oil drums.

"The hedge keeps it from being too unsightly," said the estate agent, as we crossed to it. "See—the remains of the gate."

A few half-rotten slats dangled from an upright. One still bore part of a chrome-plated name. "MI——" and, a little farther on, "K".

"Nothing worth seeing now," he said. I peered inside. "Not that there ever was much— Look out!" I felt a violent push. In the same instant something zipped past my head and crashed against the car behind. "My God! Went right at you!" gasped the agent.

It had shattered a window of the car and gone through the open door opposite. We found it in the road beyond, sizzling on the tarmac. A heavy steel nut, white-hot.

"I don't know about you,' 'the estate agent said, "but I'm rather in favour of getting out of here."

And we did. Quickly.

PHANTOMS
AND
GHOSTLY VISITATIONS

ALFRED MCLELLAND BURRAGE

THE GREEN SCARF

WHEN the Wellingford family became extinct the days of Wellingford Hall as one of the great country homes of England were already numbered. The estate passed into the hands of commercial-minded people who had no reverence for the history of a great house. The acres around the old Hall became too valuable as building sites to be allowed to remain as a park surrounding a country mansion. So the fat Wellingford sheep were driven elsewhere to pasture, and surveyors and architects heralded the coming of navvies and builders.

All this happened many years ago. The old park became crossed and criss-crossed by new roads, and perky little villas with names like "Ivyleigh" and "Dulce Domum" sprang up like monstrous red fungi. Even these have since mellowed, and grown their own ivy and Virginia creeper, and put on airs of respectable maturity. The Hall itself, forlorn and abandoned, like some poor human wretch deserted in his old age, began slowly to crumble and decay.

Wellingford Hall was no more than an embarrassment to the new owners of the estate, who were willing to let it or sell it at the prospective tenant's or purchaser's own price; but to dispose of a great house with no land attached to it and surrounded by a garden city is no easy matter. It was too big for its environment. After some vicissitudes as a private school and the home of a small community of nuns, it was abandoned to its natural fate: "for," said one of the directors of the Wellingford Estate, Limited, a gentleman not above mixing his metaphors, "what was the sense of keeping a white elephant in a state of repair?"

Three years before this present time of writing came Aubrey Vair, the painter, as poor as most other painters, a lover of old buildings and all the cobwebby branches of archaeology, and took Wellingford Hall at a weekly rental of fewer shillings than might be demanded for the use of a gardener's cottage. He knew one of the directors, and he had discovered that a few rooms in the middle of the block of buildings were still habitable. The directors, I suppose, wondered why anyone should wish to live in the damp-ridden, rat-riddled old hole, but they did not despise shillings, and they let him come.

Vair wrote me several letters, begging me to come down and rough it with him. It was just the place for a writer, he assured me; it would give me ideas. He had been searching after priests'-holes and had discovered no less than five. One of the great rooms made the finest studio he had yet painted in. And really, as regards comfort, he avowed, it wasn't so bad, so long as one came there already warned to expect only the amenities of a poor bachelor establishment. And then, he added temptingly, there were the historical associations.

I already knew something about the latter, having discovered my facts in a book dealing with old English country houses. Charles the First had spent a night there during the Great Civil War. Charles the Second was supposed to have ridden there after the battle of Worcester. But best of all was the romantic tale of the capture and execution of Sir Peter Wellingford in 1649.

Briefly, Sir Peter was a proscribed Royalist who lived hunted and in hiding after the failure of the royal arms. A wiser man would have crossed the Channel, but Sir Peter had a young wife at Wellingford Hall. He had often visited her in safety, and might have continued to do so, but for a traitor in his own household. This fellow, so the story went, betrayed his master by waving a green scarf from one of the windows, this being a prearranged signal to inform a detachment of Parliamentary troops that the head of the house was secretly in residence. The soldiers burst in at night, and ransacked the house before Sir Peter Wellingford was discovered in a hiding-hole—or "privacie", as the old chronicle described it. The cavalier was dragged outside and shot in his own courtyard.

Here was a story romantic enough to inveigle the fancy of most men with a grain of imagination. I fully intended to visit Wellingford Hall, but circumstances caused me to defer my intention for the first summer and it was not until the following May, when Vair had been in residence a full year, that I paid him my deferred visit. I journeyed by road, driving myself in my small two-seater, so that Vair had no opportunity to meet me, and I had my first view of Wellingford Hall before I could be biased by his enthusiasms.

Holy writ speaks of the abomination of desolation standing where it ought not; and here was this grim, forbidding, crumbling old ruin still surrounded by its moat and standing in the midst of jerry-built "Chumleighs" and "Rosemounts". It was like finding the House of Usher in the middle of a new garden city. In spite of its moat the Hall had never been intended for a fortress and the bridge I crossed must have been nearly as old as the house itself.

Vair heard me coming and pushed open the great nail-studded door under the archway of the main entrance to come out and greet me with a grin and a handshake. He climbed up beside me and directed me round into the yard, where there was plenty of accommodation for a dozen cars. Strangely enough, the stables and coach-houses were in better repair than the old house itself.

The hall had once been magnificent, but most of the ceiling was gone, and the oak balustrade of the staircase, having had a commercial value, had been long since removed. A trail of sacking across broken paving stones pointed the way to Vair's apartments beyond. He ushered me into a fine room, in quite a reasonable state of repair, furnished with products of his speculations at country auctions. Although the month was May the weather was none too warm, and I was glad of the sight of the log fire which lent the room an additional air of comfort. Vair laughed to hear me exclaim, and asked if I were ready for tea.

He lived there, he explained, entirely alone, except that a charwoman came each morning to do the rough work and cook his one hot meal of the day.

"You won't mind putting up with cold stuff and tinned things of an evening?" he asked anxiously.

I hate tinned foods, but, of course, I could not say so.

After tea, Vair showed me the rest of the rooms which he had made habitable, and, really, he had managed to make himself much more comfortable than I had expected. He had contrived—Heaven knows how—to learn a lot of intimate history of the old place, and knew the name by which every room had been called in the house's palmy days of dignity and prosperity. My bedroom, for instance, was known as "Lady Ursula's Nursery", although history had long since forgotten who Lady Ursula was.

It was easy to see that Vair had a boyish enthusiasm for the place. He was a queer chap, with more than the average artist's share of eccentricities, and he believed in all manner of superstitions and pseudo sciences. He was one of those ageless men who might have been anything in the twenties, thirties, or forties. I happened to know that he was nearly fifty, but his thin wiriness of figure and boyish zest for life kept him youthful. Obviously his pleasure at having me down was not so much for my own sake as his. I was somebody to whom he could "show off" the house. He was clearly as proud of it as if it had been restored to its former dignity and he were the actual owner.

"For Heaven's sake, don't go about the place by yourself," he said, "or you'll break your neck. I've nearly broken mine a dozen times, and I'm beginning to know where it isn't safe to walk. It must be rather rare to find damp-rot and dry-rot in the same house, but we've got both here."

I promised faithfully that I wouldn't move without him. Even the main staircase did not appear too safe to me, but Vair assured me that it was all right.

After tea he took me over such parts of the house as it was safe to visit, but I shall make no attempt to describe most of this pilgrimage. My memory carries dreary pictures of damp and decay, of dust and dirt, and cobwebs, mouldering walls and crumbling floors. The old place must have been a warren of secret rooms and passages, and he showed me those he had discovered. All I can say is that the refugees of the bad old days must have been very uncomfortable, and those who escaped deserved to.

One large room under the roof, which we visited, had once been a secret chamber. It was called the Chapel, and here Mass had been said in defiance of the law throughout part of the sixteenth and seventeenth centuries.

"There must be a lot more secret rooms," Vair remarked. "Little Owen, who was a master at constructing such places, is known to have spent months here during the reign of Elizabeth. The house was always being raided, and the raiders had little satisfaction."

"They got the poor old cavalier," I laughed.

"Oh, yes. But he was given away, or sold, by a servant. I've shown you the place where I'm almost sure he hid—behind where the bed-head used to be in the room called the King's Chamber. We'll see if we can find some more while you're here, if you like."

It suddenly occurred to me that Vair had always called himself "sensitive", or psychic, and it was perhaps natural of me to put on the non-committal smile of the polite sceptic and inquire if he had seen any ghosts. Rather to my surprise, he shook his head.

"No," he answered; "it isn't at all that kind of place. The house is quite friendly. I should have felt it at once if it had been otherwise."

"But I should have thought with its history—"

"Ah, it's seen troubled days, but they were always nice people who lived here. There are no dreadful legends of bloodshed and cruelty."

"There is the story of the cavalier," I objected. "Surely his ghost ought to haunt the place."

"Why? He was a good man from all accounts and he died a man's death. Only troubled or wicked people linger about the scenes of their earth-life. When he was taken out and slaughtered all the hatred and blood-lust came from *outside*. If any impressions of those spent passions remain, they're not inside the house, and I don't want them inside."

I smiled to myself, knowing that, from Vair's point of view, the house *ought* to be haunted, and his excuses for the non-appearance of a ghost or two struck me as ingenious but far-fetched.

"That's a pity," I said, tongue in cheek. "I quite hoped to be introduced to a Grey Lady or Spectre Cavalier."

He frowned, knowing that I was laughing at him.

"Well, you won't be," he said, "unless—"

"Unless what?"

"Well, unless something happens to alter present conditions. If, for instance, we were to find something which someone long forgotten desired should remain hidden."

"I see."

"I doubt if you do. And I doubt if anything could be done now to disturb any of the Wellingfords in their long sleep. They seem to have been an ideal family; I haven't been able to find a word of scandal on any page of their history. Where there has once been bitterness and hatred, there you may look for ghosts. There was none here. All that came from outside. That frenzied desire, for instance, to trap and kill a man because he had fought for his king, long after his cause was well lost; that bitter bigotry which sought to prevent folk from worshipping according to their consciences. It all came from outside, I tell you!"

Vair's voice had risen. Like most men with no particular faith he respected all creeds, and religious intolerance always moved him to violent anger. Respect for his deadly seriousness kept my face grave.

"Do you mean just outside?" I asked.

"How do I know? And so long as they remain outside what does it matter? I assure you, I don't want them brought in."

To my relief, he then veered away from a subject which was hardly within my scope of conversation. There was little of the mystic in me. All the same, when at last I retired to bed in Lady Ursula's nursery, I was glad to remember that Vair had given the house a clean bill of health in the psychic sense. By the time I had been Vair's guest for twenty-four hours I had begun to feel with him that the old ruin had a kindly and friendly atmosphere, in spite of its apparent gloom, and that this might have been the legacy of good people who had lived and died within its walls.

At the risk of giving this narrative an air of being disconnected, I must pass hurriedly over the next two or three days of my visit, for they brought forth little that is worth recording. Sometimes Vair did a little painting, and then his preoccupation drove me to my own work. We did a little fishing and sometimes walked three-quarters of a mile to the Wellingford Arms where, according to Vair, who accounted himself an expert, the bitter beer was better than the average. Sometimes we risked our necks on rickety stairs and crumbling floors, looking for more secret hiding-places, an occupation in which I soon became infected with some of Vair's schoolboy zest.

The place was quiet enough during the day, but the villas and bungalows which had marched almost to the edge of the moat made themselves audible at night. Every Lyndhurst and Balmoral seemed able to boast of a musical daughter or a powerful gramophone. The effect of sitting in one of those dignified old rooms with the windows open and hearing echoes from the musical comedies was grotesque in the extreme. Vair had evidently grown used to it, for he made no comment.

I had arrived on a Saturday, and it was on the afternoon of the Tuesday following that, between us, we made a discovery of historical interest; a discovery which we came afterwards bitterly to regret having made. We were on the first floor landing, where long windows, deep in a recess, looked out over the Wellingford Park estate, when Vair mentioned that he had never examined the window seats.

"Sliding panels," he said, "certainly have existed, but they belong mostly to fiction. They were too hard to construct and too easily discovered. Take the five hiding-places you've seen in this house. Three of them are behind fireplaces, one under the stairs, and the other must have been masked at one time by the head of a bedstead. Window-seats were very often used, and this one looks likely. Let's try it."

We rapped it with our knuckles and, although it did not sound hollow, there was obviously an empty space beneath it. We pushed and tugged and teased the surface of the wood with our fingers. And suddenly I saw a crack widen, and part of the seat which had fitted into the rest of the woodwork as neatly as a drawer came away in my hands, and we stared at each other with laughter and curiosity in our eyes.

"Hallo, what's this!" Vair exclaimed.

The cavity disclosed was very small. It was obviously not the entrance to any place of concealment capable of holding a human being. I lit a match and thrust it down into the darkness. Then cheek by jowl we peered together into a cavity no more than three feet deep.

"Nothing here," I said, breaking cobwebs as I moved my wrist to and fro.

"Isn't there!" exclaimed Vair.

He brushed me aside and his arm disappeared up to the shoulder. His hand was black when he drew it forth, and an end of something like a black rag was between his fingers. It was an old piece of silk, so rotten with age that it almost crumbled under our touch; but when we had blown on it and brushed it with our fingers we saw that it owed its present colour to the dirt of ages, and that it had once been green. On the instant the old tale leaped into the minds of both of us, and we exclaimed together:

"The Green Scarf!"

I forget what we said for the first minute or two. We were both excited and elated. There is some peculiar pleasure, difficult to analyse or explain, in discovering a relic which serves to corroborate some old tale or passage of ancient history. We neither of us doubted that we had discovered the green scarf by which Sir Peter Wellingford had been betrayed nearly three hundred years before.

"The traitor must have kept it here in readiness," said Vair, his eyes dancing, "and when he'd signalled he dropped it back again, and there it's lain from that day to this."

"And most likely," I added, taking the relic from his hands, "this is the very window he waved from."

The window was open and I leaned out and let the dingy rag flutter from my hand in the warm afternoon breeze.

"Don't!" said Vair sharply, and pulled me back.

The silk was so rotten with age that even the weak breeze tore it slightly, and I thought at the time that Vair's sharp "Don't!" was uttered because of the damage I had unwittingly done. It was a relic of treachery and bloodshed, but we both regarded it with a queer sort of reverence, as if it were associated with something sacred.

I should think an hour must have passed before we mentioned anything else. We were both agreed that one of us should write to a newspaper announcing our discovery and that the scarf should be cleaned by an expert and offered to a museum. One remark of Vair's struck me at the time as a little strange, but the full force of it did not come to me until some hours later.

"I wish you hadn't waved it out of the window," he said. "It's what that damned traitor did. That's what made you do it, of course—trying to re-enact part of an old tragedy."

"I don't see that it matters," I returned lightly. "Nobody saw."

He turned on me at once.

"How do you know?" he demanded sharply.

I could not help laughing then.

"My dear fellow," I exclaimed, "are you afraid that the wife or daughter of one of your neighbours will think—"

"I wasn't thinking of *them*," he returned curtly. "When that rag was waved out of that window nearly three hundred years ago, you know what happened, you know what it brought into the house."

I thought I had caught the drift of his meaning. Vair had always declined to walk under ladders or make the thirteenth of a party, and he was unhappy for days after he had spilled the contents of a salt-cellar.

"Oh, don't be an ass, Vair," I begged. "If there's any ill-luck about I give it leave to attack me and leave you alone."

He did not answer, and in a few minutes the incident had passed temporarily from my mind.

I have tried to tell this story so many times by word of mouth, and been compelled at this point to pause and hesitate, as now I am compelled to pause and think. It is not that my memory fails me; memory, indeed, serves me all too well. But hereabouts I am brought to realise the failure of my small command of words. A bad speaker can at least convey something otherwise unexpressed by look, gesture, hesitation, tone of voice. But with nothing but pen, ink, paper, and a limited vocabulary, I see little chance of giving an adequate account of what happened to us that night; of how, with the twilight, depression was laid upon us, straw by straw, and how with the coming of darkness horror was laid upon us, load by load.

Even before supper I found myself restless and ill at ease. Something began to weigh upon my spirit as if my mind carried the knowledge of some ordeal which I had presently to face. Of course, I put it down to an attack of "liver" and made up my mind to forget it. The intention was good, but it was unjustified by the desired result.

My discovery that Vair was suffering from a similar malaise did not help my own case. His spirits were far below normal, and I think our mutual discovery that the other was "below form" added weight to that which was already dragging at our hearts. To make matters worse we each began to act for the other's benefit, to force laughter, to crack heavy jokes, and make cumbersome epigrams. But when at twilight we lit the lamp and sat down to supper we tacitly agreed to give up pretending.

"Do you feel that there's a weight crushing you whenever there's thunder about?" Vair asked suddenly.

I was glad to think of some excuse to account for my mood and answer quickly:

"Yes, very often. And I wouldn't mind betting there's some thunder about to-night."

Vair looked at me and seemed suddenly to change his mind over what he had been about to say. He shook his head.

"The glass hasn't gone down."

I rose from the table without apology, went to the window, pulled aside the curtains, and looked out. It was just after sunset on a very perfect May evening. There was a red glow in the west, and around this glow there was an area of sky which was almost apple-green. This merged into a very deep blue in which one or two pale stars were already beginning to play hide-and-seek.

"No," I agreed grudgingly, "there isn't a cloud in the sky. Still, storms come up very quickly."

"Yes," said Vair, "and so do other things."

My lips moved to ask him what he meant, but I thought better of it. Whatever morbid imaginings he might be entertaining, they were scarcely likely to help my own mood. We ate in silence, continuing thus for a long time before I forced a laugh and exclaimed:

"Well, we're a jolly pair, aren't we? What the devil's the matter with us this evening? I only wish I knew."

"I only wish I didn't think I know," he answered strangely.

"Well, what do you think—"

"I think we ought to go out somewhere to-night and stay out."

"Why? You haven't felt like this before, have you?"

"No. And it's because I haven't felt like this before—"

He came to another sudden pause, and we looked into each other's faces for a moment before he lowered his gaze.

"Now, look here," I said, trying to keep my voice steady, "let's be as honest as we can and try to analyse this thing. I'll say it first. We're both afraid of something."

He went a step further.

"We're both afraid of the same thing," he said. "Well, what is it, then? Let's find it out and confront it. When a horse shies at a tree you lead him up to it to show him that it's only a tree."

'If it happens to be a tree or something like a tree. But if it isn't ... Look here, let's go out. Straight away now, while there's time. They've got bedrooms at the Wellingford Arms. Let's go and spend the night there."

With all my heart I wanted to. But Pride borrowed the voice of Reason and spoke for me.

"Oh, don't let's make fools of ourselves," I urged. "I for one don't want to truckle to my nerves. If we give way like this once we shall always be doing it."

He shrugged his shoulders.

"Let's have a drink."

He brought out the whisky. I am a temperate man with a weak head for spirits, and I admit that I exceeded my usual allowance, but it made no more difference to me than if it were water. We sat facing each other gloomily in a silence which became increasingly difficult to break.

The unusual quality of this silence had already begun to impress me when Vair mentioned it, as if my thought had communicated itself to him.

"Don't you notice how extraordinarily still everything seems?" he asked presently.

"Yes," I agreed, and snatched suddenly at a straw. "The silence before the storm. There *is* a storm about, you see."

He shook his head.

"No," he said. "It isn't that kind of stillness."

And then, with a little leap of the heart and a tingling of the nostrils I suddenly realised a fact which seemed to me inexpressibly ugly. This stillness was not the hush of Nature before some electrical disturbance. For some time past we had heard no sound at all from the outer world. The gramophones and pianos in the little houses around us were all silent. It was the hour when at many houses on the estate hosts and guests were parting for the night, yet there was not the faint echo of a voice, nor the comfortable workaday sound of a car droning along a road. It may seem ludicrous, but I would have given a hundred pounds just then to hear the distant shunting of a train.

Vair rose suddenly, went to the window and looked out. I followed him. For some while now it had been completely dark. Overhead in a very clear sky the stars looked peacefully into our troubled eyes.

"No storm about," said Vair shortly.

He heard me catch my breath, and a moment later he was aware of what I had already perceived.

"Look! There aren't any lights! There isn't a light anywhere!"

It was true. The hour was not late, and yet from the rows of houses which began not so many yards distant, not a light was visible, nor was it possible to discern an outline of roof or chimney against the sky. We had been cut off from the lights and sounds of the outside world as completely as if we were in a cavern miles under the ground, save that our isolation—I can think of no other word—was lateral.

Vair's voice had risen high and thin. He made no effort to disguise the terror in it.

"There must be some fog about," I said; and I was so anxious lest my voice should sound like Vair's that I spoke out of the base of my chest.

"Fog! Look, man!"

I looked. Truly there was not the least sign of fog or mist. Until we raised our eyes to the sky we stared into impenetrable, featureless darkness.

Vair let the window curtains fall from his hand. He turned to me in the oppressive stillness, and his face worked until by an effort he controlled the muscles.

"Try to tell me," he said hoarsely, "*what* you've been feeling all the evening."

"How can I? The same as you, I suppose!" A reminiscence of soldiering came back to me. "It's been like waiting to go over the top. A horrible aching anxiety. No, something more than that. A sense of being trapped, of being surrounded—"

"Surrounded!" He caught up the word with a cry. "That's just what you are! That's just what we both are!"

I drew him away from the curtained window.

"Surrounded! By what?" I made myself ask.

He spread out his hands and shook them helplessly.

"The Powers of Darkness, Hatred, Blood-lust, Intolerance—they were all waiting, waiting for the signal. Do you think these things die like spent matches? Do you think the black act of treachery, which brought them into this house, left nothing behind it? *They* were waiting—all these years—I tell you!" Suddenly he bared his teeth at me. "You fool, to have waved that rag at them!"

Just for a moment I felt my brain turning like a wheel, but I made a fight for my sanity and won it back.

"Look here," I said, "for God's sake don't let's behave like madmen. Let's get out of it if the house is going to affect us like this."

He stared back at me, giving me a look which I could not read.

"No," he muttered; "you wanted to stay."

"Let's go down to the Wellingford Arms."

"They're closed now."

"It doesn't matter. They know you. They'll open for you."

I found myself lusting for the world beyond that unnatural girdle of darkness. The Wellingford Arms, with its vulgar tin advertisement of Somebody's Beer, and Somebody Else's Whisky, and its framed Christmas Number plates—at least there was sanity there.

But Vair suddenly turned on me the eyes of a hunted animal.

"You fool!" he burst out. "It's too late! We can't pass through *Them!*"

"What do you mean?" I faltered.

"They're all around us. You know it, too. They'll break in—in their own good time—as they did before. We're trapped, I tell you!"

Against my will, and Heaven knows how hard I fought for disbelief, Vair had captured my powers of reason. In theory, if not in action, I was now prepared to follow him like a child.

"What do they want?" I stammered.

"Us! One of us or both! What did Murder and Hatred and Blood-lust ever want but sacrifice?"

He fairly spat the words at me and I seized his arm.

"Come on," I said, "we're going to get out of this. We're going to run the gauntlet."

"Ah," said Vair thickly. "If we can."

We must have crossed the hall, although I do not remember it. My next recollection is of helping Vair in his fumbling with the bolts and lock of the great door. We wrenched it open and stood looking at an opaque wall of darkness.

I tried to force myself across the threshold, only to find myself standing rigid. As in a nightmare, my legs were shackled so that I could not move a step forward, but although terror clawed at me like a wild beast, my senses were keenly and even painfully alert.

I knew that this belt of darkness around the house was alive with whisperings and movements, with all manner of stealthiness, which lurked only just beyond the horizon of vision and the limits of hearing. And as I stood straining eyes and ears I knew that the barriers must soon break and that I should both see and hear.

We stood thus a long while on the edge of the threshold we could not pass, but whether it were seconds or minutes I could not say. To us it seemed hours ere the darkness passed, melting into the living forms of men. We could *see,* and there was movement everywhere; we could *hear,* and voices were shouting orders, although the actual words eluded us. They were human voices with strange nasal intonations, snarling and shouting. Even in my extremity I remembered having heard that the soldiery of Cromwell had affected a hideous nasal accent. And now the darkness was sundered and shivered by a score of lights, the lights of naked torches which nodded to the rhythm of men marching. I saw the glint of them on the metal heads of pikes, and on the long barrels of muskets outlined clearly now against a naked sky of stars.

Terror may bind a man to the spot, but another turn of the rack may torture him back into motion. So it was with us. Blind instinct alone made me slam the great door and shoot the nearest heavy bolt. I saw Vair groping for me like a tear-blinded child and I took his arm. We ran futilely back into the room we had vacated and crouched in the corner farthest from the door, while great noises like thunder began to reverberate through the house, as pike-handles and musket-butts crashed sickeningly on the great outer door.

We must both have taken leave of reason then, for neither Vair nor I can remember anything more until the great nail-studded door, smashed off its hinges, fell on to the broken flags of the hall with the loudest crash of all. The tramp of feet, mingled with the sound of arms carelessly handled, thudding against the floor and wall, and with the sharp nasal snarling of voices. In a moment it seemed they were everywhere—in the hall, on the main staircase, in the room over our heads.

Vair had all this time the grip of a madman on my wrist, and suddenly he leaned to me and screamed into my ear:

"The Chapel ... under the roof ... it's consecrated ... there's a chance ... there's a chance, I tell you. ..."

"They're on the stairs!" I cried back in my despair.

"The back stairs! Come on!"

A second door in the old room gave access to a passage leading to the back stairs. Those stairs we knew to be unsafe, but ordinary human peril was something far beyond and beneath our consideration. I remember the rumble and murmur of sounds about the house as we rushed out into the passage. Footfalls and voices sounded everywhere, and musket-butts were smiting heavily against stairs and walls. As we stumbled and ran I expected at every step to be seized and overwhelmed by some horrible and nameless Power.

How we reached the attics I cannot say. The narrow, crumbling staircase creaked and swayed under us, and once I went down thigh deep through a rotten stair, with splinters of hard wood tearing clothes and flesh. But we were near the top ere the hunt had scented their game and sounds of pursuit began to clamour behind us.

Vair forced open the door of the little room which had once been a chapel. I blundered in over his body, which lay prone just across the threshold. He had fallen unconscious, and I had to force his legs aside before I could close the door. I slammed it to in the faces of vague forms which filled the passage to the stair-head, and drove home the wooden bolt inside. And then it seemed to me that our pursuers recoiled from that closed door like a great wave from the base of a cliff, and ugly cries outside died down to uneasy whisperings; and instinctively I knew that we were safe.

I must have fainted then, for I remember nothing more until I woke in bright sunlight. Vair was sitting beside me, watching me, with a chalk-like face. We hardly spoke, but sought each other's hands like frightened children.

Eventually we nerved ourselves to go downstairs into the ruin and disorder of the old house, through which, one might have thought, a whirlwind had passed during the night.

SEVENTH EVENING*
THE GERMAN INN
THE BENIGHTED TRAVELLER

"My story will be a very short one," said Mrs. M.; "for I must tell you that though, like everybody else, I have heard a great many ghost stories, and have met people who assured me they had seen such things, I cannot, for my own part, bring myself to believe in them; but a circumstance occurred when I was abroad, that you may perhaps consider of a ghostly nature, though I cannot.

"I was travelling through Germany, with no one but my maid—it was before the time of railways, and on my road from Leipzig to Dresden, I stopped at an inn that appeared to have been long ago part of an aristocratic residence—a castle, in short; for there was a stone wall and battlements, and a tower at one side; while the other was a prosaic-looking, square building that had evidently been added in modern times. The inn stood at one end of a small village, in which some of the houses looked so antique that they might, I thought, be coeval with the castle itself. There were a good many travellers, but the host said he could accommodate me; and when I asked to see my room, he led me up to the towers, and showed me a tolerably comfortable one. There were only two apartments on each floor; so I asked him if I could have the other for my maid, and he said yes, if no other traveller arrived. None came, and she slept there.

"I supped at the table d'hôte, and retired to bed early, as I had an excursion to make on the following day; and I was sufficiently tired with my journey to fall asleep directly.

"I don't know how long I had slept—but I think some hours, when I awoke quite suddenly, almost with a start, and beheld near the foot of the bed, the most hideous, dreadful-looking old woman, in an antique dress, that imagination can conceive. She seemed to be approaching me—not as if walking, but gliding, with her left arm and hand extended towards me.

* The title is one of several consecutive evenings on each of which the narrator details his or her experiences—*Ed.*

"'Merciful God deliver me!' I exclaimed under my first impulse of amazement; and as I said the words she disappeared."

"Then, though you don't believe in ghosts, you thought it was one when you saw it," said I.

"I don't know what I thought—I admit I was a good deal frightened, and it was a long time before I fell asleep again.

"In the morning," continued Mrs. M., "my maid knocked, and I told her to come in; but the door was locked, and I had to get out of bed to admit her—I thought I might have forgotten to fasten it. As soon as I was up, I examined every part of the room, but I could find nothing to account for this intrusion. There was neither trap nor moving panel, nor door that I could see, except the one I had locked. However, I made up my mind not to speak of the circumstance, for I fancied I must have been deceived in supposing myself awake, and that it was only a dream; more particularly as there was no light in my room, and I could not comprehend how I could have seen this woman.

"I went out early, and was away the greater part of the day. When I returned I found more travellers had arrived, and that they had given the room next to mine to a German lady and her daughter, who were at the table d'hôte. I therefore had a bed made up in my room for my maid; and before I lay down, I searched thoroughly, that I might be sure nobody was concealed there.

"In the middle of the night—I suppose about the same time I had been disturbed on the preceding one—my maid and I were awakened by a piercing scream; and I heard the voice of the German girl in the adjoining room, exclaiming, 'Ach! meine mutter! meine mutter!'

"For some time afterwards I heard them talking, and then I fell asleep—wondering, I confess, whether they had had a visit from the frightful old woman. They left me in no doubt the next morning. They came down to breakfast greatly excited—told everybody the cause—described the old woman exactly as I had seen her, and departed from the house incontinent, declaring they would not stay there another hour."

"What did the host say to it?" we asked.

"Nothing; he said we must have dreamed it—and I suppose we did."

"Your story," said I, "reminds me of a very interesting letter which I received soon after the publication of 'The Night side of Nature'. It was from a clergyman who gave his name, and said he was chaplain to a nobleman. He related that in a house he inhabited, or had inhabited, a lady had one evening gone upstairs, and seen, to her amazement, in a room, the door of which was open, a lady in an antique dress, standing before a chest of drawers, and apparently examining their contents. She stood still, wondering who this stranger could be, when the figure turned her face towards her, and, to her horror, she saw that there were no eyes. Other members of the family saw the same apparition also. I believe there were further particulars; but I unfortunately lost this letter, with some others, in the confusion of changing my residence.

"The absence of eyes I take to be emblematical of moral blindness; for in the world of spirits there is no deceiving each other by false seemings; as we are, so we appear."

"Then," said Mrs. W.C., "the apparition—if it was an apparition—that two of my servants saw lately, must be in a very degraded state.

"There is a road, and on one side of it a path, just beyond my garden wall. Not long ago two of my servants were in the dusk of the evening walking up this path, when they saw a large, dark object coming towards them. At first, they thought it was an animal; and when it got close, one of them stretched out her hand to touch it; but she could feel nothing, and it passed on between her and the garden wall, although there was no *space*, the path being only wide enough for two; and on looking back, they saw it walking down the hill behind them. Three men were coming up on the path; and as the thing approached, they jumped off into the road.

" 'Good heavens, what is that?' cried the women.

" 'We don't know,' replied the men; 'we never saw such a thing as that before.'

"The women came home greatly agitated; and we have since heard there is a tradition that the spot is haunted by the ghost of a man who was killed in a quarry close by."

"I have travelled a great deal," said our next speaker, the Chevalier de La C.G.; "and, certainly, I have never been in any country where instances of these spiritual appearances were not adduced on apparently credible authority. I have heard numerous stories of the sort, but the one that most readily occurs to me at present, was told to me not long ago, in Paris, by Count P.——, the nephew of the celebrated Count P. whose name occurs in the history of the remarkable incidents connected with the death of the Emperor Paul.

"Count P., my authority for the following story, was attached to the Russian embassy; and he told me, one evening, when the conversation turned on the inconveniences of travelling in the East of Europe, that, on one occasion, when in Poland, he found himself about seven o'clock in an autumn evening on a forest road, where there was no possibility of finding a house of public entertainment within many miles. There was a frightful storm; the road, not good at the best, was almost impracticable from the weather, and his horses were completely knocked up. On consulting his people what was best to be done, they said, that to go back was as impossible as to go forward; but that by turning a little out of the main road, they should soon reach a castle where possibly shelter might be procured for the night. The count gladly consented, and it was not long before they found themselves at the gate of what appeared a building on a very splendid scale. The courier quickly alighted and rang at the bell, and while waiting for admission, he enquired who the castle belonged to, and was told that it was Count X's.

"It was some time before the bell was answered, but at length an elderly man appeared at a wicket, with a lantern, and peeped out. On perceiving the equipage, he came forward and stepped up to the carriage, holding the light aloft to discover who was inside. Count P. handed him his card, and explained his distress.

" 'There is no one here, my lord,' replied the man, 'but myself and my family; the castle is not inhabited.'

" 'That's bad news,' said the count; 'but nevertheless, you can give me what I am most in need of, and that is—shelter for the night.'

" 'Willingly,' said the man, 'if your lordship will put up with such accommodation as we can hastily prepare.'

" 'So,' said the count, 'I alighted and walked in; and the old man unbarred the great gates to admit my carriages and people. We found ourselves in an immense *couer,* with the castle *en face,* and stables and offices on each side. As we had a *fourgon* with us, with provender for the cattle and provisions for ourselves, we wanted nothing but beds and a good fire; and as the only one lighted was in the old man's apartments, he first took us there. They consisted of a suite of small rooms in the left wing, that had probably been formerly occupied by the upper servants. They were comfortably furnished, and he and his large family appeared to be very well lodged. Besides the wife, there were three sons, with their wives and children, and two nieces; and in a part of the offices, where I saw a light, I was told there were labourers and women servants, for it was a valuable estate, with a fine forest, and the sons acted as *gardes chasse.*

" 'Is there much game in the forest?' I asked.

" 'A great deal of all sorts,' they answered.

" 'Then I suppose during the season the family live here?'

" 'Never,' they replied. 'None of the family ever reside here.'

" 'Indeed!' I said; 'how is that? It seems a very fine place.'

" 'Superb,' answered the wife of the custodian; 'but the castle is haunted.'

"She said this with a simple gravity that made me laugh; upon which they all stared at me with the most edifying amazement.

"'I beg your pardon,' I said; 'but you know, perhaps, in great cities, such as I usually inhabit, there are no ghosts.'

"'Indeed!' said they. 'No ghosts!'

"'At least,' I said, 'I never heard of any; and we don't believe in such things.'

"They looked at each other with surprise, but said nothing; not appearing to have any desire to convince me. 'But do you mean to say,' said I, 'that that is the reason the family don't live here, and that the castle is abandoned on that account?'

"'Yes,' they replied, 'that is the reason nobody has resided here for many years.'

"'But how can you live here then?'

"'We are never troubled in this part of the building,' said she. 'We hear noises, but we are used to that.'

"'Well, if there is a ghost, I hope I shall see it,' said I.

"'God forbid!' said the woman, crossing herself. 'But we shall guard against that; your seigneurie will sleep not far from this, where you will be quite safe.'

"'Oh!' said I, 'but I am quite serious; if there is a ghost, I should particularly like to see him, and I should be much obliged to you to put me in the apartments he most frequents.'

"They opposed this proposition earnestly, and begged me not to think of it; besides, they said, if anything was to happen to my lord, how should they answer for it; but as I insisted, the women went to call the members of the family who were lighting fires and preparing beds in some rooms on the same floor as they occupied themselves. When they came they were as earnest against the indulgence of my wishes as the women had been. Still I insisted.

"'Are you afraid,' I said, 'to go yourselves in the haunted chambers?'

"'No,' they answered. 'We are custodians of the castle and have to keep the rooms clean and well aired lest the furniture be spoiled—my lord talks always of removing it, but it has never been removed yet—but we would not sleep up there for all the world.'

"'Then it is the upper floors that are haunted?'

"'Yes, especially the long room; no one could pass a night there; the last that did is in a lunatic asylum now at Warsaw,' said the custodian.

"'What happened to him?'

"'I don't know,' said the man; 'he was never able to tell.'

"'Who was he?' I asked.

"'He was a lawyer. My lord did business with him; and one day he was speaking of this place, and saying that it was a pity he was not at liberty to pull it down and sell the materials; but he cannot, because it is family property and goes with the title; and the lawyer said he wished it was his, and that no ghost should keep him out of it. My lord said that it was easy for anyone to say that who knew nothing about it, and that he must suppose the family had not abandoned such a fine place without good reasons. But the lawyer said it was some trick, and that it was coiners, or robbers, who had got a footing in the castle, and contrived to frighten people away that they might keep it to themselves; so my lord said if he could prove that he should be very obliged to him, and more than that, he would give him a great sum—I don't know how much. So the lawyer said he would; and my lord wrote to me that he was coming to inspect the property, and I was to let him do anything he liked.

"'Well, he came, and with him his son, a fine young man and a soldier. They asked me all sorts of questions, and went over the castle and examined every part of it. From what they said, I could see that they thought the ghost was all nonsense, and that I and my family were in collusion with the robbers or coiners. However, I did not care for that; my lord knew that the castle had been haunted before I was born.

"'I had prepared rooms on this floor for them—the same I am preparing for your lordship, and they slept there, keeping the keys of the upper rooms to themselves, so I did not interfere with them. But one morning, very early, we were awakened by some one knocking at our bedroom door, and when we opened it, we saw Mr. Thaddeus—that was the lawyer's son—standing there half dressed and as pale as a ghost; and he said his father was very ill and he begged us to go to him; to our surprise he led us upstairs to the haunted chamber, and there we found the poor gentleman speechless, and we thought they had gone up there early and that he had had a stroke. But it was not so; Mr. Thaddeus said, that after we were all in bed, they had gone up there to pass the night. I know they thought that there was no ghost but us, and that's why they would not let us know their intention. They laid down upon some sofas, wrapped up in their fur cloaks, and resolved to keep awake, and they did so for some time, but at last the young man was overcome by drowsiness, he struggled against it, but could not conquer it, and the last thing he recollects was his father shaking him and saying 'Thaddeus, Thaddeus, for God's sake keep awake!' But he could not, and he knew no more till he woke and saw that day was breaking, and found his father sitting in a corner of the room, speechless, and looking like a corpse; and there he was when we went up. The young man thought he'd been taken ill or had a stroke, as we supposed at first; but when we found they had passed the night in the haunted chambers, we had no doubt what had happened—he had seen some terrible sight and so lost his senses.'

"He lost his senses. I should say, from terror when his son fell asleep, said I, and he felt himself alone. He could have been a man of no nerve. At all events, what you tell me raises my curiosity. Will you take me upstairs and show me those rooms?

" 'Willingly,' said the man, and fetching a bunch of keys and a light, and calling one of his sons to follow him with another, he led the way up the great staircase to a suite of apartments on the first floor. The rooms were lofty and large, and the man said the furniture was very handsome, but old. Being all covered with canvas cases, I could not judge it. 'Which is the long room?' I said.

"Upon which he led me into a long narrow room that might rather have been called a gallery. There were sofas along each side, something like a dais at the upper end; and several large pictures hanging on the walls.

"I had with me a bull dog, of a very fine breed, that had been given me in England by Lord F. She had followed me upstairs—indeed, she followed me everywhere—and I watched her narrowly as she went smelling about, but there were no indications of her perceiving anything extraordinary. Beyond this gallery there was only a small octagonal room, with a door that led out upon another staircase. When I had examined it all thoroughly, I returned to the long room and told the man, as that was the place especially frequented by the ghost, I should feel much obliged if he would allow me to pass the night there. I could take upon myself to say that Count X. would have no objection.

" 'It is not that,' replied the man; 'but the danger to your lordship,' and he conjured me not to insist on such a perilous experiment.

"When he found I was resolved, he gave way, but on condition that I signed a paper, stating that in spite of his representations I had determined to sleep in the long room.

"I confess, the more anxious these people seemed, to prevent my sleeping there, the more curious I was; not that I believed in the ghost the least in the world. I thought that the lawyer had been right in his conjectures, but that he hadn't nerve enough to investigate whatever he saw or heard; and that they had succeeded in frightening him out of his senses. I saw what an excellent place these people had got, and how much it was their interest to maintain the idea that the castle was uninhabitable. Now, I have pretty good nerves—I have been in situations that have tried them severely—and I did not believe that any ghost, if there was such a thing, or any jugglery by which a semblance of one might be contrived, would shake them. As for any real danger, I did not apprehend it; the people knew who I was, and any mischief happening to me would have led to consequences they well understood. So they lighted fires in both the grates of the gallery, and as they had abundance of dry-wood, they soon blazed up. I was determined not to leave the room after I was once in it, lest, if my suspicions were correct, they might have time to make their arrangements; so I desired my people to bring up my supper, and I ate it there.

"My courier said he had always heard the castle was haunted, but he dare say there was no ghost but the people below, who had a very comfortable berth of it; and he offered to pass the night with me, but I declined any companion and preferred trusting myself and my dog. My valet, on the contrary, strongly advised me against the enterprise, assuring me that he had lived with a family in France whose chateâu was haunted, and left his place in consequence.

"By the time I had finished my supper it was ten o'clock, and everything was prepared for the night. My bed, though an impromptu, was very comfortable, made of amply stuffed cushions and thick coverlets, placed in front of the fire. I was provided with light and plenty of wood; and I had my regimental cutlass, and a case of excellent pistols, which I carefully primed and loaded in presence of the custodian, saying, you see I am determined to fire at the ghost, so if he cannot stand a bullet, he had better not pay me a visit.

"The old man shook his head calmly, but made no answer. Having desired the courier, who said he should not go to bed, to come upstairs immediately if he heard the report of firearms, I dismissed my people and locked the doors, barricading each with a heavy ottoman besides. There was no arras or hangings of any sort behind which a door could be concealed; and I went round the room, the walls of which were panelled with white and gold, knocking every part, but neither the sound, nor Dido, the dog, gave any indications of there being anything unusual. Then I undressed and lay down with my sword and my pistols beside me; and Dido at the foot of my bed, where she always slept.

"I confess I was in a state of pleasing excitement; my curiosity and my love of adventure were roused; and whether it was ghost, or robber, or coiner, I was to have a visit from, the interview was likely to be equally interesting. It was half-past ten when I lay down; my expectations were too vivid to admit of sleep; and after an attempt at a French novel, I was obliged to give it up; I could not fix my attention to it. Besides, my chief care was not to be surprised. I could not help thinking the custodian and his family had some secret way of getting into the room, and I hoped to detect them in the act; so I lay with my eyes and ears open in a position that gave me a view of every part of it, till my travelling clock struck twelve, which being pre-eminently the ghostly hour, I thought the critical moment had arrived. But no, no sound, no interruption of any sort to the silence and solitude of the night occurred. When half-past twelve, and one struck, I pretty well made up my mind that I should be disappointed in my expectations, and that the ghost, whoever he was, knew better than to encounter Dido and a brace of well charged pistols; but just as I arrived at this conclusion, an unaccountable *frisson* came over me, and I saw Dido, who, tired with her day's journey, had lain till now quietly curled up asleep, begin to move, and slowly get up on her feet. I thought she was only going to turn, but, instead of lying down, she stood still with her ears erect and her head towards the dais, uttering a low growl.

"The dais, I should mention, was but the skeleton of a dais, for the draperies were taken off. There was only remaining a canopy covered with crimson velvet, and an arm chair covered with velvet too, but cased in canvas like the rest of the furniture. I had examined this part of the room thoroughly, and had moved the chair aside to ascertain that there was nothing under it.

"Well, I sat up in bed and looked steadily in the same direction as the dog, but I could see nothing at first, though it appeared that she did; but as I looked, I began to perceive something like a cloud in the chair, while at the same time a chill which seemed to pervade the very marrow in my bones crept through me, yet the fire was good; and it was not the chill of fear, for I cocked my pistols with perfect self-possession and abstained from giving Dido the signal to advance, because I wished eagerly to see the dénouement of the adventure.

"Gradually, this cloud took a form, and assumed the shape of a tall white figure that reached from the ceiling to the floor of the dais, which was raised by two steps. 'At him, Dido! At him!' I said, and away she dashed to the steps, but instantly turned and crept back completely cowed. As her courage was undoubted, I own this astonished me, and I should have fired, but that I was perfectly satisfied that what I saw was not a substantial human form, for I had seen it grow into its present shape and height from the undefined cloud that first appeared in the chair. I laid my hand on the dog who had crept up to my side, and I felt her shaking in her skin. I was about to rise myself and approach the figure, though I confess I was a good deal awe struck, when it stepped majestically from the dais, and seemed to be advancing. 'At him!' I said, 'At him, Dido!' and I gave the dog every encouragement to go forward. She made a sorry attempt, but returned when she had got half way and crouched beside me whining with terror. The figure advanced upon me; the cold became icy; the dog crouched and trembled; and I, as it approached, honestly confess, said Count P., that I hid my head under the bed clothes and did not venture to look up till morning. I know not what it was—as it passed over me I felt a sensation of undefinable horror, that no words can describe—and I can only say that nothing on earth would tempt me to pass another night in that room, and I am sure if Dido could speak, you'd find her of the same opinion.

"I had desired to be called at seven o'clock, and when the custodian who accompanied my valet, found me safe and in my perfect senses, I must say the poor man appeared greatly relieved; and when I descended the whole family seemed to look upon me as a hero. I thought it only just to them to admit that something had happened in the night that I felt impossible to account for, and that I should not recommend anybody who was not very sure of his nerves to repeat the experiment."

When the Chevalier had concluded this extraordinary story, I suggested that the apparition of the castle very much resembled that mentioned by the late Professor Gregory, in his letters on mesmerism, as having appeared in the Tower of London some years ago, and from the alarm it created, having occasioned the death of a lady, the wife of an officer quartered there, and one of the sentries. Everyone who had read that very interesting publication was struck by the resemblance.

THE EYES

I

We had been put in the mood for ghosts, that evening, after an excellent dinner at our old friend Culwin's, by a tale of Fred Murchard's—the narrative of a strange personal visitation.

Seen through the haze of our cigars, and by the drowsy gleam of a coal fire, Culwin's library, with its oak walls and dark old bindings, made a good setting for such evocations; and ghostly experiences at first hand being, after Murchard's opening, the only kind acceptable to us, we proceeded to take stock of our group and tax each member for a contribution. There were eight of us, and seven contrived, in a manner more or less adequate, to fulfil the condition imposed. It surprised us all to find that we could muster such a show of supernatural impressions, for none of us, excepting Murchard himself and young Phil Frenham—whose story was the slightest of the lot—had the habit of sending our souls into the invisible. So that, on the whole, we had ever reason to be proud of our seven "exhibits", and none of us would have dreamed of expecting an eighth from our host.

Our old friend, Mr. Andrew Culwin, who had sat back in his armchair, listening and blinking through the smoke circles with the cheerful tolerance of a wise old idol, was not the kind of man likely to be favoured with such contacts, though he had imagination enough to enjoy, without envying, the superior privileges of his guests. By age and by education he belonged to the stout Positivist tradition, and his habit of thought had been formed in the days of the epic struggle between physics and metaphysics. But he had been, then and always, essentially a spectator, a humorous detached observer of the immense muddled variety show of life, slipping out of his seat now and then for a brief dip into the convivialities at the back of the house, but never, as far as one knew, showing the least desire to jump on the stage and do a "turn".

Among his contemporaries there lingered a vague tradition of his having, at a remote period, and in a romantic clime, been wounded in a duel; but this legend no more tallied with what we younger men knew of his character than my mother's assertion that he had once been "a charming little man with nice eyes" corresponded to any possible reconstitution of his physiognomy.

"He never can have looked like anything but a bundle of sticks," Murchard had once said of him. "Or a phosphorescent log, rather," someone else amended; and we recognised the happiness of this description of his small squat trunk, with the red blink of the eyes in a face like mottled bark. He had always been possessed of a leisure which he had nursed and protected, instead of squandering it in vain activities. His carefully guarded hours had been devoted to the cultivation of a fine intelligence and a few judiciously chosen habits; and none of the disturbances common to human experience seemed to have crossed his sky. Nevertheless, his dispassionate survey of the universe had not raised his opinion of that costly experiment, and his study of the human race seemed to have resulted in the conclusion that all men were superfluous, and women necessary only because someone had to do the cooking. On the importance of this point his convictions were absolute, and gastronomy was the only science which he revered as a dogma. It must be owned that his little dinners were a strong argument in favour of this view, besides being a reason—though not the main one—for the fidelity of his friends.

Mentally he exercised a hospitality less seductive but no less stimulating. His mind was like a forum, or some open meeting-place for the exchange of ideas: somewhat cold and draughty, but light, spacious and orderly—a kind of academic grove from which all the leaves have fallen. In this privileged area a dozen of us were wont to stretch our muscles and expand our lungs; and, as if to prolong as much as possible the tradition of what we felt to be a vanishing institution, one or two neophytes were now and then added to our band.

Young Phil Frenham was the last, and the most interesting, of these recruits, and a good example of Murchard's somewhat morbid assertion that our old friend "liked 'em juicy". It was indeed a fact that Culwin, for all his dryness, specially tasted the lyric qualities in youth. As he was far too good an Epicurean to nip the flowers of soul which he gathered for his garden, his friendship was not a disintegrating influence: on the contrary, it forced the young idea to robuster bloom. And in Phil Frenham he had a good subject for experimentation. The boy was really intelligent, and the soundness of his nature was like the pure paste under a fine glaze. Culwin had fished him out of a fog of family dullness, and pulled him up to a peak in Darien; and the adventure hadn't hurt him a bit. Indeed, the skill with which Culwin had contrived to stimulate his curiosities without robbing them of their bloom of awe seemed to me a sufficient answer to Murchard's ogreish metaphor. There was nothing hectic in Frenham's efforescence, and his old friend had not laid even a finger-tip on the sacred stupidities. One wanted no better proof of that than the fact that Frenham still reverenced them in Culwin.

"There's a side of him you fellows don't see. *I* believe that story about the duel!" he declared; and it was of the very essence of this belief that it should impel him—just as our little party was dispersing—to turn back to our host with the joking demand: "And now you've got to tell us about *your* ghost!"

The outer door had closed on Murchard and the others; only Frenham and I remained; and the devoted servant who presided over Culwin's destinies, having brought a fresh supply of soda-water, had been laconically ordered to bed.

Culwin's sociability was a night-blooming flower, and we knew that he expected the nucleus of his group to tighten around him after midnight. But Frenham's appeal seemed to disconcert him comically, and he rose from the chair in which he had just reseated himself after his farewells in the hall.

"*My* ghost? Do you suppose I'm fool enough to go to the expense of keeping one of my own, when there are so many charming ones in my friends' closets?—take another cigar," he said, revolving towards me with a laugh.

Frenham laughed too, pulling up his slender height before the chimney-piece as he turned to face his short bristling friend.

"Oh," he said, "you'd never be content to share if you met one you really liked."

Culwin had dropped back into his arm-chair ,his shock head embedded in the hollow of worn leather, his little eyes glimmering over a fresh cigar.

"Liked—*liked?* Good Lord!" he growled.

"Ah, you *have*, then!" Frenham pounced on him in the same instant, with a side glance of victory at me; but Culwin cowered gnome-like among his cushions, dissembling himself in a protective cloud of smoke.

"What's the use of denying it? You've seen everything, so of course you've seen a ghost!" his young friend persisted, talking intrepidly into the cloud. "Or, if you haven't seen one, it's only because you've seen two!"

The form of the challenge seemed to strike our host. He shot his head out of the mist with a queer tortoise-like motion he sometimes had, and blinked approvingly at Frenham.

"That's it," he flung at us on a shrill jerk of laughter; "it's only because I've seen two!"

The words were so unexpected that they dropped down and down into a deep silence, while we continued to stare at each other over Culwin's head, and Culwin stared at his ghosts. At length Frenham, without speaking, threw himself into the chair on the other side of the hearth, and leaned forward with his listening smile....

II

"Oh, of course they're not show ghosts—a collector wouldn't think anything of them.... Don't let me raise your hopes ... their one merit is their numerical strength: the exceptional fact of their being *two*. But, as against this, I'm bound to admit that at any moment I could probably exorcise them both by asking my doctor for a prescription, or my oculist for a pair of spectacles. Only, as I never could make up my mind whether to go to the doctor or the oculist—whether I was afflicted by an optical or a digestive delusion—I left them to pursue their interesting double life, though at times they made mine exceedingly uncomfortable....

"Yes—uncomfortable; and you know how I hate to be uncomfortable! But it was part of my stupid pride, when the thing began, not to admit that I could be disturbed by the trifling matter of seeing two—

"And then I'd no reason, really, to suppose I was ill. As far as I knew I was simply bored—horribly bored. But it was part of my boredom—I remember—that I was feeling so uncommonly well, and didn't know how on earth to work off my surplus energy. I had come back from a long journey down in South America and Mexico—and had settled down for the winter near New York, with an old aunt who had known Washington Irving and corresponded with N. P. Willis. She lived, not far from Irvington, in a damp Gothic villa, overhung by Norway spruces, and looking exactly like a memorial emblem done in hair. Her personal appearance was in keeping with this image, and her own hair—of which there was little left—might have been sacrificed to the manufacture of the emblem.

"I had just reached the end of an agitated year, with considerable arrears to make up in money and emotion; and theoretically it seemed as though my aunt's mild hospitality would be as beneficial to my nerves as to my purse. But the deuce of it was that as soon as I felt myself safe and sheltered my energy began to revive; and how was I to work it off inside of a memorial emblem? I had, at that time, the illusion that sustained intellectual effort could engage a man's whole activity; and I decided to write a great book—I forget about what. My aunt, impressed by my plan, gave up to me her Gothic library, filled with classics bound in black cloth and daguerreotypes of faded celebrities; and I sat down at my desk to win myself a place among their number. And to facilitate my task she lent me a cousin to copy my manuscript.

"The cousin was a nice girl, and I had an idea that a nice girl was just what I needed to restore my faith in human nature, and principally in myself. She was neither beautiful nor intelligent—poor Alice Nowell!—but it interested me to see any woman content to be so uninteresting, and I wanted to find out the secret of her content. In doing this I handled it rather rashly, and put it out of joint—oh, just for a moment! There's no fatuity in telling you this, for the poor girl had never seen anyone but cousins. . . .

"Well, I was sorry for what I'd done, of course, and confoundedly bothered as to how I should put it straight. She was staying in the house, and one evening, after my aunt had gone to bed, she came down to the library to fetch a book she'd mislaid, like any artless heroine on the shelves behind us. She was pink-nosed and flustered, and it suddenly occurred to me that her hair, though it was fairly thick and pretty, would look exactly like my aunt's when she grew older. I was glad I had noticed this, for it made it easier for me to decide to do what was right; and when I had found the book she hadn't lost I told her I was leaving for Europe that week.

"Europe was terribly far off in those days, and Alice knew at once what I meant. She didn't take it in the least as I'd expected—it would have been easier if she had. She held her book very tight, and turned away a moment to wind up the lamp on my desk—it had a ground glass shade with vine leaves, and glass drops around the edge, I remember. Then she came back, held out her hand, and said: 'Good-bye.' And as she said it she looked straight at me and kissed me. I had never felt anything as fresh and shy and brave as her kiss. It was worse than any reproach, and it made me ashamed to deserve a reproach from her. I said to myself: 'I'll marry her, and when my aunt dies she'll leave us this house, and I'll sit here at the desk and go on with my book; and Alice will sit over there with her embroidery and look at me as she's looking now. And life will go on like that for any number of years.' The prospect frightened me a little, but at the time it didn't frighten me as much as doing anything to hurt her; and ten minutes later she had my seal ring on her finger, and my promise that when I went abroad she should go with me.

"You'll wonder why I'm enlarging on this incident. It's because the evening on which it took place was the very evening on which I first saw the queer sight I've spoken of. Being at that time an ardent believer in a necessary sequence between cause and effect I naturally tried to trace some kind of link between what had just happened to me in my aunt's library, and what was to happen a few hours later on the same night; and so the coincidence between the two events always remained in my mind.

"I went up to bed with rather a heavy heart, for I was bowed under the weight of the first good action I had ever consciously committed; and young as I was, I saw the gravity of my situation. Don't imagine from this that I had hitherto been an instrument of destruction. I had been merely a harmless young man, who had followed his bent and declined all collaboration with Providence. Now I had suddenly undertaken to promote the moral order of the world, and I felt a good deal like the trustful spectator who has given his gold watch to the conjuror, and doesn't know in what shape he'll get it back when the trick is over.... Still, a glow of self-righteousness tempered my fears, and I said to myself as I undressed that when I'd got used to being good it probably wouldn't make me as nervous as it did at the start. And by the time I was in bed, and had blown out my candle, I felt that I really *was* getting used to it, and that, as far as I'd got, it was not unlike sinking down into one of my aunt's very softest wool mattresses.

"I closed my eyes on this image, and when I opened them it must have been a good deal later, for my room had grown cold, and intensely still. I was waked by the queer feeling we all know—the feeling that there was something in the room that hadn't been there when I fell asleep. I sat up and strained my eyes into the darkness. The room was pitch black, and at first I saw nothing; but gradually a vague glimmer at the foot of the bed turned into two eyes staring back at me. I couldn't distinguish the features attached to them, but as I looked the eyes grew more and more distinct: they gave out a light of their own.

"The sensation of being thus gazed at was far from pleasant, and you might suppose that my first impulse would have been to jump out of bed and hurl myself on the invisible figure attached to the eyes. But it wasn't—my impulse was simply to lie still.... I can't say whether this was due to an immediate sense of the uncanny nature of the apparition—to the certainty that if I did jump out of bed I should hurl myself on nothing—or merely to the benumbing effect of the eyes themselves. They were the very worst eyes I've ever seen: a man's eyes—but what a man! My first thought was that he must be frightfully old. The orbits were sunk, and the thick red-lined lids hung over the eyeballs like blinds of which the cords are broken. One lid drooped a little lower than the other, with the effect of a crooked leer; and between these folds of flesh, with their scant bristle of lashes, the eyes themselves, small glassy discs with an agate-like rim, looked like sea-pebbles in the grip of a starfish.

"But the age of the eyes was not the most unpleasant thing about them. What turned me sick was their expression of vicious security. I don't know how else to describe the fact that they seemed to belong to a man who had done a lot of harm in his life, but had always kept just inside the danger lines. They were not the eyes of a coward, but of someone much too clever to take risks; and my gorge rose at their look of base astuteness. Yet even that wasn't the worst; for as we continued to scan each other I saw in them a tinge of derision, and felt myself to be its object.

"At that I was seized by an impulse of rage that jerked me to my feet and pitched me straight at the unseen figure. But of course there wasn't any figure there, and my fists struck at emptiness. Ashamed and cold, I groped about for a match and lit the candles. The room looked just as usual—as I had known it would; and I crawled back to bed, and blew out the lights.

"As soon as the room was dark again the eyes reappeared; and I now applied myself to explaining them on scientific principles. At first I thought the illusion might have been caused by the glow of the last embers in the chimney; but the fireplace was on the other side of my bed, and so placed that the fire could not be reflected in my toilet glass, which was the only mirror in the room. Then it struck me that I might have been tricked by the reflection of the embers in some polished bit of wood or metal; and though I couldn't discover any object of the sort in my line of vision, I got up again, groped my way to the hearth, and covered what was left of the fire. But as soon as I was back in bed the eyes were back at its foot.

"They were an hallucination, then: that was plain. But the fact that they were not due to any external dupery didn't make them a bit pleasanter. For if they were a protection of my inner consciousness, what the deuce was the matter with that organ? I had gone deeply enough into the mystery of morbid pathological states to picture the conditions under which an exploring mind might lay itself open to such a midnight admonition; but I couldn't fit it to my present case. I had never felt more normal, mentally and physically; and the only unusual fact in my situation—that of having assured the happiness of an amiable girl—did not seem of a kind to summon unclean spirits about my pillow. But there were the eyes still looking at me....

"I shut mine, and tried to evoke a vision of Alice Nowell's. They were not remarkable eyes, but they were as wholesome as fresh water, and if she had had more imagination—or longer lashes—their expression might have been interesting. As it was, they did not prove very efficacious, and in a few moments I perceived that they had mysteriously changed into the eyes at the foot of the bed. It exasperated me more to feel these glaring at me through my shut lids than to see them, and I opened my eyes again and looked straight into their hateful stare....

"And so it went on all night. I can't tell you what that night was like, nor how long it lasted. Have you ever lain in bed, hopelessly wide awake, and tried to keep your eyes shut, knowing that if you opened 'em you'd see something you dreaded and loathed? It sounds easy, but it's devilish hard. Those eyes hung there and drew me. I had the *vertige de l'abîme,* and their red lids were the edge of my abyss.... I had known nervous hours before: hours when I'd felt the wind of danger in my neck; but never this kind of strain. It wasn't that the eyes were awful; they hadn't the majesty of the powers of darkness. But they had—how shall I say?—physical effect that was the equivalent of a bad smell: their look left a smear like a snail's. And I didn't see what business they had with me, anyhow—and I stared and stared, trying to find out....

"I don't know what effect they were trying to produce; but the effect they *did* produce was that of making me pack my portmanteau and bolt to town early the next morning. I left a note for my aunt, explaining that I was ill and had gone to see my doctor; and as a matter of fact I did feel uncommonly ill—the night seemed to have pumped all the blood out of me. But when I reached town I didn't go to the doctor's. I went to a friend's rooms, and threw myself on a bed, and slept for ten heavenly hours. When I woke it was the middle of the night, and I turned cold at the thought of what might be waiting for me. I sat up, shaking, and stared into the darkness; but there wasn't a break in its blessed surface, and when I saw that the eyes were not there I dropped back into another long sleep.

"I had left no word for Alice when I fled, because I meant to go back the next morning. But the next morning I was too exhausted to stir. As the day went on the exhaustion increased, instead of wearing off like the fatigue left by an ordinary night of insomnia: the effect of the eyes seemed to be cumulative, and the thought of seeing them again grew intolerable. For two days I fought my dread; and on the third evening I pulled myself together and decided to go back the next morning. I felt a good deal happier as soon as I'd decided, for I knew that my abrupt disappearance, and the strangeness of my not writing, must have been very distressing to poor Alice. I went to bed with an easy mind, and fell asleep at once; but in the middle of the night I woke, and there were the eyes....

"Well, I simply couldn't face them; and instead of going back to my aunt's I bundled a few things into a trunk and jumped aboard the first steamer for England. I was so dead tired when I got on board that I crawled straight into my berth, and slept most of the way over; and I can't tell you the bliss it was to wake from those long dreamless stretches and look fearlessly into the dark, *knowing* that I shouldn't see the eyes....

"I stayed abroad for a year, and then I stayed for another; and during that time I never had a glimpse of them. That was enough reason for prolonging my stay if I'd been on a desert island. Another was, of course, that I had perfectly come to see, on the voyage over, the complete impossibility of my marrying Alice Nowell. The fact that I had been so slow in making this discovery annoyed me, and made me want to avoid explanations. The bliss of escaping at one stroke from the eyes, and from this other embarrassment, gave my freedom an extraordinary zest; and the longer I savoured it the better I liked its taste.

"The eyes had burned such a hole in my consciousness that for a long time I went on puzzling over the nature of the apparition, and wondering if it would ever come back. But as time passed I lost this dread, and retained only the precision of the image. Then that faded in its turn.

"The second year found me settled in Rome, where I was planning, I believe, to write another great book—a definitive work on Etruscan influences in Italian art. At any rate, I'd found some pretext of the kind for taking a sunny apartment in the Piazza di Spagna and dabbling about in the Forum; and there, one morning, a charming youth came to me. As he stood there in the warm light, slender and smooth and hyacinthine, he might have stepped from a ruined altar—one to Antinous, say; but he'd come instead from New York, with a letter (of all people) from Alice Nowell. The letter—the first I'd had from her since our break—was simply a line introducing her young cousin, Gilbert Noyes, and appealing to me to befriend him. It appeared, poor lad, that he 'had talent', and 'wanted to write'; and, an obdurate family having insisted that his calligraphy should take the form of double entry, Alice had intervened to win him six months' respite, during which he was to travel abroad on a meagre pittance, and somehow prove his ability to increase it by his pen. The quaint conditions of the test struck me first: it seemed about as conclusive as a medieval 'ordeal'. Then I was touched by her having sent him to me. I had always wanted to do her some service, to justify myself in my own eyes rather than hers; and here was a beautiful occasion.

"I imagine it's safe to lay down the general principle that predestined geniuses don't, as a rule, appear before one in the spring sunshine of the Forum looking like one of its banished gods. At any rate, poor Noyes wasn't a predestined genius. But he *was* beautiful to see, and charming as a comrade. It was only when he began to talk literature that my heart failed me. I knew all the symptoms so well—the things he had 'in him', and the things outside him that impinged! There's the real test, after all. It was always—punctually, inevitably, with the inexorableness of a mechanical law—it was *always* the wrong thing that struck him. I grew to find a certain fascination in deciding in advance exactly which wrong thing he'd select; and I acquired an astonishing skill at the game....

"The worst of it was that his *bêtise* wasn't of the too obvious sort. Ladies who met him at picnics thought him intellectual; and even at dinners he passed for clever. I, who had him under the microscope, fancied now and then that he might develop some kind of a slim talent, something that he could make 'do' and be happy on; and wasn't that, after all, what I was concerned with? He was so charming—he continued to be so charming—that he called forth all my charity in support of this argument; and for the first few months I really believed there was a chance for him....

"Those months were delightful. Noyes was constantly with me, and the more I saw of him the better I liked him. His stupidity was a natural grace—it was as beautiful, really, as his eyelashes. And he was so gay, so affectionate, and so happy with me, that telling him the truth would have been about as pleasant as slitting the throat of some gentle animal. At first I used to wonder what had put into that radiant head the detestable delusion that it held a brain. Then I began to see that it was simply protective mimicry—an instinctive ruse to get away from family life and an office desk. Not that Gilbert didn't—dear lad!—believe in himself. There wasn't a trace of hypocrisy in him. He was sure that his 'call' was irresistible, while to me it was the saving grace of his situation that it *wasn't*, and that a little money, a little leisure, a little pleasure, would have turned him into an inoffensive idler. Unluckily, however, there was no hope of money, and with the alternative of the office desk before him he couldn't postpone his attempt at literature. The stuff he turned out was deplorable, and I see now that I knew it from the first. Still, the absurdity of deciding a man's whole future on a first trial seemed to justify me in withholding my verdict, and perhaps even in encouraging him a little, on the ground that the human plant generally needs warmth to flower.

"At any rate, I proceeded on that principle, and carried it to the point of getting his term of probation extended. When I left Rome he went with me, and we idled away a delicious summer between Capri and Venice. I said to myself: 'If he has anything in him, it will come out now,' and it *did*. He was never more enchanting and enchanted. There were moments of our pilgrimage when beauty born of murmuring sound seemed actually to pass into his face—but only to issue forth in a flood of the palest ink. . . .

"Well, the time came to turn off his tap; and I knew there was no hand but mine to do it. We were back in Rome, and I had taken him to stay with me, not wanting him to be alone in his *pension* when he had to face the necessity of renouncing his ambition. I hadn't, of course, relied solely on my own judgement in deciding to advise him to drop literature. I had sent his stuff to various people—editors and critics—and they had always sent it back with the same chilling lack of comment. Really there was nothing on earth to say—

"I confess I never felt more shabbily than I did on the day when I decided to have it out with Gilbert. It was well enough to tell myself that it was my duty to knock the poor boy's hopes into splinters—but I'd like to know what act of gratuitous cruelty hasn't been justified on that plea? I've always shrunk from usurping the functions of Providence, and when I have to exercise them I decidedly prefer that it shouldn't be on an errand of destruction. Besides, in the last issue, who was I to decide, even after a year's trial, if poor Gilbert had it in him or not?

"The more I looked at the part I'd resolved to play, the less I liked it; and I liked it still less when Gilbert sat opposite me, with his head thrown back in the lamplight, just as Phil's is now. . . . I'd been going over his last manuscript, and he knew it, and he knew that his future hung on my verdict—we'd tacitly agreed to that. The manuscript lay between us, on my table—a novel, his first novel, if you please!—and he reached over and laid his hand on it, and looked up at me with all his life in the look.

"I stood up and cleared my throat, trying to keep my eyes away from his face and on the manuscript.

" 'The fact is, my dear Gilbert—' I began.

"I saw him turn pale, but he was up and facing me in an instant.

" 'Oh, look here, don't take on so, my dear fellow! I'm not so awfully cut up as all that!' His hands were on my shoulders, and he was laughing down at me from his full height, with a kind of mortally-stricken gaiety that drove the knife into my side.

"He was too beautifully brave for me to keep up any humbug about my duty. And it came over me suddenly how I should hurt others in hurting him: myself first, since sending him home meant losing him; but more particularly poor Alice Nowell, to whom I had so longed to prove my good faith and my desire to serve her. It really seemed like failing her twice to fail Gilbert. . . .

"But my intuition was like one of those lightning flashes that encircle the whole horizon, and in the same instant I saw what I might be letting myself in for if I didn't tell the truth. I said to myself: 'I shall have him for life'—and I'd never yet seen anyone, man or woman, whom I was quite sure of wanting on those terms. Well, this impulse of egotism decided me. I was ashamed of it, and to get away from it I took a leap that landed me straight in Gilbert's arms.

"'The thing's all right, and you're all wrong!' I shouted up at him; and as he hugged me, and I laughed and shook at his clutch, I had for a minute the sense of self-complacency that is supposed to attend the footsteps of the just. Hang it all, making people happy *has* its charms....

"Gilbert, of course, was for celebrating his emancipation in some spectacular manner; but I sent him away alone to explode his emotions, and went to bed to sleep off mine. As I undressed I began to wonder what their after-taste would be—so many of the finest don't keep! Still, I wasn't sorry, and I meant to empty the bottle, even if it *did* turn a trifle flat.

"After I got into bed I lay for a long time smiling at the memory of his eyes—his blissful eyes.... Then I fell asleep, and when I woke the room was deathly cold, and I sat up with a jerk—and there were *the other eyes*....

"It was three years since I'd seen them, but I'd thought of them so often that I fancied they could never take me unawares again. Now, with their red sneer on me, I knew that I had never really believed they would come back, and that I was as defenceless as ever against them.... As before, it was the insane irrelevance of their coming that made it so horrible. What the deuce were they after, to leap out at me at such a time? I had lived more or less carelessly in the years since I'd seen them, though my worst indiscretions were not dark enough to invite the searchings of their infernal glare; but at this particular moment I was really in what might have been called a state of grace; and I can't tell you how the fact added to their horror....

"But it's not enough to say they were as bad as before: they were worse. Worse by just so much as I'd learned of life in the interval; by all the damnable implications my wider experience read into them. I saw now what I hadn't seen before: that they were eyes which had grown hideous gradually, which had built up their baseness coral-wise, bit by bit, out of a series of small turpitudes slowly accumulated through the industrious years. Yes—it came to me that what made them so bad was that they'd grown bad so slowly....

"There they hung in the darkness, their swollen lids dropped across the little watery bulbs rolling loose in the orbits, and the puff of flesh making a muddy shadow underneath—and as their stare moved with my movements, there came over me a sense of their tacit complicity, of a deep hidden understanding between us that was worse than the first shock of their strangeness. Not that I understood them; but that they made it so clear that some day I should.... Yes, that was the worst part of it, decidedly; and it was the feeling that became stronger each time they came back....

"For they got into the damnable habit of coming back. They reminded me of vampires with a taste for young flesh, they seemed to gloat over the taste of a good conscience. Every night for a month they came to claim their morsel of mine: since I'd made Gilbert happy they simply wouldn't loosen their fangs. The coincidence almost made me hate him, poor lad, fortuitous as I felt it to be. I puzzled over it a good deal, but couldn't find any hint of an explanation except in the chance of his association with Alice Nowell. But then the eyes had let up on me the moment I had abandoned her, so they could hardly be the emissaries of a woman scorned, even if one could have pictured poor Alice charging such spirits to avenge her. That set me thinking, and I began to wonder if they would let up on me if I abandoned Gilbert. The temptation was insidious, and I had to stiffen myself against it; but really, dear boy! he was too charming to be sacrificed to such demons. And so, after all, I never found out what they wanted...."

III

The fire crumbled, sending up a flash which threw into relief the narrator's gnarled face under its grey-black stubble. Pressed into the hollow of the chair-back, it stood out an instant like an intaglio of yellowish red-veined stone, with spots of enamel for the eyes; then the fire sank and it became once more a dim Rembrandtish blur.

Phil Frenham, sitting in a low chair on the opposite side of the hearth, one long arm propped on the table behind him, one hand supporting his thrown-back head, and his eyes fixed on his old friend's face, had not moved since the tale began. He continued to maintain his silent immobility after Culwin had ceased to speak, and it was I who, with a vague sense of disappointment at the sudden drop of the story, finally asked: "But how long did you keep on seeing them?"

Culwin, so sunk into his chair that he seemed like a heap of his own empty clothes, stirred a little, as if in surprise at my question. He appeared to have half forgotten what he had been telling us.

"How long? Oh, off and on all that winter. It was infernal. I never got used to them. I grew really ill."

Frenham shifted his attitude, and as he did so his elbow struck against a small mirror in a bronze frame standing on the table behind him. He turned and changed its angle slightly; then he resumed his former attitude, his dark head thrown back on his lifted palm, his eyes intent on Culwin's face. Something in his silent gaze embarrassed me, and as if to divert attention from it I pressed on with another question:

"And you never tried sacrificing Noyes?"

"Oh, no. The fact is I didn't have to. He did it for me, poor boy!"

"Did it for you? How do you mean?"

"He wore me out—wore everybody out. He kept on pouring out his lamentable twaddle, and hawking it up and down the place till he became a thing of terror. I tried to wean him from writing—oh, ever so gently, you understand, by throwing him with agreeable people, giving him a chance to make himself felt, to come to a sense of what he *really* had to give. I'd foreseen this solution from the beginning—felt sure that, once the first ardour of authorship was quenched, he'd drop into his place as a charming parasitic thing, the kind of chronic Cherubino for whom, in old societies, there's always a seat at table, and a shelter behind the ladies' skirts. I saw him take his place as 'the poet': the poet who doesn't write. One knows the type in every drawing-room. Living in that way doesn't cost much—I'd worked it all out in my mind, and felt sure that, with a little help, he could manage it for the next few years; and meanwhile he'd be sure to marry. I saw him married to a widow, rather older, with a good cook and a well-run house. And I actually had my eye on the widow.... Meanwhile I did everything to help the transition—lent him money to ease his conscience, introduced him to pretty women to make him forget his vows. But nothing would do him: he had but one idea in his beautiful obstinate head. He wanted the laurel and not the rose, and he kept on repeating Gautier's axiom, and battering and filing at his limp prose till he'd spread it out over Lord knows how many hundred pages. Now and then he would send a barrelful to a publisher, and of course it would always come back.

"At first it didn't matter—he thought he was 'misunderstood'. He took the attitudes of genius, and whenever an opus came home he wrote another to keep it company. Then he had a reaction of despair, and accused me of deceiving him, and Lord knows what. I got angry at that, and told him it was he who had deceived himself. He'd come to me determined to write, and I'd done my best to help him. That was the extent of my offence, and I'd done it for his cousin's sake, not his.

"That seemed to strike home, and he didn't answer for a minute.

Then he said: 'My time's up and my money's up. What do you think I'd better do?'

" 'I think you'd better not be an ass,' I said.

" 'What do you mean by being an ass?' he asked.

"I took a letter from my desk and held it out to him.

" 'I mean refusing this offer of Mrs. Ellinger's to be her secretary at a salary of five thousand dollars. There may be a lot more in it than that.'

"He flung out his hand with a violence that struck the letter from mine. 'Oh, I know well enough what's in it!' he said, red to the roots of his hair.

" 'And what's the answer, if you know?' I asked.

"He made none at the minute, but turned away slowly to the door. There, with his hand on the threshold, he stopped to say, almost under his breath: 'Then you really think my stuff's no good?'

"I was tired and exasperated, and I laughed. I don't defend my laugh—it was in wretched taste. But I must plead in extenuation that the boy was a fool, and that I'd done my best for him—I really had.

"He went out of the room, shutting the door quietly after him. That afternoon I left for Frascati, where I'd promised to spend the Sunday with some friends. I was glad to escape from Gilbert, and by the same token, as I learned that night, I had also escaped from the eyes. I dropped into the same lethargic sleep that had come to me before when I left off seeing them; and when I woke the next morning, in my peaceful room above the ilexes, I felt the utter weariness and deep relief that always followed on that sleep. I put in two blessed nights at Frascati, and when I got back to my rooms in Rome I found that Gilbert had gone. . . . Oh, nothing tragic had happened —the episode never rose to *that*. He'd simply packed his manuscripts and left for America—for his family and the Wall Street desk. He left a decent enough note to tell me of his decision, and behaved altogether, in the circumstances, as little like a fool as it's possible for a fool to behave. . . ."

IV

Culwin paused again, and Frenham still sat motionless, the dusky contour of his young head reflected in the mirror at his back.

"And what became of Noyes afterwards?" I finally asked, still disquieted by a sense of incompleteness, by the need of some connecting thread between the parallel lines of the tale.

Culwin twitched his shoulders. "Oh, nothing became of him—

because he became nothing. There could be no question of 'becoming' about it. He vegetated in an office, I believe, and finally got a clerkship in a consulate, and married drearily in China. I saw him once in Hong Kong, years afterwards. He was fat and hadn't shaved. I was told he drank. He didn't recognise me."

"And the eyes?" I asked, after another pause which Frenham's continued silence made oppressive.

Culwin, stroking his chin, blinked at me meditatively through the shadows. "I never saw them after my last talk with Gilbert. Put two and two together if you can. For my part, I haven't found the link."

He rose, his hands in his pockets, and walked stiffly over to the table on which reviving drinks had been set out.

"You must be parched after this dry tale. Here, help yourself, my dear fellow. Here, Phil—" he turned back to the hearth.

Frenham made no response to his host's hospitable summons. He still sat in his low chair without moving, but as Culwin advanced towards him, their eyes met in a long look; after which the young man, turning suddenly, flung his arms across the table behind him, and dropped his face upon them.

Culwin, at the unexpected gesture, stopped short, a flush on his face.

"Phil—what the deuce? Why, have the eyes scared *you*? My dear boy—my dear fellow—I never had such a tribute to my literary ability, never!"

He broke into a chuckle at the thought, and halted on the hearth-rug, his hands still in his pockets, gazing down at the youth's bowed head. Then, as Frenham still made no answer, he moved a step or two nearer.

"Cheer up, my dear Phil! It's years since I've seen them—apparently I've done nothing lately bad enough to call them out of chaos. Unless my present evocation of them has made *you* see them; which would be their worst stroke yet!"

His bantering appeal quivered off into an uneasy laugh, and he moved still nearer, bending over Frenham, and laying his gouty hands on the lad's shoulders.

"Phil, my dear boy, really—what's the matter? Why don't you answer? *Have* you seen the eyes?"

Frenham's face was still hidden, and from where I stood behind Culwin I saw the latter, as if under the rebuff of this unaccountable attitude, draw back slowly from his friend. As he did so, the light of the lamp on the table fell full on his congested face, and I caught its reflection in the mirror behind Frenham's head.

Culwin saw the reflection also. He paused, his face level with the mirror, as if scarcely recognising the countenance in it as his own.

But as he looked his expression gradually changed, and for an appreciable space of time he and the image in the glass confronted each other with a glare of slowly gathering hate. Then Culwin let go on Frenham's shoulders, and drew back a step....

Frenham, his face still hidden, did not stir.

SIR ARTHUR T. QUILLER-COUCH ('Q')

A PAIR OF HANDS

An Old Maid's Ghost-Story

"YES," said Miss Le Petyt, gazing into the deep fireplace and letting her hands and her knitting lie for the moment idle in her lap. "Oh, yes, I have seen a ghost. In fact I have lived in a house with one for quite a long time."

"How you *could*—!" began one of my host's daughters; and "*You*, Aunt Emily?" cried the other at the same moment.

Miss Le Petyt, gentle soul, withdrew her eyes from the fireplace and protested with a gay little smile. "Well, my dears, I am not quite the coward you take me for. And, as it happens, mine was the most harmless ghost in the world. In fact"—and here she looked at the fire again—"I was quite sorry to lose her."

"It was a woman, then? Now *I* think," said Miss Blanche, "that female ghosts are the horridest of all. They wear little shoes with high red heels, and go about *tap, tap*, wringing their hands."

"This one wrung her hands, certainly. But I don't know about the high red heels, for I never saw her feet. Perhaps she was like the Queen of Spain, and hadn't any. And as for the hands, it all depends *how* you wring them. There's an elderly shopwalker at Knightsbridge, for instance—"

"Don't be prosy, dear, when you know that we're just dying to hear the story."

Miss Le Petyt turned to me with a small deprecating laugh. "It's such a little one."

"The story, or the ghost?"

"Both."

And this was Miss Le Petyt's story:

"It happened when I lived down in Cornwall, at Tresillack on the south coast. Tresillack was the name of the house, which stood quite alone at the head of a coombe, within sound of the sea but without sight of it; for though the coombe led down to a wide open beach, it wound and twisted half a dozen times on its way, and its overlapping sides closed the view from the house, which was advertised as 'secluded'. I was very poor in those days. Your father and all of us were poor then, as I trust, my dears, you will never be; but I was young enough to be romantic and wise enough to like independence, and this word 'secluded' took my fancy.

"The misfortune was that it had taken the fancy, or just suited the requirements, of several previous tenants. You know, I dare say, the kind of person who rents a secluded house in the country? Well, yes, there are several kinds; but they seem to agree in being odious. No one knows where they come from, though they soon remove all doubt about where they're 'going to', as the children say. 'Shady' is the word, is it not? Well, the previous tenants of Tresillack (from first to last a bewildering series) had been shady with a vengeance.

"I knew nothing of this when I first made application to the landlord, a solid yeoman inhabiting a farm at the foot of the coombe, on a cliff overlooking the beach. To him I presented myself fearlessly as a spinster of decent family and small but assured income, intending a rural life of combined seemliness and economy. He met my advances politely enough, but with an air of suspicion which offended me. I began by disliking him for it: afterwards I set it down as an unpleasant feature in the local character. I was doubly mistaken. Farmer Hosking was slow-witted, but as honest a man as ever stood up against hard times; and a more open and hospitable race than the people on that coast I never wish to meet. It was the caution of a child who had burnt his fingers, not once but many times. Had I known what I afterwards learned of Farmer Hosking's tribulations as landlord of a 'secluded country residence', I should have approached him with the bashfulness proper to my suit and faltered as I undertook to prove the bright exception in a long line of painful experiences. He had bought the Tresillack estate twenty years before—on mortgage, I fancy—because the land adjoined his own and would pay him for tillage. But the house was a nuisance, an incubus; and had been so from the beginning.

" 'Well, miss,' he said, 'you're welcome to look over it; a pretty enough place, inside and out. There's no trouble about keys, because I've put in a housekeeper, a widow-woman, and she'll show you round. With your leave I'll step up the coombe so far with you, and put you in your way.' As I thanked him he paused and rubbed his chin. 'There's one thing I must tell you, though. Whoever takes the house must take Mrs. Carkeek along with it.'

" 'Mrs. Carkeek?' I echoed dolefully. 'Is that the housekeeper?'

" 'Yes: she was wife to my late hind. I'm sorry, miss,' he added, my face telling him no doubt what sort of woman I expected Mrs. Carkeek to be; 'but I had to make it a rule after—after some things that happened. And I dare say you won't find her so bad. Mary

Carkeek's a sensible comfortable woman, and knows the place. She was in service there to Squire Kendall when he sold up and went: her first place it was.'

"'I may as well see the house, anyhow,' said I dejectedly. So we started to walk up the coombe. The path, which ran beside a little chattering stream, was narrow for the most part, and Farmer Hosking, with an apology, strode on ahead to beat aside the brambles. But whenever its width allowed us to walk side by side I caught him from time to time stealing a shy inquisitive glance under his rough eyebrows. Courteously though he bore himself, it was clear that he could not sum me up to his satisfaction or bring me square with his notion of a tenant for his 'secluded country residence'.

"I don't know what foolish fancy prompted it, but about halfway up the coombe I stopped short and asked:

"'There are no ghosts, I suppose?'

"It struck me, a moment after I had uttered it, as a supremely silly question; but he took it quite seriously. 'No; I never heard tell of any *ghosts*.' He laid a queer sort of stress on the word. 'There's always been trouble with servants, and maids' tongues will be runnin'. But Mary Carkeek lives up there alone, and she seems comfortable enough.'

"We walked on. By-and-by he pointed with his stick. 'It don't look like a place for ghosts, now, do it?'

"Certainly it did not. Above an untrimmed orchard rose a terrace of turf scattered with thorn-bushes, and above this a terrace of stone, upon which stood the prettiest cottage I had ever seen. It was long and low and thatched; a deep verandah ran from end to end. Clematis, Banksia roses and honeysuckle climbed the posts of this verandah, and big blooms of the Maréchal Niel were clustered along its roof, beneath the lattices of the bedroom windows. The house was small enough to be called a cottage, and rare enough in features and in situation to confer distinction on any tenant. It suggested what in those days we should have called 'elegant' living. And I could have clapped my hands for joy.

"My spirits mounted still higher when Mrs. Carkeek opened the door to us. I had looked for a Mrs. Gummidge, and I found a healthy middle-aged woman with a thoughtful but contented face, and a smile which, without a trace of obsequiousness, quite bore out the farmer's description of her. She was a comfortable woman; and while we walked through the rooms together (for Mr. Hosking waited outside) I 'took to' Mrs. Carkeek. Her speech was direct and practical; the rooms, in spite of their faded furniture, were bright and exquisitely clean; and somehow the very atmosphere of the house gave me a sense of well-being, of feeling at home and cared for; yes, *of being loved.* Don't laugh, my dears; for when I've done you may not think this fancy altogether foolish.

"I stepped out into the verandah, and Farmer Hosking pocketed the pruning-knife which he had been using on a bush of jasmine.

"'This is better than anything I had dreamed of,' said I.

"'Well, miss, that's not a wise way of beginning a bargain, if you'll excuse me.'

"He took no advantage, however, of my admission; and we struck the bargain as we returned down the coombe to his farm, where the hired chaise waited to convey me back to the market town. I had meant to engage a maid of my own, but now it occurred to me that I might do very well with Mrs. Carkeek. This, too, was settled in the course of the next day or two, and within the week I had moved into my new home.

"I can hardly describe to you the happiness of my first month at Tresillack; because (as I now believe) if I take the reasons which I had for being happy, one by one, there remains over something which I cannot account for. I was moderately young, entirely healthy; I felt myself independent and adventurous; the season was high summer, the weather glorious, the garden in all the pomp of June, yet sufficiently unkempt to keep me busy, give me a sharp appetite for meals, and send me to bed in that drowsy stupor which comes of the odours of earth. I spent the most of my time out of doors, winding up the day's work as a rule with a walk down the cool valley, along the beach and back.

"I soon found that all housework could be safely left to Mrs. Carkeek. She did not talk much; indeed her only fault (a rare one in housekeepers) was that she talked too little, and even when I addressed her seemed at times unable to give me her attention. It was as though her mind strayed off to some small job she had forgotten, and her eyes wore a listening look, as though she waited for the neglected task to speak and remind her. But as a matter of fact she forgot nothing. Indeed, my dears, I was never so well attended to in my life.

"Well, that is what I'm coming to. That, so to say, is just *it.* The woman not only had the rooms swept and dusted, and my meals prepared to the moment. In a hundred odd little ways this orderliness, these preparations, seemed to read my desires. Did I wish the roses renewed in a bowl upon the dining-table, sure enough at the next meal they would be replaced by fresh ones. Mrs. Carkeek (I told myself) must have surprised and interpreted a glance of mine. And yet I could not remember having glanced at the bowl in her presence. And how on earth had she guessed the very roses, the very shapes and colours I had lightly wished for? This is only an instance, you understand. Every day, and from morning to night, I happened on others, each slight enough, but all together bearing witness to a ministering intelligence as subtle as it was untiring.

"I am a light sleeper, as you know, with an uncomfortable knack of waking with the sun and roaming early. No matter how early I rose at Tresillack, Mrs. Carkeek seemed to have prevented me. Finally I had to conclude that she arose and dusted and tidied as soon as she judged me safely a-bed. For once, finding the drawing-room (where I had been sitting late) 'redded up' at four in the morning, and no trace of a plate of raspberries which I had carried thither after dinner and left overnight, I determined to test her, and walked through to the kitchen, calling her by name. I found the kitchen as clean as a pin, and the fire laid, but no trace of Mrs. Carkeek. I walked upstairs and knocked at her door. At the second knock a sleepy voice cried out, and presently the good woman stood before me in her nightgown, looking (I thought) very badly scared.

" 'No,' I said, 'it's not a burglar. But I've found out what I wanted, that you do your morning's work overnight. But you mustn't wait for me when I choose to sit up. And now go back to your bed like a good soul, whilst I take a run down to the beach.'

"She stood blinking in the dawn. Her face was still white.

" 'Oh. miss,' she gasped, 'I made sure you must have seen something!'

" 'And so I have,' I answered, 'but it was neither burglars nor ghosts.'

" 'Thank God!' I heard her say as she turned her back to me in her grey bedroom—which faced the north. And I took this for a carelessly pious expression and ran downstairs, thinking no more of it.

"A few days later I began to understand.

"The plan of Tresillack house (I must explain) was simplicity itself. To the left of the hall as you entered was the dining-room; to the right the drawing-room, with a boudoir beyond. The foot of the stairs faced the front door, and beside it, passing a glazed inner door, you found two others right and left, the left opening on the kitchen, the right on a passage which ran by a store-cupboard under the bend of the stairs to a neat pantry with the usual shelves and linen-press, and under the window (which faced north) a porcelain basin and brass tap. On the first morning of my tenancy I had visited this pantry and turned the tap; but no water ran. I supposed this to be accidental. Mrs. Carkeek had to wash up glassware and crockery, and no doubt Mrs. Carkeek would complain of any failure in the water supply.

"But the day after my surprise visit (as I called it) I had picked a basketful of roses, and carried them into the pantry as a handy place to arrange them in. I chose a china bowl and went to fill it at the tap. Again the water would not run.

"I called Mrs. Carkeek. 'What is wrong with this tap?' I asked. 'The rest of the house is well enough supplied.'

" 'I don't know, miss. I never use it.'

" 'But there must be a reason; and you must find it a great nuisance washing up the plate and glasses in the kitchen. Come around to the back with me, and we'll have a look at the cisterns.'

" 'The cisterns'll be all right, miss. I assure you I don't find it a trouble.'

"But I was not to be put off. The back of the house stood but ten feet from a wall which was really but a stone face built against the cliff cut away by the architect. Above the cliff rose the kitchen garden, and from its lower path we looked over the wall's parapet upon the cisterns. There were two—a very large one, supplying the kitchen and the bathroom above the kitchen; and a small one, obviously fed by the other, and as obviously leading, by a pipe which I could trace, to the pantry. Now the big cistern stood almost full, and yet the small one, though on a lower level, was empty.

" 'It's as plain as daylight,' said I. 'The pipe between the two is choked.' And I clambered on to the parapet.

" 'I wouldn't, miss. The pantry tap is only cold water, and no use to me. From the kitchen boiler I gets it hot, you see.'

" 'But I want the pantry water for my flowers.' I bent over and groped. 'I thought as much!' said I, as I wrenched out a thick plug of cork and immediately the water began to flow. I turned triumphantly on Mrs. Carkeek, who had grown suddenly red in the face. Her eyes were fixed on the cork in my hand. To keep it more firmly wedged in its place somebody had wrapped it round with a rag of calico print; and, discoloured though the rag was, I seemed to recall the pattern (a lilac sprig). Then, as our eyes met, it occurred to me that only two mornings before Mrs. Carkeek had worn a print gown of that same sprigged pattern.

"I had the presence of mind to hide this very small discovery, sliding over it some quite trivial remark; and presently Mrs. Carkeek regained her composure. But I own I felt disappointed in her. It seemed such a paltry thing to be disingenuous over. She had deliberately acted a fib before me; and why? Merely because she preferred the kitchen to the pantry tap. It was childish. 'But servants are all the same,' I told myself. 'I must take Mrs. Carkeek as she is; and, after all, she is a treasure.'

"On the second night after this, and between eleven and twelve o'clock, I was lying in bed and reading myself sleepy over a novel of

Lord Lytton's, when a small sound disturbed me. I listened. The sound was clearly that of water trickling; and I set it down to rain. A shower (I told myself) had filled the water-pipes which drained the roof. Somehow I could not fix the sound. There was a water pipe against the wall just outside my window. I rose and drew up the blind.

"To my astonishment no rain was falling; no rain had fallen. I felt the slate window-sill; some dew had gathered there—no more. There was no wind, no cloud: only a still moon high over the eastern slope of the coombe, the distant plash of waves, and the fragrance of many roses. I went back to bed and listened again. Yes, the trickling sound continued, quite distinct in the silence of the house, not to be confused for a moment with the dull murmur of the beach. After a while it began to grate on my nerves. I caught up my candle, flung my dressing-gown about me, and stole softly downstairs.

"Then it was simple. I traced the sound to the pantry. 'Mrs. Carkeek has left the tap running,' said I: and, sure enough, I found it so—a thin trickle steadily running to waste in the porcelain basin. I turned off the tap, went contentedly back to my bed, and slept.

"—for some hours. I opened my eyes in darkness, and at once knew what had awakened me. The tap was running again. Now it had shut easily in my hand, but not so easily that I could believe it had slipped open again of its own accord. 'This is Mrs. Carkeek's doing,' said I; and am afraid I added 'Bother Mrs. Carkeek!'

"Well, there was no help for it: so I struck a light, looked at my watch, saw that the hour was just three o'clock, and descended the stairs again. At the pantry door I paused. I was not afraid—not one little bit. In fact the notion that anything might be wrong had never crossed my mind. But I remember thinking, with my hand on the door, that if Mrs. Carkeek were in the pantry I might happen to give her a severe fright.

"I pushed the door open briskly. Mrs. Carkeek was not there. But something *was* there, by the porcelain basin—something which might have sent me scurrying upstairs two steps at a time, but which as a matter of fact held me to the spot. My heart seemed to stand still—so still! And in the stillness I remember setting down the brass candlestick on a tall nest of drawers beside me.

"Over the porcelain basin and beneath the water trickling from the tap I saw two hands.

"That was all—two small hands, a child's hands. I cannot tell you how they ended.

"No: they were not cut off. I saw them quite distinctly: just a pair of small hands and the wrists, and after that—nothing. They were moving briskly—washing themselves clean. I saw the water trickle and splash over them—not *through* them—but just as it would on real hands. They were the hands of a little girl, too. Oh, yes, I was sure of that at once. Boys and girls wash their hands differently. I can't just tell you what the difference is, but it's unmistakable.

"I saw all this before my candle slipped and fell with a crash. I had set it down without looking—for my eyes were fixed on the basin—and had balanced it on the edge of the nest of drawers. After the crash, in the darkness there, with the water running, I suffered some bad moments. Oddly enough, the thought uppermost with me was that I *must* shut off that tap before escaping. I *had* to. And after a while I picked up all my courage, so to say, between my teeth, and with a little sob thrust out my hand and did it. Then I fled.

"The dawn was close upon me: and as soon as the sky reddened I took my bath, dressed and went downstairs. And there at the pantry door I found Mrs. Carkeek, also dressed, with my candlestick in her hand.

"'Ah!' said I, 'you picked it up.'

"Our eyes met. Clearly Mrs. Carkeek wished me to begin, and I determined at once to have it out with her.

"'And you knew all about it. That's what accounts for your plugging up the cistern.'

"'You saw . . . ?' she began.

"'Yes, yes. And you must tell me all about it—never mind how bad. Is—is it—murder?'

"'Law bless you, miss, whatever put such horrors in your head?'

"'She was washing her hands.'

"'Ah, so she does, poor dear! But—murder! And dear little Miss Margaret, that wouldn't hurt a fly!'

"'Miss Margaret?'

"'Eh, she died at seven year. Squire Kendall's only daughter; and that's over twenty years ago. I was her nurse, miss, and I know—diphtheria it was; she took it down in the village.'

"'But how do you know it is Margaret?'

"'Those hands—why, how could I mistake, that used to be her nurse?'

"'But why does she wash them?'

"'Well, miss, being always a dainty child—and the housework, you see—'

"I took a long breath. 'Do you mean to tell me that all this tidying and dusting—' I broke off. 'Is it *she* who has been taking care of me?'

"Mrs. Carkeek met my look steadily.

"'Who else, miss?'

"'Poor little soul!'

"'Well now'—Mrs. Carkeek rubbed my candlestick with the edge of her apron—'I'm so glad you take it like this. For there isn't really nothing to be afraid of—is there?' She eyed me wistfully. 'It's my belief she loves you, miss. But only to think what a time she must have had with the others!'

"'The others?' I echoed.

"'The other tenants, miss: the ones afore you.'

"'Were they bad?'

"'They was awful. Didn't Farmer Hosking tell you? They carried on fearful—one after another, and each one worse than the last.'

"'What was the matter with them? Drink?'

"'Drink, miss, with some of 'em. There was the Major—he used to go mad with it, and run about the coombe in his nightshirt. Oh, scandalous! And his wife drank too—that is, if she ever was his wife. Just think of that tender child washing up after their nasty doings!'

"I shivered.

"'But that wasn't the worst, miss—not by a long way. There was a pair here—from the colonies, or so they gave out—with two children, a boy and gel, the eldest scarce six. Poor mites!'

"'Why, what happened?'

"'They beat those children, miss—your blood would boil!—*and* starved, *and* tortured 'em, it's my belief. You could hear their screams, I've been told, away back in the high-road, and that's the best part of half a mile. Sometimes they was locked up without food for days together. But it's my belief that little Miss Margaret managed to feed them somehow. Oh, I can see her, creeping to the door and comforting!'

"'But perhaps she never showed herself when these awful people were here, but took to flight until they left.'

"'You didn't never know her, miss. The brave she was! She'd have stood up to lions. She've been here all the while: and only to think what her innocent eyes and ears must have took in! There was another couple—' Mrs. Carkeek sunk her voice.

"'Oh, hush!' said I, 'if I'm to have any peace of mind in this house!'

"'But you won't go, miss? She loves you, I know she do. And think what you might be leaving her to—what sort of tenant might come next. For she can't go. She've been here ever since her father sold the place. He died soon after. You mustn't go!'

"Now I had resolved to go, but all of a sudden I felt how mean this resolution was.

"'After all,' said I, 'there's nothing to be afraid of.'

" 'That's it, miss; nothing at all. I don't even believe it's so very uncommon. Why, I've heard my mother tell of farmhouses where the rooms were swept every night as regular as clockwork, and the floors sanded, and the pots and pans scoured, and all while the maids slept. They put it down to the piskies; but we know better, miss, and now we've got the secret between us we can lie easy in our beds, and if we hear anything, say "God bless the child!" and go to sleep.'

" 'Mrs. Carkeek,' said I, 'there's only one condition I have to make.'

" 'What's that?'

" 'Why, that you let me kiss you.'

" 'Oh, you dear!' said Mrs. Carkeek as we embraced: and this was as close to familiarity as she allowed herself to go in the whole course of my acquaintance with her.

"I spent three years at Tresillack, and all that while Mrs. Carkeek lived with me and shared the secret. Few women, I dare to say, were ever so completely wrapped around with love as we were during those three years. It ran through my waking life like a song: it smoothed my pillow, touched and made my table comely, in summer lifted the heads of the flowers as I passed, and in winter watched the fire with me and kept it bright.

" 'Why did I ever leave Tresillack?' Because one day, at the end of five years, Farmer Hosking brought me word that he had sold the house—or was about to sell it; I forget which. There was no avoiding it, at any rate; the purchaser being a Colonel Kendall, a brother of the old Squire.'

" 'A married man?' I asked.

" 'Yes, miss; with a family of eight. As pretty children as ever you see, and the mother a good lady. It's the old home to Colonel Kendall.'

" 'I see. And that is why you feel bound to sell.'

" 'It's a good price, too, that he offers. You mustn't think but I'm sorry enough—'

" 'To turn me out? I thank you, Mr. Hosking; but you are doing the right thing.'

"Since Mrs. Carkeek was to stay, the arrangement lacked nothing of absolute perfection—except, perhaps, that it found no room for me.

" '*She*—Margaret—will be happy,' I said; 'with her cousins, you know.'

" 'Oh, yes, miss, she will be happy, sure enough,' Mrs. Carkeek agreed.

"So when the time came I packed up my boxes, and tried to be cheerful. But on the last morning, when they stood corded in the hall, I sent Mrs. Carkeek upstairs upon some poor excuse, and stepped alone into the pantry.

"'Margaret!' I whispered.

"There was no answer at all. I had scarcely dared to hope for one. Yet I tried again, and, shutting my eyes this time, stretched out both hands and whispered:

"'Margaret!'

"And I will swear to my dying day that two little hands stole and rested—for a moment only—in mine."

FATHER MACCLESFIELD'S TALE

MONSIGNOR MAXWELL announced next day at dinner that he had already arranged for the evening's entertainment. A priest, whose acquaintance he had made on the Palatine, was leaving for England the next morning; and it was our only chance, therefore, of hearing his story. That he had a story had come to the Canon's knowledge in the course of a conversation on the previous afternoon.

"He told me the outline of it," he said, "I think it very remarkable. But I had a great deal of difficulty in persuading him to repeat it to the company this evening. But he promised at last. I trust, gentlemen, you do not think I have presumed in begging him to do so."

Father Macclesfield arrived at supper.

He was a little, unimposing dry man, with a hooked nose, and grey hair. He was rather silent at supper; but there was no trace of shyness in his manner as he took his seat upstairs, and without glancing round once, began in an even and dispassionate voice:

"I once knew a Catholic girl that married an old Protestant three times her own age. I entreated her not to do so; but it was useless. And when the disillusionment came she used to write to me piteous letters, telling me that her husband had in reality no religion at all. He was a convinced infidel; and scouted even the idea of the soul's immortality.

"After two years of married life the old man died. He was about sixty years old; but very hale and hearty till the end.

"Well, when he took to his bed, the wife sent for me; and I had half-a-dozen interviews with him; but it was useless. He told me plainly that he wanted to believe—in fact he said that the thought of annihilation was intolerable to him. If he had had a child he would not have hated death so much; if his flesh and blood in any manner survived him, he could have fancied that he had a sort of vicarious life left; but as it was, there was no kith or kin of his alive; and he could not bear that."

Father Macclesfield sniffed cynically, and folded his hands.

"I may say that his death-bed was extremely unpleasant. He was a coarse old fellow, with plenty of strength in him; and he used to make remarks about the churchyard— and—and in fact the worms, that used to send his poor child of a wife half fainting out of the room. He had lived an immoral life too, I gathered.

"Just at the last it was—well—disgusting. He had no consideration; (God knows why she married him!). The agony was a very long one, he caught at the curtains round the bed; calling out; and all his words were about death, and the dark. It seemed to me that he caught hold of the curtains as if to hold himself into this world. And at the very end he raised himself clean up in bed, and stared horribly out of the window that was open just opposite.

"I must tell you that straight away beneath the window lay a long walk, between sheets of dead leaves with laurels on either side, and the branches meeting overhead, so that it was very dark there even in summer; and at the end of the walk away from the house was the churchyard gate."

"Father Macclesfield paused and blew his nose. Then he went on, still without looking at us.

"Well, the old man died; and he was carried along this laurel path, and buried.

"His wife was in such a state that I simply dared not go away. She was frightened to death; and, indeed, the whole affair of her husband's dying was horrible. But she would not leave the house. She had a fancy that it would be cruel to him. She used to go down twice a day to pray at the grave; but she never went along the laurel walk. She would go round by the garden and in at a lower gate, and come back the same way, or by the upper garden.

"This went on for three or four days. The man had died on a Saturday, and was buried on Monday; it was in July; and he had died about eight o'clock.

"I made up my mind to go on the Saturday after the funeral. My curate managed alone very well for a few days; but I did not like to leave him for a second Sunday.

"Then on the Friday at lunch—her sister had come down, by the way, and was still in the house—on the Friday the widow said something about never daring to sleep in the room where the old man had died. I told her it was nonsense, and so on; but you must remember she was in a dreadful state of nerves, and she persisted. So I said I would sleep in the room myself. I had no patience with such ideas then.

"Of course she said all sorts of things, but I had my way; and my things were moved in on Friday evening.

"I went to my new room about a quarter before eight to put on my cassock for dinner. The room was very much as it had been—

rather dark because of the trees at the end of the walk outside. There was the four-poster there with the damask curtains; the table and chairs, the cupboard where his clothes were kept, and so on.

"When I had put my cassock on, I went to the window to look out. To right and left were the gardens, with the sunlight just off them, but still very bright and gay, with the geraniums, and exactly opposite was the laurel walk, like a long green shady tunnel, dividing the upper and lower lawns.

"I could see straight down it to the churchyard gate, which was about a hundred yards away, I suppose. There were limes overhead, and laurels, as I said, on each side.

"Well—I saw someone coming up the walk; but it seemed to me at first that he was drunk. He staggered several times as I watched; I suppose he would be fifty yards away—and once I saw him catch hold of one of the trees and cling against it as if he were afraid of falling. Then he left it, and came on again slowly, going from side to side, with his hands out. He seemed desperately keen to get to the house.

"I could see his dress; and it astonished me that a man dressed so should be drunk; for he was quite plainly a gentleman. He wore a white top hat, and a grey cut-away coat, and grey trousers, and I could make out his white spats.

"Then it struck me he might be ill; and I looked harder than ever, wondering whether I ought to go down.

"When he was about twenty yards away he lifted his face; and, it struck me as very odd, but it seemed to me he was extraordinarily like the old man we had buried on Monday; but it was darkish where he was, and the next moment he dropped his face, threw up his hands and fell flat on his back.

"Well, of course I was startled at that, and I leaned out of the window and called out something. He was moving his hands, I could see, as if he were in convulsions; and I could hear the dry leaves rustling.

"Well, then I turned and ran out and downstairs."

Father Macclesfield stopped a moment.

"Gentlemen," he said abruptly, "when I got there, there was not a sign of the old man. I could see that the leaves had been disturbed, but that was all."

There was an odd silence as he paused; but before any of us had time to speak he went on.

"Of course I did not say a word of what I had seen. We dined as usual; I smoked for an hour or so by myself after prayers; and then I went up to bed. I cannot say I was perfectly comfortable, for I was not; but neither was I frightened.

"When I got to my room I lit all my candles, and then went to a big cupboard I had noticed, and pulled out some of the drawers. In the bottom of the third drawer I found a grey cut-away coat and grey trousers; I found several pairs of white spats in the top drawer; and a white hat on the shelf above. That is the first incident."

"Did you sleep there, Father?" said a voice softly.

"I did," said the priest, "there was no reason why I should not. I did not fall asleep for two or three hours; but I was not disturbed in any way; and came to breakfast as usual.

"Well, I thought about it all a bit; and finally I sent a wire to my curate telling him I was detained. I did not like to leave the house just then."

Father Macclesfield settled himself again in his chair and went on, in the same dry uninterested voice.

"On Sunday we drove over to the Catholic Church, six miles off, and I said Mass. Nothing more happened till the Monday evening.

"That evening I went to the window again about a quarter before eight, as I had done both on the Saturday and Sunday. Everything was perfectly quiet, till I heard the churchyard gate unlatch; and I saw a man come through.

"But I saw almost at once that it was not the same man I had seen before; it looked to me like a keeper, for he had a gun across his arm; then I saw him hold the gate open an instant, and a dog came through and began to trot up the path towards the house with his master following.

"When the dog was about fifty yards away he stopped dead, and pointed.

"I saw the keeper throw his gun forward and come up softly; and as he came the dog began to slink backwards. I watched very closely, clean forgetting why I was there; and the next instant something—it was too shadowy under the trees to see exactly what it was—but something about the size of a hare burst out of the laurels and made straight up the path, dodging from side to side, but coming like the wind.

"The beast could not have been more than twenty yards from me, when the keeper fired, and the creature went over and over in the dry leaves, and lay struggling and screaming. It was horrible! But what astonished me was that the dog did not come up. I heard the keeper snap out something, and then I saw the dog making off down the avenue in the direction of the churchyard as hard as he could go.

"The keeper was running now towards me; but the screaming of the hare, or of whatever it was, had stopped; and I was astonished to see the man come right up to where the beast was struggling and kicking, and then stop as if he was puzzled.

"I leaned out of the window and called to him.

" 'Right in front of you, man,' I said. 'For God's sake kill the brute.'

"He looked up at me, and then down again.

" 'Where is it, sir?' he said. 'I can't see it anywhere.'

"And there lay the beast clear before him all the while, not a yard away, still kicking.

"Well, I went out of the room and downstairs and out to the avenue.

"The man was standing there still, looking terribly puzzled, but the hare was gone. There was not a sign of it. Only the leaves were disturbed, and the wet earth showed beneath.

"The keeper said that it had been a great hare; he could have sworn to it; and that he had orders to kill all hares and rabbits in the garden enclosure. Then he looked rather odd.

" 'Did you see it plainly, sir?' he asked.

"I told him, not very plainly; but I thought it a hare too.

" 'Yes, sir,' he said, 'it was a hare, sure enough; but, do you know, sir, I thought it to be a kind of silver grey with white feet. I never saw one like that before!'

"The odd thing was that not a dog would come near, his own dog was gone; but I fetched the yard dog—a retriever, out of his kennel in the kitchen yard; and if ever I saw a frightened dog it was this one. When we dragged him up at last, all whining and pulling back, he began to snap at us so fiercely that we let go, and he went back like the wind to his kennel. It was the same with the terrier.

"Well, the bell had gone, and I had to go in and explain why I was late; but I didn't say anything about the colour of the hare. That was the second incident."

Father Macclesfield stopped again, smiling reminiscently to himself. I was very much impressed by his quiet air and composure. I think it helped his story a good deal.

'Again, before we had time to comment or question he went on.

"The third incident was so slight that I should not have mentioned it, or thought anything of it, if it had not been for the others; but it seemed to me there was a kind of diminishing gradation of energy, which explained. Well, now you shall hear.

"On the other nights of that week I was at my window again; but nothing happened till the Friday. I had arranged to go for certain next day; the widow was much better and more reasonable, and even talked of going abroad herself in the following week.

"On that Friday evening I dressed a little earlier, and went down to the avenue this time, instead of staying at my window, at about twenty minutes to eight.

"It was rather a heavy depressing evening, without a breath of wind; and it was darker than it had been for some days.

"I walked slowly down the avenue to the gate and back again; and, I suppose it was fancy, but I felt more uncomfortable than I had felt at all up to then. I was rather relieved to see the widow come out of the house and stand looking down the avenue. I came out myself then and went towards her. She started rather, when she saw me, and then smiled.

" 'I thought it was someone else,' she said. 'Father, I have made up my mind to go. I shall go to town to-morrow, and start on Monday. My sister will come with me.'

"I congratulated her; and then we turned and began to walk back to the lime avenue. She stopped at the entrance, and seemed unwilling to come any further.

" 'Come down to the end,' I said, 'and back again. There will be time before dinner.'

"She said nothing; but came with me; and we went straight down to the gate and then turned to come back.

"I don't think either of us spoke a word; I was very uncomfortable indeed by now; and yet I had to go on.

"We were halfway back, I suppose, when I heard a sound like a gate rattling; and I whisked round in an instant, expecting to see someone at the gate. But there was no one.

"Then there came a rustling overhead in the leaves; it had been dead still before. Then I don't know why, but I took my friend suddenly by the arm and drew her to one side out of the path, so that we stood on the right hand, not a foot from the laurels.

"She said nothing, and I said nothing; but I think we were both looking this way and that, as if we expected to see something.

"The breeze died, and then sprang up again; but it was only a breath. I could hear the living leaves rustling overhead, and the dead leaves underfoot; and it was blowing gently from the churchyard.

"Then I saw a thing that one often sees; but I could not take my eyes off it, nor could she. It was a little column of leaves, twisting and turning and dropping and picking up again in the wind, coming slowly up the path. It was a capricious sort of draught, for the little scurry of leaves went this way and that, to and fro across the path. It came up to us, and I could feel the breeze on my hands and face. One leaf struck me softly on the cheek, and I can only say that I shuddered as if it had been a toad. Then it passed on.

"You understand, gentlemen, it was pretty dark; but it seemed to me that the breeze died and the column of leaves—it was no more than a little twist of them—sank down at the end of the avenue.

"We stood there perfectly still for a moment or two; and when I turned, she was staring straight at me, but neither of us said one word.

"We did not go up the avenue to the house. We pushed our way through the laurels, and came back by the upper garden.

"Nothing else happened; and the next morning we all went off by the eleven o'clock train.

"That is all, gentlemen."

THE GREY PIPER AND THE HEAVY COACH OF DONALDGOWERIE HOUSE, PERTH

DONALDGOWERIE HOUSE, until comparatively recent times, stood on the outskirts of Perth. It was a long, low, rambling old place, dating back to the beginning of the seventeenth century. At the time of the narrative it was in the possession of a Mr. William Whittingen, who bought it at a very low price from some people named Tyler. It is true that it would cost a small fortune to repair, but, notwithstanding this disadvantage, Mr. Whittingen considered his purchase a bargain, and was more than satisfied with it. Indeed, he knew of no other house of a similar size, of such an imposing appearance, and so pleasantly situated, that he could have bought for less than twice the amount he had paid for this; and he was really very sorry for the Tylers, who explained to him, in confidence, that had they not been in such urgent need of money, they would never have sold Donaldgowerie House at such a ridiculously low figure. However, with them it was a question of cash—cash down, and Mr. Whittingen had only to write out a cheque for the modest sum they asked, and the house was his. It was June when Mr. Whittingen took possession of the house—June, when the summer sun was brightest and the gardens looked their best.

The Whittingen family, consisting of Mr. and Mrs. Whittingen, two sons, Ernest and Harvey, and three daughters, Ruth, Martha, and Mary, were, as one might gather from their names alone, plain, practical, genteel, and in fact very superior people, who were by no means lacking in that exceedingly useful quality of canniness, so characteristic of the Lowland Scot, to which race they belonged. Mr. Whittingen had, for years, conducted a grocery business in Jedburgh, twice filling the honoured and coveted post of mayor, and when he at length retired into private life, his friends (and it was astonishing how many friends he had) shrewdly suspected that his pockets were not only well lined but full to bursting. Acting on the advice of his wife and daughters, who were keen on social distinction, he sent Ernest to Oxford, conditionally that he should take Holy Orders in the Church of England, whilst Harvey, who, when scarcely out of the petticoat stage, displayed the regular Whittingen talent for business by covertly helping himself to the sugar in his father's shop, and disposing of it at strictly sale price to his sisters' cronies in the nursery, was sent to one of those half preparatory and half finishing schools (of course, for the sons of gentlemen only) at Edinburgh, where he was kept till he was old enough to be articled to a prosperous, exceedingly prosperous, firm of solicitors.

The girls, Ruth, Martha, and Mary, had likewise been highly educated; that is to say, they had remained so many years at an English seminary for young ladies, and had been given a final twelve months in France and Germany to enable them to obtain "the correct accent".

At the time of the story they were as yet unmarried, and were awaiting with the most laudable patience the advent of men of title. They were delighted with their new home (which Ruth had persuaded her father to christen "Donaldgowerie", after the house in a romantic novel she had just been reading), and proud of their gilded premises and magnificent tennis lawns; they had placed a gigantic and costly tray in the hall, in confident assurance that it would speedily groan beneath the weight of cards from all the gentry in Perthshire.

But please be it understood, that my one and only object in alluding to these trifling details is to point out that the Whittingens, being entirely engrossed in matters mundane, were the very last people in the world to be termed superstitious, and although imaginative where future husbands' calls and cards were concerned, prior to the events about to be narrated had not an ounce of superstition in their natures. Indeed, until then they had always smiled in a very supercilious manner at even the smallest mention of a ghost.

September came, their first September in Donaldgowerie, and the family welcomed with joy Ernest and his youthful bride.

The latter was not, as they fondly hoped (and roundly announced in Perth), the daughter of a Peer, but of a wealthy Bristol draper, the owner of a house near the Downs, whose son had been one of Ernest's many friends at Oxford. The coming of the newly-married pair to Donaldgowerie brought with it a burst of bird-like gaiety. All sorts of entertainments—musical "at homes", dinners, dances, tennis and garden parties, in fact, every variety that accorded with the family's idea of good taste—were given; and with praiseworthy "push", for which the Whittingens had fast become noted, all the County was invited. This splendid display of wealth and hospitality was not disinterested; I fear it might be not only accounted a "send off" for the immaculately-clad curate and his wife, but also a determined effort on the part of Mr. and Mrs. Whittingen to attract the right sort of lover for their girls.

It was during the progress of one of their alfresco entertainments that the scepticism of certain of the Whittingens with regard to the supernatural received a rude blow.

Martha, Mary, and two eligible young men, friend's of Harvey's, having finished a somewhat spirited game of croquet, were refreshing themselves with lemonade, whilst they continued their flirtation. Presently Mary, whose partner declared how much he should like to see some photographs she had recently taken of herself, with a well-affected giggle of embarrassment set off to the house to fetch her album. The minutes passed, and, as she did not return, Martha went in search of her. The album, she knew, was in their boudoir, which was situated at the end of the long and rather gloomy corridor of the upper storey.

Highly incensed at her sister's slowness, she was hastening along the corridor, when, to her supreme astonishment, she suddenly saw the figure of a man in kilts, with a bagpipe under his arm, emerge through the half-open door of the boudoir, and with a peculiar gliding motion advance towards her. A curious feeling, with which she was totally unfamiliar, compelled her to remain mute and motionless; and in this condition she awaited the approach of the stranger. Who was he? she asked herself, and how on earth had he got there, and what was he doing? As he drew nearer, she perceived that his face was all one hue—a ghastly livid grey—and that his eyes, which were all the time fixed on hers, were lurid and menacing; so terrible, in fact, that she turned cold with fear, and felt the very hair on her head beginning to rise on end. She opened her mouth to shriek, but found she could not ejaculate a syllable; neither could she, even with the most desperate efforts, tear her feet from the floor. On came the figure, and, without swerving either to the right or left, it glided right up to and through her; and, as she involuntarily turned round, she saw it disappear through a half-open staircase window, at least twenty feet above the ground outside. Shaking all over with terror, and not understanding in the slightest what to make of it, Martha ran to the boudoir, where her heart almost sprang out of her body at the spectacle of her sister Mary stretched at full length on the floor, her cheeks ashy pale, her lips blue. Martha at once made a frantic rush to the bell, and, in a few minutes, half the establishment, headed by Mr. Whittingen, poured into the room. With the aid of a little cold water, Mary speedily recovered, and, in reply to the anxious inquiries of her sympathetic rescuers as to what had happened, indignantly demanded why such a horrible-looking creature as "that piper" had been allowed not merely to enter the house but to come up to her room, and half frighten her to death. "I had just got my album," she added, "when, feeling someone was in the room, I turned round, and there"—she indicated a spot on the carpet—"was the piper, not ten paces away from me, regarding me with the most awful look imaginable. I was too taken aback with surprise to say anything, nor—for some unaccountable reason—could I escape, before he touched me on the shoulder with one of his icy cold hands, and then commenced playing. Up and down the floor he paced, backwards and forwards, never taking his hateful glance off my face and ever piping the same dismal dirge. At last, unable to stand the strain of it any longer, and convinced he was a madman, bent on murdering me—for who but a lunatic would behave in such a way?—I gave way to a violent fit of hysterics, and fainted. Now tell me who he was, and why he was permitted to frighten me in this manner?" And Mary stamped her feet and grew vicious, as only her class will when they are at all vexed. Her speech was followed by a silence that exasperated her. She repeated her inquiries with crimson cheeks, and then, as again no one responded, she signalled out the head footman and raved at him.

Up to this point, Mr. Whittingen had been dumb with amazement. The idea of a strange piper having the twofold effrontery to enter his house and proceed to the private and chaste sanctuary of his highly respectable daughters, almost deprived him of breath. He could scarcely believe his ears. "What—what in the name of—what does it all mean?" he at length stammered, addressing the unfortunate footman. "A piper! And without any invitation from me, how dare you let him in?"

"I did not, sir," the luckless footman replied; "no such person came to the door when I was in the hall."

"No more he did when I was there," chimed in the second footman, and all the other servants vociferated in a body, "We never saw any piper, sir, nor heard one either," and they looked at Mary reproachfully.

At this Mr. Whittingen looked exceedingly embarrassed. In the face of such a unanimous denial what could he say? He knew if he suggested the servants were untruthful they would all give notice to leave on the spot, and knowing good servants are scarce in Perth as elsewhere, he felt rather in a fix. At length, turning to Mary, he asked if she was sure it was a piper. "Sure!" Mary screamed, "why, of course I am, did I not tell you he marched up and down here playing on his disgusting bagpipes, which nearly broke the drum of my ear."

"And I saw him too, pa," Martha put in. "I met him in the corridor; he had his pipes under his arm, and the most dreadful expression in his face. I don't wonder Mary was frightened."

"But where did he go?" Mr. Whittingen cried.

"You would not believe me if I told you," Martha said, her cheeks flushing. "He seemed to pass right through me, and then to vanish through the staircase window. I have never been so terribly upset in my life," and, sinking on to the sofa, she began to laugh hysterically.

"Dear me! dear me! it is very odd!" Mr. Whittingen exclaimed, as Mary handed her sister a wineglass of sal-volatile. "They can't both have been dreaming; it must—but there, what a nonsensical notion, there are no such things as ghosts! Only children and nursemaids believe in them nowadays. As soon as you have quite recovered, my dears, we will return to the garden, and I think that under the circumstances, the rather peculiar circumstances, ahem! it will be better to say nothing to your mother. Do you understand?" Mr. Whittingen went on, eyeing the servants, "Nothing to your mistress."

The affair thus terminated, and for some days nothing further happened to disturb the peace of the family. At the end of a week, however—exactly a week after the appearance of the piper—Mary met with a serious accident. She was running across the croquet lawn to speak to her sister-in-law, when she tripped over a hoop that had been accidentally left there, and, in falling, ran a hatpin into her head. Blood poisoning ensued, and within a fortnight she was dead. Martha was the only one in the house, however, who associated Mary's accident and death with the piper; to her that sinister expression in the mysterious Highlander's eyes portended mischief, and she could not but suspect that, in some way or another, he had brought about the catastrophe.

The autumn waned, and Christmas was well within sight, when another mysterious occurrence took place. It was early one Sunday evening; tea was just over, and the Whittingen family were sitting round the fire engaged in a somewhat melancholy conversation, for the loss of Mary had affected them all very deeply, when they heard the far-away rumble of a heavy coach on the high road. Nearer and nearer it came, till it seemed to be about on a level with the front lodge gate; then to their surprise there was a loud crunching of gravel, and they heard it careering at a breakneck speed up the carriage-drive. They looked at one another in the utmost consternation.

A coach, and driven in this mad fashion! Whose was it? What did it mean? Not visitors, surely!

It pulled up at the front door, and the champing and stamping of the horses vibrated loudly through the still night air. Sounds as of one or more people descending were next heard, and then there came a series of the most terrific knockings at the door. The Whittingen family stared at one another aghast; there was something in those knockings—something they could not explain—that struck terror in their souls and made their blood run cold. They waited in breathless anxiety for the door to be opened; but no servant went to open it. The knocks were repeated; if anything, louder than before, the door swung back on its hinges, and the tread of heavy footsteps was heard slowly approaching the drawing-room. Mrs. Whittingen gave a low gasp of horror, Ruth screamed, Harvey buried his face in his hands, Mr. Whittingen rose to his feet, and made desperate efforts to get to the bell, but could not stir, whilst Martha rushed to the drawing-room door and locked it. They then with one accord began to pray. The steps halted outside the room, the door slowly opened, and the blurred outlines of a group of ghastly-looking figures, supporting a grotesquely shaped object in their midst, appeared on the threshold. For some seconds there was a grim silence. It was abruptly broken by a thud—Ruth had slipped from her chair to the floor in a dead faint; whereupon the shadowy forms solemnly veered round and made their way back again to the front door. The latter swung violently open, there was a rush of icy wind which swept like a hurricane across the hall and into the drawing-room, the front door then slammed to with a crash, and the coach drove away.

Everyone's attention was now directed to Ruth. At first sal-volatile and cold water produced no effect, but after a time she slowly, very slowly, regained consciousness. As soon as she had recovered sufficiently to speak, she expressed an earnest desire that no reference should ever be made in her presence to what had just happened. "It was for me!" she said in such an emphatic tone as filled her audience with the direst forebodings. "I know it was for me; they all looked in my direction. God help me! I shall die like Mary."

Though greatly perplexed as to what she meant, for no one excepting herself had been able to make out the phenomena with any degree of distinctness, they yielded to her entreaties, and asked her no questions. The servants had neither heard nor seen anything. A fortnight later, Ruth was taken ill with appendicitis; peritonitis speedily set in, and she died under the operation. The Whittingens now began to wish they had never come to Donaldgowerie; but, with the astuteness that had been characteristic of the family through countless generations of fair days and foul, they took the greatest precautions never to drop even as much as a hint to the servants or to anyone in the town that the house was haunted.

A year passed without any further catastrophe, and they were beginning to hope their ghastly visitors had left them, when something else occurred. It was Easter-time, and Ernest, his wife and baby, were staying with them. The baby, a boy, was fat and bonny, the very picture of health and happiness.

Mrs. Whittingen and Martha vied with one another in their devotion to him; and either one or other of them was always dancing attendance on him. It so happened that one afternoon, whilst the servants were having their tea, Martha found herself alone in the upper part of the house with her precious nephew. Mr. Whittingen had gone to Edinburgh to consult his lawyer (the head of the firm with whom Harvey was articled) on business, whilst Mrs. Whittingen had taken her son and daughter-in-law for a drive. The weather was glorious, and Martha, though as little appreciative of the beauties of nature as most commercial-minded young women, could not but admire the colouring of the sky as she looked out of the nursery window. The sun had disappeared, but the effect of its rays was still apparent on the western horizon, where the heavens were washed with alternate streaks of gold and red and pink—the colour of each streak excessively brilliant in the centre but paling towards the edges. Here and there were golden, pink-tipped clouds and crimson islets surrounded with seas of softest blue. And outside the limits of this sun-kissed pale, the blue of the sky gradually grew darker and darker, until its line was altogether lost in the black shadows of night that, creeping over the lone mountain-tops in the far east, slowly swept forward. Wafted by the gentle breeze came the dull moaning and whispering of the pine trees, the humming of the wind through the telephone wires, and the discordant cawing of the crows.

And it seemed to Martha as she sat there and peered out into the garden, that over the whole atmosphere of the place had come a subtle and hostile change—a change in the noises of the trees, the birds, the wind; a change in the flower-scented ether; a change, a most marked and emphatic change, in the shadows. What was it? What was this change? Whence did it originate? What did it portend? A slight noise, a most trivial noise, attracted Martha's attention to the room; she looked round and was quite startled to see how dark it had grown. In the old days, when she had scoffed at ghosts, she would as soon have been in the dark as in the light, the night had no terrors for her; but now—now since those awful occurrences last year, all was different, and as she peered apprehensively about her, her flesh crawled. What was there in that corner opposite, that corner hemmed in on the one side by the cupboard—how she hated cupboards, particularly when they had shiny surfaces on which were reflected all sorts of curious things—and the chest of drawers on the other. It was a shadow, only a shadow, but of what? She searched the room everywhere to find its material counterpart, and at last discovered it in the nurse's shawl which hung over the back of a chair. Then she laughed, and would have gone on laughing, for she tried to persuade herself that laughter banished ghosts, when suddenly something else caught her eyes. What was it? An object that glittered evilly like two eyes. She got up in a state of the most hideous fascination and walked towards it. Then she laughed again—it was a pair of scissors. The nurse's scissors—clean, bright and sharp. Why did she pick them up and feel the blades so caressingly with her thumb? Why did she glance from them to the baby? Why? In the name of God, why? Frightful ideas laid hold of her mind. She tried to chase them away but they quickly returned. The scissors, why were they in her fingers? Why could she not put them down? For what were they intended? Cutting! Cutting thread, and tape—and throats! *Throats!* And she giggled hysterically at the bare notion. But what was this round her waist—this shadowy arm-like object! She looked fearfully round, and her soul died within her as she encountered the malevolent, gleeful eyes of the sinister piper, pressed closely against her face. Was it she he wanted this time—she, or—or whom—in the name of all that was pitiable?

Desperately, as if all the lives in the universe and the future of her soul were at stake, did she struggle to free herself from his grasp—but in vain; every fibre, every muscle of her body, was completely at his will. On and on he pushed her, until foot by foot, inch by inch, she approached the cradle, and all the while his hellish voice was breathing the vilest of inspiration into her brain. At last she stood by the side of the baby, and bent over it. What a darling! What a dear! What a duck! A sweet, pretty, innocent, prattling duck! How like her mother—how like her handsome brother—how like herself—very, very like herself! How everyone loved it—how everyone worshipped it—how (and here the grey face beside her chuckled) everyone would miss it! How pink its toes—how fat its calves—how chubby its little palms—how bonny its cheeks—and how white, how gloriously, heavenly, snowy white—its throat! And she stretched forth one of her stubby inartistic fingers and played with its flesh. Then she glanced furtively at the scissors, and smiled.

It was soon done, soon over, and she and the grey-faced piper danced a minuet in the moonbeams; afterwards he piped a farewell dirge—a wild, weird, funereal dirge, and, marching slowly backwards, his dark, gleaming eyes fixed gloatingly on hers, disappeared through the window. Then the reaction set in, and Martha shrieked till everyone in the house flew to the rescue.

Of course, no one—saving her father and mother—believed her. Ernest, his wife, and the servants, attributed her bloody act to jealousy; the law—to madness; and she subsequently journeyed from Donaldgowerie to a criminal lunatic asylum, where the recollection of all she had done soon killed her. This was the climax. Mr. Whittengen sold Donaldgowerie, and a new house was shortly afterwards erected in its stead.

THE HOUSE OF THE GHOSTLY TAP-DANCING

Away in the distance came the faint sounds of a church clock. Welchman could not count the strokes, the wind and rain were making such a fearful noise, but he calculated that it must be twelve, because it was eleven when he left Gloucester and that must surely be a good hour ago.

His objective had been Broadway, but the weather was so infernal that, being a complete stranger in those parts and not seeing the sign posts, he had somehow missed the way. In turning a rather sharp corner at the foot of a steep incline he had collided with a wall. Result, a period of nothingness from personal contact with something rather harder than his own head, and a buckled wheel.

On recovering and realising what had happened, Welchman found some relief in profanity, and then commenced walking. He was still plodding wearily along, pushing, his damaged machine, when he heard that church clock striking. Bruised and tired, hungry and soaked to the skin, he was thinking of dropping by the wayside and trusting to luck and a fairly sound constitution to escape pneumonia, when he suddenly espied a light. It was to one side of him.

His own cycle lamp being smashed and the night being pitch dark, he could not see a yard ahead of him; consequently, in making for the light he had to go slowly. After bumping into hedges and tumbling into ditches he at last got on to what appeared to be a path of some kind. Groping his way along it he presently saw that the light proceeded from the windows of a large house.

Passing through a ruined gateway, he found himself in an avenue, bordered on either side by stately trees. The road was in an even worse condition than the one he had just quitted. It was overrun with weeds and full of holes, converted into very unpleasant miniature lakes by the heavy rain.

On getting nearer to the house he caught the sound of music. Someone, a man, was singing a sweet, melancholy air, accompanied by a tinkling piano. It was a strangely haunting air, and one he had never heard before. The words were either Spanish or Italian; the voice was a pure baritone and well-trained.

Crossing a terrace that shone wet in the bright gleams from the window, he knocked several times at the front door; and as there was no response and he kept getting colder and colder, his patience at last was exhausted. He gave the door a violent push, upon which it opened wide, creaking rustily on its hinges. To his astonishment all was dark within and absolutely still. The music had abruptly ceased.

After several attempts to find a dry match, he at last discovered one, and by its aid found his way to a table on which were several half-used wax candles. Lighting one, he saw he was in a hall. Confronting him was an oak staircase leading to a gallery overhead. There were the remains of gildings and frescoes on the walls and ceiling, but everything was decayed, and everywhere dust and cobwebs. There was a feeling of great depression in the atmosphere, and the feeble light from the candle, revealing shadows that were unpleasantly fantastic, made the surrounding gloom seem weird and full of horrible possibilities.

Considerably mystified, Welchman propped his bicycle against one of the walls and then proceeded to explore. The house, though large, was not so large as it had appeared from the outside.

Rambling and old-world, it consisted of two storeys. There were corridors and staircases and narrow winding passages where one did not expect to find them. The architecture was extraordinary and full of quaint surprises. The rooms all had very low ceilings, wide, old-world fireplaces and the same uncannny, depressing atmosphere. Nowhere was there a sign of life, and yet Welchman could feel all the time that he was being watched and followed.

In one corner of a room, which might have once been a study or library—it was on the ground floor—was a pile of wood, and in the fireplace were the remains of a wood fire. Very possibly, he thought, some other wayfarer like himself had sought refuge in the house and made himself a fire. Welchman decided to do the same, and he was soon warming himself before a very cheery blaze. What with the heat from the fire and weariness he presently dozed off, to awake with a start and the sensation of being no longer alone.

Opening his eyes and looking round he saw the shadowy form of a woman standing some few feet away from him, apparently watching him. She was standing amid the shadows of the walls, and so out of range of the flickering fire flames that he could not see her with any degree of distinctness. He called out several times, "Who are you?" but she did not reply. Losing his temper at last, he took up one of his shoes and threw it at her.

The shoe passed right through her and, striking the wall behind her, fell on the wooden floor with a thud that awoke disturbingly weird echoes. Turning round, the woman moved stealthily out of the room.

Though distinctly jarred, Welchman got up and followed her. Crossing the hall, still in the same stealthy manner, she was about half-way up the staircase when she turned slowly round and looked at Welchman. The face he saw was that of an old woman, with a white cap border, closely crumpled round her puckered, leering face. A gruesome light seemed to surround her, and Welchman could see her shrivelled lips move and her bleared eyes light up with evil glee. Shaking her skinny fist menacingly at him, she ran, with surprising swiftness for one of her age, up the stairs and disappeared in the gloom beyond.

For some seconds Welchman was too frightened to follow her, but pulling himself together, he mounted several stairs and called out, "My good woman, who are you and what is your business?" A low, chuckling laugh in answer resounded through the echoing old house. Welchman got back to the cheery blaze of the fire as fast as he could.

Again overcome with heat and weariness, he fell asleep, and, as before, he awoke with a start, this time to hear a tapping sound. Faint at first, it gradually drew nearer. A quick, very quiet, tap-tapping, on hard boards. There was something curiously familiar to Welchman about those sounds. Where, he asked himself, had he heard them before, and then, suddenly, it all came back to him.

Welchman was not a lover of the theatre or pictures. It was very rare, indeed, that he went to either, but a few days before, having nothing else to do, he had gone to the White Ladies' Road Cinema in Bristol. One of the films he had seen was a musical comedy and in it there had been a clever girl tap-dancer. That was why the sounds he now heard had seemed so familiar. It was tap-dancing, of course!

But what on earth could a tap-dancer be doing here, in this old deserted house and at such an hour? Welchman sat up and listened intently. Yes, it was tap-dancing right enough, but there was something so uncanny about it that his blood chilled.

It was now in the hall, tapping its way across the oak floor in his direction, and from the lightness of the steps he instinctively felt it was a woman. The sounds at last paused outside his door, and his heart thumped painfully as the door handle began to turn slowly, and the door, as slowly, to open. Through the aperture appeared a hand. A slim, white hand. A spurt of firelight playing on the door threw the fingers into strong relief.

They were tapering, with long, rosy filbert nails. Such hands are often to be found on dancers. Ginger Rogers has beautiful hands of this type, so have Anna Neagle and Carole Lombard, and many other dancers.

The hands Welchman now saw fascinated him by reason of their extraordinary beauty, and yet they alarmed him. There was the same jarring weirdness about them that there had been about the dancing, the leering, pucker-faced old woman, and indeed, the whole house—a weirdness born of evil.

The door kept opening, and presently there appeared in the aperture a face. The flickering fire flames threw the features into bold relief. The hands had not belied the face. It was that of a girl, beautiful in a dark Latin way. She smiled archly as her long-lashed black eyes met those of Welchman, and beckoned to him, with the gleaming forefinger of her right hand.

Again, obeying an impulse he could not resist, he got up from the floor on which he had been lying, and followed her. Across the still, shadow-laden hall she led him, to a room exactly opposite the one in which he had been sleeping. Pausing at the door with one hand on the handle, she placed her polished finger tip at her lips, as if to ensure silence, and pressed her ear against the door panel. Again came the sounds of music, the same sad, haunting air he had heard before, the same pure baritone voice.

Opening the door noiselessly the girl passed within, motioning Welchman to follow. The moment he did so the singing and music ceased.

Though he fancied he had been in all the rooms, he certainly had not been in the one he now saw. It was a boudoir. One or two paintings hung opposite the window and in a corner stood a piano. What arrested Welchman's attention, however, more than anything else, was a large chesterfield on which lay a young man with long black hair and quite startlingly white cheeks. From his regular breathing and closed eyes he appeared to be fast asleep. Of the singer and musician there was not a sign.

Obeying a sign from the girl—Welchman could not do otherwise, she had an extraordinary compelling influence—he sat down on a chair against the wall, opposite the chesterfield, and waited—waited for something terrible he intuitively felt was going to happen shortly.

Presently, from the hall, came the sounds of soft and rather struggling footsteps. They approached the boudoir and halted outside. Welchman could hear someone breathing. Then there was a faint knock. The girl, with a smile, a strange combination of archness and significance, at Welchman tiptoed to the door and opened it cautiously.

A cold thrill ran through Welchman when he saw the hideous old hag with the bleary eyes and puckered face standing outside. She had in one hand a hammer with long, gleaming claws. Entering the room, she stood whispering with the girl. Welchman could not hear what they said; it was all in some tongue unknown to him and sounded strangely far away and hollow. Every now and then they cast glances full of frightful mockery and hate at the man on the chesterfield and smiled evilly at one another.

This for some minutes, and then, moving with hideous stealth they crept noiselessly to the chesterfield. Bending over the sleeping man, the girl with the long tapering fingers gently brushed apart the hair on the top of his head. The old hag then handed her the hammer and a long shining nail.

Frozen with horror, but horribly fascinated, Welchman watched every detail. He saw the girl take the nail between her lovely thumb and forefinger, look at it for a second or two with inimical satisfaction, and then, putting it over the spot she had so carefully selected, drive it with fiendish glee into the skull of the sleeping man. Directly this was done, the room, which had been illuminated with a strong light that seemed to emanate from walls and ceiling, was plunged in absolute darkness, and there were loud peals of hellish laughter.

The spell which had hitherto kept Welchman glued to his seat broke, he sprang up in terror and made in the direction he believed the door to be. Luck favoured him. He found the door, and groping his way across the hall found his way out of the house, too. The moment he stepped out into the night, the house lit up, and he heard again tap-dancing, tap-dancing crossing the hall after him. Then, as pushing his motor bike, he stumbled forward in the blinding rain and darkness, he caught the sounds of mocking girlish laughter, hellish laughter.

When, next day, at the inn in Stow-on-the-Wold, where he was staying till his machine was mended, he casually asked the landlord if he knew anything about the empty old house of his midnight adventure, the landlord said: "Oh, that house! The people round here declare it to be haunted; not that I believe in ghosts myself. They are just imagination."

"You think so, do you?" Welchman observed quietly. "Is there any story associated with the house?"

"Why, yes," the landlord said. "There is a sad story associated with it. I often heard my old dad tell it. It happened when he was a boy. A young singer and composer, a foreigner of some kind, used to live in the house. He fell in love with the daughter of a titled man, who owned most of the property around here.

"It seems she led him on, just for fun, merely to pass the time, in the absence of better game, and when she found he was in earnest and actually wanted to marry her, she turned him down with scorn and told her father, who forbade him ever to enter the house again.

Well, he went home in a fury and out of pique, so it was said, married a girl, a tap-dancer on the Music Hall stage, who, like himself, was a foreigner. She had an old mother, and the three of them, she and her husband and her mother, lived in the house together. It was not a happy marriage, for the singer and his wife were continually quarrelling. He was always thinking of the girl who had turned him down, and she was rumoured to be carrying on with a wealthy farmer in the neighbourhood. The tragedy came when he was found one day, hanging to the railing of the hall gallery. He had committed suicide."

"What became of his wife?"

"She married the farmer, but what beats me is that all three of them, she, her old mother, and the singer, are said to haunt the house. There might be a reason for the singer haunting the place, as he put an end to himself, but why the other two? There doesn't seem any sense in it."

"Perhaps there is more reason for them to haunt the house than you imagine," Welchman said quietly, and he then, for the first time, narrated to the landlord his experience in the haunted house the previous evening.

THE CIGARETTE CASE

"A CIGARETTE, Loder?" I said, offering my case. For the moment Loder was not smoking; for long enough he had not been talking.

"Thanks," he replied, taking not only the cigarette, but the case also. The others went on talking; Loder became silent again; but I noticed that he kept my cigarette case in his hand, and looked at it from time to time with an interest that neither its design nor its costliness seemed to explain. Presently I caught his eye.

"A pretty case," he remarked, putting it down on the table. "I once had one exactly like it."

I answered that they were in every shop window.

"Oh yes," he said, putting aside any question of rarity ... "I lost mine."

"Oh ... ?"

He laughed. "Oh, that's all right—I got it back again—don't be afraid I'm going to claim yours. But the way I lost it—found it—the whole thing—was rather curious. I've never been able to explain it. I wonder if you could?"

I answered that I certainly couldn't till I'd heard it, whereupon Loder, taking up the silver case again and holding it in his hand as he talked, began:

"This happened in Provence, when I was about as old as Marsham there—and every bit as romantic. I was there with Carroll—you remember poor old Carroll and what a blade of a boy he was—as romantic as four Marshams rolled into one. (Excuse me, Marsham, won't you? It's a romantic tale, you see, or at least the setting is.) ... We were in Provence, Carroll and I; twenty-four or thereabouts; romantic, as I say; and—and this happened.

"And it happened on the top of a whole lot of other things, you must understand, the things that do happen when you're twenty four. If it hadn't been Provence, it would have been somewhere else, I suppose, nearly, if not quite as good; but this was Provence, that smells (as you might say) of twenty-four as it smells of argelasse and wild lavender and broom....

"We'd had the dickens of a walk of it, just with knapsacks—had started somewhere in the Ardèche and I tramped south through the vines and almonds and olives—Montélimar, Orange, Avignon, and a fortnight at that blanched skeleton of a town, Les Baux. We'd nothing to do, and had gone just where we liked, or rather just where Carroll had liked; and Carroll had had the *De Bello Gallico* in his pocket, and had had a notion, I fancy, of taking in the whole ground of the Roman conquest—I remember he lugged me off to some place or other, Pourrières I believe its name was, because—I forget how many thousands—were killed in a river-bed there, and they stove in the water-casks so that if the men wanted water they'd have to go forward and fight for it. And then we'd gone on to Arles, where Carroll had fallen in love with everything that had a bow of black velvet in her hair, and after that Tarascon, Nimes, and so on, the usual round—I won't bother you with that. In a word, we'd had two months of it, eating almonds and apricots from the trees, watching the women at the communal washing-fountains under the dark plane-trees, singing *Magali* and the *Qué Contes*, and Carroll yarning away all the time about Caesar and Vercingetorix and Dante, and trying to learn Provençal so that he could read the stuff in the *Journal des Félibriges* that he'd never have looked at if it had been in English....

"Well, we got to Darbisson. We'd run across some young chap or other—Rangon his name was—who was a vine-planter in those parts, and Rangon had asked us to spend a couple of days with him, with him and his mother, if we happened to be in the neighbourhood. So as we might as well happen to be there as anywhere else, we sent him a postcard and went. This would be in June or early in July. All day we walked across a plain of vines, past hurdles of wattled *cannes* and great wind-screens of velvety cypresses, sixty feet high, all white with dust on the north side of 'em, for the mistral was having its three-days' revel, and it whistled and roared through the *cannes* till scores of yards of 'em at a time were bowed nearly to the earth. A roaring day it was, I remember.... But the wind fell a little late in the afternoon, and we were poring over what it had left of our Ordnance Survey—like fools, we'd got the unmounted paper maps instead of the linen ones—when Rangon himself found us, coming out to meet us in a very badly turned-out trap. He drove us back himself, through Darbisson, to the house, a mile and a half beyond it, where he lived with his mother.

"He spoke no English, Rangon didn't, though, of course, both French and Provençal; and as he drove us, there was Carroll, using him as a Franco-Provençal dictionary, peppering him with questions about the names of things in the patois—I beg its pardon, the language—though there's a good deal of my eye and Betty Martin about that, and I fancy this Félibrige business will be in a good many places when Frédéric Mistral is under that Court-of-Love pavilion arrangement he's had put up for himself in the graveyard at Maillanne. If the language has got to go, well, it's got to go, I suppose; and while I personally don't want to give it a kick, I rather sympathise with the Government. Those jaunts of a Sunday out to Les Baux, for instance, with paper lanterns and Bengal fire and a fellow spouting *O blanche Venus d'Arles*—they're well enough, and compare favourably with our Bank Holidays and Sunday League picnics, but ... but that's nothing to do with my tale after all. ... So he drove on, and by the time we got to Rangon's house Carroll had learned the greater part of *Magali*. ...

"As you, no doubt, know, it's a restricted sort of life in some respects that a young *vigneron* lives in those parts, and it was as we reached the house that Rangon remembered something—or he might have been trying to tell us as we came along for all I know, and not been able to get a word in edgeways for Carroll and his Provençal. It seemed that his mother was away from home for some days—apologies of the most profound, of course; our host was the soul of courtesy, though he did try to get at us a bit later. ... We expressed our polite regrets, naturally; but I didn't quite see at first what difference it made. I only began to see when Rangon, with more apologies, told us that we should have to go back to Darbisson for dinner. It appeared that when Madame Rangon went away for a few days she dispersed the whole of the female side of her establishment also, and she'd left her son with nobody to look after him except an old man we'd seen in the yard mending one of these double-cylindered sulphur-sprinklers they clap across the horse's back and drive between the rows of vines. ... Rangon explained all this as we stood in the hall drinking an apéritif—a hall crowded with oak furniture and photographs and a cradle-like bread-crib and doors opening to right and left to the other rooms of the ground floor. He had also, it seemed, to ask us to be so infinitely obliging as to excuse him for one hour after dinner—our postcard had come unexpectedly, he said, and already he had made an appointment with his agent about the *vendange* for the coming autumn. ... We begged him, of course, not to allow us to interfere with his business in the slightest degree. He thanked us a thousand times.

" 'But though we dine in the village, we will take our own wine with us,' he said, 'a wine *surfin*—one of my wines—you shall see—'

"Then he showed us round his place—I forget how many hundreds of acres of vines, and into the great building with the presses and pumps and casks and the huge barrel they call the thunderbolt—and about seven o'clock we walked back to Darbisson to dinner, carrying our wine with us. I think the restaurant we dined in was the only one in the place, and our gaillard of a host—he was a straight-backed, well-set-up chap, with rather fine eyes—did us on the whole pretty well. His wine certainly was good stuff, and set our tongues going....

"A moment ago I said a fellow like Rangon leads a restricted sort of life in those parts. I saw this more clearly as dinner went on. We dined by an open window, from which we could see the stream with the planks across it where the women washed clothes during the day and assembled in the evening for gossip. There were a dozen or so of them there as we dined, laughing and chatting in low tones—they all seemed pretty—it was quickly falling dusk—all the girls are pretty then, and are quite conscious of it—*you* know, Marsham. Behind them, at the end of the street, one of these great cypress windscreens showed black against the sky, a ragged edge something like the line the needle draws on a rainfall chart; and you could only tell whether they were men or women under the plantains by their voices rippling and chattering and suddenly a deeper note.... Once I heard a muffled scuffle and a sound like a kiss.... It was then that Rangon's little trouble came out....

"It seemed that he didn't know any girls—wasn't allowed to know any girls. The girls of the village were pretty enough, but you see how it was—he'd a position to keep up—appearances to maintain—couldn't be familiar during the year with the girls who gathered his grapes for him in the autumn.... And as soon as Carroll gave him a chance, *he* began to ask *us* questions, about England, English girls, the liberty they had, and so on.

"Of course, we couldn't tell him much he hadn't heard already, but that made no difference; he could stand any amount of that, our strapping young *vigneron;* and he asked us questions by the dozen, that we both tried to answer at once. And his delight and envy! ... What! In England did the young men see the young women of their own class without restraint—the sisters of their friends *même*—even at the house? Was it permitted that they drank tea with them in the afternoon, or went without invitations to pass the *soirée*?.... He had all the later Prévosts in his room, he told us (I don't doubt he had the earlier ones also); Prévost and the Disestablishment between them must be playing the mischief with the convent system of education for young girls; and our young man was—what d'you call it?—'Co-ed' co-educationalist—by Jove, yes! ... He seemed to marvel that we should have left a country so blessed as England to visit his dusty, wild-lavender-smelling, girl-less Provence.... You don't know half your luck, Marsham....

"Well, we talked after this fashion—we'd left the dining-room of the restaurant and had planted ourselves on a bench outside with

Rangon between us—when Rangon suddenly looked at his watch and said it was time he was off to see this agent of his. Would we take a walk, he asked us, and meet him again there? he said.... But as his agent lived in the direction of his own home, we said we'd meet him at the house in an hour or so. Off he went, envying every Englishman who stepped, I don't doubt.... I told you how old—how young—we were.... Heigho! ...

"Well, off goes Rangon, and Carroll and I got up, stretched ourselves, and took a walk. We walked a mile or so, until it began to get pretty dark, and then turned; and it was as we came into the blackness of one of these cypress hedges that the thing I'm telling you of happened. The hedge took a sharp turn at that point; as we came round the angle we saw a couple of women's figures hardly more than twenty yards ahead—don't know how they got there so suddenly, I'm sure; and that same moment I found my foot on something small and white and glimmering on the grass.

"I picked it up. It was a handkerchief—a woman's—embroidered—

"The two figures ahead of us were walking in our direction; there was every probability that the handkerchief belonged to one of them; so we stepped out....

"At my 'Pardon, madame,' and lifted hat one of the figures turned her head; then, to my surprise, she spoke in English—cultivated English. I held out the handkerchief. It belonged to the elder lady of the two, the one who had spoken, a very gentle-voiced old lady, older by very many years than her companion. She took the handkerchief and thanked me....

"Somebody—Sterne, isn't it?—says that Englishmen don't travel to see Englishmen. I don't know whether he'd stand to that in the case of English-women; Carroll and I didn't.... We were walking rather slowly along, four abreast across the road; we asked permission to introduce ourselves, did so, and received some name in return which, strangely enough, I've entirely forgotten—I only remember that the ladies were aunt and niece, and lived at Darbisson. They shook their heads when I mentioned Mr. Rangon's name and said we were visiting him. They didn't know him....

"I'd never been in Darbisson before, and I haven't been since, so I don't know the map of the village very well. But the place isn't very big, and the house at which we stopped in twenty minutes or so is probably there yet. It had a large double door—a double door in two senses, for it was a big *porte-cochère* with a smaller door inside it, and an iron grille shutting in the whole. The gentle-voiced old lady had already taken a key from her reticule and was thanking us again for the little service of the handkerchief; then, with the little gesture one makes when one has found oneself on the point of omitting a courtesy, she gave a little musical laugh.

"'But,' she said with a little movement of invitation, 'one sees so few compatriots here—if you have the time to come in and smoke a cigarette ... also the cigarette,' she added, with another rippling laugh, 'for we have few callers, and live alone—'

"Hastily as I was about to accept, Carroll was before me, professing a nostalgia for the sound of the English tongue that made his recent protestations about Provençal a shameless hypocrisy. Persuasive young rascal, Carroll was—poor chap.... So the elder lady opened the grille and the wooden door beyond it, and we entered.

"By the light of the candle which the younger lady took from a bracket just within the door we saw that we were in a handsome hall or vestibule; and my wonder that Rangon had made no mention of what was apparently a considerable establishment was increased by the fact that its tenants must be known to be English and could be seen to be entirely charming. I couldn't understand it, and I'm afraid hypotheses rushed into my head that cast doubts on the Rangons—you know—whether *they* were all right. We knew nothing about our young planter, you see....

"I looked about me. There were tubs here and there against the walls, gaily painted, with glossy-leaved aloes and palms in them—one of the aloes, I remember, was flowering; a little fountain in the middle made a tinkling noise; we put our caps on a carved and gilt console table; and before us rose a broad staircase with shallow steps of spotless stone and a beautiful wrought-iron hand-rail. At the top of the staircase were more palms and aloes, and double doors painted in a clear grey.

"We followed our hostesses up the staircase. I can hear yet the sharp clean click our boots made on that hard shiny stone—see the lights of the candle gleaming on the handrail.... The young girl—she was not much more than a girl—pushed at the doors, and we went in.

"The room we entered was all of a piece with the rest for rather old-fashioned fineness. It was large, lofty, beautifully kept. Carroll went round for Miss ... whatever her name was ... lighting candles in sconces; and as the flames crept up they glimmered on a beautifully polished floor, which was bare except for an Eastern rug here and there. The elder lady had sat down in a gilt chair, Louis Fourteenth I should say, with a striped rep of the colour of a petunia; and I really don't know—don't smile, Smith—what induced me to lead her to it by the finger-tips, bending over her hand for a moment as she sat down. There was an old tambour-frame behind her chair, I remember, and a vast oval mirror with clustered candle-brackets filled the greater part of the farther wall, the brightest and clearest glass I've ever seen...."

He paused, looking at my cigarette case, which he had taken into his hand again. He smiled at some recollection or other, and it was a minute or so before he continued.

"I must admit that I found it a little annoying, after what we'd been talking about at dinner an hour before, that Rangon wasn't with us. I still couldn't understand how he could have neighbours so charming without knowing about them, but I didn't care to insist on this to the old lady, who for all I knew might have her own reasons for keeping to herself. And, after all, it was our place to return Rangon's hospitality in London if he ever came there, not, so to speak, on his own doorstep.... So presently I forgot all about Rangon, and I'm pretty sure that Carroll, who was talking to his companion of some Félibrige junketing or other and having the air of Gounod's *Mireille* hummed softly over to him, didn't waste a thought on him either. Soon Carroll—you remember what a pretty crooning, humming voice he had—soon Carroll was murmuring what they call 'seconds', but so low that the sound hardly came across the room; and I came in with a soft bass note from time to time. No instrument, you know; just an unaccompanied murmur no louder than an Æolian harp; and it sounded infinitely sweet and plaintive and—what shall I say?—weak—attenuated—faint—'pale' you might almost say—in that formal, rather old-fashioned salon, with that great clear oval mirror throwing back the still flames of the candles in the sconces on the walls. Outside the wind had now fallen completely; all was very quiet; and suddenly, in a voice not much louder than a sigh, Carroll's companion was singing *Oft in the Stilly Night*—you know it...."

He broke off again to murmur the beginning of the air. Then, with a little laugh for which we saw no reason, he went on again:

"Well, I'm not going to try to convince you of such a special and delicate thing as the charm of that hour—it wasn't more than an hour—it would be all about an hour we stayed. Things like that just have to be said and left; you destroy them the moment you begin to insist on them; we've already one of us had experiences like that, and don't say much about them. I was as much in love with my old lady as Carroll evidently was with his young one—I can't tell you why—being in love has just to be taken for granted too, I suppose. ... Marsham understands.... We smoked our cigarettes, and sang again, once more filling that clear-painted, quiet apartment with a murmuring no louder than if a light breeze found that the bells of a bed of flowers were really bells and played on 'em. The old lady moved her fingers gently on the round table by the side of her chair . . . oh, infinitely pretty it was. . . . Then Carroll wandered off into the *Qué Contes*—awfully pretty—'It is not for myself I sing, but for my friend who is near to me'—and I can't tell you how like four old friends we were, those two so oddly met ladies and Carroll and myself. . . .

"But for all the sweetness and the glamour of it, we couldn't stay on indefinitely, and I wondered what time it was, but didn't ask—anything to do with clocks and watches would have seemed a cold and mechanical sort of thing just then. . . . And when presently we both got up neither Carroll nor I asked to be allowed to call again in the morning to thank them for a charming hour. . . . And they seemed to feel the same as we did about it. There was no 'hoping that we should meet again in London'—neither an au revoir nor a good-bye—just a tacit understanding that the hour should remain isolated, accepted like a good gift without looking the gift-horse in the mouth, single, unattached to any hours before or after—I don't know whether you see what I mean. . . . Give me a match, somebody. . . .

"And so we left, with no more than looks exchanged and finger-tips resting between the back of our hands and our lips for a moment. We found our way out by ourselves, down that shallow-stepped staircase with the handsome handrail, and let ourselves out of the double door and grille, closing it softly. We made for the village without speaking a word. . . . Heigho . . . !"

Loder had picked up the cigarette case again, but for all the way his eyes rested on it I doubt whether he really saw it. I'm pretty sure he didn't; I knew when he did by the glance he shot at me, as much as to say "I see you're wondering where the cigarette case comes in." . . . He resumed with another little laugh.

"Well," he continued, "we got back to Rangon's house. I really don't blame Rangon for the way he took it when we told him, you know—he thought we were pulling his leg, of course, and he wasn't having any; not he! There were no English ladies in Darbisson, he said. . . . We told him as nearly as we could just where the house was—we weren't very precise, I'm afraid, for the village had been in darkness as we had come through it, and I had to admit that the cypress hedge I tried to describe where we'd met our friends was a good deal like other cypress hedges—and, as I say, Rangon wasn't taking any. I myself was rather annoyed that he should think we were returning his hospitality by trying to get at him, and it wasn't very easy either to explain in my French and Carroll's Provençal that we were going to let the thing stand as it was and weren't going to call on our charming friends again. . . . The end of it was that Rangon just laughed and yawned. . . .

" 'I knew it was good, my wine,' he said, 'but—' a shrug said the rest. 'Not so good as all that,' he meant....

"Then he gave us our candles, showed us to our rooms, shook hands, and marched off to his own room and the Prévosts.

"I dreamed of my old lady half the night.

"After coffee the next morning I had put my hand into my pocket for my cigarette case and didn't find it. I went through all my pockets, and then I asked Carroll if he'd got it.

" 'No,' he replied.... 'Think you left it behind at that place last night?'

" 'Yes; did you?' Rangon popped in with a twinkle.

"I went through all my pockets again. No cigarette case....

"Of course, it was possible that I'd left it behind, and I was annoyed again. I didn't want to go back, you see.... But, on the other hand, I didn't want to lose the case—it was a present—and Rangon's smile nettled me a good deal, too. It was both a challenge to our truthfulness and a testimonial to that very good wine of his....

" 'Might have done,' I grunted.... 'Well, in that case we'll go and get it.'

" 'If one tried the restaurant first—?' Rangon suggested, smiling again.

" 'By all means,' said I stuffily, though I remembered having the case after we'd left the restaurant.

"We were round at the restaurant by half-past nine. The case wasn't there. I'd known jolly well beforehand it wasn't, and I saw Rangon's mouth twitching with amusement.

" 'So we now seek the abode of these English ladies, *hein*?' he said.

" 'Yes,' said I; and we left the restaurant and strode through the village by the way we'd taken the evening before....

"That *vigneron's* smile became more and more irritating to me.. . 'It is then the *next* village?' he said presently, as we left the last house and came out into the open plain.

"We went back....

"I was irritated because we were two to one, you see, and Carroll backed me up. 'A double door, with a grille in front of it,' he repeated for the fiftieth time.... Rangon merely replied that it wasn't our good faith he doubted. He didn't actually use the word 'drunk'....

" '*Mais tiens,*' he said suddenly, trying to conceal his mirth. '*Si c'est possible ... si c'est possible ...* a double door with a grille? But perhaps that I know it, the domicile of these so elusive ladies.... Come this way.'

"He took us back along a plantain-groved street, and suddenly turned up an alley that was little more than two gutters and a crack of sky overhead between two broken-tiled roofs. It was a dilapidated deserted *nuelle,* and I was positively angry when Rangon pointed to a blistered old *porte-cochère* with a half-unhinged railing in front of it.

"'Is it that, your house?' he asked.

"'No,' says I, and 'No,' says Carroll ... and off we started again....

"But another half-hour brought us back to the same place, and Carroll scratched his head.

"'Who lives there, anyway?' he said, glowering at the *porte-cochère,* chin forward, hands in pockets.

"'Nobody,' says Rangon, as much as to say 'look at it!' 'M'sieu then meditates taking it ... ?'

'Then I struck in, quite out of temper by this time.

"'How much would the rent be?' I asked, as if I really thought of taking the place just to get back at him.

"He mentioned something ridiculously small in the way of francs.

"'One might at least see the place,' says I. 'Can the key be got?'

"He bowed. The key was at the baker's, not a hundred yards away, he said....

"We got the key. It was the key of the inner wooden door—that grid of rusty iron didn't need one—it came clean off its single hinge when Carroll touched it. Carroll opened, and we stood for a moment motioning to one another to step in. Then Rangon went in first, and I heard him murmur 'Pardon, Mesdames'....

"Now this is the odd part. We passed into a sort of vestibule or hall, with a burst lead pipe in the middle of a dry tank in the centre of it. There was a broad staircase rising in front of us to the first floor, and double doors just seen in the half-light at the head of the stairs. Old tubs stood against the walls, but the palms and aloes in them were dead—only a cabbage-stalk or two—and the rusty hoops lay on the ground about them. One tub had come to pieces entirely and was no more than a heap of staves on a pile of spilt earth. And everywhere, everywhere was dust—the floor was an inch deep in dust and old plaster that muffled our footsteps, cobwebs hung like old dusters on the walls, a regular goblin's tatter of cobwebs draped the little bracket inside the door, and the wrought-iron of the hand-rail was closed up with webs in which not even a spider moved. The whole thing was preposterous....

"'It is possible that for even a less rental—' Rangon murmured, dragging his forefinger across the hand-rail and leaving an inch-deep furrow.

"'Come upstairs,' said I suddenly....

"Up we went. All was in the same state there. A clutter of stuff came down as I pushed at the double doors of the *salon*, and I had to strike a stinking French sulphur match to see into the room at all. Underfoot was like walking on thicknesses of flannel, and except where we put our feet the place was as printless as a snowfield—dust, dust, unbroken grey dust. My match burned down....

"'Wait a minute—I've a *bougie*,' said Carroll, and struck the wax match....

"There were the old sconces, with never a candle-end in them. There was the large oval mirror, but hardly reflecting Carroll's match for the dust on it. And the broken chairs were there, all giltless, and the rickety old round table....

"But suddenly I darted forward. Something new and bright on the table twinkled with the light of Carroll's match. The match went out, and by the time Carroll had lighted another I had stopped. I wanted Rangon to see what was on the table....

"'You'll see by my footprints how far from that table *I've* been." I said. "Will you pick it up?'

"And Rangon, stepping forward, picked up from the middle of the table—my cigarette case."

Loder had finished. Nobody spoke. For quite a minute nobody spoke, and then Loder himself broke the silence, turning to me.

"Make anything of it?" he said.

I lifted my eyebrows. "Only your *vigneron's* expression—" I began, but stopped again. seeing that wouldn't do.

"*Any*body make anything of it?" said Loder, turning from one to another.

I gathered from Smith's face that he thought *one* thing might be made of it—namely, that Loder had invented the whole tale. But even Smith didn't speak.

"Were any English ladies ever found to have lived in the place—murdered, you know—bodies found and all that?" young Marsham asked diffidently, yearning for an obvious completeness.

"Not that we could ever learn," Loder replied. "We made inquiries too.... So you all give it up? Well, so do I...."

And he rose. As he walked to the door, myself following him to get his hat and stick,, I heard him humming softly the lines—they are from *Oft in the Stilly Night*—

"I seem like one who treads alone
Some banquet-hall deserted,
Whose guests are fled, whose garlands dead,
And all but he—departed!"

THOMAS BURKE

THE LONELY INN

THE tall man on the lawn outside the cottage gave the cottage a long look and nodded at it. "Seems to be a perfect week-end cottage. Just big enough for us and easy to run. Ought to have some good week-ends here."

The man with him agreed. "Yes. Hasn't got everything but almost everything. Good view from the lawn. Stream over there. Woods on the left. Even the house-agent must have strained his Arabian vocabulary in listing it."

"Yes. Village quite interesting, too. People seem a bit surly, though."

"You must give country people time. We've only been here two hours, remember. Maybe the soil's got something to do with it. Certain soils make cheerful people; others make taciturn people, or hot-tempered people."

Their wives appeared at the cottage door. "Why don't you boys go and explore a bit? There's nothing to do in here. The maid's left everything. We've only got to heat the soup. Dinner'll be eightish."

The tall man said, "Right." And then to the other—"What about it, Mac? Shall we stroll and see if we can find the local?"

Mac nodded, and they went through the gate into the lane. To the right lay the village, a mile away. They had seen it an hour ago. They turned to the left. The lane here was little more than a grass-track. By its width it appeared to have been at one time a road, but now its surface was rough grass corrugated with wheel-tracks. The grass in the ditches on either side was of somewhat stronger hue.

It was a winding lane, and at no point did it disclose more than a hundred yards of itself. The hedges stood high, and afforded no view of the surrounding country. "Almost like a shrubbery," the tall man said. "Wonder where it leads to eventually, and whether we've got to come back the same way." They followed its bends for some minutes, and then the tall man said "Ha!" explosively. And then: "The oasis. I see a sign. Let's hope it isn't a desert mirage. But I'm sure I saw a sign, just over the hedge-top." At the next turn he gave his friend a facetious pat. "There we are! Thought I wasn't mistaken. As we're in Derbyshire they ought to have some of the real Derbyshire ale. Step out, my lad."

The inn's exterior was somewhat weather-beaten; almost univiting; but it was an inn. It had known no paint for some years, and its door and windows had a bedraggled aspect. The door and its stone front bore brown and black patches. It showed a faded sign of "The White Cockade."

The two men paused. The tall and talkative man said, "H'm. Hardly one of the picture-postcard inns But that's no fair test. All its good points may be inside. I've found several like that. Anyway, it's the only one, so..."

They went in. They found the inside no compensation of the outside. They entered a dim and silent tap-room. It contained the usual fixtures of a wayside public-house—old wooden benches, old wooden trestle-tables, an old and wide fireplace with the ashes of the last fire of winter, and an old and strong smell. Nothing in the place was grey in colour; yet it offered a general feeling of greyness. The landlord, standing listlessly behind the stained bar, was a man of heavy features and sunless eyes. The very type of man who ought not to keep an inn. His physical appearance accounted for, if it did not explain, the air of lost-heart and letting-things-go which hung over everything. One light, a shaded lamp, lit a small pool about the bar. The rest of the room was a muslin of shadow which gave common objects an uncommon shape.

They ordered their drink, and the landlord served them without "Good Evening" or other word. The beer was good. They drank, and looked about them. It was then, when their eyes, fresh from the bright evening, had become adjusted to the half-light, that they noted a slight stir among the shadow. Looking more closely, they saw that the room, which they thought was empty, held company. Some half-dozen dim figures sat along the benches and on chairs. No two sat together. They sat at intervals, each self-enclosed. they were men of ordinary appearance, in soiled or ragged clothes of miscellaneous quality and style; but their silence and their attitudes made them extraordinary.

The horrific figures evoked by the lobster nightmare or the unchaining drug cannot so freeze the human mind as the sight of the ordinary creature in the extraordinary attitude or state. DeQuincey's picture of the fat man of Keswick sitting alone on his lawn in shirtsleeves on a bitter March midnight brings more of the authentic recoil than any of his laudanum visions.

And so these dumb and solitary figures affected the two visitors more than any scene of ugliness or violence. Something in their peculiar arrangement suggested that they were sitting like that with some reason. It was as though they had placed themselves like actors on a stage, awaiting the rise of the curtain. The silence of the place, which was underlined by the intermittent drip-drip of the beer-tap, also had an effect, and when the talkative visitor wanted to say something he found himself muttering.

He touched his friend. "Queer place, Mac." The other nodded. "Must be a side-entrance somewhere, I guess."

"Why?"

"Well, I didn't see anybody come in, but a minute ago I'd have said there were four people in the far corner."

"So there were."

"Well, there's six now. And there were two just behind us."

"Yes."

"There's three now."

Mac looked about him, and found that his friend was right. He found, too, that the company, without moving, was exchanging signals. He saw a head nod, and then another head respond to it. He caught his friend's eye, and together they watched the invisible message pass visibly along the room in nods. It was as though a row of Victorian mantelpiece images had been set in motion. All these people, it seemed, knew each other; yet sat apart holding no communication beyond nods.

He brought his earthenware mug sharply to the counter. He expected it to make in that silence a startling report, and had made the motion deliberately in the hope of bringing a touch of life to the room. But somehow, possibly by the shape of the room, it made only a faint noise, and the company ignored it. His friend turned to him: "Wonder if there's a deaf-and-dumb institute near here. And if this is Founder's Day." He looked at the landlord. "Customers not very talkative," he said. The landlord continued to stare at nothing. He looked at Mac, and they exchanged a smile.

It was while he was taking a cigarette from the packet held by Mac that he became aware that the silence was being very gently troubled. At first he thought it was the swishing of a curtain. Then he knew that it was a whisper. A whisper was passing along the benches and chairs, and once or twice he caught its burden. *That's him. That's him.* He saw that Mac had heard it, too, and as they turned and looked at the benches they found the dilapidated faces of the company fixed on them. It seemed to him, as he turned, that they were fixed on him, but with the next glance he saw that they were all looking beyond him, at Mac. The moment they saw that they were observed, the faces dropped, and each man resumed his former pose of looking at his knees.

Mac picked up his mug and finished it. "Fit?" His friend nodded.

They stepped out of twilight into orange sunset and scented fields and limpid light. They took some six paces from the inn; then the tall one stopped and said, expressively: *"Gawd!"* He took three deep breaths. Then: "I'd like to show that place to some of those literary blokes who write about the old village inn, and the mellow company, and the rich rustic voices, and Uncle Tom Cobleigh and all."

Mac agreed. "Still, we can't have everything. The cottage is about perfect, so we shall have to put up with the local. But what a hole. And not merely dull and dingy. Something more than that about it. We must investigate again. A place like that in this gorgeous country must have a reason for being what it is. Some story behind it. And why were they so interested in me?"

"Lord knows. Don't look as though they could be interested in *anything*—let alone an everyday specimen like you. Perhaps they'd seen you in the village, though, and were thinking of giving you the village greeting—'arf a brick."

"Huh. . . . Well, I've found some queer pubs in my ups-and-downs of England, but that's the queerest so far."

The next day, Saturday, they spent in a motor-run of exploration, and got back to the cottage between six and seven. After a little pottering, Mac said, "Coming down to the lousy local?"

"Not this evening, I think. I've got about four or five letters I want to answer, so's to have to-morrow free. You go."

"Right. I'd like to have another look at it. Something about it fascinates me. It had the feeling of something going to happen."

"Don't be long, though. I've got an appetite. Don't want to have to wait dinner."

"Needn't worry. I've got one, too. I'll be on time."

Mac stepped out of the door as the other settled himself at a table. As he passed the open window he heard his friend call, "What's the date?" He answered, "April thirty," and swung down the lane.

And dinner was late. They waited until twenty to nine, and then, as Mac had not returned, they waited no longer. "I suppose he's managed to get the deaf-and-dumb school talking, and can't tear himself away. He'll have to have what's left, and have it half-cold. Ethel can't go down and drag him out. Create a bad impression on our first week-end—wives pulling husbands out of pubs. 'Father, dear father, come home with me now.' "

Ethel was dealing with soup. "Oh, he'll turn up when it suits him. He's done it before. When he finds an interesting local, as he calls them, he forgets time."

But he did not turn up. They left the door unlocked until one o'clock; then, as he had not turned up, they went to bed. "If he turns up now he'll have to throw gravel at the window. Gone off on a binge, perhaps, with one of the deaf-and-dumbs, and staying the night. Probably turn up with a hang-over about church-time to-morrow."

But he did not turn up. He did not turn up at church-time or at any other time. The trio left at the cottage never saw their Mac again.

At about midday his friend went out to look about, and to enquire at the local and in the village. Just outside the gate he met the old man whom they had engaged to keep the garden tidy during the week.

"Morning. D'you happen to have seen anything of my friend?"

The man looked at him dully while the question sank in and wandered through his mind to pick up some association with "my friend".

"Your friend?"

"Yes; the man who came with me. You saw him yesterday."

"Ar—'im. What would he be like?"

"Stocky figure, Red hair. Horn-rimmed glasses."

"Oh ... 'im. No. I ain' seen 'im. I remember 'im. Scotty, I says to meself."

"Yes. He is a Scot. Well, he went out yesterday evening—down to the inn here—and was coming back in an hour. But he didn't come back last night. Nor this morning. I wondered whether you'd seen him or heard anything of him."

"No-o. I ain' seed 'im."

"I was just going down to the inn to ask if he'd been there. Thought perhaps you might have been there last night and seen him." He went into the lane and turned to the left. The man stopped him.

"This way, sir."

"No. This way. The inn's down here. Down the lane."

"You mean up the lane."

"I mean down the lane."

"You mean up the lane. The 'Green Man', just outside village."

"I don't. I mean down the lane." He pointed to the left.

The man stared at him. "Dinno of no public down there."

"No? I see you don't know your own country. Often happens that the stranger finds what the inhabitant misses." The man looked puzzled. He stroked the stubble of his chin. He seemed about to say something but didn't say it. He was dealing with a Londoner. Queer things, Londoners. Said what they didn't mean, and twisted words about, and called it wit. Played silly games called *pulling your leg*.

Sometimes they weren't quite right in the head. Zanies, some of 'em. This seemed to be one of that sort.

"I dinno of no—"

"Ah, but I do. I'm just going along there to ask if my friend called in last night. If you care to come along I'll show it to you. And you can sample the brew."

"I'll come along with ye, but—"

They went along. They went down the twisting lane. The gardener held his puzzled expression, but made no remark. They went along until they came to the elm, through whose branches the sign had been visible.

"Just at the next bend," the tall man said; and they made the next bend. Having made it he looked about him. "Funny. Must have been the *next* bend." They went on and followed the next bend, and this bend marked the end of the lane and its junction with a main road. The tall man now did some staring. "Well...." He looked back up the lane. "Can't have *passed* it, can we?"

"No, sir, we din pass it."

"I remember it as just this side of that elm." He took a few strides up the lane. "Yes. This side of the elm. Just opposite that gap in the hedge. I could have sworn that— And I'm certain we never left the lane. But if so, what the devil—"

The gardener watched him with blank expression. He appeared to have no interest in the proceedings. He was humouring a Londoner. The tall man turned to him. "Well, if it wasn't in the lane where was it? How did we lose ourselves? You—" Then something in the man's blank face arrested him.

"There bent no public in this lane. Nor anywheres 'bout 'ere. Nothing 'bout 'ere for four miles. Not till ye come to the Golden Lion. And that be along the road—four mile."

The tall man stared at him and then at the lane, and then shouted. "But man, we did come to a pub here. We did have drinks in it. In the lane. A dismal place."

The gardener looked sad and shook his head. With rustic civility, or polite contempt, he refrained from comment. He repeated only "Bent no public in this lane."

"But, man, I tell you—" He broke off. He realised that he could not insist on the fact of his pub, because nowhere in the lane was there any pub. There had been a pub, and now there wasn't a pub. He strode backwards and forwards. "What's happened here? What funny work's going on here? We can't both have been insane. We did come to a pub here, and we did have drinks. What do you make of it?"

The old man stared at the horizon. "If there'd been a public 'ere

I'd 'a known it. I come down 'ere twice a week. Never no public 'ere in my time. Nor in me faather's time. But I do remember me granfer telling me that 'is granfer told 'im there were a public down 'ere."

"What!"

"There *were* a public down 'ere. I do remember me granfer telling me that 'is granfer told 'im it were burnt down. It were mixed up in sommin' in 'istry. Nigh on two unnerd year ago. I dinno the rights of it, but 'e did say sommin' 'bout some kind of war. And a lot o' Scotties come 'ere. And one of 'em sold the others. And the people set fire to the place, and they was all burnt. 'Cept the one that sold 'em. And 'im they cursed with their dying breaths."

RETURN AT DUSK

"YES," I heard Drummond saying with emphasis, "for the rest of my life I shall endeavour to avoid looking into a mirror at twilight."

For a moment there was dead silence in the Common Room. We were all gazing at Drummond with surprise. That our Professor of Anthropology should be afraid of looking into a mirror at twilight seemed too absurd to be believed. And I well remember my own confused medley of thoughts in which I found myself trying to reconcile Drummond (six feet two in his socks, broad in proportion, and of noted physical courage) with a mirror and some strange masculine version of the Lady of Shalott.

Drummond must have noticed the silence. He turned round, apologetically. "But it's true," he continued, in a quieter voice; and this time speaking to all of us. "A mirror at twilight worries me. I never know what I may see in it."

"Something to do with Black Magic and your African adventures?" asked MacEwen, peering over his spectacles with excited eyes, and hoping for another of the astonishing (but well vouched-for) adventures which Drummond had experienced in his African field-work.

"No," came the unexpected answer. "Something to do with history and with a place only about a hundred miles distant from this room."

MacEwen leaned back, disappointed. But the rest of us leaned forward.

"Out with it," ordered Forrester bluntly. "You've said both too much and too little to escape saying more."

"Well, here it is then," answered Drummond, "though for reasons which you will soon appreciate you must forgive me if I change the names of persons and places."

"As you know, I was in Africa when the war broke out. The news, when it reached me, was about a fortnight old, and I promptly trekked south to join the nearest regiment I could find. It seemed the simplest thing to do. But I might just as well have made for the coast and a boat home, for, within a week of becoming a private in the South African Rifles, I was suddenly summoned to Headquarters and there told to pack my traps forthwith. Apparently some anxious G.S.O. in the War Office had sent out a 'Search all Africa' order, with the rider that as soon as I had been found I was to be returned to London with all possible speed.

"Well, to cut a long story short, I was flown to Cairo and two days later I was reporting to that selfsame anxious G.S.O. in his own doubly-guarded room in Whitehall. It was simply the old 1914–18 game once more. I was to take charge of one of the special sections devoted to counter-espionage.

"But don't jump to conclusions. What I am going to tell you has nothing to do with enemy agents. All this is simply to explain how, for some six months in the winter of 1939–40, a small group of us came to be located in such an out-of-the-way place as Cairntoul Castle in Mar. We were sent there by the War Office, that's all. Probably the choosing of Cairntoul was part of some deep-laid plan —camouflage, or what-not—I don't know. Certainly all the arrangements must have been made long before Hitler marched into Poland. The castle might be out-of-the-way, but, when we arrived there to take over, we found we were very much in touch with London and with the other sections doing similar work, and I need hardly say that our powerful transmitting and receiving set, with its aerial cunningly concealed in the old dovecot, was not installed overnight.

"In addition to our two wireless engineers, two batmen-clerks (working in that dual capacity), and one cook, there were eight of us in the section. But the unlucky number thirteen was avoided by the presence of Mrs. Lumsdaine, the old caretaker or retainer—probably an octogenarian—whom the War Office had taken over with the castle, though not, I expect, without full investigation into her character and into the characters of her forebears back to the ninth generation or more. The old lady was certainly sound enough, but whoever had had the task of taking over the castle must have found her a handful. Yet 'Mother Lum' (as we called her) kept pretty much out of our way. I could feel that she resented our intrusion into 'her' castle. To get more than two words out of her was like drawing water from a stone; but to get a cold searching look whenever our ways met was as common as porridge for breakfast on a Highland croft.

"Actually, as I was to discover later, the old lady's attachment to Cairntoul was simply part of that old loyalty so characteristic of the Highlands. *We* were aliens, but *she* had been born into the service of the castle, just as her parents and their parents before them had been born into the same service and had served and died there. In earlier days, indeed, the castle must often have seen such loyal life-long service, and, earlier still, service of a different kind when loyalty to the House probably meant dying in its defence, and dying long before the attainment of old age. The very stones emphasised that. The place was more than a castle, it was a 'strength'. Its massive structure was built in the shape of an L with the doorway in the re-entrant angle where it could be effectively defended from both wings. The old outer wooden-door had been replaced by a modern one, but the inner 'iron yett' was still there. I can tell you, I wouldn't have liked the task of breaking in, for, even when the iron yett had gone, there was what we should now call a 'baffle wall' which put the defenders in the shadow, darkened the whole entrance, and made it impossible for more than one man at a time to gain the staircase which wound upwards immediately behind the wall. Again, the staircase itself was narrow—about thirty inches wide, I should say—and, being helical, was lit only at odd intervals, so that again the defenders could choose the shadows to contest its passage. And only by that staircase could one get into the castle at all. The stone stairs, worn with age, led direct to the first floor, to a corner of the 'Hall'—a long room, full thirty-five feet long, and probably fifteen feet wide—with another staircase at its further end leading down again to the ground floor and to the vaulted kitchens below that. In the chamber, in the shorter wing, adjoining the Hall, a newel staircase led to the second floor. Thus the main staircase had to be fought for and won, step by step, before the castle itself could be won. Altogether a thoroughly interesting old place, and one ideal for security, ancient or modern.

"The ground floor and the vaulted kitchens were wholly given over to the signallers, the two batmen-clerks, and the cook; though 'Mother Lum' had kept her own room on the ground floor, in the wing. The big Hall was our general workroom (with an overflow into the adjoining chamber), and our sleeping-quarters were upstairs on the second floor where, in the main wing, all the rooms led out of one another. In the shorter wing, however, there was one room only, larger than the rest, which had a second door leading outside to a kind of beacon-turret.

"That room in the wing, called the Turret Room, was at first mine; and being one who likes to know what there may be behind doors, or where doors may lead to, I had opened the second door almost as soon as I had crossed the threshold of the room. But the turret outside was empty (save for a dead bird), and, being corbelled, it was clearly impossible for anyone to reach it from the ground below, whilst even if the impossible were achieved, an iron grille which completely enclosed the turret-top would effectively prevent the climber from entering the turret and so gaining access to the room.

"All these ancient precautions, as I have said, were ideal for security; and, to remain inconspicuous, we had no sentry or armed guard of any kind. Nevertheless our signallers had fixed an electric contact to the iron yett (which it was our practice to keep shut), and a whole battery of bells rang throughout the building whenever that gate was opened. In addition, a further press-ball was hidden in the darkness of the 'baffle-wall' and, on this, whenever any one of us had entered by the iron yett he gave a series of rings (the number being changed each day) so that the whole battery of bells again informed us that only one of our own number was entering our 'strength'.

"For a month or so after our arrival at Cairntoul we were kept busy for a good sixteen hours out of every twenty-four. As a team we worked well together; and although nominally I was in charge, our work was essentially co operative. I need not add that first spell of intensive work was not without its reward.

"Then came two or three slightly less busy days, and for the first time I was able to arrange for each of us, singly, to get out on to the moors to stretch his legs or, if he liked, to laze in the yielding heather.

"My own turn came last, and for a whole afternoon I lay deep in the heather, dozing, and drawing in physical and mental rest. Returning to Cairntoul, in the gathering twilight, I passed a few words with the others, who were busy in the Hall, before climbing the further flight of stairs to my Turret Room. I was still in a happy mood of complete content, and, once in my room, I sat down on a chair, letting my mind absorb the quietness which seemed to be all around, bringing with it an air of peace so different from the work which we had just been doing and had still to do.

"I had sat down on the chair in front of the table which served as a dressing-chest and over which an old mirror was hanging on the wall. Behind me was the door leading to the beacon-turret. Now what made me look up into the mirror, I cannot say. But look up I did, and, as I looked into the mirror, I saw that the door to the turret was slowly opening. I watched that opening door like one fascinated, and, somehow, I could neither move nor cry out. Slowly the opening grew wider and wider. Then a face appeared, peering round the side of the door. In the mirror, the face seemed to look straight into mine, but in the twilight I could recognise no features —just the blur of a face, that, and no more. Then the face withdrew, and the door began slowly to close again, as slowly and as quietly as it had opened. It shut (though I could swear I heard no click of the latch), and, as soon as it had shut, the sense of powerlessness immediately left me. I felt suddenly and strangely released and, jumping up, I rushed towards the door. But, half-way, I stopped. Surely I had imagined it all. Probably my nerves had become too tightly stretched with that recent spell of intensive work. After all, one could dream by day as well as by night. Still, I'd better look into that beacon-turret, if only to satisfy myself. I took the few remaining steps, paused, and then quickly flung open the door. Nothing! This time not even a dead bird, for I had previously removed the one that had been there on my first arrival.

"Wisely, or unwisely, I said nothing about my 'visitor'. But exactly ten days later, when the whole incident was beginning to fade from my mind, I was rudely brought back to reality (or unreality), and again at twilight. Again I was sitting in front of my dressing-chest, and this time I was certainly *not* dreaming. Actually I was brushing my hair before dinner, my mind alive and alert with the details of a pretty problem that had cropped up during the course of the day's work. And, in the midst of that simple operation of brushing my hair, my hands suddenly dropped. With a start, I had noticed in the mirror that the door to the beacon-turret was again opening, and opening as slowly and as quietly as it had opened before. Again an inquiring head peered round the side of the door. But this time it did not withdraw. The door opened wider and wider. The head was followed by a body. There was a quick movement, and my 'visitor' had entered the room: and I remember noting that the door seemed to swing-to and shut by itself.

"Now, don't ask me what my 'visitor' looked like. I simply don't know. Partly the twilight was deepening into dusk, so that the light was poor; but mainly I seemed impelled to look only at the face which was reflected in my mirror. And that face, or perhaps I should say the eyes, held me as though I had been hypnotised. Never had I seen such concentrated hate before, and I hope I shall never see it again. As I have said, I seemed to be hypnotised, or, if you prefer it that way, I felt transfixed and powerless, just as I had felt before. Slowly, very slowly, almost as though I was to be taken by surprise, 'it' began to cross the intervening space, the eyes holding mine. That slow, deliberate closing-in was horrible. I was the victim of all the evil in the world which was now closing in for the kill. And I could do nothing. I felt a peculiar 'bristling' at the back of my neck—and I can assure you that 'hair-raising' is a phrase which is used too lightly and too often. It is not a pleasant sensation. Although I had been in many tight corners in my life, I think I may say that never before had I been terrified. But I was then. Unable to move, or even to cry out, my mind raced round and round the one question—what will it do when it reaches me? Probably everything took place in a matter of seconds, but to me the torment was protracted beyond the limits of endurance. Slowly that face approached behind me. Larger and larger in the mirror grew those awful eyes. Now I became convinced I could feel its breath upon me. A pair of hands seemed to reach out and close upon my neck. And . . . and all went black.

"I am told that when I was abominably late for dinner, one of the others came up from the Hall to remind me of the time. He knocked on the door of my room and, receiving no answer, looked in. Thereafter, for a brief space, there was some bustle and confusion in Cairntoul. But, as it was, it simply transpired that for the first time in my life I had fallen to the floor in a dead faint.

"When at last they had brought me round I made some kind of feeble excuse—overwork or liver, or perhaps a combination of the two. I suppose I felt too ashamed to confess that I had fainted before a ghost. For, ponder over it as I could, no other explanation seemed possible. No alarm bell had rung; no one could reach that beacon-turret from the ground; and, above all, there was the iron grille. I remember spending that night sitting and dozing in front of the fire in the Hall, unwilling to return to my room. By morning I had ashamedly come to the conclusion that I couldn't face that room again.

"As good luck would have it, however, that very morning brought the possibility of change. Just before lunch a coded message came through calling away one of my team on an urgent, but fortunately lengthy, task in Holland. It was a bit of a rush to get his papers ready and to get him to Aberdeen in time for the London express. But it took my mind from my visitor; also, and more important so far as I was concerned, it freed a room. Taking one of the batmen-clerks with me I moved all my possessions into that providentially-provided spare room—all my possessions but two. In my old room I left two heavy filing-cases, and those, with the batman's help, I dragged across the floor to barricade the door leading to the beacon-turret. If my visitor wasn't a ghost, and if someone knew a way of gaining access to the turret, then in future he would certainly find it impossible to enter Cairntoul itself without making a noise more than sufficient to warn all those on duty in the Hall. Perhaps I was still unwilling to admit that I had been terrified by a ghost. But, and again it was my pride, the moving of the cases enabled me to say that I was changing my room only because of the appalling draught that came from the turret-door, and that those two filing-cases would alleviate the draught for anyone who might have to use the room again.

"What my team really thought, or guessed, I don't know. But a chance meeting with Mother Lum a few days later seemed to reveal that there was a 'history' to Cairntoul not unconnected with the turret and with the Turret Room. Answering my 'Good morning' with an 'Aye, it's no bad the day', followed by a keen look from her grey eyes, the old body paused as though about to say more. That was unusual, and I waited expectantly. Then apparently she changed her mind, and with the tantalising remark, 'I'm hearing Black Dougal will be back then,' she went on her way. Who 'Black Dougal' was, she left to my imagination, and I knew it would be useless to question her. Doubtless she regarded 'Black Dougal' as her own—like Cairntoul itself—and, if he were a ghost, then she was unwilling to share her ghost with other intruders who were of the solid flesh. Not unnaturally I connected him with my visitor; and, from the way Mother Lum had spoken, I gathered that to the initiated he was by no means unknown.

"For a week or two nothing disturbed the even tenor of our way. Then, unexpectedly, came a message from the War Office to say that a Mr. Mowat was on his way to fill the vacancy in my team. And at once the problem arose—where should we sleep him? If I were to suggest his sharing a room with one of the others when my old room stood empty, then perforce I would have to tell my tale. In the end I decided to stick to the old excuse: the Turret Room was a poor room, frightfully draughty, with a 'howl' from the outside grille whenever the wind blew in a certain direction, and so forth and so on. But I had reckoned without our new recruit. When he arrived, alert and confident, nothing I could say would persuade him to 'double-up' with one of the others. There was an empty room. He had slept in far worse places than a room with a draught and a howl. He was insistent. I was halting. And, in the presence of the others, pride still kept me from the truth.

"Mowat went up to the empty room, while I made a mental reservation that I would tell him of my 'visitor' as soon as I could get him alone. But although, later, I was to see him alone more than once, by then my own story had paled before his own experience.

"He had arrived late in the afternoon, and again it was twilight. Stupidly, I had been so intent on persuading him not to take over the Turret Room that I had failed to connect both *time* and *place*. And only when there came a strangled cry from above, followed by a terrific crash and then a further crash, did I curse myself for forgetting that upon both occasions my 'visitor' had come with the dusk.

"We raced to the stair and to the Room. Bursting open the door, we found Mowat lying on the floor in front of the table, almost exactly as I had been found in my 'faint'. He was lying on his back, with his arms spread eagled; but it was his face that caused us to cry out. Even in the dim light we could see that it was suffused with blood, while his eyes seemed to be sightlessly staring at us with a look in which agony and terror were horribly combined.

"Sanderson, who had taken a medical degree, and who was our 'doctor', was quickly on his knees and moving professional hands over that still body. Feeling suddenly sick, I turned away, only to trip over a large file of papers, and then over a second file. Surprised, I looked round. The two heavy filing-cases with which I had blocked the door to the beacon-turret had been flung aside as if they had been empty cardboard boxes. One had fallen one way, one the other; the drawers had fallen open, and their contents were strewn about the floor. But the door to the beacon-turret was shut.

"Mowat, mercifully, was not dead, and that same night we got him into a nursing home at Aberdeen. But it was a full three months before he was out again, when, upon my own urgent recommendation, he was posted to Southampton and given the task of coping with the many problems raised by officers coming on leave or returning overseas. I had to think of some post where he would be kept too busy to remember Cairntoul; and the R.T.O.'s office at Southampton had always seemed to me to be about the busiest of its kind.

"But I am going much too fast. Long before Mowat was out of the nursing home it had become one of my major tasks to try to induce him to tell his tale. It was clear that if only he could unburden himself, his recovery, and particularly his recovery in mind, would not be long delayed. But the terror had bitten deep, and I daren't tell my own tale first, lest, instead of encouraging him, I should only increase the torture of his mind. At long last, however, I induced him to speak, and the tale, when it came, was much the same as mine. There was this difference, however—Mowat, terrified and powerless (even as I had felt powerless), had seen the face in the mirror; he had seen it slowly draw nearer (the hate in its eyes seeming to burn into his soul); he had felt the hands at his throat; and then, suddenly, those hands had tightened into a grip, powerful, relentless and *strangling*. With that he thought he gave a cry before unconsciousness intervened. 'But what was "it"?' he asked me. 'And how did "it" get in?'

"I had noticed his use of the word 'it'. So he also had doubted the nature of his visitor. But the only answer I could give him was to tell him of my own experience, to ask him to forgive me for allowing him to use the room, and, above all, to assure him that he had finished with Cairntoul for good.

"After that unburdening, Mowat recovered quickly, and, as I have said, he was posted direct to Southampton, far removed from the

Province of Mar. Meantime, at the castle, we sedulously avoided the Room, but also we took one positive action. We smashed that mirror to fragments and, having carefully collected the fragments, we threw them into an enormous fire, specially built-up for the occasion, where we watched them melt and fuse. Later we collected the shapeless glass nodules and, with the ashes, scattered them to the winds of heaven. Later still, I had one further brief passage with Mother Lum, but her pronouncement, far from being helpful, only increased the mystery.

"I had come back from visiting Mowat in Aberdeen. Meeting her outside the iron yett, I said cheerfully, 'Well, Mr. Mowat seems to be progressing famously now.'

"'Mowat, did ye say?' she cried with a wild look in her eyes. 'A Mowat is it? May heaven save him!' And with that she hobbled away.

"'Heaven has,' I muttered, somewhat irreverently, as I cast innumerable though silent maledictions on her retreating figure.

"And that, as you can see, took me no further.

"Then, early in June 1940, the War Office suddenly decided to disband my team. We left Cairntoul and, in the urgency of new tasks, the mystery of Black Dougal and the Turret Room gradually lost its hold and became a bad memory and little more.

"With the end of Hitler and the surrender of Japan, I returned here to the humdrum labours of my Anthropology Department; and yet it was here, in the academic peace of the University, that I learned what had previously been denied.

"I had been back perhaps a week or ten days when Henderson, of the History Department, asked me if I would give a lecture to his 'medieval' students. Naturally I agreed, and, during the course of the conversation, I happened to mention that I had been stationed for a while at Cairntoul in Mar.

"'Did you see the ghost of Black Dougal?' he asked.

"I pride myself that I didn't start.

"'Why?' I said. 'Is the castle haunted?'

"'It's supposed to be,' he answered cautiously, 'and with one of the best authenticated ghosts we have. There's quite a story behind it.'

"And, to conclude, the story I got from Henderson was roughly this:

"Some time about the middle of the sixteenth century, when the Mowats of Cairntoul and the local branch of the Camerons had been long at feud, an attempt was made to end the feud by a Mowat-Cameron marriage. So Mowat of Cairntoul married the daughter of Cameron, but, after a week or so, when the Camerons had gone home, Mowat brutally strangled his wife and then sent defiance to the Camerons.

"I should add that Mowat was supposed to be mad, but naturally the Camerons were paying no attention to that. They turned out to a man, and, Cairntoul being what I have already described to you, they were wiped out to a man, and narry a footing did they get on that staircase. Wiped out to a man, yes; but there was a young brother to the murdered bride—a boy, Dougal, then about six years old. And upon Dougal fell the whole burden of a new and a more bitter feud. As he grew up, the boy, and then the man, nursed his revenge—and so came the name 'Black Dougal', from the hate that burned in his eyes.

"But there was little chance for Black Dougal in the Mowat country, unless he went there by night; and by night the mad Mowat sat and laughed in the Turret Room where he had strangled his bride. Yet mightn't that give Black Dougal his chance? One night, in the gathering dusk, and the manner of it no one knows, Dougal made that impossible climb up the castle wall, right up to the beacon-turret, only to be beaten at the end by the overhang of the turret's corbelling. Struggling to breast the corbelling he fell—a sheer forty feet at least—and was killed outright.

"At that Mad Mowat only laughed the louder. But, within a week, he had caused an iron grille to be made to enclose the open turret at its top. Within another week he was found dead in the Room—strangled, as there he had strangled his bride."

"Why then should the ghost of Black Dougal still haunt Cairntoul?" asked one of us.

"Who can answer for a ghost?" was Drummond's reply.

"Yet a Mowat in the same room would be sure to bring him back," put in another, wisely.

"Perhaps," concluded Drummond. "That sounds a possible interpretation if you believe in ghosts."

"Do *I* believe in ghosts?" he continued after a pause. "I can't tell you. But I can assure you that never again will I look into a mirror at twilight. Yet have you wondered why a ghost should need to fling aside two heavy filing-cases in order to leave a room? That point is puzzling. I thought ghosts could pass such material objects with ease.

"And there is one further point which makes it all more puzzling still. I'm convinced that no one could climb that outer wall to the beacon-turret. Yet one of our signallers, an honest, sober, and thoroughly unimaginative fellow, had other views.

"It appears that about the time when we were rushing upstairs, after hearing Mowat's strangled cry and the crashes above, this signaller was walking back to the castle after making some adjustment to the aerial in the old dovecot. Happening to look up to the turret, he was astounded to see a man hanging there by his hands. Then, to his horror, the man dropped like a stone.

"For a second our signaller stood still. Then he ran forward as fast as he could. But, to his astonishment, the climber, who should have been killed outright, picked himself up, ran round the corner of the castle, and out into the open country beyond.

"With a shout (which, of course, in our own pre-occupation we didn't hear) the signaller went in pursuit. Doggedly, in the gathering darkness, he followed his man. Before long, he could see him only against the light in the sky. The man came to a small hill, breasted it, stood silhouetted for a moment on the top, and then disappeared down the other side. In turn our signaller breasted the hill but, when he came to the top, his quarry was nowhere to be seen.

"Admittedly it was dark; and admittedly a man might easily take cover in a fold of the ground. *But later I was to discover that the Cameron country started on the far side of that hill.*"

POSSESSIONS BY SPIRIT INFLUENCES

FOR THE BLOOD IS THE LIFE

We had dined at sunset on the broad roof of the old tower, because it was cooler there during the great heat of summer. Besides, the little kitchen was built at one corner of the great square platform, which made it more convenient than if the dishes had to be carried down the steep stone steps, broken in places and everywhere worn with age. The tower was one of those built all down the west coast of Calabria by the Emperor Charles V. early in the sixteenth century, to keep off the Barbary pirates, when the unbelievers were allied with Francis I. against the Emperor and the Church. They have gone to ruin, a few still stand intact, and mine is one of the largest. How it came into my possession ten years ago, and why I spend a part of each year in it, are matters which do not concern this tale. The tower stands in one of the loneliest spots in Southern Italy, at the extremity of a curving, rocky promontory, which forms a small but safe natural harbour at the southern extremity of the Gulf of Policastro, and just north of Cape Scalea, the birthplace of Judas Iscariot, according to the old local legend. The tower stands alone on this hooked spur of rock, and there is not a house to be seen within three miles of it. When I go there I take a couple of sailors, one of whom is a fair cook, and when I am away it is in charge of a gnome-like little being who was once a miner and who attached himself to me long ago.

My friend, who sometimes visits me in my summer solitude, is an artist by profession, a Scandinavian by birth, and a cosmopolitan by force of circumstances. We had dined at sunset; the sunset glow had reddened and faded again, and the evening purple steeped the vast chain of the mountains that embrace the deep gulf to eastward and rear themselves higher and higher towards the south. It was hot, and we sat at the landward corner of the platform, waiting for the night breeze to come down from the lower hills. The colour sank out of the air, there was a little interval of deep grey twilight, and a lamp sent a yellow streak from the open door of the kitchen, where the men were getting their supper.

Then the moon rose suddenly above the crest of the promontory, flooding the platform and lighting up every little spur of rock and knoll of grass below us, down to the edge of the motionless water. My friend lighted his pipe and sat looking at a spot on the hillside. I knew that he was looking at it, and for a long time I had wondered whether he would ever see anything there that would fix his attention. I knew that spot well. It was clear that he was interested at last, though it was a long time before he spoke. Like most painters, he trusts to his own eyesight, as a lion trusts his strength and a stag his speed, and he is always disturbed when he cannot reconcile what he sees with what he believes that he ought to see.

"It's strange," he said. "Do you see that little mound just on this side of the boulder?"

"Yes," I said, and I guessed what was coming.

"It looks like a grave," observed Holger.

"Very true. It does look like a grave."

"Yes," continued my friend, his eyes still fixed on the spot. "But the strange thing is that I see the body lying on the top of it. Of course," continued Holger, turning his head on one side as artists do, "it must be an effect of light. In the first place, it is not a grave at all. Secondly, if it were, the body would be inside and not outside. Therefore, it's an effect of the moonlight. Don't you see it?"

"Perfectly; I always see it on moonlight nights."

"It doesn't seem to interest you much," said Holger.

"On the contrary, it does interest me, though I am used to it. You're not so far wrong, either. The mound is really a grave."

"Nonsense!" cried Holger incredulously. "I suppose you'll tell me that what I see lying on it is really a corpse!"

"No," I answered, "it's not. I know, because I have taken the trouble to go down and see."

"Then what is it?" asked Holger.

"It's nothing."

"You mean that it's an effect of light, I suppose?"

"Perhaps it is. But the inexplicable part of the matter is that it makes no difference whether the moon is rising or setting, or waxing or waning. If there's any moonlight at all, from east to west or overhead, so long as it shines on the grave you can see the outline of the body on top."

Holger stirred up his pipe with the point of his knife, and then used his finger for a stopper. When the tobacco burned well he rose from his chair.

"If you don't mind," he said, "I'll go down and take a look at it."

He left me, crossed the roof, and disappeared down the dark steps. I did not move, but sat looking down until he came out of the tower below. I heard him humming an old Danish song as he crossed the open space in the bright moonlight, going straight to the mysterious mound. When he was ten paces from it, Holger stopped short, made two steps forward, and then three or four backward, and then stopped again. I knew what that meant. He had reached the spot where the Thing ceased to be visible—where, as he would have said, the effect of light changed.

Then he went on till he reached the mound and stood upon it. I could see the Thing still, but it was no longer lying down; it was on its knees now, winding its white arms round Holger's body and looking up into his face. A cool breeze stirred my hair at that moment, as the night wind began to come down from the hills, but it felt like a breath from another world.

The Thing seemed to be trying to climb to its feet, helping itself up by Holger's body while he stood upright, quite unconscious of it and apparently looking towards the tower, which is very picturesque when the moonlight falls upon it that side.

"Come along!" I shouted. "Don't stay there all night!"

It seemed to me that he moved reluctantly as he stepped from the mound, or else with difficulty. That was it. The Thing's arms were still round his waist, but its feet could not leave the grave. As he came slowly forward it was drawn and lengthened like a wreath of mist, thin and white, till I saw distinctly that Holger shook himself, as a man does who feels a chill. At the same instant a little wail of pain came to me on the breeze—it might have been the cry of the small owl that lives among the rocks—and the misty presence floated swiftly back from Holger's advancing figure and lay once more at its length upon the mound.

Again I felt the cool breeze in my hair, and this time an icy thrill of dread ran down my spine. I remembered very well that I had once gone down there alone in the moonlight; that presently, being near, I had seen nothing; that, like Holger, I had gone, and had stood upon the mound; and I remembered how, when I came back, sure that there was nothing there, I had felt the sudden conviction that there was something after all if I would only look behind me. I remembered the strong temptation to look back, a temptation I had resisted as unworthy of a man of sense, until, to get rid of it, I had shaken myself just as Holger did.

And now I knew that those white, misty arms had been round me, too; I knew it in a flash, and I shuddered as I remembered that I had heard the night owl then, too. But it had not been the night owl. It was the cry of the Thing.

I refilled my pipe and poured out a cup of strong southern wine; in less than a minute Holger was seated beside me again.

"Of course there's nothing there," he said, "but it's creepy, all the same. Do you know, when I was coming back I was so sure that there was something behind me that I wanted to turn round and look? It was an effort not to."

He laughed a little, knocked the ashes out of his pipe, and poured himself out some wine. For a while neither of us spoke, and the moon rose higher and we both looked at the Thing that lay on the mound.

"You might make a story about that," said Holger after a long time.

"There is one," I answered. "If you're not sleepy, I'll tell it to you."

"Go ahead," said Holger, who likes stories.

Old Alario was dying up there in the village behind the hill. You remember him, I have no doubt. They say that he made his money by selling sham jewellery in South America, and escaped with his gains when he was found out. Like all those fellows, if they bring anything back with them, he at once set to work to enlarge his house, and as there are no masons here, he sent all the way to Paola for two workmen. They were a rough-looking pair of scoundrels—a Neapolitan who had lost one eye and a Sicilian with an old scar half an inch deep across his left cheek. I often saw them, for on Sundays they used to come down here and fish off the rocks. When Alario caught the fever that killed him the masons were still at work. As he had agreed that part of their pay should be their board and lodging, he made them sleep in the house. His wife was dead, and he had an only son called Angelo, who was a much better sort than himself. Angelo was to marry the daughter of the richest man in the village, and, strange to say, though the marriage was arranged by their parents, the young people were said to be in love with each other.

For that matter, the whole village was in love with Angelo, and among the rest a wild, good-looking creature called Cristina, who was more like a gipsy than any girl I ever saw about here. She had very red lips and very black eyes, she was built like a greyhound, and had the tongue of the devil. But Angelo did not care a straw for her. He was rather a simple-minded fellow, quite different from his old scoundrel of a father, and under what I should call normal circumstances I really believe that he would never have looked at any girl except the nice plump little creature, with a fat dowry, whom his father meant him to marry. But things turned up which were neither normal nor natural.

On the other hand, a very handsome young shepherd from the hills above Maratea was in love with Cristina, who seems to have been quite indifferent to him. Cristina had no regular means of subsistence, but she was a good girl and willing to do any work or go on errands to any distance for the sake of a loaf of bread or a mess of beans, and permission to sleep under cover. She was especially glad when she could get something to do about the house of Angelo's father. There is no doctor in the village, and when the neighbours saw that old Alario was dying they sent Cristina to Scalea to fetch one. That was late in the afternoon, and if they had waited so long it was because the dying miser refused to allow any such extravagance while he was able to speak. But while Cristina was gone matters grew rapidly worse, the priest was brought to the bedside, and when he had done what he could he gave it as his opinion to the bystanders that the old man was dead, and left the house.

You know these people. They have a physical horror of death. Until the priest spoke, the room had been full of people. The words were hardly out of his mouth before it was empty. It was night now. They hurried down the dark steps and out into the street.

Angelo, as I have said, was away, Cristina had not come back—the simple woman-servant who had nursed the sick man fled with the rest, and the body was left alone in the flickering light of the earthern oil lamp.

Five minutes later two men looked in cautiously and crept forward towards the bed. They were the one-eyed Neapolitan mason and his Sicilian companion. They knew what they wanted. In a moment they had dragged from under the bed a small but heavy iron-bound box, and long before anyone thought of coming back to the dead man they had left the house and the village under cover of the darkness. It was easy enough, for Alario's house is the last towards the gorge which leads down here, and the thieves merely went out by the back door, got over the stone wall, and had nothing to risk after that except the possibility of meeting some belated countryman, which was very small indeed, since few of the people use that path. They had a mattock and shovel, and they made their way here without accident.

I am telling you this story as it must have happened, for, of course, there were no witnesses to this part of it. The men brought the box down by the gorge, intending to bury it until they should be able to come back and take it away in a boat. They must have been clever enough to guess that some of the money would be in paper notes, for they would otherwise have buried it on the beach in the wet sand, where it would have been much safer. But the paper would have rotted if they had been obliged to leave it there long, so they dug their hole down there, close to that boulder. Yes, just where the mound is now.

Cristina did not find the doctor in Scalea, for he had been sent for from a place up the valley, halfway to San Domenico. If she had found him he would have come on his mule by the upper road, which is smoother but much longer. But Cristina took the short cut by the rocks, which passes about fifty feet above the mound, and goes round that corner. The men were digging when she passed, and she heard them at work. It would not have been like her to go by without finding out what the noise was, for she was never afraid of anything in her life, and, besides, the fishermen sometimes come ashore here at night to get a stone for an anchor or to gather sticks to make a little fire. The night was dark, and Cristina probably came close to the two men before she could see what they were doing. She knew them, of course, and they knew her, and understood instantly that they were in her power. There was only one thing to be done for their safety, and they did it. They knocked her on the head, they dug the hole deep, and they buried her quickly with the iron-bound chest. They must have understood that their only chance of escaping suspicion lay in getting back to the village before their absence was noticed, for they returned immediately, and were found half an hour later gossiping quietly with the man who was making Alario's coffin. He was a crony of theirs, and had been working at the repairs in the old man's house. So far as I have been able to make out, the only persons who were supposed to know where Alario kept his treasure were Angelo and the one woman-servant I have mentioned. Angelo was away; it was the woman who discovered the theft.

It is easy enough to understand why no one else knew where the money was. The old man kept his door locked and the key in his pocket when he was out, and did not let the woman enter to clean the place unless he was there himself. The whole village knew that he had money somewhere, however, and the masons had probably discovered the whereabouts of the chest by climbing in at the window in his absence. If the old man had not been delirious until he lost consciousness he would have been in frightful agony of mind for his riches. The faithful woman-servant forgot their existence only for a few moments when she fled with the rest, overcome by the horror of death. Twenty minutes had not passed before she returned with the two hideous old hags who are always called in to prepare the dead for burial. Even then she had not at first the courage to go near the bed with them, but she made a pretence of dropping something, went down on her knees as if to find it, and looked under the bedstead. The walls of the room were newly white-washed down to the floor, and she saw at a glance that the chest was gone. It had been there in the afternoon; it had therefore been stolen in the short interval since she had left the room.

There are no carabineers stationed in the village; there is not so much as a municipal watchman, for there is no municipality. There never was such a place, I believe. Scalea is supposed to look after it in some mysterious way, and it takes a couple of hours to get anybody from there. As the old woman had lived in the village all her life, it did not even occur to her to apply to any civil authority for help. She simply set up a howl and ran through the village in the dark, screaming out that her dead master's house had been robbed. Many of the people looked out, but at first no one seemed inclined to help her. Most of them, judging her by themselves, whispered to each other that she had probably stolen the money herself. The first man to move was the father of the girl whom Angelo was to marry; having collected his household, all of whom felt a personal interest in the wealth which was to have come into the family, he declared it to be his opinion that the chest had been stolen by the two journeymen masons who lodged in the house. He headed a search for them, which naturally began in Alario's house and ended in the carpenter's workshop, where the thieves were found discussing a measure of wine with the carpenter over the half-finished coffin, by the light of one earthen lamp filled with oil and tallow. The search-party at once accused the delinquents of the crime, and threatened to lock them up in the cellar till the carabineers could be fetched from Scalea. The two men looked at each other for one moment, and then without the slightest hesitation they put out the single light, seized the unfinished coffin between them, and using it as a sort of battering ram, dashed upon their assailants in the dark. In a few moments they were beyond pursuit.

That is the end of the first part of the story. The treasure had disappeared, and as no trace of it could be found the people naturally supposed that the thieves had succeeded in carrying it off. The old man was buried, and when Angelo came back at last he had to borrow money to pay for the miserable funeral, and had some difficulty in doing so. He hardly needed to be told that in losing his inheritance he had lost his bride. In this part of the world marriages are made on strictly business principles, and if the promised cash is not forthcoming on the appointed day, the bride or bridegroom whose parents have failed to produce it may as well take themselves off, for there will be no wedding. Poor Angelo knew that well enough. His father had been possessed of hardly any land, and now that the hard cash which he had brought from South America was gone, there was nothing left but debts for the building materials that were to have been used for enlarging and improving the old house. Angelo was beggared, and the nice plump little creature who was to have been his, turned up her nose at him in the most approved fashion. As for Cristina, it was several days before she was missed, for no one remembered that she had been sent to Scalea for the doctor, who had never come. She often disappeared in the same way for days together, when she could find a little work here and there at the distant farms among the hills. But when she did not come back at all, people began to wonder, and at last made up their minds that she had connived with the masons, and had escaped with them.

I paused and emptied my glass.

"That sort of thing could not happen anywhere else," observed Holger, filling his everlasting pipe again. "It is wonderful what a natural charm there is about murder and sudden death in a romantic country like this. Deeds that would be simply brutal and disgusting anywhere else become dramatic and mysterious because this is Italy, and we are living in a genuine tower of Charles V. built against genuine Barbary pirates."

"There's something in that," I admitted. Holger is the most romantic man in the world inside of himself, but he always thinks it necessary to explain why he feels anything.

"I suppose they found the poor girl's body with the box," he said presently.

"As it seems to interest you," I answered, "I'll tell you the rest of the story."

The moon had risen high by this time; the outline of the Thing on the mound was clearer to our eyes than before.

The village very soon settled down to its small dull life. No one missed old Alario, who had been away so much on his voyages to South America that he had never been a familiar figure in his native place. Angelo lived in the half-finished house, and because he had no money to pay the old woman-servant, she would not stay with him, but once in a long time she would come and wash a shirt for him for old acquaintance's sake. Besides the house, he had inherited a small patch of ground at some distance from the village; he tried to cultivate it, but he had no heart in the work, for he knew he could never pay the taxes on it and on the house, which would certainly be confiscated by the Government, or seized for the debt of the building material, which the man who had supplied it refused to take back.

Angelo was very unhappy. So long as his father had been alive and rich, every girl in the village had been in love with him; but that was all changed now. It had been pleasant to be admired and courted, and invited to drink wine by fathers who had girls to marry. It was hard to be stared at coldly, and sometimes laughed at because he had been robbed of his inheritance. He cooked miserable meals for himself, and from being sad became melancholy and morose.

At twilight, when the day's work was done, instead of hanging about in the open space before the church with young fellows of his own age, he took to wandering in lonely places on the outskirts of the village till it was quite dark. Then he slunk home and went to bed to save the expense of a light. But in those lonely twilight hours he began to have strange waking dreams. He was not always alone, for often when he sat on the stump of a tree, where the narrow path turns down the gorge, he was sure that a woman came up noiselessly over the rough stones, as if her feet were bare; and she stood under a clump of chestnut trees only half a dozen yards down the path, and beckoned to him without speaking. Though she was in the shadow he knew that her lips were red, and that when they parted a little and smiled at him she showed two small sharp teeth. He knew this at first rather than saw it, and he knew that it was Cristina, and that she was dead. Yet he was not afraid; he only wondered whether it was a dream, for he thought that if he had been awake he should have been frightened.

Besides, the dead woman had red lips, and that could only happen in a dream. Whenever he went near the gorge after sunset she was already there waiting for him, or else she very soon appeared, and he began to be sure that she came a little nearer to him every day. At first he had only been sure of her blood-red mouth, but now each feature grew distinct, and the pale face looked at him with deep and hungry eyes.

It was the eyes that grew dim. Little by little he came to know that some day the dream would not end when he turned away to go home, but would lead him down the gorge out of which the vision rose. She was nearer now when she beckoned to him. Her cheeks were not livid like those of the dead, but pale with starvation, with the furious and unappeased physical hunger of her eyes that devoured him. They feasted on his soul and cast a spell over him, and at last they were close to his own and held him. He could not tell whether her breath was as hot as fire or as cold as ice; he could not tell whether her red lips burned his or froze them, or whether her five fingers on his wrists seared scorching scars or bit his flesh like frost; he could not tell whether he was awake or asleep, whether she was alive or dead, but he knew that she loved him, she alone of all creatures, earthly or unearthly, and her spell had power over him.

When the moon rose high that night the shadow of that Thing was not alone down there upon the mound.

Angelo awoke in the cool dawn, drenched with dew and chilled through flesh, and blood, and bone. He opened his eyes to the faint grey light, and saw the stars still shining overhead. He was very weak, and his heart was beating so slowly that he was almost like a man fainting. Slowly he turned his head on the mound, as on a pillow, but the other face was not there. Fear seized him suddenly, a fear unspeakable and unknown; he sprang to his feet and fled up the gorge, and he never looked behind him until he reached the door of the house on the outskirts of the village. Drearily he went to his work that day, and wearily the hours dragged themselves after the sun, till at last it touched the sea and sank, and the great sharp hills above Maratea turned purple against the dove-coloured eastern sky.

Angelo shouldered his heavy hoe and left the field. He felt less tired now than in the morning when he had begun to work, but he promised himself that he would go home without lingering by the gorge, and eat the best supper he could get himself, and sleep all night in his bed like a Christian man. Not again would he be tempted down the narrow way by a shadow with red lips and icy breath; not again would he dream that dream of terror and delight. He was near the village now; it was half an hour since the sun had set, and the cracked church bell sent little discordant echoes across the rocks and ravines to tell all good people that the day was done. Angelo stood still a moment where the path forked, where it led towards the village on the left, and down to the gorge on the right, where a clump of chestnut trees overhung the narrow way. He stood still a minute, lifting his battered hat from his head and gazing at the fast-fading sea westward, and his lips moved as he silently repeated the familiar evening prayer. His lips moved, but the words that followed them in his brain lost their meaning and turned into others, and ended in a name that he spoke aloud—Cristina! With the name, the tension of his will relaxed suddenly, reality went out and the dream took him again, and bore him on swiftly and surely like a man walking in his sleep, down, down, by the steep path in the gathering darkness. And as she glided beside him, Cristina whispered strange sweet things in his ear, which somehow, if he had been awake, he knew that he could not quite have understood; but now they were the most wonderful words he had ever heard in his life. And she kissed him also, but not upon his mouth. He felt her sharp kisses upon his white throat, and he knew that her lips were red. So the wild dream sped on through twilight and darkness and moonrise, and all the glory of the summer's night. But in the chilly dawn he lay as one half dead upon the mound down there, recalling and not recalling, drained of his blood, yet strangely longing to give those red lips more. Then came the fear, the awful nameless panic, the mortal horror that guards the confines of the world we see not, neither know of as we know of other things, but which we feel when its icy chill freezes our bones and stirs our hair with the touch of a ghostly hand. Once more Angelo sprang from the mound and fled up the gorge in the breaking day, but his step was less sure this time, and he panted for breath as he ran; and when he came to the bright spring of water that rises halfway up the hillside, he dropped upon his knees and hands and plunged his whole face in and drank as he had never drunk before—for it was the thirst of the wounded man who has lain bleeding all night long upon the battlefield.

She had him fast now, and he could not escape her, but would come to her every evening at dusk until she had drained him of his last drop of blood. It was in vain that when the day was done he tried to take another turning and go home by a path that did not lead near the gorge. It was in vain that he made promises to himself each morning at dawn when he climbed the lonely way up from the shore to the village. It was all in vain, for when the sun sank burning into the sea, and the coolness of the evening stole out as from a hiding-place to delight the weary world, his feet turned towards the old way, and she was waiting for him in the shadow under the chestnut trees; and then all happened as before, and she fell to kissing his white throat even as she flitted lightly down the way, winding one arm about him. And as his blood failed, she grew more hungry and more thirsty every day, and every day when he awoke in the early dawn it was harder to rouse himself to the effort of climbing the steep path to the village; and when he went to his work his feet dragged painfully, and there was hardly strength in his arms to wield the heavy hoe. He scarcely spoke to anyone now, but the people said he was "consuming himself" for love of the girl he was to have married when he lost his inheritance; and they laughed heartily at the thought, for this is not a very romantic country.

At this time Antonio, the man who stays here to look after the tower, returned from a visit to his people, who live near Salerno. He had been away all the time since before Alario's death and knew nothing of what had happened. He has told me that he came back late in the afternoon and shut himself up in the tower to eat and sleep, for he was very tired. It was past midnight when he awoke, and when he looked out the waning moon was rising over the shoulder of the hill. He looked out towards the mound, and he saw something, and he did not sleep again that night. When he went out again in the morning it was broad daylight, and there was nothing to be seen on the mound but loose stones and driven sand. Yet he did not go very near it; he went straight up the path to the village and directly to the house of the old priest.

"I have seen an evil thing this night," he said; "I have seen how the dead drink the blood of the living. And the blood is the life."

"Tell me what you have seen," said the priest in reply.

Antonio told him everything he had seen.

"You must bring your book and your holy water to-night," he added. "I will be here before sunset to go down with you, and if it pleases your reverence to sup with me while we wait, I will make ready."

"I will come," the priest answered, "for I have read in old books of these strange beings which are neither quick nor dead, and which lie ever fresh in their graves, stealing out in the dusk to taste life and blood."

Antonio cannot read, but he was glad to see that the priest understood the business; for, of course, the books must have instructed him as to the best means of quieting the half-living Thing for ever.

So Antonio went away to his work, which consists largely in sitting on the shady side of the tower, when he is not perched upon a rock with a fishing-line catching nothing. But on that day he went twice to look at the mound in the bright sunlight, and he searched round and round it for some hole through which the being might get in and out; but he found none. When the sun began to sink and the air was cooler in the shadows, he went up to fetch the old priest, carrying a little wicker basket with him; and in this they placed a bottle of holy water, and the basin, and sprinkler, and the stole which the priest would need; and they came down and waited in the door of the tower till it should be dark. But while the light still lingered very grey and faint, they saw something moving, just there; two figures, a man's that walked, and a woman's that flitted beside him, and while her head lay on his shoulder she kissed his throat. The priest has told me that, too, and that his teeth chattered, and he grasped Antonio's arm. The vision passed, and disappeared into the shadow. Then Antonio got the leathern flask of strong liquor, which he kept for great occasions, and poured such a draught as made the old man feel almost young again; and he got the lantern, and his pick and shovel, and gave the priest his stole to put on and the holy water to carry, and they went out together towards the spot where the work was to be done. Antonio says that in spite of the rum his own knees shook together, and the priest stumbled over his Latin. For when they were yet a few yards from the mound, the flickering light of the lantern fell upon Angelo's white face, unconscious as if in sleep, and on his upturned throat, over which a very thin red line of blood trickled down into his collar; and the flickering light of the lantern played upon another face that looked up from the feast, upon two deep, dead eyes that saw in spite of death—upon parted lips, redder than life itself—upon two gleaming teeth on which glistened a rosy drop. Then the priest, good old man, shut his eyes tight and showered holy water before him, and his cracked voice rose almost to a scream; and then Antonio, who is no coward after all, raised his pick in one hand and the lantern in the other, as he sprang forward, not knowing what the end should be; and then he swears that he heard a woman's cry, and the Thing was gone, and Angelo lay alone on the mound, unconscious, with the red line on his throat and the beads of deathly sweat on his cold forehead. They lifted him, half dead as he was, and laid him on the ground close by; then Antonio went to work, and the priest helped him, though he was old and could not do much; and they dug deep, and at last Antonio, standing in the grave, stooped down with his lantern to see what he might see.

His hair used to bc dark brown, with grizzled streaks about the temples; in less than a month from that day he was as grey as a badger. He was a miner when he was young, and most of these fellows have seen ugly sights now and then, when accidents have happened, but he had never seen what he saw that night—that Thing which is neither alive nor dead, that Thing which will abide neither above ground nor in the grave. Antonio had brought something with him which the priest had not noticed. He had made it that afternoon—a sharp stake shaped from a piece of tough old driftwood. He had it with him now, and he had his heavy pick, and he had taken the lantern down into the grave. I don't think any power on earth could make him speak of what happened then, and the old priest was too frightened to look in. He says he heard Antonio breathing like a wild beast, and moving as if he were fighting with something almost as strong as himself; and he heard an evil sound also, with blows, as of something violently driven through flesh and bone; and then, the most awful sound of all—a woman's shriek, the unearthly scream of a woman neither dead nor alive, but buried deep for many days. And he, the poor old priest, could only rock himself as he knelt there in the sand, crying aloud his prayers and exorcisms to drown these dreadful sounds. Then suddenly a small iron-bound chest was thrown up and rolled over against the old man's knees, and in a moment more Antonio was beside him, his face as white as tallow in the flickering light of the lantern, shovelling the sand and pebbles into the grave with furious haste, and looking over the edge till the pit was half full; and the priest said that there was much fresh blood on Antonio's hands and on his clothes.

I had come to the end of my story. Holger finished his wine and leaned back in his chair.

"So Angelo got his own again," he said. "Did he marry the prim and plump young person to whom he had been betrothed?"

"No; he had been badly frightened. He went to South America, and has not been heard of since."

"And that poor thing's body is there still, I suppose," said Holger. "Is it quite dead yet, I wonder?"

I wonder, too. But whether it be dead or alive, I should hardly care to see it, even in broad daylight. Antonio is as grey as a badger, and he has never been quite the same since that night.

E. & H. HERON
(KATE O'BRIEN PRICHARD AND HESKETH VERNON PRICHARD)

THE STORY OF THE GREY HOUSE

MR. FLAXMAN LOW declares that only on one occasion has he undertaken, unasked, the solving of a psychical mystery. To that case he always refers as the "affair of the Grey House". The house bears a different name in the annals of more than one scientific society, and much controversy has raged over the strange details of a story that seems to open up a new province of fantastic horror. Papers and treatises have been written about it in almost every European language, and many dismaying facts of a somewhat analogous nature have thus been brought to light. There was some hesitation at first about laying this matter—backed as it is by an explanation, which, though terrible, is not altogether unsupported—before the public, but it has finally been decided to incorporate it in the present book.

During the dry summer of 19—, Mr. Low happened to be staying in a lonely village on the coast of Devon. He was deeply immersed in some antiquarian work connected with the old Norse calendars, and therefore limited his acquaintance in the neighbourhood to one individual, a Dr. Fremantle, who, besides being a medical man, was a botanist of some note.

One afternoon, when driving together, Mr. Low and Dr. Fremantle passed through a valley which nestled cup-like in the higher ground a few miles inland. As they passed along a deep, steep lane with overhanging hedges they caught a glimpse, through a break in the leaves, of a grey gable visible between the horizontal branches of a cedar.

Flaxman Low pointed it out to his companion.

"That's young Montesson's house," answered Fremantle, "and it bears a very sinister reputation. Nothing in your line, though," with a smile. "Indeed, no ghost would lend the same hideous associations to the place it now possesses as the result of a succession of mysterious murders that have occurred there."

"The grounds seem neglected. I don't remember to have seen such rank growth anywhere."

"Certainly not inside the British Isles," returned Fremantle.

"The estate is left to take care of itself, partly because Montesson won't live there, partly because it is impossible to find labourers to work near the house. Our warm, damp climate and this sheltered position give rise to extraordinary luxuriance of growth. A stream runs along the bottom, and I expect all the low-lying land, where you see that belt of yellow African grass, is little better than a morass now."

Fremantle drew up as they gained the top of the slope. From there they could overlook the tangle of vegetation, dimmed by a rising mist, which surrounded and almost hid the roof of the Grey House.

"Yes," said Freemantle, in answer to an observation of Mr. Low, "Montesson's guardian, who lived here and looked after the property for him, turned the place into a subtropical garden. It used to be one of my chief pleasures to wander about here, but since my marriage my wife objects to my doing so, on account of the tales she has heard."

"What is the danger?"

"Death!" replied Fremantle shortly.

"What form of death? Malaria?"

"No disease at all, my dear fellow. The persons who die at the Grey House are hanged by the neck until they are dead!"

"Hanged?" repeated Flaxman Low in surprise.

"Yes, hanged. Not only strangled but suspended, as the marks on the necks show. If there were any hint of a ghost in it you might investigate—Montesson would be only too grateful if you could fathom the mystery."

"Tell me something more definite."

"I'll tell you what has happened within my own knowledge. Montesson's father died some fifteen years ago and left him to the guardianship of a cousin named Lampurt, who, as I told you, was a horticulturist, and planted the place with a wonderful variety of foreign shrubs and flowers. Lampurt had a bad name in the country, and his appearance was certainly against him—a squint-eyed, pig-faced fellow, who sidled along like a crab, and could not look you in the face. He died first."

"Was he hanged? Or did he hang himself?"

"Neither, in this case. He dropped in a kind of fit, right up in front of the house, while he was engaged in planting some new acquisition. Had it not been for the evidence of the persons who were present at the time, I should have said his death resulted from some tremendous mental shock. But the gardener and his relation, Mrs. Montesson, agreed in saying that he was not exerting himself unduly, and that he had had no disturbing news. He was a healthy man and I could see no sufficient reason for his death. He was simply gardening, and had apparently pricked himself with a nail for he had a spot of blood upon his forefinger.

"After that all went well for a couple of years, when, during the summer holidays, the trouble began, Montesson must have been about sixteen at the time, and had a tutor with him. His mother and sister—a pretty girl rather older than himself—were also here. One morning the girl was found lying on the gravel under her window, quite dead. I was sent for, and, upon examination, discovered the extraordinary fact that she had been hanged!"

"Murder?"

"Of course, though we could find no trace of the murderer. The girl had been taken from her bedroom and hanged. Then the rope was removed and she was thrown in a heap under her window. The crime caused a tremendous sensation in the neighbourhood, and the police were busy for a long time, but nothing came of their inquiries.

"About a fortnight later, Platt, the tutor, sat up smoking at the open study window. In the morning he was found lying out over the sill. There could be no mistake as to how he met his death, for in addition to the deep line round his throat, his neck was broken as neatly as they could have done it at Newgate! As in the other case, there was nothing to show how he came by his death, no rope, no trace of footsteps or any struggle to lead one to suspect the presence of another person or persons. Yet from the facts it could not have been suicide."

"I see you had some suspicion of your own," said Flaxman Low.

"Well, yes, I had. But time has passed, and I now think I must have been mistaken. I must explain that the branches of the cedar you saw jut to within a few feet of the windows of the rooms occupied by Miss Montesson and Platt respectively, at the time of death. I told you there were no traces of anyone having approached the house. It therefore struck me that some active person might have leaped from the cedar into the open windows and escaped in the same way, for the windows open vertically, and when both leaves are thrown back, there is a large aperture. But the murders were so purposeless and disconnected that they suggested irresponsible agency. I recollected Poe's story of the Rue Morgue, where, you remember, the crimes were committed by an ourang-outang. It seemed to me possible that Lampurt, who was of a morose and strange temper, might, among other things, have secretly imported an ape and turned it loose in the woods. I had a thorough search made in the park and grounds, but we found nothing, and I have long ago abandoned the theory."

Low thought silently over the story for some time, then he asked for the dates of the three deaths. Fremantle answered categorically, and it appeared that all had taken place about the same season of the year—during summer, in fact. Upon this Mr. Low made an offer to investigate the affair on psychical lines, if Montesson made no objection. In answer to this message Montesson took the next train down to Devon, and begged to be allowed to accompany Mr. Low in his inquiries.

Flaxman Low quickly saw that Montesson might prove a very useful companion. He was a blond, heavily-built man, and plainly possessed of a strong will and temper. Low put aside his books and went off at once with Montesson to have a closer look at the Grey House while the daylight lasted.

It is difficult to give any adequate impression of the teeming exuberance of wild and tangled growth through which they had to cut their way. Young, lush, sappy leafage overlay and half disguised the dank rottenness of the older vegetation beneath. After wading more than breast-high through the matted reeds, below which the spreading stream was fast reducing the land to a swamp, they emerged into a fairly open space that had once been the lawn round the house.

Here brambled and lusty weeds now grew abundantly under the untended trees. Curious shrubs and plants flourished here and there. As they came up, a stoat sneaked away by a narrow footpath, nettle-grown and caked with damp, which led past blackened bushes round the house. Otherwise the place was deserted; not a leaf seemed to move in the windless heat of the afternoon. The squat, grey face of the house was scarred across by a dark-leaved creeper, hung with orchid-like blossoms, a little to the left of which Low noticed the cedar mentioned by Dr. Fremantle.

Low drew up at the weed-twisted, sunken little gate that gave upon the lawns and spoke for the first time.

"Tell me about it," and he nodded towards the house.

Montesson repeated the story already told, but added further details. "From here," went on Montesson, "you can see the exact spot where all these things took place. The upper of these two windows surrounded by the creeper and under the shadow of the cedar, belonged to my sister's room; the lower is that of the study where Platt died. The gravel path below ran the whole length of the house, but it is now over-grown.... Has Fremantle told you of Lawrence?"

Low shook his head.

"I hate the very sight of the place!" said Montesson hoarsely; "the mystery and the horror of it all seem in my blood. I can't forget!—my mother left on the day of Platt's death, and has never been here since. But when I came of age I resolved to make another attempt to live here, meaning to sift the past if I got the chance of doing so. I had the grounds cleared about the house, and after leaving Oxford, came down with a man of my own year, called Lawrence. We spent the Easter vacation here reading, and all went right enough. Meanwhile I had the house examined, thinking there might be a secret entrance or room, but nothing of the kind exists. This house is not haunted. Nothing has ever been seen or heard of a supernatural character—nothing but the same awful repetition of blind murder!"

After a few seconds he resumed.

"During the following summer Lawrence came down with me again. One hot evening we were smoking as we walked up and down the gravel under the windows. It was bright moonlight, and I remember the heavy scent of those red flowers—" Montesson glanced round him strangely.

"I went in to fetch a cigar. It took me some minutes to find the box I wanted, and to light the cigar. When I came out, Lawrence lay crumpled up as if he had fallen from a height, and he was dead. Round his neck was the same bluish line I had seen in the two other cases. You can understand what it was to leave the man not five minutes before, in health and strength, and to come back to find him dead—hanged—to judge from appearances! But, as usual, no trace of rope or struggle or murderer!"

After some further talk, Mr. Low proposed to go into the house. It had evidently been deserted in haste. In the room once occupied by Miss Montesson, her girlish treasures still lay about, dusty, moth-eaten, and discoloured. Montesson paused on the threshold.

"Poor little Fan! It's just as she left it!" he said hurriedly.

The cedar outside threw a gloomy shade into the room, and the fantastic red blossoms drooped motionless in the stagnant air.

"Was the window open when your sister was found?" inquired Low, after he had examined the room.

"Yes, it was hot weather—early in August. This room has not been occupied since. After Platt's affair, I have always avoided this side of the house, so that it was only by chance Lawrence and I came round to this part of the lawn to smoke."

"Then we may suppose that the danger, whatever it is, exists on this side of the house only?"

"So it seems," replied Montesson.

"Your sister was last seen alive in this room? Platt in the room directly below?—and your friend—what of him?"

"Lawrence was lying on the gravel path just under the study window. All of them have died under the shadow of the cedar. Did

Fremantle give you his idea? Poor Lawrence's death disposed of that theory. No big ape could live in England all those five years in the open, and in any case it must have been seen sometime in the interval."

"I think so," replied Low, abstractedly. "Now as to what we must do to try and get at the meaning of all this. Do you feel equal, considering all you have gone through in this house, do you feel equal to remaining here with me for a night or two?"

Montesson again glanced over his shoulder nervously.

"Yes," he said. "I know my nerves are not as stiff and steady as they should be, but I'll stand by you—especially as you would not find another man about here willing to run the risk. You see it is not a ghost or any fanciful trouble, it means a real danger. Think over it, Mr. Low, before you undertake so hazardous an attempt."

Low looked into the blue eyes Montesson had fixed upon him. They were weary, anxious eyes, and, taken in combination with his compressed lips and square chin, told Low of the struggle this man constantly endured between his shaken nervous system and the strong will that mastered it.

"If you'll stand by me, I'll try to get to the bottom of it," said Low.

"I wonder if I should allow you to risk your life in this way?" returned Montesson, passing his hand over his prematurely-lined forehead.

"Why not? Besides, it is my own wish. As for risking our lives—it is for the good of mankind."

"I can't say I see it in that light," said Montesson in surprise.

"If we lose our lives it will be in the effort to make another spot of earth clean and wholesome and safe for men to live on. Our duty to the public requires us to run a murderer to earth. Here we have a murderous power of some subtle kind; is it not quite as much our duty to destroy it if we can, even at risk to ourselves?"

The result of this conversation was an arrangement to pass the night at the Grey House. About ten o'clock they set out, intending to follow the path they had more or less successfully cleared for themselves in the afternoon. By Flaxman Low's advice, Montesson carried a long knife. The night was unusually hot and still, and lit only by a thin moon as they made their way along, stumbling over matted weeds and roots and literally feeling for the path, until they came to the little gate by the lawn. There they stopped a moment to look at the house, standing out among its strange sea of overgrowth, the dim moon low on the horizon, glinting palely upon the windows and over the deserted countryside. As they waited, a night-bird hooted and flapped its way across the open.

At any moment they might be at hand-grips with the mysterious power of death which haunted the place. The warm lush-scented air and the sinister shadows seemed charged with some ominous influence. As they drew near the house Low perceived a sweet, heavy odour.

"What is it?" he asked.

"It comes from those scarlet flowers, at night. It's unbearable! Lampurt imported the thing," replied Montesson irritably.

"Which room will you spend the night in?" asked Low as they gained the hall.

Montesson hesitated. "Have you ever heard the expression 'grey with fear'?" he said, laughing in the dark; "I'm that!"

Low did not like the laugh; it was only one remove, and that a very little one, from hysteria.

"We won't find out much unless we each remain alone and with open windows as they did," said Low.

Montesson shook himself.

"No, I suppose not. They were each alone when—good-night, I'll call if anything happens, and you must do the same for me. For Heaven's sake, don't go to sleep!"

"And remember," added Low, "with your knife to cut at anything that touches you." Then he stood at the study door and listened to Montesson's heavy steps as they passed up the stairs, for he had elected to pass the night in his sister's room. Low heard him walk across the floor and throw wide the window.

When Mr. Low turned into the study and tried to open the window there, he found it impossible to do so; the creeper outside had fastened upon the woodwork, binding the sashes together. There was but one thing left for him to do; he must go outside and stand where Lawrence had stood on the fatal night. He let himself out softly and went round to the south side of the house.

There he paced up and down in the shadows for perhaps an hour.

In the deceptive, iridescent moonlight, a pallid head seemed to wag at him from the gloom below the cedar, but, moving towards it, he grasped only the yellow bunched blossoms of a giant ragwort. Then he stood still and looked up into the branches above; the gnarled black branches with their fringes of black sticky leaves. Fremantle's theory of the ape passing stealthily among them to spring upon his victim found a sudden horror of possibility in Low's mind. He imagined the girl awaking in the brute's cruel hands....

Out upon the quiet brooding of the night broke a scream—or rather a roar, a harsh, jagged, pulsating roar, that ceased as abruptly as it had begun.

Without a moment's consideration, Mr. Low seized the branch nearest to him and, swinging himself up into the tree, he climbed with a frantic effort towards the window of Montesson's room, from which he was almost sure the sound had come. Being an unusually active and athletic man he leaped from the branch towards the open window, and fell headlong in upon the floor. As he did so, something seemed to pass him, something swift and sinuous that might have been a snake, and disappear out of the window!

Remembering a candle on the toilet table, he lit it when he regained his feet and looked about him.

Montesson lay on the floor "crumpled up" as he had himself described Lawrence's position. Low recalled this with misgiving as he hurried to his side. A dark smear like blood was on Montesson's cheek, but though unconscious, he was still alive. Low lifted him on to the bed and did what he could to rouse him but without success. He lay rigid, breathing the slow, almost imperceptible, respiration of deep stupor.

Low was about to go to the window, when the candle suddenly went out, and he was left in the increasing darkness, to all intents alone, to face an unknown though tangible assailant.

Silence had again fallen upon the house—that is, the silence of night, and woodlands, and many-folded leafage, and the things that go by night. He stood by the window and listened. His senses were acute and throbbing; he felt as if he could hear for miles. The scent of the scarlet blossoms rose like deadening fumes into his brain, and he drew away from the window, and, feeling strangely spent, threw himself upon a couch. Then he drew out the knife at his belt, and strung himself up to watchfulness with an effort.

He knew that the attack he had to expect would be likely to come from the direction of the window. He saw the faint, swimming moonlight that fell through the leaves and tendrils of the creeper fade slowly away. Probably clouds were coming up over the sky, for the steamy heat was even more oppressive.

The low window-sill was scarcely more than a foot above the floor, and presently he fancied something was moving along the carpet among the entangling shadows of the leaves, but the darkness was now intensified, and he could not be sure. Montesson's breathing had become quieter. It was the dead hour of the night; hardly a sound was to be heard.

Suddenly Low felt a soft touch upon his knee. His whole consciousness had been so absorbed in the act of listening that this unexpected appeal to another sense startled him Here and there, rapid, soft, and light, the touches passed over his body. It might have been some animal nosing about him in the dark. Then a smooth, cold touch fell upon his cheek.

Low sprang up, and slashed about him in the darkness with his knife.

In that instant the thing closed with him—a flexuous, snaky thing that flung its coils about his limbs and body in one swift spring like a curling whiplash!

Flaxman Low was all but helpless in the winding grasp of what?—the tentacles of some strange creature? Or was it some great snake, this sentient thing that was feeling for his throat? There was not an instant to lose. The knife was pressed against his body; with a violent effort he drew it sharply, edge outwards, against the tightening coils. A spurt of clammy fluid fell upon his hand, and the thing loosed and fell away from him into the stifling gloom.

In the morning Montesson came to himself in one of the lower rooms at the other side of the house. Fremantle was beside him.

"What's the matter?" he asked. "Ah, I remember now. There's Low. It has beaten us again, Fremantle! It is hopeless. I don't know what happened—I was not asleep, when I found myself seized, lifted up, drawn towards the window, and strangled by loving ropes. Look at Low!" he went on harshly, raising himself. "Why, man, you're all over blood!"

Flaxman Low glanced down at his hands.

"Looks like it," he said.

"It has beaten even you, Low!" went on Montesson. "There is something much more terrible and tangible than a ghost in this cursed house! See here!"

He pulled down his collar. A faint bluish circle with suffused dots was drawn round his throat.

"It is some deadly species of snake," exclaimed Fremantle.

Low sat down thoughtfully, astride a chair. "I'm sorry to disagree with both of you. But I am inclined to think it is not a snake, and on the other hand I fancy it has a great deal to do with what we may roughly call a ghost. The whole evidence points in only one direction."

"You mustn't let your prejudice in favour of psychical problems run away with your reason," said Fremantle drily. "Has a ghost actual, palpable power?—to go further, has it blood?"

Montesson, who had been looking at his neck in the glass, turned quickly. "It's some horrible thing in nature! Something between a snake and an octopus! What do you say to it, Low?"

Low looked up gravely.

"In spite of Fremantle's objections the steps from the beginning to end are very clear."

Fremantle and Montesson exchanged a glance of incredulity.

"My dear fellow, much learning has warped your mind," said Fremantle with an embarrassed laugh.

"First of all," continued Low, "we know where all the deaths have occurred."

"To speak precisely, they have all occurred in different places," interposed Fremantle.

"True; but within a strictly limited area. The slight differences have been of material help to me. In all cases they have occurred in the vicinity of one thing."

"The cedar!" cried Montesson, with some excitement.

"That was my first idea—now I refer to the wall. Will you tell me the probable weight of Lawrence and Platt at the date of death?"

"Platt was a small man—perhaps under nine stone. Lawrence, though much taller, was thin, and could not have weighed more than eleven. As for poor little Fan, she was only a slip of a girl."

"Three people have been killed—one has escaped. In what way do you differ from the others, Montesson?" asked Low.

"If you mean I'm heavier, I certainly am. I scale something like fifteen. But what has that to do with it?"

"Everything. The coils have evidently not sufficient compressive power to destroy life by strangulation simply—there must be suspension as well. You were simply too heavy for them to tackle."

"Coils of what?"

"Of this." Low held up a tapering, reddish-brown tendon or line, which had red curved triangular teeth set on it at intervals.

The two other men stared at this object, and then Montesson burst out. "The creeper on the wall!" he said, in a tone of disappointment. "It couldn't be! Besides, has a plant blood?"

"Let us go and look at it," said Low. "This creeper has never been cut because it withers away to the ground every winter and grows again in the spring. Look here!" He took out his knife and cut a leathery shoot. A crimson stain spurted out on his cuff. "The only person, as far as I can gather, who cut this plant was Mr. Lampurt in nailing it to the wall. He died of shock when he saw the red stain on his finger, as he knew something of its deadly properties. But though stupefying—as your condition last night proved, Montesson—they are not fatal. Even to stupefy they must get into the blood. Now the deaths have all occurred within reach of the tendrils of this plant. And all have happened at the same season of the year, that is to say, at the time when it attains its full annual strength and growth. Another point in favour of Montesson's escape was the dryness of the season The growth is not quite so good as usual this summer, is it?"

"No, the tendrils are thinner—a good deal thinner and smaller."

"Just so. Therefore your weight saved you, though you were stupefied by the punctures of the thorns. I feared that, and warned you to use your knife."

"But the brain of the thing?" cried Fremantle. "Why, man, has a plant will and knowledge and malevolence?"

"Not of itself, as I believe," answered Low. "Perhaps you will prefer to attribute much to the long arm of coincidence, but the explanation I can offer is one that has long been held by occultists in other countries. Pythagoras and others have taught that the forms of incarnation change as the soul raises or debases itself during each spell of life. Connect with this the belief of the Brahmins, and, I may add, of various African tribes, that an earth-bound spirit, at the moment of a premature or sudden death, may pass into plants or trees of certain species, by virtue of an inherent attraction possessed by these plants for such entities. To go further, it is said that these degraded souls have intervals during which they have power of voluntary action to do good or evil, and such action has influence on their future incarnations."

"What do you mean? What do you intend us to believe?" Montesson said, and stopped.

"It is hard to put it into words in these later days of unbelief," said Low, "but the evidence goes to show that a man—presumably not a good man—dies a sudden death near this plant, even inoculated with its sap. Fremantle knows this plant to be a Malayan creeper, belonging to a family that possess strange power and properties. I may recall the old story of the upas tree, and more lately still the murder tree discovered near Kolwe, in East Africa, by Herr Boltze. There are also other instances."

"It is incredible!" said Fremantle almost angrily.

"I don't ask you to believe it," said Flaxman Low quietly, "I only tell you such beliefs exist. Montesson can do something towards proving my theory. Let him have the plant destroyed, and judge by the results."

The tendril of the creeper severed by Mr. Low in his struggle was presented by him to the authorities at Kew.

Mr. Montesson has acted upon Mr. Flaxman Low's suggestions. The Grey House is now occupied and safe, and it is a strange fact that no plant, not even the hardy ivy, will live where the red-blossomed creeper once grew.

FEET FOREMOST

THE house warming at Low Threshold Hall was not an event that affected many people. The local newspaper, however, had half a column about it, and one or two daily papers supplemented the usual August dearth of topics with pictures of the house. They were all taken from the same angle, and showed a long, low building in the Queen Anne style flowing away from a square tower on the left which was castellated and obviously of much earlier date, the whole structure giving somewhat the impression to a casual glance of a domesticated church, or even of a small railway train that had stopped dead on finding itself in a park. Beneath the photograph was written something like "Suffolk Manor House re-occupied after a hundred and fifty years", and, in one instance, "Inset, (L.) Mr. Charles Ampleforth, owner of Low Threshold Hall; (R.) Sir George Willings, the architect responsible for the restoration of this interesting medieval relic." Mr. Ampleforth's handsome, slightly Disraelian head, nearly spiked on his own flagpole, smiled congratulations at the grey hair and rounded features of Sir George Willings who, suspended like a bubble above the Queen Anne wing, discreetly smiled back.

To judge from the photograph, time had dealt gently with Low Threshold Hall. Only a trained observer could have told how much of the original fabric had been renewed. The tower looked particularly convincing. While as for the gardens sloping down to the stream which bounded the foreground of the picture—they had that old-world air which gardens so quickly acquire. To see those lush lawns and borders as a meadow, that mellow brickwork under scaffolding, needed a strong effort of the imagination.

But the guests assembled in Mr. Ampleforth's drawing-room after dinner and listening to their host as, not for the first time, he enlarged upon the obstacles faced and overcome in the work of restoration, found it just as hard to believe that the house was old. Most of them had been taken to see it, at one time or another, in process of reconstruction; yet even within a few days of its completion, how unfinished a house looks! Its habitability seems determined in the last few hours. Magdalen Winthrop, whose beautiful, expressive face still (to her hostess's sentimental eye) bore traces of the slight disappointment she had suffered earlier in the evening, felt as if she were in an Aladdin's palace. Her glance wandered appreciatively from the Samarcand rugs to the pale green walls, and dwelt with pleasure on the high shallow arch, flanked by slender columns, the delicate lines of which were emphasised by the darkness of the hall behind them. It all seemed so perfect and so new; not only every sign of decay but the very sense of age had been banished. How absurd not to be able to find a single grey hair, so to speak, in a house that had stood empty for a hundred and fifty years! Her eyes, still puzzled, came to rest on the company, ranged in an irregular circle round the open fireplace.

"What's the matter, Maggie?" said a man at her side, obviously glad to turn the conversation away from bricks and mortar. "Looking for something?"

Mrs. Ampleforth, whose still lovely skin under the abundant white hair made her face look like a rose in snow, bent forward over the cream-coloured satin bedspread she was embroidering and smiled. "I was only thinking," said Maggie, turning to her host whose recital had paused but not died upon his lips, "how surprised the owls and bats would be if they could come in and see the change in their old home."

"Oh, I do hope they won't," cried a high female voice from the depths of a chair whose generous proportions obscured the speaker.

"Don't be such a baby, Eileen," said Maggie's neighbour in tones that only a husband could have used. "Wait till you see the family ghost."

"Ronald, please! Have pity on my poor nerves!" The upper half of a tiny, childish, imploring face peered like a crescent moon over the rim of the chair.

"If there is a ghost," said Maggie, afraid that her original remark might be construed as a criticism, "I envy him his beautiful surroundings. I would willingly take his place."

"Hear, hear," agreed Ronald. "A very happy haunting-ground. Is there a ghost, Charles?"

There was a pause. They all looked at their host.

"Well," said Mr. Ampleforth, who rarely spoke except after a pause and never without a slight impressiveness of manner, "there is and there isn't."

The silence grew even more respectful.

"The ghost of Low Threshold Hall," Mr. Ampleforth continued, "is no ordinary ghost."

"It wouldn't be," muttered Ronald in an aside Maggie feared might be audible.

"It is, for one thing," Mr. Ampleforth pursued, "exceedingly considerate."

"Oh, how?" exclaimed two or three voices.

"It only comes by invitation."

"Can anyone invite it?"

"Yes, anyone."

There was nothing Mr. Ampleforth liked better than answering questions; he was evidently enjoying himself now.

"How is the invitation delivered?" Ronald asked. "Does one telephone, or does one send a card: 'Mrs. Ampleforth requests the pleasure of Mr. Ghost's company on—well—what is to-morrow?—the eighteenth August, Moaning and Groaning and Chain Rattling. R.S.V.P.'?"

"That would be a sad solecism," said Mr. Ampleforth. "The ghost of Low Threshold Hall is a lady."

"Oh," cried Eileen's affected little voice. "I'm so thankful. I should be much less frightened of a female phantom."

"She hasn't attained years of discretion," Mr. Ampleforth said. "She was only sixteen when—"

"Then she's not 'out'?"

"Not in the sense you mean. I hope she's not 'out' in any sense," said Mr. Ampleforth, with grim facetiousness.

There was a general shudder.

"Well, I'm glad we can't ask her to an evening party," observed Ronald. "A ghost at tea-time is much less alarming. Is she what is called a 'popular' girl?"

"I'm afraid not."

"Then why do people invite her?"

"They don't realise what they're doing."

"A kind of pig in a poke business, what? But you haven't told us yet how we're to get hold of the little lady."

"That's quite simple," said Mr. Ampleforth readily. "She comes to the door."

The drawing-room clock began to strike eleven, and no one spoke till it had finished.

"She comes to the door," said Ronald with an air of deliberation, and then—don't interrupt, Eileen, I'm in charge of the cross-examination—she—she hangs about—"

"She waits to be asked inside."

"I suppose there is a time-honoured formula of invitation: 'Sweet Ermyntrude, in the name of the master of the house I bid thee welcome to Low Threshold Hall. There's no step, so you can walk straight in' Charles, much as I admire your house, I do think it's incomplete without a doorstep. A ghost could just sail in."

"There you make a mistake," said Mr. Ampleforth impressively. "Our ghost cannot enter the house unless she is lifted across the threshold."

"Like a bride," exclaimed Magdalen.

"Yes," said Mr. Ampleforth. "Because she came as a bride." He looked round at his guests with an enigmatic smile.

They did not disappoint him. "Now, Charlie, don't be so mysterious! Do tell us! Tell us the whole story."

Mr. Ampleforth settled himself into his chair. "There's very little to tell," he said, with the reassuring manner of someone who intends to tell a great deal, "but this is the tale. In the time of the Wars of the Roses the owner of Low Threshold Hall (I need not tell you his name was not Ampleforth) married *en troisièmes noces* the daughter of a neighbouring baron much less powerful than he. Lady Elinor Stortford was sixteen when she came and did not live to see her seventeenth birthday. Her husband was a bad hat (I'm sorry to have to say so of a predecessor of mine), a very bad hat. He ill-treated her, drove her mad with terror, and finally killed her."

The narrator paused dramatically but the guests felt slightly disappointed. They had heard so many stories of that kind.

"Poor thing," said Magdalen, feeling that some comment was necessary, however flat. "So now she haunts the place. I suppose it's the nature of ghosts to linger where they've suffered, but it seems illogical to me. I should want to go somewhere else."

"The Lady Elinor would agree with you. The first thing she does when she gets into the house is make plans for getting out. Her visits, as far as I can gather, have generally been brief."

"Then why does she come?" asked Eileen.

"She comes for vengeance." Mr. Ampleforth's voice dropped at the word. "And apparently she gets it. Within a short time of her appearance, someone in the house always dies."

"Nasy spiteful little girl," said Ronald, concealing a yawn. "Then how long is she in residence?"

"Until her object is accomplished."

"Does she make a dramatic departure—in a thunderstorm or something?"

"No, she is just carried out."

"Who carries her this time?"

"The undertaker's men. She goes out with the corpse. Though some say—"

"Oh, Charlie, do stop!" Mrs. Ampleforth interrupted, bending down to gather up the corners of her bedspread. "Eileen will never sleep. Let's go to bed."

"No! No!" shouted Ronald. "He can't leave off like that. I must hear the rest. My flesh was just beginning to creep."

Mr. Ampleforth looked at his wife. "I've had my orders."

"Well, well," said Ronald, resigned. "Anyhow, remember what I said. A decent fall of rain, and you'll have a foot of water under the tower there, unless you put in a doorstep."

Mr. Ampleforth looked grave. "Oh no, I couldn't do that. That would be to invite er—er—trouble. The absence of a step was a precaution. That's how the house got its name."

"A precaution against what?"

"Against Lady Elinor."

"But how? I should have thought a drawbridge would have been more effective."

"Lord Deadham's immediate heirs thought the same. According to the story they put every material obstacle they could to bar the lady's path. You can still see in the tower the grooves which contained the portcullis. And there was a flight of stairs so steep and dangerous they couldn't be used without risk to life and limb. But that only made it easier for Lady Elinor."

"How did it?"

"Why, don't you see, everyone who came to the house, friends and strangers alike, had to be helped over the threshold! There was no way of distinguishing between them. At last when so many members of the family had been killed off that it was threatened with extinction, someone conceived a brilliant idea. Can you guess what it was, Maggie?"

"They removed all the barriers and levelled the threshold, so that any stranger who came to the door and asked to be helped into the house was refused admittance."

"Exactly. And the plan seems to have worked remarkably well."

"But the family did die out in the end," observed Maggie.

"Yes," said Mr. Ampleforth, "soon after the middle of the eighteenth century. The best human plans are fallible, and Lady Elinor was very persistent."

He held the company with his glittering raconteur's eye.

But Mrs. Ampleforth was standing up. "Now, now," she said, "I gave you twenty minutes' grace. It will soon be midnight. Come along, Maggie, you must be tired after your journey. Let me light you a candle." She took the girl's arm and piloted her into the comparative darkness of the hall. "I think they must be on this table," she said, her fingers groping; "I don't know the house myself yet. We ought to have had a light put here. But it's one of Charlie's little economies to have as few lights as possible. I'll tell him about it. But it takes so long to get anything done in this out-of-the-way spot. My dear, nearly three miles to the nearest clergyman, four to the nearest doctor! Ah, here we are, I'll light some for the others. Charlie is still holding about Lady Elinor. You didn't mind that long recital?" she added, as, accompanied by their shadows, they walked up the stairs. "Charlie does so love an audience. And you don't feel uncomfortable or anything? I am always so sorry for Lady Elinor, poor soul, if she ever existed. Oh, and I wanted to say we were so disappointed about Antony. I feel we got you down today on false pretences. Something at the office kept him. But he's coming to-morrow. When is the wedding to be, dearest?"

"In the middle of September."

"Quite soon now. I can't tell you how excited I am about it. I think he's such a dear. You both are. Now which is your way, left, right, or middle? I'm ashamed to say I've forgotten."

Maggie considered. "I remember; it's to the left."

"In that black abyss? Oh, darling, I forgot; do you feel equal to going on the picnic to-morrow? We shan't get back till five. It'll be a long day: I'll stay at home with you if you like—I'm tired of ruins."

"I'd love to go."

"Good-night, then."

"Good-night."

In the space of ten minutes the two men, left to themselves, had succeeded in transforming the elegant Queen Mary drawing-room into something that looked and smelt like a bar-parlour.

"Well," observed Ronald who, more than his host, had been responsible for the room's deterioration, "time to turn in. I have a rendezvous with Lady Elinor. By the way, Charles," he went on, "have you given the servants instructions in anti-Elinor technique—told them only to admit visitors who can enter the house under their own steam, so to speak?"

"Mildred thought it wisest, and I agree with her," said Mr. Ampleforth, "to tell the servants nothing at all. It might unsettle them, and we shall have hard work to keep them as it is."

"Perhaps you're right," said Ronald. "Anyhow it's no part of their duty to show the poor lady out. Charles, what were you going to say that wasn't fit for ears polite when Mildred stopped you?"

Mr. Ampleforth reflected. "I wasn't aware—"

"Oh, yes, she nipped your smoking-room story in the bud. I asked 'Who carries Lady Elinor out?' and you said 'The undertaker's men? she goes out with the corpse', and you were going to say something else when you were called to order."

"Oh, I remember," said Mr. Ampleforth. "It was such a small point, I couldn't imagine why Mildred objected. According to one story, she doesn't go out *with* the corpse, she goes out *in* it."

Ronald pondered. "Don't see much difference, do you?"

"I can't honestly say I do."

"Women are odd creatures," Ronald said. "So long."

The cat stood by the library door, miaowing. Its intention was perfectly plain. First it had wanted to go out; then it strolled up and down outside the window, demanding to come in; now it wanted to go out again. For the third time in half an hour Antony Fairfield rose from his comfortable chair to do its bidding. He opened the door gently—all his movements were gentle; but the cat scuttled ignominiously out, as though he had kicked it. Antony looked round. How could he defend himself from disturbance without curtailing the cat's liberty of movement? He might leave the window and the door open, to give the animal freedom of exit and entrance; though he hated sitting in a room with the door open, he was prepared to make the sacrifice. But he couldn't leave the window open because the rain would come in and spoil Mrs. Ampleforth's beautiful silk cushions. Heavens, how it rained! Too bad for the farmers, thought Antony, whose mind was always busying itself with other people's misfortunes. The crops had been looking so well as he drove in the sunshine from the station, and now this sudden storm would beat everything down. He arranged his chair so that he could see the window and not keep the cat waiting if she felt like paying him another visit. The pattering of the rain soothed him. Half an hour and they would be back—Maggie would be back. He tried to visualise their faces, all so well known to him: but the experiment was not successful. Maggie's image kept ousting the others; it even appeared, somewhat grotesquely, on the top of Ronald's well-tailored shoulders. They mustn't find me asleep, thought Antony; I should look too middle aged. So he picked up the newspaper from the floor and turned to the cross-word puzzle. "Nine points of the law" in nine-ten letters. That was a very easy one: "Possession." Possession, thought Antony; I must put that down. But as he had no pencil and was too sleepy to get one, he repeated the word over and over again: Possession, Possession. It worked like a charm. He fell asleep and dreamed.

In his dream he was still in the library, but it was night and somehow his chair had got turned around so that he no longer faced the window, but he knew that the cat was there, asking to come in; only someone—Maggie—was trying to persuade him not to let it in. "It's not a cat at all," she kept saying; "it's a Possession. I can see its nine points, and they're very sharp." But he knew that she was mistaken, and really meant nine lives, which all cats have: so he thrust her aside and ran to the window and opened it. It was too dark to see, so he put out his hand where he thought the cat's body would be, expecting to feel the warm fur; but what met his hand was not warm, nor was it fur.... He woke with a start to see the butler standing in front of him. The room was flooded with sunshine.

"Oh, Rundle," he cried, "I was asleep. Are they back?"

The butler smiled.

"No, sir, but I expect them every minute now."

"But you wanted me?"

"Well, sir, there's a young lady called, and I said the master was out, but she said could she speak to the gentleman in the library? She must have seen you, sir, as she passed the window."

"How very odd. Does she know me?"

"That was what she said, sir. She talks rather funny."

"All right, I'll come."

Antony followed the butler down the long corridor. When they reached the tower their footsteps ran on the paved floor. A considerable pool of water, the result of the recent heavy shower, had formed on the flagstones near the doorway. The door stood open, letting in a flood of light; but of the caller there was no sign.

"She was here a moment ago," the butler said.

"Ah, I see her," cried Antony. "At least, isn't that her reflected in the water? She must be leaning against the door-post."

"That's right," said Rundle. "Mind the puddle, sir. Let me give you a hand. I'll have all this cleared up before they come back."

Five minutes later two cars, closely following each other, pulled up at the door, and the picnic party tumbled out.

"Dear me, how wet!" cried Mrs. Ampleforth, standing in the doorway. "What has happened, Rundle? Has there been a flood?"

"It was much worse before you arrived, madam," said the butler, disappointed that his exertions with mop, floor-cloth, scrubbing-brush, and pail were being so scantily recognised. "You could have sailed a boat on it. Mr. Antony, he—"

"Oh, has he arrived? Antony's here, isn't that splendid?"

"Antony!" they all shouted. "Come out! Come down! Where are you?"

"I bet he's asleep, the lazy devil," remarked Ronald.

"No sir," said the butler, at last able to make himself heard. "Mr. Antony's in the drawing-room with a lady."

Mrs. Ampleforth's voice broke the silence that succeeded this announcement.

"With a lady, Rundle? Are you sure?"

"Well, madam, she's hardly more than a girl."

"I always thought Antony was that sort of man," observed Ronald. "Maggie, you'd better—"

"It's too odd," interposed Mrs. Ampleforth hastily, "who in the world can she be?"

"I don't see there's anything odd in someone calling on us," said Mr. Ampleforth. "What's her name, Rundle?"

"She didn't give a name, sir."

"That is rather extraordinary. Antony is so impulsive and kind-hearted. I hope—ah, here he is."

Antony came towards them along the passage, smiling and waving his hands. When the welcoming and handshaking were over:

"We were told you had a visitor," said Mrs Ampleforth.

"Yes," said Ronald. "I'm afraid we arrived at the wrong moment."

Antony laughed and then looked puzzled. "Believe me, you didn't," he said. "You almost saved my life. She speaks such a queer dialect when she speaks at all, and I had reached the end of my small talk. But she's rather interesting. Do come along and see her: I left her in the library." They followed Antony down the passage. When they reached the door he said to Mrs. Ampleforth:

"Shall I go in first? She may be shy at meeting so many people."

He went in. A moment later they heard his voice raised in excitement.

"Mildred! I can't find her! She's gone!"

Tea had been cleared away, but Antony's strange visitor was still the topic of conversation. "I can't understand it," he was saying, not for the first time. "The windows were shut, and if she'd gone by the door we must have seen her."

"Now, Antony," said Ronald severely, "let's hear the whole story again. Remember, you are accused of smuggling into the house a female of doubtful reputation. Furthermore the prosecution alleges that when you heard us call (we were shouting ourselves hoarse, but he didn't come at once, you remember) you popped her out of that window and came out to meet us, smiling sheepishly, and feebly gesticulating. What do you say?"

"I've told you everything," said Antony. "I went to the door and found her leaning against the stonework. Her eyes were shut. She didn't move and I thought she must be ill. So I said, 'Is anything the matter?' and she looked up and said, 'My leg hurts'. Then I saw by the way she was standing that her hip must have been broken once and never properly set. I asked her where she lived, and she didn't seem to understand me; so I changed the form of the question, as one does on the telephone, and asked where she came from, and she said, A little further down', meaning down the hill, I suppose."

"Probably from one of the men's cottages," said Mr. Ampleforth.

"I asked if it was far, and she said 'No', which was obvious, otherwise her clothes would have been wet and they weren't, only a little muddy. She even had some mud on her medieval bridesmaid's head-dress (I can't describe her clothes again, Mildred; you know how bad I am at that). So I asked if she'd had a fall, and she said, 'No, I got dirty coming up', or so I understood her. It wasn't easy to understand her; I suppose she talked the dialect of these parts. I concluded (you all say you would have known long before) that she was a little mad, but I didn't like to leave her looking so rotten, so I said, 'Won't you come in and rest a minute?' Then I wished I hadn't."

"Because she looked so pleased?"

"Oh, much more than pleased. And she said, 'I hope you won't live to regret it', rather as though she hoped I should. And then I only meant just to take her hand, because of the water, you know, and she was lame—"

"And instead she flung herself into the poor fellow's arms—"

"Well, it amounted to that. I had no option! So I carried her across and put her down and she followed me here, walking better than I expected. A minute later you arrived. I asked her to wait and she didn't. That's all."

"I should like to have seen Antony doing the St. Christopher act!" said Ronald. "Was she heavy, old boy?"

Antony shifted his chair. "Oh no," he said, "not at all. Not at all heavy." Unconsciously he stretched his arms out in front of him, as though testing an imaginary weight. "I see my hands are grubby," he said with an expression of distaste. "I must go and wash them. I won't be a moment, Maggie."

That night, after dinner, there was some animated conversation in the servants' hall.

"Did you hear any more, Mr. Rundle?" asked a housemaid of the butler, who had returned from performing his final office at the dinner-table.

"I did," said Rundle, "but I don't know that I ought to tell you."

"It won't make any difference, Mr. Rundle, whether you do or don't. I'm going to give in my notice to-morrow. I won't stay in a haunted house. We've been lured here. We ought to have been warned."

"They certainly meant to keep it from us," said Rundle. "I myself had put two and two together after seeing Lady Elinor; what Wilkins said when he came in for his tea only confirmed my suspicions. No gardener can ever keep a still tongue in his head. It's a pity."

"Wouldn't you have told us yourself, Mr. Rundle?" asked the cook.

"I should have used my discretion," the butler replied. "When I informed Mr. Ampleforth that I was no longer in ignorance, he said 'I rely on you, Rundle, not to say anything which might alarm the staff'."

"Mean, I call it," exclaimed the kitchen-maid indignantly. "They want to have all the fun and leave us to die like rats in a trap."

Rundle ignored the interruption.

"I told Mr. Ampleforth that Wilkins had been tale-bearing and would he excuse it in an outdoor servant, but unfortunately we were now in possession of the facts."

"That's why they talked about it at dinner," said the maid who helped Rundle to wait.

"They didn't really throw the mask off till after you'd gone, Lizzie," said the butler. "Then I began to take part in the conversation."

He paused for a moment.

"Mr. Ampleforth asked me whether anything was missing from the house, and I was able to reply, 'No, everything was in order'."

"What else did you say?" inquired the cook.

"I made the remark that the library window wasn't fastened, as they thought, but only closed, and Mrs. Turnbull laughed and said, 'Perhaps it's only a thief, after all', but the others didn't think she could have got through the window anyhow, unless her lameness was all put on. And then I told them what the police had said about looking out for a suspicious character."

"Did they seem frightened?" asked the cook.

"Not noticeably," replied the butler. "Mrs. Turnbull said she hoped the gentlemen wouldn't stay long over their port. Mr. Ampleforth said, 'No, they have had a full day, and would be glad to go to bed'. Mrs. Ampleforth asked Miss Winthrop if she wanted to change her bedroom, but she said she didn't. Then Mr. Fairfield asked if he could have some iodine for his hand, and Miss Winthrop said she would fetch him some. She wanted to bring it after dinner, but he said, 'Oh to-morrow morning will do, darling'. He seemed rather quiet."

"What's he done to his hand?"

"I saw the mark when he took his coffee. It was like a burn."

"They didn't say they were going to shut the house up, or anything?"

"Oh Lord, no. There's going to be a party next week. They'll all have to stay for that."

"I never knew such people," said the kitchen-maid. "They'd

rather die, and us too, than miss their pleasures. I wouldn't stay another day if I wasn't forced. When you think she may be here in this very room, listening to us!" She shuddered.

"Don't you worry, my girl," said Rundle, rising from his chair with a gesture of dismissal. "She won't waste her time listening to you."

"We really might be described as a set of crocks," said Mr. Ampleforth to Maggie, after luncheon the following day. "You, poor dear, with your headache; Eileen with her nerves; I with—well—a touch of rheumatism; Antony with his bad arm."

Maggie looked troubled.

"My headache is nothing, but I'm afraid Antony isn't very well."

"He's gone to lie down, hasn't he?"

"Yes."

"The best thing. I telephoned for the doctor to come this evening. He can have a look at all of us, ha! ha! Meanwhile, where will you spend the afternoon? I think the library's the coolest place on a stuffy day like this and I did want to you to see my collection of books about Low Threshold—my Thresholdiana, I call them."

Maggie followed him into the library.

"Here they are. Most of them are nineteenth-century books, publications of the Society of Antiquaries, and so on; but some are older. I got a little man in Charing Cross Road to hunt them out for me; I haven't had time to read them all myself."

Maggie took a book at random from the shelves.

"Now I'll leave you," said her host. "And later in the afternoon I know that Eileen would appreciate a little visit. Ronald says it's nothing, just a little nervous upset, stomach trouble. Between ourselves, I fear Lady Elinor is to blame."

Maggie opened the book. It was called *An Enquiry into the Recent Tragicall Happennings at Low Threshold Hall in the County of Suffolk, with some Animadversions on the Barbarous Customs of our Ancestors.* It opened with a rather tedious account of the semi-mythical origins of the Deadham family. Maggie longed to skip this, but she might have to discuss the book with Mr. Ampleforth, so she ploughed on. Her persistence was rewarded by a highly coloured picture of Lady Elinor's husband and an account of the cruelties he practised on her. The story would have been too painful to read had not the author (Maggie felt) so obviously drawn upon a very vivid imagination. But suddenly her eyes narrowed. What was this?

—Once in a Drunken Fitt he so mishandled her that her thigh

was broken near the hip, and her screams were so loud they were heard by the servants through three closed doores; and yet he would not summon a Chirurgeon, for (quoth he)...

—Lord Deadham's reason was coarse in the extreme; Maggie hastened on.

And in consequence of these Barbarities her nature, which was soft and yielding at the first, was greatly changed, and those who sawe her now (but Pitie seal'd their lips) would have said she had a Bad Hearte.

No wonder, thought Maggie, reading with a new and painful interest how the murdered woman avenged herself on various descendants, direct and collateral, of her persecutor.

And it hath been generally supposed by the vulgar that her vengeance was directed only against members of that family from which she had taken so many Causeless Hurtes; and the depraved, defective, counterfeit records of those times have lent colour to this Opinion. Whereas the truth is as I now state it, having had access to those death-bed and testamentary depositions which, preserved in ink however faint, do greater service to verity than the relations of Pot-House Historians, enlarged by Memory and confused by Ale. Yet it is on such Testimonies that rash and sceptical Heads rely when they assert that the Lady Elinor had no hand in the late Horrid Occurrence at Low Threshold Hall, which I shall presently describe, thinking that a meer visitor and no blood relation could not be the object of her vengeance, notwithstanding the evidence of two serving-maids, one at the door and one craning her neck from an upper casement, who saw him beare her in: The truth being that she maketh no distinction between persons, but whoso admits her, on him doth her vengeance fall. Seven times she hath brought death to Low Threshold Hall; Three, it is true, being members of the family, but the remaining four indifferent Persons and not connected with them, having in common only this piece of folie, that they, likewise, let her in. And in each case she hath used the same manner of attack, as those who have beheld her first a room's length, then no further than a Lovers Embrace, from her victim have *in articulo mortis* delivered. And the moment when she is no longer seen, which to the watchers seems the Clarion and Reveille of their hopes, is in reality the knell; for she hath not withdrawn further, but approached nearer, she hath not gone out but entered in: and from her dreadful Citadel within the body rejoyces, doubtless, to see the tears and hear the groanes, of those who with Comfortable Faces (albeit with sinking Hearts), would soothe the passage of the parting Soul. Their lacrimatory Effusions are balm to her wicked

Minde; the sad gale and ventilation of their sighs a pleasing Zephyre to her vindictive spirit.

Maggie put down the book for a moment and stared in front of her. Then she began again to read.

Once only hath she been cheated of her Prey, and it happened thus. His Bodie was already swollen with the malignant Humours she had stirred up in him and his life despaired of when a kitchen-wench was taken with an Imposthume that bled inwardly. She being of small account and but lately arrived they did only lay her in the Strawe, charging the Physician (and he nothing loth, expecting no Glory or Profitt from attendance on such a wretched creature) not to Divide his Efforts but use all his skill to save their Cousin (afterwards the twelfth Lord). Notwithstanding which precaution he did hourly get worse until sodainely a change came and he began to amend. Whereat was such rejoycing (including an Ox roasted whole) that the night was spent before they heard that the serving-maid was dead. In their Revels they gave small heed to this Event, not realising that they owed His life to Hers; for a fellow-servant who tended the maid (out of charity) declared that her death and the cousin's recovery followed as quickly as a clock striking Two. And the Physician said it was well, for she would have died in any case.

Whereby we must conclude that the Lady Elinor, like other Apparitions, is subject to certain Lawes. One, to abandon her Victim and seeking another tenement to transfer her vengeance, should its path be crossed by a Body yet nearer Dissolution: and another is, she cannot possess or haunt the corpse after it hath received Christian Buriall. As witness the fact that the day after the Interment of the tenth Lord she again appeared at the Doore and being recognised by her inability to make the Transit was turned away and pelted. And another thing I myself believe but have no proof of is: That her power is circumscribed by the walls of the House; those victims of her Malignitie could have been saved but for the dreadful swiftness of the disease and the doctors unwillingness to move a Sicke man; otherwise how could the Termes of her Curse that she pronounced be fulfilled: "They shall be carried out Feet Foremost"?

Maggie read no more. She walked out of the library with the book under her arm. Before going to see how Antony was, she would put it in her bedroom where no one could find it. Troubled and oppressed, she paused at the head of the stairs. Her way lay straight ahead, but her glance automatically travelled to the right where, at the far end of the passage, Antony's bedroom lay. She looked again; the door, which she could only just see, was shut now. But she could swear it had closed upon a woman. There was nothing odd in that;

Mildred might have gone in, or Muriel, or a servant. But all the same she could not rest. Hurriedly she changed her dress and went to Antony's room. Pausing at the door she listened and distinctly heard his voice, speaking rapidly and in a low tone; but no one seemed to reply. She got no answer to her knock, so, mustering her courage, she walked in.

The blind was down and the room half dark, and the talking continued, which increased her uneasiness. Then, as her eyes got used to the darkness, she realised, with a sense of relief, that he was talking in his sleep. She pulled up the blind a little, so that she might see his hand. The brown mark had spread, she thought, and looked rather puffy, as though coffee had been injected under the skin. She felt concerned for him. He would never have gone properly to bed like that, in his pyjamas, if he hadn't felt ill, and he tossed about restlessly. Maggie bent over him. Perhaps he had been eating a biscuit: there was some gritty stuff on the pillow. She tried to scoop it up but it eluded her. She could make no sense of his mutterings, but the word 'light' came in a good deal. Perhaps he was only half asleep and wanted the blind down. At last her ears caught the sentence that was running on his lips: "She was so light." Light? A light woman? Browning. The words conveyed nothing to her, and not wishing to wake him she tiptoed from the room.

"The doctor doesn't seem to think seriously of any of us, Maggie, you'll be glad to hear," said Mr. Ampleforth, coming into the drawing-room about six o'clock. "Eileen's coming down to dinner. I am to drink less port—I didn't need a doctor, alas! to tell me that. Antony's the only casualty: he's got a slight temperature, and had better stay where he is until to-morrow. The doctor thinks it is one of those damnable horse-flies: his arm is a bit swollen, that's all."

"Has he gone?" asked Maggie quickly.

"Who, Antony?"

"No, no, the doctor."

"Oh, I'd forgotten your poor head. No, you'll just catch him. His car's on the terrace."

The doctor, a kindly, harassed, middle-aged man, listened patiently to Maggie's questions.

"The brown mark? Oh, that's partly the inflammation, partly the iodine—he's been applying it pretty liberally, you know; amateur physicians are all alike; feel they can't have too much of a good thing."

"You don't think the water here's responsible? I wondered if he ought to go away."

"The water? Oh no. No, it's a bite all right, though I confess I can't see the place where the devil got his beak in. I'll come to-morrow, if you like, but there's really no need."

The next morning, returning from his bath, Ronald marched into Antony's room. The blind went up with a whizz and a smack, and Antony opened his eyes.

"Good morning, old man," said Ronald cheerfully. "Thought I'd look in and see you. How goes the blood-poisoning? Better?"

Antony drew up his sleeve and hastily replaced it. The arm beneath was chocolate-coloured to the elbow.

"I feel pretty rotten," he said.

"I say, that's bad luck. What's this?" added Ronald, coming nearer. "Have you been sleeping in both beds?"

"Not to my knowledge," murmured Antony.

"You have, though," said Ronald. "If this bed hasn't been slept in, it's been slept on, or lain on. That I can swear. Only a head, my boy, could have put that dent in the pillow, and only a pair of muddy—hullo! The pillow's got it, too."

"Got what?" asked Antony drowsily.

"Well, if you ask me, it's common garden mould."

"I'm not surprised. I feel pretty mouldy, too."

"Well, Antony; to save your good name with the servants, I'll remove the traces."

With characteristic vigour Ronald swept and smoothed the bed.

"Now you'll be able to look Rundle in the face."

There was a knock on the door.

"If this is Maggie," said Ronald, "I'm going."

It was, and he suited the action to the word.

"You needn't trouble to tell me, dearest," she said, "that you are feeling much better, because I can see that you aren't."

Antony moved his head uneasily on the pillow.

"I don't feel very flourishing, to tell you the honest truth."

"Listen"—Maggie tried to make her voice sound casual—"I don't believe this is a very healthy place. Don't laugh, Antony; we're all of us more or less under the weather. I think you ought to go away."

"My dear, don't be hysterical. One often feels rotten when one wakes up. I shall be all right in a day or two."

"Of course you will. But all the same if you were in Sussex Square you could call in Fosbrook—and, well, I should be more comfortable."

"But you'd be here!"

"I could stay at Pamela's."

"But, darling, that would break up the party. I couldn't do it; and it wouldn't be fair to Mildred."

"My angel, you're no good to the party, lying here in bed. And as long as you're here, let me warn you they won't see much of me."

A look of irritation Maggie had never noticed before came into his face as he said, almost spitefully:

"Supposing the doctor won't allow you to come in? It may be catching, you know."

Maggie concealed the hurt she felt.

"All the more reason for you to be out of the house."

He pulled up the bedclothes with a gesture of annoyance and turned away.

"Oh, Maggie, don't keep nagging at me. You ought to be called Naggie, not Maggie."

This was an allusion to an incident in Maggie's childhood. Her too great solicitude for a younger brother's safety had provoked the gibe. It had always wounded her, but never so much as coming from Antony's lips. She rose to go.

"Do put the bed straight," said Antony, still with face averted. "Otherwise they'll think you've been sleeping here."

"What?"

"Well, Ronald said something about it."

Maggie closed the door softly behind her. Antony was ill, of course, she must remember that. But he had been ill before, and was always an angelic patient. She went down to breakfast feeling miserable.

After breakfast, at which everyone else had been unusually cheerful, she thought of a plan. It did not prove so easy of execution as she hoped.

"But, dearest Maggie," said Mildred, "the village is nearly three miles away. And there's nothing to see there."

"I love country post-offices," said Maggie; "they always have such amusing things."

"There is a post-office," admitted Mildred. "But are you sure it isn't something we could do from here? Telephone, telegraph?"

"Perhaps there'd be a picture-postcard of the house," said Maggie feebly.

"Oh, but Charlie has such nice ones," Mildred protested. "He's so house-proud, you could trust him for that. Don't leave us for two hours just to get postcards. We shall miss you so much, and think of poor Antony left alone all the morning."

Maggie had been thinking of him.

"He'll get on all right without me," she said lightly.

"Well, wait till the afternoon when the chauffeur or Ronald can run you over in a car. He and Charlie have gone into Norwich and won't be back till lunch."

"I think I'll walk," said Maggie. "It'll do me good."

"I managed that very clumsily," she thought, "so how shall I persuade Antony to tell me the address of his firm?"

To her surprise his room was empty. He must have gone away in the middle of writing a letter, for there were sheets lying about on the writing-table and, what luck! an envelope addressed to Higgins & Stukeley, 312 Paternoster Row. A glance was all she really needed to memorise the address; but her eyes wandered to the litter on the table. What a mess! There were several pages of notepaper covered with figures. Antony had been making calculations and, as his habit was, decorating them with marginal illustrations. He was good at drawing faces, and he had a gift for catching a likeness. Maggie had often seen, and been gratified to see, slips of paper embellished with portraits of herself—full-face, side-face, three-quarter-face. But this face that looked out from among the figures and seemed to avoid her glance, was not hers. It was the face of a woman she had never seen before but whom she felt she would recognise anywhere, so consistent and vivid were the likenesses. Scattered among the loose leaves were the contents of Antony's pocket-book. She knew he always carried her photograph. Where was it? Seized by an impulse, she began to rummage among the papers. Ah, here it was. But it was no longer hers! With a few strokes Antony had transformed her oval face, unlined and soft of feature, into a totally different one, a pinched face with high cheekbones, hollow cheeks, and bright hard eyes, from whose corners a sheaf of fine wrinkles spread like a fan: a face with which she was already too familiar.

Unable to look at it, she turned away and saw Antony standing behind her. He seemed to have come from the bath for he carried a towel and was wearing his dressing-gown.

"Well," he said. "Do you think it's an improvement?"

She could not answer him, but walked over to the wash-stand, and took up the thermometer that was lying on it.

"Ought you to be walking about like that," she said at last, "with a temperature of a hundred?"

"Perhaps not," he replied, making two or three goat-like skips towards the bed. "But I feel rather full of beans this morning."

Maggie edged away from his smile towards the door.

"There isn't anything I can do for you?"

"Not to-day, my darling."

The term of endearment struck her like a blow.

Maggie sent off her telegram and turned into the village street. The fact of being able to do something had relieved her mind: already in imagination she saw Antony being packed into the

Ampleforth's Daimler with rugs and hot-water bottles, and herself, perhaps, seated by the driver. They were endlessly kind, and would make no bones about motoring him to London. But though her spirits were rising her body felt tired; the day was sultry, and she had hurried. Another bad night like last night, she thought, and I shall be a wreck. There was a chemist's shop over the way, and she walked in.

"Can I have some sal volatile?"

"Certainly, madam."

She drank it and felt better.

"Oh, and have you anything in the way of a sleeping draught?"

"We have some allodanol tablets, madam."

"I'll take them."

"Have you a doctor's prescription?"

"No."

"Then I'm afraid you'll have to sign the poison book. Just a matter of form."

Maggie recorded her name idly wondering what J. Bates, her predecessor on the list, meant to do with his cyanide of potassium.

"We must try not to worry," said Mrs. Ampleforth, handing Maggie her tea, "but I must say I'm glad the doctor has come. It relieves one of responsibility, doesn't it? Not that I feel disturbed about Antony—he was quite bright when I went to see him just before lunch. And he's been sleeping since. But I quite see what Maggie means. He doesn't seem himself. Perhaps it would be a good plan, as she suggests, to send him to London. He would have better advice there."

Rundle came in.

"A telegram for Mr. Fairfield, madam."

"It's been telephoned: 'Your presence urgently required Tuesday morning—Higgins & Stukeley'. Tuesday, that's to-morrow. Everything seems to point to his going, doesn't it, Charles?"

Maggie was delighted, but a little surprised, that Mrs. Ampleforth had fallen in so quickly with the plan of sending Antony home.

"Could he go to-day?" she asked.

"To-morrow would be too late, wouldn't it?" said Mr. Ampleforth drily. "The car's at his disposal: he can go whenever he likes."

Through her relief Maggie felt a little stab of pain that they were both so ready to see the last of Antony. He was generally such a popular guest.

"I could go with him," she said.

Instantly they were up in arms. Ronald the most vehement of all. "I'm sure Antony wouldn't want you to. You know what I mean,

Maggie, it's such a long drive, in a closed car on a stuffy evening. Charlie says he'll send a man, if necessary."

Mr. Ampleforth nodded.

"But if he were ill!" cried Maggie.

The entrance of the doctor cut her short. He looked rather grave.

"I wish I could say I was satisfied with Mr. Fairfield's progress," he said, "but I can't. The inflammation has spread up the arm as far as the shoulder, and there's some fever. His manner is odd, too, excitable and apathetic by turns." He paused. "I should like a second opinion."

Mr. Ampleforth glanced at his wife.

"In that case wouldn't it be better to send him to London? As a matter of fact, his firm had telegraphed for him. He could go quite comfortably in the car."

The doctor answered immediately:

"I wouldn't advise such a course. I think it would be most unwise to move him. His firm—you must excuse me—will have to do without him for a day or two."

"Perhaps," suggested Maggie, trembling, "it's a matter that could be arranged at his house. They could send over someone from the office. I know they make a fuss about having him on the spot," she concluded lamely.

"Or, doctor," said Mr. Ampleforth, "could you do us a very great kindness and go with him? We could telephone to his doctor to meet you, and the car would get you home by midnight."

The doctor squared his shoulders: he was clearly one of those men whose resolution stiffens under opposition.

"I consider it would be the height of folly," he said, "to move him out of the house. I dare not do it on my responsibility. I will get a colleague over from Ipswich to-morrow morning. In the meantime, with your permission, I will arrange for a trained nurse to be sent to-night."

Amid a subdued murmur of final instructions, the doctor left.

As Maggie, rather late, was walking upstairs to dress for dinner she met Rundle. He looked anxious.

"Excuse me, miss," he said, "but have you seen Mr. Fairfield? I've asked everyone else, and they haven't. I took him up his supper half an hour ago, and he wasn't in his room. He'd got his dress clothes out, but they were all on the bed except the stiff shirt."

"Have you been to look since?" asked Maggie.

"No, miss."

"I'll go and see."

She tiptoed along the passage to Antony's door. A medley of sounds, footsteps, drawers being opened and shut, met her ears.

She walked back to Rundle. "He's in there all right," she said. "Now I must make haste and dress."

A few minutes later a bell rang in the kitchen.

"Who's that?"

"Miss Winthrop's room," said the cook. "Hurry up, Lettice, or you'll have Rundle on your track—he'll be back in a minute."

"I don't want to go," said Lettice. "I tell you I feel that nervous—"

"Nonsense, child," said the cook. "Run along with you."

No sooner had the maid gone than Rundle appeared.

"I've had a bit of trouble with Master Antony," he said. "He's got it into his head that he wants to come down to dinner. 'Rundle', he said to me, confidentially, 'do you think it would matter us being seven? I want them to meet my new friend'. 'What friend, Mr. Fairfield?' I said. 'Oh', he said, 'haven't you seen her? She's always about with me now'. Poor chap, he used to be the pick of the bunch, and now I'm afraid he's going potty."

"Do you think he'll really come down to dinner?" asked the cook, but before Rundle could answer Lettice rushed into the room.

"Oh," she cried, "I knew it would be something horrid! I knew it would be! And now she wants a floor cloth and pail! She says they mustn't know anything about it! But I won't go again—I won't bring it down, I won't even touch it!"

"What won't you touch?"

"That waste-paper basket."

"Why, what's the matter with it?"

"It's ... it's all bloody!"

When the word was out she grew calmer, and even seemed anxious to relate her experience.

"I went upstairs directly she rang" ("That's an untruth to start with," said the cook) "and she opened the door a little way and said, 'Oh, Lettice, I've been so scared!' And I said, 'What's the matter, miss?' And she said, 'There's a cat in here'. Well, I didn't think that was much to be frightened of, so I said, 'Shall I come in and catch him, miss?' and she said (deceitful-like, as it turned out), 'I should be so grateful'. Then I went in, but I couldn't see the cat anywhere, so I said, 'Where is he?' At which she pointed to the waste-paper basket away by the dressing-table, and said, 'In that waste-paper basket'. I said, 'Why, that makes it easier, miss, if he'll stay there'. She said, 'Oh, he'll stay there all right'. Of course I took her meaning in a moment, because I know cats do choose queer, out-of-the-way places to die in, so I said, 'You mean the poor creature's dead, miss?' and I was just going across to get him because ordinarily I don't mind the body of an animal, when she said (I will do her that justice), 'Stop a minute, Lettice, he isn't dead; he's been murdered'. I saw she was all trembling, and that made me tremble, too. And when I looked in the basket—well—"

She paused, partly perhaps to enjoy the dramatic effect of her announcement. "Well, if it wasn't our Thomas! Only you couldn't have recognised him, poor beast, his head was bashed in that cruel."

"Thomas!" said the cook. "Why, he was here only an hour ago."

"That's what I said to Miss Winthrop. 'Why, he was in the kitchen only an hour ago', and then I came over funny, and when she asked me to help her clean the mess up I couldn't, not if my life depended on it. But I don't feel like that now," she ended inconsequently. "I'll go back and do it!" She collected her traps and departed.

"Thomas!" muttered Rundle. "Who could have wished the poor beast any harm? Now I remember, Mr. Fairfield did ask me to get him out a clean shirt.... I'd better go up and ask him."

He found Antony in evening dress seated at the writing-table. He had stripped it of writing materials and the light from two candles gleamed on its polished surface. Opposite to him on the other side of the table was an empty chair. He was sitting with his back to the room; his face, when he turned it at Rundle's entrance, was blotchy and looked terribly tired.

"I decided to dine here after all, Rundle," he said. Rundle saw that the Bovril was still untouched in his cup.

"Why, your supper'll get cold, Mr. Fairfield," he said.

"Mind your own business," said Antony. "I'm waiting."

The Empire clock on the drawing-room chimney-piece began to strike, breaking into a conversation which neither at dinner nor afterwards had been more than desultory.

"Eleven," said Mr. Ampleforth. "The nurse will be here any time now. She ought to be grateful to you, Ronald, for getting him into bed."

"I didn't enjoy treating Antony like that," said Ronald.

There was a silence.

"What was that?" asked Maggie suddenly.

"It sounded like the motor."

"Might have been," said Mr. Ampleforth. "You can't tell from here."

They strained their ears, but the rushing sound had already died away. "Eileen's gone to bed, Maggie," said Mrs. Ampleforth. "Why don't you? We'll wait up for the nurse, and tell you when she comes."

Rather reluctantly, Maggie agreed to go.

She had been in her bedroom about ten minutes, and was feeling too tired to take her clothes off, when there came a knock at the door. It was Eileen.

"Maggie," she said, "the nurse has arrived. I thought you'd like to know."

"Oh, how kind of you," said Maggie. "They were going to tell me, but I expect they forgot. Where is she?"

"In Antony's room. I was coming from the bath and his door was open."

"Did she look nice?"

"I only saw her back."

"I think I'll go along and speak to her," said Maggie.

"Yes, do. I don't think I'll go with you."

As she walked along the passage Maggie wondered what she would say to the nurse. She didn't mean to offer her professional advice. But even nurses are human, and Maggie didn't want this stranger to imagine that Antony was, well, always like that—the spoilt, tiresome, unreasonable creature of the last few hours. She could find no harsher epithets for him, even after all his deliberate unkindness. The woman would probably have heard that Maggie was his fianceé; Maggie would try to show her that she was proud of the relationship and felt it an honour.

The door was still open, so she knocked and walked in. But the figure that uncoiled itself from Antony's pillow and darted at her a look of malevolent triumph was not a nurse, nor was her face strange to Maggie; Maggie could see, so intense was her vision at that moment, just what strokes Antony had used to transform her own portrait into Lady Elinor's. She was terrified, but she could not bear to see Antony's rather long hair nearly touching the floor nor the creature's thin hand on his labouring throat. She advanced, resolved at whatever cost to break up this dreadful tableau. She approached near enough to realise that what seemed a stranglehold was probably a caress, when Antony's eyes rolled up at her and words, frothy and toneless like a chain of bursting bubbles, came popping from the corner of his swollen mouth: "Get out, damn you!" At the same moment she heard the stir of presences behind her and a voice saying, "Here is the patient, nurse; I'm afraid he's half out of bed, and here's Maggie, too. What *have* you been doing to him, Maggie?" Dazed, she turned about. "Can't you see?" she cried; but she might have asked the question of herself, for when she looked back she could only see the tumbled bed, the vacant pillow, and Antony's hair trailing the floor.

The nurse was a sensible woman. Fortified by tea, she soon

bundled everybody out of the room. A deeper quiet than night ordinarily brings invaded the house. The reign of illness had begun.

A special embargo was laid on Maggie's visits. The nurse said she had noticed that Miss Winthrop's presence agitated the patient. But Maggie extracted a promise that she should be called if Antony got worse. She was too tired and worried to sleep, even if she had tried to, so she sat up fully dressed in a chair, every now and then trying to allay her anxiety by furtive visits to Antony's bedroom door.

The hours passed on leaden feet. She tried to distract herself by reading the light literature with which her hostess had provided her. Though she could not keep her attention on the books, she continued to turn their pages, for only so could she keep at bay the conviction that had long been forming at the back of her mind and that now threatened to engulf her whole consciousness: the conviction that the legend about Low Threshold was true. She was neither hysterical nor superstitious, and for a moment she had managed to persuade herself that what she had seen in Antony's room was an hallucination. The passing hours robbed her of that solace. Antony was the victim of Lady Elinor's vengeance. Everything pointed to it; the circumstances of her appearance, the nature of Antony's illness, the horrible deterioration in his character—to say nothing of the drawings, and the cat.

There were only two ways of saving him. One was to get him out of the house; she had tried that and failed; if she tried again she would fail more signally than before. But there remained the other way.

The old book about *The Tragicall Happennings at Low Threshold Hall* still reposed in a drawer; for the sake of her peace of mind Maggie had vowed not to take it out, and till now she had kept her vow. But as the sky began to pale with the promise of dawn and her conviction of Antony's mortal danger grew apace, her resolution broke down.

"Whereby we must conclude," she read, *"that the Lady Elinor, like other Apparitions, is subject to certain Lawes. One, to abandon her Victim and seeking another tenement enter into it and transfer her vengeance, should its path be crossed by a Body yet nearer Dissolution...."*

A knock, that had been twice repeated, startled her out of her reverie.

"Come in!"

"Miss Winthrop," said the nurse, "I'm sorry to tell you the patient is weaker. I think the doctor had better be telephoned for."

"I'll go and get someone," said Maggie. "Is he much worse?"

"Very much, I'm afraid."

Maggie had no difficulty in finding Rundle; he was already up.

"What time is it, Rundle?" she asked. "I've lost count."

"Half-past four, miss." He looked very sorry for her.

"When will the doctor be here?"

"In about an hour, miss, not more."

Suddenly she had an idea. "I'm so tired, Rundle, I think I shall try to get some sleep. Tell them not to call me unless ... unless ..."

"Yes, miss," said Rundle. "You look altogether done up."

About an hour! So she had plenty of time. She took up the book again. *"... transfer her vengeance ... seeking another tenement ... a Body nearer Dissolution...."* Her idle thoughts turned with compassion to the poor servant girl whose death had spelt recovery to Lord Deadham's cousin but been so little regarded: "the night was spent" before they heard that she was dead. Well, this night was spent already. Maggie shivered. "I shall die in my sleep," she thought. "But shall I feel her come?" Her tired body sickened with nausea at the idea of such a loathsome violation. But the thought still nagged at her. "Shall I realise even for a moment that I'm changing into ... into?" Her mind refused to frame the possibility. "Should I have time to do anyone an injury?" she wondered. "I could tie my feet together with a handkerchief; that would prevent me from walking." Walking ... walking.... The word let loose on her mind a new flood of terrors. She could not do it! She could not lay herself open for ever to this horrible occupation! Her tormented imagination began to busy itself with the details of her funeral; she saw mourners following her coffin into the church. But Antony was not amongst them; he was better, but too ill to be there. He could not understand why she had killed herself, for the note she had left gave no hint of the real reason, referred only to continual sleeplessness and nervous depression. So she would not have his company when her body was committed to the ground. But that was a mistake; it would not be her body, it would belong to that other woman and be hers to return to by the right of possession.

All at once the screen which had recorded such vivid images to her mind's eye went blank; and her physical eye, released, roamed wildly about the room. It rested on the book she was still holding. *"She cannot possess or haunt the corpse,"* she read, *"after it hath received Christian Buriall."* Here was a ray of comfort. But (her fears warned her) being a suicide she might not be allowed Christian burial. How then? Instead of the churchyard she saw a cross-roads, with a slanting signpost on which the words could no longer be read; only two or three people were there; they kept looking furtively about them, and the grave-digger had thrown his spade aside and was holding a stake....

She pulled herself together with a jerk. "These are all fancies," she thought. "It wasn't fancy when I signed the poison book." She took up the little glass cylinder; there were eighteen tablets and the dose was one or two. Daylight was broadening apace; she must hurry. She took some note-paper and wrote for five minutes. She had reached the words "No one is to blame" when suddenly her ears were assailed by a tremendous tearing, whirring sound: it grew louder and louder until the whole room vibrated. In the midst of the deafening din something flashed past the window, for a fraction of a second blotting out the daylight. Then there was a crash such as she had never heard in her life.

All else forgotten, Maggie ran to the window. An indescribable scene of wreckage met her eyes. The aeroplane had been travelling at a terrific pace: it was smashed to atoms. To right and left the lawn was littered with fragments, some of which had made great gashes in the grass, exposing the earth. The pilot had been flung clear; she could just see his legs sticking out from a flower-bed under the wall of the house. They did not move and she thought he must be dead.

While she was wondering what to do she heard voices underneath the window.

"We don't seem to be very lucky here just now, Rundle," said Mr. Ampleforth.

"No, sir."

There was a pause. Then Mr. Ampleforth spoke again.

"He's still breathing, I think."

"Yes, sir, he is, just."

"You take his head and I'll take his feet, and we'll get him into the house."

Something began to stir in Maggie's mind. Rundle replied:

"If you'll pardon my saying so, sir, I don't think we ought to move him. I was told once by a doctor that if a man's had a fall or anything it's best to leave him lying."

"I don't think it'll matter if we're careful."

"Really, sir, if you'll take my advice—"

There was a note of obstinacy in Rundle's voice. Maggie, almost beside herself with agitation, longed to fling open the window and cry "Bring him in! Bring him in!" But her hand seemed paralysed and her throat could not form the words.

Presently Mr. Ampleforth said:

"You know, we can't let him stay here. It's beginning to rain."

(Bring him in! Bring him in!)

"Well, sir, it's your responsibility...."

Maggie's heart almost stopped beating.

"Naturally I don't want to do anything to hurt the poor chap."

(Oh, bring him in! Bring him in!)

The rain began to patter on the pane.

"Look here, Rundle, we must get him under cover."

"I'll fetch that bit of wing, sir, and put it over him."

(Bring him in! Bring him in!)

Maggie heard Rundle pulling something that grated on the gravel path. The sound ceased and Mr. Ampleforth said:

"The very thing for a stretcher, Rundle! The earth's so soft we can slide it under him. Careful, careful!." Both men were breathing hard. "Have you got your end? Right." Their heavy, measured footfalls grew fainter and fainter.

The next thing Maggie heard was the car returning with the doctor. Not daring to go out, and unable to sit down, she stood, how long she did not know, holding her bedroom door ajar. At last she saw the nurse coming towards her.

"The patient's a little better, Miss Winthrop. The doctor thinks he'll pull through now."

"Which patient?"

"Oh, there was never any hope for the other poor fellow."

Maggie closed her eyes.

"Can I see Antony?" she said at last.

"Well, you may just peep at him."

Antony smiled at her feebly from the bed.

DENNIS YATES WHEATLEY

THE CASE OF THE LONG-DEAD LORD

"THANK God you've come," Bruce Hemmingway cried, as he gripped the hand of the little man for whom he'd been waiting on the platform at Inverness.

"Your wire interested me," Neils Orsen replied with a gentle smile. "What's this about my being a naturalist?"

"I'll tell you in a minute. Let's go over to the hotel."

As the two men walked across the street they made an oddly assorted couple. Neils Orsen was small and lightly built, with transparently pale skin and large, luminous blue eyes. His domed head with a high intelligent brow and mass of soft hair appeared too large for his diminutive body. Hatless, dressed in pale grey, carrying a basket conspicuously labelled "Live Cat", he made a striking contrast to the tall, dark-haired American by his side.

Over coffee in the hotel Bruce explained while the Siamese cat, Pāst, sat on a chair beside them, lapping cream.

"Arkon Clyde, a friend of mine from back home, has taken Castle Stuart for the shooting. I drew the lease and as the Clydes have never been in Scotland before they asked me to see them settled in. At the moment there's just the old man, who is completely absorbed in books, and his glamorous daughter Fiona; their guests don't arrive for about a week. I've known the girl for some time; she's typical of her generation; sensible, a bit hard-boiled, but full of fun. Yet, when I arrived two days after them, I found her all shot to pieces.

"Well, that puzzled me quite a bit, but the only thing I could get out of her was that for the first time in her life she was suffering from the most appalling nightmares.

"The day before yesterday I took her a walk to explore the ruins of the old castle which are some two miles away. Leading to it there's a lovely avenue of old beeches. We'd nearly got half way along it when suddenly she stopped dead, and a queer look came into her eyes: 'I've been here before,' she whispered to herself, then she began to mutter in what seemed to me like Gaelic. I took hold of her hands and shook her and she looked at me with wide, blinded eyes. As I called her name the spell seemed to snap. She just said she was tired of walking and wanted to go back.

"Maybe I'm wrong, but it didn't seem to me a case for an ordinary doctor, so I asked Arkon if I might have a friend who was a naturalist to stay for a few days, because I didn't want them to know you are a ghost-hunter, and wired you that night."

"Has anything happened since?" the little Swede asked in his careful English that held hardly a trace of accent.

"No, nothing; except that she never goes into her room if she can help it and spends most of her time wandering alone round the grounds."

"Does she strike you as an imaginative young woman?"

"Far from it. She has brains as well as looks and graduated in Law at Columbus."

Neils leaned back, placing the tips of his fingers together.

"So she doesn't like her room? Have you been into it?"

"Yes; I even spent the night before last there, but I slept like a top and yesterday she insisted on returning to it. I can't understand it—I'm sure she's terrified of it and yet she refuses to move."

"The girl may be abnormally psychic; as neither you nor, apparently, her father are in the least disturbed."

"Oh, one thing I forgot. She said that her door wouldn't stay shut. Well, the night I spent there it didn't budge an inch. I know, because I fixed a piece of cotton over the opening and it wasn't broken in the morning."

"At certain phases of the moon, perhaps," Neils hazarded, "the Force—if there is a Force—might be stronger."

"Maybe. But she didn't sleep any better in my room. It's killing her, Neils. A few days ago she was at least scared, and fighting it. Now she's just vague and won't talk. She looked like death at breakfast this morning, but of course her father didn't notice anything; he was buried in some book or other. I don't like leaving her alone. If only I could get that dog to stay with her."

"What dog?"

"The boar-hound that belongs to the place. He liked her at first, but now he runs away as soon as she appears. Can people be possessed, Neils?"

"Certainly; but we've hardly enough evidence to pre-suppose such a thing in this case. Miss Clyde sounds like a girl suffering from a species of nervous collapse. Of course, a place having the history of Castle Stuart behind it would be filled with vibrations from the past, but apart from the dog's behaviour there is nothing to suggest that her condition is the result of psychic causes."

"I know, Neils. But I'll swear something queer is going on. Ten days ago, in London, Fiona was a normal, healthy girl with bags of energy; now she's a nervous wreck and so washed out that one might

—yes, one might even think that a vampire was sapping her vitality."

Pāst closed his eyes and purred softly. "Let us go," said Neils, "to Castle Stuart."

As Bruce turned the car into the gateway the sun was brilliant over the Firth and mountain heads, and he felt a little ashamed at having summoned the famous psychic investigator for so nebulous a purpose. The Castle looked a mild architectural curiosity but no more. There was nothing sinister here where the drive wound among the sun-burnished scrub and pines. Neils, with the cat upon his knees, glanced up at the brown stone battlements.

"But this is not very old," he said, smiling.

"Oh, no, only about a hundred and fifty years. It's just a copy. The ruins of the original castle are about two miles away. It marks one boundary of the estate."

In the great hall sunlight stabbed the worn surfaces of ancient flags that hung motionless, drooping long, twisted shadows across the stairway. While the servants were taking up Orsen's luggage the Swede stood very still, his head inclined as though he listened. Bruce had left him, to look for Fiona. He brought her through the garden door into the hall, where she stood, bathed in the dusty sunlight, her golden hair responding to its caresses; but her lovely green eyes were cold and distant as she shook hands with Orsen.

Her father rushed upon them from the library, American hospitality in every gesture. He was delighted to welcome Bruce's friend. . . . Pāst was cute. . . . He had found some interesting material on the bird-life of the island . . . and the books were ready beside the sherry for the attention of Mr. Orsen.

But Neils refused the wine, and Bruce said sadly, "I'm afraid he never touches alcohol."

Throughout luncheon Neils contrived to show a surprising knowledge of his purported subject and Arkon Clyde took to him immediately; but Fiona obviously found it an effort to concentrate her attention sufficiently to appear barely civil, and directly the meal was over she excused herself abruptly.

" 'Fraid my girl doesn't take to this sort of life very easily," Clyde said in apology as the door closed behind her. "I guess she finds it a bit dull after New York."

"I'll go and see if I can amuse her," Bruce volunteered. Neils made no sign. His small, gnome-like figure remained bowed in contemplation; one hand was playing with a lock of hair.

Bruce found Fiona curled up on a garden seat behind the Castle. Sitting down, he said earnestly: "Fiona, do tell me what's wrong. It's sticking out a mile that you've got something on your mind."

"No! If I tell you, you'll say I'm crazy." She turned away from him and he saw the scarlet mouth tremble. "I'm beginning to think I must be; no sane person could feel the way I do—could"—she spoke in a hard, strained voice "—could feel *haunted*!"

As he remained silent she went on desperately. "Dammit, Bruce, the Castle *is* haunted, and you know it. Why did you let Father bring me here?"

Bruce nodded. "So I was right! Now listen, Fiona. My friend, Neils Orsen, is not really a naturalist but the world's greatest psychic investigator. I wired for him when I saw how things were with you, and I'm darned glad I did, because if anyone can help you, he can. Let me fetch him, then you can tell him all about it."

"I don't think anyone can help me, but you can get him if you promise that Father shan't be worried about me."

When Bruce returned with Orsen, she was sitting in the same position, staring at the ground. She turned her head slightly as they sat down. "Give me a cigarette, please, Bruce." Her hand shook as she held it. "There's something after me in this place," she began. "It won't let me alone. I felt odd when I first saw the Castle as we came up the drive. I knew just how it would look. That gave me a kind of shock, and I didn't tell Father, but I wanted to run away. I knew I oughtn't to go in or stay here. I lost the feeling a little until the evening—I was busy unpacking and getting the place straight. Then, when I was alone in my room before dinner, the door swung open suddenly and made me jump. It was perfectly light, and I could see nothing, but I was scared and ran out of the room. That damned door's been opening every night—except when Bruce slept there—and there's a queer, cold feeling in my head, as though I were forgetting how to think. All the time I have the idea that I know this place—that something is going to happen to me again. If only I could remember what—I might prevent it; but I can't. Wherever I go the air is full of whispers that I can't quite hear—and that was all—until last night."

"Last night," Bruce repeated.

She nodded. "Yes; I was so frightened and wretched that I decided to sleep downstairs. I waited until you and Father were in your rooms. I thought perhaps the boar-hound would be sleeping in the hall; so I stood at the head of the stairs and whistled to him. And from my room—I'd left the door open—there came the most horrible chuckle, very hoarse and—and liquid. The Thing was there—it was watching me—laughing at me. I could feel it."

"What did you do?" Orsen said quietly.

"I heard the dog growl and I ran down to him—but he was scared of something and wouldn't come near me. I stayed in the hall till about four o'clock. I couldn't sit still and I couldn't sleep, so when the light came I went for a walk. I got back about seven, had a bath and came down to breakfast. Oh, God! I'm frightened, Bruce—and I've never been frightened before. It'll get me and keep me for ever and ever. Don't let it! For God's sake don't let it!" She began to sob hysterically.

Neils stroked her hand soothingly. "I'll do my very best to help you, I promise. Meanwhile, I suggest that you come and lie down in the hall. You have nothing to fear for the moment and you might be able to get some sleep."

When they had made her comfortable Bruce offered to show Orsen his room. The man-servant had unpacked all the suitcases save one. "I kept the key," Neils smiled, "and I'll see to it later. It contains my cameras."

Bruce had already seen the cameras in Orsen's company on one strange adventure, but their process—Orsen's invention—was a mystery to him. Neils explained them only by saying that their plates were abnormally sensitive. He said the same thing of his sound-recorder, an instrument like a miniature dictaphone. Bruce wondered what his friend thought of Fiona's story but knew from past experience that he would have to wait until the little man chose to enlighten him.

"Where is Miss Clyde's room?" Orsen was asking.

"Across the passage, the second door; I'll sleep in it again if you like."

Neils shook his head. "No, Pāst and I will occupy it tonight."

He strayed towards the window and looked out across the Firth to where the blue hills melted into the horizon. "What a history those moors could tell," he said thoughtfully. "Can you hear the skirl of pipes, Bruce, or see the kilted ghosts marching up across the heather?"

"No," said Bruce uncomfortably. "All the same, I'm jolly glad I asked you to come up here. I'll leave you now, as I expect you'd like to get your things straight." Bruce was a normal practical person, but as he left his small friend, standing with arms folded, heavy head sunk forward, and eyes half-closed, he thought—Neils himself gives me the creeps at times.

Fiona was no longer in the hall, and going outside he found her lying on the grass at the entrance to the wild garden. As he approached she sat up and said coldly: "By the way, your friend is not thinking of spending the night in my room, is he?"

"He certainly is."

"Well, he won't find anything. Tell him not to fuss." She stretched her arms above her head. "*I'm* not worrying any more; I feel too tired to care."

Bruce stared at her. He could hardly believe that this calm aloof creature had been sobbing hysterically on his shoulder half an hour before. "Fiona," he pleaded, "there's one thing you must promise. Stick by me and Neils. We won't let any harm come to you."

She smiled queerly. "I think the harm has come to me already, and I'm living with it. Let me alone, Bruce; I'm not frightened any more." She turned away from him towards the house; but half an hour later through sheer inertia she had consented to move into the other wing of the Castle for the coming night.

"Everything is ready," Neils said to Bruce after dinner. "I have the cameras fixed and I've taken other precautions." He ran his fingers through his hair. "By the way, where's the girl?"

"She's in the music-room; I'll go to her, I think."

"Let me. Without her knowing it I may be able to strengthen her subconscious defences so that she gets some sleep. You go into the library and talk to Mr. Clyde." Neils was gone as quietly as a shadow.

On their way to bed he halted Bruce at the door of his own room. "I'll come in here with you for half an hour in case the servants are about." He shut the door and drew back the window curtains. Pāst watched him with colourless, unblinking eyes as he added quietly, "There *is* something here."

"What d'you think it is?"

"I can't say for certain. There are earth-bound spirits which can do great harm. You've heard me talk of such things before—of the dark places where those who have not yet passed over must lurk, and long to return. Alternatively, although this place is not old as castles go, it may have seen bloodshed. Torture or murder done for power cause vibrations and echoes that never die. If they can find some material thing to focus on they may become evil entities of great power, and even materialise at times. I have not felt any strong evil here, but when I was with Miss Clyde tonight I needed all my strength to resist a sense of bitterness, of seeking for justice, a cold and lost feeling at the heart. Perhaps that room"—he pointed across the passage—"holds the secret. We shall see."

"May I watch with you?"

'No. I want you to go to the other wing and stay beside her door until it is light."

While the hours crept by and silence held Castle Stuart as though with a mighty hand, Bruce sat leaning his head against the lintels of Fiona's door. He had no sense of the ridiculous. At times he dozed.

At times he watched the slowly gathering shadows that touched the angles of wall and stairway and crawled along the vaulted ceiling; swirling like an eddying tide around his feet. Twice the door at his cheek swung open and he heard Fiona come to shut it. Down in the well of the hall he heard the boarhound whining in its sleep, but no sound of alarm came from Fiona's room and none came from the far side of the great staircase where Orsen kept vigil. By four o'clock the short northern night was over, and having seen the cold grey dawn begin to steal through the windows, Bruce sought his bed.

He slept late and found no opportunity to be alone with Neils until Clyde retired into the library and Fiona had set out on her morning walk.

Neils looked pale and weary; his eyelids drooped. "There was nothing," he said, "nothing at all. And you?"

"Nothing. Her door opened twice, but she didn't look out."

"Did she open it?"

"I don't know. I heard her come and shut it, but this morning when I asked her how she had slept she didn't complain of anything."

"I have never passed a night in a room so free of vibrations," the Swede said slowly. "It is most perplexing. Pāst, too, felt nothing or he would certainly have shown it; and he is perhaps the severest of all tests. I think," he added, "I will spend tonight down in the hall."

They passed an uneasy day and were glad when Fiona and her father retired to bed.

Again Bruce kept watch. Again, save for the opening and shutting of the door, he was not disturbed, and in the morning Neils, too, reported an untroubled night.

Fiona had now become so far withdrawn from the three men that, to Bruce's mind at least, she seemed to move among them like a spirit. She did not appear unhappy, but her wide green eyes were heavy and shadowed, contrasting violently with the transparent pallor of her face, and her lovely hair seemed to reflect the moon rather than the sun. She made polite conversation at meals, and escaped after them. Every effort that Bruce made to talk to her was coldly received.

At dinner on the third evening Neils spoke only when addressed. For the rest of the time he was silent, his gaze fixed on Fiona. She had not changed from the tweeds she had worn all day and sat calm and composed, her eyes staring vacantly at the table.

"Only six days to the twelfth," Clyde said. "I hope I shall have the pleasure of Bruce's company and yours, Mr. Orsen, for the first few days at least."

"Not mine, I fear," Orsen said absently.

"But you won't be leaving us so soon?"

"Tomorrow, I'm afraid."

Bruce checked his astonishment. By no look, by no lift of the eyebrow or whispered word had Neils given him a hint. Fiona heard of Orsen's projected departure without speaking. She ate practically nothing. Before coffee was served she got abruptly to her feet and left the room. Her father stared after her with a worried frown creasing his forehead.

"I think Fiona must have gone *fey*," he said, "she looks mighty queer tonight."

Orsen glanced quickly at his host. "Why should she go *fey*? Only Scottish people are supposed to do that."

"Well, she is Scotch—or anyway, a good half. Her mother was a McAin."

Bruce saw that Orsen's enormous eyes were gleaming with suppressed excitement. But it was not until they had left the table and were alone that he whispered urgently:

"Her Scottish ancestry! I felt just now we should learn something important tonight. Quick! We must hunt the library for any books dealing with the history of Castle Stuart."

For an hour the two men searched, dragging out volume after volume and frantically scanning their pages for a clue; they had almost despaired, when suddenly Orsen gave a cry of relief.

"This—this should give us the link we seek. It's the history of Castle Stuart, translated into English by the Reverend Father Cox, Chaplain to the Castle from 1698 to 1717." He ran his finger down the index and turning to a page half-way through the book, began to read:

> Of all the Lordes of Castle Stuart, they do tell that Donald Stuart was the blackest of them all. He were fitter companie for men-at-arms in their drunken brawls than for the fair young maide he did bring to be his bryde.
>
> She was the Ladie Fiona McAin, own daughter to the McAin of Crath, a winsome lass of sixteen summers who did grieve most sorely to leave her mother's side.

"Good God!" Bruce broke in. "D'you realise Fiona's mother was a McAin and there's the extraordinary coincidence of the Christian names?"

"Of course," Orsen nodded impatiently. "It's something of this kind that I've been hunting for." And he read on:

> It becometh us not to linger on that mating, for of a truth it was of an eagle and a dove, contrarie to the laws of nature and a thing

offensive in the eyes of God. Poor maide, how could she find happiness with such a spouse, and who shall caste blame upon her that she did welcome the young Lorde Ninan when fresh from the Court of France and full of the gracies of the French he did come as a guest for a while beneath Black Donald's roof?

Lorde Ninan was a courtly, slender man, with smiling face and witty tongue. He did strum upon the lute for the Ladie Fiona's pleasure, write poesie for her and in the French fashion oft did kiss her hand.

Some say that no more passed between the twain than this, for well did the Ladie Fiona know the jealous heart of her own dark Lorde. Yet on a night of feasting—so the tale is told—when the women had withdrawn and the men were in their cups, Black Donald did suddenlie miss the Lorde Ninan from his board and calling for his claymore he did stagger up the stairs to his Ladie's chamber.

The lovers herde his loud approach, and knowing there to be murder in his drunken vengeful heart, the Ladie Fiona took Lorde Ninan's hande and guided him by a secret stair behind the tapestry down to the inner court.

But Black Donald knew well the secret stair, and swift for all the liquor he had drunk, followed cursing upon their heels.

They had but reached the postern gate when he espied them and shouting to his men-at-arms rushed after. Near-by the well Lord Ninan turned at bay, but the Stuart clansmen fell upon him, piercing him with a dozen pikes and skean dhus, so that he fell backwards over the well's rim, saving himself from plunging into its rockie depths onlie by the clutch of one stronge hande.

The Lady Fiona screamed for them to spare him but he knew his life was done, and as he hung there he cried aloud:

"Fiona! I'll wait for thee, m'darling!" Then with one stroke did Black Donald slice off the clutching hande and the young Lorde fell to his death in the icie water sixty feet below.

'Tis said that the Lorde Ninan's spirit doth wait there, uneasy stille, so that in passing the end of the avenue that leads up to that grim stronghold, the belated traveller yet may hear the last laugh of Black Donald when his bloodie wille was done, and that last heart-crye of the Lorde Ninan:

"Fiona! I'll wait for thee, m'darling—I'll wait for thee."

Orsen closed the book and stood up. "The whole thing is clear now. It may be a case of re-incarnation or merely the McAin strain in Fiona's blood coupled with her given name. The restless spirit of Lord Ninan still waits for his love to join him. This world is a misty, timeless place to earth-bound spirits and that of Lord Ninan cannot distinguish between our Fiona and the Fiona who lived three hundred years ago, but it has become vaguely aware of her presence in the neighbourhood and is using all the power it can command to draw her to it."

"Then her father must be told at once," Bruce said quickly, "and arrangements made for her to leave Scotland for good tomorrow."

Neils nodded. "Yes. It is she who is haunted; not the Castle or her room. That is why no manifestation occurs when she is not present. She must be got away as soon as possible, and in the meantime it's most important that she should not be allowed to go anywhere near the old ruin. The gravest possible danger awaits her there. If she were drawn to the place it's a virtual certainty that her mental resistance would be overcome and she'd feel herself compelled to throw herself down the well."

"Right," said Bruce. "I'll go and tell her that you've found the root of the trouble and warn her not to leave the house." He turned abruptly as Clyde came into the room, saying with a worried look:

"Bruce, I'm anxious about Fiona. The servants tell me she went out half an hour ago. She didn't even take a coat and it gets damp at this time of night. I wish you'd go and . . ."

Before he had time to complete his sentence Bruce leaped for the door and they heard his footsteps thunder across the hall.

Clyde had glimpsed the look of horror in Bruce's eyes and now he saw the strained expression on Orsen's face.

"What's this," he exclaimed. "What's happened?"

"We can only pray," Orsen said quietly. "Bruce can run faster than we can. Please God he will be in time."

Up the rough track with the queer grey sky overhead and the lone moors hunched and darkening on either side, Bruce ran like a man possessed. A mist had risen off the sea; rags and rafes of it danced on the air. Here and there it came down solidly. He stumbled and fell over a tuft of heather. And now the mist came more shrouding and more white. A curlew sobbed its cry somewhere in the silence, and the trees at the roadside reared their great arms heavenwards in mockery.

He ran on, his breath coming in short gasps, knowing nothing but the blind necessity to be in time. As he topped the rise above the old castle, something told him he was too late. Down into the eerie mist he plunged and instantly felt a chill, as if a cold hand grasped his throat. He fell again, staggered to his feet, and ran on desperately across the turf. His footsteps dragged as though he were wading through a bog. A cold whiteness was all about him and with its physical desolation there bore upon his brain another darkness—a sense of evil, too sickening to be borne. He was crouched and groping. He muttered a prayer that died in his throat. Out of the gloom the stones reared, spectral and forbidding. "Fiona!" he shouted. "Fiona!"

The swathes of fog beat at his face. "Fiona!" he called again. "For God's sake answer."

Cold, he thought suddenly. Cold—cold—cold. A faint wind whispered through the ruins. He passed his hand across his forehead. He did not know what thoughts they were which seized his brain and cramped it until no feeling came to him but one of intense fear. The wind whispered louder. Now he was up again and running forward. The evil mist was throttling him, but ahead he saw the figure of a girl—a girl who swayed at the edge of a dark, yawning pit. The mist had become a solid wall blocking his way; the wind rose to a shrill scream. He shut his eyes.

"Oh, Lord God, help me because"—strangely inspired the words came to his lips—"because there is none other than fighteth for us but only Thou, Oh God." Then the mist was rent as though two great hands had torn it asunder and he was at Fiona's side, dragging her back. He felt her body fall limply against him; and now where the dark pit had gaped there was only the shallow, rock-filled ruin of an old well.

Lifting his head he saw that the mist had gone. Cool and grey under the evening sky lay the stones of old Castle Stuart. He stood there for a time holding Fiona in his arms. She stirred and smiled at him:

"What happened, Bruce? ... Why are we here? ... He called me.... Why did he call me so urgently? ... Why did he want me?"

"He's gone."

"Did you send him away?" she asked faintly. "Thank you, Bruce."

"I think," he said, "we should thank Neils Orsen."

PREDICTION AND DOOM

ROBERT SMYTHE HICHENS

DEMETRIADI'S DREAM

MANY people are too stupid for the happiness of others. But there are some who are too clever, or who possess gifts which are troubling to those with whom they are brought into contact. Adrian Syke was one of these. He never posed as a Sherlock Holmes. He made no claim to the possession of the faculties which must belong to the supreme detective. He was not perpetually drawing elaborate deductions and explaining to others what they were. But it seemed that he possessed a peculiar power of gathering secret information about people from themselves. And it was often information which they were probably anxious to withhold.

Syke was well off and fond of travel. He wandered about a great deal, and usually alone—he was unmarried—staying here and there as the fancy took him. Wherever he went he got to know people. But he never seemed to care much for them. Many interested him. Few or none touched his heart. But he was a companionable man, a good talker, a very good listener. Men liked him. Yet he had this power of troubling people at times.

One autumn, coming from Italy, he found himself rather taken by a certain town in Switzerland. He meant to stay there for two or three nights. But the Palace Hotel was extraordinarily comfortable, the weather was splendid—mellow delicious autumn weather—the colour of the woods which streamed down the mountain sides to the lake edge was a marvel of copper, reds, orange, bronze, there were some pleasant people, and there was quite a decent club. So Syke stayed on for a while. And he joined the Club. There he often played bridge, generally between the hours of four-thirty and seven in the afternoon. He played with men of various nationalities. Among them was an elderly Greek, pale, melancholy, sardonic, an excellent bridge player. Indeed, he seemed to exist only for bridge.

One evening, when the last rubber had been played, this Greek, Syke, and some other men were gathered in the hall of the Club where there were easy chairs and a species of bar. And in the course of a desultory conversation in a nimbus of smoke the Greek—his name was Demetriadi—remarked that on the previous night he had

had a dream which had greatly impressed him. Now as a rule there is perhaps nothing more boring than to have to sit and listen to the relation by a man of his dream. The men gathered about Demetriadi remained silent after he had made his statement. Quite evidently they had no wish to hear anything about his dream. But Adrian Syke, after directing an apparently casual look at Demetriadi, said: "Won't you tell us your dream?"

"With pleasure," said Demetriadi, who obviously wished to share his experience, at second hand as it were. "I dreamed that I was out walking alone in the dead of night in a great city. It seemed to me such a city as modern New York is, a place of enormous buildings, of towers lifted far up into the sky. While I was passing down a broad, deserted thoroughfare I heard steps coming up behind me and was joined by an elderly man. He was tall. He looked very evil but also very sad. There was a bitterness as of satire in his face combined with acute melancholy. I felt that he was certainly wicked, but that he was somehow grieved, perhaps even shocked, at his own wickedness."

"That's very possible!" interjected Syke at this point.

The Greek looked at Syke with his dark, melancholy eyes and continued:

"On joining me this man took me by the arm and whispered in my ear, 'You must come with me.' I felt compelled to do as he wished and I went with him. He led me to the door of a vast modern hotel. As we went into it I heard a clock in a tower strike three. We passed through a deserted hall dimly lighted, and entered an automatic lift which my companion operated. The lift glided up to the third floor of the hotel. We got out and stood at the entrance to a very long corridor thickly carpeted and lit by electricity. On the left of this corridor was a line of shut doors with gilt numbers above them.

"'You think they are all sleeping in those rooms?' whispered my companion. 'Wait a moment!'

"He led me a short distance into the corridor, paused in front of a door with the number one above it, and stamped on the carpet. Directly he did this all the doors in the corridor opened, so that I was able to look into the interior of every room. In the first room I saw a young woman in pyjamas being strangled by a man in a fit of sexual fury. We passed on to the next number. Here a married couple were having a desperate quarrel. Their harsh voices uttering hideous words, the sort of words that can never be forgotten or forgiven, were audible to us. We could see black hatred imprinted on their congested faces. We went to the door of the next room. In this a child was dying in convulsions while its nurse, seated in an armchair, was smiling slyly over a love letter. We went on and on down the interminable corridor, and in every room we were witness to some indignity, some horror, some crime, some display of the desperate evil or misery hidden in humanity. At last I could bear no more and I turned to rush out into the night. But my companion caught my arm and held it firmly. He stamped again on the carpet. All the doors in the corridor shut. Then he looked deep into my eyes, and said with an accent of indescribable bitterness: 'And that's what we are!'

"I heard the clock in the tower strike four. I woke. Directly I woke I looked at my watch. The hands pointed to four o'clock."

When the Greek's thin voice—a voice without any "body" in it, a pessimistic voice—ceased there was a moment of dead silence. And in this silence I seemed to detect—I was among the men round the Greek—a creeping uneasiness.

"And that's what we are!" It wasn't a very pleasant end to the dream. I saw two or three of my companions looking furtive. I saw one—he was the British Chaplain of the place—glance round the circle quickly and look down. Then there was a slight movement, and I had the feeling that somebody was going to get up, that in a moment men would be going away with attempts at a cheery "Well, good night", or "au revoir". But then Adrian Syke spoke, and at once the movement ceased. I think we all felt that there was more to come, and that it was going to be unusual or interesting. Addressing Demetriadi, he said:

"You told us that in your dream this tall elderly man led you down the corridor and that all the doors giving on to it were open," he said.

"Yes," said Demetriadi.

"How many rooms did you look into?"

"A great many."

"You took them consecutively?"

"Consecutively?"

"I mean did you go from number to number consecutively? One, two, three, four—and so on?"

"Ah, I see. Yes, monsieur, we did."

"Did you get as far as number fourteen?"

After a quite definite pause, Demetriadi answered: "Yes."

"And number fourteen was the last room you looked into, wasn't it?"

"What—what can make you suppose that?" said the Greek, leaning forward in his chair, and staring at Syke intently.

"I just thought it might be," Syke said.

"Ah!" said the Greek.

For a moment I thought he was going to drop the subject, was not going to answer Syke's question. But I was wrong. After some hesitation he said, as if with an effort:

"Yes, the last room I looked into was numbered fourteen." We all, I think, had our eyes on Syke at this moment. I suppose all the men were astonished. Certainly I was. The Greek put the question that was probably in most of our minds. "What made you suppose that room was number fourteen?" he said.

"What made me?" said Syke in a careless sort of voice. "Oh, it just came to me. I seemed to see number fourteen and then a lot of doors shutting."

"Very—strange!" said Demetriadi.

His eyes were always fixed on Syke.

"It seems you are a thought reader," he added.

"I get impressions now and then," said Syke. "I don't claim to be a thought reader. I just get impressions occasionally."

And then as Demetriadi said nothing more, and as it was getting late, our little group broke up, separated. Men went off rather gravely that evening. A heaviness of thought seemed to have been laid upon them like a burden by the dream of Demetriadi and by Syke's reception of it.

I was staying at the Palace Hotel—I had been in the place much longer than Adrian Syke had—and that evening I asked Syke whether I should walk home with him as we were going the same way. He assented readily, and we set out together through the gay little town in the autumn evening. All the shops were brilliantly lit. A half circle of coloured lamps gleamed above the gaudy entrance to "Chez la petite Madame", as for some unknown reason the one *boîte de nuit* of our town had been named. Many elderly ladies were going discreetly home from the various tea rooms. Young girls and laughing young men came out of a restaurant where dancing went on every afternoon to the noise of a jazz band. The casino disgorged its habitual crowd. The long street, the street of an idle town, was full of the murmur of voices, the tiptap of footsteps. Above us on the right the mountains leaned, their riot of colours dying away from us in the darkness of night. On the left was the sleeping lake. A bell chimed the hour, and made me think of the Greek's dream-clock chiming three and then four in the tower of his dream. And just as that thought slipped through my brain my companion said:

"You have been here some time?"

"Yes."

"Much longer than I have?"

"Oh yes."

"Does that fellow, that Greek, Demetriadi, live in a hotel?"

"I believe he does. I think he lives in some very second-rate hotel."

"Know the name?"

"I'm not sure. But I think I heard someone say that he lives in the Hôtel des Fleurs. It's a small hotel not ten yards from the Casino and close to the lake."

"I've seen the name. Is he alone here?"

"I really don't know. I barely know him. I've always seen him alone. But then I have scarcely ever seen him except at the Club."

"I too! He seems to live solely for bridge. He plays a very good game."

"A dried-up sort of life that seems to me," I couldn't help saying. "And he looks to me a very arid individual. But I must say that I found his dream exceedingly interesting. And I'm sure I shall never forget it."

"Nor I," said Syke. "And the reason of that is that it was a dream which cut very deep. It made every man who heard it ponder on the things that go on behind the shut doors. They look so bland, those shut doors. And the silence in the great corridors is so profound. And it seems that everyone is sleeping peacefully. But not a bit of it. Life is going on behind those doors, life with its terrible activities. No wonder the silence could be felt once or twice when Demetriadi stopped speaking—the dried-up individual, the arid individual!"

"You don't think he is!" I said, detecting a sound as of sarcasm in the voice of Syke.

"I doubt if a really arid individual would ever have had that dream."

"You think men express character by their dreams?"

"Why not? We are always expressing character."

"And yet it is often difficult to read character."

Syke didn't say anything, and after a slight pause, I added: "I wish you would tell me how you knew that number fourteen was the last room that Demetriadi looked into in his dream."

"As I said in the Club, I saw fourteen and then a lot of doors shutting."

"And that was all?"

Syke gave me a rather queer sideways look. "By no means," he said.

I was silent, hoping that he would add something to his last statement, which had, I confess, greatly roused my curiosity, already excited by what had just happened at the Club. But he made no further remark and we walked on towards the Palace Hotel in silence, I feeling decidedly baffled. Yet how could I question him? I was no great friend of his. I only knew him slightly. If he wished to tell me anything more he would do so of his own accord. If he did not, well, I must put up with it and try to get rid of my curiosity.

We were turning in at the gate of the hotel garden when he at last spoke once more.

"I'm dining in the restaurant at eight-thirty," he said. "If you are alone to-night, perhaps you will dine with me."

I accepted his invitation rather eagerly.

We parted in the hall. As I was about to go to the lift the concierge came up to me and handed me a note. I opened it at once and found that it was from a distant cousin of mine, a Major Custe, and was to tell me that his wife and their daughter had just arrived for a short stay in our town and hoped to meet me. They had seen my name in the hotel list in the local paper. They were staying at the Hôtel des Fleurs near the Casino. Would I come to tea with them on the morrow? The Hôtel des Fleurs! That was the hotel where I fancied—I wasn't sure—that Demetriadi was staying. I wondered why Syke was interested to know where he lived. Syke's question about that had been put in a very casual voice. Nevertheless, I was convinced that his mind, when he put it, had not been at all casual.

And now here was I being asked to visit the Hôtel des Fleurs.

That evening at dinner in the restaurant I told Syke of my cousin's note and added that he and his wife were staying at the Hôtel des Fleurs near the Casino. (I didn't mention the daughter. I had no reason not to, but I just didn't happen to mention her.)

"Isn't that the hotel where you fancied that Demetriadi might be staying?" asked Syke.

I said it was.

"If you go there to-morrow—"

"I *am* going," I interrupted.

"Oh, then if it's not too much trouble you might do something for me there."

"Certainly. What is it?" I asked.

"If Demetriadi is staying in that hotel could you find out the number of his room for me?"

I was much intrigued by this question, which of course I couldn't help connecting with the odd conversation which had taken place between Demetriadi and Syke, after the former had related his dream.

"I see you are wondering why I take such an interest in the number of Demetriadi's room, whatever it is," said Syke.

"I must say I am."

"Well, that has something to do with that dream of his."

"I felt sure it must have."

Syke poured himself out another glass of Château Lafite. (He had told me at the beginning of dinner that he couldn't bear having really first-rate wine poured out for him by a waiter.)

"The whole thing must seem rather peculiar to you," he said, after slowly sipping and savouring his wine. "It doesn't to me, because I have long been accustomed, naturally enough, to a certain—well, suppose I call it a certain faculty which I possess and which seems to be denied to the average man. I don't pretend to be anything extraordinary. In most ways I am a very ordinary individual. But I possess—at least I believe so—a curious faculty of gathering secret information about certain people with whom I am brought into contact."

"Secret information!" I said.

"That is the name I give to it. These people are obliged to inform me of certain things about themselves without wishing or meaning to. Sometimes even against their intention, against their will."

"Am I one of those people?" I inquired abruptly.

Syke smiled.

"No, you are not," he answered.

Again he slowly and carefully sipped his wine. Then he added: "But our friend, Demetriadi, is."

"Were you gathering secret information about Demetriadi this afternoon?"

"I believe I was. That remains to be proved. But when this sort of thing occurs, I mean when it is borne in upon me, as it has been today, that such and such things are, or will be, truth is always at the bottom of it, not error."

"You said 'will be'. Do you claim to be able to read the future?"

"I am really not much given to laying claims," said Syke, rather sardonically. "But as I see you are interested I am giving you a sort of rough idea of what is up."

"Thanks very much. I am tremendously interested."

Syke went on sipping his wine.

"As you have spoken so frankly," I said, after a moment, "may I ask you something?"

"What is it?"

"Why do you want to know the number of the room in which Demetriadi is living here, either in the Hôtel des Fleurs or in some other hotel?"

"I don't think I want to tell you that just yet."

I felt snubbed, and I believe I must have reddened.

"Don't be vexed!" Syke said.

"I'm not vexed. Of course not!" I said, rather insincerely.

"Later on, perhaps, if anything comes of it!" Syke continued, enigmatically. "And now tell me something."

"Yes, if I can."

"Were you specially struck by any one thing which Demetriadi said when he told us his dream?"

I thought for a moment and then said: "I'm not sure that I was. The whole thing impressed me. Oh, wait a moment though! Yes! I think that I was specially struck by something."

"And may I ask what it was?"

"By the words the tall elderly man said at the end of the dream, 'And that's what we are!'"

"Oh that! Yes, that certainly cut down pretty deep. Yes! But no, I wasn't so much struck by that really as by something else."

He paused, but this time I was careful to ask no question. I had just had my lesson, and I hadn't forgotten it.

"You remember, of course, what Demetriadi said he saw in the first three rooms; a girl being strangled by a man, a hideous quarrel between husband and wife, a child dying in convulsions while its nurse sat smiling over a love letter. Not very pretty things, not very pretty! And then, according to his own account, he visited ten other rooms—"

"Eleven!" I corrected him.

"One moment!"

"I beg your pardon!"

"Visited ten other rooms, bringing the number of rooms visited up to thirteen. In each of these thirteen rooms he saw something hideous and frightful, some exhibition of the vileness or misery of human nature. But apparently his dream-curiosity wasn't satiated even then. No! For he went on to room number fourteen, and it was only when he looked into *that* room that he could, in his own words, 'bear no more'. It was that fact which struck me most in his curious narrative, that which riveted my attention, that which still engages my mind."

"And you knew that it was number fourteen!"

"I did know. Well, now, I was struck by this. A man has looked into thirteen rooms and seen a horror in each one of them, the first horror, the very first, which evidently didn't cause any slackening in his dream-curiosity, being the strangling of a girl by her lover. But in room number *fourteen* he sees something which makes him suddenly feel that he can't bear any more. That was what struck me—room number fourteen—the effect *that* room had on him."

He said the last words with almost tragic significance.

"But don't you think the dream-horror was simply cumulative?" I said. "That's how I took it. And isn't that natural? A man sees horror after horror, an accumulation of dreadful happenings, until at last his nerve cracks and he can't stand any more."

"You took it like that?"

"Yes."

"Well, I didn't."

There was something so definite in Syke's voice when he said that, and something so assured in his manner, that I was seized with a conviction which startled me. I looked hard at him and said: "Did you receive secret information about what Demetriadi saw happening in room number fourteen in his dream?"

"Perhaps I did," said Syke, finishing his wine and getting up from the dinner table. "But whether it was correct or not remains to be proved."

On the following day soon after four o'clock I walked to the Hôtel des Fleurs to call on my cousins. I had often seen the hotel when going to the Casino, but I had never been inside it. Although it was in a good position, described by the management in advertisements as "central", it was a second-class hotel, with a flight of steps inside the entrance leading up into a dark and rather dismal hall, where a somewhat moth-eaten hall porter crouched despondently in a shadowy nook among cinema advertisements and picture post-cards. But my cousins, I knew, were not very well off and no doubt the hotel was inexpensive.

They were at home and I was sent into a public sitting-room full of plate glass and cane chairs, where I found them waiting for me by a cane tea-table already arranged for our sustenance. After cordial greetings and the usual somewhat unmeaning inquiries, we sat down to tea and opened with bromides. But unusually soon we got to something that wasn't a bromide. I made a banal remark about hotels—something probably to the effect that in most parts of Switzerland one can find a decent hotel at a moderate price—and elicited from Derrick Custe the following piece of information.

"We chose this hotel because a friend of ours is living here."

"Really?" I said.

"Yes, a man we were with for some time in a *pension* at St. Moritz last winter, an awfully good bridge player."

"You're mad on bridge, I know," I said.

"No madder than Susie," said Custe. (Susie is Mrs. Custe.)

"An Englishman?" I asked carelessly.

"No, a Greek. His name is Demetriadi."

As my cousin said this I happened to look across at his daughter, Elise, and I thought I detected a look of self-consciousness, perhaps even of half-disguised distress, on her very pretty face. (Elise is a strikingly good-looking girl of the fair English type, tall, blooming with health and youth, blue-eyed, with bright hair and the sort of complexion that amazes the sallow and swarthy foreigner.)

During the next half-hour I was secretly considering how best to find out what was the number of Demetriadi's room. I didn't want to ask the concierge what it was, and when coming through the hall I had seen no visitors' lists stuck up. It was most unlikely that my cousins would know such a thing. Still, it was possible that they, or that one of them, might happen to know it. I wished, before I went away, to find out for certain whether any of them did know.

I told them of course that I knew Demetriadi, though but slightly, having met him at the Club. My bridge, I said, wasn't up to his. I made no allusion to the subject of his dream. But I mentioned my acquaintance, Adrian Syke, who was a far better player than I was.

On hearing of this Derrick Custe pricked up his ears.

"Hope we shall meet him," he said. "Is he up to Demetriadi?"

"Pretty much on the same level, I believe."

"Perhaps he'll come into our game some evening," said my cousin. "Demetriadi tells me the Club here doesn't open at night."

"No, it doesn't."

"We mean to get a game every night in the hotel. We are three already, but we shall have to look for a good fourth."

He didn't ask me. He knew my game. I said I should be glad to introduce him to Syke.

Tea was over, conversation was rapidly getting back to the bromide level, evening was drawing on, and I hadn't found out the number of Demetriadi's room. I couldn't stay for ever. I was getting bored and, worse still, knew I was becoming a bore. Something must be done. I began to talk about bedrooms.

"Hope you've got nice bedrooms," I said. "Which floor are you on?"

"Derrick and I are on the second floor facing towards the lake," said Susie Custe. "We've got two quite different rooms."

"And how are you off?" I asked Elise.

"Oh, I'm in clover, quite glorified in comparison to Mother and Dad."

"How's that?" I said.

"I've got a big room on the first floor that apparently doesn't let easily because people are so absurd."

"Absurd in what way?"

"Idiotically superstitious. It's numbered thirteen—I jumped at it."

Thirteen! Elise was in number thirteen. And where was Demetriadi?

At last even bromides failed and I was forced to get up to go. My cousins kindly went with me to the hall. In the hall I resolved—prompted evidently by my solicitous angel, though I didn't know it—to make a last attempt, in the dark as it were, and I said: "I wish you'd show me your rooms. I should like to feel sure you're quite comfortable here."

My cousins seemed gratified by my interest in them. They said "of course", and we all plunged into the somewhat decrepit lift and ascended asthmatically to the second floor. The bedrooms there examined and approved, we descended on foot to the first floor, and I was shown Elise's bedroom. It was, as she had said, larger and much better than the rooms of her parents. I expressed my satisfaction and commended her lack of superstition. As we left her room the door of the room beyond, number fourteen, opened and Demetriadi came out of it.

That evening before dinner I went into the cocktail bar of the Palace Hotel and having ordered a "side car" waited in the hope of presently seeing Adrian Syke. Just before half-past eight he came in. I asked him to join me, and while William was preparing another "side car" I told Syke I had some news for him. A sharp look of inquiry came into his eyes.

"You've found out about the number of Demetriadi's room?" he said.

"I have. It is number fourteen."

The look of sharp inquiry in Syke's face gave way to another look—of a satisfaction that was almost, not quite, complacent.

"Thank you," he said. "I wanted to know."

William brought him his cocktail.

"You're not much surprised, I fancy," I ventured.

(After all, hang it, I'd been busy for him!)

His reply was perhaps intended to be non-committal, but I think that a very human feeling of vanity—or shall we say of semi-vanity?—got in the way of his intention.

"Oh, his number might have been anything," he said; and then added, "Still there was no reason why it shouldn't be fourteen."

I was quite positive from that moment that he had expected it to be fourteen.

While he sipped his cocktail I told him about my cousins' passion for bridge and their wish to find a good fourth for their game with Demetriadi in the evenings.

"If you care sometimes to make a fourth I'll gladly get them to know you," I said.

"I should like it," he said, but with no eagerness.

"The hotel's very second rate," I said.

"That doesn't matter. And perhaps now and then they wouldn't mind being my guests here."

"They've got their daughter with them," I said.

"Ah!" said Syke.

And again I noticed the sharp look in his eyes.

"But I dare say she could come too, and I could look after her, she might dance while you're playing bridge."

"A good idea!" said Syke, finishing his cocktail. "Is she a pretty girl?" he added in an uninterested voice.

"Extremely pretty. At least, I think so."

As we went into dinner—we weren't dining together that night—he said: "Wonderful lot of pretty girls there are nowadays. I foresee the time when it will be considered a deadly sin on any girl's part not to be pretty."

When I left him and went to my table, I said to myself: "Why is he interested in my cousin Elise?"

There seemed absolutely no reason why he should feel the faintest interest in her. He had, I felt sure, never heard of her existence until I mentioned that she had arrived with her father and mother. But directly I did so that odd, sharply inquiring look which I was beginning to watch out for had come to his face. Then that question about her looks. Why had that been put? It had not been put idly. I was certain of that. He had really wanted to know whether Elise was pretty or not. And his slightly ironical remark about the almost universal prettiness of the girls of our day had been an attempt to throw me off the scent, as it were, had been made for the purpose of, if possible, cancelling the effect upon me of that sharp look of his, which he must have known I was wondering about.

I was completely puzzled by all this.

In order to force Syke to take the next step in this odd business I said nothing more about my cousins, made no move to make them known to Syke. Three days passed. Then Syke came up to me in the Club and said: "About those cousins of yours!"

"Yes?" I said.

"Have they got a fourth for bridge yet?"

"I believe they've found someone in the hotel," I said.

(They had, "a damned rotten player, but what are we to do?" according to Custe, who had more than once pressed me to get hold of "that friend of yours, Syke." Custe hadn't yet joined the Club, but was going to.)

Syke was silent for a moment. I felt sure he didn't wish to say anything more. But something was too strong for him and at last he said: "I should be very glad to welcome your cousins and Demetriadi here any evening if you think they would care to come and make up a rubber. Say next Friday, for instance. There's a dance in the hotel that night which might amuse the girl. We needn't stand on formalities, need we? Nobody does here."

Having got what I wanted from Syke I was charming. I went straight off to the Hôtel des Fleurs and arranged the party. On the following Friday my cousins and Demetriadi came to the Palace Hotel, and I introduced Syke.

Almost immediately the two Custes, Demetriadi and Syke sat down to bridge, while I took Elise off to find her some partners for the dance which was just beginning. As we were moving away I turned sharply and looked at the bridge players. Demetriadi and Syke were following us with their eyes. Both of them immediately looked away when I turned and became keen bridge players. But I had seen that they were both strongly interested in Elise.

She danced all the evening. I only had a few words with her when the dancing was over. It seemed to me then that she was excited, oddly excited but not happy. I asked her if she had enjoyed herself. She said, "Yes—immensely!" As she joined her parents I noticed that she sent a strange look to Demetriadi. It suggested to me two contending emotions—enticement and fear. I saw that Syke had observed it. And in that moment I realised that this odd interest in Elise, which I had wondered about, was not concentrated on Elise *qua* Elise, but on Elise as a possible object of interest to Demetriadi.

From that moment—I couldn't help it—I connected Elise with Demetriadi's dream.

There was something, there must be something, which caused Syke to find a link between this young girl, my cousin, and that most horrible dream. But what could it possibly be? I searched mind and even imagination in vain for the link. And then, baffled, I remembered that phrase of Syke's, "secret information". Could he possibly during that evening of bridge, while Elise was dancing, have gathered from her secret information of which I knew nothing? It seemed unlikely. Elise was not at all what is usually called an "interesting" girl. She was merely a typical English girl of the healthy, good-looking type. And yet perhaps she had in her some hidden strangeness. I remembered the look she had cast at the Greek which I had surprised. It certainly suggested underthings, suggested that she had some feeling for Demetriadi which she concealed. But how could that be? He was no longer young. He looked weary, "played out", devoid of zest, disenchanted, oh! very much disenchanted with life. Could such a man possibly make any appeal to a vigorous and beautiful girl? Something within me said "Impossible!" But something else replied that with women one never knows.

It was, I remember, just at this time I first became conscious of an uneasy feeling about the situation of Elise's bedroom.

After that evening at the Palace Syke became rapidly intimate with my cousins, that is intimate as a bridge player becomes with other bridge players whose game he exactly suits. Custe was enthusiastic about him and warmly thanked me for getting hold of him.

"A first-rate player, absolutely first-rate!" he said of Syke.

Susie Custe, too, was delighted with him. They met for bridge four evenings a week, twice at the Hôtel des Fleurs, twice at the Palace, and of course Demetriadi was always of the party.

I did not go to the Hôtel des Fleurs. Why should I sit among aspidistras on a cane chair doing nothing? But I was always there when they came to the Palace. And on these occasions I looked after Elise.

She danced energetically with the best of the available men, and even with me when nothing else was doing. She flirted, or seemed to flirt. She seemed to be enjoying herself. And yet I had the feeling that something was worrying her seriously and that she wasn't happy in our gay little town.

One night this feeling was so strong upon me that I spoke of it to her.

We were sitting in the great hall of the Palace Hotel. In the distance, with light nicely concentrated upon them, sat the four bridge players. Demetriadi was facing us. Syke, who was playing with Susie Custe, was in profile to us.

"Is anything bothering you?" I said.

Instantly Elise's face changed and she looked at me, I thought, with suspicion.

"Bothering me! What can you mean? What is there here to bother me?"

"I don't know. I don't see why there should be anything."

"There—isn't anything."

She said it with a touch of defiance which often accompanies a lie.

"Glad to hear it!" I said.

"Why should you think such a thing?"

Quite involuntarily my eyes went to Demetriadi. And Demetriadi was looking, was—it seemed to me—staring across the great room at us. I felt the gaze of his large black eyes just then acutely. For an instant his eyes held mine. In that instant a secret shiver went through me.

"Why? Why?" repeated Elise, with a sort of nervous irritation I had never noticed in her before.

"I have no reason except something in you."

"Something in me?" she said, as if startled.

Then she laughed. Her laugh sounded forced, artificial.

"I'm quite happy here except—"

"Ah—except?"

"Except that I don't care for the hotel. It's rather dismal and dull. I hope we shan't stay here for ever. But now that Mother and Dad have got such a marvellous four at bridge there seems no chance of our going away for a long time."

But they went away very soon.

Four nights after my little talk with Elise I dined once more with Syke in the restaurant. The Custes and Demetriadi were again coming for bridge and Elise was as usual expected.

That evening Syke seemed preoccupied. He talked, but he seemed decidedly distrait and had sometimes the peculiar look of a man who imagines himself to be alone. Several times during dinner I had the quite definite feeling that he had for the moment forgotten I was there. During these moments I kept silence. Then presently his expression changed and he would begin talking again, but without animation.

Just at the end of dinner when we were about to get up he looked at me in a quite different way, not merely like one very conscious of my presence and personality, but like one about to say something intimate. Everyone surely knows the sort of look I mean. It seems to bring one man very near to another. He was certainly going to say something intimate, confidential to me. I knew that.

"Yes?" I said.

I couldn't somehow help saying it. It was a mistake. It was premature. It must have suggested to Syke an eagerness, perhaps even a curiosity on my part which, striking unpleasantly upon his mood, shut him up. I had sounded the false note. The disharmony was manifest.

"Yes?" he echoed.

And his face had completely changed.

"I thought you were about to say something?"

"Only that I expect the bridge players must be waiting for us."

"Let's go and see," I said, concealing my discomfiture as best I could.

And we got up from the table.

The bridge players were just coming in—without Elise. Susie Custe explained that her daughter "didn't feel like coming" that night.

"She's not ill, I hope?" I said.

"Ill!" said her mother. "Elise is never ill."

I looked at Demetriadi. His eyes were on Syke. I thought he was looking horribly pale. But he was always pale; one of your bloodless men—apparently.

They went to their bridge table and I was alone. I felt disappointed. Having of course expected Elise to come with her parents I missed her. My evening was left empty. I didn't know what to do. There was dancing as usual, but I am not one of those elderly persons who have a passion for jazz. There was no one whom I particularly wanted to talk to. I didn't feel in the mood for reading. Finally I went into the hall to look at the cinema programmes.

At the Savoy Cinema, which was close to the Hôtel des Fleurs, they were giving a film with Emil Jannings in it, *Vaudeville*. I decided to go to it, put on hat and coat, took the tram, and was soon at the entrance. People were streaming in, but I didn't join them. Something enticed me away, something led me to the steps leading up into the Hôtel des Fleurs. I mounted them and came into the dismal entrance hall. The moth-eaten hall-porter was crouching among the postcards and programmes.

"Is Miss Custe at home?" I asked.

"Yes, sir," said the man.

"Can I see her? Here's my card."

"If you will wait a moment, sir, I will go and see."

He emerged and shambled away. In a few minutes he came back.

"Mademoiselle is very sorry, sir, but she can't see you to-night. She is not dressed."

"She isn't ill, I hope?"

"I don't think so, sir. She dined as usual."

I stood for a moment. I felt within me an impetus pushing me to insist on seeing my cousin. But I didn't give way to it. I said good-night to the hall-porter and left the hotel. But now I had no heart for the cinema, and I walked back to the Palace Hotel, feeling depressed, even down-hearted.

When presently I went into the big hall I found the four bridge players intent on their game. I joined them and for a while watched the play. Although I play badly I understand the game thoroughly and I was struck by the play of Demetriadi. He was, I recognised, playing marvellously well, far better than any of the others. He played, in fact, like a man inspired. Even when his cards were bad he did wonders. In his mood of that night he could have saved almost any game.

When the last rubber was finished—it was won by Demetriadi and Susie Custe—Custe said: "Monsieur Demetriadi, you're a bridge-genius! But even you, I should think, will never play again as you've played to-night. Wonderful, wasn't he?" he added, turning to Syke.

Syke didn't answer immediately. His eyes were on Demetriadi. At last he said: "It was splendid bridge. Too good for us!"

Demetriadi said nothing, only smiled slightly. When he said good-night to Syke and myself I thought that he pressed my hand rather strangely, as if he wished to express physically some feeling that he didn't choose to express in words.

But that may have been only my imagination.

When my cousins and he had gone I put a question to Syke. It was abrupt, but I had to put it that night. I said: "I wish you would tell me something."

"What is it?" he asked.

"Is my cousin, Elise, one of the people who gives you secret information?"

He looked rather surprised. But he answered without hesitation.

"Oh no!" he said. "She gives me nothing, absolutely nothing."

I knew he was speaking the truth.

By then I had been living for many weeks in the Palace Hotel and was on friendly terms with the young German-Swiss waiter who brought me my breakfast every morning at half-past eight. When he came in with it on the following day he said at once: "Monsieur, such a dreadful thing has happened!"

"What?" I said. "Wait! Was it at the Hôtel des Fleurs?"

I was out of bed in my dressing-gown standing by the breakfast table.

"Why, how did you know, monsieur?" said the waiter, surprise showing in his shallow blue eyes.

"I don't know. Tell me!"

"That poor Greek gentleman who often comes here to play cards —he was here only last night—"

"What about him?"

"He has been found dead in his bedroom—hanging, monsieur, from the curtain rod by the window."

I stood for a minute without speaking. I was horrified. And yet it seemed to me that, without being self-consciously aware of it, I had been expecting something like this.

"Horrible!" I said at last. "What was the reason?"

The young waiter looked rather embarrassed.

"I don't know for certain, monsieur. But they say—" he hesitated.

"Yes—go on!"

"They say he was in love with that young English lady, monsieur, your cousin. There is a letter left—they say."

"Thank you, Fritz. Well, I'll go round to the hotel in a few minutes."

Fritz went away.

As soon as I had dressed I went to the Hôtel des Fleurs. The body of Demetriadi had already been taken away. I didn't see Elise or her mother, but I saw Custe, who was much upset. He told me that what the waiter had said was true. Although neither he nor his wife had suspected it, Demetriadi had been madly in love with Elise ever since they had met at St. Moritz. Apparently the girl had actually been fond of him. But on the previous day, evidently realising how utterly unsuitable a marriage with him would be, and apparently also influenced by some incident which was never made public, and which my cousin refused to disclose to me, she had sent him a letter forbidding him ever to speak of love matters to her again, and threatening that if he did she would make her people take her away at once from our town.

The result of this letter was the tragedy.

Demetriadi's marvellous game of bridge at the Palace Hotel was his last.

I did not see Syke during the day. I don't know where he was. Perhaps—the weather was fine—he had gone out for some expedition. In the evening, however, he was in the restaurant as usual. After dinner I joined him.

"Can you tell me anything now?" I asked.

"Yes," he said. "Now I can! Do you know what it was Demetriadi saw in room number fourteen in his dream?"

"What was it?"

"He saw himself—hanging."

THE BAROMETER

THERE existed a few years ago, in the Yorkshire wolds, a state of affairs in which the barometer was more consulted than the Bible, and the only barometer in the district hung in the hall of the Vicarage and belonged to the parson, who scanned it daily and out of its abstruse lettering gave no hope to his pining household. The relentless needle stood ever at "set fair", and the terrible drought, which had already lasted for six whole weeks, continued. The dreary sheet of sky overhead stretched in its pitiless blueness over the baked brown earth that lay beneath, parched and cracked and yawning for rain. In between the rift set apart for their habitation, walked sad human beings, sighing and complaining, full of vague physical uneasiness and sense of stress of longing.

The Church and Vicarage of Barmoor, and the few cottages to which it ministered, made the only break in the wilderness of moorland that stretched away for miles to Pickering on the one side and Danby Moor on the other. Three trees grew near the Vicarage: the boughs of one hung over the roof of the lean-to, and made a landmark over the moor. In the early spring they had been fine bunches of verdure. Now their tattered and disconsolate foliage hung motionless, shrinking day by day into the brown semblance of what were once green leaves. A little beck ran at the bottom of the parson's garden, but it was now all but dry. Everything was dried and wasted, except the heather which sprouted and thickened and browned under the desolating shine of the pitiless sun, while the air above it quivered with refraction.

"The air is dancing!" cried the parson's boys, lying in the thick tufts and looking towards the low ridges that bounded their moor to the north. Later on it grew so hot that the very sun was veiled in mist, and the air did not dance any more, but stood still with weariness, so the children said, again. A lighted candle, held in the kitchen garden, flared straight up, like a pillar.

The children tried it—they tried everything—everything permissible under the strict system of Vicarage discipline—to amuse themselves, in these days, when their elders were too tired and cross to undertake to keep them happy. They wandered about together, their arms heavily linked round each other's shoulders, dragging their feet along the cinder paths in an irritating unison. They stood now, in their baggy little home-made clothes, on the path that led down the kitchen garden, bordered with feeble flowers. It was only bordered; the middle patch of ground was, perforce, devoted to useful vegetable cultivation. The living of Barmoor was not a rich living, and the Rev. Matthew Cooper, its incumbent, stood very low in position, birth, and education.

His gardener, who was also the sexton, was digging the potatoes for early dinner. He grunted while he dug, and his back was turned to the children, who watched, with a kind of fascination born of *ennui,* the turn of the fork and the roll of the loose mould, and the horny hand that came down every now and then and gathered up the harvest of his toil and flung it into a basket. Saunders was careless, and let several potatoes roll back into the furrow, out of the eight or so that each turn of the fork should yield.

"Oh, Saunders, look, ye've missed one!" piped the youngest child.

"Happen I have, Master John," replied the old man. "It's ower hot to be fashed!"

The child sighed.

"Won't it really rain soon, Saunders dear?" he asked wearily. He had heard so much lately of this wonderful rain that was to heal all ills and make the world a pleasant place again. Child-like, he had forgotten what rain was like, and how he hated it, since it kept him indoors, and spoiled his play.

"Happen it may, happen it mayn't!" muttered the old servant sulkily. With a sudden access of spite, he added, "Didn't the master pray for it i' church last Sunda'? But some folks has no influence with the Almighty. A'm sayin' that the Lord ought to do it for His ain sake—the bonny garden's fair perished for the want of a little kindly moisture."

"I think it will rain soon!" said the youngest child again gravely. In his blue eyes was something of the rapt look of a visionary.

"Well, it doesna' look much like it," grumbled the old fellow, pointing up with his fork to the sky that hung above, a wall of greyness, and coming very close to earth, somehow. "What for suld it rain, think'st tha'?"

"Because it must in the end," replied the child sturdily. "It wants to rain so badly. It is like me, when I want to cry and can't. Oh, Saunders, there's another potato you've left. What a lot you miss!"

"Gan awa'! Gan awa'," said Saunders impatiently, "and let me get done. Gan awa' an tew Hannah!"

He shook his pitchfork at them with playful savagery, and they turned away.

"Listen, Willie," said the child called John, confidentially taking his brother's arm, and leading him towards the kitchen, a low, one-storied outhouse attached to the house, overshadowed by the biggest of the elm trees. "Listen, Willie; I think the sky is like a great wall, very thick, and yet very brittle. There's all sorts of queer things going on the other side of it, that we can't see."

"Tell us," said the elder boy, dimly interested.

"There's great bulls roaring, and sparks flying, like in Hobbie Noble's forge, and a noise—such a noise! If there comes a hole in the wall we shall see it." His eyes dilated; he squeezed his less poetical-minded brother's hand.

"Hout!" said the listener, "I don't care for that story much. Let's go in, and bide with Hannah a bit."

The Vicarage rooms were damp and insufficiently lighted, but the Vicarage kitchen was bright and pleasant. Hannah's lime and marl floor was freshly washed, her copper vessels as bright as the mirror in Mrs. Cooper's best bedroom; but in spite of all these signs of previous activity the girl herself was sitting in a limp and weary attitude, her knees apart, and a great bowl of peas between them, which she was "podding" for dinner. Her eyes were heavy; her big lump of flaxen hair hung on one side of her head; her clumsy red hands moved among the pods lazily and inattentively. "Deary me—a deary me!" she murmured to herself at short intervals.

"Now, bairns!" She roused herself as the two slunk in. "I've not time for none of you. Gan awa' and play, there's good childer!"

"Don't be cross, Hannah!" said the eldest timidly. "We've only comed in for a sup of milk."

"The milk is all gone sour," she replied shortly. "Ye mun just content yersel's wi' a drink of water from the pump. Now be off with you!"

She gave the thin, inoffensive house-cat a hoist with her foot, and settled down to her peas again.

The pump in the garden had gone dry long since and Hannah knew it. The water they used in the household—that all the village used—came from one place, the well at the bottom of the village, which had luckily continued its functions in spite of the drought.

The children, as Hannah knew well enough, did not really want anything to drink, they wanted nothing but the antidote of human conversation to the restlessness and uneasiness that they shared with Hannah and Saunders, and what their father was apt to call "the lower animals". The house-dog was as restless as they, and would neither play with them nor stay quiet in his kennel. The hens fluttered brusquely in the henhouse, and the feverish rushing of wings that went on there made it an unpleasant abiding-place for the children. They sometimes amused themselves by going in to hunt for eggs, but they left them alone to-day, and wandered on to the open study window, where the Reverend Matthew Cooper, in hot black clothes, was working at his sermon for next Sunday, putting his hand up to his head every now and again.

The two little boys were always somewhat in awe of their stern father, and all they dared do now was to stand and watch him, until the intermittent scraping of their feet on the walk in front of the window roused him from his meditations. He looked up; his brow was pained.

"Well, my laddies, what do you want?" He spoke kindly enough, but his voice dragged with fatigue and oppression.

"Father," asked the eldest child, "Father, tell us; why don't they send rain when you pray for it?"

"You had better go and ask your mother," said the Vicar, with the sort of grim humour in which he usually dealt. He was by nature a hard, cold, God-fearing, painstaking, undeveloped man, conscious of having a wife who managed him. "What about your lessons? Willie, I gave you a chapter to write out. Go and do some work if you can't play."

"But we've got a headache, Father."

"So have I—splitting. Run away now, and let me go on with my sermon. I haven't even chosen my text yet.... *'Who doeth great things and unsearchable ... Behold, He withholdeth the waters and they dry up ... He bindeth the waters in His thick clouds, and the cloud is not rent under them ... He destroyeth the perfect and the wicked ... If the scourge slay suddenly, He will laugh at the trial of the innocent!'* "

The children left him, in desperation, and, going down to the bottom of the garden, took off their socks and sat with their feet in the diminished brook. The dog would not come with them, but snapped and growled at John when he tried to make overtures to it. Hannah, who came to look for them to fetch them to early dinner, could not find them, though they were only under the shade of the big rowan-bush near the brook head. But she did not trouble herself to look very far; she herself could not have told you what ailed her.

"I cannot find them, mistress," she said to their mother sitting, carving-knife in one hand and fork in the other, before the family joint, which Hannah had set before her, previous to going in search of the truants.

"Oh, very well! If they don't choose to come in to their meals!"

Mrs. Cooper helped her husband to a plateful, and sent it to him in his study, which he had intimated he was too busy to leave. She ate a small portion herself—not much—it was too hot to be hungry. She was a hard woman, and the absence of her two little sons did not affect her appetite in the least.

The kind-hearted maid gave them what she called "a bite and a sup" later on, when they came and put their apprehensive heads round the door cheek. She did not scold them. The youngest boy looked very pale and white, and avoided her eyes.

"Poor bairn!" she said, "he wants setting up with the sea air."

The two children lay down after they had eaten, and slept on a heap of sacking, very clean and dry, near the woodstack. Their little bedroom was over the kitchen, and easy of access, but very dreary in the daytime because of the huge tree that overshadowed it. Hannah did not think of sending them up there, but flung a sack over their bare legs as they lay, and did not disturb them.

As the afternoon wore on to evening the hush became oppressive. Not a breath, not a sound of birds twittering, of fowls fluttering. Only the far-away moo of a discontented cow in an outhouse somewhere in the hills sounded like a faint trumpet call, and emphasised the stillness. The sky seemed nearer than ever now, oppressively near, and all encompassing.

As Hannah crossed the yard, just before supper, to throw a pail of scrapings into the pig-trough, she heard a noise. It was not Hodgson's cow.... It might have been the grinding of one of Miller Farsyde's flour wagons on the quartz that sprinkled the road up there beyond the brow—half a mile away. She did not know what it was—a very faint rumble. She thought no more of it, but as she crossed the courtyard on her way back something dropped on to the back of her hand which she could have sworn was a rain-drop ... !

The thought passed. Her country mind again was a blank. She gave the boys a shake as she passed in. "Come now, wake up! 'Tis supper time!"

The youngest boy stirred and frowned.

"Is it come?" he said—"the hole in the wall?"

"Whatten hole? Whatten wall? Whatten rubbish is the child talking about?" she said carelessly, brushing the loose straws off his jacket with strong sideway pats, and leading him in to the dining-room where supper was spread. Willie, the elder and more prosaic of the two, manifested some interest in the items of the meal. It was beans and bacon and porridge, too solid fare for such a day as this had been. The Vicar had finished his sermon, and was sitting in his place, as pale as his white tie, but otherwise placable enough. The eldest child went round to his own high chair in silence, but the youngest crossed the room to his mother's side and pulled her by the sleeve.

"What ails ye, laddie?" she asked , not unkindly.

"Will you give me a kiss, Mammy?" he asked shamefacedly and in a low voice, lest his brother should hear, and taunt him for being a "mammy pet".

"What nonsense!" Mrs. Cooper said, with all the helpless shyness of a hard woman. She stooped down and kissed her little appealing son, nevertheless. "Now, sit down, and eat your supper quietly. Well, Mr. Cooper, how have ye got on with your sermon?"

"Badly!" replied her husband. "I seem to have such a weight on my brain—an oppression! It is quite dreadful. It is so bad, it really can't last—something must happen. Eat your supper, John, and don't stare."

For the youngest child's eyes were constantly fixed on his father, and little questions seemed to be trembling on his lips. He said nothing until supper was over, when he begged his mother to read to them, in which request he was seconded by his elder brother.

She got the big family Bible and reverently flirted the pages....

"Read the Israelites and the Plagues of Egypt," suggested Willie.

"Very well," the mother said equably. Her day's work was done, she had time now, and was willing to please the children in their own way.

"'And Moses stretched forth his rod towards the heaven, and the Lord sent thunder and hail—'"

"I wish He would," murmured the Vicar.

"'And the fire ran along the ground, and the Lord rained hail upon the land of Egypt....'"

She was going on in her monotonous, uneducated voice, when the youngest child suddenly screamed and hid his face in the cushions of the sofa.

"Whisht, whisht!" she called out, by way of soothing him. "Why, you silly body, haven't ye heard it all before?"

The child continued to sob.

His face remained hidden. Sternly his parent ignored his hysterical outburst.

"How old were the children of Israel?" asked Willie, by way of distracting the attention of his elders from this bad conduct on his brother's part, which would assuredly end in both being sent off to bed. (Crying was never allowed.) "Were they as old as me, or only as old as John?"

Mrs. Cooper now gave her mind to the destruction of this erroneous impression under which her children had been labouring, and when it was done she raised her voice, and called "Hannah!" to the maid, who was to be heard moving heavily about in the passage.

John raised his tear-stained face from the sofa, a wild terror in his eyes. Willie clasped his hands together, and together they pleaded with an unaccountable vehemence....

"Oh, no, no, Mother; please, Mother—we don't want to go to bed. We can't! We can't!" both wailed.

"And what for no?" asked the mother, raising her strongly marked black eyebrows. "Why not to bed, to-night, same as other nights?"

"Because—because—oh, Mother! Because we want another story. We want Abram and Isaac," pleaded William. It was only an excuse, and the mother knew it.

"One story is quite enough for one evening," she answered severely; "and John did not behave particularly well over that; I won't hear any fond nonsense. Now you just trot along, both of you! You are both as cross and sleepy as you can be. Bed's the safest place for you!"

Her rough soothing was of no value. The children's faces, as Hannah came in, were blanched with terror. John ran up to the kindly servant-maid, and hid his face in the folds of her linsey gown.

"I want to speak to you," he sobbed.

"Noo, what then, ma honey?" said Hannah good-hunouredly, stooping, till her smooth head touched his tousled one. "Well!"—as she raised her head—"did ye ever hear the like? What sets ye asking that? Mistress, he wants to know if they mayn't creep in aside of father and mother to-night?"

"Please let us, Mother," they murmured, almost inaudibly.

"I never heard anything so fond!" exclaimed Mrs. Cooper laughing grimly. "Be off with ye both quietly, now, and let me hear no more nonsense."

"We did once, Mother!"

"Once! Yes! When they were mending the roof of your bedroom; but the roof's safe and sound over your heads now, at any rate. Why," she laughed, "why, when I give ye a nice big bed to yourselves, should I go and cram my own and the master's bed with two tiresome children, to kick me black and blue before morning? What are ye afeared of, I say?"

But they would own to nothing, and averted their eyes. A little under-swell of sobbing, whimpering breaths testified to their distress.

"What's come to the bairns, I wonder?" She was puzzled, through her thick mental hide of unsympathy. "They're as fractious! It's this unked weather sets us all out of our wits."

"It *must* break," said her husband, "there's no sense in it. We may have rain to-morrow. I forgot to look at the glass as I passed in to-night. There may be a change soon, nay, there must be.... Come here, children, and say your prayers, and let's have no more crying."

They all at once realised the hopelessness of it all, and came meekly to his knee, Hannah folded her hands and looked on approvingly at the two flaxen heads, as in their innocent, pretty, piping voices they begged blessings on their hardened elders, and murmured deep contrition for the sins they had not yet committed. They wound up as usual with the prayer—

"*'Lighten our darkness, we beseech Thee, O Lord, and by Thy great mercy defend us from all perils and dangers of this night; for the love of Thine only Son, our Saviour Jesus Christ. Amen.*'"

Sadly they rose and kissed their parents, who had so carelessly crossed them in their strong instinctive desire, and murmured inaudible good-nights. Then Hannah, taking a little submissive hand of each, led them out of the room.

They went past the weather-glass in the hall, whose strongly marked signs and signals of change they were too young, and Hannah too ignorant, to understand, and walked round by half roofless passages to the kitchen. Then Hannah, laughingly propelling "mischief in front of her", inducted them up the shaky wooden staircase that led into the large room where they always slept, brooded over by the enormous over-arching elm-tree. Its branches tapped the little skylight pane when it was windy, but now they hung still like a drooping banner in a calm.

"I do believe it's that ugly, girt tree they're feared of!" Hannah thought to herself.

During the passage towards their sleeping place they said nothing, but the fingers of the younger child closed and unclosed round the maid's stout thumb, and the touch struck her as very cold.

"I'd let ye both creep in aside o' me," she said, "only I'm that fleyed o' the mistress! She'd find us out, as sure as my name is Hannah Cawthorne."

She set down the candle on the chest in the long, low, empty loft-room. The chest and the bed were almost the only articles of furniture in it. The wooden rafters that supported the roof made fanciful bars and arches over the white dimity quilt. The bed was large, clean and comfortless.

When the two children had undressed and lain down, Hannah Cawthorne, of a gloomy North Country turn of mind that ran continually on omens and predestinations, could not help thinking how like two corpses laid out they looked, lying so straight, their little bodies outlined under the quilt, their eyes wide open and staring at the roof. It made her uncomfortable.

"There's nought to be afeared on," she thought, trying to bring comfort to herself merely, for the children were still, submissive and past all repining now. "It's as safe as a church, but all the same.... Now shut your eyes," she said aloud, "there's good lads, and say 'Gentle Jesus' till ye feel the sleep coming on ye. Oh, ye'll sleep fine, trust me. Shall I leave ye the light?"

This was a wild stretch of authority. She might have lost her place over it. She was relieved when they shook their heads and declined it.

"See here," she went on, producing an apple from her pocket. "See here, ye can munch this atween ye."

She laid it down on the coverlet, but no little hand came forth to take it.

"Poor bairns, they're sad-like.... Eh, she's a hard woman, is the mistress! If they were mine, shouldn't I like them to nestle in aside o' me! This room is fair lonesome. Naebody could hear them if they were to shrike out...."

"What are ye looking at, my honey?" she asked John curiously, for the child's eyes remained obstinately fixed on the roof, as if he saw something there.

"He's looking at the hole in the wall," volunteered the eldest boy at last. "He's shiverin'."

"Hap him up in your arms, ma bonny bairn, that'll soon warm him.... Now I must be going, lads.... Good-night to ye both...."

Hesitating, reluctant, she took up the candle and made a start for the door.

"I don't half like leaving them," she murmured, as she stole out casting a last look at the two children, lying clasped, according to her recommendation, in each other's arms. Their faces were hidden in each other's necks, their sad apprehensive eyes were closed, obediently summoning sleep.

Gently snecking the door, she blundered down the rickety staircase, and made her way back into the other, safer part of the house. Ignorant, she passed by the mysterious oracle hanging in the hall, unable to read or understand the plain meaning which its hands now bore.

"Eh, but she's a right hard woman, is the mistress, and master follows her in all things. *He'd* have let the poor childer come in aside him, when they begged and prayed fit to turn a heart of stone...."

She did not toss on her hard pallet, but lay stupefied in the heavy slumber that was the mead of her arduous existence. Upstairs, in the best bedroom, the Reverend Matthew Cooper slept off his headache. His wife did not drowse, but lay by her husband's side, straight and still as she had laid down, congratulating herself on the great healing storm that was even now breaking over the Vicarage, gloating over its promise of recomfiture and peace.... It thundered and lightened for two hours.

When morning dawned the great drought was over, and the air was refreshed.

Hannah, the maid, rose and went about her duties with a light heart, and presently, having started the kitchen fire, called the parson and his wife to resume theirs.

When it was time, she pulled her dirty kitchen apron aside, put the kettle where it could not for the moment boil over, and went to call the parson's children.

She went up the crooked stair and opened the door gently, "not to waken them sudden". The first thing she saw, before she screamed, was the wide, jagged hole on the rafters above the bed where they still lay in each other's arms. The lightning that, guided by the tree which hung over the roof, had passed through to the innocent children and dealt them their unearned and undeserved death, had not divided them. They were quiet and unchanged in appearance except for some little blue marks like shot in the forehead of the one and the breast of the other.

THE BUS-CONDUCTOR

My friend, Hugh Grainger, and I had just returned from a two days' visit in the country, where we had been staying in a house of sinister repute which was supposed to be haunted by ghosts of a peculiarly fearsome and truculent sort. The house itself was all that such a house should be, Jacobean and oak-panelled, with long dark passages and high vaulted rooms. It stood also, very remote, and was encompassed by a wood of sombre pines that muttered and whispered in the dark, and all the time that we were there a south-westerly gale with torrents of scolding rain had prevailed, so that by day and night weird noises moaned and fluted in the chimneys, a company of uneasy spirits held colloquy among the trees, and sudden tattoes and tappings beckoned from the window-panes. But in spite of these surroundings, which were sufficient in themselves, one would almost say, to spontaneously generate occult phenomena, nothing of any description had occurred. I am bound to add, also, that my own state of mind was peculiarly well adapted to receive or even to invent the sights and sounds we had gone to seek, for I was, I confess, during the whole time that we were there, in a state of abject apprehension, and lay awake both nights through hours of terrified unrest, afraid of the dark, yet more afraid of what a lighted candle might show me.

Hugh Grainger, on the evening after our return to town, had dined with me, and after dinner our conversation, as was natural, soon came back to these entrancing topics.

"But why you go ghost-seeking I cannot imagine," he said, "because your teeth were chattering and your eyes starting out of your head all the time you were there, from sheer fright. Or do you like being frightened?"

Hugh, though generally intelligent, is dense in certain ways; this is one of them.

"Why, of course, I like being frightened," I said. "I want to be made to creep and creep and creep. Fear is the most absorbing and luxurious of emotions. One forgets all else if one is afraid."

"Well, the fact that neither of us saw anything," he said, "confirms what I have always believed."

"And what have you always believed?"

"That these phenomena are purely objective, not subjective, and that one's state of mind has nothing to do with the perception that perceives them, nor have circumstances or surroundings anything to do with them either. Look at Osburton. It has had the reputation of being a haunted house for years, and it certainly has all the accessories of one. Look at yourself, too, with all your nerves on edge, afraid to look round or light a candle for fear of seeing something! Surely there was the right man in the right place then, if ghosts are subjective."

He got up and lit a cigarette, and looking at him—Hugh is about six feet high, and as broad as he is long—I felt a retort on my lips, for I could not help my mind going back to a certain period in his life, when, from some cause which, as far as I knew, he had never told anybody, he had become a mere quivering mass of disordered nerves. Oddly enough, at the same moment and for the first time, he began to speak of it himself.

"You may reply that it was not worth my while to go either," he said, "because I was so clearly the wrong man in the wrong place. But I wasn't. You for all your apprehensions and expectancy have never seen a ghost. But I have, though I am the last person in the world you would have thought likely to do so, and, though my nerves are steady enough again now, it knocked me all to bits."

He sat down again in his chair.

"No doubt you remember my going to bits," he said, "and since I believe that I am sound again now, I should rather like to tell you about it. But before I couldn't; I couldn't speak of it at all to anybody. Yet there ought to have been nothing frightening about it; what I saw was certainly a most useful and friendly ghost. But it came from the shaded side of things; it looked suddenly out of the night and the mystery with which life is surrounded."

"I want first to tell you quite shortly my theory about ghost-seeing," he continued, "and I can explain it best by a simile, an image. Imagine then that you and I and everybody in the world are like people whose eye is directly opposite a little tiny hole in a sheet of cardboard which is continually shifting and revolving and moving about. Back to back with that sheet of cardboard is another, which also, by laws of its own, is in perpetual but independent motion. In it, too, there is another hole, and when, fortuitously it would seem, these two holes, the one through which we are always looking, and the other in the spiritual plane, come opposite one another, we see through, and then only do the sights and sounds of the spiritual world become visible or audible to us. With most people these holes never come opposite each other during their life.

But at the hour of death they do, and then they remain stationary. That, I fancy, is how we 'pass over'.

"Now, in some natures, these holes are comparatively large, and are constantly coming into opposition. Clairvoyants, mediums, are like that. But, as far as I knew, I had no clairvoyant or mediumistic powers at all. I therefore am the sort of person who long ago made up his mind that he never would see a ghost. It was, so to speak, an incalculable chance that my minute spy-hole should come into opposition with the other. But it did; and it knocked me out of time."

I had heard some such theory before, and though Hugh put it rather picturesquely, there was nothing in the least convincing or practical about it. It might be so, or again it might not.

"I hope your ghost was more original than your theory," said I, in order to bring him to the point.

"Yes, I think it was. You shall judge."

I put on more coal and poked up the fire. Hugh has got, so I have always considered, a great talent for telling stories, and that sense of drama which is so necessary for the narrator. Indeed before now, I have suggested to him that he should take this up as a profession, sit by the fountain in Piccadilly Circus, when times are, as usual, bad, and tell stories to the passers-by in the street, Arabian fashion, for reward. The most part of mankind, I am aware, do not like long stories, but to the few, among whom I number myself, who really like to listen to lengthy accounts of experiences, Hugh is an ideal narrator. I do not care for his theories, or for his similes, but when it comes to facts, to things that happened, I like him to be lengthy.

"Go on, please, and slowly," I said. "Brevity may be the soul of wit, but it is the ruin of story-telling. I want to hear when and where and how it all was, and what you had for lunch and where you had dined and what—"

Hugh began:

"It was the 24th of June, just eighteen months ago," he said. "I had let my flat, you may remember, and came up from the country to stay with you for a week. We had dined alone here—"

I could not help interrupting.

"Did you see the ghost here?" I asked. "In this square little box of a house in a modern street?"

"I was in the house when I saw it."

I hugged myself in silence.

"We had dined alone here in Graeme Street," he said, "and after dinner I went out to some party, and you stopped at home. At dinner your man did not wait, and when I asked where he was, you told me he was ill, and, I thought, changed the subject rather abruptly. You gave me your latch-key when I went out, and on coming back, I found you had gone to bed. There were, however, several letters for me, which required answers. I wrote them there and then, and posted them at the pillar-box opposite. So I suppose it was rather late when I went upstairs.

"You had put me in the front room, on the third floor, overlooking the street, a room which I thought you generally occupied yourself. It was a very hot night, and though there had been a moon when I started to my party, on my return the whole sky was cloud-covered, and it both looked and felt as if we might have a thunder-storm before morning. I was feeling very sleepy and heavy, and it was not till after I had got into bed that I noticed by the shadows of the window-frames on the blind that only one of the windows was open. But it did not seem worth while to get out of bed in order to open it, though I felt rather airless and uncomfortable, and I went to sleep.

"What time it was when I awoke I do not know, but it was certainly not yet dawn, and I never remembered being conscious of such an extraordinary stillness as prevailed. There was no sound either of foot-passengers or wheeled traffic; the music of life appeared to be absolutely mute. But now, instead of being sleepy and heavy, I felt, though I must have slept an hour or two at most, since it was not yet dawn, perfectly fresh and wide-awake, and the effort which had seemed not worth making before, that of getting out of bed and opening the other window, was quite easy now, and I pulled up the blind, threw it wide open, and leaned out, for somehow I parched and pined for air. Even outside the oppression was very noticeable, and though, as you know, I am not easily given to feel the mental effects of climate, I was aware of an awful creepiness coming over me. I tried to analyse it away, but without success; the past day had been pleasant, I looked forward to another pleasant day to-morrow, and yet I was full of some nameless apprehension. I felt, too, dreadfully lonely in this stillness before the dawn.

"Then I heard suddenly and not very far away the sound of some approaching vehicle; I could distinguish the tread of two horses walking at a slow foot's pace. They were, though yet invisible, coming up the street, and yet this indication of life did not abate that dreadful sense of loneliness which I have spoken of. Also in some dim unformulated way that which was coming seemed to me to have something to do with the cause of my oppression.

"Then the vehicle came into sight. At first I could not distinguish what it was. Then I saw that the horses were black and had long tails, and that what thev dragged was made of glass, but had a black frame. It was a hearse. Empty.

"It was moving up this side of the street. It stopped at your door.

"Then the obvious solution struck me. You had said at dinner that your man was ill, and you were, I thought, unwilling to speak more about his illness. No doubt, so I imagined now, he was dead, and for some reason, perhaps because you did not want me to know anything about it, you were having the body removed at night. This, I must tell you, passed through my mind quite instantaneously, and it did not occur to me how unlikely it really was, before the next thing happened.

"I was still leaning out of the window, and I remember also wondering, yet only momentarily, how odd it was that I saw things—or rather the one thing I was looking at—so very distinctly. Of course, there was a moon behind the clouds, but it was curious how every detail of the hearse and the horses was visible. There was only one man, the driver, with it, and the street was otherwise absolutely empty. It was at him I was looking now. I could see every detail of his clothes, but from where I was, so high above him, I could not see his face. He had on grey trousers, brown boots, a black coat buttoned all the way up, and a straw hat. Over his shoulder there was a strap, which seemed to support some sort of little bag. He looked exactly like—well, from my description what did he look exactly like?"

"Why—a bus-conductor," I said instantly.

"So I thought, and even while I was thinking this, he looked up at me. He had a rather long thin face, and on his left cheek there was a mole with a growth of dark hair on it. All this was as distinct as if it had been noonday, and as if I was within a yard of him. But—so instantaneous was all that takes so long in the telling—I had not time to think it strange that the driver of a hearse should be so unfunereally dressed.

"Then he touched his hat to me, and jerked his thumb over his shoulder."

" 'Just room for one inside, sir,' he said.

"There was something so odious, so coarse, so unfeeling about this that I instantly drew my head in, pulled the blind down again, and then, for what reason I do not know, turned on the electric light in order to see what time it was. The hands of my watch pointed to half-past eleven.

"It was then for the first time, I think, that a doubt crossed my mind as to the nature of what I had just seen. But I put out the light again, got into bed, and began to think. We had dined; I had gone to a party, I had come back and written letters, had gone to bed and had slept, So how could it be half-past eleven? ... Or—*what* half-past eleven was it?

"Then another easy solution struck me; my watch must have stopped. But it had not; I could hear it ticking.

"There was stillness and silence again. I expected every moment to hear muffled footsteps on the stairs, footsteps moving slowly and smally under the weight of a heavy burden, but from inside the house there was no sound whatever. Outside, too, there was the same dead silence, while the hearse waited at the door. And the minutes ticked on and ticked on, and at length I began to see a difference in the light in the room, and knew that the dawn was beginning to break outside. But how had it happened then that if the corpse was to be removed at night it had not gone, and that the hearse still waited, when morning was already coming?

"Presently I got out of bed again, and with the sense of strong physical shrinking. I went to the window and pulled back the blind. The dawn was coming fast; the whole street was lit by that silver hueless light of morning. But there was no hearse there.

"Once again I looked at my watch. It was just a quarter-past four. But I would swear that not half an hour had passed since it had told me that it was half-past eleven.

"Then a curious double sense, as if I was living in the present and at the same moment had been living in some other time, came over me. It was dawn on June 25th, and the street, as natural, was empty. But a little while ago the driver, of a hearse had spoken to me, and it was half-past eleven. What was that driver, to what plane did he belong? And again *what* half-past eleven was it that I had seen recorded on the dial of my watch?

"And then I told myself that the whole thing had been a dream. But if you ask me whether I believed what I told myself, I must confess that I did not.

"Your man did not appear at breakfast next morning, nor did I see him again before I left that afternoon. I think if I had, I should have told you about all this, but it was still possible, you see, that what I had seen was a real hearse, driven by a real driver, for all the ghastly gaiety of the face that had looked up to mine and the levity of his pointing hand. I might possibly have fallen asleep soon after seeing him, and slumbered through the removal of the body and the departure of the hearse. So I did not speak of it to you."

There was something wonderfully straightforward and prosaic in all this; here were no Jacobean houses oak-panelled and surrounded by weeping pine-trees, and somehow the very absence of suitable surroundings made the story more impressive. But for a moment a doubt assailed me.

"Don't tell me it was all a dream," I said.

"I don't know whether it was or not. I can only say that I believe myself to have been wide awake. In any case the rest of the story is—odd."

"I went out of town again that afternoon," he continued, "and I may say that I don't think that even for a moment did I get the haunting sense of what I had seen or dreamed that night out of my mind. It was present to me always as some vision unfulfilled. It was as if some clock had struck the four quarters, and I was still waiting to hear what the hour would be.

"Exactly a month afterwards I was in London again, but only for the day. I arrived at Victoria about eleven, and took the underground to Sloane Square in order to see if you were in town and would give me lunch. It was a baking hot morning, and I intended to take a bus from the King's Road as far as Graeme Street. There was one standing at the corner just as I came out of the station, but I saw that the top was full, and the inside appeared to be full also. Just as I came up to it the conductor who, I suppose, had been inside, collecting fares or what not, came out on to the step within a few feet of me. He wore grey trousers, brown boots, a black coat buttoned, a straw hat, and over his shoulder was a strap on which hung his little machine for punching tickets. I saw his face, too; it was the face of the driver of the hearse, with a mole on the left cheek. Then he spoke to me, jerking his thumb over his shoulder.

" 'Just room for one inside, sir,' he said.

"At that a sort of panic-terror took possession of me, and I knew I gesticulated wildly with my arms, and cried, 'No, no!' But at that moment I was living not in the hour that was then passing, but in that hour which had passed a month ago, when I leaned from the window of your bedroom here just before the dawn broke. At this moment, too, I knew that my spy-hole had been opposite the spy-hole into the spiritual world. What I had seen there had some significance, now being fulfilled, beyond the significance of the trivial happenings of to-day and to-morrow. The Powers of which we know so little were visibly working before me. And I stood there on the pavement shaking and trembling.

"I was opposite the post-office at the corner, and just as the bus started my eye fell on the clock in the window there. I need not tell you what the time was.

"Perhaps I need not tell you the rest, for you probably conjecture it, since you will not have forgotten what happened at the corner of Sloane Square at the end of July, the summer before last. The bus pulled out from the pavement into the street in order to get round a van that was standing in front of it. At that moment there came down the King's Road a big motor going at a hideously dangerous pace. It crashed full into the bus, burrowing into it as a gimlet burrows into a board."

He paused.

"And that's my story," he said.

SIR ANDREW CALDECOTT, G.C.M.G., C.B.E.

SEATED ONE DAY AT THE ORGAN

I

While playing out the last hymn at Evensong in the Abbey yesterday the organist was seen to collapse and fall forward over the console. A churchwarden and two choirmen hastened to his assistance; and, having announced that the collection would be taken at the doors, Canon Glenside closed the service forthwith by pronouncing the Benediction. Since his appointment to the organ last year Mr. R. Fulstowe, F.R.C.O., has effected great improvement in the Abbey music, and we are happy to record that his condition last night was reported as one of rapid recovery.

THUS the *Scarminster Mercury* of 15th October, 1931. A dull enough paragraph! Little description and no story. Indeed the Canon had himself written and communicated it, in an anxiety to forestall the curiosity of reporters. For the happening had been ugly; and of a sort that none who were present can ever forget.

Hell had been loosed on their ears by a sprawling, immobile, surpliced body whose hands, elbows and forehead lay over, and at many points upon, the keys of three manuals. In its lunge forward a knuckle had knocked against the pneumatic piston that gives voice to the full organ, and the resultant blare was insufferable. A volume of Bach's fugues, too, had fallen on to the pedals and depressed half an octave of them. The whole church was aquake; the pews quivered. Many of their occupants pressed fingers into their ears; all of them glared protestingly towards the console, and at the inert sagging figure there huddled. The startled faces of the choristers resembled those of gargoyles. Although to sit still among such pandemonium was horrible, nobody stirred. Except for one man: and he, mercifully, with the sense and knowledge to act. Tearing apart the transept curtains, verger Rustley pounced upon and turned the stopcock of the hydraulic bellows. A second later the mad fury of sound wailed into thudding silence. Thudding, because every ear throbbed with a quickened and disordered heart-beat. Then it was that Canon Glenside stuttered out his notice about the offertory and gave the Benediction. The choir retreated to the vestry in distracted groups of three or four, forgetting to form file, while the congregation hurried to the doors without waiting for its recession. Never had the stately order of an Abbey service been so interrupted and truncated.

II

Canon Glenside called on his organist early next morning. "But you *must* tell me, Fulstowe," he was saying, "what overtook you so suddenly. The doctor, you say, cannot account for it. Well, naturally I have to satisfy myself, and you, I suggest, yourself, that there is no possibility of another such exhibition; for I can call it no less. It was quite horrible; the worst sort of advertisement for our Abbey services. Hints are already abroad, no doubt unjustly, of a lapse from sobriety. Surely you must see, don't you, the necessity of a full understanding between us, whatever is said to or by the public?"

Fulstowe rose from his chair, walked to the fireplace and kicked a large lump of coal that lay in the grate. Then, turning slowly round, he faced the Canon with an expression at once unhappy and quizzical. "Why, of course, Canon, I want to explain; very much so. But the difficulty is that I can't explain the explanation. In point of fact I saw and felt something that couldn't have been there!"

"H'm," grunted the Canon. "Well, anyhow, you'd better tell me what you thought you saw and felt. Though, mind you, I don't at all like the idea of a person having hallucinations in a consecrated building."

"Very well, I'll try. As it happens, the source of my hallucinations—if you like to call them that, and I hope to goodness you're right—was something that has never been consecrated. I know that as a fact, for it wasn't in the Abbey until Saturday."

"Do you mean that Sapstead memorial tablet? It's to be dedicated in the near future. I didn't realise that you could see it from the organ."

"One can't. No, I was alluding to the mirror above the console. You will remember my telling you that the mercury was perishing at the back of the old one, and that you suggested my looking around for a cheap replacement. Walking down Raymond Street on Thursday I saw the very thing we needed, in that second-hand furniture shop—Mortimer's, isn't it?—and I bought it for only eighteen-and six. Rustley helped me to screw it up after lunch on Saturday. It fitted almost exactly; even Rustley approved, and you know what he is."

"My wife has picked up a good thing or two at Mortimer's," the Canon remarked, "but what has your purchase to do with your collapse yesterday?"

"I was just coming to that. At Matins on Sunday I was at once struck by the clearness of the reflections in the glass; they seemed to me almost what shall I say?—three-dimensional. My own image looked as though it were some actual person peering down at me through the frame. The face was rather unshaven too, but on touching my chin I found it as smooth as usual. As a matter of fact, I'd put a new blade in my safety razor that morning. Then, during the prayer for the church militant, the reflection appeared to shake its head at me, although I felt myself to be sitting quite motionless. The thing had begun to get on my nerves, so I made up my mind not to look at the glass again. I didn't, either, until the service was over and I was locking up the keyboard."

"And what then?" the Canon rapped out, for the organist had ceased speaking and appeared to be lost in thought.

"What then? Why, it smiled at me and—and it had a gold filling in one of the front teeth." At this point Fulstowe jerked his head up and round with a forced laugh. "Well, as you can see, Canon, *I* haven't! If you will excuse me a moment I will slip into the dining-room for a nip of brandy. I don't feel too good."

The Canon's face reddened at this interruption. He was a teetotaller. Would he have to look for a new organist? Most unfortunate, if so; for this one played well and got so much out of the choir. Still, if the fellow took to seeing things in the Abbey and to nips of brandy within half an hour of breakfast, it would become a plain duty to. . . .

At this point the clerical conscience was relieved by the reappearance of its disturber and an immediate resumption of his tale.

"Sorry, Canon, but I never got a wink of sleep last night, and am all to pieces this morning. Well, at evensong I couldn't help throwing an occasional glance at the mirror while playing the first voluntary. It's my habit to do so. To begin with, everything was as usual Then gradually there seemed to be reflected in it a sort of view."

"The choir-stalls, I presume," the Canon muttered impatiently, shuffling his feet on the rug.

"No; an outdoor view. The front of some country house with turrets at either end and a square tower in the middle. I saw the outline first during the Absolution, and it gained in distinctness every time I glanced at it. By the middle of the first lesson it was as though I peeped through a small window on to a real scene. It was a terribly queer sensation, and during the second lesson a curious development took place My own reflection, which was in the forefront of what I saw, began to recede; to be becoming part of the picture, as it were. I felt, too, as though I were being dragged forward. It was only by a great effort of concentration that I managed to accompany the anthem, and I dared not trust myself to look at the glass during the following prayers and hymn. When you began the sermon, however, I gave way to my curiosity and took another look. As I did so, the whole prospect seemed to move towards me; and as a result, the two end turrets passed out of view and the central tower grew larger and larger. At its middle first-floor window I could now see my own head and surpliced shoulders, small at first but returning to life-size as the window came nearer and nearer; so near at last that the top and bottom of the tower were out of sight and only the window remained. It was then that I became aware that the figure was no longer mine. Surplices do not have collars and buttons; what it was wearing was an old-fashioned nightshirt. Nor was the face mine, or I hoped not. There were dark rings under the eyes, the cheeks were yellowish and the eyebrows grey; the chin was unshaven. Through the crack between the lips I could just see the gold-stopped tooth that I had seen after Matins. Its hands were now visible, the fingers clutching the window-sill with tips bent over it. Suddenly two things gripped my attention. First, that the fingertips protruded not merely over the window-sill but over the frame of the mirror itself. They were nearer to me than the reflecting surface! Second, that the head which had usurped the place of mine was bleeding profusely from the neck. Before I had time to consider these developments, which nevertheless set me shivering, you were ending your sermon with the doxology and giving out the hymn. As I began playing it out I noticed what looked like a splash of blood in the swell manual, and in my surprise glanced upwards at the mirror. I saw there a throat slit from ear to ear and oozing great clots of blood. I gave a gasp, and at that very moment the clawing hands shot forward from the mirror frame and downward to clutch my shoulders. It was then that I must have fainted; I felt an icy clamp round my neck and everything went black. Oh God! I must have another drink."

III

The Canon rose with a frown and stared aimlessly out of the window. He was thankful that Fulstowe had left the room, though disapproving his purpose. It afforded time to think of what to say. He must not be too sympathetic, for the possible necessity of the organist's dismissal pressed uncomfortably on his mind. On the other hand he must not appear callous or offhand, for the man had obviously suffered a catastrophe of imagination for which he deserved pity. Really, a most difficult situation to find oneself in! What should, what *could* he say? In his quandary he grabbed and crushed with his right hand a frond of a fern that languished in a flower-pot on the window table. A knock at the hall door caused him to turn round with a start; he tore the leaf right off and dropped it, crumpled, on to the carpet.

The knock also brought Fulstowe back from the dining-room, apparently quite recomposed. "Who's there?" he said. "Come in."

Verger Rustley did so; and, seeing the Canon, addressed him obsequiously.

"I beg your pardon, Sir, but I didn't know as your reverence were here. I wanted a short word with Mr. Fulstowe; but it can well wait, and I'll step in later when he's disengaged."

"No, Rustley, don't go," the Canon smiled, grateful for the interruption, "you'll be pleased, I'm sure, to find Mr. Fulstowe so quickly recovered from his collapse yesterday evening."

"Indeed I am Sir; especially as having been and had a collapse myself, a thing that's never happened before. Yes, Sir, this very morning. When I was opening up the Abbey, it was. 'Why, you're looking as white as a corpse,' said Mrs. Rustley to me when I got back to breakfast. Couldn't eat much of it either."

"I'm very sorry to hear it, Rustley," the Canon rejoined with some asperity. "I had always regarded you as dependable. Faints and collapses denote a lack of self-control, you know. One has to keep a grip on things."

"I'm far from boasting of it, your reverence; but anyone who saw what I saw—or what Mr. Fulstowe saw yesterday, if I may make a guess—would come near to fainting. I feel sure of that."

At this the organist broke in with eager interest. "What did you see, Rustley? Nothing to do with the looking glass we screwed up on Saturday, I hope?"

"Ah! Then you *did* see it. I thought as much and said so to Mrs. Rustley. Yes, Sir, blood dripping from that glass and splashed all over the organ lid. Leastways that's what it looked like, but when I came to from my fainting—for I never could abear the sight of blood— it was all gone and no mess at all to clean up. Optical illusion is what Mrs. Rustley calls it. Anyhow, it wasn't that as I came to see Mr. Fulstowe about, though it has to do with the mirror. Mortimer's have taken it back."

"Taken it back?" exclaimed Fulstowe. "Why, I paid them for it and have got the receipt."

"Yes, Sir, but it appears that it wasn't theirs to sell. Young Mr. Clarence Mortimer came along himself to explain, and asked me to hand you back the money. Here it is, Sir, seven half-crowns and two sixpences; that's right, I think? His men were taking it down as I came away, and they'll put the old one back till we get a better."

"Thank God for that," Fulstowe muttered under his breath, and then aloud: "What explanation did young Mortimer give? It seems a funny way of doing business."

"He said as it wasn't *their* fault but that of the auctioneer at the Curdlestone sale. He'd never had the glass removed from Sir Peregrine's dressing-room, though it was one of the pieces to be reserved. So Mortimer's men took it away, thinking it part of the suite they'd bought. And a rare shindy Sir Peregrine kicked up, he said, when he found it gone. His favourite shaving-glass, as he'd used since at college and had given orders to be sent down to Rodneybury! That's the family seat in Northshire, as you know, Sir; where Sir Peregrine's now gone to."

Canon Glenside, not relishing the role of listener and much annoyed that two of his staff should have been seeing things in the Abbey, had been restive throughout the preceding conversation and now seized the opportunity for interruption and contradiction. "You are quite wrong, Rustley," he said, "in speaking of Rodneybury as the Randhams' family seat. The family was at Curdlestone long before Rodneybury was built. His ancestors would turn in their graves if they knew of the ruin which Sir Peregrine has brought on his inheritance. He will only have plunged deeper into disaster by selling the old estate and retaining such a big place as Rodneybury. However, that's no affair of ours; and I want you, Rustley, to come down with me to the Abbey and point out the places where the south aisle roof is said to be leaking. It wouldn't be good for you and Mr. Fulstowe to get talking together about your optical illusions. The sooner foolish things are forgotten the better. What do you keep looking at your wrists for?"

Mr. Rustley appeared uneasy. "I was afraid for a moment, Sir, that blood had got on to the cuffs."

"Nonsense," snapped the Canon, now righteously indignant; "come along with me at once. And as for you, Fulstowe, I advise you to put in some hard practice on Bach's fugues. You'll find them a wholesome antidote to hallucinations. Good evening."

IV

Seven years later Dr. Richard Fulstowe, Mus. Doc., F.R.C.O., was appointed organist of Wintonbury Cathedral. In his rooms above the gateway to the cloisters we find him one morning sitting at breakfast, with the *Morning Courier* on the table beside his coffee-cup. Having helped himself to porridge, he glanced at the pictures on the front page. There are two of them; one of a country mansion and the other of an elderly man. "Good God!" he mutters; for he instantly recognises both, though he has known neither. The headline underneath is BANKRUPT BARONET DEAD, and the letterpress runs as follows:

> The inquest is being held to-day on the body of Sir Peregrine Randham, Bart., which was found yesterday morning on the floor of his dressing-room at Rodneybury Towers (pictured above), with the throat cut. It lay before his accustomed shaving-mirror and was clad only in a nightshirt. The deceased Baronet (photo inset) had been involved in bankruptcy proceedings, as recently reported in these columns. Sir Peregrine will be remembered as a staunch patron of the Turf, and as owner of "Red Blade", the winner of the Grinfield Plate in 1929.

It chanced that on the afternoon of the day when Dr. Fulstowe read this at breakfast, Canon Glenside was also in Wintonbury, attending a synod. Thus it was that the two happened to meet at tea-time in the lounge of the Caius Hotel. The Canon having a *Morning Courier* in his hand, Dr. Fulstowe's conversational gambit was inevitable.

"But, my dear Fulstowe," the Canon remonstrated after five minutes, "surely you cannot ask me to believe that you saw the ghost of a man who had more than seven years yet to live?"

"Not exactly his ghost, perhaps."

"Or that a mirror could reflect a place two hundred miles distant from it and an event seven years before its occurrence?"

"Well, Canon, again not exactly."

AUGUST HEAT

PENISTONE ROAD, CLAPHAM,
August 20th, 190–

I HAVE had what I believe to be the most remarkable day in my life, and while the events are still fresh in my mind, I wish to put them down on paper as clearly as possible.

Let me say at the outset that my name is James Clarence Withencroft.

I am forty years old, in perfect health, never having known a day's illness.

By profession I am an artist, not a very successful one, but I earn enough money by my black-and-white work to satisfy my necessary wants.

My only relative, a sister, died five years ago, so that I am independent.

I breakfasted this morning at nine, and after glancing through the morning paper I lighted my pipe and proceeded to let my mind wander in the hope that I might chance upon some subject for my pencil.

The room, though door and windows were open, was oppressively hot, and I had just made up my mind that the coolest and most comfortable place in the neighbourhood would be the deep end of the public swimming bath, when the idea came.

I began to draw. So intent was I on my work that I left my lunch untouched, only stopping work when the clock of St. Jude's struck four.

The final result, for a hurried sketch, was, I felt sure, the best thing I had done.

It showed a criminal in the dock immediately after the judge had pronounced sentence. The man was fat—enormously fat. The flesh hung in rolls about his chin; it creased his huge, stumpy neck. He was clean shaven (perhaps I should say a few days before he must have been clean shaven) and almost bald. He stood in the dock, his short, clumsy fingers clasping the rail, looking straight in front of him. The feeling that his expression conveyed was not so much one of horror as of utter, absolute collapse.

There seemed nothing in the man strong enough to sustain that mountain of flesh.

I rolled up the sketch, and without quite knowing why, placed it in my pocket. Then with the rare sense of happiness which the knowledge of a good thing well done gives, I left the house.

I believe that I set out with the idea of calling upon Trenton, for I remember walking along Lytton Street and turning to the right along Gilchrist Road at the bottom of the hill where the men were at work on the new tram lines.

From there onwards I have only the vaguest recollection of where I went. The one thing of which I was fully conscious was the awful heat, that came up from the dusty asphalt pavement as an almost palpable wave. I longed for the thunder promised by the great banks of copper-coloured cloud that hung low over the western sky.

I must have walked five or six miles, when a small boy roused me from my reverie by asking the time.

It was twenty minutes to seven.

When he left me I began to take stock of my bearings. I found myself standing before a gate that led into a yard bordered by a strip of thirsty earth, where there were flowers, purple stock and scarlet geranium. Above the entrance was a board with the inscription—

CHS. ATKINSON. MONUMENTAL MASON.
WORKER IN ENGLISH AND ITALIAN MARBLES

From the yard itself came a cheery whistle, the noise of hammer blows, and the cold sound of steel meeting stone.

A sudden impulse made me enter.

A man was sitting with his back towards me, busy at work on a slab of curiously veined marble. He turned round as he heard my steps and I stopped short.

It was the man I had been drawing, whose portrait lay in my pocket.

He sat there, huge and elephantine, the sweat pouring from his scalp, which he wiped with a red silk handkerchief. But though the face was the same, the expression was absolutely different.

He greeted me smiling, as if we were old friends, and shook my hand.

I apologised for my intrusion.

"Everything is hot and glary outside," I said. "This seems an oasis in the wilderness."

"I don't know about the oasis," he replied, "but it certainly is hot, as hot as hell. Take a seat, sir!"

He pointed to the end of the gravestone on which he was at work, and I sat down.

"That's a beautiful piece of stone you've got hold of," I said.

He shook his head. "In a way it is," he answered; "the surface here is as fine as anything you could wish, but there's a big flaw at the back, though I don't expect you'd ever notice it. I could never make really a good job of a bit of marble like that. It would be all right in a summer like this; it wouldn't mind the blasted heat. But wait till the winter comes. There's nothing quite like frost to find out the weak points in stone."

"Then what's it for?" I asked.

The man burst out laughing.

"You'd hardly believe me if I was to tell you it's for an exhibition, but it's the truth. Artists have exhibitions: so do grocers and butchers; we have them too. All the latest little things in headstones, you know."

He went on to talk of marbles, which sort best withstood wind and rain, and which were easiest to work; then of his garden and a new sort of carnation he had bought. At the end of every other minute he would drop his tools, wipe his shining head, and curse the heat.

I said little, for I felt uneasy. There was something unnatural, uncanny, in meeting this man.

I tried first to persuade myself that I had seen him before, that his face, unknown to me, had found a place in some out-of-the-way corner of my memory, but I knew that I was practising little more than a plausible piece of self-deception.

Mr. Atkinson finished his work, spat on the ground, and got up with a sigh of relief.

"There! What do you think of that?" he said, with an air of evident pride.

The inscription which I read for the first time was this—

SACRED TO THE MEMORY

OF

JAMES CLARENCE WITHENCROFT.

BORN JAN. 18TH, 1860.

HE PASSED AWAY VERY SUDDENLY

ON AUGUST 20TH, 190–

"In the midst of life we are in death."

For some time I sat in silence. Then a cold shudder ran down my spine. I asked him where he had seen the name.

"Oh, I didn't see it anywhere," replied Mr. Atkinson. "I wanted some name, and I put down the first that came into my head. Why do you want to know?"

"It's a strange coincidence, but it happens to be mine."

He gave a long, low whistle.

"And the dates?"

"I can only answer for one of them, and that's correct."

"It's a rum go!" he said.

But he knew less than I did. I told him of my morning's work. I took the sketch from my pocket and showed it to him. As he looked, the expression on his face altered until it became more and more like that of the man I had drawn.

"And it was only the day before yesterday," he said, "that I told Maria there were no such things as ghosts!"

Neither of us had seen a ghost, but I knew what he meant.

"You probably heard my name," I said.

"And you must have seen me somewhere and have forgotten it! Were you at Clacton-on-Sea last July?"

I had never been to Clacton in my life. We were silent for some time. We were both looking at the same thing, the two dates on the gravestone, and one was right.

"Come inside and have some supper," said Mr. Atkinson.

His wife is a cheerful little woman, with the flaky red cheeks of the country-bred. Her husband introduced me as a friend of his who was an artist. The result was unfortunate, for after the sardines and watercress had been removed, she brought out a Doré Bible, and I had to sit and express my admiration for nearly half an hour.

I went outside, and found Atkinson sitting on the gravestone smoking.

We resumed the conversation at the point we had left off.

"You must excuse me asking," I said, "but do you know of anything you've done for which you could be put on trial?"

He shook his head.

"I'm not a bankrupt, the business is prosperous enough. Three years ago I gave turkeys to some of the guardians at Christmas, but that's all I can think of. And they were small ones, too," he added as an afterthought.

He got up, fetched a can from the porch, and began to water the flowers. "Twice a day regular in the hot weather," he said, "and then the heat sometimes gets the better of the delicate ones. And ferns, good Lord! They could never stand it. Where do you live?"

I told him my address. It would take an hour's quick walk to get back home.

"It's like this," he said. "We'll look at the matter straight. If you go back home to-night, you take your chance of accidents. A cart may run over you, and there's always banana skins and orange peel, to say nothing of falling ladders."

He spoke of the improbable with an intense seriousness that

would have been laughable six hours before. But I did not laugh.

"The best thing we can do," he continued, "is for you to stay here till twelve o'clock. We'll go upstairs and smoke; it may be cooler inside."

To my surprise I agreed.

We are sitting now in a long, low room beneath the eaves. Atkinson has sent his wife to bed. He himself is busy sharpening some tools at a little oilstone, smoking one of my cigars the while.

The air seems charged with thunder. I am writing this at a shaky table before the open window. The leg is cracked, and Atkinson, who seems a handy man with his tools, is going to mend it as soon as he has finished putting an edge on his chisel.

It is after eleven now. I shall be gone in less than an hour.

But the heat is stifling.

It is enough to send a man mad.

SPIRITUALISM
AND
MAGIC

THE REALM OF THE UNREAL

I

FOR a part of the distance between Auburn and Newcastle the road —first on one side of a creek and then on the other—occupies the whole bottom of the ravine, being partly cut out of the steep hillside, and partly built up with boulders removed from the creek-bed by the miners. The hills are wooded, the course of the ravine is sinuous. In a dark night careful driving is required in order not to go off into the water. The night that I have in memory was dark, the creek a torrent, swollen by a recent storm. I had driven up from Newcastle and was within about a mile of Auburn in the darkest and narrowest part of the ravine, looking intently ahead of my horse for the roadway. Suddenly I saw a man almost under the animal's nose, and reined in with a jerk that came near setting the creature upon its haunches.

"I beg your pardon," I said; "I did not see you, sir."

"You could hardly be expected to see me," the man replied civilly, approaching the side of the vehicle; "and the noise of the creek prevented my hearing you."

I at once recognised the voice, although five years had passed since I had heard it. I was not particularly well pleased to hear it now.

"You are Dr. Dorrimore, I think," said I.

"Yes; and you are my good friend Mr. Manrich. I am more than glad to see you—the excess," he added, with a light laugh, "being due to the fact that I am going your way, and naturally expect an invitation to ride with you."

"Which I extend with all my heart."

That was not altogether true.

Dr. Dorrimore thanked me as he seated himself beside me, and I drove cautiously forward, as before. Doubtless it is fancy, but it seems to me now that the remaining distance was made in a chill fog; that I was uncomfortably cold; that the way was longer than ever before, and the town, when we reached it, cheerless, forbidding, and desolate. It must have been early in the evening, yet I do not recollect a light in any of the houses nor a living thing in the streets. Dorrimore explained at some length how he happened to be there.

and where he had been during the years that had elapsed since I had seen him. I recall the fact of the narrative, but none of the facts narrated. He had been in foreign countries and had returned—this is all that my memory retains, and this I already knew. As to myself I cannot remember that I spoke a word, though doubtless I did.

Of one thing I am distinctly conscious: the man's presence at my side was strangely distasteful and disquieting—so much so that when I at last pulled up under the lights of the Putnam House I experienced a sense of having escaped some spiritual peril of a nature peculiarly forbidding. This sense of relief was somewhat modified by the discovery that Dr. Dorrimore was living at the same hotel.

II

In partial explanation of my feelings regarding Dr. Dorrimore I will relate briefly the circumstances under which I had met him some years before. One evening a half-dozen men of whom I was one were sitting in the library of the Bohemian Club in San Francisco. The conversation had turned to the subject of sleight-of-hand and the feats of the *prestidigitateurs,* one of whom was then exhibiting at a local theatre.

"These fellows are pretenders in a double sense," said one of the party; "they can do nothing which it is worth one's while to be made a dupe by. The humblest wayside juggler in India could mystify them to the verge of lunacy."

"For example, how?" asked another, lighting a cigar.

"For example, by all their common and familiar performances—throwing large objects into the air which never come down; causing plants to sprout, grow visibly and blossom, in bare ground chosen by spectators; putting a man into a wicker basket, piercing him through and through with a sword while he shrieks and bleeds, and then—the basket being opened, nothing is there; tossing the free end of a silken ladder into the air. mounting it and disappearing."

"Nonsense!" I said, rather uncivilly, I fear. "You surely do not believe such things?"

"Certainly not; I have seen them too often."

"But I do," said a journalist of considerable local fame as a picturesque reporter. "I have so frequently related them that nothing but observation could shake my conviction. Why, gentlemen, I have my own word for it."

Nobody laughed—all were looking at something behind me. Turning in my seat I saw a man in evening dress who had just entered the room. He was exceedingly dark, almost swarthy, with a thin face, black-bearded to the lips, an abundance of coarse black hair in some disorder, a high nose and eyes that glittered with as soulless an expression as those of a cobra. One of the group rose and introduced him as Dr. Dorrimore, of Calcutta. As each of us was presented in turn he acknowledged the fact with a profound bow in the Oriental manner, but with nothing of Oriental gravity. His smile impressed me as cynical and a trifle contemptuous. His whole demeanour I can describe only as disagreeably engaging.

His presence led the conversation into other channels. He said little—I do not recall anything of what he did say. I thought his voice singularly rich and melodious, but it affected me in the same way as his eyes and smile. In a few minutes I rose to go. He also rose and put on his overcoat.

"Mr. Manrich," he said, "I am going your way."

"The devil you are!" I thought. "How do you know which way I am going?" Then I said, "I shall be pleased to have your company."

We left the building together. No cabs were in sight, the street cars had gone to bed, there was a full moon and the cool night air was delightful; we walked up the California Street Hill. I took that direction thinking he would naturally wish to take another, towards one of the hotels.

"You do not believe what is told of the Hindu jugglers," he said abruptly.

"How do you know that?" I asked.

Without replying he laid his hand lightly upon my arm and with the other pointed to the stone sidewalk directly in front. There, almost at our feet, lay the dead body of a man, the face upturned and white in the moonlight! A sword whose hilt sparkled with gems stood fixed and upright in the breast; a pool of blood had collected on the stones of the sidewalk.

I was startled and terrified—not only by what I saw, but by the circumstances under which I saw it. Repeatedly during our ascent of the hill my eyes, I thought, had traversed the whole reach of that sidewalk, from street to street. How could they have been insensible to this dreadful object now so conspicuous in the white moonlight?

As my dazed faculties cleared I observed that the body was in evening dress; the overcoat thrown wide open revealed the dress-coat, the white tie, the broad expanse of shirt front pierced by the sword. And—horrible revelation!—the face, except for its pallor, was that of my companion! It was to the minutest detail of dress and feature Dr. Dorrimore himself. Bewildered and horrified, I turned to look for the living man. He was nowhere visible, and with an added terror I retired from the place, down the hill in the direction whence I had come. I had taken but a few strides when a strong grasp upon my shoulder arrested me. I came near crying out with terror: the dead man, the sword still fixed in his breast, stood beside me! Pulling out the sword with his disengaged hand, he flung it from him, the moonlight glinting upon the jewels of its hilt and the unsullied steel of its blade. It fell with a clang upon the sidewalk ahead and—vanished! The man, swarthy as before, relaxed his grasp upon my shoulder and looked at me with the same cynical regard that I had observed on first meeting him. The dead have not that look—it partly restored me, and turning my head backward, I saw the smooth white expanse of sidewalk, unbroken from street to street.

"What is all this nonsense, you devil?" I demanded, fiercely enough, though weak and trembling in every limb.

"It is what some are pleased to call jugglery," he answered, with a light, hard laugh.

He turned down Dupont Street and I saw him no more until we met in the Auburn ravine.

III

On the day after my second meeting with Dr. Dorrimore I did not see him: the clerk in the Putnam House explained that a slight illness confined him to his rooms. That afternoon at the railway station I was surprised and made happy by the unexpected arrival of Miss Margaret Corray and her mother, from Oakland.

This is not a love story. I am no storyteller, and love as it is cannot be portrayed in a literature dominated and enthralled by the debasing tyranny which "sentences letters" in the name of the Young Girl. Under the Young Girl's blighting reign—or rather under the rule of those false Ministers of the Censure who have appointed themselves to the custody of her welfare—Love

> veils her sacred fires,
> And, unaware, Morality expires,

famished upon the sifted meal and distilled water of a prudish purveyance.

Let it suffice that Miss Corray and I were engaged in marriage. She and her mother went to the hotel at which I lived, and for two weeks I saw her daily. That I was happy needs hardly be said; the only bar to my perfect enjoyment of those golden days was the presence of Dr. Dorrimore, whom I had felt compelled to introduce to the ladies.

By them he was evidently held in favour. What could I say? I knew absolutely nothing to his discredit. His manners were those of a cultivated and considerate gentleman; and to women a man's manner is the man. On one or two occasions when I saw Miss Corray walking with him I was furious, and once had the indiscretion to protest. Asked for reasons, I had none to give, and fancied I saw in her expression a shade of contempt for the vagaries of a jealous mind. In time I grew morose and consciously disagreeable, and resolved in my madness to return to San Francisco the next day. Of this, however, I said nothing.

IV

There was at Auburn an old, abandoned cemetery. It was nearly in the heart of the town, yet by night it was as gruesome a place as the most dismal of human moods could crave. The railings about the plots were prostrate, decayed, or altogether gone. Many of the graves were sunken, from others grew sturdy pines, whose roots had committed unspeakable sins. The headstones were fallen and broken across; brambles overran the ground; the fence was mostly gone, and cows and pigs wandered there at will; the place was a dishonour to the living, a calumny on the dead. a blasphemy against God.

The evening of the day on which I had taken my madman's resolution to depart in anger from all that was dear to me found me in that congenial spot. The light of the half moon fell ghostly through the foliage of trees in spots and patches, revealing much that was unsightly, and the black shadows seemed conspiracies withholding to the proper time revelations of darker import. Passing along what had been a gravel path, I saw emerging from shadow the figure of Dr. Dorrimore. I was myself in shadow, and stood still with clenched hands and set teeth, trying to control the impulse to leap upon and strangle him. A moment later a second figure joined him and clung to his arm. It was Margaret Corray!

I cannot rightly relate what occurred. I know that I sprang forward, bent upon murder; I know that I was found in the grey of the morning, bruised and bloody, with finger marks upon my throat. I was taken to the Putnam House, where for days I lay in a delirium. All this I know, for I have been told. And of my own knowledge I know that when consciousness returned with convalescence I sent for the clerk of the hotel.

"Are Mrs. Corray and her daughter still here?" I asked.

"What name did you say?"

"Corray."

"Nobody of that name has been here."

"I beg you will not trifle with me," I said petulantly. "You see that I am all right now; tell me the truth."

"I give you my word," he replied with evident sincerity, "we have had no guests of that name."

His words stupefied me. I lay for a few moments in silence; then I asked: "Where is Dr. Dorrimore?"

"He left on the morning of your fight and has not been heard of since. It was a rough deal he gave you."

V

Such are the facts of this case. Margaret Corray is now my wife. She has never seen Auburn, and during the weeks whose history as it shaped itself in my brain I have endeavoured to relate, was living at her home in Oakland, wondering where her lover was and why he did not write. The other day I saw in the *Baltimore Sun* the following paragraph:

> Professor Valentine Dorrimore, the hypnotist, had a large audience last night. The lecturer, who has lived most of his life in India, gave some marvellous exhibitions of his power, hypnotising anyone who chose to submit himself to the experiment, by merely looking at him. In fact, he twice hypnotised the entire audience (reporters alone exempted), making all entertain the most extraordinary illusions. The most valuable feature of the lecture was the disclosure of the methods of the Hindu jugglers in their famous performances, familiar in the mouths of travellers. The professor declares that these thaumaturgists have acquired such skill in the art which he learned at their feet that they perform their miracles by simply throwing the "spectators" into a state of hypnosis and telling them what to see and hear. His assertion that a peculiarly susceptible subject may be kept in the realm of the unreal for weeks, months, and even years, dominated by whatever delusions and hallucinations the operator may from time to time suggest, is a trifle disquieting.

PLAYING WITH FIRE

I CANNOT pretend to say what occurred on the 14th of April last at No. 17 Badderly Gardens. Put down in black and white, my surmise might seem too crude, too grotesque, for serious consideration. And yet that something did occur, and that it was of a nature which will leave its mark upon every one of us for the rest of our lives, is as certain as the unanimous testimony of five witnesses can make it. I will not enter into any argument or speculation. I will only give a plain statement, which will be submitted to John Moir, Harvey Deacon, and Mrs. Delamere, and withheld from publication unless they are prepared to corroborate every detail. I cannot obtain the sanction of Paul Le Duc, for he appears to have left the country.

It was John Moir (the well-known senior partner of Moir, Moir and Sanderson) who had originally turned our attention to occult subjects. He had, like many very hard and practical men of business, a mystic side to his nature, which had led him to the examination, and eventually to the acceptance, of those elusive phenomena which are grouped together with much that is foolish, and much that is fraudulent, under the common heading of spiritualism. His researches, which had begun with an open mind, ended unhappily in dogma, and he became as positive and fanatical as any other bigot. He represented in our little group the body of men who have turned these singular phenomena into a new religion.

Mrs. Delamere, our medium, was his sister, the wife of Delamere, the rising sculptor. Our experience had shown us that to work on these subjects without a medium was as futile as for an astronomer to make observations without a telescope. On the other hand, the introduction of a paid medium was hateful to all of us. Was it not obvious that he or she would feel bound to return some result for money received, and that the temptation to fraud would be an overpowering one? No phenomena could be relied upon which were produced at a guinea an hour. But, fortunately, Moir had discovered that his sister was mediumistic—in other words, that she was a battery of that animal magnetic force which is the only form of energy that is subtle enough to be acted upon from the spiritual plane as well as from our own material one. Of course, when I say this, I do not mean to beg the question; but I am simply indicating the theories upon which we were ourselves, rightly or wrongly, explaining what we saw. The lady came, not altogether with the approval of her husband, and though she never gave indications of any very great psychic force, we were able, at least, to obtain those usual phenomena of message-tilting which are at the same time so puerile and so inexplicable. Every Sunday evening we met in Harvey Deacon's studio at Badderly Gardens, the next house to the corner of Merton Park Road.

Harvey Deacon's imaginative work in art would prepare anyone to find that he was an ardent lover of eveything which was *outré* and sensational. A certain picturesqueness in the study of the occult had been the quality which had originally attracted him to it, but his attention was speedily arrested by some of those phenomena to which I have referred, and he was coming rapidly to the conclusion that what he had looked upon as an amusing romance and an after-dinner entertainment was really a very formidable reality. He is a man with a remarkably clear and logical brain—a true descendant of his ancestor, the well-known Scotch professor—and he represented in our small circle the critical element, the man who has no prejudices, is prepared to follow facts as far as he can see them, and refuses to theorise in advance of his data. His caution annoyed Moir as much as the latter's robust faith amused Deacon, but each in his own way was equally keen upon the matter.

And I? What am I to say that I represented? I was not the devotee. I was not the scientific critic. Perhaps the best that I can claim for myself is that I was the dilettante man about town, anxious to be in the swim of every fresh movement, thankful for any new sensation which would take me out of myself and open up fresh possibilities of existence. I am not an enthusiast myself, but I like the company of those who are. Moir's talk, which made me feel as if we had a private pass-key through the door of death, filled me with a vague contentment. The soothing atmosphere of the séance with the darkened lights was delightful to me. In a word, the thing amused me, and so I was there.

It was, as I have said, upon the 14th of April last that the very singular event which I am about to put upon record took place. I was the first of the men to arrive at the studio, but Mrs. Delamere was already there, having had afternoon tea with Mrs. Harvey Deacon. The two ladies and Deacon himself were standing in front of an unfinished picture of his upon the easel. I am not an expert in art, and I have never professed to understand what Harvey Deacon meant by his pictures; but I could see in this instance that it was all very clever and imaginative, fairies and animals and allegorical figures of all sorts. The ladies were loud in their praises, and indeed the colour effect was a remarkable one.

"What do you think of it, Markham?" he asked.

"Well, it's above me," said I. "These beasts—what are they?"

"Mythical monsters, imaginary creatures, heraldic emblems—a sort of weird, bizarre procession of them."

"With a white horse in front!"

"It's not a horse," said he, rather testily—which was surprising, for he was a very good-humoured fellow as a rule, and hardly ever took himself seriously.

"What is it, then?"

"Can't you see the horn in front? It's a unicorn. I told you they were heraldic beasts. Can't you recognise one?"

"Very sorry, Deacon," said I, for he really seemed to be annoyed.

He laughed at his own irritation.

"Excuse me, Markham!" said he; "the fact is that I have had an awful job over the beast. All day I have been painting him in and painting him out, and trying to imagine what a real live, ramping unicorn would look like. At last I got him, as I hoped; so when you failed to recognise it, it took me on the raw."

"Why, of course it's a unicorn," said I, for he was evidently depressed at my obtuseness. "I can see the horn quite plainly, but I never saw a unicorn except beside the Royal Arms, and so I never thought of the creature. And these others are griffins and cockatrices, and dragons of sorts?"

"Yes, I had no difficulty with them. It was the unicorn which bothered me. However, there's an end of it until to-morrow." He turned the picture round upon the easel, and we all chatted about other subjects.

Moir was late that evening, and when he did arrive he brought with him, rather to our surprise, a small, stout Frenchman, whom he introduced as Monsieur Paul Le Duc. I say to our surprise, for we held a theory that any intrusion into our spiritual circle deranged the conditions, and introduced an element of suspicion. We knew that we could trust each other, but all our results were vitiated by the presence of an outsider. However, Moir soon reconciled us to the innovation. Monsieur Paul Le Duc was a famous student of occultism, a seer, a medium, and a mystic. He was travelling in England with a letter of introduction to Moir from the President of the Parisian brothers of the Rosy Cross. What more natural than that he should bring him to our little séance, or that we should feel honoured by his presence?

He was, as I have said, a small, stout man, undistinguished in appearance, with a broad, smooth, clean-shaven face, remarkable only for a pair of large, brown, velvety eyes, staring vaguely out in front of him. He was well dressed, with the manners of a gentleman, and his curious little turns of English speech set the ladies smiling. Mrs. Deacon had a prejudice against our researches and left the room, upon which we lowered the lights, as was our custom, and drew up our chairs to the square mahogany table which stood in the centre of the studio. The light was subdued, but sufficient to allow us to see each other quite plainly. I remember that I could even observe the curious, podgy little square-topped hands which the Frenchman laid upon the table.

"What a fun!" said he. "It is many years since I have sat in this fashion, and it is to me amusing. Madame is medium. Does madame make the trance?"

"Well, hardly that," said Mrs. Delamere. "But I am always conscious of extreme sleepiness."

"It is the first stage. Then you encourage it, and there comes the trance. When the trance comes, then out jumps your little spirit and in jumps another little spirit, and so you have direct talking or writing. You leave your machine to be worked by another. *Hein?* But what have unicorns to do with it?"

Harvey Deacon started in his chair. The Frenchman was moving his head slowly round and staring into the shadows which draped the walls.

"What a fun!" said he. "Always unicorns. Who has been thinking so hard upon a subject so bizarre?"

"This is wonderful!" cried Deacon. "I have been trying to paint one all day. But how could you know it?"

"You have been thinking of them in this room."

"Certainly."

"But thoughts are things, my friend. When you imagine a thing you make a thing. You did not know it, *hein*? But I can see your unicorns because it is not only with my eye that I can see."

"Do you mean to say that I create a thing which has never existed by merely thinking of it?"

"But certainly. It is the fact which lies under all other facts. That is why an evil thought is also a danger."

"They are, I suppose, upon the astral plane?" said Moir.

"Ah, well, these are but words, my friends. They are there—somewhere—everywhere—I cannot tell myself. I see them. I could touch them."

"You could not make *us* see them."

"It is to materialise them. Hold! It is an experiment. But the power is wanting. Let us see what power we have, and then arrange what we shall do. May I place you as I wish?"

"You evidently know a great deal more about it than we do," said Harvey Deacon; "I wish that you would take complete control."

"It may be that the conditions are not good. But we will try what we can do. Madame will sit where she is, I next, and this gentleman beside me. Meester Moir will sit next to madame, because it is well to have blacks and blondes in turn. So! And now with your permission I will turn the lights all out."

"What is the advantage of the dark?" I asked.

"Because the force with which we deal is a vibration of ether and so also is light. We have the wires all for ourselves now—*hein?* You will not be frightened in the darkness, madame? What a fun is such a séance!"

At first the darkness appeared to be absolutely pitchy, but in a few minutes our eyes became so far accustomed to it that we could just make out each other's presence—very dimly and vaguely, it is true. I could see nothing else in the room—only the black loom of the motionless figures. We were all taking the matter much more seriously than we had ever done before.

"You will place your hands in front. It is hopeless that we touch, since we are so few round so large a table. You will compose yourself, madame, and if sleep should come to you you will not fight against it. And now we sit in silence and we expect—*hein?*"

So we sat in silence and expected, staring out into the blackness in front of us. A clock ticked in the passage. A dog barked intermittently far away. Once or twice a cab rattled past in the street, and the gleam of its lamps through the chink in the curtains was a cheerful break in that gloomy vigil. I felt those physical symptoms with which previous séances had made me familiar—the coldness of the feet, the tingling in the hands, the glow of the palms, the feeling of a cold wind upon the back. Strange little shooting pains came in my forearms, especially as it seemed to me in my left one, which was nearest to our visitor—due no doubt to disturbance of the vascular system, but worthy of some attention all the same. At the same time I was conscious of a strained feeling of expectancy which was almost painful. From the rigid, absolute silence of my companions I gathered that their nerves were as tense as my own.

And then suddenly a sound came out of the darkness—a low, sibilant sound, the quick, thin breathing of a woman. Quicker and thinner yet it came, as between clenched teeth, to end in a loud gasp with a dull rustle of cloth.

"What's that? Is all right?" someone asked in the darkness.

"Yes, all is right," said the Frenchman. "It is madame. She is in her trance. Now, gentlemen, if you will wait quiet you will see something, I think, which will interest you much."

Still the ticking in the hall. Still the breathing, deeper and fuller now, from the medium. Still the occasional flash, more welcome than ever, of the passing lights of the hansoms. What a gap we were bridging, the half-raised veil of the eternal on the one side and the cabs of London on the other. The table was throbbing with a mighty pulse. It swayed steadily, rhythmically, with an easy swooping, scooping motion under our fingers. Sharp little raps and cracks came from its substance, file-firing, volley-firing, the sounds of a faggot burning briskly on a frosty night.

"There is much power," said the Frenchman. "See it on the table!"

I had thought it was some delusion of my own, but all could see it now. There was a greenish-yellow phosphorescent light—or I should say a luminous vapour rather than a light—which lay over the surface of the table. It rolled and wreathed and undulated in dim glimmering folds, turning and swirling like clouds of smoke. I could see the white, square-ended hands of the French medium in this baleful light.

"What a fun!" he cried. "It is splendid!"

"Shall we call the alphabet?" asked Moir.

"But no—for we can do much better," said our visitor. "It is but a clumsy thing to tilt the table for every letter of the alphabet, and with such a medium as madame we should do better than that."

"Yes, you will do better," said a voice.

"Who was that? Who spoke? Was that you, Markham?"

"No, I did not speak."

"It was madame who spoke."

"But it was not her voice."

"Is that you, Mrs. Delamere?"

"It is not the medium, but it is the power which uses the organs of the medium," said the strange, deep voice.

"Where is Mrs. Delamere? It will not hurt her, I trust."

"The medium is happy in another plane of existence. She has taken my place, as I have taken hers."

"Who are you?"

"It cannot matter to you who I am. I am one who has lived as you are living, and who has died as you will die."

We heard the creak and grate of a cab pulling up next door. There was an argument about the fare, and the cabman grumbled hoarsely down the street. The green-yellow cloud still swirled faintly over the table, dull elsewhere, but glowing into a dim luminosity in the direction of the medium. It seemed to be piling itself up in front of her. A sense of fear and cold struck into my heart. It seemed to me that lightly and flippantly we had approached the most real and august of sacraments, that communion with the dead of which the fathers of the Church had spoken.

"Don't you think we are going too far? Should we not break up this séance?" I cried.

But the others were all earnest to see the end of it. They laughed at my scruples.

"All the powers are made for use," said Harvey Deacon. "If we *can* do this, we *should* do this. Every new departure of knowledge has been called unlawful in its inception. It is right and proper that we should inquire into the nature of death."

"It is right and proper," said the voice.

"There, what more could you ask?" cried Moir, who was much excited. "Let us have a test. Will you give us a test that you are really there?"

"What test do you demand?"

"Well, now—I have some coins in my pocket. Will you tell me how many?"

"We come back in the hope of teaching and of elevating, and not to guess childish riddles."

"Ha, ha, Meester Moir, you catch it that time," cried the Frenchman. "But surely this is very good sense what the Control is saying."

"It is a religion, not a game," said the cold, hard voice.

"Exactly—the very view I take of it," cried Moir. "I am sure I am very sorry if I have asked a foolish question. You will not tell me who you are?"

"What does it matter?"

"Have you been a spirit long?"

"Yes."

"How long?"

"We cannot reckon time as you do. Our conditions are different."

"Are you happy?"

"Yes."

"You would not wish to come back to life?"

"No—certainly not."

"Are you busy?"

"We could not be happy if we were not busy."

"What do you do?"

"I have said that the conditions are entirely different."

"Can you give us no idea of your work?"

"We labour for our own improvement and for the advancement of others."

"Do you like coming here to-night?"

"I am glad to come if I can do any good by coming."

"Then to do good is your object?"

"It is the object of all life on every plane."

"You see, Markham, that should answer your scruples."

It did, for my doubts had passed and only interest remained.

"Have you pain in your life?" I asked.

"No; pain is a thing of the body."

"Have you mental pain?"

"Yes; one may always be sad or anxious."

"Do you meet the friend whom you have known on earth?"

"Some of them."

"Why only some of them?"

"Only those who are sympathetic."

"Do husbands meet wives?"

"Those who have truly loved."

"And the others?"

"They are nothing to each other."

"There must be a spiritual connection?"

"Of course."

"Is what we are doing right?"

"If done in the right spirit."

"What is the wrong spirit?"

"Curiosity and levity."

"May harm come of that?"

"Very serious harm."

"What sort of harm?"

"You may call up forces over which you have no control."

"Evil forces?"

"Undeveloped forces."

"You say they are dangerous. Dangerous to body or mind?"

"Sometimes to both."

There was a pause, and the blackness seemed to grow blacker still, while the yellow-green fog swirled and smoked upon the table.

"Any questions you would like to ask, Moir?" said Harvey Deacon.

"Only this—do you pray in your world?"

"One should pray in every world."

"Why?"

"Because it is the acknowledgment of forces outside ourselves."

"What religion do you hold over there?"

"We differ exactly as you do."

"You have no certain knowledge?"

"We have only faith."

"These questions of religion," said the Frenchman, "they are of interest to you serious English people, but they are not so much fun. It seems to me that with this power here we might be able to have some great experience—*hein?* Something of which we could talk."

"But nothing could be more interesting than this," said Moir.

"Well, if you think so, that is very well," the Frenchman answered peevishly. "For my part, it seems to me that I have heard all this before, and that to-night I should weesh to try some experiment with all this force which is given to us. But if you have other questions, then ask them, and when you are finish we can try something more."

But the spell was broken. We asked and asked, but the medium sat silent in her chair. Only her deep, regular breathing showed that she was there. The mist still swirled upon the table.

"You have disturbed the harmony. She will not answer."

"But we have learned already all that she can tell—*hein?* For my part I wish to see something that I have never seen before."

"What then?"

"You will let me try?"

"What would you do?"

"I have said to you that thoughts are things. Now I wish to *prove* it to you, and to show you that which is only a thought. Yes, yes, I can do it and you will see. Now I ask you only to sit still and say nothing, and keep ever your hands quiet upon the table."

The room was blacker and more silent than ever. The same feeling of apprehension which had lain heavily upon me at the beginning of the séance was back at my heart once more. The roots of my hair were tingling.

"It is working! It is working!" cried the Frenchman, and there was a crack in his voice as he spoke which told me that he also was strung to his tightest.

The luminous fog drifted slowly off the table, and wavered and flickered across the room. There in the farther and darkest corner it gathered and glowed, hardening down into a shining core—a strange, shifty, luminous, and yet non-illuminating patch of radiance, bright itself, but throwing no rays into the darkness. It had changed from a greenish-yellow to a dusky sullen red. Then round this centre there coiled a dark, smoky substance, thickening, hardening, growing denser and blacker. And then the light went out, smothered in that which had grown round it.

"It has gone."

"Hush—there's something in the room."

We heard it in the corner where the light had been, something which breathed deeply and fidgeted in the darkness.

"What is it? Le Duc, what have you done?"

"It is all right. No harm will come." The Frenchman's voice was treble with agitation.

"Good heavens, Moir, there's a large animal in the room. Here it is, close by my chair! Go away! Go away!"

It was Harvey Deacon's voice, and then came the sound of a blow upon some hard object. And then ... And then ... how can I tell you what happened then?

Some huge thing hurtled against us in the darkness, rearing, stamping, smashing, springing, snorting. The table was splintered. We were scattered in every direction. It clattered and scrambled amongst us, rushing with horrible energy from one corner of the room to another. We were all screaming with fear, grovelling upon our hands and knees to get away from it. Something trod upon my left hand, and I felt the bones splinter under the weight.

"A light! A light!' someone yelled.

"Moir, you have matches, matches!"

"No, I have none. Deacon, where are the matches? For God's sake, the matches!"

"I can't find them. Here, you Frenchman, stop it!"

"It is beyond me. Oh, *mon Dieu,* I cannot stop it. The door! Where is the door?"

My hand, by good luck, lit upon the handle as I groped about in the darkness. The hard-breathing, snorting, rushing creature tore past me and butted with a fearful crash against the oaken partition. The instant that it had passed I turned the handle, and next moment we were all outside, and the door shut behind us. From within came a horrible crashing and rending and stamping.

"What is it? In Heaven's name, what is it?

"A horse. I saw it when the door opened. But Mrs. Delamere—?"

"We must fetch her out. Come on, Markham; the longer we wait the less we shall like it."

He flung open the door and we rushed in. She was there on the ground amidst the splinters of her chair. We seized her and dragged her swiftly out, and as we gained the door I looked over my shoulder into the darkness. There were two strange eyes glowing at us, a rattle of hoofs, and I had just time to slam the door when there came a crash upon it which split it from top to bottom.

"It's coming through! It's coming!"

"Run, run for your lives!" cried the Frenchman.

Another crash, and something shot through the riven door. It was a long white spike, gleaming in the lamplight. For a moment it shone before us, and then with a snap it disappeared again.

"Quick! Quick! This way!" Harvey Deacon shouted. "Carry her in! Here! Quick!"

We had taken refuge in the dining-room, and shut the heavy oak door. We laid the senseless woman upon the sofa, and as we did so,

Moir, the hard man of business, drooped and fainted across the hearthrug. Harvey Deacon was as white as a corpse, jerking and twitching like an epileptic. With a crash we heard the studio door fly to pieces, and the snorting and stamping were in the passage, up and down, shaking the house with their fury. The Frenchman had sunk his face on his hands, and sobbed like a frightened child.

"What shall we do?" I shook him roughly by the shoulder. "Is a gun any use?"

"No, no. The power will pass. Then it will end."

"You might have killed us all—you unspeakable fool—with your infernal experiments."

"I did not know. How could I tell that it would be frightened? It is mad with terror. It was his fault. He struck it."

Harvey Deacon sprang up. "Good heavens!" he cried.

A terrible scream sounded through the house.

"It's my wife! Here, I'm going out. If it's the Evil One himself I am going out!"

He had thrown open the door and rushed out into the passage. At the end of it, at the foot of the stairs, Mrs. Deacon was lying senseless, struck down by the sight which she had seen. But there was nothing else.

With eyes of horror we looked about us, but all was perfectly quiet and still. I approached the black square of the studio door, expecting with every slow step that some atrocious shape would hurl itself out of it. But nothing came, and all was silent inside the room. Peeping and peering, our hearts in our mouths, we came to the very threshold, and stared into the darkness. There was still no sound, but in one direction there was also no darkness. A luminous, glowing cloud, with an incandescent centre, hovered in the corner of the room. Slowly it dimmed and faded, growing thinner and fainter, until at last the same dense, velvety blackness filled the whole studio. And with the last flickering gleam of that baleful light the Frenchman broke into a shout of joy.

"What a fun!" he cried. "No one is hurt, and only the door broken, and the ladies frightened. But, my friends, we have done what has never been done before."

"And as far as I can help," said Harvey Deacon, "it will certainly never be done again."

And that was what befell on the 14th of April last at No. 17, Badderly Gardens. I began by saying that it would seem too grotesque to dogmatise as to what it was which actually did occur; but I give my impressions, *our* impressions (since they are corroborated by Harvey Deacon and John Moir), for what they are worth. You may, if it pleases you, imagine that we were the victims of an elaborate and extraordinary hoax. Or you may think with us that we underwent a very real and a very terrible experience. Or perhaps you may know more than we do of such occult matters, and can inform us of some similar occurrence. In this latter case a letter to William Markham, 146M, The Albany, would help to throw a light upon that which is very dark to us.

JOHN BOYNTON PRIESTLEY

THE OTHER PLACE

A SHORT walk beyond Buckden, in Upper Wharfedale, is Hubberholme, one of the smallest and pleasantest places in the world. It consists of an old church, a pub, and a bridge, set in a dale among high moors. In summer, long after the snows have melted, there is rarely much water in the river, so that it glitters and winks; and a man who has been walking for an hour or two can loiter on that bridge for quite a time, waiting for the pub to open and staring at the river. He was already there when I arrived—a big-boned dark fellow about forty—and he was looking down at the water in a glum fashion, without troubling to re-light the cigar he was chewing. Something had disappointed him, and I found it hard to believe Hubberholme had not come up to his expectations; so I spoke to him.

We agreed that it was a fine day, that this was good country; after which I thought I might try to satisfy my curiosity. So I told him how fond I was of Hubberholme, and how I rarely let a couple of years pass without taking another look at it. He said I was quite right, that he could easily imagine himself feeling the same way about it.

"But if you don't mind my saying so," I said, "you looked as if you'd found this place disappointing."

"Well, I guess I did," he said slowly. He had a deep voice and an accent that might have been American or Canadian. "But not in the way you mean, sir. Nothing wrong with this at all. Couldn't be better. But from the way a fellow described it to me, I thought it might be a place I've been trying to find. And it isn't, that's all." And now, perhaps because he did not want to say any more, he did re-light his cigar. But to show me that he was not unfriendly, he asked me where I was staying.

We discovered then that we were both spending the night in the admirable village of Kettlewell, further down the Dale, but had booked ourselves at different inns. After some further chat we agreed not only to walk back to Kettlewell together but to dine too; and after pointing out that I was the older man and this was my country and not his, I made him agree to be my guest. On our walk back I learnt that his name was Harvey Lindfield, that he was an engineer from Toronto, that he had been married but was now divorced and had a small daughter at present living with his sister. He talked readily enough, and was clearly glad of company, but somewhere behind his talk there was a cloud, a shadow, which might be disappointment or bewilderment. It was not, however, until after dinner, when we lit our cigars in the little sitting-room we had to ourselves and drank the excellent rye whisky that he had brought over as his contribution to the evening's hospitality, that I ventured to suggest that something was troubling him. And I admitted that I was curious.

"You'll remember," I told him, "you said that Hubberholme might be a place you were trying to find." I left it at that, but looked at him expectantly.

"It's the damnedest thing," he confessed, staring at the frilled paper in the fire grate. "I can hardly believe it myself, so why should you? I tried telling it once and got stuck about halfway through. If you weren't a writer, I wouldn't risk it now. But you get around, you talk to people, you must know a lot of things happen that can't be explained. Okay—this is one of 'em. The damnedest thing ever. And don't think I could make it up," he continued, regarding me earnestly. "I wouldn't know where to start. Now if you were telling it to me, that 'ud be different. I wouldn't believe you. But I'm no writer, just a plain engineer, and you've got to believe me. I'll just freshen these drinks, then I'll tell it to you the best way I can." And this was the story he told me.

My company (Lindfield began) had ordered a machine from a firm in Blackley, and I was sent over to make sure this machine was what we wanted. Well, it wasn't. Do you want to know about this machine? No, I thought not. The point is—there wasn't a hell of a lot wrong with it, but just enough to keep me there in Blackley making sure they put it right. So there I was, stuck with the Blackley Electrical Engineering Company, and with Blackley. I forgot to say, this was last November.

Do you know Blackley? Yes—well, going through it is about as much as anybody'd want of Blackley. Especially last November, when it rained and rained and rained and if the sun ever rose and shone, I missed it. When they built that place, they must have wanted to punish themselves. It didn't matter how dark and wet a November might be, Blackley was ready to meet it halfway. It was still dark when I got up in the morning, and by four o'clock it was dark again, and in between it rained. Even when you went inside somewhere, pulled down the blinds and turned on the lights, you didn't feel you'd got any illumination. I thought at first my eyesight was going.

I stayed at the Railway Hotel, next to the station and with a nice view of the tracks and sidings. It was darkish and wettish in there too. I changed my room three times, thinking I'd get something better, but I never did. We ate in the Coffee Room, which had sideboards and dish covers and cruets and knives and forks big enough for a roasted ox, only we never had the roasted ox, just a few sad bits of meat and a lot of drowned vegetables. There was an old waiter, blue in the face from heart disease, and two sour-faced waitresses, one long and thin and the other short and thick, and both of 'em dead against us. The only time they looked pleased was when they could tell you something was "off" or you were too late to have anything. The other fellows there were travelling salesmen, all oldish and defeated, not smart enough to use a car so that they wouldn't have to spend the night in the Railway Hotel, Blackley. After supper they used to sit in a gloomy little hole called the Residents' Lounge, writing long reports explaining why they hadn't taken any orders. It wasn't much better downstairs in the bar. All the customers down there were either earnestly whispering or just sitting staring at nothing. They made you feel somebody important had just died.

I'm not saying the whole town was really like that, but it did seem like that to me. Dark, wet, and dismal. Nothing to do, nowhere to go. It's not that I expected two miles of neon lighting every night and a Big City atmosphere. I've lived in small towns before, and anyhow Blackley wasn't that small—about seventy-five thousand people, I guess. But it hadn't anything for me that I wanted, except that machine I stared at every day, up at the Blackley Electrical Engineering works. On the inside, for somebody who'd properly settled there, the place might have been all right, but on the outside, where I was, it was a living death. If any people there were having a good time, they were doing it behind locked doors. Oh—there were amusements of a sort— a crummy little vaudeville theatre, three or four movie houses, a café where a lot of kids sat about with steaming clothes, and one gaudy big pub where a lot of middle-aged dough-faced whores waited for custom and listened to a blind pianist. I went home with one of 'em one night, but even with the load of gin and whisky I was carrying I couldn't make it, and had to tell her I was meeting a late train. What I did meet—and it took some facing—was that bedroom, cold as organised charity, in the Railway Hotel. I'd have met anybody, getting off any train, just for a change. It was bad enough during the week but Sunday was worse. If I'm ever sent to Hell, it won't be all flames and sulphur and roaring devils; it'll be the Railway Hotel, Blackley, on a wet November Sunday that lasts for ever.

I know what you're thinking—that I didn't give the place a chance, never tried to make the best of it. But I did. Yet somehow I'd no luck. The fellows up at the works were friendly enough—after all, I represented a big order they wanted badly—but even when we all tried, we never got going. The two I saw most of, on the job, Butterworth and Dawson, nice fellows about my own age, took me home and gave me dinner or supper, introduced me to some neighbours, made me talk about Canada, turned on their TV or arranged some bridge. They did their best and so did their wives, but it didn't really work out, perhaps because by that time I felt so dam' lonely and lost I wanted more than I'd a right to expect. I still felt way off on the outside, and couldn't break through. If I tried, got a bit personal, I felt they drew back. It was like calling somewhere when all the people in the house are worried about something, an illness they don't want you to know about or a daughter who's got herself engaged to the wrong man, and they're polite and doing their best but can't really attend to you with most of their minds. So I'd leave 'em feeling more out of it than when I went. Yet I had the notion even then—and you'll understand soon why I say *even then*—that fellows like Butterworth and Dawson might have been real friends if we could only have got rid of the glass wall between us.

I'm no chaser—and as I told you this afternoon I'd had one marriage I was glad to get out of—but it's only natural, especially when a man feels so lonely and out of it, to see if there isn't a woman who might help. And that doesn't just mean a package of sex, as too many people seem to think. There's more in being with a woman than that, though it has to find its place of course. Well, I got to know a woman—she was personnel manager at another works and happened to step across to the Blackley Electrical Engineering place when I was there. Her name was Mavis Gilbert and she was in her early thirties, tallish, dark, good profile, with something pleasant and sensible about her. I took her to the movies once or twice or we met for a drink, and one night she gave me supper where she lived. But that didn't work out either. In fact it made things worse, not better. There was some fellow she couldn't forget, and when she'd had a couple of drinks or had been softened up by a sentimental movie, she didn't even try to forget him. Round about ten-thirty a little lost puppy would come and look out of her eyes. I dare say she'd have let me make love to her, if I'd made an issue of it; but I knew there wouldn't have been anything gay about it, just awkwardness and apologies and then some quiet sobbing after I'd gone;

so I didn't press her, which must have been a relief to her but didn't do me much good. In fact, just because she was a nice girl who ought to have been fairly happy and wasn't, who could feel herself getting drearier and couldn't stop it, she made me feel worse; and by the third week I wasn't seeing her any more but killing the nights with a mixture of hard liquor and fairly soft reading matter. And it still rained, and, as far as I could tell, the sun went out altogether. Sometimes I wondered if I was dead.

Then, just when I'd decided nothing could ever happen again, something happened. One afternoon about five, on my way back from the works, I was crossing the square in front of the railway station, to reach the hotel, when I saw a little old fellow slip and fall with a truck almost on top of him. If he'd been fifty pounds heavier I couldn't have done it, but he couldn't have weighed more than a hundred and twenty; and I jerked him out of the way just in time. I took him into the hotel, made them give him some brandy, and helped to clean the mud off him. He told me he was Sir Alaric Foden; and he was a baronet, though he didn't look like my idea of a baronet. He'd spent most of his life, before he came into the title and the family property, out in India and the Far East; and I'd say that either his mother or one of his grandmothers had been a native of those parts, because his eyes were like black beads floating in yellow oil and looked about as English as the Taj Mahal. His wispy hair and little beard were white, and his face might have been a withered leaf. He always spoke very slowly and with an effort, as if his talking mechanism had got rusted up, and while he kept you waiting for the next word he fixed his black little eyes on you, with hardly a blink, until you began to feel you were already in India or China or somewhere. He was obviously grateful and made a fuss about what I'd done, yet at the same time he didn't give me the impression of being really friendly, though perhaps by then Blackley had made me morbid on the subject. When he found out I wasn't doing anything the next night—and that didn't take long—he asked me to go out to his house and dine with him. He lived about ten miles out, but there was a bus service within a few minutes' walk. I would have to leave about nine-forty-five to get the bus back, but he thought that would give me long enough with him. And so did I.

From now on it's a peculiar story, and I'll have to slow up a bit and take it steady. As I said earlier, I've never told it yet all the way through. I can't decide yet whether I ought to rattle off everything I can remember or sort it out and just give you the high spots. Yes, being a writer you must understand the kind of difficulty, so you won't mind if I stop now and again to see where I'm going and whether I'm putting too much in or leaving too much out. And help yourself to a drink, won't you? Yes, I might as well. Thanks.

Well, sir, the next night I went out by bus and found my way to the country mansion of Sir Alaric Foden, Bart. If I was making this up I'd tell you now what a wonderful place it was and what a fine reception I had, with footmen waiting on us and caviare and champagne cooling nicely in buckets. But it wasn't like that. Oh—it was a mansion all right, though I never saw most of it, and I doubt if Sir Alaric had for some time. But what I did see was damp, chilly and shabby, and you couldn't have paid me to live there. No footmen, not even a butler, only a wheezy old woman to wait on us. And the dinner might have been sent out from the Railway Hotel, all except the wine, which Sir Alaric said was one of his best clarets. He took only about half a glass and made me finish the rest, which I did, not in the dining-room, all cold and cheerless, but upstairs in the library, where there was a fire. It was a big room, and must have had thousands of books in it as well as enough Oriental stuff to stock a curio shop. All through dinner and just afterwards up there he told me very little about himself, but made me talk, chiefly by asking me what I thought about Blackley and how I was doing there. I'm not going to tell you what I said because you've heard most of it already.

"So, Mr. Lindfield," he said when I had talked myself out, "you are—unhappy—in Blackley. Or—at least—bored—depressed—lonely. You would like—to visit—some other place—humph?"

I said I would, but pointed out that just then I hadn't the time or opportunity, having to keep an eye on that machine.

"The time—that is nothing," he said; and he waved a claw at a lacquered grandfather clock as if to abolish it and time. "The opportunity—might be here. Yes—in this room. That is—if you are ready—to take the risk—of visiting—not *some* other place—but *the* Other Place."

"I don't follow you, Sir Alaric." And I wondered if I ought to clear out, although it was only just after nine. But I had to say something. "What's the difference between *some* other place and *the* other place?"

He giggled. I know that sounds all wrong for a little old fellow who must have been at least seventy-five; but you couldn't call it a laugh, and it wasn't hard enough for a cackle, and if it wasn't a giggle then I haven't a word for it. He got up now, and as he talked he began rummaging in a chest of drawers just behind his chair. "The Other Place—is round—a different kind of corner, Mr. Lindfield. You turn a corner—you didn't know was there. Something of a risk. But if you should decide—to pay it a visit—I'll be delighted—to oblige you." Evidently he'd found what he wanted, for now he turned quite sharply. There above the top of his chair were those ebony eyes, with no meaning in them that I could read, staring at me. "I will make it—simple for you—Mr. Lindfield. Yes—a door. You will go—to the Other Place—merely by opening a door. And there—you see, set in the bookshelves—is the door—you will use. Yes—that is the door. You still wish—to visit—the Other Place?"

"Why not?" I said, to humour him. I'd known one man who had a lavatory in his library, behind a door covered with false book backs, and he had worked various gags with it. "What do I do?"

Now he showed me what he had taken out of the drawer. It was a shiny black piece of stone, rather like a large pebble. He sat down, leant forward, resting his elbows on his knees, and held out the stone. "It is simple. Look at this stone—stare into it—while you count—a hundred—quite slowly."

I stared at it and into it, and began counting. I could feel myself starting to squint. After I had counted twenty or so the surface of the stone turned into a hollow darkness that spread and spread as I kept on counting. I heard the grandfather clock chime quarter-past nine, but it seemed a long way off. By the time I had reached eighty my eyes ached and soon after that I began to feel dizzy.

"A hundred," I heard myself say out loud.

"Now, Mr. Lindfield," said Sir Alaric, who might have been telephoning from New Zealand, "get up—go straight to that door—open it—go through."

I felt cock-eyed as I marched towards the bookshelves, but I spotted the door at once and I'd sense enough left to realise it was similar to the one I'd seen before, covered with false book backs. As I opened it I thought I heard Sir Alaric telling me to enjoy my visit. Then I went through and closed the door behind me. I was in a narrow dark place, like a passage, lit at the end by three or four bars of gold. When I moved forward, I saw that these were bright streaks of sunlight coming through a rough broken sort of door on the right. I opened this door—and even now I can remember exactly how it creaked—and then I was staring, dazzled after the long gloom of Blackley, at a garden in full sunlight, in a high summer that looked as if it might go on for ever.

Now let's get one thing straight. It wasn't like a dream. All the dreams I've had have been patchy, with one sketchy sort of scene turning into another, as if there wasn't enough stuff around to make up even one solid background. And in a dream, I've found, you only notice what you want to notice, so to speak, and if a thing isn't in the centre of your focus then it isn't there at all; there aren't a lot of things, as there are in real life, waiting to be properly noticed all round the edge of your consciousness. This garden wasn't like that at all. It was solidly there, with nothing unfinished and patchy about it. You knew it couldn't begin melting away, change into a room or a ship or a workshop. In fact, it seemed to have an extra solidity, as if it had stayed longer exactly like that than any ordinary garden could do.

A stone-flagged path went through a sort of tunnel of old-fashioned climbing roses. At the other end was a small lawn, bright in the sun, and beyond that some flower beds, burning with colour, set against a rough stone wall. When I reached the lawn I could just see the far bank of a river, not unlike the river at Hubberholme but broader and deeper. Beyond were fields rising sharply, then hanging woods and scree and rocks, and above them the hazy summits of high hills. It was a beautiful place, and you knew at once it was a long way from any trouble. And there was another thing, hard to describe. Have you ever known a room where there was a busy little clock, ticking your life away? And have you ever gone into that room when the clock wasn't there or had stopped, so that your life wasn't being ticked away? Well, arriving at this place was like that, only more so. The busy little clock inside you had stopped or wasn't there any more. The old *tick-tock-tick-tock-hurry-up-must-go* had gone. Nothing was wasting away, running down, draining out. I felt this at once, and it seemed to make everything sharper, more distinct, more itself and waiting to be noticed, whether it was the flame of the flowers or the blue of the sky.

I'd got some bearings now. The rough broken door I'd opened to let myself into this garden belonged to some sort of woodshed at the back of an inn. As I walked down the lawn I was coming round to the front of the inn, which was a longish low building with smooth walls washed in a faded pink. The lawn curved round there, losing its trim look, and became an outside drinking place. There were stout wooden tables and seats. A path led up to the open door of the inn. But I turned my back on that door and went to look over the bottom wall at the river. The nearer bank was quite close, with only a narrow strip of meadow, thick with buttercups and daisies, between it and the wall. A young man was fishing down there, and lying by his side, her head resting against him, was a dark young woman, in a green dress. She caught sight of me, and as people do when they're feeling relaxed and happy, she gave me a smile and a wave of the arm that didn't mean anything in particular. And then I saw it was Mavis Gilbert.

Well, that didn't make any particular sense, but there was nothing wrong with it; and I was glad to see her there, looking so happy, complete—and that stuck out a mile—with the fellow she'd always been thinking about when I'd been with her. Good luck to them! I waved back; and then she made her chap turn round, and he waved too and made drinking motions before watching his rod again.

"It's about time too, Lindfield," somebody said, punching me in the back. That was Butterworth. Dawson was just coming out of the inn, carrying a tray with pots of beer on it. He gave a shout when he saw me; you'd have thought the two of them were the oldest friends I had, and had been waiting for me. They were dressed in old shirts and pants, and as brown and merry as sailors home from the sea. We drank the beer and then went loafing on the river bank, smoking and telling tales and watching the water slide by. No glass wall between us now—not on your life!

Their wives were around somewhere and afterwards I met them, all relaxed and friendly, not looking as if they were thinking about something else when they were talking to you. There were other people, of course. and some I'd met at Blackley, only they were quite different now; and others I hadn't, though I can't be sure. You said anything that came into your head, because anything that came into your head there was all right and not likely to hurt anybody; and so did the other people. It was a long day, not because it was dull but because there seemed time for everything, like summer days when you're a kid. And everybody there seemed a bit larger than life, not smaller as they do in places like Blackley. But I can't give you a proper idea of it. Don't think it was paradise or fairyland or anything fancy like that; it wasn't. But don't go too far the other way and think I was having something like a nice fine day at a holiday camp. It was out of this world all right, but it oughtn't to have been, if you see what I mean.

It wasn't until evening that I met her. She was the daughter of the genial fat old boy who kept the inn, and she'd been away from it all day. Her name was Paula, and she showed me the room I had to sleep in, at the end of the landing at the back. My bag was there too, though how it had got there God only knows. And I didn't care, all I cared about was Paula. She looked about thirty, and she was fairly tall for a woman but not scraggy, but broad and firmly set, and she'd a rather broad calm face, with darkish brown hair and grey eyes; and as soon as I saw her I knew I'd been looking for her all my life. There wasn't much light up in that bedroom then, for it was just after sunset and the hills overshadowed the back of the inn, and the room was settling into a green dusk that seemed to put us at the bottom of the sea. But there was light enough for me to see the look on her face, when she waited a moment after showing me the room. I guessed then she knew I felt as if I'd been looking for her all my life. You know that look of tender amusement women have when they're fond of you and sure of you too.

"All day I've been missing you," I said, though I couldn't have explained why I said it. "Everything's been grand, wonderful, just what I needed—except I've been missing you. Now you're here, Paula."

"Yes, Harvey," she said, as if she'd been giving me my first name for the last ten years. "Here I am."

I don't know whether she made a move or I did or we both moved together, but then I had my arms round her—all so snug and easy that I might have done it ten thousand times before—and we kissed. And not one of those fighting, let's-get-on-with-it kisses neither; but one of the other sort you only find when everything else is dead right.

"And now I can't let you go," I told her.

But she pulled away gently, smiling at me. "You know you must. I'll be busy now until half-past ten. Come to me then—to my little sitting-room, through the green door at the far end of the kitchen—you remember? But not before half-past ten. You won't forget that, will you, Harvey?" And she looked at me anxiously, the only time she ever gave me that particular look.

I promised, and off she went then, a busy woman. Well, for the next hour or two, during supper and afterwards, when now and again she and I would exchange a look that was like a clasp of hands, everything was wonderful. It would have been good anyhow—the food and drink with friends so easy and happy, the jokes, the yarns, the songs and dancing after supper—but the idea of having her to myself later on raised everything another two thousand feet into the air. You know how you feel at those times, and this was a whole lot of those times rolled into one.

How long I'd have been there if I hadn't got impatient and turned nasty, I don't know; perhaps for ever. What got into me, what did the dirty on me, beats me, and you might say it's been beating me ever since. But when people began to move off, mostly two by two, and I didn't see her around inside, and the night outside, with no moon but a glitter of stars, was too big and lonely for me, I got impatient and didn't want to join in anything or talk to anybody, except to her of course, while the minutes went by like sick elephants. And I worked up some anger too, the way you do when you must have trouble. To hell with it! Why should she fix a time like that, as if everything had to be done her way? If I was good enough for her to see at half-past ten, I was good enough for quarter-past—what was the difference? I stuck it out a few minutes more, but all the time stoking my impatience like a furnace, and then made a dash for that green door at the far end of the kitchen, daring anybody to try and stop me.

Nobody did, of course; they never do when you're so hell-bent on trouble. There was the kitchen, empty and washed and swept out but still warm and heavy with the smell of food, and only a little lamp burning; but enough light to show me the green door at the opposite end. And now for Paula, who, if she didn't like it, because there were still ten minutes to go before the half-hour, could lump it—after all she belonged to me, and she knew it and knew I knew it. The green door opened easily—they always do, those doors—and there I was.

But not in any little sitting-room with Paula, of course. I was back in Sir Alaric's library, with my heart a lump of lead. I didn't even try to turn back, because I knew I hadn't a hope in hell. And I hated Sir Alaric and his library, which looked like a crummy old junk shop, and I hated myself.

I didn't want to look at Sir Alaric, so I looked at the grandfather clock. The time was nine-twenty; which meant that my day there had lasted about three minutes in here.

"Can I get back there?" I asked him.

"Not tonight, Mr. Lindfield." He seemed amused, and that didn't make me like him any better.

"Why not? I've only been out of this room for three minutes. And I didn't intend to come back so soon. That was a mistake."

"It always is. Perhaps—I ought—to have warned you. But I did—tell you—there was some risk—"

More in despair than hoping for anything, I went to that door and tore it open. There were shelves of odds and ends and wash-hand basin in the cupboard. I thought I could hear Sir Alaric having a soft giggle. I felt like throwing the big paste-pot at him.

"I take it—Mr. Lindfield—that our little experiment—was successful. You arrived—at the Other place—humph?"

"I arrived where I'd still like to be," I told him sourly.

"Then—clearly—it was the Other Place." He waited a moment. "You met—friends—there—humph?"

I made my reply a nod. Though he was responsible for getting me there, I didn't want to talk about it to him. But there was something else I had to talk about. "What's that black stone you asked me to stare at, Sir Alaric? And how does it do the trick?"

"It would be—just as sensible—to ask me—how the door—did the trick" he said reproachfully.

"Okay then, how did *you* do the trick?"

I don't know whether he was sleepy or just bored with me, but after he had shaken his head, to show me there was no reply coming, he began to yawn.

But I had to know *something*. "You said it was just a matter of getting round a corner, though of course a different kind of corner.

More dimensions or something. Now—look, Sir Alaric, I don't want to keep bothering you, so tell me—could I do it for myself, sit in my hotel bedroom and get round that corner somehow?"

"You—could try, Mr. Lindfield." He sounded very cagey.

I couldn't leave it at that. "I suppose any door would do, wouldn't it, Sir Alaric?"

"Certainly. Any door."

"And that black polished stone was only something to stare at and concentrate on, wasn't it?"

"You—must have something—Mr. Lindfield—to stare at—certainly." Still cagey. And now he got up, and I knew the evening was over, even though it was only about half-past nine. Somehow my going to the Other Place—and I'd decided I might as well call it that—had finished things between us. Perhaps he felt that now he didn't owe me anything for saving him from that truck; we were quits. Perhaps he just didn't like me. I'd decided I didn't take to him, so all was fair and square between us.

"I seemed to be there about ten hours at least," I said, just to keep the conversation going. "But actually I was spending three minutes in that cupboard. That happens in dreams, of course. Yet this didn't seem like a dream."

"It wasn't."

"What was it then?"

He gave me another yawn. "Forgive me—Mr. Lindfield—sometimes I cannot sleep—but tonight—as you can see—" In other words, Clear out, Lindfield.

There was more fog than rain that night, and the journey back to Blackley in the bus seemed very long and quite hopeless. At the end of it the Railway Hotel was waiting for me and was ready to do all it could to prove it was very different from the inn in the Other Place. I was in bed by about ten-forty-five and then spent the next four hours hearing railway waggons bumped and banged among the sidings. The following morning, Blackley looked darker and wetter and more dismal than ever.

Up at the Electrical Engineering Works that day I lost my temper because they hadn't yet completed a new bearing they'd promised me, and finally Butterworth was sent for, to explain the delay.

"And that's how it is, old man," he said, at the end of a long explanation, bristling with ministries and permits. "We keep asking them to get cracking, but if they won't move, there isn't a thing we can do. What's the matter? Don't you believe me?"

"Yes," I said, and then, taking a chance, went on: "But I was wondering what happened the other night—or was it last night?—after I left you and Dawson to go and see Paula."

"The other night? Paula?" Obviously he hadn't a clue.

There was no point in going on with it, but I had one more shot. "It was the same day you and I and Dawson drank beer in front of the inn and then went down to the river."

Butterworth had his share of brains but he was one of those Englishmen who never look as if they have any sense at all. He had a big moon-face made of underdone sirloin with some indeterminate features clustering together in the middle of it. And it looked so blank at that moment, I wanted to slug him. "I'm sorry, Lindfield, old man," he said, "but there's some mistake."

"Yes, there is," I told him. "So please forget it. I was thinking of some other fellows. But do get that bearing in as soon as you can."

"We will, we will," he said, relieved to discover I'd returned to sanity. "Hate to keep you hanging about like this. Look here, old man, come out and dine with us tomorrow. There'll be eight of us—two tables of bridge."

Well, I went, and Dawson and his wife were there, and Mavis Gilbert; and even the other two, a couple called Jennings, I remembered having seen in the Other Place. So there we were, eight of us, and we'd all been in the Other Place, some of us spending hours together, living the life of Reilly. And although I hadn't much hope even then, I had to try them out. I started first with Mrs. Butterworth, who'd put me next to her at dinner. Did she, I asked, know a delightful little spot with an inn among the hills near a river; and I described the Other Place in some detail. I didn't even feel she was listening properly, because she was one of those anxious hostesses with half their minds in the kitchen; but when I'd finished and had felt a droning bore, she surprised me by saying: "No, I don't know that place. Where is it? Oh—you don't know." And then her eyes widened, and instead of being merely colourless, screwed-up and anxious they were blue, young and alive. "Mr. Lindfield, let's go and find it, shall we?" she whispered; and for a second she was almost the woman I had seen in the Other Place.

During a break in the bridge I was playing with them, I tried the Dawsons and Mrs. Jennings, concentrating on the inn this time, and telling them I had stayed there years ago and had now forgotten where it was. Dawson said it was in North Devon, his wife was sure that it was in Gloucestershire and had been pulled down, and Mrs. Jennings told us she knew a much nicer little pub in Dorset; and I knew that I had drawn a blank from the three of them. There wasn't a peep out of them to suggest they'd ever been near the Other Place. And what made it ten times worse was that I could still remember them there, which made this social evening of ours look as if we were playing charades about zombies.

We finished fairly, so Mavis Gilbert, who was running me down town in her little car, suggested we stopped at her flat for a drink. When we'd tasted it and were feeling easy, she said: "Something's happened to you. I noticed it, and so did Mrs. Butterworth. What is it—or can't you tell?"

"I can tell some of it," I said, "but you won't know what I'm talking about. I saw you by a river—it was a bright warm morning—and you were wearing a green dress."

"Did I look nice?" she asked, smiling to show me she knew I was talking about a dream.

"You looked fine. Very happy too. You were with a fellow—I think I can describe him—"

"Go on. You must."

"He was a stiffish gingerish fellow with the greeny eyes his sort always have—and a scar on the left side of his face—"

"Rodney!" Then she was staring at me, white and angry. "I don't think that's funny. Somebody's been gossiping to you—and now you think this is an amusing way of telling me you know about Rodney and me. Well, I don't think it is."

"Look, Mavis, you've got it all wrong." I took her hand and wouldn't let her snatch it away. "I haven't been discussing you. I never heard of Rodney until now. I simply described the fellow I saw you with, when you were wearing a green dress, down by the river."

"What river?"

"I don't know what river. I wish I did," I told her.

"There were lots of people there, the Butterworths and Dawsons included, and you were there with this fellow. There was also a girl called Paula—her father kept the inn where we were all staying." And I described Paula, trying to remember every detail of her appearance. "Do you know anybody like that?"

"She sounds rather like a girl I used to know called Norma Blake," said Mavis. "But she'd nothing to do with an inn. She went in for occupational therapy. It can't be the same girl. I can see this Paula was very special. But where was all this happening?"

So then I had to describe the inn and the river and the hills, and I gave her a sketch of what happened there. But I didn't explain about Sir Alaric and the black stone and the door.

"I don't know any place quite like that," she said slowly, looking rather foggy-eyed. "I was never anywhere like that with Rodney—worse luck! But do you mean to say you dreamt it all?" That's one thing about women, they take this sort of thing seriously, none of your "Come off it old man" stuff about them.

But, even so, I didn't feel like telling her the whole story. "I can't explain," I said, "but I don't think I did dream it. Somehow I went there—I met all you people, happy as kings—I found Paula—and then, because I was in a hurry, I lost her. And all you people who were there don't seem to know what I'm talking about, which means either that you weren't there and I was making it all up or that you go there and then forget—"

"Oh—I can't bear that," she cried. "I wish you hadn't told me now. It's the sort of thing I've imagined—being somewhere like that with Rodney—yes, night after night, here in this room, I've imagined it. And now you say you saw me there. You're making me feel miserable."

"I've made myself feel miserable. Let's change the subject."

"No," she said, "I must tell you about Rodney now."

And of course she did, with intervals for laughing and crying, and to her it was a wonderful heart-breaking story, enough to keep anybody on the edge of his seat, but to me, though I liked her and didn't mind what I'd seen of Rodney, it was nothing but two hours of trying to keep awake. I got back to the Railway Hotel, which didn't want to let me in, feeling rather worse than when I'd left it to enjoy this night out.

Well, the next few days were like walking across a wet ploughed field wearing lead boots. I tried hard not to be sorry for myself—and about time, you'll say, and I agree; but when you're such a long way from home it's not so easy—and I went to the Reference Library to see if I could get a line on Sir Alaric's magic, and couldn't, and I also made some enquiries about Sir Alaric himself. But the people I asked either had never heard of him or knew he existed but weren't interested. Come to think of it, people in Blackley last winter didn't seem to be much interested in anything. They just went on living for something but didn't quite know what. Sometimes I felt they'd have been better off in the long run if they'd set fire to the place and then started all over again.

Then one night—as a matter of fact it was Monday, and I think living through another Blackley Sunday night might have had something to do with what happened—I had a few slugs of gin, because the whisky had given out, and told myself it was time for action. After all, Sir Alaric had shot me into the Other Place, and now he could shoot me there again, if only to stop me wandering round this grimy dump like a lost soul. He wasn't on the telephone, so I took a chance on his being in and caught a bus out there. It must have been one of the last, because it was late then for Blackley, round about ten o'clock. How I was to get back didn't worry me at all, not in the state of mind I was in then. And if Sir Alaric had gone to bed, I was ready to make such a commotion that he'd have to get up and let me in. I don't say I was plastered but I wasn't exactly sober.

But he hadn't gone to bed and he invited me in politely enough, though I didn't feel he was pleased to see me. He took me up to his library, where he'd been drowsing over the fire, and then he asked me, with no old-world courtesy at all, what I wanted. And obviously it was no use my pretending I'd gone there to enquire about his health; he'd spotted the mood I was in at once, so there was no point in trying to fool him.

"I want to get back to the Other Place," I told him. "And don't tell me to go away and try to go there on my own, because I've already tried and it doesn't work. Apart from that, I'm having a bad time. I've talked to the people I met there—all except the most important one—and they don't know what I'm talking about. I've even tried putting the place out of my mind, but it won't stay out more than a few minutes. So now, Sir Alaric, with your help, I'm going back."

"Mr. Lindfield—you take—too much—for granted."

"That's because I'm a desperate man, Sir Alaric."

"Desperate men—Mr. Lindfield—should not attempt—to go anywhere. They should—stay at home—and begin to lose—their desperation."

"You're probably right, and we won't argue about it. In fact, we won't argue about anything. I'm going back there, Sir Alaric, and don't try to stop me. Where's that black stone?" And I got up and stood over him. I'm not proud of all this but I might as well tell you everything.

But if I thought I could frighten him, I was a mile out. All he did was to shake his head at me, as if I was ten years old. "You are behaving—very stupidly—Mr. Lindfield. You come here—uninvited—half drunk, I suspect—"

"About that, I'd say," I told him. "And you're quite right, I'm behaving badly. I've a lot of excuses but I won't bore you with them. Just bring out that black stone, Sir Alaric, and I'll do the rest. *Come on*," I shouted, when he hadn't made a move.

We stared at one another for what seemed quite a long time—and I thought I saw a flicker of flame in those black beady eyes of his—then he went to the chest of drawers and brought out the stone. This time he handed it to me instead of keeping it himself. "Do as you did before," he said coldly. "But be careful—to put down—the stone—before you go—to the door. If you will take—my advice—you will not—attempt this."

"I'm not taking your advice." And I began staring at the stone and counting up to a hundred. Everything happened just as it did the first time—the squinting, the hollow darkness that spread and spread, the dizziness. I put the stone down on the rug and went slowly over to the door in the bookshelves. I opened the door very carefully, as if something might break, probably because I was afraid the magic wouldn't have worked and that all I would see behind the door was the cupboard of odds and ends and its wash-hand basin. But no, I was back all right. There I was in that narrow dark passage with the streaks of sunlight at the end, coming through the rough broken door. Down I went, banged open the door, and hurried out into the garden, where I waited a moment, by the edge of the stone-flagged path among the roses, just to catch my breath.

I don't think I'm cheating when I tell you that even then, right at the start, I guessed something was wrong. But I'll admit I'm not sure what gave me the idea. Let me try and sort it out while you give yourself some more whisky. Okay, thanks, I'll join you. That's fine—thanks. Well, to begin with, everything I could see—and that wasn't much, remember—seemed narrower, not quite the right shape. And the sunshine had a kind of sting to it, wasn't mellow like the other sunshine I remembered. And then the time trick wasn't working right. I felt time had stopped, as it had done before, but it had stopped *in the wrong way*. Don't ask me just what I mean by that, because I'll be damned if I know. But it seemed to have stopped in a sinister way. Anyhow that's as near as I can get to what I felt.

I went through the tunnel of climbing roses and came out on to the lawn, and of course now I knew what to expect—the river, the hills, the drinking place in front of the inn itself. At a first glance, nothing had changed, except that I had an idea the colours were sharper and the shapes not quite the same, a bit meaner somehow. Like a copy of a picture that just missed it, if you see what I mean. And I didn't feel happy, not a bit.

Then it really got to work on me. That river, for instance. When I saw it out of the corner of my eye, not really paying attention to it, it looked just as it had done before, a full smooth stream. But as soon as I really looked at it, to take some pleasure in it, then it shrank to a mere trickle among cracked cakes of brown mud. So I'd look away, and at once I'd know it was an easy broad stretch of water again. Another proper look, and it had dwindled again.

But the people were worse. As I stood there on the lawn, playing hide-and-seek with the river, I knew that where the tables and seats were, in front of the inn, to my left, people were drinking and talking and laughing, just as they'd done before. But when I turned that way, to shout "Hello!" and let them know I was there, they all froze up and were still as waxworks. And what put the finishing touch on it and gave me the creeps was that they were all looking at me, not with any particular expression on their faces but just looking, like dummies. I went towards them, half angry, half terrified. Not a sound. Not a move. Waxworks under an angry sun. I stopped, turned towards the river, and there it was, a miserable trickle again, while at the corner of my eye I could just catch a glimpse of the people coming to life again and could hear them talking and laughing. I whirled round on them, frantic now, and there they were, frozen, staring at me, silent as death.

"What the hell do you think you're playing at?" I shouted at them. Not a sound, not a quiver. And every goddam thing was wrong—the blue of the sky, the feel of the sun, the flowers that withered at a look. I felt I was outside time again, but out now on the wrong side. I had to make something happen in that place even if it meant being flattened by some giant dead hand that would drop from the sky.

I went charging through the gap in the stone wall to the staring dummies in the drinking place. The first one I reached was standing up and I saw that it was Jennings, who'd been dining with me at the Butterworths.

"Now look, Jennings," I cried, putting a hand on his shoulder, "you know me—Lindfield." And now that I'd concentrated upon him the rest of them were all lively again, and Jennings was the only staring dummy there, unless you count me. "What's the idea? What's the matter with you people?"

He didn't say a thing, never gave so much as a twitch, and I felt that if I didn't take my hand off his shoulder I might push him over. So I took it away, but the next moment, in a blind fury because I couldn't get any response from him, I gave him a sharp slap across the cheek. And the next moment after that—and how it happened I can't tell you—I was down on the grass, out for the count, having taken the hardest punch I'd known since I'd boxed as a light-heavy for the University of Toronto. And while I was down there, waiting for the counting and the bell, I could hear, as if from far away, all those people talking and laughing over their drinks. Harvey Lindfield couldn't pay attention, so off they were again, enjoying themselves.

After a few minutes, feeling dazed and rather sick, I got on to my feet again and looked round. This time they weren't all completely frozen. They moved a little, like weeds under water, and they made some noise—but it wasn't a noise I was glad to hear, for they were laughing in a slow dim under-water fashion, and laughing at me. And then I wondered why I'd wasted any time on these people, if you could still call them people, when I didn't really care about them and had come back to find only one person—Paula. And I knew she wasn't out here. My only chance of finding her was somewhere inside the inn.

She was there, standing alone in the long room that was now as quiet and nearly as dark as a vault. She was no staring dummy but it might have been better if she had been, because the very sight of her standing there turned my heart into ice water. As I went up to her I saw that she was slowly shaking her head and that her cheeks were wet with tears. Everything that's ever been wrong between men and women, all the old long heartbreak, was there between us.

"Paula," I said, "I know it was my fault last time, but now I'm back and I came back, forced my way here, just because of you." I'd have gone on but I knew she wasn't going to talk to me, that she'd do nothing but shake her head and cry, the way they do when at last they feel it's hopeless.

Finally she moved away, and I followed her, wanting to say something but not knowing what to say. There was nobody else about; the place was empty, silent, a mile deep in misery. She went into the kitchen, which was cold and hadn't an appetising smell left, and she walked the length of it until she came to that green door. There she stopped long enough to give me a look and what might have been the shadow of a smile. The door was slowly closing behind her when I arrived—the big masterful type, God help me! I flung open that door and marched through like Alexander the Great.

But of course Sir Alaric wasn't impressed, and I don't blame him. I'd only been away a minute and a half this time, and he didn't care if I came out of his cupboard marching like Alexander the Great or crawling like the Hunchback of Notre Dame. All he cared about was getting me out of his house before I turned ugly and began kicking things around. So he told me in a hurry that a man who lived quarter of a mile down the road would run me into Blackley for about a pound. As a matter of fact he needn't have worried, because this last visit to the Other Place—if it was the Other Place—had taken all the fight out of me.

Once he had got me as far as his front door, Sir Alaric felt he could relax. "It was not—so pleasant—this time, Mr. Lindfield—humph?"

"It was very unpleasant," I told him grumpily. "But it probably serves me right for insisting upon going again. I've not behaved very well. But, come to that, neither have you."

"No, Mr. Lindfield," he said earnestly—and I can see him now, a little white-and-brown wisp of an old fellow, very English up to a point but with India or China looking out of his eyes, "you wrong me—as well as yourself. You have been—to the Other Place. Forget—this last visit—remember the first one. Now—of course—you are dissatisfied. But you have something—I imagine—to be dissatisfied about—now."

"I had before," I grumbled. "We all have. They're almost dying of it in Blackley. All you've done for me, in return for not leaving you in front of that truck, is to add to my dissatisfaction."

"No," he said softly, "there is no addition. Not in—the long run—I think. No—a subtraction. You will see."

Well, I don't know that I have seen, though now and again I think I know what he meant. No, I never saw him again. I called at his house again, a few nights later, but it was all shut up and dark and then I was told he'd gone away, perhaps to stand on his head in Bombay or turn a prayer wheel in Tibet. I took that fellow Jennings out to lunch, just to see how he'd react when I told him that a few nights before, in a place where people turned into staring dummies when you looked hard at them, he'd knocked me cold with a right hook I never even saw. And of course he didn't react at all, just told me he'd stopped dreaming now that he didn't eat cheese in the evening and went on to say that British boxing or any other sport wasn't what it had been.

I had a night out with Mavis Gilbert before I left Blackley, and she told me more about Rodney and made me describe Paula, though I left out the Other Place; and we got rather tight and sentimental and tried to console one another with some messy half-hearted love-making and were about as clever at it as a couple of short-sighted bears. In fact the night ended just as I'd imagined it would when I'd tried to avoid it.

Then the Blackley Electrical Engineering Company completed the machine to our specification, and after having it run and testing it for a couple of days, I watched them take it down and crate it and send it to Liverpool, ready for the next boat. By this time my company was screaming for me, so I booked a passage by plane, and on one of those muffled sad winter afternoons I found myself at London Airport. I mention this because it was there I saw Paula.

You know the way they shepherd you around in airports, as if an idiot school was having a day's outing. Well, my lot was being herded out to the plane just as another lot was being herded in from one, so that a string of us passed each other. And there was Paula—no question about it, I'd doubt my own name sooner.

"Paula!" I shouted, and hurried across to her.

She stopped but looked surprised, and not pleasantly surprised either. "There's some mistake," she said. "I'm Mrs. Endersley—and my name's not Paula and I don't know you."

"What's this?" And the big fellow behind her frowned at me. He owned her. He owned nearly everything. He was one of those men.

"Just a mistake, darling," she said to him, and then she gave me an apologetic little smile, probably because I was looking like a lost dog.

I don't know what I stammered at them, because what I'd suddenly seen in her eyes, like a sort of signal from miles away in their grey depths, had turned me upside down and inside out. And what it had seemed to say was something like this: *Yes, I was Paula when I was there, and now I remember you too, Harvey Lindfield, but where we were and what we can do about it, God knows!* And the next minute I was straggling along with the rest of the sheep, going towards the plane.

So here I am, back again at the first chance I had, but of course taking a holiday this time, with no more Blackley in the rain and the Railway Hotel. And I keep on describing the Other Place to people, and when they tell me they know something like it I go and have a look, which takes me to some of your nicest places, like this Hubberholme where we met this afternoon. Cornwall, Devon, Dorset, Cotswolds, Lake District—I've been all over. Oh—yes—I tried Sir Alaric again, but he died last February—somewhere abroad. Yes—and I asked about that black stone, but everything he had has been sold or given away, and nobody seems to know anything about it. I know—I might try to track it down, I've thought of that.

There's just one other thing that worries me from time to time. You must have noticed this yourself. Now and again you meet people who look at you eagerly and cry "Haven't we met before somewhere?" And when you tell 'em you haven't, you see a light go out of their faces. Well, what worries me now about those people is that they may have been to some Other Place of their own and met me there, the way I did with those Blackley people—and of course with Paula. It's the damnedest thing, you know, if we all keep meeting in some Other Place and then can't make other people understand. My God!—look at the time. And I'm running up to Northumberland in the morning, because I've heard of a place there that might possibly be It—you never know, do you?

WITCHCRAFT AND SATANISM

THE ASH-TREE

EVERYONE who has travelled over Eastern England knows the smaller country-houses with which it is studded—the rather dank little buildings, usually in the Italian style, surrounded with parks of some eighty to a hundred acres. For me they have always had a strong attraction: with the grey paling of split oak, the noble trees, the meres with their reed-beds, and the line of distant woods. Then, I like the pillared portico—perhaps stuck on to a red-brick Queen Anne house which has been faced with stucco to bring it into line with the "Grecian" taste of the end of the eighteenth century; the hall inside, going up to the roof, which hall ought always to be provided with a gallery and a small organ. I like the library, too, where you may find anything from a Psalter of the thirteenth century to a Shakespeare quarto. I like the pictures, of course; and perhaps most of all I like fancying what life in such a house was when it was first built, and in the piping times of landlords' prosperity, and not least now, when, if money is not so plentiful, taste is more varied and life quite as interesting. I wish to have one of these houses, and enough money to keep it together and entertain my friends in it modestly.

But this is a digression. I have to tell you of a curious series of events which happened in such a house as I have tried to describe. It is Castringham Hall in Suffolk. I think a good deal has been done to the building since the period of my story, but the essential features I have sketched are still there—Italian portico, square block of white house, older inside than out, park with fringe of woods, and mere. The one feature that marked out the house from a score of others is gone. As you looked at it from the park, you saw on the right a great old ash-tree growing within half a dozen yards of the wall, and almost or quite touching the building with its branches. I suppose it had stood there ever since Castringham ceased to be a fortified place, and since the moat was filled in and the Elizabethan dwelling-house built. At any rate, it had wellnigh attained its full dimensions in the year 1690.

In that year the district in which the Hall is situated was the scene of a number of witch-trials. It will be long, I think, before we arrive at a just estimate of the amount of solid reason—if there was any—which lay at the root of the universal fear of witches in old times. Whether the persons accused of this offence really did imagine that they were possessed of unusual powers of any kind; or whether they had the will at least, if not the power, of doing mischief to their neighbours; or whether all the confessions, of which there are so many, were extorted by the mere cruelty of the witch-finders—these are questions which are not, I fancy, yet solved. And the present narrative gives me pause. I cannot altogether sweep it away as mere invention. The reader must judge for himself.

Castringham contributed a victim to the *auto-da-fé*. Mrs. Mothersole was her name, and she differed from the ordinary run of village witches only in being rather better off and in a more influential position. Efforts were made to save her by several reputable farmers of the parish. They did their best to testify to her character, and showed considerable anxiety as to the verdict of the jury.

But what seems to have been fatal to the woman was the evidence of the then proprietor of Castringham Hall—Sir Matthew Fell. He deposed to having watched her on three different occasions from his window, at the full of the moon, gathering sprigs "from the ash-tree near my house". She had climbed into the branches, clad only in her shift, and was cutting off small twigs with a peculiarly curved knife, and as she did so she seemed to be talking to herself. On each occasion Sir Matthew had done his best to capture the woman, but she had always taken alarm at some accidental noise he had made, and all he could see when he got down to the garden was a hare running across the park in the direction of the village.

On the third night he had been at the pains to follow at his best speed, and had gone straight to Mrs. Mothersole's house; but he had had to wait a quarter of an hour battering at her door, and then she had come out very cross, and apparently very sleepy, as if just out of bed; and he had no good explanation to offer of his visit.

Mainly on this evidence, though there was much more of a less striking and unusual kind from other parishioners, Mrs. Mothersole was found guilty and condemned to die. She was hanged a week after the trial, with five or six more unhappy creatures, at Bury St. Edmunds.

Sir Matthew Fell, then Deputy-Sheriff, was present at the execution. It was a damp, drizzly March morning when the cart made its way up the rough grass hill outside Northgate, where the gallows stood. The other victims were apathetic or broken down with misery; but Mrs. Mothersole was, as in life so in death, of a very different temper. Her "poysonous Rage", as a reporter of the time puts it, "did so work upon the Bystanders—yea, even upon the Hangman—that it was constantly affirmed of all that saw her that she presented the living Aspect of a mad Divell. Yet she offer'd no Resistance to the Officers of the Law; onely she looked upon those that laid Hands upon her with so direfull and venomous an Aspect that—as one of them afterwards assured me—the meer Thought of it preyed inwardly upon his Mind for six months after".

However, all that she is reported to have said was the seemingly meaningless words: "There will be guests at the Hall." Which she repeated more than once in an undertone.

Sir Matthew Fell was not unimpressed by the bearing of the woman. He had some talk upon the matter with the Vicar of his parish, with whom he travelled home after the assize business was over. His evidence at the trial had not been very willingly given; he was not specially infected with the witch finding mania, but he declared, then and afterwards, that he could not give any other account of the matter than that he had given, and that he could not possibly have been mistaken as to what he saw. The whole transaction had been repugnant to him, for he was a man who liked to be on pleasant terms with those about him; but he saw a duty to be done in this business, and he had done it. That seems to have been the gist of his sentiments, and the Vicar applauded it, as any reasonable man must have done.

A few weeks after, when the moon of May was at the full, Vicar and Squire met again in the park, and walked to the Hall together. Lady Fell was with her mother, who was dangerously ill, and Sir Matthew was alone at home; so the Vicar, Mr. Crome, was easily persuaded to take a late supper at the Hall.

Sir Matthew was not very good company that evening. The talk ran chiefly on family and parish matters, and, as luck would have it, Sir Matthew made a memorandum in writing of certain wishes or intentions of his regarding his estates, which afterwards proved exceedingly useful.

When Mr. Crome thought of starting for home, about half-past nine o'clock, Sir Matthew and he took a preliminary turn on the gravelled walk at the back of the house. The only incident that struck Mr. Crome was this: they were in sight of the ash-tree which I described as growing near the windows of the building, when Sir Matthew stopped and said:

"What is that that runs up and down the stem of the ash? It is never a squirrel? They will all be in their nests by now."

The Vicar looked and saw the moving creature, but he could make nothing of its colour in the moonlight. The sharp outline, however, seen for an instant, was imprinted on his brain, and he could have sworn, he said, though it sounded foolish, that, squirrel or not, it had more than four legs.

Still, not much was to be made of the momentary vision, and the two men parted. They may have met since then, but it was not for a score of years.

Next day Sir Matthew Fell was not downstairs at six in the morning, as was his custom, nor at seven, nor yet at eight. Hereupon the servants went and knocked at his chamber door. I need not prolong the description of their anxious listenings and renewed batterings on the panels. The door was opened at last from the outside, and they found their master dead and black. So much you have guessed. That there were any marks of violence did not at the moment appear; but the window was open.

One of the men went to fetch the parson, and then by his directions rode on to give notice to the coroner. Mr. Crome himself went as quick as he might to the Hall, and was shown to the room where the dead man lay. He has left some notes among his papers which show how genuine a respect and sorrow was felt for Sir Matthew, and there is also this passage, which I transcribe for the sake of the light it throws upon the course of events, and also upon the common beliefs of the time:

"There was not any the least Trace of an Entrance having been forc'd to the Chamber: but the Casement stood open, as my poor Friend would always have it in this Season. He had his Evening Drink of small Ale in a silver vessel of about a pint measure, and tonight had not drunk it out. This Drink was examined by the Physician from Bury, a Mr. Hodgkins, who could not, however, as he afterwards declar'd upon his Oath, before the Coroner's quest, discover that any matter of a venomous kind was present in it. For, as was natural, in the great Swelling and Blackness of the Corpse, there was talk made among the Neighbours of Poyson. The Body was very much Disorder'd as it laid in the Bed, being twisted after so extream a sort as gave too probable Conjecture that my worthy Friend and Patron had expir'd in great Pain and Agony. And what is as yet unexplain'd, and to myself the Argument of some Horrid and Artfull Designe in the Perpetrators of this Barbarous Murther, was this, that the Women which were entrusted with the laying-out of the Corpse and washing it, being both sad Persons and very well Respected in their Mournfull Profession, came to me in a great Pain and Distress both of Mind and Body, saying, what was indeed confirmed upon the first View, that they had no sooner touch'd the Breast of the Corpse with their naked Hands than they were sensible of a more than ordinary violent Smart and Acheing in their Palms, which, with their whole Forearms, in no time swell'd so immoderately, the Pain still continuing, that, as afterwards proved, during many weeks they were forc'd to lay by the exercise of their Calling; and yet no mark seen on the Skin.

"Upon hearing this, I sent for the Physician, who was still in the House, and we made as careful a Proof as we were able by the Help of a small Magnifying Lens of Crystal of the condition of the Skinn on this Part of the Body: but could not detect with the Instrument we had any Matter of importance beyond a couple of small Punctures or Pricks, which we then concluded were the Spotts by which the Poyson might be introduced, remembering that Ring of *Pope Borgia*, with other known Specimens of the Horrid Art of the Italian Poysoners of the last age.

"So much is to be said of the Symptoms seen on the Corpse. As to what I am to add, it is meerly my own Experiment, and to be left to Posterity to judge whether there be anything of Value therein. There was on the Table by the Beddside a Bible of the small size, in which my Friend—punctuall as in Matters of less Moment, so in this more weighty one—used nightly, and upon his First Rising, to read a sett Portion. And I taking it up—not without a Tear duly paid to him which from the Study of this poorer Adumbration was now pass'd to the contemplation of its great Originall—it came into my Thoughts, as at such moments of Helplessness we are prone to catch at any the least Glimmer that makes promise of Light, to make trial of that old and by many accounted Superstitious Practice of drawing the *Sortes*: of which a Principall Instance, in the case of his late Sacred Majesty the Blessed Martyr King *Charles* and my Lord *Falkland*, was now much talked of. I must needs admit that by my Trial not much Assistance was afforded me: yet, as the Cause and Origin of these Dreadfull Events may hereafter be search'd out, I set down the Results, in the case it may be found that they pointed the true Quarter of the Mischief to a quicker Intelligence than my own.

"I made, then, three trials, opening the Book and placing my Finger upon certain Words: which gave in the first these words, from Luke xiii. 7, *Cut it down*; in the second, Isaiah xiii. 20, *It shall never be inhabited*; and upon the third Experiment, Job xxxix. 30, *Her young ones also suck up blood*."

This is all that need be quoted from Mr. Crome's papers. Sir Matthew Fell was duly coffined and laid into the earth, and his funeral sermon, preached by Mr. Crome on the following Sunday, has been printed under the title of "The Unsearchable Way; or, England's Danger and the Malicious Dealings of Antichrist", it being the Vicar's view, as well as that most commonly held in the neighbourhood, that the Squire was the victim of a recrudescence of the Popish Plot.

His son, Sir Matthew the second, succeeded to the title and estates. And so ends the first act of the Castringham tragedy. It is to be mentioned, though the fact is not surprising, that the new Baronet did not occupy the room in which his father had died. Nor, indeed, was it slept in by anyone but an occasional visitor during the whole of his occupation. He died in 1735, and I do not find that anything particular marked his reign, save a curiously constant mortality among his cattle and live-stock in general, which showed a tendency to increase slightly as time went on.

Those who are interested in the details will find a statistical account in a letter to the *Gentleman's Magazine* of 1772, which draws the facts from the Baronet's own papers. He put an end to it at last by a very simple expedient, that of shutting up all his beasts in sheds at night, and keeping no sheep in his park. For he had noticed that nothing was ever attacked that spent the night indoors. After that the disorder confined itself to wild birds, and beasts of chase. But as we have no good account of the symptoms, and as all-night watching was quite unproductive of any clue, I do not dwell on what the Suffolk farmers called the "Castringham sickness".

The second Sir Matthew died in 1735, as I said, and was duly succeeded by his son, Sir Richard. It was in his time that the great family pew was built out on the north side of the parish church. So large were the Squire's ideas that several of the graves on that unhallowed side of the building had to be disturbed to satisfy his requirements. Among them was that of Mrs. Mothersole, the position of which was accurately known, thanks to a note on a plan of the church and yard, both made by Mr. Crome.

A certain amount of interest was excited in the village when it was known that the famous witch, who was still remembered by a few, was to be exhumed. And the feeling of surprise, and indeed disquiet, was very strong when it was found that, though her coffin was fairly sound and unbroken, there was no trace whatever inside it of body, bones, or dust. Indeed, it is a curious phenomenon, for at the time of her burying no such things were dreamt of as resurrection-men, and it is difficult to conceive any rational motive for stealing a body otherwise than for the uses of the dissecting-room.

The incident revived for a time all the stories of witch-trials and of the exploits of the witches, dormant for forty years, and Sir Richard's orders that the coffin should be burnt were thought by a good many to be rather foolhardy, though they were duly carried out.

Sir Richard was a pestilent innovator, it is certain. Before his time the Hall had been a fine block of the mellowest red brick; but Sir Richard had travelled in Italy and became infected with the Italian taste, and, having more money than his predecessors, he determined to leave an Italian palace where he had found an English house. So stucco and ashlar masked the brick; some indifferent Roman marbles were planted about in the entrance-hall and gardens; a reproduction of the Sibyl's temple at Tivoli was erected on the opposite bank of the mere; and Castringham took on an entirely new, and, I must say, a less engaging, aspect. But it was much admired, and served as a model to a good many of the neighbouring gentry in after-years.

One morning (it was in 1754) Sir Richard woke after a night of discomfort. It had been windy, and his chimney had smoked persistently, and yet it was so cold that he must keep up a fire. Also something had so rattled about the window that no man could get a moment's peace. Further, there was the prospect of several guests of position arriving in the course of the day, who would expect sport of some kind, and the inroads of the distemper (which continued among his game) had been lately so serious that he was afraid for his reputation as a game-preserver. But what really touched him most nearly was the other matter of his sleepless night. He could certainly not sleep in that room again.

That was the chief subject of his meditations at breakfast, and after it he began a systematic examination of the rooms to see which would suit his notions best. It was long before he found one. This had a window with an eastern aspect, and that with a northern; this door the servants would be always passing, and he did not like the bedstead in that. No, he must have a room with a western look-out, so that the sun could not wake him early, and it must be out of the way of the business of the house. The housekeeper was at the end of her resources.

"Well, Sir Richard," she said, "you know that there is but one room like that in the house."

"Which may that be?" said Sir Richard.

"And that is Sir Matthew's—the West Chamber."

"Well, put me in there, for there I'll lie to-night," said her master. "Which way is it? Here, to be sure"; and he hurried off.

"Oh, Sir Richard, but no one has slept there these forty years. The air has hardly been changed since Sir Matthew died there."

Thus she spoke, and rustled after him.

"Come, open the door, Mrs. Chiddock. I'll see the chamber, at least."

So it was opened, and, indeed, the smell was very close and earthy. Sir Richard crossed to the window, and, impatiently, as was his wont, threw the shutters back and flung open the casement. For this end of the house was one which the alterations had barely touched, grown up as it was with the great ash-tree, and being otherwise concealed from view.

"Air it, Mrs. Chiddock, all to-day, and move my bed-furniture in in the afternoon. Put the Bishop of Kilmore in my old room."

"Pray, Sir Richard," said a new voice, breaking in on this speech, "might I have the favour of a moment's interview?"

Sir Richard turned round and saw a man in black in the doorway, who bowed.

"I must ask your indulgence for this intrusion, Sir Richard. You will, perhaps, hardly remember me. My name is William Crome, and my grandfather was Vicar here in your grandfather's time."

"Well, sir," said Sir Richard, "the name of Crome is always a passport to Castringham. I am glad to renew a friendship of two generations' standing. In what can I serve you? For your hour of calling—and, if I do not mistake you, your bearing—shows you to be in some haste."

"That is no more than the truth, sir. I am riding from Norwich to Bury St. Edmunds with what haste I can make, and I have called in on my way to leave with you some papers which we have but just come upon in looking over what my grandfather left at his death. It is thought you may find some matters of family interest in them."

"You are mighty obliging, Mr. Crome, and, if you will be so good as to follow me to the parlour, and drink a glass of wine, we will take a first look at these same papers together. And you, Mrs. Chiddock, as I said, be about airing this chamber.... Yes, it is here my grandfather died.... Yes, the tree, perhaps, does make the place a little dampish.... No; I do not wish to listen to any more. Make no difficulties, I beg. You have your orders—go. Will you follow me, sir?"

They went to the study. The packet which young Mr. Crome had brought—he was then just become a Fellow of Clare Hall in Cambridge, I may say, and subsequently brought out a respectable edition of Polyaenus—contained among other things the notes which the old Vicar had made upon the occasion of Sir Matthew Fell's death. And for the first time Sir Richard was confronted with the enigmatical *Sortes Biblicae* which you have heard. They amused him a good deal.

"Well," he said, "my grandfather's Bible gave one prudent piece of advice—*Cut it down*. If that stands for the ash-tree, he may rest assured I shall not neglect it. Such a nest of catarrhs and agues was never seen."

The parlour contained the family books, which, pending the arrival of a collection which Sir Richard had made in Italy, and the building of a proper room to receive them, were not many in number.

Sir Richard looked up from the paper to the bookcase.

"I wonder," says he, "whether the old prophet is there yet? I fancy I see him."

Crossing the room, he took out a rumpy Bible, which, sure enough, bore on the flyleaf the inscription: "To Matthew Fell, from his Loving Godmother, Anne Aldous, 2 September, 1659."

"It would be no bad plan to test him again, Mr. Crome. I will wager we get a couple of names in the Chronicles. H'm!—what have we here? 'Thou shalt seek me in the morning, and I shall not be'. Well, well! Your grandfather would have made a fine omen of that, hey? No more prophets for me! They are all in a tale. And now, Mr. Crome, I am infinitely obliged to you for your packet. You will, I fear, be impatient to get on. Pray allow me—another glass."

So with offers of hospitality, which were genuinely meant (for Sir Richard thought well of the young man's address and manner), they parted.

In the afternoon came the guests—the Bishop of Kilmore, Lady Mary Hervey, Sir William Kentfield, and the rest. Dinner at five, wine, cards, supper, and dispersal to bed.

Next morning Sir Richard is disinclined to take his gun with the rest. He talks with the Bishop of Kilmore. This prelate, unlike a good many of the Irish Bishops of his day, had visited his see, and, indeed, resided there for some considerable time. This morning, as the two were walking along the terrace and talking over the alterations and improvements in the house, the Bishop said, pointing to the window of the West Room:

"You could never get one of my Irish flock to occupy that room, Sir Richard."

"Why is that, my lord? It is, in fact, my own."

"Well, our Irish peasantry will always have it that it brings the worst of luck to sleep near an ash-tree, and you have a fine growth of ash not two yards from your chamber window. Perhaps," the Bishop went on, with a smile, "it has given you a touch of its quality already, for you do not seem, if I may say it, so much the fresher for your night's rest as your friends would like to see you."

"That, or something else, it is true, cost me my sleep from twelve to four, my lord. But the tree is to come down to-morrow, so I shall not hear much more from it."

"I applaud your determination. It can hardly be wholesome to have the air your breathe strained, as it were, through all that leafage."

"Your lordship is right there, I think. But I had not my window open last night. It was rather the noise that went on—no doubt from the twigs sweeping the glass—that kept me open-eyed."

"I think that can hardly be, Sir Richard. Here—you see it from this point. None of these nearest branches even can touch your casement unless there were a gale, and there was none of that last night. They miss the panes by a foot."

"No, sir, true. What, then, will it be, I wonder, that scratched and rustled so—ay, and covered the dust on my sill with lines and marks?"

At last they agreed that the rats must have come up through the ivy. That was the Bishop's idea, and Sir Richard jumped at it.

So the day passed quietly, and night came, and the party dispersed to their rooms, and wished Sir Richard a better night.

And now we are in his bedroom, with the light out and the Squire in bed. The room is over the kitchen, and the night outside still and warm, so the window stands open.

There is very little light about the bedstead, but there is a strange movement there; it seems as if Sir Richard were moving his head rapidly to and fro with only the slightest possible sound. And now you would guess, so deceptive is the half-darkness, that he had several heads, round and brownish, which move back and forward, even as low as his chest. It is a horrible illusion. Is it nothing more? There!—something drops off the bed with a soft plump, like a kitten, and is out of the window in a flash; another—four—and after that there is quiet again.

"Thou shalt seek me in the morning, and I shall not be."

As with Sir Matthew, so with Sir Richard—dead and black in his bed!

A pale and silent party of guests and servants gathered under the window when the news was known. Italian poisoners, Popish emissaries, infected air—all these and more guesses were hazarded, and the Bishop of Kilmore looked at the tree, in the fork of whose lower boughs a white tom-cat was crouching, looking down the hollow which years had gnawed in the trunk. It was watching something inside the tree with great interest.

Suddenly it got up and craned over the hole. Then a bit of the edge on which it stood gave way, and it went slithering in. Everyone looked up at the noise of the fall.

It is known to most of us that a cat can cry; but few of us have heard, I hope, such a yell as came out of the trunk of the great ash. Two or three screams there were—the witnesses are not sure which—and then a slight and muffled noise of some commotion or struggling was all that came. But Lady Mary Hervey fainted outright, and the housekeeper stopped her ears and fled till she fell on the terrace.

The Bishop of Kilmore and Sir William Kentfield stayed. Yet even they were daunted, though it was only at the cry of a cat; and Sir William swallowed once or twice before he could say:

"There is something more than we know of in that tree, my lord. I am for an instant search."

And this was agreed upon. A ladder was brought, and one of the gardeners went up, and, looking down the hollow, could detect nothing but a few dim indications of something moving. They got a lantern, and let it down by a rope.

"We must get at the bottom of this. My life upon it, my lord, but the secret of these terrible deaths is there."

Up went the gardener again with the lantern, and let it down the hole cautiously. They saw the yellow light upon his face as he bent over, and saw his face struck with an incredulous terror and loathing before he cried out in a dreadful voice and fell back from the ladder—where, happily, he was caught by two of the men—letting the lantern fall inside the tree.

He was in a dead faint, and it was some time before any word could be got from him.

By then they had something else to look at. The lantern must have broken at the bottom, and the light in it caught upon dry leaves and rubbish that lay there, for in a few minutes a dense smoke began to come up, and then flame; and, to be short, the tree was in a blaze.

The bystanders made a ring at some yards' distance, and Sir William and the Bishop sent men to get what weapons and tools they could; for, clearly, whatever might be using the tree as its lair would be forced out by the fire.

So it was. First, at the fork, they saw a round body covered with fire—the size of a man's head—appear very suddenly, then seem to collapse and fall back. This, five or six times; then a similar ball leapt into the air and fell on the grass, where after a moment it lay still. The Bishop went as near as he dared to it, and saw—what but the remains of an enormous spider, veinous and seared! And, as the fire burned lower down, more terrible bodies like this began to break out from the trunk, and it was seen that these were covered with greyish hair.

All that day the ash burned, and until it fell to pieces the men stood about it, and from time to time killed the brutes as they darted out. At last there was a long interval when none appeared, and they cautiously closed in and examined the roots of the tree.

"They found," says the Bishop of Kilmore, "below it a rounded hollow place in the earth, wherein were two or three bodies of these creatures that had plainly been smothered by the smoke; and, what is to me more curious, at the side of this den, against the wall, was crouching the anatomy or skeleton of a human being, with the skin dried upon the bones, having some remains of black hair, which was pronounced by those that examined it to be undoubtedly the body of a woman, and clearly dead for a period of fifty years."

THE SANCTUARY

I

FRANCIS ELTON was spending a fortnight's holiday one January in the Engadine, when he received the telegram announcing the death of his uncle, Horace Elton, and his own succession to a very agreeable property: the telegram added that the cremation of the remains was to take place that day, and it was therefore impossible for him to attend, and there was no reason for his hurrying home.

In the solicitor's letter that reached him two days later Mr. Angus gave fuller details: the estate consisted of sound securities to the value of about £80,000, and there was as well Mr. Elton's property just outside the small country town of Wedderburn in Hampshire. This consisted of a charming house and garden and a small acreage of building land. Everything had been left to Francis, but the estate was saddled with a charge of £500 a year in favour of the Reverend Owen Barton.

Francis knew very little of his uncle, who for a long time had been much of a recluse; indeed he had not seen him for nearly four years, when he had spent three days with him at this house at Wedderburn. He had vague but slightly uneasy memories of those days, and now on his journey home, as he lay in his berth in the rocking train, his brain, rummaging drowsily among its buried recollections, began to disinter these. There was nothing very definite about them: they consisted of suggestions and side-lights and oblique impressions, things observed, so to speak, out of the corner of his eye, and never examined in direct focus.

He had only been a boy at the time, having just left school, and it was in the summer holidays, hot sultry weather of August, he remembered, that he had paid him this visit, before he went to a crammer's in London to learn French and German.

There was his Uncle Horace, first of all, and of him he had vivid images. A grey-haired man of middle age, large and extremely stout with a cushion of jowl overlapping his collar, but in spite of this obesity, he was nimble and light in movement, and with a merry blue eye that was equally alert, and seemed constantly to be watching him. Then there were two women there, a mother and daughter, and, as he recalled them, their names occurred to him, too: they were Mrs. Isabel Ray and Judith. Judith, he supposed, was a year or two older than himself, and on the first evening had taken him for a stroll in the garden after dinner. She had treated him at once as if they were old friends, had walked with her arm round his neck, had asked him many questions about his school, and whether there was any girl he was keen on. All very friendly, but rather embarrassing. When they came in from the garden, certainly some questioning signal had passed between the mother and the girl, and Judith had shrugged her shoulders in reply.

Then the mother had taken him in hand; she made him sit with her in the window-seat, and talked to him about the crammer's he was going to: he would have much more liberty, she supposed, than he had at school, and he looked the sort of boy who would make good use of it. She tried him in French and found he could speak it very decently, and told him that she had a book which she had just finished, which she would lend him. It was by that exquisite stylist Huysman and was called *Là-Bas*. She would not tell him what it was about: he must find out for himself. All the time those narrow grey eyes were fixed on him, and when she went to bed, she took him up to her room to give him the book. Judith was there, too: she had read it, and laughed at the memory of it. "Read it, darling Francis," she said, "and then go to sleep immediately, and you will tell me to-morrow what you dreamed about, unless it would shock me."

The vibrating rhythm of the train made Francis drowsy, but his mind went on disinterring these fragments. There had been another man there, his uncle's secretary, a young fellow, perhaps twenty-five years old, clean-shaven and slim and with just the same gaiety about him as the rest. Everyone treated him with an odd sort of deference, hard to define but easy to perceive. He sat next to Francis at dinner that night, and kept filling his wine-glass for him whether he wanted it or not, and next morning he had come into his room, sat on his bed, looked at him with odd questioning eyes, had asked him how he got on with his book, and then taken him to bathe in the swimming-pool behind the belt of trees at the bottom of the garden.... No bathing-costume, he said, was necessary, and they raced up and down the pool and lay basking in the sun afterwards. Then from the belt of trees emerged Judith and her mother, and Francis, much embarrassed, draped himself in a towel. How they all laughed at his delightful prudery.... And what was the man's name? Why, of course, it was Owen Barton, the same who had been mentioned in Mr. Angus's letter as the Reverend Owen Barton. But why "reverend", Francis wondered. Perhaps he had taken Orders afterwards.

All day they had flattered him for his good looks, and his swimming and his lawn-tennis: he had never been made so much of, and all their eyes were on him, inviting and beckoning. In the afternoon his uncle had claimed him: he must come upstairs with him and see some of his treasures. He took him into his bedroom, and opened a great wardrobe full of magnificent vestments. There were gold-embroidered copes, there were stoles and chasubles with panels of needlework enriched with pearls, and jewelled gloves, and the use of them was to make glorious the priests who offered prayer and praise to the Lord of all things visible and invisible. Then he brought out a scarlet cassock of thick shimmering silk, and a cotta of finest muslin trimmed round the neck and the lower hem with Irish lace of the sixteenth century. These were for the vesting of the boy who served at the Mass, and Francis, at his uncle's bidding, stripped off his coat and arrayed himself, and took off his shoes and put on the noiseless scarlet slippers which were called sanctuary shoes. Then Owen Barton entered, and Francis heard him whisper to his uncle, "God! What a server!" and then he put on one of those gorgeous copes and told him to kneel.

The boy had been utterly bewildered. What were they playing at, he wondered. Was it charades of some sort? There was Barton, his face solemn and eager, raising his left hand as if in blessing: more astonishing was his uncle, licking his lips and swallowing in his throat, as if his mouth watered. There was something below all this dressing-up, which meant nothing to him, but had some hidden significance for the two men. It was uncomfortable: it disquieted him, and he wouldn't kneel, but disrobed himself of the cotta and cassock. "I don't know what it's about," he said: and again, as between Judith and her mother, he saw question and answer pass between them. Somehow his lack of interest had disappointed them, but he felt no interest at all : just a vague repulsion.

The diversions of the day were renewed: there was more tennis and bathing, but they all seemed to have lost the edge of their keenness about him. That evening he was dressed rather earlier than the others, and was sitting in a deep window-seat of the drawing room, reading the book Mrs. Ray had lent him. He was not getting on with it; it was puzzling, and the French was difficult: he thought he would return it to her, saying that it was beyond him. Just then she and his uncle entered: they were talking together, and did not perceive him.

"No, it's no use, Isabel," said his uncle. "He's got no curiosity, no leanings: it would only disgust him and put him off. That's not the way to win souls. Owen thinks so, too. And he's too innocent: why, when I was his age.... Why, there's Francis. What's the boy reading? Ah, I see! What do you make of it?"

Francis closed the book.

"I give it up," he said. "I can't get on with it."

Mrs. Ray laughed.

"I agree, too, Horace," she said. "But what a pity!"

Somehow Francis got the impression, he remembered, that they had been talking about him. But, if so, *what* was it for which he had no leanings?

He had gone to bed rather early that night, encouraged, he thought, to do so, leaving the rest at a game of Bridge. He soon slept, but awoke, thinking he heard the sound of chanting. Then came three strokes of a bell, and a pause and three more. He was too sleepy to care what it was about.

Such, as the train rushed through the night, was the sum of his impressions about his visit to the man whose substance he had now inherited, subject to the charge of £500 a year to the Reverend Owen Barton. He was astonished to find how vivid and how vaguely disquieting were these memories, which now for four years had been buried in his mind. As he sank into sounder sleep they faded again, and he thought little more of them in the morning.

He went to see Mr. Angus as soon as he got to London. Certain securities would have to be sold in order to pay death duties, but the administration of the estate was a simple matter. Francis wanted to know more about his benefactor, but Mr. Angus could tell him very little. Horace Elton had, for some years, lived an extremely sequestered life down at Wedderburn, and his only intimate associate was his secretary, this Mr. Owen Barton. Beyond him, there were two ladies who used often to stay with him for long periods. Their names?—and he paused, searching his memory.

"Mrs Isabel Ray and her daughter Judith?" suggested Francis.

"Exactly. They were often there. And, not infrequently, a number of people used to arrive rather late in the evening, eleven o'clock or even later, stay for an hour or two and then be off again. A little mysterious. Only a week or so before Mr. Elton died, there had been quite a congregation of them, fifteen or twenty, I believe."

Francis was silent for a moment: it was as if pieces of jig-saw puzzle were calling for their due location. But their shapes were too fantastic....

"And about my uncle's illness and death," he said. "The cremation of his body was on the same day as that on which he died; at least so I understood from your telegram."

"Yes; that was so," said Mr. Angus.

"But why? I should instantly have come back to England in order to be present. Was it not unusual?"

"Yes, Mr. Elton, it was unusual. But there were reasons for it."

"I should like to hear them," he said. "I was his heir, and it would have been only proper that I should have been there. Why?"

Angus hesitated a moment.

"That is a reasonable question," he said, "and I feel bound to answer it. I must begin a little way back.... Your uncle was in excellent physical health apparently, till about a week before his death. Very stout, but very alert and active. Then the trouble began. It took the form at first of some grievous mental and spiritual disturbance. He thought for some reason that he was going to die very soon, and the idea of death produced in him an abnormal panic terror. He telegraphed me, for he wanted to make some alteration in his will. I was away and could not get down till the next day, and by the time I arrived he was too desperately ill to give any sort of coherent instructions. But his intention, I think, was to cut Mr. Owen Barton out of it."

Again the lawyer paused.

"I found," he said, "that on the morning of the day I got down to Wedderburn, he had sent for the parson of his parish, and had made a confession to him. What that was I have not, of course, the slightest idea. Till then he had been in this panic fear of death, but was physically himself. Immediately afterwards some very horrible disease invaded him. Just that: invasion. The doctors who were summoned from London and Bournemouth had no idea what it was. Some unknown microbe, they supposed, which made the most swift and frightful havoc of skin and tissue and bone. It was like some putrefying internal corruption. It was as if he was dead already.... Really, I don't know what good it will do to tell you this."

"I want to know," said Francis.

"Well: this corruption. Living organisms came out as from a dead body. His nurses used to be sick. And the room was always swarming with flies; great fat flies, crawling over the walls and the bed. He was quite conscious, and there persisted this frantic terror of death, when you would have thought that a man's soul would have been only too thankful to be quit of such a habitation."

"And was Mr. Owen Barton with him?" asked Francis.

"From the moment that Mr. Elton made his confession, he refused to see him. Once he came into the room, and there was a shocking scene. The dying man screamed and yelled with terror. Nor would he see the two ladies we have mentioned: why they continued to stop in the house I can't imagine. Then on the last morning of his life—he could not speak now—he traced a word or two on a piece of paper, and it seemed that he wanted to receive the Holy Communion. So the parson was sent for."

The old lawyer paused again; Francis saw that his hand was shaking.

"Then very dreadful things happened," he said. "I was in the room, for he signed to me to be near him, and I saw them with my own eyes. The parson had poured the wine into the chalice, and had put the bread on the paten, and was about to consecrate the elements, when a cloud of those flies, of which I have told you, came about him. They filled the chalice like a swarm of bees, they settled in their unclean thousands on the paten, and in a couple of minutes the chalice was dry and empty and they had devoured the bread. Then like drilled hosts, you may say, they swarmed on to your uncle's face, so that you could see nothing of it. He choked and he gasped: there was one writhing convulsion, and, thank God, it was all over."

"And then?" asked Francis.

"There were no flies. Nothing. But it was necessary to have the body cremated at once and the bedding with it. Very shocking indeed! I would not have told you, if you had not pressed me."

"And the ashes?" asked he.

"You will see that there is a clause in his will, directing that his remains should be buried at the foot of the Judas-tree beside the swimming pool in the garden at Wedderburn. That was done."

Francis was a very unimaginative young man, free from superstitious twitterings and unprofitable speculations, and this story, suggestive though it was, of ghastly sub-currents, did not take hold of his mind at all or lead to the fashioning of uneasy fancies. It was all very horrible, but it was over. He went down to Wedderburn for Easter with a widowed sister of his and her small boy, aged eleven, and they all fairly fell in love with the place. It was soon settled that Sybil Marsham should let her house in London for the summer months, and establish herself here. Dickie, who was a delicate boy, rather queer and elfin, would thus have the benefit of country air, and Francis the benefit of having the place run by his sister and occupied and in commission whenever he was able to get away from his work.

The house was of brick and timber, with accommodation for half a dozen folk, and stood on high ground above the little town. Francis made a tour of it, as soon as he arrived, rather astonished to find how the sight of it rubbed up to clearness in the minutest details his memory of it. There was the sitting-room with its tall bookcases and its deep window-seats overlooking the garden, where he had sat unobserved when his uncle and Mrs. Ray came in talking together. Above was his uncle's panelled bedroom, which he proposed to occupy himself, with the big wardrobe containing vestments. He opened it: they were under their covering sheets of tissue paper, shimmering with scarlet and gold and finest lawn foamed with Irish lace: a faint smell of incense hung about them. Next that was his uncle's sitting-room, and beyond that the room which he had slept in before, and was now appropriated to Dickie. These rooms lay on the front of the house, looking westwards over the garden, and he went out to renew acquaintance with it. Flower-beds gay with spring blossoms ran below the windows; then came the lawn, and beyond the belt of trees that enclosed the swimming-pool. He passed along the path that threaded it between tapestries of primrose and anemone, and came out into the clearing that surrounded the water. The bathing shed stood at the deep end of it by the sluice that splashed riotously into the channel below, for the stream that supplied the pool was running full with the rains of March. In front of the copse on the far side stood a Judas-tree decked gloriously with flowers, and the reflection of it was cast waveringly on the rippled surface of the water. Somewhere below those red-blossoming boughs, there was buried a casket of ashes. He strolled round the pool: it was quite sheltered here from the April breeze, and bees were busy in the red blossoms. Bees, and large fat flies, a quantity of them.

He and Sybil were sitting in the drawing-room with the deep window-seats as dusk began to fall. A servant came in to say that Mr. Owen Barton had called. Certainly they were at home, and he entered, and was introduced to Sybil.

"You will hardly remember me, Mr. Elton," he said, "but I was here when you paid a visit to your uncle: four years ago it must have been."

"But I remember you perfectly," Francis said. "We bathed together, we played tennis; you were very kind to a shy boy. And are you living here still?"

"Yes: I took a house in Wedderburn after your uncle's death. I spent six very happy years with him as his secretary, and I got much attached to the country. My house stands just outside your garden palings opposite the latched gate leading into the woods round the pool."

The door opened and Dickie came in. He caught sight of the stranger and stopped.

"Say 'how do you do' to Mr. Barton, Dickie," said his mother.

Dickie performed this duty with due politeness and stood regarding him. He was a shy boy usually; but, after this inspection, he advanced close to him, and laid his hands on his knees.

"I like you," he said confidently, and leant up against him.

"Don't bother Mr. Barton, Dickie," she said rather sharply.

"But indeed he's doing nothing of the kind," said Barton, and he drew the boy towards him so that he stood clipped between his knees.

Sybil got up.

"Come, Dick," she said. "We'll have a walk round the garden before it gets dark."

"Is he coming, too?" asked the boy.

"No; he's going to stop and talk to Uncle Francis."

When the two men were alone Barton said a word or two about Horace Elton, who had always been so generous a friend to him. The end, mercifully short, had been terrible, and terrible to him personally had been the dying man's refusal to see him during the last two days of his life.

"His mind, I think, must have been affected," he said, "by his awful sufferings. It happens like that sometimes: people turn against those with whom they have been most intimate. I have often mourned over that, and deeply regretted it.... And I owe you a certain word of explanation, Mr. Elton. No doubt you were puzzled to find in your uncle's will that I was entitled 'the Reverend'. It is quite true, though I do not call myself so. Certain spiritual doubts and difficulties caused me to give up my orders, but your uncle always held that if a man is once a priest he is always a priest. He was very strong about that, and no doubt he was right."

"I didn't know my uncle took any interest in ecclesiastical affairs," said Francis. "Ah, I had forgotten about his vestments. Perhaps that was only an artistic taste."

"By no means. He regarded them as sacred things, consecrated to holy uses. ... And may I ask you what happened to his remains? I remember he once expressed a wish to be buried by the swimming pool."

"His body was cremated," said Francis, "and the ashes were buried there."

Barton stayed but little longer, and Sybil on her return was frankly relieved to find he had gone. Simply, she didn't like him. There was something queer, something sinister about him. Francis laughed at her; quite a good fellow, he thought.

Dreams, of course, are a mere hash-up of recent mental images and associations, and a very vivid dream that came to Francis that night could easily have arisen from such topics. He thought he was swimming in the bathing pool with Owen Barton, and that his uncle, stout and florid, was standing underneath the Judas-tree watching them. That seemed quite natural, as is the way of dreams: merely he was not dead at all. When they came out of the water he looked for his clothes, but found that there was laid out for him a scarlet cassock and a white lace-trimmed cotta. This again was quite natural; so, too, was the fact that Barton put on a gold cope.

His uncle, very merry and licking his lips, joined them, and each of them took an arm of his and they walked back to the house together, singing a hymn. As they went the daylight died, and by the time they crossed the lawn it was black night, and the windows of the house were lit. They walked upstairs, still singing, into his uncle's bedroom which was now his own. There was an open door, which he had never noticed before, opposite his bed, and there came a very bright light from it. Then the sense of nightmare began, for his two companions, gripping him tightly, pulled him along towards it, and he struggled with them, knowing there was something terrible within. But step by step they dragged him, violently resisting, and now out of the door there came a swarm of large fat flies that buzzed and settled on him. Thicker and thicker they streamed out, covering his face, and crawling into his eyes, and entering his mouth as he panted for breath. The horror grew to breaking-point, and he woke sweating with a hammering heart. He switched on the light, and there was the quiet room and the dawn beginning to be luminous outside, and the birds just tuning up.

Francis's few days of holiday passed quickly. He went down to the village to see Barton's house, and found it a most pleasant little dwelling, and its owner an exceedingly pleasant fellow. Barton dined with them one evening, and Sybil went so far as to admit that her first judgment of him was hasty. He was charming with Dickie, too, and that disposed her in his favour, and the boy adored him. Soon it was necessary to find some tutor for him, and Barton readily agreed to undertake his education, and every morning Dickie trotted across the garden and through the wood where the swimming pool lay to Barton's house. His ill-health made him rather backward in his studies, but he was now eager to learn and to please his instructor, and he got on quickly.

II

It was now that I first met Francis, and during the next few months in London we became close friends. He told me that he had lately inherited this place at Wedderburn from his uncle, but for the present I knew no more than that of the previous history which I have just recorded. Sometime during July he told me he was intending to spend the month of August there. His sister, who kept house for him, and her small boy would be away for the first week or two, for she had taken him off to the seaside. Would I then come and share his solitude, and get on there, uninterrupted, with some work I had on hand. That seemed a very attractive plan, and we motored down together one very hot afternoon early in August, that promised thunder. Owen Barton, he told me, who had been his uncle's secretary, was coming to dine with us that night.

It wanted an hour or so yet to dinner-time when we arrived, and Francis directed me, if I cared for a dip, to the bathing pool among the trees beyond the lawn. He had various household businesses to look into himself, so I went off alone. It was an enchanting place, the water still and very clear, mirroring the sky and the full-foliaged trees, and I stripped and plunged in. I lay and floated in the cool water, I swam and dived again, and then I saw, walking close to the far bank of the pool, a man of something more than middle-age, and extremely stout. He was in dress clothes, dinner-jacket and black tie, and instantly it struck me that this must be Mr. Barton coming up from the village to dine with us. It must therefore be later than I thought, and I swam back to the shed where my clothes were. As I climbed out of the water, I glanced round. There was no one there.

It was a slight shock, but very slight. It was odd that he should have come so unexpectedly out of the wood and disappeared again so suddenly, but it did not concern me much. I hurried home, changed quickly and came down, expecting to find Francis and his guest in the drawing-room. But I need not have been in such haste for now my watch told me that there was still a quarter of an hour before dinner time. As for the others, I supposed that Mr. Barton was upstairs with Francis in his sitting-room. So I picked up a chance book to beguile the time, and read for a while, but the room grew rather dark, and, rising to switch on the electric light, I saw standing outside the French window into the garden the figure of a man, outlined against the last of a stormy sunset, looking into the room.

There was no doubt whatever in my mind that he was the same person as I had seen when I was bathing, and the switching on of the light made this clear, for it shone full on his face. No doubt then Mr. Barton, finding he was too early, was strolling about the garden till the dinner-hour. But now I did not look forward at all to this evening; I had had a good look at him and there was something horrible about him. Was he human, was he earthly at all? Then he quietly moved away, and immediately afterwards there came a knock at the front door just outside the room, and I heard Francis coming downstairs. He went to the door himself; there was a word of greeting, and he came into the room accompanied by a tall, slim fellow whom he introduced to me.

We had a very pleasant evening: Barton talked fluently and agreeably, and more than once he spoke of his friend and pupil Dickie. About eleven he rose to go, and Francis suggested to him that he should walk back across the garden which gave him a short cut to his house. The threatening storm still held off, but it was very dark overhead, as we stood together outside the French window. Barton was soon swallowed up in the blackness. Then there came a bright flash of lightning, and in that moment of illumination I saw that there was standing in the middle of the lawn, as if waiting for him, the figure I had seen twice already. "Who is that?" was on the tip of my tongue, but instantly I perceived that Francis had seen nothing of it, and so I was silent, for I knew now what I had already half-guessed, that this was no living man of flesh and blood whom I had seen. A few heavy drops of rain plopped on the flagged walk, and, as we moved indoors, Francis called out "Good night, Barton!" and the cheery voice answered.

Before long we went up to bed, and he took me into his room as we passed, a big panelled chamber with a great wardrobe by the bed. Close to it hung an oil-portrait of kit-cat size.

"I'll show you what's in that wardrobe to-morrow," he said. "Rather wonderful things.... That's a picture of my uncle."

I had seen that face before this evening.

For the next two or three days I had no further glimpse of that dreadful visitant, but never for a moment was I at ease, for I was aware that he was about. What instinct or what sense perceived that, I have no idea: perhaps it was merely the dread I had of seeing him again that gave rise to the conviction. I thought of telling Francis that I must get back to London; what prevented me from so doing was the desire to know more, and that made me fight this cold fear. Then very soon I perceived that Francis was no more at ease than I was. Sometimes as we sat together in the evening he was oddly alert: he would pause in the middle of a sentence as if some sound had attracted his attention, or he would look up from our game of bezique and focus his eyes for a second on some corner of the room or, more often, on the dark oblong of the open French window. Had he, I wondered, been seeing something invisible to me, and, like myself, feared to speak of it?

These impressions were momentary and infrequent, but they kept alive in me the feeling that there was something astir, and that something, coming out of the dark, and the unknown, was growing in force. It had come into the house, and was present everywhere....

And then one awoke again to a morning of heavenly brightness and sunshine, and surely one was disquieting oneself in vain.

I had been there about a week when something occurred which precipitated what followed. I slept in the room which Dickie usually occupied, and awoke one night feeling uncomfortably hot. I tugged at a blanket to remove it, but it was tucked very tightly in between the mattresses on the side of the bed next to the wall. Eventually I got it free, and as I did so I heard something drop with a flutter on to the floor. In the morning I remembered that, and found underneath the bed a little paper notebook. I opened it idly enough, and within were a dozen pages written over in a round childish handwriting, and these words struck my eye:

"Thursday, July 11th. I saw great-uncle Horace again this morning in the wood. He told me something about myself which I didn't understand, but he said I should like it when I got older. I mustn't tell anybody that he's here, nor what he told me, except Mr. Barton."

I did not care one jot whether I was reading a boy's private diary. That was no longer a consideration worth thinking about. I turned over the page and found another entry.

"Sunday, July 21st. I saw Uncle Horace again. I said I had told Mr. Barton what he had told me, and Mr. Barton had told me some more things, and that he was pleased, and said I was getting on and that he would take me to prayers some day soon."

I cannot describe the thrill of horror that these entries woke in me. They made the apparition which I had seen infinitely more real and more sinister. It was a spirit corrupt and malign and intent on corruption that haunted the place. But what was I to do? How could I, without any lead from Francis, tell him that the spirit of his uncle—of whom at present I knew nothing—had been seen not by me only, but by his nephew, and that he was at work on the boy's mind? Then there was the mention of Barton. Certainly that could not be left as it was. He was collaborating in that damnable task. A cult of corruption (or was I being too fantastic?) began to outline itself. Then what did that sentence about taking him to prayers mean? But Dickie was away, thank goodness, for the present, and there was time to think it over. As for that pitiful little notebook, I put it into a locked despatch case.

The day, as far as outward and visible signs were concerned, passed pleasantly. For me there was a morning's work, and for both of us an afternoon on the golf-links. But below there was something heavy; my knowledge of that diary kept intervening with mental telephone-calls asking "What are you going to *do*?" Francis, on his side, was troubled; there were sub-currents, and I did not know what they were. Silences fell, not the natural unobserved silences between those who are intimate, which are only a symbol of their intimacy, but the silences between those who have something on their minds of which they fear to speak. These had got more stringent all day; there was a growing tenseness; all common topics were banal, for they only cloaked a certain topic.

We sat out on the lawn before dinner on that sultry evening, and breaking one of these silent intervals, he pointed at the front of the house.

"There's an odd thing," he said. "Look! There are three rooms, aren't there, on the ground floor: dining-room, drawing-room, and the little study where you write. Now look above. There are three rooms there: your bedroom, my bedroom, and my sitting-room. I've measured them. There are twelve feet missing. Looks as if there was a sealed-up room somewhere."

Here, at any rate, was something to talk about.

"Exciting," I said. "Mayn't we explore?"

"We will. We'll explore as soon as we've dined. Then there's another thing; quite off the point. You remember those vestments I showed you the other day? I opened the wardrobe, where they are kept, an hour ago, and a lot of big fat flies came buzzing out. A row like a dozen aeroplanes overhead. Remote but loud, if you know what I mean. And then there weren't any."

Somehow I felt that what we had been silent about was coming out into the open. It might be ill to look upon....

He jumped from his chair.

"Let's have done with these silences," he cried. "He's here, my uncle, I mean. I haven't told you yet, but he died in a swarm of flies. He asked for the Sacrament, but before the wine was consecrated the chalice was choked with them. And I know he's here. It sounds damned rot, but he is."

"I know that, too," I said. "I've seen him."

"Why didn't you tell me?"

"Because I thought you would laugh at me."

"I should have a few days ago," said he. "But I don't now. Go on."

"The first evening I was here I saw him at the bathing pool. That same night, when we were seeing Owen Barton off, a flash of lightning came, and he was there again standing on the lawn."

"But how did you know it was he?" asked Francis.

"I knew it when you showed me the portrait of him in your bedroom that same night. Have you seen him?"

"No; but he's here. Anything more?"

This was the opportunity not only natural but inevitable.

"Yes, much more," I said. "Dickie has seen him too."

"That child? Impossible."

The door out of the drawing-room opened, and Francis's parlourmaid came out with the sherry on a tray. She put the decanter and glasses down on the wicker table between us, and I asked her to bring out the despatch case from my room. I took the paper notebook out of it.

"This slipped out from beneath my mattresses last night. It's Dickie's diary. Listen:" and I read him the first extract.

Francis gave one of those swift disconcerting glances over his shoulder.

"But we're dreaming," he said. "It's a nightmare. God, there's something awful here! And what about Dickie not telling anybody except Barton what he told him? Anything more?"

"Yes. 'Sunday, July 21st. I saw Uncle Horace again. I said I had told Mr. Barton what he told me, and Mr. Barton told me some more things, and that he was pleased and said I was getting on, and that he would take me to prayers some day soon.' I don't know what that means."

Francis sprang out of his chair.

"What?" he cried. "Take him to prayers? Wait a minute. Let me remember about my first visit here. I was a boy of nineteen, and frightfully, absurdly innocent for my age. A woman staying here gave me a book to read called *Là-Bas*. I didn't get far in it then, but I know what it's about now."

"Black Mass," said I. "Satan worshippers."

"Yes. Then one day my uncle dressed me up in a scarlet cassock, and Barton came in and put on a cape and said something about my being a server. He used to be a priest, did you know that? And one night I awoke and heard the sound of chanting and a bell rang. By the way, Barton's coming to dine to-morrow. . . ."

"What are you going to do?"

"About him? I can't tell yet. But we've got something to do to-night. Horrors have happened here in this house. There must be some room where they held their Mass, a chapel. Why, there's that missing space I spoke of just now."

After dinner we set to work. Somewhere on the first floor on the garden front of the house there was this space unaccounted for by the dimensions of the rooms there. We turned on the electric light in all of them, and then going out into the garden we saw that the windows in Francis's bedroom and in his sitting-room next door were far more widely spaced than they should have been. Somewhere, then, between them lay the area to which there was no apparent access and we went upstairs. The wall of his sitting-room seemed solid, it was of brick and timber, and large beams ran through it at narrow intervals. But the wall of his bedroom was panelled, and when we tapped on it, no sound came through into the other room beyond.

We began to examine it.

The servants had gone to bed, and the house was silent, but as we moved about from garden to house and from one room to another there was some presence watching and following us. We had shut the door into his bedroom from the passage, but now as we peered and felt about the panelling, the door swung open and closed again, and something entered, brushing my shoulder as it passed.

"What's that?" I said. "Someone came in."

"Never mind that," he said. "Look what I've found."

In the border of one of the panels was a black stud like an ebony bell-push. He pressed it and pulled, and a section of the panelling slid sideways, disclosing a red curtain cloaking a doorway. He drew it aside with a clash of metal rings. It was dark within, and out of the darkness came a smell of stale incense. I felt with my hand along the frame of the doorway and found a switch, and the blackness was flooded with a dazzling light.

Within was a chapel. There was no window, and at the West end of it (not the East) there stood an altar. Above it was a picture, evidently of some early Italian school. It was on the lines of the Fra Angelico picture of the Annunciation. The Virgin sat in an open loggia, and on the flowery space outside the angel made his salutation. His spreading wings were the wings of a bat, and his black head and neck were those of a raven. He had his left hand, not his right, raised in blessing. The virgin's robe of thinnest red muslin was trimmed with revolting symbols, and her face was that of a panting dog with tongue protruding.

There were two niches at the East end, in which were marble statues of naked men, with the inscriptions "St. Judas" and "St. Gilles de Raies". One was picking up pieces of silver that lay at his feet, the other looked down leering and laughing at the prone figure of a mutilated boy. The place was lit by a chandelier from the ceiling: this was of the shape of a crown of thorns and electric bulbs nestled among the woven silver twigs. A bell hung from the roof, close beside the altar.

For the moment, as I looked on these obscene blasphemies, I felt that they were merely grotesque and no more to be regarded seriously than the dirty inscriptions written upon empty wall-spaces in the street. That indifference swiftly passed, and a horrified consciousness of the devotion of those who had fashioned and assembled these decorations took its place. Skilled painters and artificers had wrought them and they were here for the service of all that is evil; that spirit of adoration lived in them dynamic and active. And the place was throbbing with the exultant joy of those who had worshipped here.

"And look here!" called Francis. He pointed to a little table standing against the wall just outside the altar-rails.

There were photographs on it, one of a boy standing on the header-board at the bathing pool about to plunge.

"That's me," he said. "Barton took it. And what's written underneath it? 'Ora pro Francisco Elton'. And that's Mrs. Ray, and that's my uncle, and that's Barton in a cope. Pray for him, too, please. But it's childish!"

He suddenly burst out into a shout of laughter. The roof of the chapel was vaulted and the echo that came from it was loud and surprising, the place rang with it. His laughter ceased, but not so the echo. There was someone else laughing. But where? Who? Except for us the chapel was empty of all visible presences.

On and on the laughter went, and we stared at each other with panic stirring. The brilliant light from the chandelier began to fade, dusk gathered, and in the dusk there was brewing some hellish and deadly force. And through the dimness I saw, hanging in the air, and oscillating slightly as if in a draught, the laughing face of Horace Elton. Francis saw it too.

"Fight it! Withstand it!" he cried as he pointed to it. "Desecrate all that it holds sanctified! God, do you smell the incense and the corruption?"

We tore the photographs, we smashed the table on which they stood. We plucked the frontal from the altar and spat on the accursed table: we tugged at it till it toppled over and the marble slab split in half. We hauled from the niches the two statues that stood there, and crash they went on to the paved floor. Then, appalled at the riot of our iconoclasm, we paused. The laughter had ceased and no oscillating face dangled in the dimness. Then we left the chapel and pulled across the doorway the panel that closed it.

Francis came to sleep in my room, and we talked long, laying our plans for next day. We had forgotten the picture over the altar in our destruction, but now it worked in with what we proposed to do. Then we slept, and the night passed without disturbance. At the least we had broken up the apparatus that was hallowed to unhallowed uses, and that was something. But there was grim work ahead yet, and the issue was unconjecturable.

Barton came to dine that next evening, and there hung on the wall opposite his place the picture from the chapel upstairs. He did not notice it at first, for the room was rather dark, but not dark enough yet to need artificial light. He was gay and lively as usual, spoke amusingly and wittily, and asked when his friend Dickie was to return. Towards the end of dinner the lights were switched on, and then he saw the picture. I was watching him, and the sweat started out on his face that had grown clay-coloured in a moment. Then he pulled himself together.

"That's a strange picture," he said. "Was it here before? Surely not."

"No: it was in a room upstairs," said Francis. "About Dickie? I don't know for certain when he'll come back. We have found his diary, and presently we must speak about that."

"Dickie's diary? Indeed!" said Barton, and he moistened his lips with his tongue.

I think he guessed then that there was something desperate ahead, and I pictured a man condemned to be hanged waiting in his cell with his warders for the imminent hour, as Barton waited then. He sat with an elbow on the table and his hand propping his forehead. Immediately, almost, the servant brought in our coffee and left us.

"Dickie's diary," said Francis quietly. "Your name figures in it. Also my uncle's. Dickie saw him more than once. But, of course, you know that."

Barton drank off his glass of brandy.

"Are you telling me a ghost story?" he said. "Pray go on."

"Yes, it's partly a ghost story, but not entirely. My uncle—his ghost if you like—told him certain stories and said he must keep them secret except from you. And you told him more. And you said he should come to prayers with you some day soon. Where was that to be? In the room just above us?"

The brandy had given the condemned man a momentary courage.

"A pack of lies, Mr. Elton," he said. "That boy has got a corrupt mind. He told me things that no boy of his age should know; he giggled and laughed at them. Perhaps I ought to have told his mother."

"It's too late to think of that now," said Francis. "The diary I spoke of will be in the hands of the police at ten o'clock to-morrow morning. They will also inspect the room upstairs where you have been in the habit of celebrating the Black Mass."

Barton leant forward towards him.

"No, no," he cried. "Don't do that! I beg and implore you! I will confess the truth to you. I will conceal nothing. My life has been a blasphemy. But I'm sorry: I repent. I abjure all those abominations from henceforth: I renounce them all in the name of Almighty God."

"Too late," said Francis.

And then the horror that haunts me still began to manifest itself. The wretched man threw himself back in his chair, and there dropped from his forehead on to his white shirt-front a long grey worm that lay and wriggled there. At that moment there came from overhead the sound of a bell, and he sprang to his feet.

"No!" he cried again. "I retract all I said. I abjure nothing. And my Lord is waiting for me in the sanctuary. I must be quick and make my humble confession to him."

With the movement of a slinking animal he slid from the room, and we heard his steps going swiftly upstairs.

"Did you see?" I whispered. "And what's to be done? Is the man sane?"

"It's beyond us now," said Francis.

There was a thump on the ceiling overhead as if someone had fallen, and without a word we ran upstairs into Francis's bedroom. The door of the wardrobe where the vestments were kept was open; some lay on the floor. The panel was open, too, but within it was dark. In terror at what might meet our eyes, I felt for the switch and turned the light on.

The bell which had sounded a few minutes ago was still swinging gently, though speaking no more. Barton, clad in the gold-embroidered cope, lay in front of the overturned altar, with his face twitching. Then that ceased, the rattle of death creaked in his throat, and his mouth fell open. Great flies, swarms of them, coming from nowhere, settled on it.

ALGERNON BLACKWOOD

MAY DAY EVE

I

IT was the spring when I at last found time from the hospital work to visit my friend, the old folk-lorist, in his country isolation, and I rather chuckled to myself, because in my bag I was taking down a book that utterly refuted all his tiresome pet theories of magic and the powers of the soul.

These theories were many and various, and had often troubled me. In the first place, I scorned them for professional reasons, and, in the second, because I had never been able to argue quite well enough to convince or to shake his faith in even the smallest details, and any scientific knowledge I brought to bear only fed him with confirmatory data. To find such a book, therefore, and to know that it was safely in my bag, wrapped up in brown paper and addressed to him, was a deep and satisfactory joy, and I speculated a good deal during the journey how he would deal with the overwhelming arguments it contained against the existence of any important region outside the world of sensory perceptions.

Speculative, too, I was, whether his visionary habits and absorbing experiments would permit him to remember my arrival at all, and I was accordingly relieved to hear from the solitary porter that the "professor" had sent a "veeckle" to meet me, and that I was thus free to send my bag and walk the four miles to the house across the hills.

It was a calm, windless evening, just after sunset, the air warm and scented, and delightfully still. The train, already sinking into distance, carried away with it the noise of crowds and cities and the last suggestions of the stressful life behind me, and from the little station on the moorland I stepped at once into the world of silent, growing things, tinkling sheep-bells, shepherds, and wild, desolate spaces.

My path lay diagonally across the turfy hills. It slanted a mile or so to the summit, wandered vaguely another two miles among gorse-bushes along the crest, passed Tom Bassett's cottage by the pines, and then dropped sharply down on the other side through rather thin woods to the ancient house where the old folk-lorist lived and dreamed himself into his impossible world of theory and fantasy. I fell to thinking busily about him during the first part of the ascent, and convinced myself, as usual, that, but for his generosity to the poor, and his benign aspect, the peasantry must undoubtedly have regarded him as a wizard who speculated in souls and had dark dealings with the world of faery.

The path I knew tolerably well. I had already walked it once before—a winter's day some years ago—and from the cottage onwards felt sure of my way; but for the first mile or so there were so many cross cattle-tracks, and the light had become so dim, that I felt it wise to inquire more particularly. And this I was fortunately able to do of a man who, with astonishing suddenness, rose from the grass where he had been lying behind a clump of bushes, and passed a few yards in front of me at a high pace downhill towards the darkening valley.

He was in such a state of hurry that I called out loudly to him, fearing to be too late, but on hearing my voice he turned sharply, and seemed to arrive almost at once beside me. In a single instant he was standing there, quite close, looking, with a smile and a certain expression of curiosity, I thought, into my face. I remember thinking that his features, pale and wholly untanned, were rather wonderful for a countryman, and that the eyes were those of a foreigner; his great swiftness, too, gave me a distinct sensation—something almost of a start—though I knew my vision was at fault at the best of times, and of course especially so in the deceptive twilight of the open hillside.

Moreover—as the way often is with such instructions—the words did not stay in my mind very clearly after he had uttered them, and the rapid, panther-like movements of the man as he quickly vanished down the hill again left me with little more than a sweeping gesture indicating the line I was to follow. No doubt his sudden rising from behind the gorse-bush, his curious swiftness, and the way he peered into my face, and even touched me on the shoulder, all combined to distract my attention somewhat from the actual words he used; and the fact that I was travelling at a wrong angle, and should have come out a mile too far to the right, helped to complete my feeling that his gesture, pointing the way, was sufficient.

On the crest of the ridge, panting a little with the unwonted exertion, I lay down to rest a moment on the grass beside a flaming yellow gorse-bush. There was still a good hour before I should be looked for at the house; the grass was very soft, the peace and silence soothing. I lingered, and lit a cigarette. And it was just then, I think, that my subconscious memory gave back the words, the actual words, the man had spoken, and the heavy significance of the personal pronoun, as he had emphasised it in his odd foreign voice, touched me with a sense of vague amusement: "The safest way *for you* now," he had said, as though I was so obviously a townsman and might be in danger on the lonely hills after dark. And the quick way he had reached my side, and then slipped off again like a shadow down the steep slope, completed a definite little picture in my mind. Then other thoughts and memories rose up and formed a series of pictures, following each other in rapid succession, and forming a chain of reflections undirected by the will and without purpose or meaning. I fell, that is, into a pleasant reverie.

Below me, and infinitely far away, it seemed, the valley lay silent under a veil of blue evening haze, the lower end losing itself among darkening hills whose peaks rose here and there like giant plumes that would surely nod their great heads and call to one another once the final shadows were down. The village lay, a misty patch, in which lights already twinkled. A sound of rooks faintly cawing, of sea-gulls crying far up in the sky, and of dogs barking at a great distance rose up out of the general murmur of evening voices. Odours of farm and field and open spaces stole to my nostrils, and everything contributed to the feeling that I lay on the top of the world, nothing between me and the stars, and that all the huge, free things of the earth—hills, valleys, woods, and sloping fields—lay breathing deeply about me.

A few sea-gulls—in daytime hereabouts they fill the air—still circled and wheeled within range of sight, uttering from time to time sharp, petulant cries; and far in the distance there was just visible a shadowy line that showed where the sea lay.

Then, as I lay gazing dreamily into this still pool of shadows at my feet, something rose up, something sheet-like, vast, imponderable, off the whole surface of the mapped-out country, moved with incredible swiftness down the valley, and in a single instant climbed the hill where I lay and swept by me, yet without hurry, and in a sense without speed. Veils in this way rose one after another, filling the cups between the hills, shrouding alike fields, village, and hillside as they passed, and settled down somewhere into the gloom behind me over the ridge, or slipped off like vapour into the sky.

Whether it was actually mist rising from the surface of the fast-cooling ground, or merely the earth giving up her heat to the night, I could not determine. The coming of darkness is ever a series of mysteries. I only know that this indescribable vast stirring of the landscape seemed to me as though the earth were unfolding immense sable wings from her sides, and lifting them for silent, gigantic strokes so that she might fly more swiftly from the sun into the night. The darkness, at any rate, did drop down over everything very soon afterwards, and I rose up hastily to follow my pathway, realising with a degree of wonder strangely new to me the magic of twilight, the blue open depths into the valley below, and the pale yellow heights of the watery sky above.

I walked rapidly, a sense of chilliness about me, and soon lost sight of the valley altogether as I got upon the ridge proper of these lonely and desolate hills.

It could not have been more than fifteen minutes that I lay there in reverie, yet the weather, I at once noticed, had changed very abruptly, for mist was seething here and there about me, rising somewhere from smaller valleys in the hills beyond, and obscuring the path, while overhead there was plainly a sound of wind tearing past, far up, with a sound of high shouting. A moment before it had been the stillness of a warm spring night, yet now everything had changed; wet mist coated me, raindrops smartly stung my face, and a gusty wind, descending out of cool heights, began to strike and buffet me, so that I buttoned my coat and pressed my hat more firmly upon my head.

The change was really this—and it came to me for the first time in my life with the power of a real conviction—that everything about me seemed to have become suddenly *alive*.

It came oddly upon me—prosaic, matter-of-fact, materialistic doctor that I was—this realisation that the world about me had somehow stirred into life; oddly, I say, because Nature to me had always been merely a more or less definite arrangement of measurement, weight, and colour, and this new presentation of it was utterly foreign to my temperament. A valley to me was always a valley; a hill, merely a hill; a field, so many acres of flat surface, grass or ploughed, drained well or drained ill; whereas now, with startling vividness, came the strange, haunting idea that after all they could be something more than valley, hill, and field: that what I had hitherto perceived by these names were only the veils of something that lay concealed within, something alive. In a word, that the poetic sense I had always rather sneered at in others, or explained away with some shallow physiological label, had apparently suddenly opened up in myself without any obvious cause.

And, the more I puzzled over it, the more I began to realise that its genesis dated from those few minutes of reverie lying under the gorse-bush (reverie, a thing I had never before in all my life indulged in!), or, now that I came to reflect more accurately, from my brief interview with that wild-eyed, swift-moving, shadowy man of whom I had first inquired the way.

I recalled my singular fancy that veils were lifting off the surface of the hills and fields, and a tremor of excitement accompanied the memory. Such a thing had never before been possible to my practical intelligence, and it made me feel suspicious—suspicious about myself. I stood still a moment—I looked about me into the gathering mist, above me to the vanishing stars, below me to the hidden valley, and then sent an urgent summons to my individuality, as I had always known it, to arrest and chase these undesirable fancies.

But I called in vain. No answer came. Anxiously, hurriedly, confusedly too, I searched for my normal self, but could not find it; and this failure to respond induced in me a sense of uneasiness that touched very nearly upon the borders of alarm.

I pushed on faster and faster along the turfy track among the gorse-bushes with a dread that I might lose the way altogether, and a sudden desire to reach home as soon as might be. Then, without warning, I emerged unexpectedly into clear air again, and the vapour swept past me in a rushing wall and rose into the sky. Anew I saw the lights of the village behind me in the depths, here and there a line of smoke rising against the pale yellow sky, and stars overhead peering down through thin wispy clouds that stretched their wind-signs across the night.

After all, it had been nothing but a stray bit of sea-fog driving up from the coast, for the other side of the hills, I remembered, dipped their chalk cliffs straight into the sea, and strange lost winds must often come a-wandering this way with the sharp changes of temperature about sunset. None the less, it was disconcerting to know that mist and storm lay hiding within possible reach, and I walked on smartly for a sight of Tom Bassett's cottage and the lights of the Manor House in the valley a short mile beyond.

The clearing of the air, however, lasted but a brief while, and vapour was soon rising about me as before, hiding the path and making bushes and stone walls look like running shadows. It came, driven apparently by little independent winds up the many side gullies, and it was very cold, touching my skin like a wet sheet. Curious great shapes, too, it assumed as the wind worked to and fro through it: forms of men and animals: grotesque, giant outlines; ever shifting and running along the ground with silent feet, or leaping into the air with sharp cries as the gusts twisted them inwardly and lent them voice. More and more I pushed my pace, and more and more darkness and vapour obliterated the landscape. The going was not otherwise difficult, and here and there cowslips glimmered in patches of dancing yellow, while the springy turf made it easy to keep up speed; yet in the gloom I frequently tripped and plunged into prickly gorse near the ground, so that from shin to knee was soon a-tingle with sharp pain. Odd puffs and spits of rain stung my face, and the periods of utter stillness were always followed by little shouting gusts of wind, each time from a new direction. Troubled is perhaps too strong a word, but flustered I certainly was; and though I recognised that it was due to my being in an environment so remote from the town life I was accustomed to, I found it impossible to stifle altogether the feeling of malaise that had crept into my heart, and I looked about with increasing eagerness for the lighted windows of Bassett's cottage.

More and more, little pin-pricks of distress and confusion accumulated, adding to my realisation of being away from streets and shop-windows, and things I could classify and deal with. The mist, too, distorted as well as concealed, played tricks with sounds as well as with sights. And, once or twice, when I stumbled upon some crouching sheep, they got up without the customary alarm and hurry of sheep, and moved off slowly into the darkness, but in such a singular way that I could almost have sworn they were not sheep at all, but human beings crawling on all-fours, looking back and grimacing at me over their shoulders as they went. On these occasions—for there were more than one—I never could get close enough to feel their woolly wet backs, as I should have liked to do; and the sound of their tinkling bells came faintly through the mist, sometimes from one direction, sometimes from another, sometimes all round me as though a whole flock surrounded me; and I found it impossible to analyse or explain the idea I received that they were *not* sheep-bells at all, but something quite different.

But mist and darkness, and a certain confusion of the senses caused by the excitement of an utterly strange environment, can account for a great deal. I pushed on quickly. The conviction that I had strayed from the route grew, nevertheless, for occasionally there was a great commotion of sea-gulls about me, as though I had disturbed them in their sleeping-places. The air filled with their plaintive cries, and I heard the rushing of multitudinous wings, sometimes very close to my head, but always invisible owing to the mist. And once, above the swishing of the wet wind through the gorse-bushes, I was sure I caught the faint thunder of the sea and the distant crashing of waves rolling up some steep-throated gully in the cliffs. I went cautiously after this, and altered my course a little away from the direction of the sound.

Yet, increasingly all the time, it came to me how the cries of the sea-birds sounded like laughter, and how the everlasting wind blew and drove about me with a purpose, and how the low bushes persistently took the shape of stooping people, moving stealthily past me, and how the mist more and more resembled huge protean figures escorting me across the desolate hills, silently, with immense footsteps. For the inanimate world now touched my awakened poetic sense in a manner hitherto unguessed, and became fraught with the pregnant messages of a dimly concealed life. I readily understood, for the first time, how easily a superstitious peasantry might people their world, and how even an educated mind might favour an atmosphere of legend. I stumbled along, looking anxiously for the lights of the cottage.

Suddenly, as a shape of writhing mist whirled past, I received so direct a stroke of wind that it was palpably a blow in the face. Something swept by with a shrill cry into the darkness. It was impossible to prevent jumping to one side and raising an arm by way of protection, and I was only just quick enough to catch a glimpse of the sea-gull as it raced past, with suddenly altered flight, beating its powerful wings over my head. Its white body looked enormous as the mist swallowed it. At the same moment a gust tore the hat from my head and flung the flap of my coat across my eyes. But I was well trained by this time, and made a quick dash after the retreating black object, only to find on overtaking it that I held a prickly branch of gorse. The wind combed my hair viciously. Then, out of a corner of my eye, I saw my hat still rolling, and grabbed swiftly at it; but just as I closed on it, the real hat passed in front of me, turning over in the wind like a ball, and I instantly released my first capture to chase it. Before it was within reach, another one shot between my feet so that I stepped on it. The grass seemed covered with moving hats, yet each one, when I seized it, turned into a piece of wood, or a tiny gorse bush, or a black rabbit hole, till my hands were scored with prickles and running blood. In the darkness, I reflected, all objects looked alike, as though by general conspiracy.

I straightened up and took a long breath, mopping the blood with my handkerchief. Then something tapped at my feet, and on looking down, there was the hat within easy reach, and I stooped down and put it on my head again. Of course, there were a dozen ways of explaining my confusion and stupidity, and I walked along wondering which to select. My eyesight, for one thing—and under such conditions why seek further? It was nothing, after all, and the dizziness was a momentary effect caused by the effort and stooping.

But for all that, I shouted aloud, on the chance that a wandering shepherd might hear me; and of course no answer came, for it was like calling in a padded room, and the mist suffocated my voice and killed its resonance.

It was really very discouraging: I was cold and wet and hungry; my legs and clothes torn by the gorse, my hands scratched and bleeding; the wind brought water to my eyes by its constant buffetings, and my skin was numb from contact with the chill mist. Fortunately I had matches, and after some difficulty, by crouching under a wall, I caught a swift glimpse of my watch, and saw that it was but little after eight o'clock. Supper I knew was at nine, and I was surely over half-way by this time. But here again was another instance of the way everything seemed in a conspiracy against me to appear otherwise than ordinary, for in the gleam of the match my watch-glass showed as the face of a little old grey man, uncommonly like the folk-lorist himself, peering up at me with an expression of whimsical laughter. My own reflection it could not possibly have been, for I am clean-shaven, and this face looked up at me through a running tangle of grey hair. Yet a second and a third match revealed only the white surface with the thin black hands moving across it.

II

And it was at this point, I well remember, that I reached what was for me the true heart of the adventure, the little fragment of real experience I learned from it and took back with me to my doctor's life in London, and that has remained with me ever since, and helped me to a new sympathetic insight into the intricacies of certain curious mental cases I had never before really understood.

For it was sufficiently obvious by now that a curious change had been going forward in me for some time, dating, so far as I could focus my thoughts sufficiently to analyse, from the moment of my speech with that hurrying man of shadow on the hillside. And the first deliberate manifestation of the change, now that I looked back, was surely the awakening in my prosaic being of the "poetic thrill"; my sudden amazing appreciation of the world around me as something alive. From that moment the change in me had worked ahead subtly, swiftly. Yet, so natural had been the beginning of it, that although it was a radically new departure for my temperament, I was hardly aware at first of what had actually come about; and it was only now, after so many encounters, that I was forced at length to acknowledge it.

It came the more forcibly too, because my very commonplace ideas of beauty had hitherto always been associated with sunshine and crude effects; yet here this new revelation leaped to me out of wind and mist and desolation on a lonely hillside, out of night, darkness, and discomfort. New values rushed upon me from all sides. Everything had changed, and the very simplicity with which the new values presented themselves proved to me how profound the change, the readjustment, had been. In such trivial things the evidence had come that I was not aware of it until repetition forced my attention: the veils rising from valley and hill; the mountain tops as personalities that shout or murmur in the darkness; the crying of the sea birds and of the living, purposeful wind; above all, the feeling that Nature about me was instinct with a life differing from my own in degree rather than in kind; everything, from the conspiracy of the gorse-bushes to the disappearing hat, showed that a fundamental attitude of mind in me had changed—and changed, too, without my knowledge or consent.

Moreover, at the same time the deep sadness of beauty had entered my heart like a stroke; for all this mystery and loveliness, I realised poignantly, was utterly independent and careless of *me*, as me; and that while I must pass, decay, grow old, these manifestations would remain for ever young and unalterably potent. And thus gradually had I become permeated with the recognition of a region hitherto unknown to me, and that I had always depreciated in others and especially, it now occurred to me, in my friend the old folk-lorist.

Here surely, I thought, was the beginning of conditions which, carried a little further, must become pathogenic. That the change was real and pregnant I had no doubt whatever. My consciousness was expanding, and I had caught it in the very act. I had of course read much concerning the changes of personality, swift, kaleidoscopic—had come across something of it in my practice—and had listened to the folk-lorist holding forth like a man inspired upon ways and means of reaching concealed regions of the human consciousness, and opening it to the knowledge of things called magical, so that one became free of a larger universe. But it was only now for the first time, on these bare hills, in touch with the wind and the rain, that I realised in how simple a fashion the frontiers of consciousness could shift this way and that, or with what touch of genuine awe the certainty might come that one stood on the borderland of new, untried, perhaps dangerous, experiences.

At any rate, it did now come to me that my consciousness had shifted its frontiers very considerably, and that whatever might happen must seem not abnormal, but quite simple and inevitable, and of course utterly true. This very simplicity, however, doing no violence to my being, brought with it none the less a sense of dread and discomfort; and my dim awareness that unknown possibilities were about me in the night puzzled and distressed me perhaps more than I cared to admit.

III

All this that takes so long to describe became apparent to me in a few seconds. What I had always despised ascended the throne.

But with the finding of Bassett's cottage as a sign-post close to home, my former *sang-froid*, my stupidity, would doubtless return, and my relief was therefore considerable when at length a faint gleam of light appeared through the mist, against which the square dark shadow of the chimney line pointed upwards. After all, I had not strayed so very far out of the way. Now I could definitely ascertain where I was wrong.

Quickening my pace, I scrambled over a broken stone wall, and almost ran across the open bit of grass to the door. One moment the black outline of the cottage was there in front of me, and the next, when I stood actually against it—there was nothing! I laughed to think how utterly I had been deceived. Yet not utterly, for as I groped back again over the wall, the cottage loomed up a little to the left, with its windows lighted and friendly, and I had only been mistaken in my angle of approach after all. Yet again, as I hurried to the door, the mist drove past and thickened a second time—and the cottage was not where I had seen it!

My confusion increased a lot after that. I scrambled about in all directions, rather foolishly hurried, and over countless stone walls it seemed, and completely dazed as to the true points of the compass. Then suddenly, just when a kind of despair came over me, the cottage stood there solidly before my eyes, and I found myself not two feet from the door. Was ever mist before so deceptive? And there, just behind it, I made out the row of pines like a dark wave breaking through the night. I sniffed the wet resinous odour with joy, and a genuine thrill ran through me as I saw the unmistakable yellow light of the windows. At last I was near home and my troubles would soon be over.

A cloud of birds rose with shrill cries off the roof and whirled into the darkness when I knocked with my stick on the door, and human voices, I was almost certain, mingled somewhere with them, though it was impossible to tell whether they were within the cottage, or outside. It all sounded confusedly with a rush of air like a little whirlwind, and I stood there rather alarmed at the clamour of my knocking. By way, too, of further proof that my imagination had awakened, the significance of that knocking at the door set something vibrating within me that most surely had never vibrated before, so that I suddenly realised with what atmosphere of mystical suggestion is the mere act of knocking surrounded—*knocking at a door*—both for him who knocks, wondering what shall be revealed on opening, and for him who stands within, waiting for the summons of the knocker. I only know that I hesitated a lot before making up my mind to knock a second time.

And, anyhow, what happened subsequently came in a sort of haze. Words and memory both fail me when I try to record it truthfully, so that even the faces are difficult to visualise again, the words almost impossible to hear.

Before I knew it the door was open, and before I could frame the words of my first brief question, I was within the threshold, and the door was shut behind me.

I had expected the little dark and narrow hall-way of a cottage, oppressive of air and odour, but instead I came straight into a room that was full of light and full of—people. And the air tasted like the air about a mountain top.

To the end I never saw what produced the light, nor understood how so many men and women found space to move comfortably to and fro and pass each other as they did within the confines of those four walls. An uncomfortable sense of having intruded upon some private gathering was, I think, my first emotion; though how the poverty-stricken countryside could have produced such an assemblage puzzled me beyond belief. And my second emotion—if there was any division at all in the wave of wonder that fairly drenched me—was feeling a sort of glory in the presence of such an atmosphere of splendid and vital *youth*. Everything vibrated, quivered, shook about me, and I almost felt myself as an aged and decrepit man by comparison.

I know my heart gave a great fiery leap as I saw them, for the faces that met me were fine, vigorous, and comely, while burning everywhere through their ripe maturity shone the ardours of youth and a kind of deathless enthusiasm. Old, yet eternally young they were, as rivers and mountains count their years by thousands, yet remain ever youthful; and the first effect of all those pairs of eyes lifted to meet my own was to send a whirlwind of unknown thrills about my heart and make me catch my breath with mingled terror and delight. A fear of death, and at the same time a sensation of touching something vast and eternal that could never die, surged through me.

A deep hush followed my entrance as all turned to look at me. They stood, men and women, grouped about a table, and something about them—not their size alone—conveyed the impression of being *gigantic,* giving me strangely novel realisations of freedom, power, and immense existences more or less than human.

I can only record my thoughts and impressions as they came to me and as I dimly now remember them. I had expected to see old Tom Bassett crouching half asleep over a peat fire, a dim lamp on the table beside him, and instead this assembly of tall and splendid men and women stood there to greet me, and stood in silence. It was little wonder that at first the ready question died upon my lips, and I almost forgot the words of my own language.

"I thought this was Tom Bassett's cottage!" I managed to ask at length, and looked straight at the man nearest me across the table. He had wild hair falling about his shoulders and a face of clear beauty. His eyes, too, like all the rest, seemed shrouded by something veil-like that reminded me of the shadowy man of whom I had first inquired the way. They were *shaded*—and for some reason I was glad that they were.

At the sound of my voice, unreal and thin, there was a general movement throughout the room, as though everyone changed places, passing each other like those shapes of fluid sort I had seen outside in the mist. But no answer came. It seemed to me that the mist even penetrated into the room about me and spread inwardly over my thoughts.

"Is this my way to the Manor House?" I asked again louder, fighting my inward confusion and weakness. "Can *no one* tell me?"

Then apparently everyone began to answer at once, or rather, not to answer directly, but to speak to each other in such a way that I could easily overhear. The voices of the men were deep, and of the women wonderfully musical, with a slow rhythm like that of the sea, or of the wind through the pine trees outside. But the unsatisfactory nature of what they said only helped to increase my sense of confusion and dismay.

"Yes," said one; "Tom Bassett *was* here for a while with the sheep, but his home was not here."

"He asks the way to a house when he does not even know the way to his own mind!" another voice said, sounding overhead it seemed.

"And could he recognise the signs if we told him?" came in the singing tones of a woman's voice close beside me.

And then, with a noise more like running water, or wind in the wings of birds, than anything else I could liken it to, came several voices together:

"And what sort of way does he seek? The splendid way, or merely the easy?"

"Or the short way of fools!"

"But he must have *some* credentials, or he never could have got as far as this," came from another.

A laugh ran round the room at this, though what there was to laugh at I could not imagine. It sounded like wind rushing about the hills. I got the impression, too, that the roof was somehow open to the sky, for their laughter had such a spacious quality in it, and the air was so cool and fresh, and moving about in currents and waves.

"It was I who showed him the way," cried a voice belonging to someone who was looking straight into my face over the table. "It was the safest way for him once he had got so far—"

I looked up and met his eye, and the sentence remained unfinished. It was the hurrying, shadowy man of the hillside. He had the same shifting outline as the others now, and the same veiled and shaded eyes, and as I looked the sense of terror stirred and grew in me. I had come in to ask for help, but now I was only anxious to be free of them all and out again in the rain and darkness on the moor. Thoughts of escape filled my brain, and I searched quickly for the door through which I had entered. But nowhere could I discover it again. The walls were bare; not even the windows were visible. And the room seemed to fill and empty of these figures as the waves of the sea fill and empty a cavern, crowding one upon another, yet never occupying more space, or less. So the coming and going of these men and women always evaded me.

And my terror became simply a terror that the veils of their eyes might lift, and that they would look at me with their clear, naked sight. I became horribly aware of their eyes. It was not that I felt them evil, but that I feared the new depths in me their merciless and terrible insight would stir into life. My consciousness had expanded quite enough for one night! I must escape at all costs and claim my own self again, however limited. I must have sanity, even if with limitations, but sanity at any price.

But meanwhile, though I tried hard to find my voice again, there came nothing but a thin piping sound that was like reeds whistling where winds meet about a corner. My throat was contracted, and I could only produce the smallest and most ridiculous of noises. The power of movement, too, was far less than when I first came in, and every moment it became more difficult to use my muscles, so that I stood there, stiff and awkward, face to face with this assemblage of shifting, wonderful people.

"And now," continued the voice of the man who had last spoken, "and now the safest way for him will be through the other door, where he shall see that which he may more easily understand."

With a great effort I regained the power of movement, while at the same time a burst of anger and a determination to be done with it all and to overcome my dreadful confusion drove me forward.

He saw me coming, of course, and the others indeed opened up and made a way for me, shifting to one side or the other whenever I came too near them, and never allowing me to touch them. But at last, when I was close in front of the man, ready both to speak and act, he was no longer there. I never saw the actual change—but instead of a man it was a woman! And when I turned with amazement, I saw that the other occupants, walking like figures in some ancient ceremony, were moving slowly towards the far end of the room. One by one, as they filed past, they raised their calm, passionless faces to mine, immensely vital, proud, austere, and then, without further word or gesture, they opened the door I had lost and disappeared through it one by one into the darkness of the night beyond. And as they went it seemed that the mist swallowed them up and a gust of wind caught them away, and the light also went with them, leaving me alone with the figure who had last spoken.

Moreover, it was just here that a most disquieting thought flashed through my brain with unreasoning conviction, shaking my personality, as it were, to the foundations: viz., that I had hitherto been spending my life in the pursuit of false knowledge, in the mere classifying and labelling of effects, the analysis of results, scientific so called; whereas it was the folk-lorist, and such like, who with their dreams and prayers were all the time on the path of real knowledge, the trail of causes; that the one was merely adding to the mechanical comfort and safety of the body, ultimately degrading the highest part of man, and never advancing the type, while the other—but then I had never yet believed in a soul—and now was no time to begin, terror or no terror. Clearly, my thoughts were wandering.

IV

It was at this moment the sound of the purring first reached me—deep, guttural purring—that made me think at once of some large concealed animal. It was precisely what I had heard many a time at the Zoological Gardens, and I had visions of cows chewing the cud, or horses munching hay in a stall outside the cottage. It was certainly an animal sound, and one of pleasure and contentment.

Semi-darkness filled the room. Only a very faint moonlight, struggling through the mist, came through the window, and I moved back instinctively towards the support of the wall against my back. Somewhere, through openings, came the sound of the night driving over the roof, and far above I had visions of those everlasting winds streaming by with clouds as large as continents on their wings. Something in me wanted to sing and shout, but something else in me at the same time was in a very vivid state of unreasoning terror. I felt immense, yet tiny; confident, yet timid; a part of huge, universal forces, yet an utterly small, personal, and very limited being.

In the corner of the room on my right stood the woman. Her face was hid by a mass of tumbling hair, that made me think of living grasses on a field in June. Thus her head was partially turned from me, and the moonlight, catching her outline, just revealed it against the wall like an impressionist picture. Strange hidden memories stirred in the depths of me, and for a moment I felt that I knew all about her. I stared about me quickly, nervously, trying to take in everything at once. Then the purring sound grew much louder and closer, and I forgot my notion that this woman was no stranger to me and that I knew her as well as I knew myself. That purring thing was in the room close beside me. Between us two, indeed, it was, for I now saw that her arm nearest to me was raised, and that she was pointing to the wall in front of us.

Following the direction of her hand, I saw that the wall was transparent, and that I could see through a portion of it into a small square space beyond, as though I was looking through gauze instead of bricks. This small inner space was lighted, and on stooping down I saw that it was a sort of cupboard or cell-like cage let into the wall. The thing that purred was there in the centre of it.

I looked closer. It was a being, apparently a *human* being, crouching down in its narrow cage, feeding. I saw the body stooping over a quantity of coarse-looking, piled-up substance that was evidently food. It was like a man huddled up. There it squatted, happy and contented, with the minimum of air, light, and space, dully satisfied with its prisoned cage behind the bars, utterly unconscious of the vast world about it, grunting with pleasure, purring like a great cat, scornfully ignorant of what might lie beyond. The cell, moreover, I saw was a perfect masterpiece of mechanical contrivance and inventive ingenuity—the very last word in comfort, safety, and scientific skill. I was in the act of trying to fix in my memory some of the details of its construction and arrangement, when I made a chance noise, and at once became too agitated to note carefully what I saw. For at the noise the creature turned, and I saw that it *was* a human being—a man. I was aware of a face close against my own as it pressed forward, but a face with embryonic features impossible to describe and utterly loathsome, with eyes, ears, nose, and skin, only just sufficiently alive and developed to transfer the minimum of gross sensation to the brain. The mouth, however, was large and thick-lipped, and the jaws were still moving in the act of slow mastication.

I shrank back, shuddering with mingled pity and disgust, and at the same moment the woman beside me called me softly *by my own name*. She had moved forward a little so that she stood quite close to me, full in the thin stream of moonlight that fell across the floor, and I was conscious of a swift transition from hell to heaven as my gaze passed from that embryonic visage to a countenance so refined, so majestic, so divinely sensitive in its strength, that it was like turning from the face of a devil to look upon the features of a goddess.

At the same instant I was aware that both beings—the creature and the woman—were moving rapidly towards me.

A pain like a sharp sword dived deep down into me and twisted horribly through my heart, for as I saw them coming I realised in one swift moment of terrible intuition that they had their life in me, that they were born of my own being, and were indeed *projections of myself*. They were portions of my own consciousness projected outwardly into objectivity, and their degree of reality was just as great as that of any other part of me.

With a dreadful swiftness they rushed towards me, and in a single second had merged themselves into my own being; and I understood in some marvellous manner beyond the possibility of doubt that they were symbolic of my own soul: the dull animal part of me that had hitherto acknowledged nothing beyond its cage of minute sensations, and the higher part, almost out of reach, and in touch with the stars, that for the first time had feebly awakened into life during my journey over the hill.

V

I forgot altogether how it was that I escaped, whether by the window or the door. I only know I found myself a moment later making great speed over the moor, followed by screaming birds and shouting wind, straight on the track downhill towards the Manor House. Something must have guided me, for I went with the instinct of an animal, having no uncertainties as to turnings, and saw the welcome lights of windows before I had covered another mile. And all the way I felt as though a great sluice gate had been opened to let a flood of new perceptions rush like a sea over my inner being, so that I was half ashamed and half delighted, partly angry, yet partly happy.

Servants met me at the door, several of them, and I was aware at once of an atmosphere of commotion in the house. I arrived breathless and hatless, wet to the skin, my hands scratched and my boots caked with mud.

"We made sure you were lost, sir," I heard the old butler say, and I heard my own reply, faintly, like the voice of someone else:

"I thought so too."

A minute later I found myself in the study, with the old folk-lorist standing opposite. In his hands he held the book I had brought down for him in my bag, ready addressed. There was a curious smile on his face.

"It never occurred to me that you would dare to *walk*—to-night of all nights," he was saying.

I stared without a word. I was bursting with the desire to tell him something of what had happened and try to be patient with his explanations, but when I sought for words and sentences my story seemed suddenly flat and pointless, and the details of my adventure began to evaporate and melt away, and seemed hard to remember.

"I had an exciting walk," I stammered, still a little breathless from running. "The weather was all right when I started from the station."

"The weather's all right still," he said, "though you may have found some evening mist on the top of the hills. But it's not that I meant."

"What then?"

"I meant," he said, still laughing quizzically, "that you were a very brave man to walk to-night over the enchanted hills, because this is May Day eve, and on May Day eve, you know, *They* have power over the minds of men, and can put glamour upon the imagination—"

"Who—*'they?'* What do you mean?"

He put my book down on the table beside him and looked quietly for a moment into my eyes, and as he did so the memory of my adventure began to revive in detail, and I thought quickly of the shadowy man who had shown me the way first. What could it have been in the face of the old folk-lorist that made me think of this man? A dozen things ran like flashes through my excited mind, and while I attempted to seize them I heard the old man's voice continue. He seemed to be talking to himself as much as to me.

"The elemental beings you have always scoffed at, of course; they who operate ceaselessly behind the screen of appearances, and who fashion and mould the moods of the mind. And an extremist like you—for extremes are always dangerously weak—is their legitimate prey."

"Pshaw!" I interrupted him, knowing that my manner betrayed me hopelessly, and that he had guessed much. "Any man may have subjective experiences, I suppose—"

Then I broke off suddenly. The change in his face made me start; it had taken on for the moment so exactly the look of the man on the hillside. The eyes gazing so steadily into mine had shadows in them, I thought.

"Glamour!" he was saying, "all glamour! One of them must have come very close to you, or perhaps touched you." Then he asked sharply, "Did you meet anyone? Did you speak with anyone?"

"I came by Tom Bassett's cottage," I said. "I didn't feel quite sure of my way and I went in and asked."

"All glamour," he repeated to himself, and then aloud to me, "And as for Bassett's cottage, it was burnt down three years ago, and nothing stands there now but broken, roofless walls—"

He stopped because I had seized him by the arm. In the shadows of the lamp-lit room behind him I thought I caught sight of dim forms moving past the book-shelves. But when my eye tried to focus them they faded and slipped away again into ceiling and walls. The details of the hill-top cottage, however, started into life again at the sight, and I seized my friend's arm to tell him. But instantly, when I tried, it all faded away again as though it had been a dream, and I could recall nothing intelligible to repeat to him.

He looked at me and laughed.

"They always obliterate the memory afterwards," he said gently, "so that little remains beyond a mood, or an emotion, to show how profoundly deep their touch has been. Though sometimes part of the change remains and becomes permanent—as I hope in your case it may."

Then, before I had time to answer, to swear, or to remonstrate, he stepped briskly past me and closed the door into the hall, and then drew me aside farther into the room. The change that I could not understand was still working in his face and eyes.

"If you have courage enough left to come with me," he said, speaking very seriously, "we will go out again and see more. Up till midnight, you know, there is still the opportunity, and with me perhaps you won't feel so—so—"

It was impossible somehow to refuse; everything combined to make me go. We had a little food and then went out into the hall, and he clapped a wide-awake on his grey hairs. I took a cloak and seized a walking-stick from the stand. I really hardly knew what I was doing. The new world I had awakened to seemed still a-quiver about me.

As we passed out on to the gravel drive the light from the hall windows fell upon his face, and I saw that the change I had been so long observing was nearing its completeness, for there breathed about him that keen, wonderful atmosphere of eternal youth I had felt upon the inmates of the cottage. He seemed to have gone back forty years; a veil was gathering over his eyes; and I could have sworn that somehow his stature had increased, and that he moved beside me with a vigour and power I had never seen in him before.

And as we began to climb the hill together in silence I saw that the stars were clear overhead and there was no mist, that the trees stood motionless without wind, and that beyond us on the summit of the hills there were lights dancing to and fro, appearing and disappearing like the reflection of stars in water.

A COLLECTOR'S COMPANY

THE story which follows was told to me rather more than thirty years ago. The narrator was elderly then. He died very soon after the end of the last war with Germany, so there can be no harm in repeating it now. His name, if you want to know, was Arthur Harberton. As he was a young man when it happened to him I suppose it must be dated not long after the year 1870. I made notes of it at the time, and reproduce it now as nearly as I can in his own words.

Three years after my ordination I was offered a post as a college lecturer at Cambridge. That was the kind of work which I had always thought that I should like, at any rate for a few years, so I accepted the offer very gladly. I have never regretted that I did so; nor that I did not devote the rest of my life to academic work.

I was not dean of the college, and as in those days the number of Fellows in Holy Orders was much larger than it is now it was very seldom necessary for me to be in the Chapel on a Sunday. Accordingly I used to go about the diocese a good deal, visiting the country churches. I don't think that I was under any illusion as to my powers as a preacher, even then. But I thought, without, I hope, undue vanity, that it might be good for village congregations to hear a fresh voice occasionally, and even for the incumbent if he were present. That was not always the case, for I was always willing to take the whole duty of the day if I were asked, so that the incumbent might secure a short holiday.

As a rule I enjoyed these expeditions thoroughly. They began with a short train journey, followed by a drive from the station, sometimes of as much as ten miles. Country lanes were country lanes then. They had not been blackened with tar macadam and motor-cars were, of course, unknown. An occasional traction engine, preceded by a man on foot carrying a red flag, was the only disagreeable object likely to be encountered. From a dog-cart, which was usually the vehicle which came to meet me, it was possible to see over the hedges and to get a very fair idea of the country as you went along at eight to ten miles an hour.

My hosts were generally interesting. For the most part they were country-bred men who belonged naturally to their surroundings. Many of them had a wide variety of interests (and sometimes a store of real knowledge) on which they were ready to discourse to a stranger. When I had the house to myself it was amusing to try to deduce what manner of man the owner might be from his books and pictures.

Most of the churches and a good many of the houses presented features of architectural interest, which appealed to me strongly. Besides, I used to enjoy such conversations as I might have with rural churchwardens, sextons and other parish officials. I remember one churchwarden (a farmer, I think) who had heard that Huntingdon was a fine town. Personally he had never penetrated farther than St. Neots. When I told him that I lived at Cambridge I might as well have said Peking, or Timbuctoo.

In another place the village schoolmaster was opposed to elementary education in the abstract: not merely to the particular form of it which he was required to administer. He thought it unsettled children and took them off the land. There was, no doubt, something to be said on behalf of his views; but I couldn't help wondering whether he was *quite* the right man in the right place. Well—no doubt the countryside is more sophisticated now, and I won't bore you with speculations as to whether the gains outweigh the losses or not.

So, as you see, I had good reason to look forward to these excursions. In fact, I only once got to a place which I should not care to visit again, and that is the one which I am going to tell you about now. All the same, I don't entirely regret that I did go there. Anyhow, it was a unique experience.

Towards the end of one October term I got a letter from the bishop's chaplain, asking me if I could preach twice on the following Sunday at a village about twenty-five miles from Cambridge—I don't think I will tell you in what direction. The incumbent, it appeared, was not very well, and, having no curate, was doubtful of his ability to get through the day single-handed. As it would be the second Sunday in Advent it would not be difficult for me to preach at short notice. The collect and epistle for the day provided me with a subject ready-made: a subject, moreover, which I have always found particularly congenial.

I discovered that there was a convenient train to the nearest station on the Saturday afternoon, and from it on the Monday morning; so I telegraphed Yes, and wrote to my prospective host to say when I might be expected.

It was a little after three when I got out at a wayside station. I was met by a groom with a dog-cart who brought a note from his master apologising for not having come in person. As I had understood that he wasn't well I hadn't expected him. I will call him Melrose.

As we drove away from the station I said to the groom, "I hope Mr. Melrose has nothing serious the matter with him?"

"No," he replied, "but he *du* come over all queer-like at times—so he du. When he have one of his turns—well, it's not for me to be explaining of it, if you take my meaning, Sir."

I was not at all sure that I did, but thought it would be ill-bred on my part to ask for details. Also I was inclined to suspect that they might be copious rather than enlightening. However, as my companion seemed inclined to talk I did not feel bound to try to suppress him.

I gathered that Mr. Melrose was wealthy and a bachelor. He had "travelled furren", which was regarded locally as a hazardous proceeding, on the ground that all foreigners are well known to be black, and that "they blackamoors" might be up to anything. He was much "took up" with reading: also in my companion's opinion a dubious proceeding. For if there was good in some books there was bad in others, and "how'd you know which till arterwards", and then it was done.

The general impression left on my mind was that while Mr. Melrose might be loved by his parishioners he was certainly feared. I thought that I might look forward to an unusually interesting weekend. As it turned out, this expectation was not unduly sanguine, as I think you will agree when you have heard the rest of my story.

After a drive of about seven miles we arrived. The light was failing, but I could see that the house was an old one. It was rather larger than the average, and I judged that there was probably a considerable garden behind it. I looked forward to examining both more closely between services on Sunday.

Mr. Melrose made me very welcome. He was a tall man who stooped a little. I set him down as about seventy; probably over rather than under. He had abundant white hair and very prominent white eyebrows. His eyes were dark and his nose aquiline. The general effect was scholarly and striking. He would have been noticeable in any company, and, once seen, would always be remembered. My first impression was that he was very handsome.

Here Mr. Harberton paused for a minute or two and then said rather abruptly, "Did you ever see Thompson, the Master of Trinity?"

"No," I said. "He was some years before my time. But I know the portrait; by Richmond, I think."

"No, of course you didn't," he went on. "Stupid of me. But one forgets how time passes. I don't think the portrait really does him justice. However, if you know it you'll understand what I am going to say.

"I knew him very well by sight and he was one of the most distinguished-looking men I have ever seen. He was handsome if you like, and you couldn't doubt his ability or force of character. You had only to look at him to see that he was a great man. Yet somehow I never could think his face a pleasing one. It always seemed to me to contain great possibilities of evil. I could believe him to be capable of absolutely diabolical conduct."

"Well," I said, "I believe that when Richmond painted Lightfoot he declared that he had never had a sitter whose jaw was so obviously and unmistakably that of a murderer. And I have been told by people who knew the Bishop well that they could believe that he had a naturally violent temper, and that his complete mastery of it was part of his greatness. The same may have been true of Thompson."

"Yes," said Mr. Harberton, "it may. Anyhow, this was the effect which Mr. Melrose produced on me. However, I tried to dismiss it from my mind as foolishness."

After tea, which we had in a square hall by a log fire, Mr. Melrose asked me to excuse him until dinner-time as he had some letters to write and the post went out at six-thirty. He had a small study on the first floor opening out of his bedroom to which he proposed to betake himself. The library, which was on the ground floor and opened out of the hall, was at my disposal and there were writing materials there if I wanted them.

The library was a large room, completely lined with bookcases. A cursory inspection of these showed that my host was a man of wide and miscellaneous reading. He seemed to be particularly interested in the later Neoplatonists and to be well supplied with Orphic literature. On a glass-topped table by the window was a collection of Gnostic gems. An Egyptian mummy-case stood upright in a corner. On a table by the fire was a book which he had presumably been reading when I arrived. I picked it up and found that it was Philostratus' *Life of Apollonius of Tyana*. It had been interleaved and was copiously annotated. I should have liked to read some of the notes, but thought that would be impertinent.

Evidently I was in the house of a scholar whose interests were out of the common run, and the possessor of means which enabled him to indulge them freely.

At dinner he proved very good company. He had travelled widely and had visited places which were then very much off the beaten track, such as Sicily and Transylvania. He had spent some considerable time in the latter country and had made a careful study of its grim folk-lore.

The dinner was good, and my host exerted himself to be pleasant. Interesting he undoubtedly was, but I was not at all sure how much I liked him. I had a vague feeling that in some way he was playing a part. But I could find no rational ground for my suspicion. And, after all, why should he think it worth while to try to impress anyone so much younger than himself?

It struck me as curious that a man of his calibre should be content to bury himself in so obscure a place. Of course the country was much more prosperous then than it is now and rural life offered more interests than I fear it does to-day. But this particular neighbourhood was not specially attractive in any way. Most of the land had belonged to the see of Ely and was now administered by the Ecclesiastical Commissioners. I believe that they are always considered to be good landlords, but naturally there are seldom any country-houses other than farms on their estates. I could hardly see my host at ease in the society of farmers, nor could I imagine that they would be able to make much of him. (I had discovered that he did not shoot or hunt, and in those days a man who did neither was very much out of it in the country.)

When he told me that he had been rector of the parish for more than thirty years I could not help expressing surprise—rather clumsily, I fear, and perhaps not too politely, but I was very young then—and saying something about the solitariness of the life which he led.

"Yes," he said; "I don't wonder that it strikes you like that. The road from the station is rather desolate. But I have plenty of occupation and interests here; and do you know, I find some of my neighbours more companionable than you would expect."

The last sentence struck me as rather odd, not only in itself but in the way he said it. I felt that there was more behind the remark than I was meant to understand, and did not like the feeling. I liked the laugh which followed it even less. However, there was obviously no more to be said about that. Perhaps he thought I had been rather impertinent, and perhaps he was right.

After dinner we went into the library for coffee, and somehow our talk drifted to witchcraft, necromancy and kindred topics. I had always taken an interest in such matters, if not a very serious one, and have often wondered what foundation, if any, there is or was for the belief that the powers to which witches lay claim have any real existence.

At this distance of time I do not mind admitting that as an undergraduate I had once made an essay in Invultuation. The object was the Vice-Chancellor of the day, whom I did not know by sight. He had annoyed me by refusing to allow a play which I had written to be acted publicly by the A.D.C., on the ground that it was disrespectful to authority. I adopted the only method of retaliation which seemed to be open. I made a waxen image and placed it on my mantelpiece. After some incantations which I thought appropriate (*Flectere si nequeo superos Acheronta movebo** is the only line which I remember now) I inserted a pin into one leg. The very next day I heard that the Vice-Chancellor had slipped going downstairs in his lodge and had sprained one of his ankles. I felt that my cause had been vindicated and took no further steps. But, as you will understand, I had not been serious in the matter. I never pretended to think that the accident had been more than a coincidence for which I need not reproach myself. The story leaked out somehow, and one comment on it which came to my ears was "Whole religions have been founded upon less evidence". I will not name the author, but I still think he ought to have known better.

Mr. Melrose's discourse seemed to me to be a very different story. I could not help thinking that he knew more than he ought about a great deal which was very undesirable. And he spoke with an air of inside knowledge which I found disquieting. His tone was that of a lecturer on a subject which he had really made his own, and he gave the impression of having verified at least some of his knowledge by experiment. I felt that there was something malign about him, as well as creepy.

Finally, I came to the conclusion that he was like an evil caricature of Dr. Hans Emmanuel Bryerley, the Swedenborgian teacher in *Uncle Silas.** Altogether I was extremely glad when he suggested a move bedwards, and was at pains to lock the door of my room. Perhaps that would not avail much if it came to the point. But the illusion of security it produced was comforting.

I do not know how long I had been asleep when I awoke with the impression which one sometimes has of having been disturbed by a loud and sudden noise. Probably the church clock, I thought, though I had not noticed its strike earlier in the evening. I was just disposing myself for a renewed period of slumber when it struck me that although my fire had burned low the room was curiously light; not with firelight either. I had drawn back the window curtains before going to bed, as I usually did, and the light was coming from the window.

* Aeneid, vii, 12.
* By J. Sheridan Le Fanu.

"Moonlight," you will say. But I knew that it was not. In the first place, the moon was several days short of full, and in the second, the light was not coming from a particular point. It was evenly diffused, like daylight on a cloudy day; and no moon could have produced so much light from behind clouds. It seemed to me to have a bluish tinge which was unnatural and unpleasant. I went to the window and looked out. It commanded a view of a good-sized lawn flanked by dark shrubberies of some sort—rhododendrons, I found out subsequently.

This lawn sloped slightly upwards away from the house, and at the farther end was a low wall with a gateway in it leading to the churchyard. This and the church itself were as plainly visible as if it had been midday instead of just after midnight in December. But everything to right and left was in darkness. I felt as if I were looking down an illuminated tunnel, and it seemed obvious that something would appear at the upper end. I took my courage in both hands and waited. I did not have to wait long. Through the gate in the churchyard wall came my host. He seemed to be wearing a cassock with a long black cloak over it. On his head was a high-pointed cap, something like a mitre, and he carried a short rod in his right hand. He came straight down the lawn towards the house. I wondered whether I was as visible to him as he was to me; and hoped not. Anyhow I felt bound to see the performance through. He was followed by a number of figures: I think about twelve, but I could not be sure.

Although there seemed to be plenty of light they were somehow curiously indistinct. They may have dodged behind each other from time to time in some odd fashion. Anyhow I found that it was no use to try to count them. They were dressed in long black cloaks with hoods, which prevented their faces from being seen. On the whole I felt glad of that. They moved rather stiffly, like marionettes. Of course their feet made no sound upon the grass. But I was conscious of a faint creaking, the source of which was not easy to determine. It might have been produced by the breeze in the shrubbery; but I did not think that it was.

The procession advanced until it had reached the middle of the lawn. Then the leader stopped and the others formed a circle round him. Still I could not be sure how many they were. Every time I tried to count them I became confused and arrived at a different result.

Then they began to dance while he beat time or conducted, however you like to put it, with his wand. They moved more quickly than I should have expected, though they still suggested marionettes. The faint creaking which I had heard before was more audible.

There could be no doubt now that it came from the dancing figures.

Do you remember a story told by one of the minor characters in Stevenson's *Catriona*? About Tod Lapraik, the warlock weaver of Leith. He used to fall into a dwam* in his house and once, while he was in that state, he, or something in his likeness, was seen dancing alone on the Bass Rock "in the black glory of his heart". Those words rose in my mind now. The performance which I was watching seemed to be inspired by an unholy—well, *joie de vivre*, I suppose I must call it, though I don't know how far the dancers could be considered to be alive. The whole effect was abominably, indescribably evil. Yet, curiously enough, I did not feel afraid. I have never considered myself a particularly courageous person, and have not had many opportunities of discovering whether I am or not. But anyhow I was not conscious of any fear then. Partly, perhaps, I was too deeply interested in what I was watching to think of anything else. Also, youth and a good digestion will carry their possessor securely through many of the changes and chances of this mortal life.

The dance grew faster, and the ring of dancers contracted. As it did so, the mysterious light contracted too. I could no longer see the church, or the greater part of the lawn. Only the tall stationary figure with his black-shrouded companions whirling—it had come to that now—whirling round him. The group was illuminated as a particular figure sometimes is upon the stage (spotlight, I think they call it), but, as before, the light did not seem to be coming from any particular direction. Perhaps this was why I could see no shadow upon the grass.

In another minute the dancers seemed to have closed in, and then (as was perhaps to be expected) the light went out. I could neither see nor hear anything. The garden seemed to be as dark and deserted as you might expect between midnight and 1 a.m. on a moonless night in December. As I turned away from the window I heard the discordant cry of a night-jar (at least, that was what I thought it sounded like) very loud and apparently very close to my window. Immediately afterwards I heard a low chuckle. It was not a pleasant one. I felt pretty sure that whatever the joke might be I should prefer not to meet the author of it. I made certain that my door was locked, made up my fire to last until daylight, got into bed, and rather to my surprise fell asleep almost immediately.

It was getting light when I woke. I got out of bed and unlocked my door. As I waited to be called I naturally thought of my experience of a few hours earlier. The more I considered it the less

* A swoon or sudden sickness (Scot.).

confident did I become that I had not dreamed the whole thing. I have always been an active and vivid dreamer, but have never had a vision of my head upon my bed worth taking seriously; even by the most nasty-minded psycho-analyst who ever came out of Vienna or anywhere else.

At eight o'clock the butler brought me tea and hot water. On the tray was a note from Mr. Melrose, saying that he regretted that he was unable to leave his room. The clerk would show me where everything was in the church. Would I make myself at home in the house and ask for anything I wanted, etc.

"Is your master seriously ill?" I asked the man. "Ought a doctor to be sent for, or can you look after him?"

"No, Sir, not serious. But he don't come down as a rule, after one of his nights, not for a day or two."

For a moment I thought he was going to say more, but he turned away and began laying out my clothes. So I said something to the effect that old people often slept badly and that no doubt a wakeful night was very exhausting.

To this he merely replied, "Yes, Sir," and left the room.

While I was drinking my tea I thought I would look at the lessons for the day, as I should probably have to read them myself. There was a Bible beside my bed and I opened it at *Isaiah* (the first lesson was Chapter 5, as you probably remember), and it so happened that the first words which caught my eye were from Chapter 8, verse 19—

Seek unto them that have familiar spirits
and unto the wizards that peep and that mutter.

No doubt a coincidence. But as I dressed I became more and more inclined to think that I had not been dreaming.

The day passed uneventfully. Evensong was at three, as was not unusual in the country then, during the winter months; I must confess that I was glad of this as I did not relish the prospect of coming down the lawn from the church in the dark. Of course it was getting dark by the time service was over, and as I went through the gate leading from the churchyard I had an uncomfortable feeling that my movements were being watched by some person or persons whom I could not see—and not with any amiable solicitude for my welfare.

However, nothing untoward happened then or during the evening. I went to bed early and slept soundly all night. Next morning the butler brought another note from my host, expressing his regret that he would be unable to see me before I left, the disappointment which he felt at having had so little of my society, and a hope that I had been made comfortable.

I replied to the first two heads of this communication as politely as was consistent with the truth. As regards the third I could reassure him honestly. I left the house soon after breakfast. The butler had not seemed disposed to be communicative, nor was the groom who drove me to the station. Three days later I went down for the Christmas vacation.

Mr. Harberton was silent for a minute or two, so I asked—I must admit with a feeling of disappointment—"Is that all?"

"Not quite," he replied. "But for the conclusion of the story you had better read this."

He handed me a cutting from a newspaper, probably a local weekly, which he took from a large old-fashioned pocket-book. I had seen the book before, as it was his practice to carry it with him. The cutting was from the bottom of a column, so no date was visible. I judged it to be about thirty years old. It ran as follows:

RECTOR'S STRANGE DEATH

A PAINFUL sensation was produced at (the name of the place was carefully erased) on Christmas morning.

As soon as it was light the sexton, Mr. Jonas Day, had gone to the church to make up the fire in the stove. As he approached the south door he was horrified to observe the body of the rector lying face downwards on a flight of four steps leading from the churchyard to the rectory garden. He went at once to the house and summoned the butler, Mr. Thomas Blogg, and the groom, Mr. Henry Meekin. They carried the reverend gentleman to his room, but it was all too evident that the vital spark had ceased to pulsate. Dr. Horridge was sent for and arrived a little before ten o'clock. He reported that the neck of the deceased was broken, and that death must have intervened some hours before.

It may be presumed that the unfortunate gentleman had gone to the church at a late hour to satisfy himself that everything was in order for the morrow. The steps were slippery with frost and he did not appear to have taken a lantern.

The Rev. (name erased) had held the rectory for thirty-two years, and the sad occurrence cast a deep aroma of gloom over the festivities naturally incidental to the day.

The inquest was held at the *Fox and Grapes* on the 30th ult., Dr. Horridge presiding as Coroner. Mr. Blogg deposed that his master not infrequently went to the church late at night. When asked by one of the Jury if he knew for what purpose, he replied that he had never demeaned himself to curiosity in his master's business. He was warmly commended by the Coroner for his reply.

Mr. Day deposed that when he approached the body he saw some curious marks on the back of the coat. When pressed to describe them he said "Like muddy claws". Neither Mr. Blogg nor Mr. Meekin had noticed these. The coat was sent for, but it had been brushed. The Coroner thought that they might easily have been made by an owl or some other bird of the night perching upon the body after life was extinct, and by his direction the Jury returned a verdict of *Death by Misadventure*.

The funereal obsequies were celebrated on the 2nd instant.

"May I take a copy of this?" I asked.

"Yes, if you like," said Mr. Harberton. And I did.

THE LATE MRS. FOWKE

THE Reverend Barnabas Fowke, though he live to reach a century, will never forget the death-bed of his wife. Most widowers can probably say the same thing; though few, it may be hoped, have similar cause to recollect it.

Mr. Fowke, at the time of the event referred to, was a man of middle age, and the incumbent of G., a small agricultural town on the edge of one of our Northern moors. He was a hard-working, honest parson, of no great strength of character and of no particular ability, nor had he had any special experience with the more subtle side of life. He had been educated at a good second class public school and a small Oxford College, whence he had gone in due course to take up a curacy in one of our lesser manufacturing towns.

After serving some years in this capacity, he had been promoted, on the death of the Vicar, to take charge of the living, in which position he had remained till a few weeks before his marriage to Stella Farnleigh, at whose instigation he had exchanged his town living at R. for the country one at G., which he still occupied at the time of this story. The reverend gentleman's history is thus commonplace and uninteresting, as, I fear, are the histories of many of our clergy, which it resembled save that, unlike most of his cloth, he had remained unmarried till he fell a victim at the age of forty to the charms of Miss Stella Farnleigh.

This lady requires a closer study. She was the only child of a certain Mr. Farnleigh, who for many years was a merchant of, and acted as, British Consul in Z., a town in Hungary, where by hard work and close attention to business he amassed a fair-sized fortune. Somewhat late in life he had met a beautiful and attractive woman, whose nationality even was uncertain, but who boasted of a considerable admixture of gipsy blood in her veins. Exactly who she was or where she came from is at this distance of time impossible to ascertain. At the time she met Mr. Farnleigh she was giving music lessons, by which she gained a small pittance, and her marriage to the well-to-do English merchant may well be considered a very fortunate event for her.

However, her married life did not last long, for Mr. Farnleigh died very suddenly within six months of the wedding day, leaving his widow his sole executrix and legatee. It is not known whether Mrs. Farnleigh had any relatives; if she had, she never kept up any connection with them, and after her husband's death she acquired a small and lonely estate on the banks of the River Theiss and removed there to dwell in complete retirement. Here in due course Stella was born, and here the child lived with her mother until about the age of twenty-five, when Mrs. Farnleigh died, leaving her fortune entirely to the girl.

The latter at first appeared to be inclined to remain on in her old home, but it would seem as if neither she nor her mother had been popular in the district, and apparently some pretty strong hints were conveyed to the young lady that she had best betake herself elsewhere. Mr. Fowke knew nothing of all this at the time he married Stella, and for reasons which will transpire he did not care to make any investigations into the matter later on. Therefore the history of mother and daughter in Hungary and the reasons why the latter left that country are buried in an obscurity which will never be lightened. Whatever they may have been, Stella no doubt felt that it would be difficult for her to settle down by herself in any new country, and she accordingly put herself into communication with the only relative she knew herself possessed of, a Miss Farnleigh, the elderly sister of her father, with a view to taking up her abode with her as a paying-guest.

The elder Miss Farnleigh was a poor woman, living in solitude at R. She was a worthy soul, narrow-minded, unintelligent, devoted to clergymen and church work; in fact, an absolute type of thousands of middle-aged, middle-class English spinsters. The proposal of her niece, whom she had never seen and with whom she had but rarely corresponded, was a welcome one, as the young lady would certainly provide some much needed cash for the household, and would probably, as she fondly believed, provide a pleasant companion for herself also. Besides, she was sorry for the orphaned girl, and altogether it was with pleasure she made the preliminary arrangements and welcomed the arrival of the traveller.

However, these high hopes were doomed to disappointment. Stella and her aunt quickly found that they were uncongenial in nearly every respect. Miss Farnleigh I have described, and when I say that Stella was a young woman of considerable though rather peculiar literary accomplishments, and that she had a strong will which she frequently exercised in the pursuit of some highly unconventional purpose, I think it will be clear why the two ladies did not agree together. Stella had brought with her from Hungary a considerable library of foreign books, none of which her aunt could understand, but which actually dealt largely with occult subjects, and she also brought with her a habit of going away alone every few weeks for a night on the moors not far from R., a custom which she said she found necessary for her health and happiness. To these occasional expeditions Miss Farnleigh at first took great exception, but after a stormy scene with her niece the elder lady felt herself worsted and, as she had ceased to take any affectionate interest in the younger woman, she also ceased to care greatly as to what she did or thought. Stella, therefore, went on her own way undisturbed but conscious of perpetual criticism, and no doubt was eager to escape from an atmosphere so uncongenial to her. At the same time she realised the conventions that bound her and that her best hope for the future lay in marrying some man, weaker than herself, whom she could bend to her will. This, no doubt, actuated her in encouraging the somewhat timid suit of Mr. Fowke, and in astonishing as well as delighting that gentleman when she accepted his rather diffident offer of marriage.

The young lady showed herself of an obliging disposition in the arrangements made prior to the wedding, her only stipulation being that Mr. Fowke should change his present living for one nearer the moors. In accordance with this Mr. Fowke negotiated an exchange with the Vicar of G., and after a short honeymoon took possession of his new cure. Here he settled down to what he anticipated would prove a peaceful and happy life. He was devoted to his new wife, and she, while less demonstratively happy, appeared to be contented both with her husband and her new surroundings.

The first flaw in their married life showed itself a few months after their arrival at G., when one day, Mr. Fowke, having occasion to speak to his wife, went upstairs to the room which she had selected as her private sitting-room and in which she had installed her voluminous library. On reaching it he heard from within a sound of low chanting in a language that he did not understand, and at the same time became aware of a singular smell as of the burning of some aromatic herb. He tried the door and, finding it locked, called to his wife. The chanting ceased immediately and his wife's voice told him to wait a few minutes and she would admit him. On the door being opened he found the room filled with the pungent smell emanating from some herbs, which were burning in a small brazier set upon the table.

"Whatever are you doing, my dear?" he asked.

Stella replied that she was suffering from a severe headache, which she was trying to cure by inhaling the smoke; it was a Hungarian remedy, she added, but she did not explain the singing. Mr. Fowke remained somewhat puzzled, and his astonishment was considerably increased when a little later his wife informed him that she intended to go to I.—a tiny hamlet far up on the fells—that afternoon and would spend the night there, returning the following day. It was the first time that Mr. Fowke had heard of Stella's solitary visits to the moorland and he not unnaturally sought an explanation of them, which his wife refused to give in any greater detail than the mere statement that she had for long been accustomed to make these periodical trips into solitude. He asked to be allowed to accompany her, but she positively refused to permit this, and it was with a heavy and worried heart that he watched her leave the house later in the day.

The following afternoon she returned, tired and with muddy clothes, but seemingly exhilarated by her expedition. She refused all information about it, save that during these trips she was in the habit of staying at the *Three Magpies*, a small inn at I., and making thence expeditions on the higher fells. With this slender explanation Mr. Fowke had to be satisfied.

A few weeks passed, when again one day Mr. Fowke detected the odour of burning herbs and again learnt that his wife was on the point of starting for I. She again declined his proferred company and left the house as before.

Mr. Fowke had never been to I., which is a remote hamlet, not distant as far as mileage is concerned from G., but only approachable by a branch line of railway with an infrequent service of trains. He was, however, acquainted with its Vicar, to whom he presently wrote to inquire as to the standing of the *Three Magpies*, since he was not overpleased that his wife, a foreigner ignorant of our ways, should elect to stay alone at an absolutely unknown inn. The reply he received was not at all reassuring, for the Vicar of I. wrote that the *Three Magpies* was a public house of poor repute, kept by an old couple of more than doubtful respectability.

This letter decided Mr. Fowke and, when for the third time his wife announced her intention of proceeding to I. and for the third time refused his company, he determined to follow her there secretly and observe her movements and surroundings. It was not difficult for him to arrange to do this, since he could easily reach I. on his motor-cycle long before her slow train could land her there, even if he did not start until after she had left the parsonage. He carried out his programme and in due course reached I. and made his way to the *Three Magpies*. Here he found that the old man was very nearly bedridden and quite senile, whilst his wife regarded her clerical visitor with almost open hostility. However, the gift of a sovereign and the promise of another effected a great change and unlocked the old woman's tongue, so that she poured forth volubly all she knew.

Yes, she knew the lady quite well. She had been in the habit of coming to I. once every few weeks for a long time. No; she always came alone and had never spoken to anyone except herself, to her knowledge.

"What does she do?"

"Oh, she always goes straight up to her room and shuts herself in, then she sings to herself something I cannot make out and burns something that smells sweet and strong. Then about dark like, sometimes sooner, sometimes later, she comes down and goes out towards the Fells."

"Have you ever followed her?"

"No, never, nor anybody else as I know of. A shepherd once saw her walking all alone in a wild part of the moor but he did not follow her or speak to her."

"How long is she out?"

"Well, that depends, but generally till near morning. She takes the key of the house with her and lets herself in, but I hear her come in once in a while."

"What does she do then?"

"Why, goes up to her room and stays there quietly and has breakfast and then goes to the train."

This was about all that Mr. Fowke could find out, except the curious detail that his wife never wore a hat on her nocturnal rambles, but went draped in a hooded grey cloak.

By the time this catechism was finished it was nearly time for Mrs. Fowke to arrive, and the Reverend Barnabas accordingly ensconced himself in a room into which he was ushered by the old woman, which commanded the front door of the inn. In a short time he saw his wife arrive. After exchanging a few words with the old woman she went upstairs, and husband and wife remained in their respective seclusions till dusk fell.

Then Mr. Fowke heard Stella descending the stairs and in a few moments he saw her emerge from the house clad, as described, in a long hooded grey cloak, and walking swiftly and resolutely. Giving her a short start, he followed, and as he left the inn the well-known smell of burning, aromatic herbs was in his nostrils. His wife was by now a few hundred yards away and had nearly cleared the little hamlet, heading for the open moor. As she proceeded a singular episode occurred. Mr. Fowke thought little of it at the time, but much, later.

A sheep-dog was lying asleep by the roadside, and as Mrs. Fowke drew near it suddenly started up and, with back upraised and tail depressed, uttered a melancholy howl and darted through the hedge.

Mrs. Fowke paid not the least attention to the dog, but pursued her way steadily through the rapidly falling dusk. Her husband followed as steadily, and thus for a long time they wound their way upwards towards the loneliest and wildest part of the fells. It was by now night, but the moon had risen and flooded the landscape with her rays. The couple, one about two hundred yards behind the other, were now mounting the side of a steep hill, and hitherto Mr. Fowke had remained in the pleasant belief that his presence was unsuspected by his wife. He was to be undeceived. The lady passed round a corner of the hill, thereby disappearing from sight; Mr. Fowke hastened after her and on passing the corner in his turn found himself confronted by his wife, who stood watching for his appearance with a sarcastic smile. She greeted him:

"Well, Mr. Spy, are you very much puzzled?"

He remained silent, dumb with astonishment and chagrin, and she went on:

"I have been wondering what to do with you ever since you left home, but I have decided at last. You shall see all there is to see; I don't think you can do any harm and you may be useful by and by. Follow me." And she turned and went on again.

Mr. Fowke followed silently and abashed. Presently he became aware of a rosy light shining in front of them, and after walking a few yards more he found himself standing by the side of his wife on the edge of a small, cup-shaped hollow in the hills. In the centre of this hollow a large fire was burning and near the fire Mr. Fowke could make out a pile of stones, shaped like a rough altar. A group of about half a dozen people, all clad in the same grey, hooded cloaks, were sitting silently near the fire; and towards these his wife now began to descend, first telling him in a low, imperious voice to stay where he was. As Stella advanced down the declivity the group by the fire became aware of her approach and, rising, moved to meet her with gestures of greeting and respect. Stella passed through them, haughtily returning their salutations and, slowly ascending the stone altar, seated herself on a rock near its summit. As soon as she had taken up her position, she gave a signal, and the others forming round the fire commenced a slow and stately dance to the accompaniment of their own low chanting.

Mr. Fowke watched absorbed. Gradually the dance grew quicker and wilder and the chanting louder, the whirling forms flung themselves into grotesque attitudes and shrieked ejaculations, the meaning of which Mr. Fowke began dimly to divine, though the words were strange. Suddenly they were silent and still and at the same moment Stella rose from her seat and, throwing back her hood and turning towards the summit of the altar, began in her turn to take up the chant. As she sang and bowed towards the topmost stone, her face and figure seemed transformed. In the flickering firelight and pale moonshine she seemed to grow weirdly and horribly beautiful and to grow statelier and taller in her person. Slowly, too, as the song progressed, the horrified watcher saw another change. A grey cloud formed on the summit of the altar, diminishing, thickening and turning into a Shape, a Shape of evil and fear. The silent group by the fire once more broke forth into wild gesticulations and cries, Stella prostrated herself, the Form on the altar grew clearer, and with a cry of horror Mr. Fowke turned away and rushed madly across the moor.

He never knew where he went or what he did. When he once more recovered his senses it was broad day and he was alone and lost on the moors. It was late afternoon before, broken and exhausted, he reached his own home, where the first person to greet him was his wife, cool and collected as ever. She led him into his study.

"Well," she said, "and what are you going to do now? Are you going to go about telling a cock-and-bull story of the moors, or are you going to be a good little man and hold your tongue? Don't imagine I care," she went on, "the Great One can protect his servants and destroy his enemies."

Mr. Fowke groaned.

"It was true then," he said, "not a horrid dream."

"You had better call it that," she answered with a laugh and left him.

Mr. Fowke was utterly perplexed and, like many men of weak character, could decide on nothing. So matters drifted on: he had little or no communication with his wife, who was, however, invariably civil and pleasant when they met, with a kind of mocking courtesy which maddened him. At last came the day when she announced her intention of again going to I.

"And perhaps you would like to go with me," she said. "*You* will be ready for the grey robe soon."

She went, and he spent the night in an agony of prayer.

The next day Stella returned and came immediately to his study. This time, however, she had no look of exhilaration on her face; she was troubled and angry.

"How dare you interfere with us," she began, "with your paltry little prayers and tears? You disturbed us last night. The Great One was angry—" She stopped and then went on, "I shall have to find a means of silencing you; it was a mistake to show you what I did."

He looked at her.

"So it is not too late, is it?" he said. "I can perhaps save you and drag you away from—"

She interrupted him.

"Silence," she cried violently, "or I will take steps to quiet you; I will blast you; I will call upon the Powers of the Air. I will—" she was going on madly in her excitement when suddenly she became rigid, her face blanched and she fell senseless to the floor in a fit.

Mr. Fowke raised the prostrate body, laid it on a sofa and summoned help. The unfortunate woman was carried to her bedroom, still unconscious, and the doctor sent for. He was an ordinary country practitioner and the case seemed to be clearly beyond his powers to deal with, but he emphasised the need of a trained nurse; and, one being fortunately available in the village, she was presently duly installed at the Parsonage.

After having seen all done that was possible, Mr. Fowke, utterly worn out, retired to rest. Towards midnight he was awakened by a knocking at his door and, opening it, found the nurse pale and trembling on the threshold. She instantly assured him that she must throw up the case and leave the house at once. She could, or would, give no clear reasons for her action, but repeated again and again that she would sacrifice her whole professional career rather than remain in that sick room. Things had happened there, she said, things she could not tell of, but the place was accursed. In vain Mr. Fowke tried to reassure her; she would not remain and so, bidding her go to her room till morning without disturbing the household, Mr. Fowke went to his wife's room to take up the vigil himself.

When he entered the sick room all was still. Stella was lying motionless, breathing gently and at intervals murmuring a few words in her native tongue. Mr. Fowke settled himself down in an armchair and gradually fell into a doze.

He woke suddenly as the clock struck three and glanced around him. The lamp had burnt low and the room was very cold. His wife still lay quietly in her bed, muttering softly to herself, but as Mr. Fowke watched her, by the dim light, he fancied he noticed a horrible change in her. Gone were the full rounded outlines of a woman's form; the figure on the bed had become angular and misshaped. Her hand and arm, which lay outside the coverlet were also changed and looked like a claw. Her face, too, was changing. As he watched, her beauty faded, the features altered, they ran together, became distorted, misplaced, and, with a shudder, he found himself gazing on the lineaments of an unknown, hideous beast. Paralysed with horror, he could not stir.

All at once there was a movement. The figure on the bed shivered violently, lifted itself up and sat gazing out beyond the foot of the bed. Mr. Fowke followed the direction of its eyes and saw, growing up slowly at the end of the room, a grey shapeless form, of which the burning eyes alone were distinct.

The creature on the bed moved and, slipping back the bedclothes, stepped suddenly to the floor. Mr. Fowke saw that the lower limbs and, in fact, every part of it save the face that he could see were covered with a thick, grey fur. It moved again and passed swiftly across the room towards the grim shape in the corner; he heard its hoofs tap on the bare floor as it passed. It reached the motionless watcher, whose eyes seemed to blaze as it approached, and with a swift movement the two forms met, intermingled and—Mr. Fowke could bear no more; he fainted.

It was daylight when he regained his senses. He glanced towards the bed; Mrs. Fowke lay there, calm, beautiful—and dead.

THE HILL

It was one of those hard, precise evenings when, before sunset, everything seems to become flat: the fields that lay just in front of me were cut out of cardboard, the long road down to Broad Oak appeared to stretch, not to the country, but to a backcloth; and the trees that overarched the lane to Symondsbury were untouched by any breeze that might give them the illusion of reality. For, when the country takes the decorative note, it is reality which is the illusion: one almost imperceptibly flattens oneself along the hedgerows in order to avoid breaking the perfect truth of the theatre which Nature contrives so much more skilfully than man.

I was tired and walked a little listlessly. I had business to do in Bridport; but I knew I should be there long before seven, and I enjoyed sauntering down the road, while the decadent sun of early April made green tinsel out of the budding larches, while soft little puddles of brown glowed from the ruts and hoof-marks in the sandy soil. I was feeling well in a genially tired way, and quite ready for the walk home again; feeling, however, singularly un-sharp. I mean that my senses, after the exertions of the week, were rather sleep-haunted—I had caught Nature's lesson, and felt all this activity of limb and thought to be the substance of nothing but a rather beautiful dream. My mind was as casual as my walk, and was occupied, so far as I remember, with nothing more arresting than some vaguely pleasant remembrance of a youthful affection.

I dwell on all this because I want to insist that I was not in an observant mood, not at all in the state to make the adventure I had likely. Those to whom I have told this story have all insisted that my "imagination" or "fancy" has made more of the facts than they warrant; that I was deceived by shadows, or misled by reflections; that my eyes were tired and played me tricks, that my memory is false and ill suited to exact accuracy. So I would insist that such imagination as I have was almost quiescent, that my mind was singularly unalert, and that nothing can explain the extreme vividness of my recollection of that night of April 3rd, except the truth of what I saw. Its very incongruity, not only with my mental condition, but with the actual character of the evening, with the verdant artificiality of that

Dorset springtime, when the countryside is rather less actual than the contours on an ordnance map, is a witness to the reality of that experience.

I had indeed forgotten the Hill. I generally used to look out for the first sight of it, when the road begins to run under the shoulder of the wooded height, and to skirt the Hill of Sacrifice. I don't know who gave it that name: whether, indeed, it is more than a modern device of some local journalist; but it suits the Hill. Everyone who passes along the main road from Chideock to Bridport must see it; but its most characteristic aspect is only caught from the road between North Chideock and Symondsbury. It is a curious, conical hill, covered with green grass and generally delivered over to innumerable sheep. It reminds one instantly of those high places on which the ancient Hebrews honoured other gods than Jehovah, the places where Solomon built temples for the family godlings of his heathen queens. Everyone felt this about the Hill, so it does not show any preoccupation of mine that I, too, always connected it with sacrifice, and the stone, square altars of the old faiths. I had never been up the Hill. I never met anyone who had. It was out of the way, and would be, though an easy, an unnecessary little climb for one whom Fleet Street had left without the wind of his youth. The sheep which grazed there belonged to a farm in the valley, and found their own way up and down.

Well, as I said, on that night I had forgotten the Hill; and when I caught my first glimpse of it, I had a shock. I thought at first the shock was due to the vision of a familiar but forgotten object. I think when one, so to speak, re-sees a perfectly familiar object, it has a more active and energising effect on the nerves than contact with something entirely new. Certainly the Hill made me jump. I stood and stared at it. As I stared I realised that the shock I had received was not entirely due to the Hill's re-assertion of its presence to my forgetful mind.

The Hill was different.

I glanced hastily back along the road, and over to my left where the fields stretched idly away; they were the same as they had been a minute ago, comfortable, artificial, flat, with no more atmosphere than a landscape in a modern painting. Then I swerved back to the Hill. It was ominous, alive, clamant with some mystery that I had not guessed. I should explain that though it was the Hill of Sacrifice, no one had associated it with anything mysterious or unusual. It was obviously the servant of some settled, rather courtly, religion, where the priests of the second-century Roman, journeying from Dorchester, had made polite augury at dawn. This evening, all that was changed. The Hill threatened. It quarrelled vehemently with the rest of the landscape. It stood like something or somebody naked and hairy in the middle of a crowd of modish and courtly figures; it was like some primitive, pre-Gothic idol in a French classical temple; or as if you sundered a picture of Watteau's with one of those brown, watchful Tahitians of Gauguin's.

I stood and stared at the Hill. And as I stared I became aware of two things. First, there were no sheep on the Hill. Their absence aided the strange, nude look of the thing. And I began to think that perhaps, after all, the change in the Hill was my fancy. Then, as I looked, the Hill lurched: that, of course, is an exaggeration; but it was the effect made on me by the movement of something that was almost up on the round crown at the top. With that movement the power of the Hill became active: suddenly and as by antagonism, I, too, leapt into mental alertness. The Hill and I were there, enemies, but akin in this, that we were the players in the set scene; still the green fields spread away to the backcloth; still the road ran as a stage road runs to the wings; still the sun, though now faintlier, flickered on green and brown, and turned them to paper and canvas —but now there were two lives on the stage, and the play was begun.

Before starting for the Hill—it is noteworthy that no other course but that of immediate access to my antagonist ever seemed possible —I looked at it once more, for I knew when I had scrambled through the hedge and across the first field, I should lose sight, for a while, of the top: I looked at the spot where the Hill had shuddered, and I saw that it was a figure, apparently human, and heavily burdened, which was now on the top and against the blue-black clouds which the sun was even now burning into angry gold. I was now much too far away—I have always suffered from short-sightedness—to make out clearly whether it was man or woman, or what it was that the figure carried; nor indeed did I greatly care, but I got through the hedge and started as quickly as I could for the summit of the Hill.

In the second field it was darker; and I felt that the atmosphere was a trifle oppressive; and there was a heavy, hot smell in the air, like musk. Of course, by now my imagination was at work; but I was not consciously inventing any explanation of what I saw or felt. I was simply bringing to bear on facts that were obtrusive all I had of perception and sensitiveness. I had not even then definitely decided whether what was evil or not. I knew it was an enemy—but it was inimical, at present, only in the sense of demanding effort and conflict. I could not proclaim that it was evil. As I climbed towards the lower slopes of the Hill, still hidden from view by a thick hedge, I was not conscious of any definite aim. I knew where I had to go; but

I had no idea of what I should find, or what I should do. Just before I reached the final hedge something happened which removed all doubt as to the nature of that which I had to fight. Abruptly, and beginning on one long piercing note, a strange music clove the surrounding silence. After the first shrill rending of the evening's solitary quiet, the music went on with a wicked and luxuriant abandon that recalled to me all that I knew of the vague power of harmony for evil. It was not vulgarly lascivious or alluring; it had in it that higher note of defiance, that keener note of pride and power and of certain, though dishonourable, rule which distinguishes the realm of the devil from that of the world and the flesh. It had in it that perverse ascetic note, that strain of rapture and endeavour and adventure which the sons of Satan achieve no less than the sons of Christ. It gave out no single note of compromise or concession: it was music of the airless heights, of the wilderness, of the great wastes of sand, or the interminable vastness of evil waters where the greater devils meditate and morosely scheme.

When I heard it, all doubt dropped from me. There dropped, too, everything of the present. I knew the music: I knew, somehow, the player; and I knew his instrument. And as I went up the Hill I knew what task lay before me, and with Whom I was to wrestle. I felt no fear and no confidence. No fear as to the terror or extent of the conflict, and no confidence as to the result. The whole incident, though still to come, seemed a part of my life, not something that I could do, or could not do, so much as something without which I would not be I.

When I was through the hedge the sun was set, but it was still quite light, and I hoped it would not be dark for almost another hour. I looked up to the top of the Hill, and there was the figure I had seen, kneeling and piling stones on one another. He—for it was a young lad—was half turned towards me; but he was stooping over his work, and evidently had no idea of my approach. The music, which was getting louder every moment, seemed to come from the top of the Hill; but I could see no signs of the player: nor, indeed, had expected to.

I looked carefully to my stick, and wished it had been of some stouter wood than cherry; and then started rapidly up the Hill. As I went on the music altered in character: from defiance it passed to menace, and from menace to a curious thin anger that somehow seemed intended for other ears than mine. It was. The lad looked up, puzzled, and I saw him distinctly say something towards the sound of the music. Then he saw me, recognised me, I think, and started down the Hill. The music stopped.

I went on, and after a few minutes the lad and I met. We were both a little out of breath, and stood for a moment at gaze. He was a singularly beautiful boy, with one of those faces in which it is so hard to discover the lines which will afterwards coarsen and harden. He was about seventeen, and I remember that I had seen him working on some job between Allington and Eype. At the moment his beauty was almost unearthly: it had no intellectual qualities, and little of character, but just that even bloom which marks young animals. There was in his eyes, however, a look far from animal—a look of exultation, of absorption, and combined with it a hardness that showed me my task would not be easy. What he said was in curious contrast with his appearance, and in even odder discordance with what was in our hearts, and in the heart of the Hill, and in the heart of that old musician who this night, at least, was claiming the worship of his ancient altar.

"You be trespassing, Mr. O'Brien."

"I suppose I am," I answered. "It's so jolly to be in a country where trespassing doesn't do any harm. It's why I like Dorset, and these great grazing fields."

He looked at me as the country folk do when they don't quite catch what you say, and yet don't want to confess to it.

"No one be allowed up here. I must ask you to go down again, Sir."

His tone was very polite; but his eyes were set, and I saw his fingers twitching, and noticed the tremor of his shirt above his scurrying heart.

"Nonsense," I said. "I'm going to the top. Good night to you," and I started to get past him, rather hurriedly and with little dignity, I am afraid.

With a sharp cry he stepped in front of me. Before he could say anything more, I spoke again, as sharply as I could—for I would have given anything just then to avoid the fight, and for the lad to go home— "What on earth are you doing, boy? You know perfectly well Mr. Goodere doesn't mind where I go on his land. Besides, you have no business here: you are not in his employ, and I don't know that he would allow you here. Get out of my way."

For the moment my tone of ordinary annoyance staggered him. He became—for a minute—an ordinary good-looking lad who, through clumsiness, had offended "one of the gentry", and made a fool of himself. I kept hold on myself and waited to see him go away, apologetic and abashed. If this was the fight, I had feared unnecessarily. He began to turn on his heel, muttering some excuse, and I went on upwards, when suddenly the music began again, insistent, defiant, challenging. In a second he rushed round; and with hot, hurried words, clung to my arm, impeding my way— "I was not to go—he was meeting his girl—he wouldn't let me—he would break me if I did—he would—" lies, and appeals, and foul threats followed each other as swift as sin; his face once more took on that strange look of unearthly beauty, of curious exultation, as he asked me not to go up the Hill.

And the music played faster and faster.

After a struggle that lasted, I suppose, but for a few minutes, I broke away from him and ran towards the summit. All pretence was now thrown aside. The lad knew that I was aware of his purpose: knew that I knew Who his companion would be, and what that awful music meant, as it broke the evening quiet of the spring fields with a challenge older and more hideous than any voice of cities or of civilisation.

I got to the top of the Hill, with the lad close on my heels: and when I was at the top I realised suddenly that it was night. Not, I think, that the ordinary world was yet dark, but a mist, acrid and pungent, hung over the top of the Hill, and seemed to settle on the rude altar which the boy had built.

I could not see him, but I heard his breathing close on my right. I thought I would try one last chance to avoid the conflict—for now fear had entered my very marrow. "Come down," I said, trying to make my voice as self-possessed as possible, and as ordinary. "Come down and I'll go too."

There was no answer but his quick breathing; and then, on a note of the music, he began to sing. When he sang there was little trace of Dorset in his speech, and his voice was a beautiful treble, that of a boy whose voice is going to break later than usual. What he sang I cannot put down here. It soared up in unimaginable wickedness, clear and pure as crystal, full of thoughts and words that we believe to have forsaken our world. The music adapted itself to his song and grew subtly and insolently wicked. The psalm of Satan rose up, invitatory, clarion, ascending to heights of sin that I did not know had ever been expressed in human words. The air grew hotter, and the mist glowed with a strange blurred light. The keen, acrid smell grew more intense, and the music shrieked more and more riotously, as though preluding some monstrous apocalypse.

Then, with no warning, there was silence.

I could hear nothing, not even my own breathing; and I could see nothing but the blurred glow that was, I judged, just over the altar. Then I heard a sound. It was a voice, but of an accent not human, and the words it spoke were not English. I remember how, even then, it struck me as odd that one should hear a voice in a Dorset field speaking in tones that belonged neither to the place nor to the age I lived in. It sounded very low, very sure, and very old; old not with any quavering, but with that sacerdotal certainty of age-long experience which people who are very old, or of a great tradition, so frequently possess. Yet any certainty I had caught in human voices seemed but a shadow beside the deep, awful solemnity of this utterance. The voice was magical, ecstatic, assured with an eternal assurance. I strained my ears to listen during the few seconds while the voice continued, but I could distinguish nothing except what I thought possibly was the syllable "Pai", and I wondered if the sentence was in Greek.

My senses by now were singularly acute: I had passed through fear into that strong, wine-glowing condition when one watches everything securely, oneself being external even to the dangers that are threatening one's body or soul. In this state, and in the boldness engendered by it, I took one step towards the glow that still shone over the altar. Long before I could approach, however, I was smitten —or rather not so much smitten as involved in a thick, palpable, and hideous atmosphere. Never have I been so submerged by anything external. The sensation was partly like that caused by a quicksand, which will wrestle with one's leg or arm as though the sand were endowed with life, and when one pulls out the endangered limb, it is as if one sprung out of some being's lively jaws. So with an automatic movement of repulsion, I leapt back and was released. Then the light glowed more brightly and I saw my companion. He was standing stark naked, with his arms outstretched like an Orante's on a Catacomb fresco. His lips were still moving, and his gaze fixed intently on the glow above the rude stones he had piled up. Every moment the glow increased; I was only just over three yards from the altar, but the glow gave no heat, neither was there any smoke. Then as the light grew, in the centre of it there appeared a figure, and yet not so much a figure as a face, nor so much a face as a presence. It had the same beauty, that intolerable and sinful beauty which the boy had; or rather it seemed to *be* that beauty. It was, however, never still, but passed with incredible rapidity from the expression of one sensation to that of another; it had that most singular quality which can occasionally be seen on earthly faces, a complete lack of unity—there was no central and availing character in which the details might inhere, and it was this lack which gave the Presence its extraordinary sense of wrongness, of wickedness, of sin. It is a vulgar comparison, but the mode of its loveliness, the mode of its very expression, reminded me of nothing so much as a cinematograph, that dreadful invention in which the mimicry of Life treads breathlessly and continuously on the heels of Life itself, and yet never attains it. The same absolute lack of peace, of joy, of truth, shone at me from the glow on the Hill of Symondsbury.

As I was looking, feeling numbed and rather sick from my effort to penetrate that infernal barrier which surrounded the altar, the boy stooped down and picked up something which had escaped my notice. When he stood up again I saw it was a spaniel which from the droop of its head was either drugged or dead—I guessed the former. Round its neck was a cord, and at the end of the cord a knife, whose blade glanced in the strange glow, gleaming uneasily in the shadow of the night. Carrying the spaniel the boy stepped forward. I waited anxiously. He, when he was within the circle of the light, not only appeared to feel no discomfort, but looked lighter, more at ease, supremely healthy. If it had not been for the look on his face, and the careless way he carried the dog, one would have judged him walking towards some celestial, instead of an infernal, revelation. As he approached the altar the Presence over it retreated, or rather ascended, and hovered, ominous, giving a sort of benison to what was going to be done.

For the strangest thing about that strange evening was not, perhaps, the events so much as my unhesitating acceptance of them. As I said, I was in no expectant mood when I first saw that movement on the Hill; yet I never doubted that what I saw on the Hill was an altar, never even questioned myself as to what the boy's purpose was, nor Whom it was he was going to worship; nor did he, in spite of the assumed ordinariness of our conversation, ever doubt that I was come to prevent his rites, if and how I could. Why this was I leave to others; I have only to record the facts.

As he stepped up to the altar, I felt once more that I must take some action, I knew not what. It seemed useless to approach any nearer to the circle of the sacrifice, and it was evident I could do nothing with the boy except by force; and he had on his side powers greater than I had on mine.... But, had he? Ashamed, I remembered my faith. Since this ghastly business had begun I had uttered no conscious prayer, taken no steps to set in motion that vast spiritual machinery which is on the side of beauty and holiness. I made quick, in my foolish flurry, to remedy my mistake. Hurriedly I scampered through an "our Father" and "Hail Mary", and, making the Sign of the Cross, walked towards the altar. Once more I was sucked in—though this time with greater force—and it needed considerable effort, as well as natural revulsion, to pull myself out of the circle; and then I fell back on the clean, dark grass, trembling with futile excitement.

As I stumbled out, the Presence laughed, and the boy echoed it. Anything more horrible in its perfection, and more cruel in its note of absolute and casual conquest I never expect to hear. I felt not only beaten and baffled, but silly and childish; I felt as though some huge force had been not so much victorious, as possessive, over me. The boy knew, it seemed, that I could offer no resistance, let alone any active interference. Maddened by the laughter, I dashed once more towards the altar, and again was first absorbed and then, by the strong reaction of my body, flung out of the ring, weak and helpless. As I was thus beaten for a third time, the music began again.

This time it had lost its note of gay sinfulness, and was more ceremonial and evocative; but it still kept its undertone of essential vice; the grey of its formal progress was still marked by passages of scarlet and phrases of deep black. With the beginning of the music the boy stooped, laid the dog on the altar, untied the knife, and swiftly cut some string that bound its legs together. As he did so, either because the effect of the drug had passed off or because he touched the poor animal with the knife, the dog gave a little moan. I cannot hope to convey the effect on me of the dog's cry. Quite suddenly I felt that what I had to do was to save the dog. That possibly I should have to struggle with the boy, and to fight that Presence which still hung over the altar and glowed in the darkness of the night; but that everything else was incidental to saving the dog.

The boy had now begun a new hymn, and this time he, too, used a language which was not English. Once more I stepped forward, and as I moved the dog shrieked loudly, horribly. I rushed forward, and in a moment was involved in the atmosphere of terror and power. This time, however, instead of fighting against it, I tried to ignore it, and simply kept in mind the fact that I must save the dog. I caught the boy's arm just as the knife was about to come down behind the animal's shoulder, and with a quick jerk twisted his wrist, so that the knife flew out of his hand. With a snarl of fury he turned on me—still ignoring him, I caught at the dog and rushed towards the darkness. Then something caught me: the glow buzzed like a million bees, the face of the Thing became altogether blurred with the rapidity of its changes, and loomed once more imminent and horrible. Hands that were not hands plucked at the spaniel, feet that were not feet tried to trip mine; whatever I caught changed and swelled and shrunk and changed until I found myself again and again digging my fingers into my own palms, or clutching in foiled futility at the thick, obscene air. The smell was now rank and poisonous, and though there was no heat I felt the sweat running down my brow. The boy had fallen, apparently in a fit, but still clung tightly to my ankles; and as I pushed and heaved and struggled through the light, I dragged his body with me. At first, as I say, the Thing which was there had seemed to attack me; but after a moment this stopped, and, instead of any active attack, I had to contend with what felt like a crushing, inchoate and slime-covered mass. I was near the end of my resources, and there was still more than a yard and a half of that atrocious glow to get through. As I fought on, the dog in my arms moved, gave a little bark and snapped furiously at the air. Strangely enough, the effort of the animal gave me extra strength. I burst out of the clutch that was holding me, and, the dog still barking excitedly, fell exhausted but outside the light. As I fell, my head struck something cold and sharp, and I fainted away.

I woke in the morning to find a small spaniel anxiously licking my hand.

I sat up, and saw some farm-hands approaching with a hurdle. I feebly waved my hand, and noticed that it was covered with blood. My head ached intolerably, and I put up my hand to it and found my hair was caked with dried blood. Then on the ground I saw a knife, with blood on the blade. The men came up. "Are you better, Mr. O'Brien?" "Yes, I'm all right," and I tried to struggle to my feet, but my head swam and I had to sit down again, rather ignominiously, on the ground.

"I shan't need that hurdle, I don't think—but thanks very much. How on earth did I—" then I recollected what my last conscious experience had been, and I could still smell that acrid stench.

"How did 'ee get here? Why, we don't know. Farmer Goodere's spaniel bitch brought us up here. She were in a terr'ble to-do. Don't 'ee remember ought?"

I did: but nothing I could tell these men. I muttered something about having fallen against a stone; and they looked puzzled.

I got up again, and found I could stand.

Yes; there was the altar, or rather its ruins, for the stones had fallen. I began to walk along with the men, when I noticed some pebbles arranged rather curiously round the altar. I looked more closely at them—and spelled out in Greek letters the words *ΠΑΝ*, *ΠΡΙΑΠΟΣ*, *ΑΠΟΛΛΩ;* and then I knew under what titles the boy had come to sacrifice to Evil, and with Whom I had fought that night. I stooped and caressed the dog, who was frisking at my side in extravagant pleasure.

" 'Ee must have have a pup of hers, Mr. O'Brien—she won't be long now," said one of the men.

That afternoon there was a caller—or rather two—at my cottage. My little maid came and told me that Mrs. Toogood would like to see me, and a woman entered whom I knew well by sight. She was evidently in great distress. When she was a little calmer she told me how her boy—who had just begun work as a railway porter—had been rather odd lately, humming to himself, and looking, as she expressed it, "all overish". This morning she had gone to wake him, and found him looking dead white; no effort of hers could rouse him from a slumber that seemed deeper than natural. She made up her mind to send some excuse to the station, and ran round for the doctor. When he came the boy was awake. "He seemed, Mr. O'Brien, to be a child again. He just put his arms round me and kissed me—which he hasn't done for three weeks—but he can't speak."

"Can't speak," I echoed.

"Not a word," she sobbed. "The doctor says he's had a shock." Here she broke down again and wept.

I sat wondering. "I suppose, Mrs. Toogood, you don't know whether he was out last night?"

"Out? No, sir. I still go up and see him after he's in bed—and he was in at half past nine. He was very curious, though, and didn't say a word to me, though I knew he was awake."

"Ah! But earlier in the evening—about sunset?"

"No, sir. He was home to supper, though he didn't eat a bit and wouldn't speak a word. But it's this morning, sir. Though he's so kind and nice and happy, he has such odd ideas. He got a slate and wrote on it, 'I belong to Mr. O'Brien'—"

"What," I said—"I belong—!"

"Yes, sir; that's what I'm telling you. And the doctor said we mustn't excite him, though he doesn't get annoyed like he used; and so I've brought him up here. I thought you might help me, sir."

"Where is he?"

"Outside, sir." She rose eagerly. "May I have him in?"

"Yes," I answered.

In a minute she was back with her son. There was no doubt about it. It was the same boy. He was not less beautiful than I had thought; but this morning there was nothing sinister or evil about his beauty. He saw me and then, with a grace very rare in an English boy, knelt and kissed my hand. I hastily drew it away, and asked him—

"What do you want?"

With a smile that was quite jolly and boylike, he darted into a corner, where there was a pair of old boots of mine, and went through the motions of polishing them. Then looked, first at me, then at his mother, with an air of plaintive request.

Well, after some discussion that lasted longer than it needed, the boy became my servant. He was perfectly sane, though more child-like than most country boys. He has never recovered his voice, but is so quick that one hardly realises his dumbness. I can give no explanation of how he was on the Hill of Sacrifice at the same time that he was at home eating his supper; but would suggest that there is more than modern incredulity will admit in those old stories of the Sabbath when demons assumed the places of men and women who were temporarily absent from their homes, entangled in the lures of the Devil.

Farmer Goodere had to give me, not a puppy, but Jessie herself: for she ran to my cottage that evening, and has lived with me ever since.

THE HAUNTER OF THE DARK

I have seen the dark universe yawning
  Where the black planets roll without aim—
Where they roll in their horror unheeded,
  Without knowledge or lustre or name.
—NEMESIS

CAUTIOUS investigators will hesitate to challenge the common belief that Robert Blake was killed by lightning, or by some profound nervous shock derived from an electrical discharge. It is true that the window he faced was unbroken, but nature has shown herself capable of many freakish performances. The expression on his face may easily have arisen from some obscure muscular source unrelated to anything he saw, while the entries in his diary are clearly the result of a fantastic imagination aroused by certain local superstitions and by certain old matters he had uncovered. As for the anomalous conditions at the deserted church of Federal Hill—the shrewd analyst is not slow in attributing them to some charlatanry, conscious or unconscious, with at least some of which Blake was secretly connected.

For after all, the victim was a writer and painter wholly devoted to the field of myth, dream, terror, and superstition, and avid in his quest for scenes and effects of a bizarre, spectral sort. His earlier stay in the city—a visit to a strange old man as deeply given to occult and forbidden lore as he—had ended amidst death and flame, and it must have been some morbid instinct which drew him back from his home in Milwaukee. He may have known of the old stories despite his statements to the contrary in the diary, and his death may have nipped in the bud some stupendous hoax destined to have a literary reflection.

Among those, however, who have examined and correlated all this evidence, there remain several who cling to less rational and commonplace theories. They are inclined to take much of Blake's diary at its face value, and point significantly to certain facts such as the undoubted genuineness of the old church record, the verified existence of the disliked and unorthodox Starry Wisdom sect prior to 1877, the recorded disappearance of an inquisitive reporter named

Edwin M. Lillibridge in 1893, and—above all—the look of monstrous, transfiguring fear on the face of the young writer when he died. It was one of these believers who, moved to fanatical extremes, threw into the bay the curiously angled stone and its strangely adorned metal box found in the old church steeple—the black windowless steeple, and not the tower where Blake's diary said those things originally were. Though widely censured both officially and unofficially, this man—a reputable physician with a taste for odd folklore—averred that he had rid the earth of something too dangerous to rest upon it.

Between these two schools of opinion the reader must judge for himself. The papers have given the tangible details from a sceptical angle, leaving for others the drawing of the picture as Robert Blake saw it—or thought he saw it—or pretended to see it. Now studying the diary closely, dispassionately, and at leisure, let us summarise the dark chain of events from the expressed point of view of their chief actor.

Young Blake returned to Providence in the winter of 1934–5, taking the upper floor of a venerable dwelling in a grassy court off College Street—on the crest of the great eastward hill near the Brown University campus and behind the marble John Hay Library. It was a cosy and fascinating place, in a little garden oasis of village-like antiquity where huge, friendly cats sunned themselves atop a convenient shed. The square Georgian house had a monitor roof, classic doorway with fan carving, small-paned windows, and all the other earmarks of early nineteenth century workmanship. Inside were six-panelled doors, wide floor-boards, a curving colonial staircase, white Adam-period mantles, and a rear set of rooms three steps below the general level.

Blake's study, a large south west chamber, overlooked the front garden on one side, while its west windows—before one of which he had his desk—faced off from the brow of the hill and commanded a splendid view of the lower town's outspread roofs and of the mystical sunsets that flamed behind them. On the far horizon were the open countryside's purple slopes. Against these, some two miles away, rose the spectral hump of Federal Hill, bristling with huddled roofs and steeples whose remote outlines wavered mysteriously, taking fantastic forms as the smoke of the city swirled up and enmeshed them. Blake had a curious sense that he was looking upon some unknown, ethereal world which might or might not vanish in dream if ever he tried to seek it out and enter it in person.

Having sent home for most of his books, Blake bought some antique furniture suitable to his quarters and settled down to write and paint—living alone, and attending to the simple housework himself. His studio was in a north attic room, where the panes of the monitor roof furnished admirable lighting. During that first winter he produced five of his best-known short stories—*The Burrower Beneath, The Stairs in the Crypt, Shaggai, In the Vale of Pnath,* and *The Feaster from the Stars*—and painted seven canvases; studies of nameless, un-human monsters, and profoundly alien, non-terrestrial landscapes.

At sunset he would often sit at his desk and gaze dreamily off at the outspread west—the dark towers of Memorial Hall just below, the Georgian court-house belfry, the lofty pinnacles of the downtown section, and that shimmering, spire-crowned mound in the distance whose unknown streets and labyrinthine gables so potently provoked his fancy. From his few local acquaintances he learned that the far-off slope was a vast Italian quarter, though most of the houses were remnant of older Yankee and Irish days. Now and then he would train his field-glasses on that spectral, unreachable world beyond the curling smoke; picking out individual roofs and chimneys and steeples, and speculating upon the bizarre and curious mysteries they might house. Even with optical aid Federal Hill seemed somehow alien, half fabulous, and linked to the unreal, intangible marvels of Blake's own tales and pictures. The feeling would persist long after the hill had faded into the violet, lamp-starred twilight, and the court-house floodlights and the red Industrial Trust beacon had blazed up to make the night grotesque.

Of all the distant objects on Federal Hill, a certain huge, dark church most fascinated Blake. It stood out with especial distinctness at certain hours of the day, and at sunset the great tower and tapering steeple loomed blackly against the flaming sky. It seemed to rest on especially high ground; for the grimy façade, and the obliquely seen north side with sloping roof and the tops of great painted windows, rose boldly above the tangle of surrounding ridgepoles and chimney-pots. Peculiarly grim and austere, it appeared to be built of stone, stained and weathered with the smoke and storms of a century and more. The style, so far as the glass could show, was that earliest experimental form of Gothic revival which preceded the stately Upjohn period and held over some of the outlines and proportions of the Georgian age. Perhaps it was reared around 1810 or 1815.

As months passed, Blake watched the far-off, forbidding structure with an oddly mounting interest. Since the vast windows were never lighted, he knew that it must be vacant. The longer he watched, the more his imagination worked, till at length he began to fancy curious things. He believed that a vague, singular aura of desolation hovered over the place, so that even the pigeons and swallows shunned its smoky eaves. Around other towers and belfries his glass would reveal great flocks of birds, but here they never rested. At least, that is what he thought and set down in his diary. He pointed the place out to several friends, but none of them had even been on Federal Hill or possessed the faintest notion of what the church was or had been.

In the spring a deep restlessness gripped Blake. He had begun his long-planned novel—based on a supposed survival of the witch-cult in Maine—but was strangely unable to make progress with it. More and more he would sit at his westward window and gaze at the distant hill and the black, frowning steeple shunned by the birds. When the delicate leaves came out on the garden boughs the world was filled with a new beauty, but Blake's restlessness was merely increased. It was then that he first thought of crossing the city and climbing bodily up that fabulous slope into the smoke-wreathed world of dream.

Late in April, just before the aeon-shadowed Walpurgis time, Blake made his first trip into the unknown. Plodding through the endless downtown streets and the bleak, decayed squares beyond, he came finally upon the ascending avenue of century-worn steps, sagging Doric porches, and blear-paned cupolas which he felt must lead up to the long-known, unreachable world beyond the mists. There were dingy blue-and-white street signs which meant nothing to him, and presently he noted the strange, dark faces of the drifting crowds, and the foreign signs over curious shops in brown, decade-weathered buildings. Nowhere could he find any of the objects he had seen from afar; so that once more he half fancied that the Federal Hill of that distant view was a dream-world never to be trod by living human feet.

Now and then a battered church façade or crumbling spire came in sight, but never the blackened pile that he sought. When he asked a shopkeeper about a great stone church the man smiled and shook his head, though he spoke English freely. As Blake climbed higher, the region seemed stranger and stranger, with bewildering mazes of brooding brown alleys leading eternally off to the south. He crossed two or three broad avenues, and once thought he glimpsed a familiar tower. Again he asked a merchant about the massive church of stone, and this time he could have sworn that the plea of ignorance was feigned. The dark man's face had a look of fear which he tried to hide, and Blake saw him make a curious sign with his right hand.

Then suddenly a black spire stood out against the cloudy sky on his left, above the tiers of brown roofs lining the tangled southerly alleys. Blake knew at once what it was, and plunged towards it through the squalid, unpaved lanes that climbed from the avenue. Twice he lost his way, but he somehow dared not ask any of the patriarchs or housewives who sat on their doorsteps, or any of the children who shouted and played in the mud of the shadowy lanes.

At last he saw the tower plain against the south-west, and a huge stone bulk rose darkly at the end of an alley. Presently he stood in a wind-swept open square, quaintly cobblestoned, with a high bank wall on the farther side. This was the end of his quest; for upon the wide, iron-railed, weed-grown plateau which the wall supported—a separate, lesser world raised fully six feet above the surrounding streets—there stood a grim, titan bulk whose identity, despite Blake's new perspective, was beyond dispute.

The vacant church was in a state of great decrepitude. Some of the high stone buttresses had fallen, and several delicate finials lay half lost among the brown, neglected weeds and grasses. The sooty Gothic windows were largely unbroken, though many of the stone mullions were missing. Blake wondered how the obscurely painted panes could have survived so well, in view of the known habits of small boys the world over. The massive doors were intact and tightly closed. Around the top of the bank wall, fully enclosing the grounds, was a rusty iron fence whose gate—at the head of a flight of steps from the square—was visibly padlocked. The path from the gate to the building was completely overgrown. Desolation and decay hung like a pall above the place, and in the birdless eaves and black, ivyless walls Blake felt a touch of the dimly sinister beyond his power to define.

There were very few people in the square, but Blake saw a policeman at the northerly end and approached him with questions about the church. He was a great wholesome Irishman, and it seemed odd that he would do little more than make the sign of the cross and mutter that people never spoke of that building. When Blake pressed him he said very hurriedly that the Italian priests warned everybody against it, vowing that a monstrous evil had once dwelt there and left its mark. He himself had heard dark whispers of it from his father, who recalled certain sounds and rumours from his boyhood.

There had been a bad sect there in the old days—an outlaw sect that called up awful things from some unknown gulf of night. It had taken a good priest to exorcise what had come, though there did be those who said that merely the light could do it. If Father O'Malley were alive there would be many the thing he could tell. But now there was nothing to do but let it alone. It hurt nobody now, and those that owned it were dead or far away. They had run away like rats after the threatening talk in '77, when people began to mind the way folks vanished now and then in the neighbourhood. Some day the city would step in and take the property for lack of heirs, but little good would come of anybody's touching it. Better it be left alone for the years to topple, lest things be stirred that ought to rest for ever in their black abyss.

After the policeman had gone Blake stood staring at the sullen steepled pile. It excited him to find that the structure seemed as sinister to others as to him, and he wondered what grain of truth might lie behind the old tales the bluecoat had repeated. Probably they were mere legends evoked by the evil look of the place, but even so, they were like a strange coming to life of one of his own stories.

The afternoon sun came out from behind dispersing clouds, but seemed unable to light up the stained, sooty walls of the old temple that towered on its high plateau. It was odd that the green of spring had not touched the brown, withered growths in the raised, iron-fenced yard. Blake found himself edging nearer the raised area and examining the bank wall and rusted fence for possible avenues of ingress. There was a terrible lure about the blackened fane which was not to be resisted. The fence had no opening near the steps, but round on the north side were some missing bars. He could go up the steps and walk round on the narrow coping outside the fence till he came to the gap. If the people feared the place so wildly, he would encounter no interference.

He was on the embankment and almost inside the fence before anyone noticed him. Then, looking down, he saw the few people in the square edging away and making the same sign with their right hands that the shopkeeper in the avenue had made. Several windows were slammed down, and a fat woman darted into the street and pulled some small children inside a rickety, unpainted house. The gap in the fence was very easy to pass through, and before long Blake found himself wading amidst the rotting, tangled growths of the deserted yard. Here and there the worn stump of a headstone told him that there had once been burials in this field; but that, he saw, must have been very long ago. The sheer bulk of the church was oppressive now that he was close to it, but he conquered this mood and approached to try the three great doors in the façade. All were securely locked, so he began a circuit of the Cyclopean building in quest of some minor and more penetrable opening. Even then he could not be sure that he wished to enter that haunt of desertion and shadow, yet the pull of its strangeness dragged him on automatically.

A yawning and unprotected cellar window in the rear furnished the needed aperture. Peering in, Blake saw a subterrene gulf of cobwebs and dust faintly litten by the western sun's filtered rays. Debris, old barrels, and ruined boxes and furniture of numerous sorts met his eye, though over everything lay a shroud of dust which softened all sharp outlines. The rusted remains of a hot-air furnace showed that the building had been used and kept in shape as late as mid-Victorian times.

Acting almost without conscious initiative, Blake crawled through the window and let himself down to the dust-carpeted and debris-strewn concrete floor. The vaulted cellar was a vast one, without partitions; and in a corner far to the right, amid dense shadows, he saw a black archway evidently leading upstairs. He felt a peculiar sense of oppression at being actually within the great spectral building, but kept it in check as he cautiously scouted about—finding a still-intact barrel amid the dust, and rolling it over to the open window to provide for his exit. Then, bracing himself, he crossed the wide, cobweb-festooned space towards the arch. Half-choked with the omnipresent dust, and covered with ghostly gossamer fibres, he reached and began to climb the worn stone steps which rose into the darkness. He had no light, but groped carefully with his hands. After a sharp turn he felt a closed door ahead, and a little fumbling revealed its ancient latch. It opened inward, and beyond it he saw a dimly illumined corridor lined with worm-eaten panelling.

Once on the ground floor, Blake began exploring in a rapid fashion. All the inner doors were unlocked, so that he freely passed from room to room. The colossal nave was an almost eldritch place with its drifts and mountains of dust over box pews, altar, hour-glass pulpit, and sounding-board, and its titanic ropes of cobweb stretching among the pointed arches of the gallery and entwining the clustered Gothic columns. Over all this hushed desolation played a hideous leaden light as the declining afternoon sun sent its rays through the strange, half-blackened panes of the great apsidal windows.

The paintings on those windows were so obscured by soot that Blake could scarcely decipher what they had represented, but from the little he could make out he did not like them. The designs were largely conventional, and his knowledge of obscure symbolism told him much concerning some of the ancient patterns. The few saints depicted bore expressions distinctly open to criticism, while one of the windows seemed to show merely a dark space with spirals of curious luminosity scattered about in it. Turning away from the windows, Blake noticed that the cobwebbed cross above the altar was not of the ordinary kind, but resembled the primordial ankh or crux ansata of shadowy Egypt.

In a rear vestry room beside the apse Blake found a rotting desk and ceiling-high shelves of mildewed, disintegrating books. Here for the first time he received a positive shock of objective horror, for the titles of those books told him much. They were the black, forbidden things which most sane people have never even heard of, or have heard of only in furtive, timorous whispers; the banned and dreaded repositories of equivocal secret and immemorial formulae which have trickled down the stream of time from the days of man's youth, and the dim, fabulous days before man was. He had himself read many of them—a Latin version of the abhorred *Necronomicon,* the sinister *Liber Ivonis,* the infamous *Cultes des Gaules* of Comte d'Erlette, the *Unaussprechlichen Kulten* of von Junzt, and old Ludwig Prinn's hellish *De Vermis Mysteriis.* But there were others he had known merely by reputation or not at all—the *Pnakotic Manuscripts,* the *Book of Dzyan,* and a crumbling volume of wholly unidentifiable characters yet with certain symbols and diagrams shudderingly recognisable to the occult student. Clearly, the lingering local rumours had not lied. This place had once been the seat of an evil older than mankind and wider than the known universe.

In the ruined desk was a small leatherbound record-book filled with entries in some odd cryptographic medium. The manuscript writing consisted of the common traditional symbols used today in astronomy and anciently in alchemy, astrology, and other dubious arts—the devices of the sun, moon, planets, aspects, and zodiacal signs—here massed in solid pages of text, with divisions and paragraphings suggesting that each symbol answered to some alphabetical letter.

In the hope of later solving the cryptogram, Blake bore off this volume in his coat pocket. Many of the great tomes on the shelves fascinated him unutterably, and he felt tempted to borrow them at some later time. He wondered how they could have remained undisturbed so long. Was he the first to conquer the clutching, pervasive fear which had for nearly sixty years protected this deserted place from visitors?

Having now thoroughly explored the ground floor, Blake ploughed again through the dust of the spectral nave to the front vestibule, where he had seen a door and staircase presumably leading up to the blackened tower and steeple—objects so long familiar to him at a distance. The ascent was a choking experience, for dust lay thick, while the spiders had done their worst in this constricted space. The staircase was a spiral with high, narrow wooden treads, and now and then Blake passed a clouded window looking dizzily out over the city. Though he had seen no ropes below, he expected to find a bell or peal of bells in the tower whose narrow, louvre-boarded lancet windows his field-glasses had studied so often. Here he was doomed to disappointment; for when he attained the top of the stairs he found the tower chamber vacant of chimes ,and clearly devoted to vastly different purposes.

The room, about fifteen feet square, was faintly lighted by four lancet windows, one on each side, which were glazed within their screening of decayed louvre-boards. These had been further fitted with tight, opaque screens, but the latter were now largely rotted away. In the centre of the dust-laden floor rose a curiously angled stone pillar some four feet in height and two in average diameter, covered on each side with bizarre, crudely incised and wholly unrecognisable hieroglyphs. On this pillar rested a metal box of peculiarly asymmetrical form; its hinged lid thrown back, and its interior holding what looked beneath the decade-deep dust to be an egg-shaped or irregularly spherical object some four inches through. Around the pillar in a rough circle were seven high-backed Gothic chairs still largely intact, while behind them, ranging along the dark-panelled walls, were seven colossal images of crumbling, black-painted plaster, resembling more than anything else the cryptic carven megaliths of mysterious Easter Island. In one corner of the cobwebbed chamber a ladder was built into the wall, leading up to the closed trap door of the windowless steeple above.

As Blake grew accustomed to the feeble light he noticed odd bas-reliefs on the strange open box of yellowish metal. Approaching, he tried to clear the dust away with his hands and handkerchief, and saw that the figurings were of a monstrous and utterly alien kind; depicting entities which, though seemingly alive, resembled no known life-form ever evolved on this planet. The four-inch seeming sphere turned out to be a nearly black, red-striated polyhedron with many irregular flat surfaces; either a very remarkable crystal of some sort or an artificial object of carved and highly polished mineral matter. It did not touch the bottom of the box, but was held suspended by means of a metal band around its centre, with seven queerly designed supports extending horizontally to angles of the box's inner wall near the top. This stone, once exposed, exerted upon Blake an almost alarming fascination. He could scarcely tear his eyes from it, and, as he looked at its glistening surfaces he almost fancied it was transparent, with half-formed worlds of wonder within. Into his mind floated pictures of alien orbs with great stone towers, and other orbs with titan mountains and no mark of life, and still remoter spaces where only a stirring in vague blacknesses told of the presence of consciousness and will.

When he did look away, it was to notice a somewhat singular mound of dust in the far corner near the ladder to the steeple. Just why it took his attention he could not tell, but something in its contours carried a message to his unconscious mind. Ploughing towards it, and brushing aside the hanging cobwebs as he went, he began to discern something grim about it. Hand and handkerchief soon revealed the truth, and Blake gasped with a baffling mixture of emotions. It was a human skeleton, and it must have been there for a very long time. The clothing was in shreds, but some buttons and fragments of cloth bespoke a man's grey suit. There were other bits of evidence—shoes, metal clasps, huge buttons for round cuffs, a stickpin of bygone pattern, a reporter's badge with the name of the old *Providence Telegram,* and a crumbling leather pocket-book. Blake examined the latter with care, finding within it several bills of antiquated issue, a celluloid advertising calendar for 1893, some cards with the name "Edwin M. Lillibridge", and a paper covered with pencilled memoranda.

This paper held much of a puzzling nature, and Blake read it carefully at the dim westward window. Its disjointed text included such phrases as the following;

Prof. Enoch Bowen home from Egypt May 1844—buys old Free-Will Church in July—his archaeological work & studies in occult well known.

Dr. Drowne of 4th Baptist warns against Starry Wisdom in sermon Dec. 29, 1844.

Congregation 97 by end of '45.

1846—3 disappearances—first mention of Shining Trapezohedron.

7 disappearances 1848—stories of blood sacrifice begin.

Investigation 1853 comes to nothing—stories of sounds.

Fr. O'Malley tells of devil-worship with box found in great Egyptian ruins—says they call up something that can't exist in light. Flees a little light, and banished by strong light. Then has to be summoned again. Probably got this from deathbed confession of Francis X. Feeney, who had joined Starry Wisdom in '49. These people say the Shining Trapezohedron shows them heaven & other worlds, & that the Haunter of the Dark tells them secrets in some way.

Story of Orrin B. Eddy 1857. They call it up by gazing at the crystal, & have a secret language of their own.

200 or more in cong. 1863, exclusive of men at front.

Irish boys mob church in 1869 after Patrick Regan's disappearance.

Veiled article in J. March 14, '72, but people don't talk about it.

6 disappearances 1876—secret committee calls on Mayor Doyle.

Action promised Feb. 1877—church closes in April.
May.

Gang—Federal Hill Boys—threaten Dr.—— and vestrymen in

181 persons leave city before end of '77—mention no names.

Ghost stories begin around 1880—try to ascertain truth of report that no human being has entered church since 1877.

Ask Lanigan for photograph of place taken 1851....

Restoring the paper to the pocketbook and placing the latter in his coat, Blake turned to look down at the skeleton in the dust. The implications of the notes were clear, and there could be no doubt but that this man had come to the deserted edifice forty-two years before in quest of a newspaper sensation which no one else had been bold enough to attempt. Perhaps no one else had known of his plan—who could tell? But he had never returned to his paper. Had some bravely suppressed fear risen to overcome him and bring on sudden heart failure? Blake stopped over the gleaming bones and noted their peculiar state. Some of them were badly scattered, and a few seemed oddly *dissolved* at the ends. Others were strangely yellowed, with vague suggestions of charring. This charring extended to some of the fragments of clothing. The skull was in a very peculiar state—stained yellow, and with a charred aperture in the top as if some powerful acid had eaten through the solid bone. What had happened to the skeleton during its four decades of silent entombment here Blake could not imagine.

Before he realised it, he was looking at the stone again, and letting its curious influence call up a nebulous pageantry in his mind. He saw processions of robed, hooded figures whose outlines were not human, and looked on endless leagues of desert lined with carved, sky-reaching monoliths. He saw towers and walls in nighted depths under the sea, and vortices of space where wisps of black mist floated before thin shimmerings of cold purple haze. And beyond all else he glimpsed an infinite gulf of darkness, where solid and semisolid forms were known only by their windy stirrings, and cloudy patterns of force seemed to superimpose order on chaos and hold forth a key to all the paradoxes and arcana of the worlds we know.

Then all at once the spell was broken by an access of gnawing, indeterminate panic fear. Blake choked and turned away from the stone, conscious of some formless alien presence close to him and watching him with horrible intentness. He felt entangled with something—something which was not in the stone, but which had looked through it at him—something which would ceaselessly follow him with a cognition that was not physical sight. Plainly, the place was getting on his nerves—as well it might in view of his gruesome find. The light was waning too, and since he had no illuminant with him he knew he would have to be leaving soon.

It was then, in the gathering twilight, that he thought he saw a faint trace of luminosity in the crazily angled stone. He had tried to look away from it, but some obscure compulsion drew his eyes back. Was there a subtle phosphorescence of radio-activity about the thing? What was it that the dead man's notes had said concerning a *Shining Trapezohedron?* What, anyway, was his abandoned lair of cosmic evil? What had been done here, and what might still be luring in the bird-shunned shadows? It seemed now as if an elusive touch of fetor had arisen somewhere close by, though its source was not apparent. Blake seized the cover of the long-open box and snapped it down. It moved easily on its alien hinges, and closed completely over the unmistakably glowing stone.

At the sharp click of that closing a soft stirring sound seemed to come from the steeple's eternal blackness overhead, beyond the trap-door. Rats, without question—the only living things to reveal their presence in this accursed pile since he had entered it. And yet that stirring in the steeple frightened him horribly, so that he plunged almost wildly down the spiral stairs, across the ghoulish nave, into the vaulted basement, out amidst the gathering dusk of the deserted square, and down through the teeming, fear-haunted alleys and avenues of Federal Hill towards the sane central streets and the home-like brick sidewalks of the college district.

During the days which followed, Blake told no one of his expedition. Instead, he read much in certain books, examined long years of newspaper files downtown, and worked feverishly at the cryptogram in that leather volume from the cobwebbed vestry room. The cipher, he soon saw, was no simple one; and after a long period of endeavour he felt sure that its language could not be English, Latin, Greek, French, Spanish, Italian, or German. Evidently he would have to draw upon the deepest wells of his strange erudition.

Every evening the old impulse to gaze westwards returned, and he saw the black steeple as of yore amongst the bristling roofs of a distant and half-fabulous world. But now it held a fresh note of terror for him. He knew the heritage of evil lore it masked, and with the knowledge his vision ran riot in queer new ways. The birds of spring were returning, and as he watched their sunset flights he fancied they avoided the gaunt, lone spire as never before. When a flock of them approached it, he thought, they would wheel and scatter in panic confusion—and he could guess at the wild twitterings which failed to reach him across the intervening miles.

It was in June that Blake's diary told of his victory over the cryptogram. The text was, he found, in the dark Aklo language used by certain cults of evil antiquity, and known to him in a halting way through previous researches. The diary is strangely reticent about what Blake deciphered, but he was patently awed and disconcerted by his results. There are references to a Haunter of the Dark awaked by gazing into the Shining Trapezohedron, and insane conjectures about the black gulfs of chaos from which it was called. The being is spoken as of holding all knowledge, and demanding monstrous sacrifices. Some of Blake's entries show fear lest the thing, which he seemed to regard as summoned, stalk abroad; though he adds that the streetlights form a bulwark which cannot be crossed.

Of the Shining Trapezohedron he speaks often, calling it a window on all time and space, and tracing its history from the days it was fashioned on dark Yuggoth, before ever the Old Ones brought it to earth. It was treasured and placed in its curious box by the crinoid things of Antarctica, salvaged from their ruins by the serpent-men of Valusia, and peered at eons later in Lemuria by the first human beings. It crossed strange lands and stranger seas, and sank with Atlantis before a Minoan fisher meshed it in his net and sold it to swarthy merchants from nighted Khem. The Pharaoh Nephren-Ka built around it a temple with a windowless crypt, and did that which caused his name to be stricken from all monuments and records. Then it slept in the ruins of that evil fane which the priests and the new Pharaoh destroyed, till the delver's spade once more brought it forth to curse mankind.

Early in July the newspapers oddly supplement Blake's entries, though in so brief and casual a way that only the diary has called general attention to their contribution. It appears that a new fear had been growing on Federal Hill since a stranger had entered the dreaded church. The Italians whispered of unaccustomed stirrings and bumpings and scrapings in the dark windowless steeple, and called on their priests to banish an entity which haunted their dreams. Something, they said, was constantly watching at a door to see if it were dark enough to venture forth. Press items mentioned the long-standing local superstitions, but failed to shed much light on the earlier background of the horror. It was obvious that the young reporters of today are no antiquarians. In writing of these things in his diary, Blake expresses a curious kind of remorse, and talks of the duty of burying the Shining Trapezohedron and of banishing what he had evoked by letting daylight into the hideous jutting spire. At the same time, however, he displays the dangerous extent of his fascination, and admits a morbid longing—pervading even his dreams—to visit the accursed tower and gaze again into the cosmic secrets of the glowing stone.

Then something in the *Journal* on the morning of July 17 threw the diarist into a veritable fever of horror. It was only a variant of the other half-humorous items about the Federal Hill restlessness, but to Blake it was somehow very terrible indeed. In the night a thunderstorm had put the city's lighting system out of commission for a full hour, and in that black interval the Italians had nearly gone mad with fright. Those living near the dreaded church had sworn that the thing in the steeple had taken advantage of the street lamps' absence and gone down into the body of the church, flopping and lumping around in a viscous, altogether dreadful way. Towards the last it had bumped up to the tower, where there were sounds of the shattering of glass. It could go wherever the darkness reached, but light would always send it fleeing.

When the current blazed on again there had been a shocking commotion in the tower, for even the feeble light trickling through the grime-blackened, louvre-boarded windows was too much for the thing. It had bumped and slithered up into its tenebrous steeple just in time—for a long dose of light would have sent it back into the abyss whence the crazy stranger had called it. During the dark hour praying crowds had clustered round the church in the rain with lighted candles and lamps somehow shielded with folded paper and umbrellas—a guard of light to save the city from the nightmare that stalks in darkness. Once, those nearest the church declared, the outer door had rattled hideously.

But even this was not the worst. That evening in the *Bulletin* Blake read of what the reporters had found. Aroused at last to the whimsical news value of the scare, a pair of them had defied the frantic crowds of Italians and crawled into the church through the cellar window after trying the doors in vain. They found the dust of the vestibule and of the spectral nave ploughed up in a singular way, with pits of rotted cushions and satin pew-linings scattered curiously around. There was a bad odour everywhere, and here and there were bits of yellow stain and patches of what looked like charring. Opening the door to the tower, and pausing a moment at the suspicion of a scraping sound above, they found the narrow spiral stairs wiped roughly clean.

In the tower itself a similarly half-swept condition existed. They spoke of the heptagonal stone pillar, the overturned Gothic chairs, and the bizarre plaster images; though strangely enough the metal box and the old mutilated skeleton were not mentioned. What disturbed Blake the most—except for the hints of stains and charring and bad odours—was the final detail that explained the crashing glass. Every one of the tower's lancet windows was broken, and two of them had been darkened in a crude and hurried way by the stuffing of satin pew-linings and cushion-horsehair into the spaces between the slanting exterior louvre-boards. More satin fragments and bunches of horsehair lay scattered around the newly swept floor, as if someone had been interrupted in the act of restoring the tower to the absolute blackness of its tightly curtained days.

Yellowish stains and charred patches were found on the ladder to the windowless spire, but when a reporter climbed up, opened the horizontally-sliding trap-door and shot a feeble flashlight beam into the black and strangely fetid space, he saw nothing but darkness, and a heterogeneous litter of shapeless fragments near the aperture. The verdict, of course, was charlatanry. Somebody had played a joke on the superstitious hill-dwellers, or else some fanatic had striven to bolster up their fears for their own supposed good. Or perhaps some of the younger and more sophisticated dwellers had staged an elaborate hoax on the outside world. There was an amusing aftermath when the police sent an officer to verify the report. Three men in succession found ways of evading the assignment, and the fourth went very reluctantly and returned very soon without adding to the account given by the reporters.

From this point onwards Blake's diary shows a mounting tide of insidious horror and nervous apprehension. He upbraids himself for not doing something, and speculates wildly on the consequences of another electrical breakdown. It has been verified that on three occasions—during thunderstorms—he telephoned the electric light company in a frantic vein and asked that desperate precautions against a lapse of power be taken. Now and then his entries show concern over the failure of the reporters to find the box and stone, and the strangely marred old skeleton, when they explored the shadowy tower room. He assumed that these things had been removed—whither, and by whom or what, he could only guess. But his worst fears concerned himself, and the kind of unholy rapport he felt to exist between his mind and that lurking horror in the distant steeple—that monstrous thing of night which his rashness had called out of the ultimate black spaces. He seemed to feel a constant tugging at his will, and callers of that period remember how he would sit abstractedly at his desk and stare out of the west window at that far off spire-bristling mound beyond the swirling smoke of the city. His entries dwell monotonously on certain terrible dreams, and of a strengthening of the unholy rapport in his sleep. There is mention of a night when he awakened to find himself fully dressed, outdoors, and headed automatically down College Hill towards the west. Again and again he dwells on the fact that the thing in the steeple knows where to find him.

The week following July 30 is recalled as the time of Blake's partial breakdown. He did not dress, and ordered all his food by telephone. Visitors remarked the cords he kept near his bed, and he said that sleep-walking had forced him to bind his ankles every night with knots which would probably hold or else waken him with the labour of untying.

In his diary he told of the hideous experience which had brought the collapse. After retiring on the night of the 30th, he had suddenly found himself groping about in an almost black space. All he could see were short, faint, horizontal streaks of bluish light, but he could smell an overpowering fetor and hear a curious jumble of soft, furtive sounds above him. Whenever he moved he stumbled over something, and at each noise there would come a sort of answering sound from above—a vague stirring, mixed with the cautious sliding of wood on wood.

Once his groping hands encountered a pillar of stone with a vacant top, whilst later he found himself clutching the rungs of a ladder built into the wall, and fumbling his uncertain way upwards towards some region of intenser stench where a hot, searing blast beat down against him. Before his eyes a kaleidoscopic range of fantasmal images played, all of them dissolving at intervals into the picture of a vast, unplumbed abyss of night wherein whirled suns and worlds of an even profounder blackness. He thought of the ancient legends of Ultimate Chaos, at whose centre sprawls the blind idiot god Azathoth, Lord of all Things, encircled by his flopping hoard of mindless and amorphous dancers, and lulled by the thin monotonous piping of a demoniac flute held in nameless paws.

Then a sharp report from the outer world broke through his stupor and roused him to the unutterable horror of his position. What it was, he never knew—perhaps it was some belated peal from the fireworks heard all summer on Federal Hill as dwellers hail their various patron saints, or the saints of their native villages in Italy. In any event he shrieked aloud, dropped frantically from the ladder, and stumbled blindly across the obstructed floor of the almost lightless chamber that encompassed him.

He knew instantly where he was, and plunged recklessly down the narrow spiral staircase, tripping and bruising himself at every turn. There was a nightmare flight through a vast cobwebbed nave whose ghostly arches reached up to realms of leering shadow, a sightless scramble through a littered basement, a climb to regions of air and street lights outside, and a mad racing down a spectral hill of gibbering gables, across a grim, silent city of tall black towers, and up the steep eastward precipice to his own ancient door.

On regaining consciousness in the morning he found himself lying on his study floor fully dressed. Dirt and cobwebs covered him, and every inch of his body seemed sore and bruised. When he faced the mirror he saw that his hair was badly scorched, while a trace of strange evil odour seemed to cling to his upper outer clothing. It was then that his nerves broke down. Thereafter, lounging exhaustedly about in a dressing-gown, he did little but stare from his west window, shiver at the threat of thunder, and make wild entries in his diary.

The great storm broke just before midnight on August 8th. Lightning struck repeatedly in all parts of the city, and two remarkable fireballs were reported. The rain was torrential, while a constant fusillade of thunder brought sleeplessness to thousands. Blake was utterly frantic in his fear for the lighting system, and tried to telephone the company around one a.m., though by that time service had been temporarily cut off in the interests of safety. He recorded everything in his diary—the large, nervous, and often undecipherable, hieroglyphs telling their own story of growing frenzy and despair, and of entries scrawled blindly in the dark.

He had to keep the house dark in order to see out of the window, and it appears that most of his time was spent at his desk, peering anxiously through the rain across the glistening miles of downtown roofs at the constellation of distant lights marking Federal Hill. Now and then he would fumblingly make an entry in his diary, so that detached phrases such as "The lights must not go"; "It knows where I am"; "I must destroy it"; and "It is calling to me, but perhaps it means no injury this time"; are found scattered down two of the pages.

Then the lights went out all over the city. It happened at 2.12 a.m. according to power-house records, but Blake's diary gives no indication of the time. The entry is merely, "Lights out—God help me." On Federal Hill there were watchers as anxious as he, and rain-soaked knots of men paraded the square and alleys around the evil church with umbrella-shaded candles, electric flashlights, oil lanterns, crucifixes, and obscure charms of the many sorts common to southern Italy. They blessed each flash of lightning, and made cryptical signs of fear with their right hands when a turn in the storm caused the flashes to lessen and finally cease altogether. A rising wind blew out most of the candles, so that the scene grew threateningly dark. Someone roused Father Merluzzo of Spirito Santo Church, and he hastened to the dismal square to pronounce whatever helpful syllables he could. Of the restless and curious sounds in the blackened tower, there could be no doubt whatever.

For what happened at 2.35 we have the testimony of the priest, a young, intelligent, and well-educated person; of Patrolman William J. Monohan of the Central Station, an officer of the highest reliability who had paused at that part of his beat to inspect the crowd; and of most of the seventy-eight men who had gathered around the church's high bank wall—especially those in the square where the eastward façade was visible. Of course there was nothing which can be proved as being outside the order of nature. The possible causes of such an event are many. No one can speak with certainty of the obscure chemical processes arising in a vast, ancient, ill-aired, and long deserted building of heterogeneous contents. Mephitic vapours—spontaneous combustion—pressure of gases born of long decay—any one of numberless phenomena might be responsible. And then, of course, the factor of conscious charlatanry can by no means be excluded. The thing was really quite simple in itself and covered less than three minutes of actual time. Father Merluzzo, always a precise man, looked at his watch repeatedly.

It started with a definite swelling of the dull fumbling sounds inside the black tower. There had for some time been a vague exhalation of strange, evil odours from the church, and this had now become emphatic and offensive. Then at last there was a sound of splintering wood and a large, heavy object crashed down in the yard beneath the frowning easterly façade. The tower was invisible now that the candles would not burn, but as the object neared the ground the people knew that it was the smoke-grimed louvre-boarding of that tower's east window.

Immediately afterwards an utterly unbearable fetor welled forth from the unseen heights, choking and sickening the trembling watchers, and almost prostrating those in the square. At the same time the air trembled with a vibration as of flapping wings, and a sudden east-blowing wind more violent than any previous blast snatched off the hats and wrenched the dripping umbrellas of the crowd. Nothing definite could be seen in the candleless night, though some upward-looking spectators thought they glimpsed a great spreading blur of denser blackness against the inky sky—something like a formless cloud of smoke that shot with meteorlike speed towards the east.

That was all. The watchers were half numbed with fright, awe, and discomfort, and scarcely knew what to do, or whether to do anything at all. Not knowing what had happened, they did not relax their vigil; and a moment later they sent up a prayer as a sharp flash of belated lightning, followed by an earsplitting crash of sound, rent the flooded heavens. Half an hour later the rain stopped, and in fifteen minutes more the street lights sprang on again, sending the weary, bedraggled watchers relievedly back to their homes.

The next day's papers gave these matters minor mention in connection with the general storm reports. It seems that the great lightning flash and deafening explosion which followed the Federal Hill occurrence were even more tremendous farther east, where a burst of the singular fetor was likewise noticed. The phenomenon was most marked over College Hill, where the crash awoke all the sleeping inhabitants and led to a bewildered round of speculations. Of those who were already awake only a few saw the anomalous blaze of light near the top of the hill, or noticed the inexplicable upward rush of air which almost stripped the leaves from the trees and blasted the plants in the gardens. It was agreed that the lone, sudden lighting-bolt must have struck somewhere in this neighbourhood, though no trace of its striking could afterwards be found. A youth in the Tau Omega fraternity house thought he saw a grotesque and hideous mass of smoke in the air just as the preliminary flash burst, but his observation has not been verified. All of the few observers, however, agree as to the violent gust from the west and the flood of intolerable stench which preceded the belated stroke, whilst evidence concerning the momentary burned odour after the stroke is equally general.

These points were discussed very carefully because of their probable connection with the death of Robert Blake. Students in the Psi Delta house, whose upper rear windows looked into Blake's study, noticed the blurred white face at the westward window on the morning of the ninth, and wondered what was wrong with the expression. When they saw the same face in the same position that evening they felt worried, and watched for the lights to come up in his apartment. Later they rang the bell of the darkened flat, and finally had a policeman force the door.

The rigid body sat bolt upright at the desk by the window, and when the intruders saw the glassy, bulging eyes, and the marks of stark, convulsive fright on the twisted features, they turned away in sickened dismay. Shortly afterwards the coroner's physician made an examination, and despite the unbroken window, reported electrical shock, or nervous tension induced by electrical discharge, as the cause of death. The hideous expression he ignored altogether, deeming it a not improbable result of the profound shock as experienced by a person of such abnormal imagination and unbalanced emotions. He deduced these latter qualities from the books, paintings, and manuscripts found in the apartment, and from the blindly scrawled entries in the diary on the desk. Blake had prolonged his frenzied jottings to the last, and the broken-pointed pencil was found clutched in his spasmodically contracted right hand.

The entries after the failure of the lights were highly disjointed, and legible only in part. From them certain investigators have drawn conclusions differing greatly from the materialistic official verdict, but such speculations have little chance for belief among the conservative. The case of these imaginative theorists has not been helped by the action of superstitious Doctor Dexter, who threw the curious box and angled stone—an object certainly self-luminous as seen in the black windowless steeple where it was found—into the deepest channel of Narragansett Bay. Excessive imagination and neurotic unbalance on Blake's part, aggravated by knowledge of the evil bygone cult whose startling traces he had uncovered, form the dominant interpretation given those final frenzied jottings. These are the entries—or all that can be made of them:

Lights still out—must be five minutes now. Everything depends on lightning. Yaddith grant it will keep up! ... Some influence seems beating through it.... Rain and thunder and wind deafen.... The thing is taking hold of my mind....

Trouble with memory. I see things I never knew before. Other worlds and other galaxies.... Dark.... The lightning seems dark and the darkness seems light....

It cannot be the real hill and church that I see in the pitch-darkness. Must be retinal impression left by flashes. Heaven grant the Italians are out with their candles if the lightning stops!

What am I afraid of? Is it not an avatar of Nyarlathotep, who in antique and shadowy Khem even took the form of man? I remember Yuggoth, and more distant Shaggai, and the ultimate void of the black planets....

The long, winging flight through the void ... cannot cross the universe of light ... re-created by the thoughts caught in the Shining Trapezohedron ... send it through the horrible abysses of radiance....

My name is Blake—Robert Harrison Blake of 620 East Knapp Street, Milwaukee, Wisconsin.... I am of this planet....

Azathoth have mercy!—the lightning no longer flashes—horrible—I can see everything with a monstrous sense that is not sight—light is dark and dark is light ... those people on the hill ... guard ... candles and charms ... their priests....

Sense of distance gone—far is near and near is far. No light—no glass—see that steeple—that tower—window—can hear—Roderick Usher—am mad or going mad—the thing is stirring and fumbling in the tower—I am it and it is I—I want to get out ... must get out and unify the forces.... It knows where I am....

I am Robert Blake, but I see the tower in the dark. There is a monstrous odour ... senses transfigured ... boarding at that tower window cracking and giving way ... Iä ... ngai ... ygg....

I see it—coming here—hell-wind—titan blur—black wings—Yog-Sothoth save me—the three-lobed burning eye....